The Emperor's Lady

The EMPEROR'S LADY

by F. W. Kenyon

A novel based on the life
of the Empress Josephine

THOMAS Y. CROWELL COMPANY

NEW YORK

To

Awdrey Kenyon

CONTENTS

The Emperor's Lady

Part One
The Little Vicomtesse

YOUNG ALEXANDRE-FRAN-çois-Marie, Vicomte de Beauharnais, paused outside the library. With a frown on his brow he tapped lightly on the door. A sharp though not unpleasant female voice bade him enter. The frown deepened. His father had sent for him, but as usual, whatever reason his father might have for wanting to see him, Madame Renaudin had issued the order—issued it in a manner as imperious as if she were the Queen, Marie Antoinette of Austria, herself.

Alexandre entered the library, bowed stiffly to Madame Renaudin and addressed himself solely to his father, the marquis.

"I believe you wished to see me, Father."

The elderly Marquis de Beauharnais smiled eagerly—too eagerly, Alexandre thought. "Yes, yes, my boy. You—er—you may be seated if you wish."

Alexandre bowed but remained standing. Madame Renaudin cleared her throat sharply. The marquis gave a little start, like a horse that had been prodded gently but firmly with the spurs, and smiled eagerly again.

"Alexandre," he said, in his low and pleasant voice, "we have something of the utmost importance to discuss with you. You are now eighteen and I—" he glanced quickly at the watchful Madame Renaudin—"that is *we*," he amended hastily, "consider it time a wife was found for you."

Alexandre inclined his head. "I have been of that opinion for some little time myself, Father."

The slight pomposity in the boy's voice made Madame Renaudin smile. She had never been fond of the marquis's younger son, but since he was necessary to her plans she was prepared to overlook a characteristic which, in less happy circumstances, would certainly have repelled her.

The marquis fingered the lace edge of his cravat nervously and turned appealingly to Madame Renaudin.

"My dear Marie," he beseeched her, "what we have to say would, I feel sure, come more aptly from your lips."

"Just as you wish, François." With a smile she turned to the young man. "Alexandre, I have often spoken to you of my three nieces in Martinique, and quite possibly, since you were there yourself as a child, you remember them."

"I remember little more than their names," he said, and with a suspicious gravity he repeated them slowly, "Marie-Joseph-Rose, Catherine-Désirée and Marie-Françoise."

"I am happy," Madame Renaudin said drily, "to know that your interest is deep enough for you to have remembered the names correctly."

"They happen to be pretty names," he murmured condescendingly, "and in consequence easily remembered."

"And the girls themselves," the marquis broke in happily, "are even prettier than their names."

"Pretty," Madame Renaudin said severely, "is an inept description. Creole girls are never merely *pretty.*"

"I do admit," Alexandre said smoothly, "that a dash of color, while the Creole girl is young, of course, is apt to make her boldly handsome."

"A dash of color?" She looked at him pityingly. "My poor Alexandre, such ignorance in a young man of your education is amazing. Surely you know that a Creole is not a person of mixed blood, but one born in the islands of French parents. You were born there. You, therefore, are a Creole."

Alexandre bit his lip in annoyance. "I stand corrected, madame," and he added quickly, "am I to understand that you wish to arrange a marriage between me and one of your—er—colonial nieces?"

"But naturally!"

"How old is the eldest?" he asked.

"Sixteen," the marquis said, "and by all accounts, a graceful child with a lovely voice."

"Sixteen?" Alexandre shook his head. "A little too old. I should prefer my future wife to be more than two years younger than myself."

"Catherine-Désirée," Madame Renaudin said promptly, "is barely fourteen."

"And the youngest, Marie-Françoise?"

"Not yet twelve."

"Ah, a little too young, I fear."

"Tell Alexandre more about Catherine-Désirée," the marquis suggested.

"Catherine-Désirée," Madame Renaudin said promptly, "is a beautiful child. But not only is she beautiful. She combines in her character the gracefulness of Marie-Joseph-Rose and the sweetness of nature possessed by Marie-Françoise."

Alexandre, well aware that Madame Renaudin had left Martinique while her nieces were still very young, controlled an impulse to argue the point. Instead he asked a question of far greater importance to his studious, book-loving nature.

"What of her education, madame?"

"Her education? My dear Alexandre, she has enjoyed all the advantages that Martinique can give."

Alexandre raised his eyebrows. "The advantages of an island so far removed from France are surely limited. However, let me make myself clear. The fewer the educational advantages enjoyed by Catherine-Désirée the better I shall be pleased."

Madame Renaudin and the marquis exchanged a look of surprise.

"It so happens, madame," Alexandre went on, "that I hold certain positive ideas as to how a wife should act and speak. If a man is to influence the mental development of his future wife the young lady in question must be young enough not to have been ruined by education and environment. That is why I look more favorably on Catherine-Désirée than on Marie-Joseph-Rose."

"Then you have a definite preference for Catherine-Désirée?" the marquis asked.

"If it is your wish," Alexandre said gravely, "that I should be compelled to marry one of Madame Renaudin's nieces, yes."

"It is indeed my wish!" the marquis said, in an attempt at sternness, and having noted Madame Renaudin's frown at his son's use of the word 'compelled.'

Alexandre bowed, first to Madame Renaudin, then to his father. "Then my choice is Catherine-Désirée."

The marquis rose and embraced him.

"You make a wise decision," he said. "Now leave us, my boy. We have a letter to write to Martinique."

*　　*　　*　　*　　*

The discussion of this proposed marriage for the young Vicomte de Beauharnais had taken place at Madame Renaudin's country house, a present from the marquis, near Noisy-le-Grand, and while

Madame Renaudin and the marquis were congratulating themselves on the unexpected ease with which they had influenced Alexandre's choice, Alexandre himself was pacing quickly up and down the garden, raging inwardly at the control exercised over his life by Madame Renaudin.

It must be admitted that Marie Renaudin had found her association with the marquis, an association of almost twenty years' duration, a most profitable one. A Creole by birth, she had first met François de Beauharnais in Martinique when, in the year 1757, he had arrived from France with his wife and child to take up the position of governor of the colony. The marquis, a man of weak but amiable character, was at that time forty-two; Marie, then Mademoiselle Tascher de la Pagerie, was half that age. Due to her father's influence with the new governor, Marie soon entered Government House in the capacity of companion to the governor's wife. Within a few months gossip was suggesting that however pleasant a companion she might be to the wife she was an even pleasanter companion to the susceptible husband. As a result of this, and in a vain attempt to refute the gossip, the governor brought about a speedy marriage between Marie and Alexis Renaudin, a son of one of the best families in Martinique.

This over-eager matchmaking had one disastrous result. More concerned with the marriage celebrations than the fact that he should have been leading reinforcements against the English, who were attacking the island of Guadaloupe, he gaily forgot the urgency of his military duties for a period of six weeks, by which time the French commander of Guadaloupe had thrown up his hands in despair and surrendered. The governor did the best he could to blame the commander for this catastrophe, but in the end the true story reached Paris and in spite of his influence at court the marquis was replaced at Government House.

By this time a second son had been born to him and his wife. This child was given the name of Alexandre-François-Marie, and at his christening Madame Renaudin kindly consented to stand as godmother. This occasioned many raised eyebrows and much polite sniggering, and when Madame Renaudin left for France some years later (and several months in advance of the marquis and his wife) nobody, save Madame de Beauharnais, was deceived. Renaudin himself, unreasonable enough to object to this arrangement, remained in Martinique, and Marie never saw him again.

Once in Paris, and while awaiting the arrival of the marquis, Madame Renaudin made a beautiful gesture. She sought the shelter of a convent from which, after due meditation and reflection, she emerged to take up her old position in the marquis's household. The faint and tremulous protests of the belatedly suspicious wife had only one result. Madame Renaudin became more firmly established in the affections of her lover, while the marquise, with gratifying promptness, left to take up residence with her mother, under whose roof she died a few years later.

With the departure of the marquise, Madame Renaudin's influence over the marquis and his affairs increased to such an extent that presently she came to hold a position of complete authority, a position resented, as we have already seen, by the younger son.

While pacing up and down in the garden Alexandre admitted to himself that he had no real objection to a wife being found for him. (There were certain theories concerning the training of a young wife which it would give him a great deal of pleasure to prove.) What he actually objected to was that a wife should be chosen by Madame Renaudin, and that the choice should fall upon one of the daughters of her impoverished brother in Martinique. However, as he was eventually obliged to tell himself, there was little he could do but submit—submit with as much grace as possible and wait patiently for the day when the opportunity of getting the better of Madame Renaudin might present itself.

* * * * *

In the library the marquis, twisting the quill pen in his fingers and scowling at the sheet of writing paper before him, made an impatient gesture and turned to Madame Renaudin.

"Marie, you might have the goodness to help me with this letter to your brother."

With the feeling of satisfaction which his helplessness always gave her, Madame Renaudin joined him at the writing bureau and looking over his shoulder read what he had already written.

Dear Friend,
It is with great pleasure and satisfaction that I set myself the task of writing to you today. Because of the friendship I bear you and the attachment I feel to you and your family I should be deeply honored if the ties which already bind us could be more intimately secured.

"A very suitable opening," she said, resisting the impulse to pat him on the shoulder as if he were a well-trained house-dog.

After a moment her manner grew grave. "There is one thing I think I ought to mention, François. My brother, as you know, was never a wealthy man, and of late he has suffered reverses." She looked at the marquis obliquely and then continued: "My nieces are therefore in the unhappy position of being obliged to face the world without the support of dowries."

The marquis, dismissing this with a pleasant laugh, responded as she had hoped he would. "My dear Marie, any one of your nieces would be acceptable, with or without a dowry. Alexandre is well provided for. A dowry is of no importance whatever."

She kissed him lightly on the brow. "You put my mind at rest François. However, I think your attitude in the matter should be made quite clear to my brother."

"Certainly, certainly. You could perhaps write to him separately and tell him in your own words that no dowry will be expected."

"I could, if you insist."

"I do, my dear, I do! And I insist that you help me finish my own letter too!"

She smiled and kissed him on the brow again. "You rely on me far too much, François. However, take up your pen and we will see what we can do between us."

And so, with Madame Renaudin dictating and the marquis writing slowly and diligently, the letter to Madame Renaudin's brother, Joseph-Gaspard Tascher de la Pagerie, was eventually completed.

CHAPTER II

THE GIRL, KICKING LAZILY, swam from the center of the stream to the moss-covered bank.

"Marion!" she called.

The mulatto woman came forward from the shade of the mango trees and stooping held out her fat brown hands. Marie-Joseph-Rose grasped them and drew herself up. For a moment, her body gleaming whitely in the sunlight, the water tracing little shimmering lines down her abdomen and thighs, she stood there breathing deeply. Then she turned her head and looked back towards the deeper water of the stream.

"Tercier," she said, "would you say that my body is beautiful?"

The young man, floating on his back and kicking against the slight pull of the current, laughed derisively.

"M'm'selle Tascher de la Pagerie," he pronounced flatly, "is much too fat."

The girl thrust out her tongue.

"Pig of a pig," she said, "and you, my friend, are much too thin."

A grunt, which was in reality a laugh, came from the mulatto woman. She slapped the girl lightly across the buttocks and poked her playfully in the stomach.

"Fat," she said. "Everywhere, fat."

Marie-Joseph-Rose laughed good-naturedly. "You shall give me some of those herbs you brew," she said, "and perhaps it will disappear. Come, Marion, my clothes."

"And not before time," Marion commented. "If your poor Papa came and found you like this, bathing naked with a young man—" and she threw up her hands eloquently.

The girl looked puzzled. "What harm is there in it?" she asked.

"None," Tercier complained, "with Marion standing guard like this."

"Harm or not," Marion grumbled, "M'sieur Tascher would have me whipped for permitting it." She pointed a quivering finger at the young man in the stream. "And the *sous-lieutenant*, what would happen to him?"

Marie-Joseph-Rose laughed merrily. "Poor Tercier would be sent back to France in disgrace, or else—" for a moment she looked thoughtful—"or else Papa would insist upon my marrying him."

Marion snorted. "You would then be ruined, both of you."

"Ruined? *Both* of us?"

"The *sous-lieutenant*," said Marion, not unacquainted with the ways of the fashionable world, "is a young man of good family but no money. For him to marry the daughter of a poor planter, that would be disaster."

The girl stamped her foot angrily. "My father may be poor but Tercier will be a general some day. He will win many battles against the English and will be rich, and then—" She saw that Tercier was now floating downstream on the current to the place where his clothes were hidden. "Tercier!" she called.

He turned his head.

"Tonight?" she asked. "At this same place? Tonight when the moon is up?"

"Tonight!" he agreed, "when the moon is up."

When Marion had dressed her, Marie-Joseph-Rose sat on the bank of the stream and dangled her feet in the water. Marriage with Tercier— Strange that until now such a thought had never occurred to her. A pity that his family in France was as poor as her own, for he was quite a good-looking fellow and, contrary to her accusation about thinness, well-built and nicely proportioned. As for his becoming a general some day, who knew, there might be a possibility of that. She sprang to her feet.

"Marion, the old hag who reads the future, the one who predicted

7

poor little Catherine-Désirée's death—you will take me to her at once."

The Martinique estate of Joseph-Gaspard Tascher de la Pagerie stood on the outskirts of the small township of Trois-Ilets which lay on the opposite side of the bay from Fort-Royal. To the north of the house, but hidden from it by a plantation of mango trees, was a little group of native huts inhabited by a handful of the Tascher slaves and their families. Seated in a squatting position at the door of one of these huts, and attended by a naked Negro child who fanned her lazily, was the aged Negress fortune-teller. While the girl stood back hesitantly Marion exchanged a few words with the old hag in the native jargon, upon which Marie-Joseph-Rose was invited to draw closer. She did so, averting her head as the warm, sickly stench which rose from the old woman's body assailed her nostrils.

"Let her speak without delay," she commanded faintly.

After a moment of silence a spate of guttural words tumbled from the Negress's mouth.

"What does she say?" Marie-Joseph-Rose asked.

Marion, looking owlish, began to translate.

"M'm'selle Rose," she said, "is born for greater things than to remain in Martinique and make an unimportant local marriage. First, a long voyage across the water and then a splendid alliance with a family of great consequence."

"I am to go to France?" (Poor Tercier, undoubtedly he was to play but a small part in her life.)

"Where else does one go across the water from Martinique but to France?"

Despite the offensive smell, and the feeling of nausea with which it was filling her, the girl leaned eagerly forward. Suddenly the old hag grew greatly excited and began to shout. Marion, listening, grew excited too.

"Child," she said, "it is the decree of fate that you will become the Queen of France."

Marie-Joseph-Rose's eyes grew big and round. For the moment she was speechless.

"Queen of France!" she managed to whisper at last.

The old hag was still speaking, but her excitement had faded. Marion listened, shook her head sadly, and solemnly added: "The Crown of France will be placed on your head, but you will die, perhaps in sorrow, and without your crown."

Marie-Joseph-Rose turned suddenly and was immediately sick. Marion came to her side in some concern. The girl smiled wanly.

"It was not the thought of losing my crown," she said, "but the terrible smell." She retched again until the tears ran down her cheeks, then she said: "Queen of France! I almost don't believe it."

* * * * *

It was dusk when Marie-Joseph-Rose and Marion returned to the house. This building, surrounded by unkempt shrubberies and neglected lawns, was in reality a converted sugar refinery. In 1766, shortly after Marie-Joseph-Rose's third birthday, one of the worst storms in the memory of the islanders had swept Martinique. This, followed by an earthquake, had destroyed the Tascher sugar plantation and partially demolished the original house. With this disaster, the family had taken up residence in the undamaged refinery—a residence which, in consequence of the decline in the Tascher fortunes, had become permanent.

Entering the house and ascending to the first floor, Marie-Joseph-Rose found her father and mother on the gallery which had been erected along the southern side of the building. Her father, waving an opened letter in his hand, was pacing up and down the gallery in evident agitation while her mother, as the girl could see at a glance, was on the point of tears. She shrugged philosophically. The creditors, quite obviously, were pressing poor Papa once again, and this time, no doubt, a little more insistently than usual.

"To argue," Madame Tascher said sadly, "is of no avail. You can do nothing, Joseph, but reply to the Marquis de Beauharnais's letter at once and tell him that had Catherine-Désirée not died of the fever a marriage between her and his son would have given us the greatest pleasure in the world."

"Bah!" Monsieur Tascher exclaimed, "the thought of missing such a splendid opportunity is more than I can bear."

In a moment, her mind working rapidly, Marie-Joseph-Rose had grasped the full significance of what she had heard. She stepped forward eagerly.

"As far as I can see, Papa," she cried, "there's no reason in the world why the opportunity *should* be missed!"

Her father and mother looked at her in silence and she added triumphantly: "Papa, let *me* take poor little Catherine-Désirée's place. Let *me* go to France to marry the marquis's son."

"You have the look of a Paris street urchin," her father said. "Go to your room and, in the name of heaven, find yourself a dress that is at least clean."

"But Papa——!"

"You will do as I order, Yeyette."

The use of the stupid pet name brought a tinge of angry color to the girl's cheeks. She folded her arms stubbornly.

"Please listen to me, Papa," she pleaded. "I'm no longer a child. I'm sixteen, and what difference could it possibly make to the marquis's son, whether I take her place or not?"

"Alexandre was born in Martinique," Monsieur Tascher said. "As a child he played with you and your sisters. Undoubtedly he will remember Catherine-Désirée."

"Oh come," Madame Tascher protested, "she was only a baby when Alexandre was taken home to France."

Tascher ceased his agitated pacing and stared at his wife thoughtfully. What difference indeed would such a substitution make to the young man? And in any case— But his next thought was voiced by Marie-Joseph-Rose herself.

"From what I've heard you say of Aunt Marie she regulates the life of the Marquis de Beauharnais to so great an extent that if *she* decides that I am to marry Alexandre the marriage will be an accomplished fact."

Her mother smiled happily. "Yeyette is perfectly correct."

Tascher smiled also, but not so happily. "The child is, as you say, perfectly correct, but unfortunately the young man himself has already declared her too old."

"Too *old*, Papa?" Marie-Joseph-Rose exclaimed. "But how extraordinary!"

Tascher picked up his sister's letter, which he had dropped, and glanced through it quickly.

"By 'too old,'" he went on, "I mean too near his own age. Your aunt discussed you yourself, Catherine-Désirée and Marie-Françoise with Alexandre. You, he said, were too old; Marie-Françoise was too young, but Catherine-Désirée was just the right age." A new thought struck him. "One moment! Marie-Françoise, too young at the moment, will naturally grow. After all, need a marriage take place immediately?"

"Your sister," his wife reminded him, "stresses the point that the sooner it takes place the better."

"Well, yes," he was forced to admit, "she does."

"There's only one thing to be said," Marie-Joseph-Rose declared with decision, "Alexandre de Beauharnais must marry me."

Her father chuckled. He tapped her playfully on the cheek.

"You rogue," he laughed, "I do believe you're right!"

"My dear Joseph," his wife reminded him tartly, "the decision is hardly yours to make."

"No," he agreed, "only one person can make it, my sister Marie. I shall write to her at once and within three months, or possibly less——"

"I shall be on my way to France," Marie-Joseph-Rose concluded.

Tascher tapped her playfully again. "We shall see, little Yeyette, we shall see."

* * * * *

Lying on her back Marie-Joseph-Rose could see the moon through a gap in the topmost branches of the trees. A beautiful sight, but how much more beautiful if the moon were riding in the sky of Paris instead of that of Martinique! She glanced at Tercier. He was lying with his elbows planted firmly in the ground and his chin cupped in his upturned palms. Was Alexandre de Beauharnais as handsome as he? Not that it mattered, of course, for even if Alexandre were the ugliest young man in the world there would be many compensations. He was, to begin with, a vicomte. "Madame la Vicomtesse. . . ." She framed the words with her lips without actually uttering them. And in addition, or so her father had assured her, he enjoyed an income of forty thousand livres a year. Forty thousand! That indeed was riches!

Tercier laughed suddenly.

"Queen of France!" he cried, derisively.

"You may jeer," she said, with dignity, "but Marion has every faith in the prediction."

"Then why this eagerness," he muttered sulkily, "to marry Alexandre de Beauharnais? He's only a vicomte, isn't he? What possibility is there of a vicomte's wife becoming a queen?"

"Alexandre will be a marquis some day," she retorted.

"Nonsense. He's only a younger son, isn't he?"

"His elder brother will undoubtedly die."

"Even a marquise has little chance of becoming a queen."

"The fates have decreed it," she insisted, resisting the temptation to shake him. "I shall become the Queen of France. I know it. I *believe* it."

"And what will that profit you, m'm'selle, if you die in sorrow and lose your crown?"

She rose to a sitting position and looked down at him with flashing eyes. "You're only jealous, Tercier—jealous because I'm going to France to marry Alexandre de Beauharnais."

"My poor little Rose," he said lazily, "your precious vicomte might decide in your sister's favor, or might even reject both of you."

"That isn't possible," she cried, regretting that she had confided in him so deeply, "not with Aunt Marie there to make up his mind for him!"

11

This thought, despite the alarm with which Tercier's words had filled her, did much to restore her dwindling confidence. Aunt Marie was a very clever woman. Both her father and mother had agreed on that. Some day she, Marie-Joseph-Rose, would model herself on Aunt Marie, would become just as clever, or cleverer; would learn how to gain power over men, how to gain it and wield it to the very greatest advantage. Madame la Vicomtesse de Beauharnais, *patronne* of a fashionable Parisian *salon*, possibly even a notorious court favorite. What little she remembered of history lessons came back to her vividly. A court favorite—a second Madame Pompadour, or perhaps a du Barry. Or why not—

"Tercier," she asked, not quite certain of her facts, "who was Madame de Maintenon?"

"The wife of a poet," he said, "until Louis the Fourteenth saw her and took her to court."

"She became his mistress?"

"Naturally. And later he was even stupid enough to marry her and make her queen."

"Ah!" That was all Marie-Joseph-Rose wanted to know.

"Louis the Sixteenth," Tercier said indulgently, "a fool in many things, will never prove himself as capable of setting up mistresses as his famous ancestor."

"That," she said curtly, "remains to be seen."

Tercier sat up abruptly and pulled her roughly towards him. She averted her face with a gesture of distaste and made to rise to her feet. The pressure of his hands on her shoulders forced her down again. She felt the weight of his body above her and the warmth of his breath on her face. She tried to turn her head away again, but without success. His lips brushed hotly against her own, and so harshly that she felt the sharp edge of his teeth. His breath, she noticed, was heavy and labored. A giggle escaped her, and then she began to shake with suppressed laughter. He released her quickly and sat back on his haunches.

"That," he said sulkily, "is worse than laughing in church."

"But I often laugh in church," she cried, "especially when——"

"Bah," he said, "bah!"

Impulsively she took his hands in hers. "I'm sorry, Tercier, really I am."

He leaned forward eagerly.

"No, no," she protested. "You will only make me laugh again."

He rose to his feet and looked down at her moodily. "What a queer girl you are, Rose. When you bathed with me this morning, and then asked me to meet you here tonight, I naturally thought——"

"You naturally thought I was ready to become your mistress."

"Of course I did!"

"Perhaps I was," she said, reflectively, "but between this morning and tonight so much has happened. The fortune-telling, the news from Paris— Quite obviously," she concluded sententiously, "my virtue is something that can hardly be sacrificed so lightly, *now*."

"Your virtue?" His voice rose on a note of surprise. "Would you have me believe that any Creole girl of sixteen is still a virgin?"

"I don't think even *one* of my friends is," she said candidly, "and that was why, when I met you a week ago, and asked you to meet me here tonight—but as I say, between this morning and tonight——"

"But surely," he broke in quickly, "a girl who is determined to become a court favorite would have a greater chance of success if—" He kneeled at her side again. "I do assure you," he said earnestly, and not without a touch of adolescent pride, "that I have the reputation of being a most proficient lover."

She pursed her lips. His argument, in all conscience, was a reasonable one, and her curiosity, stimulated from time to time by the whispered stories of her friends, was undeniably strong. She placed her hands behind her head and stretched languorously.

"Sweetheart—" he whispered hoarsely.

His breath, warm on her face again, was heavier and more labored than before. Fearing that she might laugh a second time she sprang to her feet and struck a dignified attitude.

"I thank you for your offer," she said, "but coming as it does from a mere *sous-lieutenant*, how can I, a future queen of France, accept it?"

CHAPTER III

ONCE AGAIN ALEXANDRE, Vicomte de Beauharnais, stood before his father and Madame Renaudin in the library at Noisy-le-Grand. He had arrived only that morning from Paris where he had been spending several weeks with the Duc de la Rochefoucauld, whose two nephews, the de Rohan boys, were his closest friends.

"Is that a new uniform you're wearing?" the marquis asked.

"Yes, Father."

Alexandre squared his shoulders and threw out his chest. At the age of fifteen, through the influence of de la Rochefoucauld, he had become a *sous-lieutenant* in one of the household regiments of the King. The position being of greater significance socially than militarily, he had seen little of actual army life, and what little he had experienced had appealed to him scarcely at all.

"The uniform," said Madame Renaudin, who was looking at him in amusement, "of a full lieutenant. Or am I mistaken?"

Alexandre bowed stiffly. "Of a full lieutenant, madame. M'sieur le Duc has been gracious enough to arrange my promotion." He turned to his father. "You think the uniform smart?"

"Who made it for you?" the marquis asked cautiously.

"Remadier, of course."

"Ah, one of the best military tailors in Paris. Without hesitation I can say that I think it *very* smart." The marquis laughed gently at his own joke for a moment, then he grew grave. "Alexandre, bad news has reached us from Martinique. Madame Renaudin's niece, Catherine-Désirée, is dead. Indeed, poor child, the fever had carried her off before my letter left France."

"Naturally," Madame Renaudin said briskly, before Alexandre had time to make any comment, "neither your father nor I expect you to be very deeply affected by the death of a girl you only knew as a child and scarcely remember, though of course——"

"Ah, but madame," he broke in smoothly, "if only because of the love and affection I feel for you, the poor child's aunt, this news affects me a great deal more deeply than you might think."

Suspecting sarcasm beneath these courteous words, Madame Renaudin looked at him sharply. His face was expressionless, his eyes were downcast.

"I shall write to Martinique at once," he added, "and commiserate with the bereaved father."

"That would be a touching gesture," she said drily.

At this point the marquis took a hand himself. "The situation, my boy, is not entirely hopeless. It is true, you have lost one prospective bride but there remain two others."

Alexandre, who had been waiting for this, made no reply.

"There remain," the marquis continued, "two singularly attractive young women, Marie-Joseph-Rose and Marie-Françoise."

"Am I to understand," Alexandre asked, with a hint of rising indignation, "that I am now asked to choose between Madame Renaudin's two remaining nieces?"

"Most certainly you are!"

"The choice is a difficult one, Father. If I am successfully to influence the mental development of my future wife she must be much the same age as Catherine-Désirée was." He sighed deeply. "I had set my heart on marrying Catherine-Désirée."

"You are trying to make things difficult, Alexandre!"

"No, Father. You misunderstand me."

"Perhaps," Madame Renaudin said quietly, "you will be able to make up your mind after a little thought."

"I very much doubt it, madame."

The marquis began to lose his temper. "Are you refusing to marry either of them, sir?"

"No, Father. I am not in a position to do that."

"Then you are being purposely blockheaded!"

Alexandre gave his father a pained look. "I merely find it impossible to make up my mind."

The marquis rose to his feet. "Then leave us, Alexandre, leave us and we will see what we can do about making it up for you."

For a moment Alexandre hesitated; then, with a scowl clouding his good-looking face, he left the room. Once again there was nothing he could do save submit, but the resolve to get the better of Madame Renaudin some day cemented itself more firmly in his mind.

With Alexandre out of the room the marquis turned to Madame Renaudin. "Well, my dear, which of the two girls do you choose for Alexandre?"

She laughed wryly. "I'm afraid I am rather at a loss myself. It would be much easier for us if he could take them both and have done with it."

"It certainly would!"

They laughed for a moment.

"Wait!" Madame Renaudin cried. "I have an idea!"

"A good one, I hope!"

"As good as any. Come, François, get pen and paper. We'll write to Martinique at once. Enough time has been wasted in this matter as it is."

* * * * *

Marion held the cup firmly to the girl's mouth.

"Come, M'm'selle Rose, it must be drained while hot, otherwise the quality of the mixture will be lost."

Marie-Joseph-Rose distended her nostrils and shuddered. The smell which rose from the mysterious brew, a smell both sickly and bitter, reminded her strongly of the stench which had risen from the body of the aged fortune-teller.

"Be resolute," the mulatto woman commanded. "Instead of sipping, take the draught at a single gulp."

The girl closed her eyes and opened her mouth. The cup was tilted forward. She spluttered and coughed. Save for the little dribbles that ran down each side of her mouth, she swallowed most of the nauseating liquid.

Marie-Françoise, a solemn child, asked in wonder: "Will it really make you thin, Yeyette?"

"Much of the fat has already gone," Marion said.

"Ah yes," Marie-Joseph-Rose wailed, "but at what a price. And not much of it, Marion, only a *little*."

She stripped off her old mousseline dress and slipped out of the worn chemise. Naked she stepped onto a little velvet-covered footstool.

"The mirror, Marion," she commanded.

Marion took the only mirror from the wall, oval in shape and less than three hand-spans in length. First the girl viewed her legs, then standing down from the stool, her torso, then finally, in a kneeling position, her shoulders and neck. That nowhere in the house could a larger mirror be found was a sign of poverty indeed, but in Paris—ah, in Paris one would insist on a boudoir the entire walls of which would be lined with mirrors.

"When I grow up," Marie-Françoise asked, pointing a steady finger, "will I have lumps on my chest like that?"

"Without doubt," Marion assured her, "though not such large ones, let us pray."

"Pig!" Marie-Joseph-Rose cried. "Large they may be, but firm too, with the nipples pointing upwards, whereas yours remind me of overripe mangoes that somebody has forgotten to pick."

"The bearing of many children," Marion said composedly, "will do the same to yours." She put the mirror back on the wall.

"Well, M'm'selle Rose, is it not the truth that I spoke?"

The girl pouted. "A little of the fat may be gone, but only because the taste of your wretched herbs, remaining in my mouth day after day, has prevented me from eating."

"And therein," Marion said sagely, "lies the secret."

The sound of hoof-beats brought a shout of excitement from Marie-Joseph-Rose.

"Papa!" she cried, and flew to the window.

She caught a glimpse of her father dismounting. He had left that morning for Fort-Royal, intending to spend a week there. His return the same day could only mean that the *Île de France* had reached Martinique in advance of her expected time, and that letters from Paris had been received.

She dressed hurriedly and was downstairs in time to throw herself at Tascher as he entered the house. Two opened letters were in his hand, but he refused to say more than: "From the marquis and your aunt," until he had joined his wife on the gallery.

"Papa, is it good news?" Marie-Joseph-Rose demanded.

He smiled at her eagerness. "It is more than that, *chérie*, it is excellent."

"Then I go to France!"

"Now, now, I didn't say that. *One* of my daughters goes to France, but which daughter has yet to be decided."

"What do you mean, Joseph?" his wife asked.

"It seems that neither the marquis, Alexandre nor Marie herself could make up their minds, so—" he laughed—"they have left it to me. The marquis has even sent me an order authorizing me to publish the banns here in Martinique, an order on which there is a blank space where the name of the bride should be. *I* have the privilege of filling in the name."

"That should be easy, Papa!" Marie-Joseph-Rose almost shouted. "You have only to take the order and write *my* name in the blank space!"

"It isn't as easy as you think, my dear. Alexandre wants a girl, a *young* girl, whose mind is flexible and adaptable enough to be trained along the lines he has in mind. You are too old for him; Marie-Françoise, on the other hand, is too young."

"And yet one of us must be chosen!"

"Yes, thanks to your aunt, one of you must be chosen."

"I promise you, Papa, that in spite of my age my mind will be flexible and adaptable enough to please Alexandre."

"I wish I could be sure of that. It would be wise, I think, for me to decide on Marie-Françoise."

Marie-Joseph-Rose sighed deeply and looked up at her father with soulful eyes.

"Poor little Marie-Françoise," she said softly.

"What in the name of heaven do you mean?"

"Marie-Françoise is so young, Papa—so much younger than her actual years. To be separated from Mama would kill her."

There was a pause. Tascher looked at his wife questioningly. Inspired still further Marie-Joseph-Rose added:

"Why, the poor little darling might die of grief before the ship reached France."

"Really, Rose," her mother said, "are you trying to frighten me?"

"No, Mama. I am trying to warn you, and Papa too. You both know what a sensitive child Marie-Françoise is."

By this time Madame Tascher was beginning to look thoroughly upset. In agitation she declared that Rose was right. Marie-Françoise *was* a sensitive child and, as Rose said, much younger than her actual years.

"Rose," Tascher said tartly, "is a cunning little devil. In spite of what she says I'm going to write Marie-Françoise's name in the blank space."

Marie-Joseph-Rose caught her breath and looked down at the floor. Two big tears splashed over her cheeks. With a sob she said: "Oh, Papa, if only you knew what you're doing. Poor little Marie-Françoise, she will be desolated. I only hope you'll be able to forgive yourself if your decision is the cause of her death."

"Nonsense, she isn't going to die."

"We hope not, Papa. We pray not!"

"My mind is made up," he said weakly. "Tears are wasted on me."

"These tears are not for myself, Papa. They are for my poor little sister. Oh, Papa, think well, think well!"

"Yes," Madame Tascher implored, tears rolling down her own cheeks, "think well, Joseph, think well. If I should lose Marie-Françoise after having lost Catherine-Désirée I—I think I should die also."

For a moment mother and daughter wept in unison, Marie-Joseph-Rose none the less watching her father's face warily out of the corner of her eye. Presently he made an impatient gesture and appeared to curse under his breath.

"You are behaving with the utmost foolishness, both of you, but perhaps there is something in what you say. Come, dry your eyes. Marie-Françoise shall remain in Martinique; Marie-Joseph-Rose shall go to France."

"You give your word, Papa?"

"I give my solemn word." He looked at his wife and daughter in disgust. "For the love of heaven, must you *still* weep? Bah! This is no place for a man, two females flooding the room with tears!" And with quick steps he left the room.

After a moment Madame Tascher blew her nose and turned to her daughter.

"Have you quite finished, Rose?"

"Y-yes, Mama."

"Splendid. I want to tell you something. You weep with a grace that is quite irresistible."

Marie-Joseph-Rose smiled in delight. "Do I really, Mama?"

"Irresistible, I mean, to men," her mother added. "It might be worth your while to remember it."

"You suggest that it might be a useful weapon where men are concerned?"

"You understand me perfectly, Rose. Nevertheless I should advise you not to use the weapon too frequently with the same man." Madame Tascher rose from her chair. "And now, my dear, I think we had better begin our preparations for your voyage to France."

CHAPTER IV

M ARIE-JOSEPH-ROSE STOOD on the foredeck of the *Île de France* with the captain and stared intently at the horizon.

"It isn't just a cloud?" she asked. "It really *is* the coast of France?"

The captain smiled. "No, M'm'selle Rose, it isn't just a cloud. It really is the coast of France."

"When do we arrive?"

"Before nightfall you'll step ashore at Brest."

"Thank heaven for that," she murmured.

She would never have thought it possible that the sea could make anybody so ill. Day after day she had lain in the bunk in agony, afraid to sit up, and when actually doing so on the rare occasions she had attempted to take a little nourishment, afraid to lie down again. And poor Papa! Even now, when most people had struggled to the deck for their first glimpse of France, he was still too ill to move. What a mercy it had not been possible for Mama to make the journey too!

She looked again at the hazy outline of the land on the horizon which was France. Brest before nightfall! Brest within a few short hours, Paris itself within a few short days! No, what was the matter with her geography—Paris within two days at least! Paris, not only the city of her dreams, but the greatest city in the world!

Unhappily for her hopes it was discovered, on disembarking at Brest, that her father was too ill to set out at once for Paris. Accordingly father and daughter found accommodation at a gaunt and dismal hotel and a letter was dispatched to Madame Renaudin in Paris. A week later, for it was winter and the road was almost impassable in parts, a reply was received announcing that the marquis, Alexandre and Madame Renaudin intended to leave for Brest without delay, but another week passed before they arrived.

In the half-light of the late afternoon Marie-Joseph-Rose, peering between the drawn curtains of her window, watched the coach draw up. First a lady with a very straight back and an imperious manner was handed down—Aunt Marie, undoubtedly! Then an elderly gentleman with a stoop, and so stiff that he had to be assisted by the porters—the Marquis de Beauharnais, surely! And finally, after Aunt Marie had turned and looked back into the interior of the coach, a slender young man, who sprang out and strode forward without a backward glance. The girl's heart missed a beat. Alex-

19

andre? She hoped not, for there was something about his attitude that made her tremble with apprehension.

The meeting between Tascher and his sister Marie was cordial, each congratulating the other in Marie-Joseph-Rose's presence on the unexpected smoothness with which the marriage plans had so far progressed. The marquis and his son, it seemed, had gone straight to their rooms to make themselves presentable.

When mutual greetings were over Tascher looked inquiringly and a trifle anxiously at his sister.

"You—approve of your niece, I hope, Marie?"

Marie-Joseph-Rose was subjected to a critical scrutiny under which, unaccountably, she quailed and finally, in a fit of sheer nervousness, began to giggle. She saw her father's face freeze with horror and then, searching desperately for some reasonable explanation for her conduct, she found her eyes resting on the most amazing sight in the world, the massive, towering structure that was Aunt Marie's hat.

"Forgive me, Aunt Marie," she spluttered, "but your *hat!*"

Madame Renaudin's face broke into a smile. "When I wore it for the first time and saw myself in the mirror I too, I must confess, was inclined to a similar mirth. Fortunately we traveled in a large coach, otherwise I couldn't possibly have worn it. Come, child, help me remove it."

Still giggling, Marie-Joseph-Rose obeyed the command.

"Carefully," Madame Renaudin cautioned, "carefully."

With the delicate operation completed and the hat standing erect on a table, the girl was able to make a close inspection. It was like a model of some fantastic building, three stories in height, with miniature flower-pots in the 'windows' of each story, while the flat 'roof' of the third story was thick with tropical shrubs, clinging to the branches of which were exotic birds and—yes, and tiny monkeys!

"An English fashion," Madame Renaudin commented, "the very latest, I understand, in London, but with certain modifications which, being French, are naturally in better taste."

"Formidable," Tascher murmured.

Madame Renaudin was looking at her niece again.

"Child," she said, "is that the smartest dress you have?"

"Perhaps not the smartest, Aunt Marie, but certainly the warmest."

"Yeyette," Tascher told his sister, "is finding France the coldest country in the world."

"Let me see your other dresses," Madame Renaudin commanded.

After a moment's hesitation Marie-Joseph-Rose obeyed.

Madame Renaudin gave an exclamation of surprise. "You have

but three in all? These two and the impossible gown you are wearing now?"

The girl bit her lip and tears sprang to her eyes.

"My circumstances," Tascher explained quietly, "made the purchase of a new wardrobe impossible. In order to cover the expenses of the journey it was necessary for me to sell my best slaves. Fortunately slaves are bringing a high price in Martinique at the moment, otherwise—" and he shrugged eloquently.

Madame Renaudin was fingering the thin material of Marie-Joseph-Rose's white mousseline. "You should have let me know, Joseph. The marquis is rich. Ample provision could easily have been made." She turned to her niece. "Underclothes are scarcely important, but have you many?"

"Three shifts only, Aunt Marie, and four petticoats. One of the petticoats," the girl added quickly, "is silk."

"Let me see them."

Marie-Joseph-Rose lifted the hem of her dress. "The weather is so cold, Aunt Marie——"

"I understand. With the exception of these two pitiful little dresses, your entire wardrobe is on your back."

The girl bit her lip again but was quite unable to stop the tears from flowing.

"Oh come, child," Madame Renaudin said gently, "the fault is hardly yours. I myself shall buy you a complete new wardrobe before the wedding."

"I take it," Tascher said, "that whatever you may think of her clothes, you do approve of the girl herself."

"Well, yes, but in appearance she is a great deal older than I expected."

"Girls mature quickly in Martinique. She is very like you at the same age."

Madame Renaudin brushed the intended compliment aside with a laugh. "I should be deceiving myself if I claimed that my skin was ever as good as hers." She took her niece by the shoulders and spun her round. "A lovely skin, my dear. So soft to touch, and so white. But heavens, your mature appearance. You look at least two years older than your actual age."

The girl made a wry face and thought, with a touch of regret, of the young *sous-lieutenant*, Tercier. "Really, but this is the first time my maturity has been held against me."

Madame Renaudin laughed with understanding. "I'm sure it is, my dear Rose. However, the main thing to guard against is the betrayal of *mental* maturity. Alexandre, you see, has decided that it is his mission in life to influence your mental development. He has, I understand, a plan. You are to be *trained*."

"I know how to say 'yes' when 'yes' is required," the niece said demurely, "and 'no' when 'no' is required."

The older woman laughed drily. "Alexandre will require much more than 'yes' and 'no.' His intention, I suspect, is to set you lessons and then question you deeply on what you have learned."

"*Lessons*, Aunt Marie?"

"Your future husband, my dear, has a flair for philosophy, history, geography, and heaven alone knows what else. At the moment he is deep in a study of the essays of Montaigne."

"Montaigne!" Tascher echoed, with a laugh.

"Yes," his sister assured him, with a shudder, "Montaigne."

"Poor little Yeyette," he said, half-seriously.

Marie-Joseph-Rose merely shrugged. It looked as if she were going to marry a school teacher and that she would need to be merely a good pupil. What an extraordinary young man Alexandre must be, and how different from Tercier! Ah well, aided by her 'lovely skin,' she would be able to change all that.

As if reading her thoughts, Madame Renaudin remarked: "Let me warn you not to thrust your feminine charm on Alexandre too suddenly. And now, before you meet him, which of your three dresses would be the most suitable?"

"Perhaps the white mousseline?" Marie-Joseph-Rose suggested. "I look my best in white, and——"

"If by that you mean 'more virginal,' by all means the white mousseline. Come now! Alexandre, who sulked during the entire journey, will be growing impatient. Quickly, child, let me help you change—"

*　　*　　*　　*　　*

Alexandre stood back from the mirror and clicked his heels sharply together.

"Yes," he said, "an excellent choice."

He had changed from his traveling clothes into the new dress uniform which he had worn once only, during a recent visit to the Tuileries with the Duc de la Rochefoucauld. He particularly liked the silver-grey facings of the white tunic.

He turned to the marquis. "You agree, Father?"

"The tunic is excellent, but—" here the marquis frowned—"surely the breeches are a little *too* tight?"

"His Majesty himself," Alexandre reproved, "has set the fashion for the tightest of tight breeches."

"Well, providing no very great strain is placed upon them——"

"You like the new shade, I hope?"

"Ah, so it's a new shade, is it? I thought it was merely dark plum."

"A brownish purple, really. The court has decreed that it shall be known as—er—flea's belly."

The marquis flinched. "Really, my boy!"

"An unusual name, you must admit, Father," Alexandre said, haughtily.

"Unusual indeed. Is one permitted to ask the reason for the court's remarkable decree?"

"It came about this way," Alexandre explained, with a lack of humor that was in itself amusing. "His Majesty, while at the Italian opera some weeks ago, complained of a most distressing irritation. He was even seen, on several occasions, to scratch himself violently. Later that night, in the royal bedchamber, the gentleman in attendance was horrified to discover a flea of amazingly large proportions. He was about to—er—crack it between his thumbnails when His Majesty stopped him. 'What a delightful shade,' the King said. 'Call Her Majesty and have the Court tailor summoned immediately.'"

"Well, well," was all the marquis could say, and very weakly.

"And so," Alexandre concluded, "the new shade was—er—perpetuated." He turned from the mirror abruptly. "How much longer do we have to wait to be formally introduced to Madame Renaudin's niece?"

"Patience, my boy, patience," the marquis said archly. "The longer you wait for a glimpse of the young lady the greater will be your delight when the moment comes."

"I sincerely hope so!" Alexandre snapped.

"You don't sound very sure of it, Alexandre!"

"How *can* I be sure of it, Father? All we have been told of Madame Renaudin's niece seems very much to her credit, but that is no guarantee that I shall like her."

The marquis made a weak gesture. "Alexandre, if you're going to take up a pigheaded attitude at this stage——"

"I have only one wish," Alexandre interrupted coldly, "and that is to please you, but you must admit that one cannot answer for two people who have never met liking each other." He paused and then added: "No one would regret more than I that the young lady and her father should have made the journey to France in vain."

"Enough of this nonsense, Alexandre!" the marquis stormed. "The marriage has been arranged. Whether you like the girl or not you are going to marry her. Do you understand?"

"The marriage would never have been arranged," Alexandre pointed out, "had it not been for Madame Renaudin. You know that as well as I——"

"Silence, Alexandre!"

"Much as I respect my godmother," Alexandre went on unheedingly, "I cannot restrain myself from drawing your attention to the fact that at times she appears to take complete control of your affairs."

The marquis sprang to his feet. "How dare you, sir!"

"I merely feel it my duty, Father, to——"

"Silence! Silence, sir!"

Alexandre sighed. "Very well, Father."

There was a pause, and then the marquis, feeling called upon to defend himself a little, made a number of laudatory comments on the sterling qualities of his mistress.

"Madame Renaudin," he wound up, "is a very dear friend and a constant source of—er—of help to me. If she should seem to take command of my affairs from time to time she does so with my heartiest approval. You understand?"

Alexandre looked at the ceiling. "Yes, Father."

"She is a clever woman," the marquis added warmly, "with an uncommonly fine head for business, an uncommonly fine head indeed!"

Alexandre was still looking at the ceiling.

"You should deem yourself fortunate," the marquis declared, "to be marrying her niece."

Alexandre examined his finger-nails. "Yes, Father."

"If, even in the slightest degree, the niece grows to resemble the aunt, you will be able to count yourself among the happiest of young husbands."

"Yes, Father."

"The *happiest* of young husbands!"

Alexandre repressed a yawn. "Yes, Father."

With this last monotonous repetition the marquis lost his temper. "In the name of heaven, Alexandre, is that all you can say, '*Yes, Father*'?"

Alexandre looked at the ceiling again. "Yes, Father."

* * * * *

"You find it satisfactory, Aunt Marie?"

Marie-Joseph-Rose had changed into the white mousseline and stood stiffly, and a little awkwardly, before her aunt.

24

"It robs you of a little of your maturity," Madame Renaudin admitted, "but not as much as one might have hoped."

"Perhaps if we took it in here," the girl said gravely, "and let it out *here*, it might rob me of a little more."

"It might," Madame Renaudin laughed, "but we haven't time for that."

Marie-Joseph-Rose laughed quietly. Doubtless it was just as well they hadn't. She had no real wish to look flat-chested, even for Alexandre, who would inevitably discover the truth and quite possibly blame her for having tried to deceive him.

"What a strange young man he is," she remarked. "Is he a woman-hater?"

Madame Renaudin laughed drily. "Dear me, no, otherwise he would never have been received at court. It is only because you're to be his wife, rather than his mistress, that he wants you young, childish and unsophisticated. Take my advice, my dear, make the best you can of his strangeness and remember that he is a vicomte with the handsome income of forty thousand livres a year."

The girl nodded wisely. "That has been kept well in mind from the first, Aunt Marie." Then she laughed gaily. "Perhaps if I could cultivate a slightly empty expression it would help the white mousseline. Something like this, for instance!"

She did her best to drain her face of all animation, but Madame Renaudin raised her hands in horror and declared that an expression of that sort was quite idiotic and would frighten Alexandre away.

"However," she said, "if you could blush now and again and make your conversation slightly confused and school-girlish, you might impress him deeply."

Marie-Joseph-Rose nodded eagerly. "And as a last resort I could burst into tears. I assure you, Aunt Marie, I cry most appealingly. Mama once told me that my tears would always be a useful weapon when dealing with men."

Madame Renaudin laughed drily. "A useful weapon when dealing with *some* men—men like the marquis, for instance—but you would have to cry very skilfully indeed if you wanted to move Alexandre."

"We shall see," the girl said confidently.

"Yes, my dear, we shall see. But come, we have talked enough. I must take you to Alexandre. Give me your arm and cling to me nervously. And look down—look down and for heaven's sake do your very best to blush."

With Tascher bringing up the rear the little procession moved out of the room. Unable to blush when the formal introduction was made, Marie-Joseph-Rose succeeded in looking confused. She also clung shyly to her aunt and was wise enough to laugh nervously when that resourceful lady said teasingly: "Come, come, child, it's no use trying to hide behind my skirts." Nevertheless the nervousness of her laugh was not entirely feigned, for Alexandre, in spite of his youthfulness, had such an elderly look. He held himself so stiffly, too, and the faint smile which crossed his face for a moment was that of a soldier unbending against his will in a lady's drawing room. And then there was the dazzling splendor of his attire which, humbling her, made her feel like a very poor relation from the provinces.

"You must forgive my niece," Madame Renaudin said, "if she appears speechless. She is not, as you must have guessed, accustomed to meeting strange young men."

Alexandre inclined his head graciously. "I trust you enjoyed a pleasant voyage, m'm'selle."

"It was a wretched voyage," Madame Renaudin replied, determined to maintain her niece's speechlessness as long as possible. "So wretched that she nearly died."

Alexandre inclined his head again. "The sea can be most unkind."

"Rose," Madame Renaudin said sharply, "must I tell you again not to hide behind my skirts?" She turned to Alexandre with a challenging smile. "Such a shy creature, but then, that is only natural in one so young and inexperienced."

"Quite," he agreed drily.

"You must try to forgive her, Alexandre, if you find her a trifle gauche."

"But of course."

The conversation became general and Marie-Joseph-Rose was able to study her prospective father-in-law, the marquis. She liked him instantly. His softly spoken greeting and his gentle encouraging smile put her at her ease, and she wondered, looking from him to Alexandre, how he had come to have such a son. There was a slight family resemblance, certainly, but one could see at a glance that that was all they had in common.

Presently, with her father and the marquis deep in conversation, and at Madame Renaudin's suggestion, Alexandre offered Marie-Joseph-Rose his arm and led her to the balcony of the room from which, according to Madame Renaudin, an excellent view of the coast could be obtained.

On the balcony an awkward silence was broken by Alexandre who said, surprisingly enough: "Permit me to remark, m'm'selle, that I find the simplicity of your dress most becoming."

She made him a clumsy little bow. "Thank you, m'sieur."

At first she had thought him handsome and a little like Tercier, but now, catching a glimpse of his face in profile she was strongly reminded of a ferret. And his voice, there was an edge to it which filled her with an unaccountable misgiving.

"It would be just as well," he said, "if we dispensed with the formal 'm'sieur' and 'm'm'selle.' I shall call you Rose; you may call me Alexandre."

"Just as you wish—Alexandre."

"You may, of course, prefer me to call you Marie."

"No, I always liked Rose better than Marie, and the pet name Papa uses, Yeyette, I hate with all my heart."

There was another awkward silence, during which Alexandre stared slowly and deliberately at this colonial girl whom Madame Renaudin had decided he was to marry. He wondered why he had made the remark about the simplicity of her dress, which was in reality impossible and proclaimed the poverty of her father with a blatancy which was almost indecent. His eyes travelled down to her shoes, the worn cloth tips of which were just visible beneath the hem of the dress, then up again to linger for an uncertain moment on the full round contours of her breasts—she was much too old, much too *mature*!—till they came to rest on her face and hair. The eyes, meeting his for a moment before they wavered and fell, were certainly remarkable—if the king were to see them a new shade of blue would become the latest fashion immediately!—but the hair, hanging loosely about her face and over her shoulders, was unfit to be seen, even in the privacy of a boudoir. He must speak to Madame Renaudin. If not a fashionable head-dress, surely at very least a modest *pouf*! He pulled himself up sharply. His chief concern was her mental capacity, not her physical appearance.

"Madame Renaudin tells me that you are fond of music," he said.

"Oh yes, very fond, and—and I play the guitar a little."

"The *guitar*?" he echoed, in a pained voice. "But surely such an instrument is a little barbaric?"

With this she saw an opportunity to convince him of her ignorance.

"You will probably think me very lacking in education," she murmured, "but what does 'barbaric' mean?"

"You mean you don't really know?"

"I'm afraid I don't, Alexandre."

"My dear child," he said, almost in delight, "it means rude and un-civilized. Er—not in the best of taste. Lacking in refinement. Yes, especially lacking in refinement."

"Thank you," she said gravely, as if memorizing the little lesson. "I will do my best to remember." She looked down and sighed gently. "You will have to be patient with me. You see, I haven't had the advantage of an education in France, like you."

She looked at him out of the corner of her eye to see how this was being received, and concluded by the smile now flooding his face that it was being very well received indeed.

"Oh, I shall never hold that against you," he said benevolently. "I prefer you to be uneducated. And by the way, you said, 'I haven't had the advantage of an education in France, like you.' It would be more correct to say—'an education in France, *such as you have had.*' Please try to remember."

"*Such as you have had,*" she repeated solemnly.

"You will please me very much if you take care in these small matters," he went on, almost genially, "for I value correctness of speech very highly. But come, tell me about the little education you succeeded in gaining in Martinique. You attended some local convent, of course?"

"Yes. The Convent des Dames de la Providence."

"That was the extent of your education?" he asked anxiously. "There was no private tutor?"

She nodded her head to the first part of his question and shook it to the second.

"Dear me, dear me!" His delight was unmistakable. "Well, so much the better. You will have all the less to unlearn. What did they teach you at the convent, apart from music?"

She contracted her brows in an effort to remember, an effort entirely unfeigned.

"There was religious instruction, naturally, and a little history and geography, some singing and—oh yes, Alexandre, and dancing."

"Dancing?" His voice rose in amusement. "Dancing, my dear Rose, in a *convent*?"

"But why not?" she asked in surprise.

"Such freedom," he laughed, "such license! What else did they teach you? English, perhaps, and Italian?"

"Oh no, there was only French grammar," and she refrained from adding, "fortunately." She looked at him with big eyes. "You speak different languages yourself, Alexandre?"

He smiled indulgently. "I flatter myself that I speak English moderately well."

"How clever you are!" she breathed.

"I merely happen to have a flair for study," he said negligently.

"How splendid," she said earnestly, "to meet a young man who takes life seriously like you."

"It would be more correct," he said gently, "to say—*as you do.*"

"As you do," she repeated, obediently. And then, her zeal getting the better of her, she almost made a serious slip. "None of the young men I ever met in Martinique was in the least studious."

"You knew many young men there?" he asked, in a tone that warned her instantly.

"Hardly any at all," she said quickly.

"You had no childish love-affairs?"

"I——"

She stopped, inhaled her breath quickly, and held it. She felt herself growing hot and wondered if the trick would succeed. Alexandre, at any rate, was looking at her curiously.

"Is anything the matter?" And then he smiled. "Why, my dear, you're blushing. I must have embarrassed you. Pray forgive me."

Looking down to hide her satisfaction, she murmured, "I was too young to be interested in anything like that, Alexandre."

"But of course. Nothing could be more obvious!"

"I was too young to even have a thought for young men."

He took her hands in his. "My dear Rose, never say 'to even have.' It is most incorrect. You should say, 'too young to have even a thought for young men,' or 'too young even to have a thought for young men.' "

"Yes, Alexandre," she said faintly.

"Never, whatever you do, separate the verb from its infinitive. 'To even have' is a split infinitive. You quite understand?"

"Quite, Alexandre."

He released her hands, gave her cheek a little pat and suggested that it was time to rejoin the others, but first he made her a little speech.

"I can see that there are many things which you will have to learn, but you may rest assured that I will do everything within my power to teach you. Your education has been sadly neglected." He smiled happily. "We may even say that there has been no education at all. However, if I am zealous enough, and patient enough, it will not be too long before that lamentable fact is partially remedied."

Marie-Joseph-Rose listened in silence. At the end of it all she was too overcome even to murmur a polite 'Thank you.' At times during this interview she had found it difficult not to laugh, but now she found it difficult not to burst into tears.

*　　　*　　　*　　　*　　　*

That night, before he retired to bed, Alexandre made another and even more pompous speech, this time to his father.

"Yes, Father, I think I am satisfied with what little I have seen of Madame Renaudin's niece. She is not exactly pretty, but on the whole there is something appealing and promising about her."

29

He squared his shoulders and went on. "Her education has been shockingly neglected, and I am greatly distressed at the vacancy of her mind. However, after a few months of association with me she will, I believe, show a marked improvement. I have decided to marry her, Father, if only for the satisfaction which I shall find in supervising her education."

It would seem that for the moment he had forgotten his resentment, his resolve to get the better of Madame Renaudin. As for the marquis, he could only stare at his son in amazement and silently repeat the words he had uttered earlier in the day to the effect that there was something a little inhuman in the boy's attitude.

'Poor little Rose,' he thought, 'if this marriage brings her unhappiness I shall never be able to forgive myself.'

CHAPTER V

"AND WHAT," SAID MADame Renaudin, "is this?"

Her sharp eyes had fastened themselves on the small packet which was among the few belongings Marie-Joseph-Rose had brought with her from Martinique, and now, fingering it curiously, she held it in her hands. The girl blushed in confusion and remained silent. With a shrug Madame Renaudin opened it.

"Why, it looks like dried grass," she said. "Some native herb, perhaps?"

Marie-Joseph-Rose nodded. "Marion insisted on my bringing it. One pours boiling water over it and drinks it while it is still hot."

"In heaven's name why?"

"In order to reduce one's weight, Aunt Marie. Marion considered me too fat, and I thought that if Alexandre was displeased with my figure——"

"Too fat?" Madame Renaudin cried. "Nonsense! Thinness, I admit, was fashionable until very recently, but the men never liked it. The new style in dresses, as you must have noticed yourself, is designed to make thin women look plump. The best thing you can do is throw away your silly herbs and forget them."

Marie-Joseph-Rose smiled happily. "Nothing could please me more. The brew has a most nauseating flavor."

A week had now passed since the arrival in Paris where the girl and her father were guests at the marquis's house in the rue Thévenot, and where they would remain until the marriage ceremony, which was to take place quietly in the parish church at Noisy-le-Grand.

Paris! It was still difficult for Marie-Joseph-Rose to believe that she had actually reached this city about which she had dreamed so much, and impossible for her to believe that the rue Thévenot, close to the rue Saint-Denis, was situated in one of the most fashionable quarters of Paris. She would never forget her first glimpse of the house. The arrival had been at night after an uncomfortable journey over rough and often snow-bound roads. Half asleep she had been assisted from the coach into a house which seemed like a veritable dream palace. Servants, moving swiftly over thickly carpeted floors, had sprung up everywhere with candles, while the two massive chandeliers in the impressive dining-hall had already been lighted in anticipation of the little party's arrival. The next day, when she had gained her first real glimpse of Paris, she had realized that her dream palace was one of the smaller houses of the district, but the first impression had remained and she still felt that her feet, poorly shod as they were, had been firmly placed on the first step of the magic stairway which was to lead her to the Tuileries itself.

A servant entered the room and stood waiting for permission to speak.

"Well?" Madame Renaudin said.

He bowed respectfully. "The carriage is waiting, madame."

Excitement rose in Marie-Joseph-Rose's breast and caught her by the throat. This meant another expedition to the amazing shops of Paris. Already a dozen visits had been made to dressmakers, milliners and hosiers, where countless consultations and fittings had taken place with bewildering rapidity.

"Where do we go today, Aunt Marie?" she asked.

"The dressmaker's, my dear."

"But surely," the girl demurred, "enough dresses have been ordered already."

"By no means, and we completely forgot the riding-dress. I particularly want to see you in that new English style, 'The Amazon,' I think they call it. I myself would look ridiculous wearing it, especially with that long pig-tail down my back, but on you it will look most becoming."

Marie-Joseph-Rose had seen 'The Amazon' only that morning. A haughty young woman attended by two grooms had ridden down the rue Thévenot wearing a little hat with high feathers, a long tight skirt, a fancy waistcoat covered in bright buttons and an overcoat cut sharply away over the hips. " 'The Amazon,' " one of the maids had told her, and when Marie-Joseph-Rose had laughed at the long and ridiculous pig-tail, the girl had said: "It is Madame la

Duchesse de Bourbon at whom m'm'selle laughs." Marie-Joseph-Rose had been suitably awed, but still, the pig-tail, thick as a man's wrist at the top and tapering down to nothing in the small of the Bourbon back. . . .

"Aunt Marie," she frowned, "my own hair is too thin for such a formidable pig-tail."

"Naturally, and so is any woman's. The hairdresser will provide you with the necessary false hair. Come now, the carriage is waiting and so, my child, am I!"

*　　*　　*　　*　　*

Alexandre, attired in an elaborate seagreen dressing-gown replete with gold facings, was seated at the writing bureau in the bedroom which he and Marie-Joseph-Rose were to share at Noisy-le-Grand. His leather-bound diary, the massive type fitted with a substantial lock, was open before him. After a moment he laid down the pen and read what he had already written.

Madame Renaudin has at last succeeded in bringing her most cherished scheme to a successful conclusion. Today her eldest niece, Marie-Joseph-Rose Tascher de la Pagerie, and I were married here at Noisy-le-Grand, after hurried preparations in Paris and the buying of an elaborate trousseau.

Alexandre paused and frowned. He took up the pen and in the margin he scribbled:

This said trousseau was bought by Madame Renaudin, but with money provided by my father.

He smiled thinly and added:

Better that the money should have come from my father's income than from mine. It will not be necessary for me to spend any money on my wife for some time to come.

He laid down the pen again and continued to read.

My wife, though she wears her new clothes awkwardly, is, I must admit, quite good material—too good, I think to be wasted. Otherwise I should have refused point-blank to marry her. If, in the end, I am able to make a cultured, accomplished lady fit to be presented

32

at court out of this gauche and timid colonial girl I shall have nothing with which to reproach myself.

Satisfied with this Alexandre took up the pen again and wrote:

My father, who has permitted a colorful imagination to run away with him, declares that Rose is a sweet, charming and graceful young lady; in short, a veritable treasure. He has even exhorted me to treat her with the utmost gentleness. I myself, however, have yet to be convinced that gentleness is always the wisest course. Come what may, whether I treat her gently or harshly, I have made up my mind to begin her education afresh, and, by my zeal, make up for the shameful neglect of the early years of her life.

After a moment he sanded the page, closed the diary and locked it away in the bottom drawer of the bureau. Then, taking up a leather-bound copy of the essays of Montaigne, he rose and crossed to the bed. While waiting for his wife to join him he would relax and enjoy the beautiful prose of the man who, for the moment, was his favorite author.

$$* \quad * \quad * \quad * \quad *$$

"Come," Madame Renaudin said, "Alexandre will be growing impatient."

Marie-Joseph-Rose smiled nervously and glanced at herself once more in the mirror. Surely that was a stranger staring back at her, never the girl who had come from far-off Martinique! The figure reflected in the mirror wore a low-cut nightgown the silk of which was so fine and thin that one could see right through it. And the figure's hair! How odd it looked, gathered up on the top of her head in a high, almost pointed *pouf*, and crowned by what Aunt Marie called a 'simple' frilled-edged head-dress, but which was nothing more or less than a silly night-cap.

Madame Renaudin, who had dismissed the maid, held out a heavy fur-trimmed wrap. Placing it round her niece's shoulders she noticed that the girl was trembling.

"Nervous, child?" she asked gently.

"Nervous and a little frightened too, Aunt Marie."

"Of that stupid Alexandre?"

Marie-Joseph-Rose nodded. Actually, since that first meeting at Brest, she and Alexandre had been alone together on four occasions only, but brief as those occasions had been they had filled her with an indefinable apprehension. Each time he had approached her, not as the girl who was to become his wife, but as one who was to become his pupil. With a little shudder she recalled that he had corrected her grammar at least twenty times and that once, when he had made her read aloud to him, he had almost lost his temper.

"I wonder," she asked her aunt, "if I shall ever please him?"

"That will depend on how clever you are, child. Unhappy as you may feel at the moment, try to remember that you are really a very fortunate girl."

"I wish I could look at it like that, Aunt Marie, but try as I do I can't. I came to France with so much hope, with so many dreams. I came expecting romance. Romance! Think of it," she said with heat, "I expected romance and all I found was a young man who seems more interested in educating me than in making love to me."

"My dear Rose," Madame Renaudin told her, "a man never makes love to the girl he intends to marry until after the marriage ceremony. It would be most improper, I assure you, if he did."

For a moment Marie-Joseph-Rose forgot her nervousness enough to giggle.

"Alexandre," Madame Renaudin went on, hiding a smile, "is eager for you to become accomplished. He wants to be proud of you. Try to please him, and remember that marriage is something quite different from a romantic love-affair."

"This sort of marriage seems to be, certainly!"

"This sort of marriage," Madame Renaudin said sharply, "is the only sort that a girl in your position could possibly make. Remember, please, that it gives you everything—security, social position, the opportunity of being presented at court, and later, if you are clever enough, it might even give you love."

"I understand," the girl said quietly, "love, if it comes at all, comes last."

Madame Renaudin made an impatient gesture. "I know that Alexandre regards you as a child who is first to be educated, but he is not, as I must have told you already, inexperienced. Tonight, my dear, you make a delightful bride. No man could resist you. No man could possibly prefer a grammar lesson at this moment with you at his side, offering him so much." She smiled at a secret thought. Not for nothing had she chosen a night-gown which would reveal the deep red of her niece's somewhat prominent nipples. "Keep that in your mind," she concluded, "and when you go to him in a moment you will have nothing to be afraid of."

Marie-Joseph-Rose looked puzzled. "But Aunt Marie, you warned me not to thrust my feminine charm on Alexandre too suddenly."

"I naturally meant before the marriage, but heavens, *this* is your wedding night!"

There was a tap on the door and when Madame Renaudin said "Come in," the marquis entered, looking very smart and distinguished with his white hair and still wearing the ribbon of his order which Marie-Joseph-Rose had seen for the first time at the wedding ceremony. He took her hands in his and looked down at her a trifle anxiously.

"You are—happy, my dear?" he said.

"I—I think so, M'sieur le Marquis."

He tweaked her nose playfully. "You are my daughter now, the new little vicomtesse. You must learn to call me 'Father.'"

Her heart warmed to him. "Thank you. I should like that."

"Then remember, or I shall be obliged to retaliate by calling you 'Madame la Vicomtesse,' which, delightful as it may sound on the lips of the servants, is a most uncomfortable mouthful."

She laughed almost happily.

"Before you go to Alexandre," he said, "let me say something that I have wanted to say all day. It isn't always easy, adjusting oneself to a new situation—a new situation such as marriage, for instance. Should you feel unhappy at any time and in need of advice, remember that I am your friend as well as your father-in-law, and will be ready to help you if I can."

"Thank you—Father," she said, the tears springing to her eyes, "thank you!"

* * * * *

Alexandre looked at his wife with a little frown. "You seem to have been a long time, Rose."

She stood irresolute in the middle of the room, staring at him as he rearranged the pillows and propped up the book in a more comfortable position in front of him.

"I'm sorry," she stammered.

He yawned. "Never mind. That you have come at last is all that really matters." He yawned again. "Dear me, I seem to have grown quite sleepy waiting. Ah well, it has been a long and tiring day. Are you sleepy yourself, my dear?"

"Oh no, I—" she found it impossible to control the heavy beating of her heart—"I feel quite wide awake!"

"You do? Then you may as well read aloud to me for a while. I feel too tired to go on reading myself. The words were beginning to run into each other. Had you been any longer I might have fallen asleep over the book. Here, take it."

She went forward obediently. The nervous beating of her heart had ceased and there was a hint of rebellion in her voice when she said: "Are you sure you want me to read, Alexandre?"

"Sure? Of course I am," he said mildly.

A little titter came up in her throat. To spend one's wedding night reading aloud! It was ludicrous, ludicrous. She leaned over him to take the book, conscious of the fact that her breasts would thus be warmly revealed. She saw him give a little start and waited for his breath to become heavy and labored, as Tercier's certainly would had he been lying there instead of Alexandre.

"Did you laugh?" he asked, with a frown.

"Laugh? Oh no, Alexandre, I—I merely cleared my throat."

He looked at her suspiciously. His breathing, she noted, was perfectly even and untroubled. "Come," he said at last, "take the book."

Her heart began to beat heavily again, but this time in anger.

"You can read much better than me," she said.

"Much better than *me!*" he repeated, his voice rising shrilly. "Really, my dear Rose, what language is this?"

"Much better than I," she corrected herself hastily.

"There!" he cried in triumph. "You know! You know all the time but grow lazy and careless."

"I'm sorry, Alexandre."

"Reading aloud," he told her weightily, "will be good practice for you, practice in modulation and phrasing. Your voice, I think, is, or could be, your best point. All it needs is training."

"Where shall I begin?" she asked, her voice low.

"At the new paragraph near the top of the page. I was reading, as you see, Montaigne's essay on the inconstancy of our actions. Er—" he glanced at her vaguely. "Get into bed if you think you'll be more comfortable."

She stepped back from the bed and drew up a chair quickly. "I shall be quite comfortable here, thank you!"

"Just as you wish." There was a little pause. "Well, are you ready?"

"Yes," she said, and there were tears of anger in her throat.

"Proceed, then, proceed!"

She began to read in a low voice, and so hurriedly that after a moment he stopped her.

"Not so quickly, please!"

She began again, more slowly. The words made little sense to her but Alexandre, by the look of his face, was drinking them in with rapture. Once he nodded his head wisely and said: "True, very true indeed," and after she had read a full page he declared that she was reading much better than he had expected. With that she stopped.

"No, no," he said, with a yawn, "proceed, my dear, proceed."

She sighed and went on, fighting the while to keep back her tears. She remembered what her mother had said about tears being a useful weapon, but remembering also what her aunt had said she fought the harder to keep them back.

At the end of another page she noticed that Alexandre's head had fallen back and that his eyes were closed. She stopped and waited breathlessly, but without opening his eyes, and bringing up his hands until the fingers formed an apex above his chest, he said drowsily:

"Proceed, my dear Rose, proceed."

She turned the page and went on:

There is nothing I so hardly believe to be in a man as constancy, and nothing so easy to be found in him as inconstancy. He that should distinctly and part by part judge of him, should often jump to speak truth. View all antiquity over and you shall find. . . .

On and on she went until, glancing up again, she saw that Alexandre's hands had collapsed and his head had fallen farther back. She stopped reading once more. She waited for one moment, two moments, and then, with shattering clearness, a snore rose from the bed.

The book dropped from her hands with a clatter. Alexandre snored again. In a fit of uncontrollable anger she sprang to her feet.

"Alexandre!"

There was no response.

"*Alexandre!*" she shouted.

He stirred slightly and moved his head away from her.

Crying his name again she threw herself face downward on the bed. She drew the pillow over her head to muffle her sobbing, but her shoulders shook. 'Pig,' she thought, 'pig, pig, *pig!*' Her heart, she felt sure, was broken.

CHAPTER VI

THE GIRL SAT ALONE IN the gloomy library of the Marquis de Beauharnais's house in the rue Thévenot, an unopened history book on her lap. Accompanied by her father, Aunt Marie and the marquis, she and Alexandre had come to Paris after the period which it pleased the world to call a honeymoon. At first the idea of her and her husband becoming permanent guests at the rue Thévenot, instead of taking a house of their own, had disappointed her, but now, with her father having taken his departure for Martinique, she was grateful for the presence of Aunt Marie and her kindly father-in-law.

The three months since her wedding day had not been happy ones. Apart from all else she had never been able to efface from her mind the memory of that first night with Alexandre. Awaking to find her sobbing at his side he had obviously judged her tears to be nothing more serious than an outward expression of virginal modesty and nervousness. At first, with kindly intent, he had tried to take her in his arms and soothe her, but with the failure of gentleness his sudden anger, combined with the rising tide of passion, had forced her to a cold, impersonal surrender. 'I have one regret,' she had told herself many times. 'To have refused Tercier as I did was not only cruel but stupid.'

With a sigh she opened the history book, but weary of the endless lessons set by Alexandre she put it aside with a gesture of distaste and went to stare out of the window. It was a dull day. Heavy clouds raced across the sky and the wind moaned faintly. Even on a sunny day—and there had been few such days since the arrival from Martinique—the rue Thévenot filled her with depression, but today the sight of its bleak, characterless houses was more than she could bear. "And to think," she said aloud, "that I once thought the marquis's house a dream palace!" A longing to see the little stream at Trois-Ilets again brought the tears to her eyes. What heaven it would be to lounge for a moment in that lazy freedom! Oh, she was miserable, miserable! Life in Paris, which she had been so eager to grasp with both hands, was the greatest disappointment she had ever suffered.

She pressed her face against the glass of the window and fought back her tears. After all, life in Paris, with anybody else but Alexandre, would be all she had ever dreamed. Married to any other man she would possess a salon of her own. There would be an endless round of social activities. There would be parties and balls, and exciting visits to the court. There would be laughter, and music, witty conversation and admiring young men to bow before her. . . .

"My dear Rose," a voice said, "to flatten one's nose against a window is a child's trick. The passers-by will think my wife a half-wit."

She swung round from the window and faced Alexandre, who had come silently into the room.

"As usual you were wasting your time dreaming," he said coldly. "What have you done with the book I gave you to read?"

"My eyes were tired," she lied, "so I put it down."

"Your eyes are always tired," he said, "you force me to conclude that you really want to remain ignorant."

He sat down and motioned to her to do the same. For a moment they faced each other in silence.

"Well," he said at last, "have you nothing to say?"

She folded her hands in her lap. "Nothing that would interest you, Alexandre."

He leaped to his feet and strode to the window. "Of all the exasperating things to say!"

"It's perfectly true," she defended herself. "The things that interest me never seem to interest you. They're too commonplace, I suppose!"

"Commonplace?" he echoed. "Oh yes, I'm well aware of that! But why in the name of heaven should your interests *remain* commonplace? No one strives more diligently than I to create in you an intelligent interest in the topics of the day."

She made no reply.

"No one strives more diligently than I, but I am quickly coming to the conclusion that my efforts are being wasted. Like all Creoles you are hopelessly lazy and indolent."

"I—I'm sorry, Alexandre."

"You give me little evidence of it!"

He strode back from the window and sat down again. There was a long pause. Presently he broke out afresh.

"Say something, Rose! Say *anything!* The veriest commonplace would be better than a long dull silence!"

She looked down at her fingers and braced herself. "Alexandre, we've been married for three months and you haven't yet presented me at court. I—I keep wondering when you will."

He laughed sharply. "I shall only present you at court, my dear Rose, when I feel sure that you will not disgrace me."

His tone implied that he would never feel sure of that, and looking about him for the discarded history book he picked it up from the floor, opened it and thrust it into her unwilling hands.

"Come, I think it time we learned something about the reign of Louis the Ninth."

She laughed suddenly, hysterically.

He looked at her coldly. "Well?"

"It says here that Louis the Ninth was a saint and once wore a hair-shirt before going on a crusade. Would you like me to wear one, Alexandre, would you—*would* you?"

"My dear Rose," he said crushingly, "if anyone should wear a hair-shirt it is I, not you, for a hair-shirt, I imagine, would be less difficult to sustain than a stupid and ignorant wife."

∗   ∗   ∗   ∗   ∗

The hairdresser, no less a person than Léonard who was summoned from time to time to the Queen, stood back from Madame Renaudin and studied his handiwork with satisfaction.

"The foundation is complete, madame," he said. "We may now proceed."

Marie-Joseph-Rose, who had been granted the privilege of sitting quietly in her aunt's dressing-closet to watch the great Léonard at work, looked curiously at the 'foundation.' Madame Renaudin's hair, instead of being mounted high and dressed with waving feathers and numerous strange flowers, had been swept back flatly and padded out with false hair until it resembled a thick pancake.

While she studied this odd structure, Léonard busied himself with the opening of the large and mysterious parcel a servant had brought in and laid reverently before him.

"La, la!" he cried, when the wrappings fell away at last.

Madame Renaudin looked at the object thus revealed.

"Magnificent," she said.

"An exact replica," Léonard assured her.

It was, Marie-Joseph-Rose decided, a beautiful piece of work. She could see the name, *La Belle Poule,* painted on the bow. *La Belle Poule* . . . Alexandre had spoken of such a vessel only yesterday. A frigate of the French navy, it had fought a terrible battle with an English vessel by the name of *Arethusa,* a battle which had ended with the sinking of the enemy.

"What a beautiful model," she said, and laughed at the sight of the miniature sailors on the decks and in the riggings. "A present for Alexandre, or M'sieur le Marquis, perhaps?"

Léonard and Madame Renaudin shook their heads at the girl's amazing ignorance, and then, at a nod from Madame Renaudin, the hairdresser placed *La Belle Poule* squarely in the middle of her 'foundation'. Once it was secured with little strands of wire, more false hair was laid about it and teased into tiny waves to resemble the ocean.

"There!" Léonard cried, his task completed, "how better could so great a victory be celebrated!"

Madame Renaudin surveyed her head-dress in the mirror. "You give me your word, m'sieur, that this style was invented by the Queen herself?"

"My solemn word, madame."

When Léonard had bustled away to his coach, which was waiting

40

to take him to his next client in the rue Saint-Denis, Madame Renaudin turned to her niece.

"Come, Rose, help me complete my *toilette*."

Obediently Marie-Joseph-Rose took up a large paper bag from the side-table and placed it carefully over her aunt's face. Then, the face thus protected, she dusted white powder over hair and head-dress alike.

"Now the rouge," Madame Renaudin said, when the bag had been removed.

"You go to the Tuileries, perhaps?" the girl asked, as she painted the rouge on her aunt's cheeks.

"Why, no," Madame Renaudin said airily. "My position being what it is in the marquis's household I am naturally never received at court." She looked at the deep circles beneath her niece's eyes, and was aware, for the first time, of the deathly paleness of her cheeks. "Child," she said gently, "are you very unhappy?"

Unable to speak, but smiling wanly, the girl nodded.

"You sometimes wish that you had never left Martinique?"

"Oh, yes, Aunt Marie, often. Paris is so gloomy, so very gloomy."

"How foolish," Madame Renaudin said quietly, "for you to crave for the past when in reality the future holds so much for you."

"Oh, no. All that the future holds is the dreary round of trying to please Alexandre. Of trying, and failing."

"You must try to have a little patience. Heavens, my dear, but this head-dress is woefully heavy!"

"Patience!" Marie-Joseph-Rose exclaimed. "If that was all I needed I should be well content."

"Nevertheless, I say it again. Try to have a little patience, and remember that this period of adjustment is a difficult one in any marriage."

"It would be less difficult if I had married a man instead of a wretched school-teacher. Alexandre expects too much of me. He wants to turn me from a woman into a bookworm. Every day he gives me a new book to read—a dry history or an even drier political discourse. Then he goes out with his friends and enjoys himself, and when he returns he questions me, always he questions me. I tell you, Aunt Marie, a hundred times a day I wish I were dead!"

Madame Renaudin felt an inclination to laugh, but the tragedy in her niece's voice drove all thought of laughter from her mind. "The fault is mine," she told herself, "the fault is mine!" Hastily she thrust this thought aside.

"The best thing you can do," she said, feeling suddenly inspired, "is have a baby soon, and then your time will be too full for history books and political discourses."

41

"A—a baby, Aunt Marie?"

"But of course. Alexandre, I presume, is still an attentive husband?"

Marie-Joseph-Rose looked down modestly and nodded.

"You would like to have a baby?" her aunt asked.

"Yes I—I think I would."

Till now she had never thought of such a possibility, but if escape from Alexandre lay in that direction she would gladly welcome a dozen babies.

"Perhaps the future *does* hold more for me than I believe," she agreed. "At all events, that is what I shall try to tell myself."

*   *   *   *   *

"My dear child," the marquis said gently, "you've been weeping."

Unable to deny so obvious a fact Marie-Joseph-Rose tried to smile up at him through her tears.

Having observed his daughter-in-law's all-too-evident unhappiness for some time now the marquis had been deeply troubled. He had discussed the matter apologetically with Madame Renaudin, and had only been partly convinced when she had assured him that in the course of time all would be well.

He took her hands in his. "My dear, it hurts to see you unhappy like this. Why not confide in me? Who knows, I might be able to help a little."

"It's nothing, really. I'm just weak and silly."

"Nonsense, Rose. I could never bring myself to believe that."

"It's true, all the same, M'sieur le Marquis."

"You once promised to call me Father," he reproved her. "Had you forgotten. Or do you find me too forbidding?"

"No, I hadn't forgotten."

"That means you really do find me forbidding?"

"No, no, of course not!"

"Splendid! You even like me a little, perhaps?"

She laughed tremulously. "Oh, yes, I like you very much!"

"Splendid! We are friends, good friends, and you are going to tell me what it is that makes you so unhappy."

She hesitated for a moment. "There—there's nothing to tell you."

"I think there is. Alexandre, I feel sure, is responsible. My stupid son has been bullying you."

"No, please—!" she protested.

"I have eyes and ears, and moreover I know my son a little better than you do. There are times when I think myself a criminal for permitting you to marry him."

42

"Please don't say that. The fault is mine. I am a constant disappointment to him. I—I am too stupid to learn."

"You are young and sweet. Whether you are 'too stupid to learn' is a point no other man but Alexandre would consider." An idea occurred to him. "If Alexandre could see other men gathering about you, if he could see them admiring you and hear them paying you compliments, he might be roused to jealousy!" Oh, yes, it was a splendid idea! "My dear, you haven't been about in society much since you came to France, have you?"

"Hardly at all."

"Alexandre has seen to that, of course! He has kept you at home, doing his utmost to cram political theories, history and the unutterably dull essays of Montaigne into your delightful little head. However, we are now going to change all that. We——"

The girl gave a sudden start and stared in horror at the door. Alexandre, having entered noiselessly, came forward with anger written plainly on his face.

"I should be interested to know, Father," he said coldly, "just how you propose to change 'all that'!"

The marquis swung round on him. "By heavens, sir, you were eavesdropping!"

"Nonsense. You were speaking loudly. The door was open. I heard you distinctly for some time as I came down the passage." He turned furiously to his wife. "So you have come running to my father with your complaints and have gained his misplaced sympathy!"

The marquis stepped angrily between them. "Alexandre, there are times when I would give my soul to thrash you soundly."

Alexandre looked at his father with raised eyebrows. "That would be both rash and undignified, Father. You were about to 'change all that.' Pray continue."

"I was about to tell Rose," said the marquis, controlling himself with difficulty, "that just as soon as it can be arranged I intend to give a ball in her honor." He turned to the girl. "Does the idea appeal to you, my dear?"

It was obvious from the light in her eyes and the smile that had come to her face that it did, but before she could reply Alexandre said cuttingly:

"You are surely not serious, Father."

"I was never more serious in my life. It is time our friends saw something of your charming wife."

Alexandre shrugged his shoulders disdainfully. "Then I must warn you that if you continue with such a preposterous idea I shall cause a scandal by refusing to be present myself." He paused, waited for his father to speak, and added: "And now, would you be kind enough to leave us? There are several things I want to say to my wife."

The marquis attempted to speak but failed. He looked weakly from his son to his daughter-in-law.

"Without wishing to seem ill-mannered," Alexandre went on, "I must point out that Rose is *my* wife, not yours. What she does is *my* concern, not yours. Please, Father, leave us."

Fearing that a more painful scene might develop and sensing the marquis's irresolution, Marie-Joseph-Rose intervened herself.

"Please do as Alexandre wishes, Father." Her voice softened. "And thank you for thinking of such a lovely idea. I shall always remember it."

"Sentimentality," Alexandre said harshly, "is quite uncalled for."

The marquis hesitated for a moment, looked helplessly at his son and finally left the room with rapid, nervous steps. A look of satisfaction crossed Alexandre's face. A moment later he swung round angrily on Marie-Joseph-Rose.

"To go crying to my father! That is more than I can bear!"

She made no attempt to deny the charge.

"From now on," Alexandre continued, "I wash my hands of you. You wish to remain ignorant—as far as I am concerned you *shall* remain ignorant."

She gave a low, stricken cry and tears began to roll down her cheeks.

"Snivelling," he almost shouted, "is useless."

He looked at her steadily for a moment, hating her, and through her, Madame Renaudin, who was the cause of all this.

Marie-Joseph-Rose did her best to check her tears.

"I have tried so hard to please you," she said.

"I find that difficult to believe!"

"I—I have never pleased you at all, then?"

"There have been odd moments," he admitted, "when you have lain in my arms and I have permitted myself to forget your shortcomings."

"I wish I could hate you!" she cried.

"That," he retorted, "is a remark worthy of your intelligence."

There was a moment's intolerable silence.

"What are you going to do?" the girl asked.

His thin lips parted in a bleak smile. "I imagine that army life will be a pleasant change from the sort of married life I have been forced to endure. Tomorrow, therefore, I shall make arrangements to rejoin my regiment. To save you the pain of meeting me again I shall spend tonight with friends." He turned on his heels and went to the door. "There is only one more thing to be said, and that is good-bye."

CHAPTER VII

MARIE-JOSEPH-ROSE STOOD before the long, gilt-edged mirror in her dressing-closet. Gravely she turned left on her heels, then right, and finally she brought her heels sharply together as if she were a soldier on parade.

"Madame la Vicomtesse is satisfied?" the maid, a little peasant girl from Brittany, asked anxiously.

"Yes, Marie, I think I am. The fit is indeed perfect."

For the first time the riding-dress, the fashionable 'Amazon,' was being worn. She remembered Madame la Duchesse de Bourbon, the only woman she had yet seen wearing the new style. 'And I surely,' she told herself with satisfaction, 'look just as smart, if not a little smarter.' Would Alexandre, now at Verdun with his regiment, agree? Or would he make some rude remark about the pig-tail, the thick ridiculous pig-tail, hanging down her back?

"And now the hat," she commanded.

When the hat was set at the right angle, so that the high feather bobbed jauntily, she made her way down to the hall, not quickly, for the tight skirt made all but short steps impossible, but slowly, even a little mincingly, with the hips, exaggerated by the cut of the over-coat, undulating voluptuously.

"In the name of heaven, child," said a voice, "where are you going?"

She turned to find herself confronted by Madame Renaudin and the marquis. It was Aunt Marie, of course, who had spoken.

"It's a beautiful spring day," she said, "I asked Jacques to prepare a horse for me." She turned to the marquis. "Do you like my riding-dress, Father?"

"Charming," he said, "utterly charming. Of course you must go riding if you want to. This will be the first time, won't it?"

"Yes, Father, the first time, and since it wasn't necessary to ask Alexandre's permission. . . ." Her voice trailed away, for Aunt Marie, she saw, was looking at her in horror.

"You must be mad," Madame Renaudin said at last. "Have you no consideration whatever for your state of health? Have you forgotten your condition?"

"My state of health? My condition?" Then, understanding, she laughed merrily. "But it isn't yet the third month, and see, my riding-dress is still a perfect fit."

"Nevertheless, child, the risk would be too great," Madame Renaudin said with decision. "This afternoon, if you wish, you shall ride with me in the new cabriolet, but horseback riding, no, no, that is out of the question."

Marie-Joseph-Rose sighed deeply. "Very well, Aunt Marie."

"Madame Renaudin is undoubtedly right," the marquis said kindly. "Would you come to the library, my dear? Your aunt and I have something we wish to discuss with you.

"We have only one desire," he went on, when they were in the library, and that is to see you happy. No one was more distressed than I when Alexandre left Paris. His conduct has been——"

"To come to the point," Madame Renaudin said sharply, "it is high time the young man came back from Verdun."

"Came back?" the girl echoed, almost in alarm.

"Surely, child, you want him to return to you?"

Marie-Joseph-Rose hesitated. She had been lonely, certainly, during the last few weeks, but she had not been as desperately unhappy as she had imagined a deserted wife should be. With Alexandre no longer present to treat her like a backward schoolgirl the house had seemed once again like a dream palace and a not unpleasant tranquility had settled about her aimless life. Aimless? Well, hardly, since she was going to have a baby. Or *was* she? Menstruation, certainly, had ceased, but the sickness which she had always understood to be inseparable from pregnancy had passed her by.

"Alexandre," she said at last, "has no intention of coming back, so the question hardly arises."

"Alexandre is your husband," Madame Renaudin snapped. "He has a duty to you, a duty to the child you're going to have. And you, Rose, have a duty to him. He must be made to see reason. He *shall* be made to see it."

"You *do* want him to come back?" the marquis asked.

"I don't know, Father." She hesitated again, seeking the words with which to state clearly how she felt. "I—I'm still a little miserable, now that he's gone, but I was a great deal more miserable when he was here."

"How many times have you written to him?" Madame Renaudin demanded.

"Twice only, but each time there was no reply."

"Did you tell him about your condition?"

"Well, no, Aunt Marie."

"So much the better. If he can be induced to come back by other means, well and good. If not, your condition, our last card, shall be skilfully played."

"You think, Marie," the marquis asked, "that Rose should write again?"

"Indeed I do."

He took the girl's hands in his and looked at her with a smile. "There, my dear, you must write again, and your aunt, who is very clever when it comes to composing letters, will help you." He laughed reminiscently. "As a matter of fact, she dictated the letters I wrote to your father when we were arranging the marriage. If I had been left entirely to myself——"

"If you had been left entirely to yourself," Madame Renaudin said acidly, "there might have been no marriage at all!"

"That would have been far better for all of us," Marie-Joseph-Rose remarked, looking steadily at her aunt.

"Nonsense, child!" Madame Renaudin declared, uneasy under her niece's gaze. "In my experience even an unhappy marriage is better than no marriage at all!" She paused to give full weight to her following words: "You want to make a place for yourself in society, don't you?"

"Well, yes, if that is possible."

"Very well! Be guided by me, then."

"Yes," the marquis put in, realizing that as spokesman he was rapidly losing his grip on the conversation, "be guided by your aunt."

"A woman today," Madame Renaudin went on, "has two chances of making a place for herself in fashionable society—either through inheriting a fortune or through a good marriage. Since the first was out of the question as far as you were concerned, I saw to it that you made a good marriage. But come, get pen and paper and we will see what we can do about this third letter to Alexandre."

And so, guided by Madame Renaudin, Marie-Joseph-Rose wrote again to Alexandre. She told him, with complete duplicity, that during his absence she was persisting doggedly with her studies. Not that she hoped to achieve much, but if she only achieved a little there would be cause for satisfaction. She told him that she was missing him desperately and she added a few smooth words about his good looks. "Intellectual as his leanings might be," said Madame Renaudin, "he is still man enough to be susceptible to flattery." Finally she hoped that he would find her penmanship neat and legible and her grammar less faulty than formerly.

"The main thing," Madame Renaudin said, when the letter was addressed and sealed, "is to induce him to reply. If that happens we will have made a little progress and should soon persuade him to return to you."

Marie-Joseph-Rose, however, felt ill at ease about the whole thing. "If we persuade him to come back," she said, "because he believes that in his absence I am becoming accomplished and intellectual he will soon discover how much we have deceived him."

Madame Renaudin chuckled. "My dear child, you must be clever enough to make him *think* that you are becoming accomplished and intellectual. Alexandre likes to talk, to air his ridiculous views. The elderly type of youth always does. Once you get him back you must do all you can to encourage him in that and then he won't have quite so much time to waste on instructing and questioning you."

Marie-Joseph-Rose began to take heart. "I can at least try, Aunt Marie."

"Splendid, my dear! You can at least try, and while trying, remember that a woman's slogan should sometimes read, *Be a good listener.*" She chuckled again. "It is only a question of time, I think, before we turn this stupid, conceited young man into quite a good, obedient husband!"

*   *   *   *   *

After a lapse of several days a reply, much to Marie-Joseph-Rose's surprise, arrived from Verdun. With a flush of triumph on her face Madame Renaudin brought the letter to her niece and together they opened it. The first sentence came as something of a shock.

If I could be sure, my dear Rose, that you alone had handled the pen I would feel more pleasure in reading the flattering things that you say. I would feel more pleasure and I would be able to persuade myself more easily that they came from your heart.

Marie-Joseph-Rose looked at her aunt in dismay. "So he guessed that you helped me!"

"Pooh! What of it? He has been induced to reply. That is the main thing."

They read the next paragraph.

If you are persisting as doggedly with your studies as you say the acquirements which will eventually be yours will raise you far above other women and make you a wife to be envied.

Marie-Joseph-Rose shook her head doubtfully. "Aunt Marie, I suspect sarcasm there."

"So do I, but read on, read on!"

The next sentence brought a gasp of surprise from both of them.

*It is possible that within the next few days I shall be free to pay
you a visit, but whether that visit will be paid depends on what I
think of your letter when I have had time to read it again.*

Madame Renaudin clapped her hands. "Better and better!"

Give my respects to Madame Renaudin, the closing sentence read,
*and let her know that I suspect that she was at your elbow when
you sat down to write to me.*

At this Madame Renaudin merely chuckled. "Alexandre has replied and might even come to see you. If that happens it will be
up to you to see that he stays."

Marie-Joseph-Rose, however, remained silent. The phrasing of the
letter and the general tone had turned her heart to ice. Alexandre
was not a man, he was a soulless encyclopedia and the letter had
brought her nearer to hating him than she had ever been.

*   *   *   *   *

Alexandre strode jauntily into his wife's dressing-closet. The sight
of him caused her to start so violently that the curling tongs which
the maid was using expertly on her hair gave her a sudden little
burn. Alexandre dismissed the maid with a wave of his hand.

"Well, my dear," he said, "can you do nothing more than stare at
me?"

Since her feelings about his letter were still unchanged she faced
him now with considerable apprehension, though his mood, while
condescending, seemed heavily playful.

"To be frank, Alexandre," she stammered, "I hardly expected you
to come."

"But surely, after my letter——!"

"Your letter was—indefinite."

"Well perhaps it was," he said loftily, "but I may as well admit that
I really did intend to come." He threw out his chest. "My dear Rose,
rightly or wrongly, I have made up my mind to be magnanimous."

"Magnanimous?"

"You understand the meaning of the word, I hope?"

She brushed this aside with a show of irritation which amazed her
and made her catch her breath in apprehension afterwards.

"You mean to leave your regiment and come back to me?" she
asked.

49

There was a calm self-assurance in her manner, an indifference almost, and for a moment he hardly knew how to deal with it.

"Do you want me to leave my regiment and come back to you?" he parried.

"Only if you want to yourself," she replied.

He looked at her oddly. "You mentioned in your letter that you were persisting doggedly with your studies. If I come back I shall expect you to show proof of that."

"Tell me one thing, Alexandre," she said, "why did you marry me? Was it merely for the pleasure of trying to educate me?"

"Pleasure!" he cried. "There's been little pleasure in it in all conscience!"

"That isn't answering my question, Alexandre."

Her continued self-assurance, slight as it was, unsteadied him. "Tell me first why *you* married *me*."

"Very well," she said quietly. "I married you because our parents arranged the marriage, and because I wanted to come to France. I felt that if I stayed in Martinique life would hold nothing for me. I knew, at least I *thought* I knew, that if I came to France life would hold everything for me. Now please answer my question!"

"I agreed to the marriage," he said, still looking at her oddly, "because I imagined that with training you would become a wife of whom I could be proud."

"And I disappointed you."

"And you disappointed me!" he said, with heat.

"One other question, Alexandre. Have you never loved me, even a little?"

"Perhaps," he said, jauntily, "but no doubt it was merely youthful passion and the novelty of a new possession."

Stung by this she said: "If I loved you now, Alexandre, my love would have little hope of surviving."

"By heavens!" he cried, "this is a fine way to talk when I come to you willing to make a reconciliation!"

She considered this for a moment. "Are you telling the truth? Are you really willing to make a reconciliation?"

"Yes, but only if you are prepared to continue your studies with sincerity and intelligence!"

She looked at him in disgust. What a pompous fool he was! Ignorant and unaccomplished as she might be, in *his* estimation, she felt many years his senior. For a fleeting moment she even found it in her heart to feel sorry for him, to pity him.

"Alexandre," she said at last, "you may come back if you wish, but I shall never again submit to your bullying attempts to educate me."

He looked at her pale set face in complete astonishment. He had expected and looked forward to tears and stammered apologies, never to a self-assurance that amounted to sheer impertinence.

"Very well," he said coldly, "the best thing I can do is return to the happier and more congenial atmosphere of army life."

She inclined her head gravely. "Just as you wish, Alexandre, but before you go——"

"Yes?"

"Before you go I think you ought to know that I am going to have a child."

"You—!" He looked at her narrowly. "Is this a trick? A trick to force me to an unwilling reconciliation?"

"If it were a trick you would soon find me out."

"Then why wasn't I told before?" he stormed. "I had a right to be told!"

He began to pace up and down the room. Agitation and indecision were clearly marked in his every movement. This news, he admitted to himself, made a considerable difference to his attitude. To have children, to watch over their mental growth, to influence their ever-widening intellectual pursuits—that was a pleasure he had always hoped would be in store for him. He came to a quick decision.

"My dear," he said briskly, "I will come back to you. I will give you a last chance. But mind you, I make this gesture, not for you, not for myself, but for the child that is to be born to us." He paused dramatically. "Is that perfectly clear?"

She gave a shrug of distaste. "Yes, Alexandre, perfectly."

Later, when she was alone, the strain of the interview reduced her to tears, but very soon, in a calmer frame of mind, she began to feel that she had scored something of a victory. Undoubtedly Aunt Marie would have disapproved of the attitude she had adopted, but it had been quite involuntary, and Aunt Marie, had she been present, would have been struck by the fact that Alexandre, perhaps for the first time in his life, had been severely shaken.

With a feeling of wonder Marie-Joseph-Rose looked at herself in the mirror. No, her appearance had changed in no way, no way whatever. And yet, she felt different, very different. She laughed almost gaily and looked herself straight in the eye.

"Madame la Vicomtesse," she said aloud, "you must have been inspired," and she added in wonder: "Inspired by the knowledge that a new life is taking shape within you."

CHAPTER VIII

BREATHLESS WITH EXCITE-
ment Marie-Joseph-Rose glanced eagerly about her. So this was the
famous Comédie Française, and here she was, seated in a box with
Madame Renaudin on her right and the marquis on her left. She
glanced slily at Aunt Marie whose face beneath the shadow of the
lofty head-dress was set in stern and disapproving lines. With a little
giggle she recalled the scene which had taken place when her desire
to visit the theater had been made known.

"Nothing," Madame Renaudin had pronounced, "could be more
unseemly. If you persist in this nonsense I shall be forced, like Alexandre, to forbid you to leave the house."

Marie-Joseph-Rose had stamped her foot in a little burst of anger
To be forbidden to leave the rue Thévenot by Alexandre, who was
making her pregnancy an excuse for forcing a continued social ostra-
cism upon her, was one thing; to be forbidden by Aunt Marie was
quite another.

"Unseemly, Aunt Marie?" she'd questioned. "Why do you call it
that?"

"Because of your condition. For a girl of your station to appear in
public in an advanced state of pregnancy would be quite unthinkable. Try to remember, Rose, that there is such a thing as good
taste."

She'd stamped her foot again and laughed derisively. "What do
I, who have never appeared in society, even for a moment, care for
good taste? Besides, with Alexandre at Versailles I want to make
the most of the freedom his absence gives me."

"Nevertheless, I still consider—" Madame Renaudin had begun.

"I shall go to the theater," Marie-Joseph-Rose had said firmly, "even
if you force me to go alone and unattended."

And so, wearing the most voluminous dress Madame Renaudin
had been able to select, she had had her way, and the box she now
occupied was the one which Alexandre had been renting for some
time, not for the use of his wife—oh dear no!—but for himself and
the friends to whom he had never introduced her.

"Aunt Marie," she whispered, slipping a warm hand into Madame
Renaudin's, "what a study Alexandre's face would be if he could see
me now!"

Madame Renaudin relaxed for a moment and a smile came to her
lips. "Thank heaven the wretched young man is at Versailles."

The girl frowned and withdrew her hand. Versailles, where the court was in residence, and where Alexandre, still refusing to present his colonial wife, was doubtless playing the gay and carefree bachelor at this very moment. She tossed her head. Better not to think of such things. She had achieved at least a little. She had had her way in one small thing. She had come to the Comédie Française.

She leaned forward in the box. It was on the third tier and next to the gallery, but even though a massive pillar limited her vision she had a good view of the boxes on the opposite side and by straining forward a little more could look down into the pit. The thing that amazed her the most was that though the curtain had been up for quite some time and the first act of the new *Le Mariage de Figaro* was well established it was impossible to hear a single word for the chatter and laughter of the gossiping audience. Many people, especially those standing in the pit, actually had their backs to the stage.

"Is it always like this?" she asked.

"No," the marquis told her, "though the audience is generally noisy during the first act."

Madame Renaudin laughed drily. "By all accounts this is a very daring play, so it's just as well that you can hear nothing."

There was a slight stir behind them. The curtains of the box had been parted and a man and woman, unrecognizable in the dim light, were entering.

"Forgive me," a voice said, "but some little mistake has undoubtedly occurred. This box, I assure you, is mine."

Marie-Joseph-Rose sprang to her feet.

"Alexandre!" she cried.

There was a little silence. Madame Renaudin and the marquis rose, the latter in considerable agitation. At length Alexandre, drawing back the curtains again and standing aside, spoke two words.

"Permit me," he said, bowing briefly.

Madame Renaudin took her niece firmly by the arm. "Come," she said.

"Alexandre—" the marquis began.

"Please, François!" Madame Renaudin said, fixing him steadily with her eyes. Then she returned Alexandre's bow curtly. "Yes, indeed, m'sieur, some little mistake, but yours, I suspect, rather than ours."

Impelled by the pressure of her aunt's grip Marie-Joseph-Rose found herself in the foyer. Dimly she heard the porter's voice calling: "My Lord Marquis's carriage! Hurry there, my Lord Marquis's carriage!"

Only when they were seated in the carriage did Madame Renaudin permit the marquis to speak his mind.

"Shameful," he said, "shameful! Had I known, had I suspected——"

"You should have known," Madame Renaudin told him sharply, "you should have suspected."

"That woman," Marie-Joseph-Rose asked quietly, "is she Alexandre's mistress?"

"You saw her for yourself, child. Need you ask? I may as well tell you now what has been known to me for some time. Alexandre has taken a house in the rue de l'Université. He has been there apparently during the past few days, not at Versailles. His life since shortly after he returned from Verdun has been one of such exaggerated gaiety that even the court, corrupt as it is, is beginning to frown on him."

Marie-Joseph-Rose laughed hysterically. "My success in turning him into a good, obedient husband has been amazing, hasn't it!"

For the first time in her life she felt a pang of jealousy. Perhaps it was unreasonable, she admitted to herself, but there it was—deep, primitive and inescapable. She had never loved her husband; now, though she supposed she hated him, the only thing she really felt was jealousy.

Much to her surprise Alexandre returned to the rue Thévenot that night. He stormed into the house at midnight, less than an hour after the theater would have closed and when most theater-goers would be taking supper as a prelude to spending the rest of the night at the card tables.

"I demand an explanation for this blatant flaunting of my wishes," he cried.

She looked at him with a calmness that surprised her. "I wanted to go to the play. You, I knew, would never take me. Even if your father and my aunt had refused to accompany me I would still have gone."

Her calmness left him speechless.

"Do you propose to remain here," she asked, "or is this merely a brief visit on your way to the rue de l'Université?"

"What do you know about the rue de l'Université?" he demanded.

"Very little," she admitted, "but after what I saw tonight, enough, surely!" She laughed shakily. "Tonight, before we entered the theater, I saw what I believe is a common sight in Paris, a prostitute ogling the men who passed her. An hour later I saw what is apparently another common sight, a husband parading his mistress in public."

He raised his hands in exasperation. "By all the saints in heaven, is it necessary to make me a scene like this?"

"You admit," she asked, "that the house in the rue de l'Université has been taken for the purpose of keeping a mistress?"

"Yes, yes, I admit it!" he shouted. Then, more calmly, he said: "A wise woman, my dear Rose, neither looks for nor expects what the world is pleased to call faithfulness in a husband."

"As if any woman could be wise in such a matter!" she was stung to exclaim.

He stared at her in amazement. "One moment, Rose. Do you actually expect me to be faithful to you?"

"Perhaps not," she admitted, "but at least you might show me the kindness of practicing a little discretion."

"Discretion," he said, with an effeminate simper, "is hardly fashionable. My conduct is not exceptional. Among the men of my class it is the accepted thing."

She looked at him in silence. He was almost strutting, and she noticed in surprise that he had grown stouter during the last few months. His face had filled out and there were little pockets of loose skin beneath his eyes. She decided on a new line of attack.

"To ask you to reform, Alexandre, to be faithful to me, would be stupid, but for the sake of the child that is to be born to us I do ask that we might be friends."

"Friends! What a thing to ask. What have we in common to make us friends? Nothing. Nothing in the world!"

"We—we could try to create something, however small."

"Whether we create anything or not is a matter that rests entirely with you. It has always rested with you." His voice rose on a high note. "I have always been willing to place the happiness of home life first, always. Why, I once even dreamed of a well-ordered household. How dear it has cost my heart to renounce that dream only I will ever know."

With that he swung on his heels and left the room. A few moments later, after the outer door had slammed, she heard the sound of hoof-beats and carriage wheels in the street below. Alexandre, apparently, was on his way to the rue de l'Université.

∗　　∗　　∗　　∗　　∗

Marie-Joseph-Rose gazed with frightened eyes at the doctor, but not without some little curiosity. He was, she thought, the most elegant man she had ever seen, more elegant even than the hairdresser Léonard. True, he carried no sword, but he wore black silk lined with ermine and his hair was both powdered and scented. At the moment, his lace cuffs turned neatly back, he was making yet another examination with firm and probing fingers, pausing every now and then to exchange a word of gossip with Madame Renaudin who stood watchfully at hand. The girl shuddered and felt the hot blood rise in her cheeks. Horrible and humiliating it was, but even more horrible and humiliating to know that soon, when the pains grew worse, the silent *accoucheur* would step forward and take the doctor's place. A male midwife! Such an outrage had never even been heard of in Martinique!

"A matter of perhaps an hour," the doctor said, drawing up the bedclothes and flicking his cuffs back into place. "And by the way, Madame Renaudin, it reached my ears only this morning, and from the Queen's personal physician too. . . ." And off he went on yet another daring tidbit of gossip.

Another and more violent spasm gripped the girl. She bit her lip, fighting back the scream which rose in her throat. If only the senseless gossip would cease, if only she could be left alone for a moment, for one little moment!

The door opened and she heard another voice, Alexandre's voice, she noted dully. She laughed stupidly. How considerate of him to have come hurrying to her side from the rue de l'Université. His mistress, was she with child too? Not that it really mattered, but was she? For a moment she caught sight of Alexandre's face hovering grotesquely in the haze above her.

"Who," she heard him say, "is this?"

There was a mumbled explanation and then, from Alexandre: "Nonsense! I refuse to permit it! Fashionable as these men may be these days I insist on your fetching a woman!"

For the next few moments two voices—Madame Renaudin's and Alexandre's—rose against each other. The girl heard her aunt laugh drily and say: "You object to the man as if he were your wife's prospective lover instead of merely a very skilled *accoucheur!*"

"I assure you, M'sieur le Vicomte," the doctor's voice came softly, "that since the introduction of the *accoucheurs* there have been fewer deaths. The midwives, generally, are women of great ignorance and lamentable carelessness. Because of them there are too many maimed and crippled children in Paris, too many unfortunate imbeciles. In addition, the *accoucheur* is skilled in the use of oils and ointments and can, by the administration of the new narcotics, make the most difficult birth well-nigh painless. By the employment of an *accoucheur* Madame la Vicomtesse will find the bearing of this child as pleasant, almost, as the conceiving of it."

Marie-Joseph-Rose forced herself to a half-sitting position and laughed hysterically. As pleasant, almost, as the conceiving of it!

"I assure you, M'sieur le Docteur," she cried, "that I found small pleasure in that!"

Before she sank back on the pillows she saw the black hatred of Alexandre's eyes and watched the flush of anger and embarrassment which suffused his cheeks. A moment later she heard the violent slam of the door.

There was a deep chuckle from Madame Renaudin.

"And now, M'sieur l'Accoucheur," that lady said briskly, "you may proceed."

✳   ✳   ✳   ✳   ✳

Alexandre gazed fixedly at his son's features.

"A little pleasanter to look at," he remarked. "Two weeks ago he was, to me, the most nauseating little animal I ever saw."

Marie-Joseph-Rose took the baby more closely in her arms. "To me he was beautiful even then and grows more so every day."

"To a mother," Alexandre conceded grandly, "the ugliest child is always beautiful."

This was only the second time that Alexandre had seen his son. After the birth, for which he had waited impatiently, he had expressed satisfaction that the child was a boy, had commanded that the name Eugene should be given to him and had hurried away to the rue de l'Université.

Marie-Joseph-Rose looked at him thoughtfully.

"Alexandre," she asked, almost incuriously, "have you come home to stay, or is this merely another brief visit?"

He cleared his throat. "You—er—you spoke of our becoming friends——"

She shrugged, feeling little more than indifference now. "Ah, yes, so I did."

"For the sake of our child," he added.

"Yes, for the sake of our child."

"Eugene, of course, is an infant in arms," he said. "Whether we become friends or not could make little difference to him."

"None whatever, at present," she agreed, "though when he grows and begins to take notice of things——"

"Precisely, Rose, and because of that I am willing, providing you agree to my wishes, to make what will naturally be an unpleasant sacrifice."

"Your wishes, Alexandre?"

"Your ignorance is still as pronounced as when you first set foot on French soil. Therefore——"

57

She stopped him impatiently. "So you want to set yourself up as a school-teacher again! What a great fool you are, Alexandre! What a great pompous fool!"

Though his eyes flashed anger at her choice of words he drew himself up with a semblance of dignity and was not displeased, she suspected, at her attitude.

"Very well," he said, "I shall return to the rue de l'Université. As for my son, though he will be a woman's concern for some considerable time the day will come when he will be a man's concern, *my* concern, Rose. When he grows, when his intelligence begins to develop, I shall take control of him, complete control. I have already made up my mind what his place in life is to be. Step by step I shall guide him towards a political career. It will not be *my* fault if he is not regarded by his contemporaries as one of the most learned men of his day."

Marie-Joseph-Rose sighed heavily. "Poor little Eugene."

"Oh, I know that you would pamper him, if you got the opportunity, pamper him shamefully!"

"At all events," she said spiritedly, "I shall do my best to protect him from too much of your ridiculous learning!"

Alexandre looked at her menacingly. "You would actually oppose me in the matter of my son's education?"

"For Eugene's good I would oppose anybody!"

They were both shouting now.

"And once I said you were timid!" he exclaimed.

"I once was, just as I was once afraid of you. Perhaps I still am, but not nearly so much as when I first came to France."

She could see by the way his eyes fell weakly when they met hers that she was getting the better of him. He made one more attempt to assert himself.

"I must say that this is a high and mighty attitude to take up!"

"Yes," she agreed. "A year ago I would never have thought it possible. Perhaps I have gained courage from being a mother."

"Courage!" he shouted. "I have another word for it, *two* words! Disrespect! Impudence!"

"Impudence?" she took him up. "No, no, I can't allow that. Disrespect? Well perhaps, since I find it impossible to feel respect for you."

"Silence!" he screamed. "Silence!"

She thought for a moment that he was going to strike her.

"Please remember this," he said, in a choking voice, "*I* am the master of my own household. *I* shall say what my son shall do and what he shall not do. And remember this too!—if you oppose me too much I shall exercise my full right and take him from you!"

* * * * *

A few months after the birth of Eugene, Alexandre called at the rue Thévenot and announced that he was about to leave France on an extended tour of Italy. Quite naturally Marie-Joseph-Rose suspected that she and her 'opposition' were the cause of this unexpected departure, but later, after he had left Paris, she learned the true reason, first from indefinite hints dropped by the marquis, then in a more concrete form from Madame Renaudin.

"In plain language, my dear," Madame Renaudin said, "Alexandre has gone to Italy because he is in disgrace at court."

"In disgrace because of his unfaithfulness to me?"

"Partly, but chiefly because he has carried dissipation and debauchery a little too far, even for the Queen. There are limits, it seems, even with that woman. Of course, when the scandal of his conduct is forgotten he will come back." Madame Renaudin's eyes twinkled. "In the meantime he is improving his mind in Florence and Rome, is indulging, in fact, in a veritable orgy of culture."

Marie-Joseph-Rose smiled. The smile turned into a broad grin. "A veritable orgy of culture!" she echoed, and burst into laughter.

"My dear," her aunt said, laughing also, "it does me good to see that you have a sense of humor. To know how to laugh is one of the greatest comforts in life."

That Alexandre was indulging in a veritable orgy of culture became evident as his absence lengthened. He wrote a surprising number of letters. They were formal, of course, and pompous, and so typical that when reading them Marie-Joseph-Rose had difficulty in convincing herself that her husband was not in the room towering menacingly above her. Apart from that she derived a certain amount of grim amusement from such sentences as: "I am finding my travels so intellectually stimulating that I propose to continue them for two or three months longer." And she was even able to laugh a little at his remarks on her own dutiful replies: "I must admit that you write a better letter now, though the precision of your phrasing is not as consistent as I should like it to be."

When Alexandre judged that he was no longer in serious disgrace at court he returned, heralding himself by a brief and again typical letter.

This should reach you perhaps a week before my own arrival. I may as well admit that I feel an unreasonably strange excitement at the prospect of seeing you and little Eugene again. I even dare to dream that the happiness of domestic peace and conjugal felicity lie temptingly ahead of me. However, whether such a dream remains a dream, or is transformed into pleasing reality, rests entirely with you.

And so Alexandre, Vicomte de Beauharnais, the house in the rue de l'Université being apparently forgotten, returned to his wife. He was in excellent spirits and even a little amorous, and for the first few weeks he made it quite clear what had been in his mind when he had written the words, 'conjugal felicity.' As for the other words, 'domestic peace,' there was little of that, and what little there was evaporated with the satiation of Alexandre's appetite for 'conjugal felicity.' Within a month there was another and more serious estrangement. Within two months Alexandre was announcing his decision to rejoin his regiment.

"Well," he said, when Marie-Joseph-Rose received his news in silence, "have you nothing to say?"

She shrugged. "What do you want me to say, Alexandre?"

"Nothing, since you seem determined to remain indifferent to my actions!"

She judged it wiser not to open an argument and merely asked if his regiment was still stationed at Verdun.

"Yes," he said, "but it will shortly proceed to Brest. I shall join it there and embark with it on an expedition to Martinique."

This came as a surprise. "Why to Martinique?"

"Because, my dear Rose, whether you know it or not, Martinique is besieged by the cursed English. It is the purpose of the expedition to drive them off." He threw out his chest and appeared to stand stiffly at attention. "And by God, I can promise you they will be driven off!"

Before he left for the coast Marie-Joseph-Rose discovered, with mixed feelings, that the short period of 'conjugal felicity' had resulted in a second pregnancy. She expected Alexandre to be angry at the news, but instead he declared himself to be delighted.

"Ah," he said, dramatically, "if I should die fighting the English there will be two children left to carry on my name!"

When Madame Renaudin and the marquis were told, Madame Renaudin, unknown to her niece, had a word in private with Alexandre.

"I will come to the point at once," she said, "now that your wife is to have a second child your place is surely in France, *not* in Martinique."

In an instant all Alexandre's hatred flared up.

"Madame Renaudin," he said, "you are my father's dearest friend. You are also my godmother. For both reasons I owe you respect.

I give it gladly, but if you continue to meddle in my affairs I shall be obliged to speak to you plainly."

"To my mind, Alexandre, you speak plainly enough now!"

"Regarding the expedition to Martinique, I am a soldier, madame, and it is a soldier's duty to make every sacrifice for his country."

Madame Renaudin found it impossible not to smile. "It is refreshing to hear you speak so patriotically, Alexandre."

"Madame," he said sternly, "I am before all else a patriot!"

"Bravo!" she cried, "bravo!"

He looked at her oddly. "Are you by any chance laughing at me?"

"But of course not. Why should I laugh at such an admirable display of patriotism?"

He still looked at her oddly.

"As for this second child," he said, clearing his throat, "I am delighted to hear of it. I trust the added responsibility of another child will develop in my wife a better sense of decorum and responsibility. And now, madame, if you will excuse me, I have much to do."

And with an air of tremendous importance he bustled out of the room.

✳ ✳ ✳ ✳ ✳

Fate, as things turned out, crowned Alexandre's vaunting patriotism with an unkind climax. By the time he reached Martinique the fighting was over and a peace had been signed. His letters from the island were brief and infrequent, while those from his father-in-law, Joseph-Gaspard Tascher de la Pagerie, brief and infrequent also, hinted vaguely that M'sieur le Vicomte was not a very welcome visitor at Trois-Ilets.

Some seven months after his departure, and while he was still in Martinique, Marie-Joseph-Rose gave birth to her second child, a girl, for whom, unhampered by the interference of Alexandre, she chose the name Hortense. Since in his first letter from the island he had expressed his delight again that he was to be a father a second time, and had instructed her to pray for another son, she was afraid that Hortense would displease him. Nevertheless a letter was dispatched at once to Martinique acquainting him with the news, a letter to which an amazing answer was received.

I tell you coldly, Alexandre wrote, *that in my eyes you are the vilest of beings. I wish you to understand that I have discovered the full extent of the abominable life you led here in Martinique before you became my wife. I cannot bring myself to contemplate the shame*

61

with which you and I, as well as your children, will be covered when all is told. And yet all must be told, for no man in my position could do otherwise than what I shall do when I return to France, and that is to divorce you.

CHAPTER IX

WHEN WORD CAME OF Alexandre's return to France, Marie-Joseph-Rose and Madame Renaudin were at Noisy-le-Grand with the children. Leaving them there with their nurse, aunt and niece hurried back to Paris to see Alexandre and demand an explanation, but he had not yet put in an appearance at the rue Thévenot. However, a letter presently arrived, a letter in which Alexandre ordered his wife to leave his father's roof and retire in shame to a convent. When questioned closely the marquis admitted that he had seen Alexandre for a few moments but had been unable to obtain any satisfaction out of what had clearly been a stormy interview.

"But where is he?" Madame Renaudin demanded. "Where is he staying?"

"He appears to have taken a house in the rue de l'Université."

"He took a house there before," Madame Renaudin said sharply, "for one of his mistresses."

"This is a different house, I think."

"And a different mistress, I presume!"

The marquis shook his head. "He seems to be alone at the moment, Marie."

"Well, whether he is or not hardly matters. Come, François, call the carriage. We must go to him at once."

"We? You mean——?"

"I mean you and I, of course. Rose shall remain here. She will have to see him eventually, but first we must get to the bottom of his extraordinary attitude. The carriage, François, the carriage!"

At the rue de l'Université, Madame Renaudin insisted on the marquis' waiting in the carriage while she entered the house and saw Alexandre alone. At first, after she had gained admittance with difficulty, he refused to see her, but finally she succeeded in coming face to face with him. His appearance shocked her. His eyes, she thought, had the light of madness in them; his voice when he spoke was too level and controlled.

"You might have saved yourself the trouble of this visit, madame."

"I might, but while there is the faintest chance of making you see reason I mean to take it. Your father and I——"

He stopped her with a harsh laugh. "My God, the number of times I've heard you use that opening—*Your father and I!* Why not be honest for once and leave my father out of it?"

Taken slightly aback, Madame Renaudin had nothing to say.

"I have never been blind to the fact that he rarely speaks for himself," Alexandre went on. "From my earliest years my father has been a mere mouthpiece, uttering your views and wishes."

"How *dare* you!" she cried, stung by the truth of this.

"*You* made this marriage of mine, not my father. You made it because you saw a chance of bestowing wealth and position on the child of your impoverished brother." He laughed harshly again. "You saw the chance and you took it, irrespective of whether your niece or I were suited to each other. You took it, I suggest, knowing well enough that Rose would never please me."

"I had certain doubts," Madame Renaudin admitted, "but I never dreamed that you would subject a girl to such inhuman treatment. First you tried to turn her into a pretentious intellectual of your own kidney. Then——"

Alexandre tried to interrupt her but she silenced him with a savage glance.

"Then, when you failed, you began to neglect her. You neglected her to such an extent that you got into trouble at court and were forced to hide for a while in Italy. You have a fine name in Paris, Alexandre, a name to be proud of!" For a moment her indignation almost choked her. "And yet," she went on, scathingly, "the moment you hear some distorted story of your wife's early life in Martinique you come raging home to France demanding a divorce. You sicken me, Alexandre, you sicken me!"

She saw that he was now trembling with rage.

"You will live to regret your words," he said.

"Not I!" She dropped her voice and said more gently: "Alexandre, before you go further with this, please see your wife and tell her what she is accused of, and give her a chance to put things right. Whatever it is she will have some explanation."

"But of course she will!" he sneered. "Being your niece, she will certainly have some explanation!"

"Then you refuse to see her?"

He considered the point for a moment. An instinct, which he refused to recognize as fear, warned him to keep away from his wife; another instinct, which he refused to recognize as vanity, whispered that a meeting with her would give him the chance to dramatize the situation with a host of fine ringing phrases.

"No," he said at last, "I don't refuse to see her. I think I know my duty, but I warn you, madame, my heart is hardened."

"Your heart," Madame Renaudin said, getting in a last thrust, "was always hardened!"

* * * * *

When Alexandre visited Marie-Joseph-Rose at the rue Thévenot the meeting took place in the library, the scene of so much unhappiness in the young girl's married life. Alexandre took up a position at the window and bade her, with exaggerated politeness, to sit down. He appeared to be in a highly nervous state. His eyes were restless and a nerve twitched in his left cheek. For want of something to say Marie-Joseph-Rose asked him if he would like to see Hortense. The question seemed to infuriate him.

"I never want to see her!" he said.

"But why?" she asked, her voice quivering.

"You shall learn that in good time."

There was a silence. Marie-Joseph-Rose, who had felt brave before he arrived, was now on the point of tears.

"Your letter," she said, trying to control her tears, "was horrible."

"Horrible?" he echoed. "Let me tell you, if I had written in the first moment of my anger my pen would have scorched the paper. I waited three weeks before I wrote—three weeks of hell!"

"But tell me what you accuse me of," she begged. "Give me a chance to defend myself."

"Your conscience should tell you the thing of which I accuse you."

"My conscience tells me nothing."

"Then you have no conscience."

"But Alexandre——"

He shrugged his shoulders elaborately. "Very well, if you insist on keeping up this ridiculous pretense, does the name Tercier mean anything to you?"

"Tercier?" she repeated, her hand going involuntarily to her mouth.

"I see that it does!" he cried. "You knew him in Martinique. Come, come, admit it. You knew him in Martinique!"

"Naturally I knew him," she said, "though only for a short time. He was a *sous-lieutenant* in the Martinique Regiment. I was barely sixteen at the time and——"

"Yes," he broke in, dramatically, "to your lasting shame you were barely sixteen!"

"You mean—? You think—?" And she burst into hysterical laughter.

"Tercier," he went on, "is now a captain. I met him at Fort-Royal, and there, when he had taken a little too much wine one day, he made a certain boast. Apparently it was your habit, madame, to bathe with him, to bathe with him in a state of complete nakedness."

"My mulatto maid was present on the only occasion it ever happened," she said quickly. "There was no harm in it, no harm whatever."

"Thank you," he said, with a little bow of mock politeness, "for making no attempt to deny the *affaire*." And he added scornfully: "The fact that you bathed naked with a young man in the presence of a third person is complete proof of your depravity."

She leaped forward instinctively and struck him across the face with her open palm. Then, frightened at what she had done, she fell back in horror.

"So you would strike me!" he gasped.

"I think I would kill you if I could," she whispered.

"This show of temper," he said coldly, "is additional proof of your guilt."

She saw that it was useless to argue with him, to try to convince him of her innocence. And nor, she thought reasonably, could she blame him for believing the worst.

"Tercier," she said, "was obviously piqued because I refused to become his mistress. He told you this story to make trouble between us."

"Ah," he said quickly, "but it so happens that his claim is substantiated by the evidence of a third person."

"Not Marion," she gasped. "She, surely, would have told you the truth."

"No, not your precious mulatto nurse. Someone else. Someone who knew that you met Tercier by appointment, met him many times, and always late at night."

She was watching him closely. The faint smile which had come to his face and the look in his eyes gave her a flash of intuition.

"I think I understand, Alexandre. Your 'third person' is a woman, a woman you met in Martinique and with whom you had an *affaire*. A woman who was jealous of my apparently good marriage, and who has convinced you, perhaps, that you should now set me aside and marry her."

"Very clever," he commented, looking startled, "very clever indeed!"

"Is it possible that I have discovered the truth?"

"If it gives you any satisfaction," he said jauntily, "the third person of whom I spoke was a woman."

"Tell me her name! Tell me her name, Alexandre!"

"Her name is of no consequence, Rose, and storming at me, let me warn you, is useless. I have made my accusation and am prepared to maintain it before any court."

"You must be mad. No judge would attach importance to gossip."

"The gossip can be substantiated. I advise you not to defend yourself, but should you be unwise enough to do so when I present my petition I shall be obliged to bring forward my witness."

"You mean that the woman is actually in France—in Paris?"

"Yes." He bit his lip and cursed himself under his breath. He had never meant to let this fact slip out, but he had been trapped into it, yes, trapped into it. "To help me," he said weakly, "she has made the journey to France."

There was a little silence.

"But this charge you make," Marie-Joseph-Rose broke out at last, "it concerns my life before I met you. Even if what you claim were true——"

"I am well aware of that." He strode forward from the window, affecting a stern, judicial attitude. "In court I shall make it chiefly because it supports and bears out the greater charge I have to bring against you."

"The—*greater* charge?"

"Yes, the greater charge!" He struck a tragic attitude. "You wonder why I refuse to see Hortense. Now you shall know. I am forced to accept this second child of yours, but I swear before God that I am not her father!"

* * * * *

A week after Alexandre had called at the rue Thévenot a briefly worded communication was received from the lawyer who had been engaged to act on his behalf. In this communication Marie-Joseph-Rose was informed that her husband was determined to bring his charges before the courts in an attempt to obtain a divorce, or nullification of the marriage. By this time the wild assertion that he was not Hortense's father had ceased to affect her very deeply, and since, during his absence in Martinique, he had become almost a stranger to her, she had begun to feel that this ridiculous young man, this Alexandre, Vicomte de Beauharnais, had little or nothing to do with her.

"If he wants to divorce me," she told her aunt and the marquis, "let him. I really feel that I have never been his wife, and I know I shall be much happier without him."

"You must be out of your mind," Madame Renaudin said.

"But I never want to live with him again, Aunt Marie."

"I can well imagine that, but——"

"You surely don't think I ought to do so?"

"Certainly not!"

"Then——"

"Whatever happens, my dear Rose, Alexandre must not be permitted to bring his charges before the courts. At least," she amended, "not unopposed. The marquis shall consult with the family adviser at once and discuss the preparation of a counter-case."

"A counter-case? That would really be possible?"

"Unfair as the law is in respect of a wife, yes. Alexandre is in the wrong, shockingly in the wrong, and we can prove it, or so I believe, with the utmost ease."

Marie-Joseph-Rose considered this unexpected aspect thoughtfully. To oppose Alexandre in a court of law, to oppose him and get the better of him, that indeed would be a triumph.

"But wouldn't that mean that I should be obliged to live with him again?" she asked anxiously.

"By no means," the marquis told her. "Prove my stupid son to be in the wrong and a judicial separation will then be possible."

"A judicial separation in your own favor," Madame Renaudin stressed. "I tell you, Rose," she went on, her voice shaking with anger, "Alexandre shall be made to smart for what he has done to you."

It was then suggested by the marquis that Marie-Joseph-Rose would be advised to obey Alexandre in one respect and retire, not in shame, of course, but with dignity, to a convent.

"It happens to be the convention of the day," Madame Renaudin explained. "The retirement, naturally, will only be temporary. I myself shall accompany you and there, in the tranquil atmosphere of a convent, you will be able to rest and—" here she looked obliquely at her niece—"and should you feel so disposed, pray."

An impish light flashed into Marie-Joseph-Rose's eyes. "Pray for Alexandre, you mean?"

"For his confusion, at all events!" Madame Renaudin said, with a laugh.

*　　*　　*　　*　　*

Marie-Joseph-Rose had not been many days at the Abbaye de Panthemont in the rue de Grenelle before she realized that though a convent, the *abbaye* was pervaded by a distinct air of social elegance. Received immediately with sympathy and understanding by numerous women of her own class who, for one reason and another,

67

had become separated from their husbands, she obtained her first real introduction to high Parisian society.

"Just think," she said, with a chuckle, "it was necessary to come to a convent to make my début!"

After only a week at the *abbaye* she became fully conscious of a new and mature dignity. This contact with women of her own class, who chatted freely about their affairs, treated her as an equal and on occasion repeated a naughty story, made her feel more grown up than the birth of her two children could ever have made her feel.

'It would seem,' she told herself with satisfaction, 'that Marie-Joseph-Rose, Vicomtesse de Beauharnais, is a woman of considerable importance.'

After three months at the *abbaye*, three carefree, happy months, she received the marquis and the family lawyer, a prosy old gentleman who discussed the main points of the counter-case and, with many an apologetic cough, asked her a number of searching questions. In the end she gathered that her defense was based chiefly on the fact that Alexandre, when first told of her second pregnancy, had expressed delight, not only to her but to his father and Madame Renaudin, and that later he had expressed this delight again in a letter. The entire weight of the counter-case, it seemed, was contained in this letter which, fortunately, was still in existence.

"We may then conclude," said Madame Renaudin, addressing the lawyer, "that you have every confidence in the success of our counter-case?"

Wagging a playful finger at her he refused to be hustled into a hasty judgment.

"However," he vouchsafed, "I consider it possible that M'sieur le Vicomte's lawyer, when confronted with the sober facts of the counter-case, will advise his client that his over-confidence has led him to make a charge which will be difficult to—er—substantiate."

"In short," Madame Renaudin smiled, "the young man will be advised to change his mind and gracefully withdraw."

"Possibly, possibly," was all the old gentleman would admit.

"You lawyers," she laughed, "you're all the same!"

During the stay at the *abbaye* Madame Renaudin spoke many times of her own share in bringing about her niece's unhappiness.

"If you wished," she said one day, "you could blame me for everything. I was determined to make a wealthy marriage for one of my nieces, and make it I did, but with results more disastrous than I would ever have thought possible."

Marie-Joseph-Rose sighed gently. "I wanted the marriage as much as you did, Aunt Marie. To me it was the one chance of freeing myself from the dullness of life in Martinique. I imagined that if

I could once reach Paris life would take on a great importance, a tremendous richness. I was young and enthusiastic, and very, very ignorant."

"My poor child!" Madame Renaudin exclaimed, emotionally.

Her niece looked at her calmly. "It isn't really necessary to pity me. In spite of everything I am here in Paris, and still young enough to be hopeful."

"You astonish me, Rose, but you please me also."

"It's something I find hard to explain, and yet something that has seemed to grow more certain since I came to the Abbaye de Panthemont. I have the children, of course. They, perhaps, are part of it."

She laughed lightly, dismissing the matter. Nevertheless the impression of impending greatness persisted and she thought of the words of the old hag at Trois-Ilets who had told her fortune. The crown of France indeed! She laughed a little derisively at the memory, a memory which, for the moment, brought tears to her eyes. If, in those far-off days she had believed the talk of a crown, she had the good sense to scoff at it now. She might become a leader of society, the possessor of a famous *salon*, the power behind the political ambitions of many men who were yet to meet and admire her—naturally to admire her!—but a queen, that surely was laughable!

*   *   *   *   *

"Alexandre," Madame Renaudin announced with satisfaction, "has presented himself and wishes to see you."

Marie-Joseph-Rose frowned. "I don't think I want to see him, but his visit, I confess, makes me curious. How does he look, Aunt Marie?"

Madame Renaudin chuckled. "A trifle harassed. Oh, his manner is as pompous as ever, but I suspect a slight uneasiness beneath it all. Naturally you will refuse to receive him."

"Refuse?" The frown deepened, not at the thought of Alexandre but at Madame Renaudin's manner. *Naturally you will refuse to receive him.* It was an order, and as an order, intolerable. She had asserted herself once before in the matter of going to the theater; it was time she asserted herself again.

"Tell me exactly what he said," she demanded.

"Oh, he muttered something about wanting to see you before the legal proceedings are permitted to go any farther."

"Ah, then perhaps he comes from an unpleasant interview with his lawyer." And without further hesitation she said: "Very well, Aunt Marie, I'll receive him at once."

Madame Renaudin began to protest but was quickly silenced.

"I'm not in the least frightened of him. I'm brave enough, I think, and strong enough, to face anything now."

When Alexandre was admitted and Madame Renaudin, at his request, had been dismissed, Marie-Joseph-Rose saw at once that there was certainly a slight uneasiness beneath his pompous exterior. It was more than uneasiness; it was irresolution and something amounting almost to shiftiness.

"I must say," were his first words, "that you appear to be in excellent health."

She watched him guardedly. "I feel better than I have felt for some time, thank you."

He came closer. "Forgive my mentioning the fact, but you look more charming than I have ever seen you look."

She raised her eyebrows. "Really, Alexandre, a compliment at this unhappy stage of our affairs!"

"Even if it is a little out of place," he said sententiously, "I speak the truth. When I married you, you were a child. You are a woman now, a woman whose gracefulness must be envied by many other women."

"Well, well," she said, unable to hide her mirth, "another compliment!"

He frowned. "You ought to know that it is not my habit to pay compliments unless they are fully deserved."

She bowed mockingly. "Then I should be deeply honored indeed!"

A look of irritation crossed his face. "You should be but you're not!" There was a sharp edge to his voice. "That would be clear to the dullest intelligence!"

There was a silence. Marie-Joseph-Rose was the first to break it.

"If you're here simply to pay me compliments, Alexandre, you are wasting your time."

He cleared his throat. "I am here for another purpose."

She waited politely for him to continue.

"It is my duty," he said, "to speak to you once more before the legal proceedings go too far."

"Your—*duty*?"

He drew himself up to his full height. "My duty, Rose, as a husband and a father."

"As a father?" she looked at him squarely. "As a father of one child or—two?"

"As a father of two children." He strode across the room and back.

She saw that a self-righteous look had settled over his face. "I am determined," he went on grandly, "that the child Hortense shall never know, either by the education or treatment I give her, that she owes her existence to some one other than me."

She turned from him with an exclamation of disgust. "For a moment, Alexandre, I believed that you were about to suggest a reconciliation."

"But I was!" he cried. "I——"

"You astound me, Alexandre. You suggest a reconciliation yet persist in making that unspeakable accusation."

"Certainly I persist in making it, but I am nevertheless magnanimous enough to agree to regard Hortense as my own." He struck a lofty attitude. "You fell to temptation, but we are all human and could all sustain a similar fall. I am here today willing to forgive and forget. I am here today to offer you a last chance."

For a moment Marie-Joseph-Rose was speechless. His effrontery was monstrous. Once before, after he had neglected and humiliated her, he had come to her like this, generously offering her a last chance. His conceit was even more monstrous than his effrontery.

"I assure you," he went on, "that I come to you motivated by the tenderest of feelings, and——"

"Motivated by the tenderest of feelings!" she echoed. "Motivated, you mean, by the sudden fear that your case against me might suddenly collapse!"

He made a furious move towards her and then controlled himself.

"I will be patient with you," he said. "I will make my offer once more. Confess that you were unfaithful to me, that Hortense is not mine, and I will say no more about it and—and take you back."

She went swiftly to the door and flung it open. "I have only one thing to say, Alexandre. Please go."

"Go?" he said dumbly.

"Since you don't seem to appreciate plain language I'll say it again. Please go, Alexandre."

With that he gave way to blind anger.

"Henceforth, madame," he raged, "you will find me the most pitiless of tyrants."

"The most pitiless of tyrants?" she repeated. "You speak of the past, surely. You possess no tyrant's power now. I am no longer afraid of you. Please go, Alexandre. You can do no good by remaining. *You* planned this separation. *You* forced it upon me. *I* am determined to maintain it to the best of my ability. Go back to your lawyer. Think of some additional insult. Do your worst. I am not *afraid*!"

* * * * *

It soon became clear that the counter-case was not only strong but unshakable. It even seemed likely that the matter might not be brought before the courts and that Alexandre would be forced to agree to a judicial separation.

Had Marie-Joseph-Rose been present at a meeting between Alexandre and his lawyer she would have seen that this assumption was correct. It was pointed out to Alexandre that, while accusing his wife of improper conduct before marriage with him, it would be obvious to the courts that the woman he proposed to bring forward to substantiate the accusation had been and probably still was his mistress. It was further pointed out that while accusing her of unfaithfulness he was unable to substantiate this more serious accusation with the evidence of a single reliable witness.

And finally it was pointed out that his denial of paternity in respect of Hortense was destroyed before it was made by the letter in which he had expressed delight at the prospect of becoming a father a second time.

"How the devil do you know that I wrote such a letter?" Alexandre demanded.

His lawyer replied by showing him a copy of the letter which had been thoughtfully supplied by his wife's legal adviser. Alexandre sprang to his feet in rage and humiliation and declared that he would take the case to another lawyer.

"You may please yourself," was the reply, "but I warn you that no reputable lawyer will listen to you. Take my advice, m'sieur, and show yourself willing to accept your wife's terms."

"My wife's terms?" Alexandre gasped. "You mean that she has the temerity to suggest *terms*?"

"Yes, indeed, and very generous terms they are, I assure you."

"Monstrous!" Alexandre raged. "I won't listen to them!" His voice rose to a scream. "I won't listen to them!"

The lawyer shrugged and went on to inform his client in a steady voice that a meeting had been suggested at which it was proposed that the already mentioned terms should be discussed.

"A meeting," he added, "to take place on a date mutually agreeable to you and madame your wife."

Alexandre declared weakly that such a meeting was out of the question, but he was advised curtly to give a little calm thought to the matter and warned that if he insisted on taking the case before the courts he would be ruined, socially if not financially. This shook the young man badly.

"Ruined!" he whispered to himself—"impossible, *impossible!*"

The lawyer rose to his feet. "And now, m'sieur, shall we say *au revoir?*"

Alexandre was, of course, unwilling to admit himself to be in the wrong. Nor was it possible for him, in his present frame of mind, to give even a little calm thought to the prospect of meeting Marie-Joseph-Rose in her lawyer's chambers and discussing her terms. The very thought of such a meeting brought a return of the brainstorm which had caused him to make his accusations in the first place. In the end, however, and moved chiefly by fear, he came round to taking his lawyer's advice and intimated, with very bad grace, that he was prepared to meet his wife when and where she wished.

And so, with a sober sense of triumph, Marie-Joseph-Rose, attended by the marquis and Madame Renaudin, came face to face with Alexandre on the afternoon of 3rd March, 1785. Alexandre's lawyer was also present and made it perfectly clear by an occasional sniff and a whole battery of disdainful glances that he was entirely out of sympathy with his client.

"So you are here to gloat over your victory!" Alexandre greeted his wife.

"Hold your tongue, sir!" the marquis said sternly. "This meeting is no easier for Rose than it is for you!"

"No, but it is more profitable!" Alexandre sneered.

Marie-Joseph-Rose turned to her husband's lawyer. "M'sieur, if you are ready I think we could begin."

Her own lawyer invited Alexandre to take a seat.

"I prefer to stand, thank you!" he snapped.

His lawyer stepped forward with a forced smile. "My client is a little—er—distraught. Pray forgive him."

"We are not here to discuss my mood," Alexandre said acidly, "but to transact business of an extremely objectionable nature. Shall we proceed?"

With that the terms of the proposed judicial separation were read out. Marie-Joseph-Rose was to receive an income of five thousand livres a year. Eugene was to remain in her custody until he reached the age of five, when he would pass to his father, while Hortense, maintained entirely by Alexandre, was to remain permanently with her mother. During the reading of these terms Alexandre made several half-hearted attempts to interrupt and from time to time he glanced in fury at his wife.

"All that we require of you now, M'sieur le Vicomte," said the lawyer, when he had finished reading, "is your signature."

Everybody looked at Alexandre. For a moment, while he hesitated, there was a strained silence. Marie-Joseph-Rose felt sure that he was about to refuse to sign the document, but at last, with a wild flourish, he snatched up the pen which was offered to him.

"You see, all of you!" he cried—"I sign! You see, Rose, I sign! Your triumph is complete!" He threw down the pen. "Well, have you nothing to say?"

Marie-Joseph-Rose looked at him gravely. "There is only one thing to say, Alexandre, and that is good-bye."

"Yes, there is that!" he cried. "Good-bye, Rose. Good-bye, and may I never see you again!"

Without a backward glance he flung himself from the room.

The marquis mopped his brow heavily. "Thank God he signed. Frankly, knowing my son, I anticipated a dreadful scene."

Marie-Joseph-Rose herself remained silent. She should, she supposed, feel happy, or at all events satisfied. Alexandre, who had caused her so much unhappiness, had gone out of her life, presumably forever. She sighed deeply. The only thing she was capable of feeling at the moment was a strange tranquillity—that and something else, something which was perhaps independence. Five thousand livres a year! Only a small portion of Alexandre's own income, but still, a sum pleasingly large when up to now she had never enjoyed any real private means of her own.

Madame Renaudin embraced her warmly and she remembered that once she had resolved to model herself on her clever aunt. Now, of course, that would be preposterous. She wanted only to be herself, Madame la Vicomtesse de Beauharnais, and nobody else. The past was the past and too unpleasant to contemplate. Therefore she refused to contemplate it. The future, that was all that could possibly matter.

Sure of one important thing she smiled faintly, secretly; the life she had come to France to live was just about to begin.

Part Two
Independence

ALEXANDRE DE BEAUHAR-
nais was a little bored with the fashionable crowd in the elegant *salon*
of the Princess Amalie of Hohenzollern-Sigmaringen. He stood
in a corner with a refined scowl on his face and glanced languidly
from one chattering group to another. He had come with the princess's brother, the Prince of Salm-Kyrbourg, a young man he had
known casually for several years but with whom he had recently
become more closely acquainted.

Presently Alexandre caught sight of a strange young woman standing with her back to him at the other side of the *salon*. More than
a little tired of his present mistress (the girl he had brought from
Martinique had long since been replaced), he stared speculatively
at the straight back of the stranger, and then at her waist, the slim-
ness of which was emphasized by the fashionable dress she wore.
He moved a little closer. The dress was white, cool and flimsy, and
though she wore a monstrous hat, rather like a Norman castle in
structure (but a Norman castle idiotically bedecked with feathers
and bows), there was an air about her which marked her as a woman
of good taste and, what was more important, good breeding. The
best-dressed woman here, he concluded, and moved closer still. At
that moment she laughed gaily at something Charlotte Robespierre
had said, and turned. Seeing her face, recognizing it in complete
amazement, he uttered a savage little curse, swung on his heels in
exasperation and went quickly from the room.

This was the first time that Alexandre and Marie-Joseph-Rose had
seen each other since the judicial separation a year ago. Having
caught a glimpse of him as he fled, she chuckled in delight, though
a moment later, for some unaccountable reason, she began to feel a
little sorry for him. Poor Alexandre, how woebegone he'd looked,

retreating from the room like that. She sighed gently and felt more than a trifle self-righteous. What a mercy it was that the suffering imposed upon her by Alexandre in the past had failed to embitter her. 'A fool,' she summed up, 'that's what I am, a tender-hearted fool.'

During this year of separation Marie-Joseph-Rose had made many friends. The women she had met at the Abbaye de Panthemont had introduced her to others, the most celebrated being the Princess Amalie, now her close friend. In a very short time she had been made welcome in many of the fashionable *salons* and was now able to consider herself an accepted member of that stratum of society known as *le monde*. No more cultured than on the first day of her marriage, she had nevertheless found this place for herself without the dubious advantages of culture. Schooling herself carefully she had become what Madame Renaudin had advised her to become, a good listener. Bored though she might be with their conversation, she had learned the art of giving all the men she met the impression that she was drinking in and understanding every word they uttered. And in addition she now knew how to encourage and flatter the most tedious talker (and heavens how full *le monde* was of tedious talkers!) by throwing in a wise little comment or question every now and then.

And yet, her great ambition—the ambition to rule over a *salon* of her own—had not been realized, for five thousand livres a year, as she had soon learned, was not the large and magnificent fortune she had first thought it.

On leaving the *abbaye* she and her aunt had joined the marquis at a new house in the rue Charles—a house which was smaller, less imposing and less expensive than the house in the rue Thévenot. At first the marquis had eagerly discussed the possibility of setting up a *salon* for his daughter-in-law, but since his Government pension had been reduced and some of his investments in Saint Domingo had failed, nothing further had been said of so exciting a project. "Economy," Madame Renaudin had warned, "is a necessary evil." She herself had sold the house at Noisy-le-Grand and was now encouraging the marquis to buy a small country residence at Fontainebleau where, with the rising cost of living, expenses would be lighter than in Paris.

"Rose, my dear——"

The voice was Charlotte Robespierre's. She was coming forward now with a strange young man, a tall, dark-eyed young man attired in the new English clothes which every man of fashion was now affecting.

"Permit me," Charlotte said. "M'sieur Edouard Lacoste. M'sieur, the Vicomtesse de Beauharnais."

Marie-Joseph-Rose inclined her head graciously; Lacoste took her hand in his and bowed over it.

"My duty, madame," he murmured.

She looked at him with faint interest. Not only his dress, but his manners also, were English.

She inclined her head again.

"Madame," he remarked, "smiles with her lips but not with her eyes, and that, when madame possesses such splendid eyes, is regrettable."

She freed her hand and laughed gaily.

"Ah," he breathed, "and now, as if by magic, the eyes light up." He clicked his heels and slapped his beautiful, rounded calf with the little riding whip he carried. "I am overcome, madame, with gratitude." He bowed stiffly. "Your servant, madame."

Charlotte's brother, the sombre and frighteningly austere Maximilien Robespierre, approached and engaged Lacoste in conversation.

"What a quaint little man," Marie-Joseph-Rose remarked.

"Hardly 'little,'" Charlotte laughed, "and let me tell you, Rose, he admires you deeply."

Marie-Joseph-Rose giggled. "My duty, madame," she imitated him. "Your servant, madame. Who is he, Charlotte? Or rather, *what* is he? You made no reference to a title of any sort."

Charlotte smiled. "Title or not, M'sieur Lacoste is a young man of considerable wealth."

The faint interest Marie-Joseph-Rose had first felt began to expand.

"A—bachelor?"

"Presumably, and a very close friend, a confederate, one might almost say, of the formidable Necker."

Marie-Joseph-Rose felt a sudden excitement. Necker! Lacoste a very close friend, a confederate, one might say, of His Majesty's Director-General of Finance! She glanced at him quickly as he talked with Charlotte's brother. "Your servant, madame," she heard him say again. Your *servant*! Was this the opportunity for which she had waited? Was Lacoste to be the means of bringing her nearer to her long-cherished goal, the Court of Marie Antoinette?

She picked up her hooped skirt hurriedly, but not, she hoped, *too* hurriedly.

"Excuse me, Charlotte," she murmured. "I feel a little faint. This dreadful crowd. . . ."

She began to move towards the balcony and in passing Lacoste brushed lightly against him. As she left the room she glanced back. Lacoste had already broken away from Robespierre. She smiled, with her eyes this time if not with her mouth, and sailed with dignity towards the balcony. . . .

*   *   *   *   *

Madame Renaudin chuckled. "So Alexandre fled the moment he recognized you. How very amusing!"

Marie-Joseph-Rose, still thinking of Lacoste and the conversation on the balcony, was barely listening.

"Alexandre," the marquis remarked, "is newly back from a tour of the provinces. They tell me that he's beginning to take an interest, an active interest, in politics. He made a speech at Lyon, a speech in which he gave expression to some amazingly republican ideas."

"More fool he," Madame Renaudin snapped. "Republican ideas will hardly maintain the favor he still enjoys at court."

"Possibly not," said the marquis, wagging his head sagely, "but Alexandre, I suspect, is merely acting shrewdly."

"Shrewdly?" Marie-Joseph-Rose questioned, forced, in spite of her preoccupation, to take an interest in the conversation.

"I mean, my dear, that he must see how badly things are going with the monarchy. He must realize, as many do, that the restlessness in France today, particularly in the provinces, is only the beginning."

Madame Renaudin pursed her lips. "So you think there's more than meets the eye in this wild talk one hears of a coming revolution?"

"I do indeed, though I must admit that Necker, with his many economies, may yet avert what some people insist on regarding as inevitable."

Marie-Joseph-Rose smiled. So that was the reason behind Alexandre's opposition to the monarchy! She laughed scornfully. Revolution! Could anything be more impossible!

Her thoughts returned to Lacoste. Could any man have been more amazingly frank? "I am," he'd said, "a man who shuns marriage, a man who runs from it. Therefore, when I pay court to a woman I choose one who is either unlikely, or unable, to make marriage a tiresome condition." That, in all conscience, had been clear enough!

"What," Aunt Marie was saying, "does Charlotte Robespierre think of the political situation?"

Marie-Joseph-Rose shrugged lazily. "I haven't asked her, Aunt Marie. She and I have more interesting things to discuss than politics, which, I'm afraid, are something of a bore to me."

78

"No one would think so when a politician talks to you, my dear."

"Our little Rose," the marquis laughed, "is an exceedingly clever young woman these days."

She smiled her thanks. She had been prepared, of course, to listen to a political discourse from Lacoste, but he, thank heaven, had spoken of anything but politics. She frowned. Politics, nevertheless, would have been a safer, less disconcerting subject. Then she repressed a giggle. "M'sieur," she'd said with tremendous dignity when he had boldly proposed an assignation, "separated as I am from my husband, I have never yet been unfaithful to him," and with a wicked little laugh Lacoste had asked her if she were on the point of taking the veil.

"You know," Aunt Marie was saying thoughtfully, "had you dealt with Alexandre as skilfully as you now deal with the men you meet there might never have been a separation."

"That is possible," she agreed.

Had she, she wondered, dealt skilfully with Lacoste? When he'd pressed her still further for an assignation she'd told him indignantly that she wasn't the sort of woman he might find on the pavement outside the Opera House. And then, when he'd tweaked her nose— tweaked it really hard—and called her a provocating little witch, she'd fallen into a confused and blushing silence. Finally he'd said: "That Madame la Vicomtesse has had no experiences in love, save those which the good God granted her during her married life with Alexandre de Beauharnais, is all too evident. Madame la Vicomtesse, however, is still young, still in possession of a tempting charm." And with a bow and an unmistakable gleam in his eye he'd added: "Your servant, madame, when and where you choose."

"If you really wished it, my dear," the marquis said brightly, "the relationship between you and Alexandre could be very different now."

She looked in amazement from him to Madame Renaudin.

"Is it possible," she gasped, "that you would like to see us reconciled?"

"If a reconciliation could be achieved on your own terms, yes, I think we would." It was Madame Renaudin who spoke. "After all, you must think of your children. Hortense will never be taken from you, but Eugene, remember, is fast approaching the age when he will pass to his father's care."

Marie-Joseph-Rose gave an exclamation of annoyance. That Eugene would soon be five and taken from her was a fact which she had been trying to ignore for weeks now. She loved her son. She wanted to keep him, but to keep him at the price of a reconciliation with Alexandre, always providing Alexandre himself could be brought to such an agreement, was a thought which filled her with horror. She sighed. Was ever a poor woman more harassed than she! A reconciliation with Alexandre or an intrigue with Lacoste, the friend of Necker—which was it to be? In the name of heaven, *which* was it to be?

There was, of course, the alternative of turning her back on both Alexandre and Lacoste and justifying her independence completely by setting up house on her own account. This she had thought of many times, but her income of five thousand livres, scrape and save as she might, would hardly be sufficient. *Hardly* sufficient! Indeed not at all, for wasn't she, though living at no cost to herself with the marquis and Madame Renaudin, a little in debt already?

"What am I to do?" she asked herself, "what in the world am I to do?"

*   *   *   *   *

Madame la Comtesse de Beauharnais, Alexandre's aunt, was giving a hunt. It was, of course, a very fashionable occasion, since Madame Fanny, as she was known to her large circle of friends, was a very fashionable lady. She herself, Marie-Joseph-Rose took note at once, was wearing the latest style in riding-dresses. Like 'The Amazon,' which Marie-Joseph-Rose had taken such pride in wearing when first she'd come to Paris, it was English in origin, but the skirt, instead of being tight, was full and loose, the whole effect being much less austere than one might have expected from those prim and somewhat gloomy English. "Most certainly," she decided, feeling wretchedly out-moded in her own still well-preserved Amazon, "I must order a new riding-dress at once." She glanced swiftly about her, ignoring the men, the horses, the joyously barking dogs, and concentrated solely on the women. She smiled almost happily. What a mercy that most of them were dressed as she was dressed in the same old style.

Madame Fanny (really, the woman was much too old to wear *any* sort of riding-dress!) approached and embraced her warmly.

"My dear Rose, such a pleasure to see you here."

"Such a pleasure to be able to come," Marie-Joseph-Rose murmured.

"Alexandre is expected—" the old woman's eyes danced mischievously—"you knew that, of course?"

"Yes, I knew."

"And yet, it didn't deter you?"

"Certainly not," Marie-Joseph-Rose replied with hauteur.

"The question, of course, is whether your being invited will deter Alexandre, for naturally I thought it only fair to warn him."

Marie-Joseph-Rose laughed lightly. "So very considerate of you, Madame Fanny."

A bitch, Madam Fanny, for all her breeding, to be sure, a bitch!

"Ah!" cried the old harridan, "there he is now. See, my dear, to the left of the Princess Amalie and in conversation with that fascinating M'sieur Lacoste."

Marie-Joseph-Rose glanced hastily at her husband and Lacoste. Lacoste, stifling a yawn, was clearly bored with Alexandre's all-too-evident earnestness. Both were dressed in the same style which, like the female riding-dress, was also English in origin, but Lacoste, undoubtedly a better figure of a man than Alexandre, looked the smarter. Such broad shoulders, such a lovely chest, such delightful thighs and well-turned calves.

"The recalcitrant husband," Madame Fanny tittered, "and the prospective lover."

Taken off her guard for a moment, Marie-Joseph-Rose began to protest. Her, "But Madame Fanny, M'sieur Lacoste and I have met on one occasion only," was cut short by another and undoubtedly lewd titter.

"One occasion only, my dear Rose, should be sufficient for a man like Lacoste."

"How disgusting," Marie-Joseph-Rose said weakly, "that people, having seen me in conversation with M'sieur Lacoste several days ago, should have begun to gossip already."

She moved away, paused for a moment to speak to the Princess Amalie and then, turning, found herself face to face with Alexandre. Lacoste, who withdrew a few paces but remained at a distance to watch sardonically, she completely ignored.

Alexandre, who for a moment showed signs of fleeing once again from the sight of her, controlled himself visibly and mumbled a polite greeting. Inclining her head graciously she agreed that it was indeed a pleasant day for Madame Fanny's hunt.

Perhaps the devil was in her, or perhaps it was the new self which independence and a measure of social success had bred, or perhaps again it was the contemplation of a profitable reconciliation —whatever the reason she found herself leading Alexandre on to talk of his political interests. At first he looked at her suspiciously, but soon, obviously deciding that she was absolutely sincere in her attitude, he became expansive. While he talked her mind strayed to a hundred things and her eyes kept an alert watch on Lacoste, but she schooled herself to listen with an air of expectancy and nodded her neat little head energetically every now and again.

"And so," she said, at exactly the right moment, "you're beginning to make yourself *felt*, Alexandre."

His face glowed foolishly with pleasure. "Indeed I am, my dear Rose, indeed I am!"

"But not in court circles, I gather," she remarked, with unintentional wickedness.

He gave a contemptuous snort. "Certainly not! My views are a little too drastic, a little too revolutionary, for the ordinary court idler."

She reflected with amusement that Alexandre himself was no longer a court idler, ordinary or otherwise. And for no reason at all she thought: 'Forty thousand livres a year and all he allows me is five thousand.'

"France," he went on, staring prophetically into space, "is on the eve of a tremendous change, a change that even Necker and his friend Lacoste are too blind to foresee. Wherever you go throughout the length and breadth of the country you find restlessness and dissatisfaction. True, the people have been restless before, but this time their restlessness arises from the fact that their stomachs as well as their pockets are empty. And yet, how many worthy members of the Assembly can see the signs, can grasp their significance?"

"How many indeed!" she sighed, looked prophetically into space too, and then, in a flash of sheer inspiration she added: "You should be in the Assembly yourself, Alexandre."

He laughed triumphantly. "I should be, Rose, and indeed I shall be soon." And he told her proudly that he was even now preparing to stand as a candidate at a coming by-election at Blois. Mildly surprised and feeling a more serious interest than formerly in a possible reconciliation, she allowed him to enlarge at length on the coming revolutionary speeches he intended to make. Supposing he *were* elected, supposing he became prominent in the Assembly, became, in fact, a leader of some consequence? If a revolution did take place Alexandre de Beauharnais the anti-monarchist would be a man of considerable importance. It made one think, merciful heavens it did!

Presently, when Alexandre became aware that the Prince of Salm-Kyrbourg was waiting for him, he withdrew reluctantly and Lacoste strolled up to take his place.

"Your servant, madame," he said.

She evaded him with a frown as he made to take her arm.

"Madame la Vicomtesse," he murmured, "is a tantalizing creature, but I, I assure her, am a man of infinite patience." He bowed. "I repeat, your servant, madame, when and where you choose." And with that he was gone.

She stared broodingly after his handsome figure. Alexandre or Lacoste? Would she ever be able to make up her mind?

CHAPTER XI

Y OUR CHIEF TROUBLE," Madame Renaudin remarked, a trifle acidly, "is that you buy anything and everything that takes your fancy and never dream of asking the price."

They were discussing the tiresome subject of money. For some time now Marie-Joseph-Rose's debts had been mounting steadily. An uncontrollable extravagance allied with a characteristic carelessness in money matters had brought her to this unfortunate pass and neither Madame Renaudin nor the marquis, it seemed, was able to offer her much in the way of material assistance.

"Precisely how much do you owe?" Madame Renaudin demanded.

"Oh, a few hundred livres here," Marie-Joseph-Rose said vaguely, "a few hundred there. Perhaps a thousand livres altogether. I couldn't possibly give you the exact figure off-hand."

"The matter appears to rest anything but heavily on your mind."

"It rests a great deal more heavily on it than you imagine, Aunt Marie. Are you sure you can't help me over this temporary embarrassment?"

Madame Renaudin laughed drily. "Between us, my dear child, François and I can raise little more than a few hundred livres."

"Dear me, are things as bad as that?"

"They are. Fortunately a convenient house has been found at Fontainebleau, to which we shall retire permanently just as soon as a good price can be obtained for this Paris house, but even so, rigid economy will be unavoidable for all of us in the future."

Marie-Joseph-Rose sighed deeply. How utterly tiresome this money question was. She was desperately in need of three or four new dresses and at least two new hats. If only styles changed less frequently these days!

"Have you never thought," Madame Renaudin said, "of asking Alexandre for an increased allowance?"

An increased allowance? But of course! That would solve everything—temporarily, at all events. Besides, Alexandre was now a member of the Assembly, having succeeded in getting himself elected as one of the two deputies for Blois. With his forty thousand livres a year and the perquisites of his office, surely— After all, an increased allowance would be better than a reconciliation, and even if she did reach an understanding with Lacoste, ten thousand livres a year from her husband instead of the present five would give her the security of a substantial independence.

She laughed merrily. The next time she met Alexandre she'd set him talking about his precious political aspirations and listen more attentively than she had listened to anybody else before. And then, when he was in a magnanimous mood, she would weep quietly, force back her tears with a brave effort, and tell him just how hard it was for a poor woman to manage alone with two children to keep in times as difficult and trying as these.

She laughed again. Her cares had melted away. It would not be long, she felt, before she could order not simply four new dresses but twelve, which was actually the number she needed.

* * * * *

"A pity," Alexandre said gallantly, "that our meetings these days should be so infrequent and haphazard."

She looked at him gravely. "Indeed yes, Alexandre, a pity."

She and Alexandre were at a ball, an elaborate and gay affair given by the Princess Amalie. Since Lacoste was absent she had devoted the entire evening to Alexandre, boring as it undoubtedly was. She had even danced with him to the exclusion of all others and now, having been led to a secluded corner of the ballroom, was prepared to put her little plan into action.

"I wonder," she said, with a gay laugh, "whether this is really proper, our retiring together like this?"

"You think we ought to be chaperoned?" he asked archly.

"Perhaps," she replied, with mock gravity.

Alexandre coughed and, though looking at her speculatively, turned the subject of the conversation to the children.

"Tell me about them, Rose. Are they well and happy?"

"Oh yes," she said. "Hortense especially, but your father thinks she should be inoculated and I'm a little in doubt about giving my consent. Inoculation, I know, has become all the rage, but one hears such dreadful stories about it, really one does."

"Inoculation," Alexandre pronounced authoritatively, "is a splendid thing. You would be well advised to fall in with my father's suggestion."

"You really think so, Alexandre?"

"I do indeed."

"Then in that case—" She gave a little sigh. "It's so very hard for a woman in my position to know just what to do for the best." She dismissed the subject with a gesture of resignation. "But tell me about yourself, Alexandre, and your political activities. I can't say how pleased I was to hear of your election to the Assembly."

Delighted by this he began a long and detailed account of what he had done since becoming a deputy, and what he intended to do in the immediate future. Presently, however, he recollected with an effort that they were at a ball and asked her half-heartedly if she would care to dance again.

She shook her head decisively. "I would much rather stay here and talk, if you don't mind, Alexandre."

"Mind!" he cried, and her heart sank a little. "I prefer it." He looked at her searchingly. "But surely I shall bore you if I talk *too* much?"

She shook her head again—thank heaven the light was too dim for him to see her eyes!

"Oh no, my dear," she said. "So few men today have anything worthwhile to talk about. Please tell me more of the work you're doing for France. I am deeply, *very* deeply, interested."

"My dear Rose—" his voice was warm and rich—"you astonish me. Why, in the past——"

She stopped him quickly. "Let's not talk of the past, Alexandre. Neither our own past nor our country's. For those who love France—" how grand it sounded, how very grand!—"it is the future that matters."

"The future, yes!" With which he began to enlarge on what he had already said. "I have many plans and hopes for the future of our country, but before the plans can be executed and the hopes realized, unheard-of reforms must be brought about. For any man who has studied Rousseau as I have, for any man who knows the lamentable conditions of present-day France as I do, for any man who. . . ."

And so, he ran on, repeating phrase after phrase for additional emphasis and flinging himself to his feet every now and again in a vertible fervor of political and patriotic zeal. At midnight he was still talking.

"Revolution is an ugly word, Rose, but so blind and wilful are those who uphold the monarchy in its present manifestation that revolution may yet burst upon a startled France in all its ugliness. I tell you, my dear, there is just one course open to any man who is a patriot, one bold and dangerous course. . . ."

What that course was she never learned, for soothed rather than irritated by the rise and fall of his voice she had fallen for a few moments into a fitful doze. Fortunately she was wide awake again before Alexandre discovered what had happened, and by that time it was seen that the Princess Amalie's guests were beginning to take their leave.

Going home to the rue Charles in the carriage she wondered how on earth she had managed to hide her boredom. Alexandre was the most tedious man in the world, and the most conceited. All this fiery talk of a coming revolution, surely it was lunacy, sheer lunacy.

She was satisfied, however, that she had made an even bigger impression than previously—for hadn't Alexandre kissed her hand on bidding her *au revoir* and uttered the hope that he would have the pleasure of her company again very soon? That was why, while taking the lateness of the hour into consideration also, she had decided against confiding in him this time. It would be wiser to wait just a little longer before bringing up the subject of her financial troubles. In the end—why, in the end he would have been flattered and sweetened to such an extent that he would be willing to treble her allowance, yes *treble* it!

✳   ✳   ✳   ✳   ✳

The packet which Lacoste's valet had delivered at the rue Charles was small, so small that it looked ridiculous lying on the pale yellow expanse of the letter which had accompanied it. A present? Without doubt, but—what?

Ignoring the letter, Marie-Joseph-Rose tore open the packet. A slim gold chain fell out, and attached to it a small cross formed exquisitely in jet. She frowned. A cross? In the name of heaven why a cross? She opened the letter. The handwriting was elegant and sloping. As she read she was torn between indignation and a desire to giggle.

Madame,

I present my duty, and with it this trifling gift. The cut of a woman's gown becoming lower with each new style, many dear creatures these days have taken to wearing crosses as a sign of purity and chastity. We are to be fellow-guests, I understand, at Madame Fanny's a week from today when the chief attraction of the evening will be the celebrated Doctor Mesmer. Should you choose to wear my little offering I shall, naturally, be obliged to commend your chaste pretensions; should you choose not to wear it, but to treasure it in your jewel casket, unused, I shall prepare myself with all speed to take advantage of the invitation so delicately issued.

Your servant, Madame,
Edouard Lacoste.

A footman entered.

"M'sieur le Vicomte de Beauharnais," he announced.

Marie-Joseph-Rose gave a little gasp of surprise. She caught up the cross and the letter, hiding them in the folds of her dress just as Alexandre, following on the heels of the servant, came forward to greet her. He had come, he said, not without a show of embarrassment, to see the children, and to discuss the matter of Eugene's approaching fifth birthday.

"Naturally," he said, "you will hardly relish the thought of parting with the boy."

"Naturally." Her face clouded and she went on bravely. "But since I agreed that he should pass to your care at the age of five there's little I can do, save hope that he will be as happy with you as he has been with me."

Alexandre pursed his lips. "I understand how you feel, my dear, but I want my son. I want to give him the father's care so necessary to a boy. You will still have Hortense, you know."

"Of course." And she asked if he intended to engage a tutor for Eugene.

"No," Alexandre said, "I shall send him to school. I should like a tutor for him but school will be cheaper."

"Cheaper?" Marie-Joseph-Rose echoed in surprise.

"Yes, cheaper. Economy, I fear, is a necessary evil with me these days."

She looked at him sharply. *School would be cheaper—economy was a necessary evil!* And here she was about to ask Alexandre for an increased allowance!

"I should advise you to practice a little economy too," he went on. "You will be sure to feel the pinch sooner or later."

"I'm afraid I'm beginning to feel it already, Alexandre."

He raised his eyebrows. "Already? But there has been no decrease in your allowance up to now."

The word 'decrease' made her heart miss a beat.

"I find it terribly hard," she confessed, "to manage in these difficult times. The cost of living is always going up—" little she knew about the cost of living, but it was a grand phrase!—"and the price of clothes is simply staggering. Really Alexandre, one's money goes nowhere at all."

He looked at her steadily. "Are you by any chance trying to tell me that you are in debt?"

She made her eyelids flutter for a moment, then she looked down in apparent embarrassment. "I'm ashamed to admit it, Alexandre, but I really am in debt."

He looked at her for a moment in grim silence.

"Confound it all, Rose, five thousand livres a year——!"

"Please don't misunderstand me," she broke in quickly, "I have merely over-spent myself a little. The next payment of your allowance is due soon. I shall be able to liquidate my debts then."

"I sincerely hope so, Rose!"

"I happened to think," she went on, in her sweetest manner, "that you might help me by making an advance."

"An advance? Er—how much would you need?"

This was a little better than she had expected after the use of the word 'decrease.'

"Let me see, now," she pondered—"a thousand livres, perhaps."

"A *thousand!*" he echoed, and laughed as if it were a good joke. "Tell me how much you owe."

She looked at him apologetically. "More than a thousand, I'm afraid. Honestly, I can't imagine how I got so badly in debt. I suspect my creditors of cheating me on every hand, just because I am a poor defenseless woman."

Alexandre chose not to see the tears that had come to her eyes and asked her again how much she owed.

She took a deep breath and said in a whisper, "Almost three thousand livres."

This was too much for him and he began to pace up and down in agitation. "Shameful!" he kept muttering, "shameful." Finally he sat down at her side.

"Three thousand livres," he said severely, "is more than half your yearly income."

She found a little lace handkerchief. "Yes, Alexandre." She touched her eyes gently with the handkerchief. "Isn't it terrible? That is the worst of being a poor defenseless woman. Do you—do you think you can come to my rescue?"

He frowned at the repetition of the phrase *a poor defenseless woman,* and murmured that he would like very much to come to her rescue.

"After our last two meetings," he said, "when you showed such a surprisingly sound understanding of the political situation, I began to feel a real friendship for you. I said to myself, 'Rose has changed: Rose has gained wisdom and balance.' In short, I began to see that you had grown up at last."

"You flatter me, Alexandre," she said earnestly.

"That is not my intention." He sprang to his feet. "However, I am too deep in financial difficulties myself to be of any real help to you. As a matter of fact—" he looked at her obliquely and coughed—"as a matter of fact, I was about to approach you on the subject of reducing your yearly allowance."

Her first impulse was to remind him that he was legally bound by the deed of separation to pay her five thousand livres a year, and that even the smallest reduction was out of the question, but she was wise enough to check this impulse and wait for him to continue.

"Things have come to such a pass," he said, "that I shall have extreme difficulty in making you the full payment this year. When we were first married I had forty thousand livres a year, but every year since then a thousand or so has fallen off. In addition I have made bad investments recently and the family estates in Saint Domingo, as my father must have told you, are showing little or no return."

"Then you can give me no help whatever?"

"I can let you have four hundred livres now, not a sou more. Later I will do my best to meet my obligations, but please try not to count on me too much."

"But only four hundred livres!"

He looked at her hopefully. "Perhaps you think the amount too small to accept?"

"Oh no," she said hastily, "I shall accept it gladly!"

"I imagined you would," he sighed.

A few moments later, there being little more to say, he bade her a grave *au revoir* and took his departure, a departure that was almost hurried. For some time she remained seated, staring gloomily into space. Four hundred livres was no doubt better than nothing at all. Distributed carefully among her creditors it might keep them quiet for a little while, but surely not for long, and *then* what? On second thoughts it would be foolish to give the creditors any of the money. Better by far to hoard it jealously against the possibility of even more difficult times, and——

Suddenly she laughed aloud, and in considerable relief. Lacoste! She'd completely forgotten Lacoste. Fingering the little black cross she read his letter again, and no longer inclined to indignation she giggled and chuckled freely. Alexandre or Lacoste, that had been the question, but now the miserable, poverty-stricken Alexandre had been eliminated. The question was simply Lacoste or not Lacoste, and there was, she saw clearly, but one answer. She swung the cross on its chain and smiled faintly. Nevertheless, when she went to Madame Fanny's to meet the amazing Doctor Mesmer—at least people *said* he was amazing—she would wear the 'trifling gift,' the 'little offering' and await with interest the next move of the obviously resourceful Edouard Lacoste.

CHAPTER XII

THE FOOTMAN JACQUES

entered the room.

"The hired carriage is waiting, madame," he announced.

Marie-Joseph-Rose looked at the man suspiciously. His face was impassive but surely there'd been a hint of superciliousness in his voice when uttering the word 'hired.'

"Very well," she said, dismissing him.

Save for two servants she was alone in the house. The marquis and Madame Renaudin, taking the children with them and accompanied by the other servants, had left that morning for Fontainebleau, travelling, of course, in the family coach. The house had been sold and tomorrow the men would come to remove the furniture, most of which was to be disposed of by auction. Permanent retirement to Fontainebleau—the thought, now that it was an actual reality, was more intolerable than ever. Ah well, there was still Lacoste. A hateful alternative, no doubt, but nonetheless a very necessary evil.

She gave a final glance at herself in the mirror. The head-dress decorated with only a few small feathers would be the least elaborate to be seen at Madame Fanny's tonight, but though the other women might sneer behind their fans, Lacoste, she felt sure, would be struck by its appealing simplicity. The dress, though old—she had worn it at least *four* times!—was a dainty white mousseline, cut extremely low and very full in the skirt. She pirouetted before the mirror. Yes, she still looked her best in white, and the little black cross—she smiled mischievously as she looked at it—gave her an air of becoming innocence.

Satisfied, she made her way down to the hall where the waiting Jacques, his face still impassive, opened the door for her and assisted her into the hired carriage.

"To the hotel of Madame la Comtesse de Beauharnais," he told the driver.

The whip cracked and the horses leaped forward with such suddenness that Marie-Joseph-Rose fell back heavily on the soiled and faded velvet cushions. It was nine o'clock and all the fashionable world, it seemed, was abroad in equally fashionable carriages. A shower of rain had fallen earlier, so that the lights from the shop windows and the street lamps flickered and gleamed in the wet pavements.

Suddenly she noticed that the carriage, turning sharply, had entered a narrow and darkened alley. Cut-throats were thick in such alleys and the driver, quite likely, was in league with them. She leaned out of the window and called to him to stop.

"This is not the way," she cried. "You've taken the wrong turning."

"A riot which began at the Pont Neuf," he told her, "is spreading rapidly. A detour is therefore necessary."

"A riot?" she questioned, disbelieving him instantly.

"The price of bread has risen again," he said, laconically. "The people cry out for the blood of M'sieur Necker."

The carriage passed out of the alley into a wide and lighted thoroughfare, a thoroughfare which, in an instant, was full of shouting, jeering people, and she realized that the driver had indeed spoken the truth. In a moment the carriage was brought to a halt and surrounded. She withdrew deeper into it, while faces, distorted in anger, loomed up about her and a woman, whose painted cheeks and exposed breasts marked her as a prostitute, flung open the door and leaped in beside her.

"Ah!" the creature cried, "a pretty lady, a marquise, one would think, on her way to the Tuileries to visit the Queen."

"In a hired carriage?" Marie-Joseph-Rose, despite her fear, had the presence of mind to retort. "You make a grave mistake, m'm'selle."

There was a loud laugh from the crowd, a laugh which changed to a low and threatening cry as a detachment of mounted soldiers entered the street at the gallop and with drawn swords. In a moment a path was cleared, the prostitute was dragged from the carriage and the frightened, whinnying horses were whipped into motion again.

When the carriage reached Madame Fanny's and a porter sprang forward to help her alight, she found that her knees were weak and shaky and that her heart was palpitating heavily. She turned to the driver.

"You are acquainted, perhaps," she said impulsively, "with certain poor people who find it impossible to buy bread at the new price?"

"Assuredly, madame."

Her heart melted in sudden pity. "Present yourself, then, at the rue Charles early tomorrow morning and you shall have fifty livres to distribute."

Feeling calmer she entered the brilliantly lighted hall, and preceded by Madame Fanny's *major-domo*, passed into the big *salon*, which was crowded with people and so dimly lit that it was impossible to recognize but a few faces. A man stepped forward.

"Ah, Lacoste," she murmured, and turned to greet her hostess who, wagging a podgy forefinger accusingly, had bustled towards her from the shadows.

"How late you are, Rose," she said. "The proceedings, as you see, have already begun."

Lacoste took Marie-Joseph-Rose's arm in a firm grip and together they moved towards the centre of the *salon*.

"How very gratifying," he whispered, "to see that Madame la Vicomtesse has decided not to wear my little present."

She clutched at her throat. The cross indeed was no longer there. It must have been lost when the crowd had surrounded her carriage, or snatched by that wretched painted woman.

"I assure you, m'sieur," she said earnestly, "that I was wearing it when I left the rue Charles."

He chuckled softly. "The catch, no doubt, was a little insecure."

She looked at him sharply. So! A faulty catch!

"You rogue!" she cried.

He chuckled again. "Whatever the reason, Madame la Vicomtesse has appeared before me unadorned and unprotected by the little cross, and I am well content."

She laughed lightly. So very sure of himself, this Edouard Lacoste! And of course, a charming gentleman. Already she was beginning to like him, to admire his bearing and powerful physique. In time it might even be possible to fall in love with him, otherwise—for a moment she had a shattering thought—otherwise what difference would there be between Madame la Vicomtesse de Beauharnais and the nameless creature who had invaded her carriage not ten minutes ago?

"An amazing sight, all this," Lacoste remarked, gazing idly round the room.

She followed his eyes. Amazing indeed, especially the little circle of people in the centre of the *salon*. They were grouped about what appeared to be a large covered bath-tub, out of which iron rods extended and were hooped about the legs and arms, and in some cases the necks, of Madame Fanny's guests.

"Mesmer," Lacoste told her, "calls it a *baquet*. The inside is full of wine bottles, each filled with supposedly magnetized water. Before the lid was adjusted water was poured into the *baquet* until the bottles were completely submerged, and iron filings, said to increase the magnetism, were scattered thickly on the surface."

"But the iron rods?" she asked.

"According to our worthy doctor the magnetism flows through them into one's body and cures one of whatever ills and pains one might be suffering."

"Then all these solemn people are in pain?"

"Hardly," he laughed scornfully. "But since the fashion to patronize our little charlatan has been set by the Queen herself—" and leaving the sentence unfinished he laughed again.

A moan, followed by a cry of ecstasy, caused Marie-Joseph-Rose to turn suddenly. There, lying full length on a couch, was an elderly woman, while Mesmer himself, dressed in a long black gown, was bending over her.

"Madame la Marquise de Bausset," Lacoste said, "and suffering, one would imagine, from a cancer in the stomach."

Mesmer, it seemed, was making curious passes in the air with an iron wand, but what was more amazing was the actions of one of Mesmer's assistants. While Mesmer waved his wand this man, fingers extended like talons, was massaging the lady's abdomen in a manner that was surely quite indecent.

"Mesmer contends," Lacoste was explaining, "that there is sufficient animal magnetism in his body to cure almost any ill. That such a thing exists is, of course, undeniable, but Mesmer, to my mind, is a quack of the most dangerous order." He smiled reminiscently. "I myself have found it possible on occasion to induce in a suitable subject a deep and lasting trance."

"By a suitable subject," Marie-Joseph-Rose murmured, "m'sieur undoubtedly means some poor and weak-willed female."

"Undoubtedly, madame."

Leaving Madame la Marquise to his assistant, Mesmer turned to Madame Fanny who, with many an arch glance, was complaining loudly of a headache.

"Music!" Mesmer commanded, in his harsh Austrian accent.

Madame Fanny clapped her hands. "Music!" she ordered.

An orchestra, which Marie-Joseph-Rose had failed to notice earlier, began to play softly. Mesmer, dispensing with his wand, made several mysterious passes in the air, creeping closer every moment to his hostess.

"Watch," Lacoste whispered.

Madame Fanny was already beginning to sway drunkenly.

"You will sleep," Mesmer ordered softly.

Madame Fanny uttered a little shriek and fell on her back, her heels tapping sharply on the floor.

"Sleep," Mesmer repeated, "sleep, sleep, sleep. . . ."

And Madame Fanny fell obediently into a deep slumber.

Mesmer turned to Marie-Joseph-Rose. "Madame suffers from a headache also, yes?"

"No!" She shrank away from him, clutching violently at Lacoste's arm. "Merciful heavens, no."

"I myself," Lacoste informed the waiting Mesmer, "will attend to Madame la Vicomtesse."

He led her to a corner of the room, turned her sharply about to face him and stood back from her.

"Really, Lacoste—" she protested weakly.

He laughed gaily. "In the interests of this strange new science a little experiment is surely permissible."

He tweaked her nose and made several rapid passes in the air. "Look into my eyes," he commanded sternly.

"What utter nonsense," she said, but she looked.

"Sleep," he whispered, "sleep," and his voice sounded strangely like Mesmer's.

The music faded and the people about her grew hazy. All she was conscious of was Lacoste's eyes, large and brilliant, the pupils contracted to tiny flame-like points. She tried to cry out, to look away, but her body, tingling not unpleasantly, had grown suddenly heavy. Her eyelids fluttered. She fought to keep them open. They fluttered again and the last thing she heard, as a sea of blackness enveloped her, was a little chuckle from Lacoste.

* * * * *

Marie-Joseph-Rose sat up suddenly. Dimly she had heard a voice saying, "Wake, wake!" or had she dreamed it? She looked about her wildly.

"Where am I?" she cried.

"At the rue Charles, and perfectly safe," a voice said.

"Lacoste!"

"Your servant, madame."

And then she remembered and looked about her once again. The flickering light of a single candle revealed the fact that she was indeed at the rue Charles, though not in one of the reception rooms downstairs, as she might have expected, but in her own apartment, and in bed, at that!

"How did I get here?" she demanded.

"I brought you myself an hour ago."

"I—I have been in a trance since you began your wretched experiment?"

"Assuredly."

She gave a little shriek, for there, thrown carelessly over the back of a chair, was her white mousseline dress. And close by it— Her hands, making rapid, searching movements, went up and down her body. Merciful heavens, she was stark naked!

"It was necessary," Lacoste murmured, "since Madame la Vicomtesse's breathing had become alarmingly labored, to reduce her to a state of nature. My powers, it seems, are greater than I suspected."

This last remark filled her mind with a terrible thought.

"Lacoste, what precisely have you done to me?"

"Nothing that need alarm you," he said reassuringly, and added significantly, "In making good her invitation I would naturally prefer madame's actions to be voluntary."

She saw then that he was fully and immaculately clothed, and though she drew the sheet up to her chin she began to breathe more freely. She looked at him with big eyes.

"What a foolish risk you took in bringing me here."

He laughed softly. "I was informed this morning that M'sieur le Marquis and Madame Renaudin had departed for Fontainebleau."

A glimmer of admiration came to her eyes. His resourcefulness was quite formidable.

"I find," he said accusingly, "that Madame la Vicomtesse is in the habit of wearing heavy black under-breeches."

She averted her eyes in embarrassment. "I was born, as you know, in Martinique, and still feel the cold winds of France."

"Only old ladies wear under-breeches," he teased her. "A young lady of fashion should be prepared to suffer a few little draughts."

She pouted. "What an impossible man you are."

He leaned forward and kissed her full on the lips, forcing her head back painfully, and while supporting her with one hand tugged gently at the sheet with the other.

She pushed him away quickly. "M'sieur——"

He silenced her with a little laugh. "My deepest apologies, madame. It had escaped me in my ardor that before madame departs from the path of continence she must be assured of certain worthwhile compensations."

"Naturally," she said, hot with shame and comparing herself once again with the painted prostitute.

"And—madame's terms?"

"A *salon* of my own," she said, in a voice she failed to recognize, "and—and presentation at court."

"In short, the two things which madame's husband has never made possible."

"In short, yes," she echoed faintly.

He rose and bowed. "Nothing, madame, could be more easily granted."

He unbuckled his sword, and his shadow dancing grotesquely on the wall in the candlelight, he began, with the nonchalance of a long-married husband, to undress.

*　　*　　*　　*　　*

She opened her eyes and blinked, then shielded them with her hand from the light of the sun which was flooding the room. There was a cough. The maid Marie, standing by the window, had obviously just drawn the curtains.

"The driver of the hired carriage is below," the girl said. "He claims that madame promised him the sum of fifty livres."

Marie-Joseph-Rose looked at her curiously. How much did she know? How much had she heard or seen? And what time had Lacoste taken his departure? Not even she, so deep was the slumber into which she had fallen, could answer that.

"Tell the man to wait," she said. "I must have been mad to make the promise, but make it I did."

She rose, stretched like a cat and went sleepily to her boudoir. For some unaccountable reason she felt desolate and utterly depressed. Frowning, she thought of Lacoste, thought of him not without bitterness. Stripped of his fine clothes, which had been cunningly padded to disguise the disgusting truth of his narrow shoulders and spindly legs, the powerful physique had melted away in a flash. *That* had been her first disappointment, the second— But why think of it? Passionate he'd been, no doubt, but hurried and ungentle, leading a poor woman up to a fever of expectation and then—poof, nothing, just as if he'd been Alexandre himself. And after his earlier display of animal magnetism too! If that was all there was in love-making—and with Alexandre and Lacoste to justify the suspicion it certainly seemed that it was—a woman might just as well renounce the world and take the veil.

Her eyes fell on a sheet of paper which was held down on her dressing-table by a pile of glittering coins. She snatched up the paper and saw that it was covered with the familiar sloping writing of Lacoste's penmanship.

Madame, she read, *I present my duty and with it the regret that affairs of state make it necessary for me to leave Paris—alas, to leave France itself—without a further moment of delay. Should it be my misfortune never to see you again your kindness will live forever in my heart.*

Your servant, Madame,
Edouard Lacoste.

The letter dropped from her fingers. *Alas to leave France itself. . . . Should it be my misfortune never to see you again. . . .* No

96

mention whatever of the money, which any lady would rightly regard as an insult. Fingering the coins, which were *louis d'or*, she counted them hurriedly. Twenty, there were. Better in all conscience than merely twenty livres. . . .

Marie entered and began dutifully and stolidly to dress her mistress, and for no reason whatever was soundly scolded, not once but several times.

"Forgive me, Marie," Marie-Joseph-Rose said contritely, "but my nerves still suffer from the outrage I was exposed to last night."

The maid's eyes glinted for a moment.

"I refer to the dreadful riots," Marie-Joseph-Rose said sternly. "I myself——"

"Ah yes, madame, the riots. Poor M'sieur Necker has been sent into exile by the King."

So that was what Lacoste meant by 'affairs of state.' Necker had been sent into exile and with him, naturally, his close friend Lacoste.

"The rat!" she said aloud. "He knew of this when he made his promise, a promise he could never keep."

"I beg madame's pardon?" the maid said, holding out a clean pair of under-breeches.

"Not those wretched things," Marie-Joseph-Rose stormed at her. "If I die of the cold I shall never wear under-breeches again."

Marie shrugged impassively. "Then perhaps an additional petticoat, madame?" she suggested.

Dressed at last, powdered, scented and rouged, she went downstairs to the waiting driver of the hired carriage. To have promised him fifty livres—the utter madness of it. And then she remembered the twenty *louis d'or* which, though she had no memory of taking them up, were clutched hotly in her hand. A *louis d'or* was worth twenty livres. Twenty times twenty— But her mind failed to grapple with such a complicated piece of arithmetic.

"My man," she said grandly, "I shall give you more than I promised."

And she counted out ten of the golden pieces, which he took in amazement and made off with, obviously thinking her out of her mind.

Watching him go she sank into a chair in the hall. 'I am,' she told herself, 'no better, and quite possibly worse, than that painted woman I saw last night.' Quite possibly worse? Yes, yes, but in one respect more fortunate. The *salon* she had dreamed of, the presentation at court—both were now lost, but by last night's adventure, unsatisfactory as it had been, she was twenty *louis d'or* the richer. No, not twenty, since her generosity had so unreasonably got the better of her, but at least ten, and no prostitute in Paris—she chuckled at the thought—could command a fee as high as that!

CHAPTER XIII

Q UITE AN EVENTFUL day," Madame Renaudin said drily. "If I were you, my dear, I should call it Creditors' Day."

"An excellent suggestion," Marie-Joseph-Rose agreed.

She was at Fontainebleau and a month had passed since her last meeting with Lacoste. During that month Eugene, attaining his fifth birthday, had passed to Alexandre's care, and though she had the four-year-old Hortense with whom to console herself she missed her son most dearly. During that month also the four hundred livres advanced by Alexandre, and which she had intended to hoard so carefully, had slipped through her fingers without her even noticing it and only a little more had been obtained from the same source.

"Six creditors in one day," Madame Renaudin said, "and each succeeding one more wrathful than his predecessor."

Marie-Joseph-Rose sighed mournfully. "You dealt with them skilfully, Aunt Marie. I thank you from the bottom of my heart."

"I merely lied to them, telling them that you were still in Paris," Madame Renaudin said. "Sooner or later they will corner you here and then what will you do?"

Marie-Joseph-Rose shuddered. "What indeed, Aunt Marie!"

"Have you written to your father?" Madame Renaudin asked.

"Yes, but you know how desperate his own position is. No help, I fear, is likely to come from Martinique. Just imagine what will happen when those wretched tradespeople smell me out. Why, they might even insist on my arrest."

"They might," Madame Renaudin agreed.

Her niece pouted. "How unsympathetic you sound!"

"If I do, my dear foolish Rose, it is only because the fault is yours. To fall into debt on the income allowed you by Alexandre is disgraceful."

"How unfair you are, Aunt Marie. Instead of reproaching me you might at least try to help me by making some sensible suggestion."

"Very well. The only suggestion I can think of is that you should escape from France and place the Atlantic between yourself and your creditors as speedily as possible."

"You mean that I should return to Martinique?"

"I do indeed."

Marie-Joseph-Rose was appalled. Paris, unkind as it had been to her, was the most wonderful city in the world. After Paris, Martinique, or more correctly Trois-Ilets, would be deadly. And yet, even if she did remain in France, what hope was there, poverty-stricken and isolated here at Fontainebleau, of her ever seeing Paris again?

"Even if I did decide to go to Martinique," she sighed, "what hope would I have of raising the passage money?"

"Ill-afford it as I can," Madame Renaudin said promptly, "I could advance it to you."

"Lend me the same amount now," her niece begged, "and I shall be well content."

Madame Renaudin shook her head. "The passage money to be used for that purpose only, or nothing at all."

Marie-Joseph-Rose sniffed loudly. What a hard and cruel woman her aunt was.

"Thank you for your offer," she said, "but while ever possible, I shall remain in France."

*　　*　　*　　*　　*

Marie-Joseph-Rose, sitting at her dressing-table, stared at her mirrored reflection in horror. It couldn't be possible, and yet, fantastic as it seemed, it was more than possible. She made a laborious calculation, counting painfully on her fingers. Four weeks, five, six, seven and now the eighth week. She made the calculation a second time, bringing the total, not to eight, but to nine. Merciful heavens yes, *more* than possible.

"Alexandre is to blame," she said aloud. "He accused me of unfaithfulness when I was innocent, entirely innocent; he disowned Hortense when the child, without a doubt, is his. It was tempting fate too much, *much* too much!"

She avoided her eyes in the mirror and wondered hopefully if it would be possible to have the child secretly here at Fontainebleau. Sheer nonsense, of course. Aunt Marie would have to be told and the servants, however great the caution taken, would soon suspect the truth and be whispering among themselves.

For no reason whatever she found herself thinking of her many creditors. Only that morning news had come from Paris that three of the less sympathetic ones, their patience exhausted, had issued writs against her. In no time at all the bailiff would be knocking at the door and she would be thrown into prison.

To give birth to a child in prison—imagine what that would mean!

No doctor, no *accoucheur*, only some wretched old midwife who would probably be drunk. Possibly not even *that* concession.

She rose quickly. There was only one thing—Martinique. Martinique where, while hiding from her creditors, the baby could be born in secret and left there on her return to France.

"If I ever *do* return!" she wailed.

Two days later, days spent in constant fear of the bailiff, Marie-Joseph-Rose and the little Hortense set out for the coast. They were accompanied by Madame Renaudin who, once they reached Le Havre, not only procured suitable lodgings, but went down to the docks to inquire about shipping. Eventually it was discovered that two ships were preparing to sail for the West Indies, and in due course mother and child embarked in one of them. At the last moment, her nerve failing her, Marie-Joseph-Rose begged her aunt to make the journey with her.

Madame Renaudin shook her head.

"I shall remain in France," she said drily, "if only for the purpose of closing the door firmly in the face of your creditors."

"But the journey may prove too much for me," her niece pressed. "I might even die, and then what would happen to poor little Hortense?"

But Aunt Marie, heartless creature that she was, merely laughed. "I think it certain, my dear, that not even a dozen voyages to Martinique could kill you. You are destined, I suspect, to torment various poor creditors for many, many years to come."

When the ship was on the point of putting out of Le Havre the weather changed and a severe storm sprang up. To Marie-Joseph-Rose's dismay the captain insisted on sailing, and for a moment she was tempted to let him sail without her. Reflection, however, convinced her that to miss this opportunity of escaping from France would be foolish.

"I have no choice whatever," she cried tragically. "After all, I may as well die in a storm as languish in a prison!"

The storm, as it turned out, was only the forerunner of a series of even greater storms, during which the ship, a tiny merchant vessel with inadequate passenger accommodation, mounted waves which seemed as high as mountains, quivered on their summits and then plunged perilously into deep and threatening valleys.

So violent was her sickness that the second day of menstruation had begun before she grasped its full significance. Ill as she was she laughed aloud in her delight and then fell to wondering whether it had been a mere irregularity or whether the extreme violence of the seasickness had brought about so timely a salvation. Irregularity, in a woman who had never been irregular, was surely out of the question, and certainly the pain she had suffered could hardly be attributed to mere seasickness. She laughed again. If ever again she found herself with child by a strange man she'd know what to do. She— Or *would* she? Rather than face such a voyage again it might be better, far better, to preserve a strict and rigid continence. . . .

✳   ✳   ✳   ✳   ✳

Changes at Martinique had been many. Her mother and father had grown older and both were in failing health. Little Marie-Françoise had grown up and instead of being the companion one might reasonably have expected was sulky, unfriendly and strangely full of envy.

"Martinique," she said bitterly, "is a miserable island from which escape is impossible. Had it not been for you, Rose, I might now be in France and the wife of Alexandre de Beauharnais."

And when Marie-Joseph-Rose pointed out that her marriage with Alexandre had brought her nothing but unhappiness the girl said sharply: "You have no one but yourself to blame. Had *I* been chosen I would have been clever enough to have kept my husband."

The house, the old sugar-refinery, was a disappointment also. It looked less than half the size she had always imagined it to be and was disgracefully shabby, while the estate had grown more neglected than ever.

Even Marion, older now and fat and dirty, was a disappointment, while her father's financial troubles were the greatest disappointment of all. Not that she had expected much help from Papa, but after only two days at Trois-Ilets it had become woefully obvious that no help whatever would be forthcoming.

"You know that I would help you if I could," he said pathetically, "but the most I can offer you, or will ever be able to offer you, is a home here at Trois-Ilets."

A home at Trois-Ilets—for the rest of her life, she presumed her father meant! Who, in the name of heaven, would be content with that after Paris and a taste, restricted and tantalizing as it had been, of *le monde*! To have come to Martinique was the most foolish thing she had ever done, and like Marie-Françoise she felt trapped and desperate.

There was one thing, however, that gave her pleasure. Hortense, now five years of age, was wide-eyed with wonder at all the strange sights she saw, so that for a time, taking an interest in the child's unquestioning delight, Marie-Joseph-Rose forgot a little of her own unhappiness. Together they made many excursions in the neigh-

101

borhood of Trois-Ilets, gathering tropical flowers and fruit, while hours on end were spent bathing in the little stream which had been Marie-Joseph-Rose's greatest childhood delight.

Inevitably, while lying in the sun on the moss-covered bank, she thought of the young *sous-lieutenant*, Tercier, who was now, she remembered having been told by Alexandre, a captain. She wondered whether he was still in Martinique, and her curiosity getting the better of her, she questioned Marion. The mulatto woman gave her a knowing look and nodded, and though disconcerted by the look, which was undoubtedly lewd, Marie-Joseph-Rose was conscious of a pleasurable thrill of expectancy. To see him again would surely bring one a little relief from boredom.

"Does he ever come to Trois-Ilets?" she asked.

"On occasion, but if the matter is urgent one could find him easily at Fort-Royal."

"And why should the matter be urgent, you black wretch?"

Nevertheless she laughed and began to think that Marion, despite her dirt and obesity, was still her friend.

"I think," she said softly, "that I shall pay a little visit to Fort-Royal."

*　*　*　*　*

The streets of Fort-Royal were surprisingly busy. Two vessels, it was true, had arrived from France that morning and were lying at anchor in the bay, but from the look of the black faces one saw on every hand the Negroes and not the Europeans had come to town to meet them.

The carriage, hampered for some time already by the jostling crowd, was brought to a sudden halt. "Whip up the horses," Marie-Joseph-Rose commanded, but all the slave did was grin foolishly back at her.

"Mama, I'm frightened," Hortense cried, clutching at her mother's hand.

"Nonsense, child. What is there to be frightened of? Nobody is going to hurt you."

Nevertheless, the negroes who blocked their passage had an ugly look. What was that Papa had said only yesterday about the unrest in France having spread to the slaves and made them insolent? Not their own few slaves, of course, for they had always been well treated and would remain faithful, whatever happened in France, but other people's.

The crowd pressed closer about the carriage until Hortense began to whimper and Marie-Joseph-Rose herself began to feel a mounting alarm. She searched hurriedly in her reticule, found a few sou-pieces and flung them at the nearest Negroes. Instead of the scramble she expected not a man or woman moved. They simply stood there staring, some with grins on their faces but the majority with hatred in their eyes.

Panic gripped her heart. If only Papa had been well enough to accompany her. (In the alarm of the moment she quite forgot that she had insisted on coming to Fort-Royal unchaperoned, just in case —by the merest chance, of course!—she should meet with Tercier.)

Hearing approaching hoof-beats she looked round wildly, and then, catching sight of a detachment of mounted soldiers approaching, she breathed more freely. In a moment the street was cleared, and while the soldiers rode in pursuit of the scattering slaves the young lieutenant in charge reined in his horse by the carriage.

"Lieutenant Dumourier at your service, madame," he said gallantly.

"Thank you, Lieutenant." By this time she was sufficiently recovered to flutter her eyelashes and smile coquettishly. "Those horrible slaves were beginning to alarm us."

"Madame," he said sternly, and blushing to the very roots of his thick curly hair, "was most unadvised to venture abroad without attendants."

She protested that she had never expected to find anything in Martinique so amazing as a large group of hostile slaves.

"The latest news from France," he said gravely, "has increased their boldness."

She fluttered her eyelashes again—he really was a handsome young man and so like Tercier as she remembered him—and asked what this latest news from home was.

His gravity increased. "Madame, the revolution, so long expected, is now a sober fact. On the fourteenth of July a great mob rose in Paris and attacked the Bastille. There was much fighting and in the end the Bastille fell."

She thought instantly of Alexandre and his revolutionary ideas. Had he been in the fighting, she wondered— Then she laughed. That was hardly possible. Alexandre, though a soldier and a politician, was both in theory only—a tedious windbag who, when action was called for, would do little more than talk and talk.

"Lieutenant Dumourier," she said, "you remind me very much of an old friend, a certain Captain Tercier. Is he known to you?"

"Very well indeed, madame."

"Ah, then if you would be so kind as to give him my regards——?"

"Gladly, madame, if one may be permitted to ask your name."

"My name and title are of little consequence, but tell him—" she laughed gaily—"tell him that the girl whose name was Rose has not entirely forgotten him, and that an old haunt at Trois-Ilets is frequented once again with pleasure."

She inclined her head graciously—a great lady of *le monde* whether the wretched Bastille had fallen or not!—gave a signal to the slave and, as the carriage moved forward, caught a final glimpse of a lieutenant who, though he sat his horse like a gentleman, stared after her with dazed eyes and a gaping mouth.

"He thought me beautiful," she told herself, and added candidly, "and indeed I think he was right."

*   *   *   *   *

"Thank God you left Paris when you did," Tascher said, when his daughter gave him the news of the storming of the Bastille. "You are at all events safe here."

"I very much doubt it," she exclaimed, and told him of her experience that day in Fort-Royal.

A look of alarm crossed his face for a moment, but on the whole he was inclined to make light of her encounter with the excited slaves.

"The natives will never rise in Martinique," he said.

"I sincerely hope not," his wife said anxiously, "but they do outnumber us very greatly, Joseph."

"That is true," he admitted, "but the Martinique Regiment is strong, and we have the additional protection, remember, of a naval squadron."

He went on to say that the slaves, on the whole, were treated leniently by the French colonials, were in consequence indolent and lazy and would never, whatever happened in France, have the energy to make an organized and serious rising, but Marie-Joseph-Rose was barely listening. Her mind still retained a vivid picture of the young lieutenant's face. Had Tercier received her message yet, she wondered.

After the evening meal, which was made in gloomy silence, restlessness took her out of doors. It was a beautiful night with a half-moon riding high in the dark indigo of the heavens and the warm scent of the tropical flowers, though a little sickly, had never been so pleasant.

She stretched her arms above her head in lazy abandon. Whether she would be safer here than in Paris hardly seemed to matter, and the fact that her return to Martinique had been a bitter disappointment was temporarily forgotten. For the first time since her encounter with Lacoste a man, even though his gaze had been fixed and his mouth agape, had paid her homage with his eyes.

She passed through the untidy growth of vegetation which surrounded the house and made her way by the well-beaten track to the stream. In the distance she heard a sudden burst of Negro chatter and hesitated, but a moment later, when a rich voice rose in song, she smiled and continued.

The scent of the flowers was stronger now, heavier and more sickly, yet she drank it in with a little sigh of pure happiness. Paris, naturally, was her real love, but Martinique, she knew, was still in her blood.

"If only I could have them both," she said aloud.

The snapping of a twig underfoot some little distance behind her brought her to a sudden halt. She remembered then that as she'd left the house the sound of approaching hoof-beats had vaguely crossed her consciousness. Her heart began to palpitate wildly. Had it been one horse, or a dozen? Was it the first step in a Negro rising? She laughed shakily. Few slaves had free access to horses—unless, of course, they'd rioted in Fort-Royal and taken them by force. Another twig snapped, closer. She picked up her skirts and hurried forward. The footsteps behind her were distinct now and heavy. The singing had ceased and the chatter had burst out again, threateningly, she fancied. She began to run, stumbling in the darkness of the mango plantation that led to the bank of the stream. There was a crash in the darkness nearby. Whoever was pursuing her had stumbled too, but was forcing his way forward again. She reached the bank and stopped on the very edge of the stream. A moment later she was uncertain whether, in her agitation, she had fallen, or whether, in a last desperate effort to escape, she had dived involuntarily.

A sudden laugh came from the darkness of the bank.

"Her Majesty the Queen of France, I presume," a voice remarked.

"Merciful heavens," she cried—"Tercier!"

"At your service, madame," he said.

"Then make good your words," she snapped, "and help me out."

Fully clothed as she was she had difficulty in swimming against the current—and what a sight she must look with her skirts floating about her neck like an army tent! A hand reached out, gripped her own strongly, and the next moment, water falling from her like a torrent, she was face to face with Tercier.

He drew her farther up the bank and tilted up her face to his. His hand, cupping her chin in a firm grip, made it impossible for her to turn away. His lips were amazingly soft and the tang of strong wine on his breath was not entirely unpleasant. She relaxed, pressing herself against him. His arms went round her and his lips hardened, forcing open her own until the day's growth of beard on his chin scraped her wet face harshly.

"Ugh!" she cried, and wriggled free.

"Slippery little water-rat," he said, "but, as water-rats go, delightful."

She laughed softly. He was a boy no longer but a man, and one so pleasingly sure of himself.

"Since you must have expected me to come," he said, "was it necessary to flee before me, even to the extent of taking refuge in the stream?"

"Why should I have expected it," she countered, "when you must have known of my presence here all this time, yet made no move to see me?"

There was no reply.

"You *did* know that I was at Trois-Ilets?" she pressed.

"Yes, I knew."

"Then why, in the name of heaven——"

"I felt sure that you could never have brought yourself to forgive me."

"To forgive you? But for what?"

"That boast I made to your husband."

She frowned. "Ah yes, of course." Then she laughed gaily. "It was understandable, and I really had forgotten it."

"And remembering it now are you willing to forgive it also?"

"Why not? The past is the past, and even though you were partly responsible for my separation from Alexandre, it was a separation which brought me freedom."

"Your majesty," he murmured, "is very gracious."

Her face clouded. "To remind me that I once dreamed of becoming Queen of France is hardly kind. If you and I are to be friends, Tercier, you will please refrain from sneering."

"Friends?" he said, unperturbed. "We were friends before. We shall be more than that this time or nothing at all."

She thought of Lacoste and made a quick comparison. Hastily she reached out and touched his chest with a searching finger, then his shoulders. No padding, she decided happily, and gracious, what formidable muscles!

"Well, which is it to be?" he asked.

She shivered, conscious of the wet clothes clinging dankly to her body.

"I shall catch my death of cold," she said.

"On a night as warm as this?" he scoffed.

"The water was cooler than you think, and my clothes——"

"Take them off," he chuckled, "and you'll dry in a moment—with my assistance."

She looked at him quickly, seeing little more than the gleam of his eyes in the darkness and the dim outline of his head and shoulders. A delicious weakness spread from her body to her limbs. Alexandre, Lacoste and now Tercier. Alexandre, because of the marriage that had been arranged; Lacoste because of the use he might have been to her, Tercier, oh surely Tercier because in this moment she had fallen in love with him. She held out her arms, remembering as she did so the roughness of his chin. She must tell him that gentlemen were in the habit of shaving twice a day, certainly she must tell him—afterwards.

*   *   *   *   *

Once again the excitement of the arrival of mails from France had subsided, though Tascher himself, reading sentences out loud from time to time, was going through the letters a second time. Poor Papa, his daughter thought, what else had he in life to look forward to but letters from France.

She listened with scant attention while he spoke of the shattered economy of France, of attempted political *coups*, of the ineffectual actions of the King and the extravagances, curtailed but still ruinous, of the Queen. Politics, the revolution itself, had never interested her less, even though Tercier, a great deal more excited than her father, spoke of little else these days.

"What folly," Tascher exclaimed, "for my sister to say that the revolution is now over. It has spread from Paris to the towns and from the towns to the villages. A lull may be taking place at present but this is only the beginning."

She shrugged. Tercier had said much the same, she remembered vaguely, but did it really matter? Naturally it didn't, for she was happy, happy for the first time in her life. So happy that when reminded that she had been in Martinique for almost two years she could scarcely believe it and most certainly didn't care. Why, with Tercier at her side, she would be happy and carefree for the rest of her life.

"So Alexandre de Beauharnais is becoming prominent in the Assembly," Madame Tascher said.

Tascher nodded vigorously. "According to Marie, very prominent." He turned to Marie-Joseph-Rose. "All things considered, my dear, you would be better off in Paris these days than here in Martinique."

"And safer, Rose," her mother added.

"Nonsense, Mama," she said sharply. "Papa was right. The slaves are too lazy to make a serious rising."

"The last little rising," Madame Tascher said timidly, "was very nearly successful."

"Only because the regiment was unprepared," Tascher reminded her. "In the end the ringleaders were caught and shot." He turned to his daughter again. "Nevertheless, my dear, if you were to decide to return to France——"

She interrupted him almost angrily. "Please remember, Papa, that however prominent Alexandre might be in the Assembly, he and I are legally separated."

"But doesn't he write to you occasionally, Rose?" her mother asked.

That was true enough, but the letters, typical of Alexandre, were pompous, extremely scholarly and utterly tedious. The only interest they held for her were the casual references to Eugene which they contained. With a frown she thought of her son, thought of him really hard. Though her love for him would grow deeper year by year it was dreadfully difficult, after all this time and when France was so far away, even to remember what he looked like.

Madame Tascher repeated her question.

"Oh yes," Marie-Joseph-Rose replied, "he writes now and again."

"And he sends you a little money, I hope?"

"None whatever, Mama, though he mentioned in his last letter that he had deposited certain amounts for me with Aunt Marie."

She rose, excused herself and went out of the room. Within an hour, when the swift tropical night had descended, she would hear the now familiar hoof-beats and Tercier, exhilarated after his long ride round the bay from Fort-Royal, would meet her at the old rendezvous by the stream. A surge of impatience and longing flooded her heart, as it always did when she was waiting for Tercier. "I am, of course, in love with him," she told herself, perhaps for the hundredth time.

The furtive meetings, satisfying as they were, were not enough. She wanted more, she wanted—and admitted it to herself for the first time now—the permanence of marriage. A splendid lover—how right he'd been, years ago, in his boastful claim of proficiency!—Tercier would surely make an even more splendid husband. Marriage with him, of course, would mean an end to the dream of greatness in France, but would that really matter? Despite the poverty which such a marriage would impose, life in Martinique with Tercier would be heavenly.

Her mind full of such thoughts she went to the stream to wait, and when finally Tercier appeared she had made up her mind to speak of a possible divorce from Alexandre. There would be no difficulties, she felt sure; Alexandre would be only too happy to free himself of all responsibility. After all, for a man as mean as Alexandre, a saving of five thousand livres a year would be a tremendous inducement.

"Tercier," she said, "you haven't kissed me yet."

Absent-mindedly he took her in his arms and his kiss, the merest peck, was alarmingly perfunctory.

"Is—is anything the matter?" she asked.

He cleared his throat.

"My dear," he said abruptly, "I'm afraid these secret meetings will have to cease."

She was speechless for a moment.

"But why?" she managed to ask.

"I—" He hesitated.

"You—you mean you've grown tired of me?"

He took her hands in his. "I love you dearly, Rose, but I happen to be on the point of marrying."

"Marrying! *You*?"

He cleared his throat again. "A long-standing arrangement between my family and—er—my *fiancée's*."

"Your *fiancée*!" She was unspeakably shocked. "You never spoke of such a creature, never!"

"To be frank it never seemed necessary."

"Are you in love with her?" she asked quickly.

He shrugged. "She'll make a good wife and her dowry will be quite substantial."

She withdrew her hands quickly. "I quite understand. Her dowry will be quite substantial, whereas mine, if you were to marry me, would be non-existent."

"If I were to marry *you*?" he said, in amazement.

"Alexandre could be induced to divorce me. I—" the long-delayed tears were close now—"I was making plans only a moment ago before you came." She turned quickly. "Oh, Tercier, I love you so much. I—I'm sure I could never live without you."

"Nonsense," he said sharply, and taking her by the shoulders, swung her round to face him again. "Our little *affaire* has been pleasant, I admit, but would never have lasted all this time in the more practical atmosphere of Parisian life. Once married to me you'd grow restless and begin to look about for another lover."

"Oh no, Tercier, never. I swear it, I *swear* it! I love you. Please understand, I love you and could never love anybody else."

Tercier laughed shortly. "What you mean, *chérie*, is that since no man ever taught you the full meaning of love, the full physical expression, you've fallen in love with love, have even been given a taste for it. Have no fear, you'll find someone in Paris just as proficient as I."

"What a loathsome thing to say!"

"Truth, in many cases, *is* loathsome."

"And Paris—why do you say 'someone in Paris'? Do you actually order me, m'sieur, to return there?"

He took her arm in a firm grip.

"Come," he said, and led her away from the stream to a high clearing from which a view of the bay could be obtained.

"Look," he said, and pointed in the direction of Fort-Royal.

Dumbly, she looked and dumbly she saw the red haze in the sky, a haze reflected in the still waters of the bay.

"The Negroes are out of hand," he said. "The burning and pillaging is not as serious as it might have been, but what *is* serious is the fact that, led by a handful of revolutionaries from Paris, they've captured the shore batteries and have issued an order commanding the naval squadron to remain in port."

"What is that to me?" she said sadly.

"The order, naturally, will not be obeyed. I know the commander. I met him secretly before I came to Trois-Ilets and he kindly agreed to take you aboard the *Sensible*. The *Sensible*, if not the other vessels, will sail for France."

"When?" she asked listlessly.

"At dawn tomorrow. Go back to the house. Tell your father what has happened and prepare yourself, and Hortense too, for the voyage."

She made no attempt to move. He shook her roughly by the shoulders.

"Do as I say, Rose."

"Very well," she said, like an obedient child. "Go back to the house. Tell Papa. Prepare for the journey. . . ."

She had barely reached the house and found her father when Tercier, making a hasty apology for his rudeness, entered the room. Lieutenant Dumourier, he said, had ridden out in haste from Fort-Royal with the news that the *Sensible* was to sail, not at dawn, but at midnight. Therefore not a moment was to be lost. A hurried explanation was made to the bewildered Tascher who agreed instantly that his daughter must embark on the *Sensible*.

"But Papa," Marie-Joseph-Rose pleaded, "I don't want to go to France."

"You might not want to go now," Tascher said, "but if you change your mind later you will find yourself stranded here."

"There will be little or no shipping between Martinique and France after the *Sensible* sails," Tercier stressed.

"Ah," she cried. "You want to get rid of me, both of you!"

"No," her father said, glancing quizzically for a moment at Tercier, "all we want is to do the best we can for you. Remember Alexandre's prominence in the Assembly. Remember what I said about your being better off in Paris than in Martinique."

"But I should feel like a traitor, leaving you and Mama and Marie-Françoise behind. Why not—why not come with me, all of you?"

Tascher shook his head. "I should be penniless in Paris. What little income I have is dependent on my estate here at Trois-Ilets."

"But the danger, Papa!"

"The danger is slight, my dear. We ourselves are well loved by the slaves, and from a political point of view, how many of the revolutionary leaders on the island would dare to harm the father-in-law of so staunch a republican as Alexandre de Beauharnais?"

And so, realizing that she was being hustled away to France chiefly because Tercier had grown tired of her, she allowed herself to be persuaded. A few belongings were hastily gathered together and packed. There was a dry-eyed and utterly unreal farewell with Madame Tascher and Marie-Françoise, and then the nightmare journey to Fort-Royal began.

"This," she told herself, as she sat in the swaying, jolting carriage which her father himself was driving, "is not me, and I, surely, am not Marie-Joseph-Rose, Vicomtesse de Beauharnais."

By the time they reached Fort-Royal the fires in the center of the town had died away to smouldering embers, but the streets were still full of prowling slaves, many of whom, having broken into the shops, had arrayed themselves in the latest fashions from Paris. Hortense was frightened and whimpered piteously in her mother's arms, but Marie-Joseph-Rose herself, shaken out of her lethargy for a moment, laughed till the tears rolled down her cheeks at the sight of a coal-black Negro dressed in an English style riding coat—that and nothing else!—and a fat and ancient Negress, stumbling down the street in a hooped velvet skirt. "I wonder," she cried hysterically, "if she is wearing under-breeches!"

Aboard the *Sensible*—dimly she remembered the tears which had been on her father's cheeks when he had bade her good-bye—the captain was waiting for her, but it was not until she felt the deck rising and falling beneath her and she saw the dim outline of Fort-Royal receding astern that she became fully conscious of what had happened. It was not until then, while the inaccurately fired shots from the rebel-held shore batteries fell to the right and left of the *Sensible*, that all the the pent-up emotion of the past few hours relieved itself in a flood of the bitterest tears she had ever shed.

111

CHAPTER XIV

THE MAIL-COACH WAS UN-
comfortably crowded and the weather, for it was November, was
bitterly cold. Marie-Joseph-Rose shivered and drew her cloak more
closely round herself and Hortense. This second arrival in France
was little different from the first, save that she was older, sadder
and unhappily wiser, and was obliged, since her arrival had been
unheralded, to travel to Paris in a public conveyance.

That great changes had taken place in France during her absence
was evident from the excited conversation of her fellow travelers,
a drab assortment of middle-class merchants and their wives and
children, though the only visible change she noticed when the coach
entered the capital itself was the red, white, and blue cockades
worn by the men who, one of the passengers told her, were members
of the newly formed National Guard.

Descending from the coach and standing forlorn on the pavement, she wondered hopelessly what she should do and where she
should go. She thought of Alexandre. Was he still at the rue de
l'Université, and would it be wise to visit him there in her present
shabby and poverty-stricken condition? She decided that it wouldn't
and was on the point of hiring a carriage to drive her out to Fontainebleau (she had insufficient money for this but it wouldn't be
necessary to admit it until Fontainebleau was reached), when she
remembered Madame Fanny de Beauharnais.

At Madame Fanny's house the first person she saw when the
major-domo announced her was Aunt Marie. She could hardly believe her eyes, and Hortense, after the first glad cry of recognition,
clung like a mad thing at her great-aunt's skirts.

"And to think," Marie-Joseph-Rose cried, "that a few moments ago
I was on the point of making straight for Fontainebleau."

She then learned that during the last few months her aunt's long-
forgotten husband, Alexis Renaudin, had died, and that Madame
Renaudin and the Marquis de Beauharnais (almost in the manner
of an afterthought, one might imagine) had found it possible to legal-
ize their relationship.

For the first time since she had left Martinique Marie-Joseph-
Rose laughed without restraint.

"Just think of it, Aunt Marie, to become a respectable woman
at *your* age!"

"What is more to the point," the new Marquise de Beauharnais said drily, "I am now, in addition to being your aunt, your step-mother-in-law."

"Merciful heavens, yes—" the tears were rolling down her cheeks—"and what a formidable thought!"

Later, when the marquis himself had joined them, and Marie-Joseph-Rose had learned that the newly married couple were spending a few days in Paris to celebrate the event, she gave them all the details of her flight from Martinique, all the details, that is, save the more intimate ones concerning Tercier.

"My poor child," the marquis said, "how very deeply you must have suffered."

She noticed then that both he and Aunt Marie had aged considerably, though neither had the look of feebleness worn by her father when last she had seen him. Poor Papa, what had happened to him and Mama and Marie-Françoise since her departure?

Later still, when Madame Fanny had invited her to remain for a few days, and while the marquis and Hortense were in happy conversation, she retired to the privacy of her aunt's room and asked for news of Alexandre.

The marquise laughed. "Your husband, my dear, is more prominent than ever in the Assembly. Only recently, after being appointed to the Military Committee, he became one of the three secretaries of the Assembly." She laughed again. "Every day he makes yet another patriotic speech. Every day he swells a little more. If ever a politician talked himself into power Alexandre certainly did."

Marie-Joseph-Rose pursed her lips thoughtfully. Perhaps Papa had been right. She might indeed be better off in Paris than Martinique. She looked up suddenly, conscious that her aunt was staring at her.

"What is it, Aunt Marie?"

"The change in you, my dear, is striking."

"Can I help it," Marie-Joseph-Rose cried dramatically, "if I was forced to leave Martinique with little more than the clothes I was wearing? Can I help it if the revolution has made me shabby, ill-dressed and wretched?"

"I was referring, Rose, to you yourself; not to your clothes."

"Merciful heavens, you mean that I'm beginning to look old and worn?"

Her aunt laughed. "Hardly that, but your eyes have a look of maturity—of wisdom, I was almost tempted to say."

"My sufferings have not been confined solely to those caused by the revolution," Marie-Joseph-Rose said sadly.

"Ah, I begin to smell a disastrous love-affair!"

"Oh, Aunt Marie, does it show as clearly as that in my eyes?"

"Was it our little Captain Tercier?"

"Yes, but I can't imagine how you——"

"I merely placed myself in your own position, Rose, and I know what the demoralizing air of the tropics can do to one. He responded to your advances, of course, and then——"

"*My* advances! You really suggest that I——!"

"*You* responded to *his*, then, and later he began to grow tired of you, and for the time being your heart was broken."

"And still is broken, Aunt Marie, and still *is*!"

That, she admitted to herself, was something of an exaggeration. She neither loved him now nor hated him.

"All I really feel," she said, "is a great emptiness."

"I know it well, my dear. It resembles a lasting bout of mild indigestion."

"Whatever it resembles," Marie-Joseph-Rose said, shaking her head sadly at her aunt's unsympathetic levity, "I know that I shall never be able to fall in love again. Not *really* in love." She raised her hands in a dramatic gesture. "Life has forced me at last to harden my heart."

"A hard heart should serve you well in your future dealings with Alexandre," her aunt commented.

"Why do you say that?"

"Your patriotic husband, my dear, is deeply in arrears with your allowance."

"But he wrote and told me that certain sums had been deposited with you."

"Yes, but only two thousand livres, when actually he owes you the best part of two years' payments."

Though she had expected a larger amount she smiled almost happily. Two thousand livres was quite a lot of money, and with it she could set herself up (and Hortense too, of course) with the new clothes she so badly needed.

"May I have the money now, Aunt Marie?"

"You may have five hundred livres only. The rest, the fifteen hundred, I paid to your creditors, thus saving you, the moment you showed your face in Paris again, from arrest."

Marie-Joseph-Rose scowled. Those wretched creditors, to be reminded of them now when for months she'd succeeded in forgetting them.

"You owed over three thousand livres," the marquise said. "You might at least thank me for having appeased them with half that amount."

"Oh I do, Aunt Marie, I do!" And then, her mind beginning to

114

envisage a plan for the future, she asked sharply: "When did you last see Alexandre?"

"Two days ago."

"And Eugene?"

"At the same time, but he was to leave that day for a new school."

"An expensive one?"

"Not a cheap one, at all events."

"Ah! Then Alexandre can hardly be as poor as you would have me believe."

Her aunt looked at her thoughtfully. "I believe you contemplated a reconciliation before you went to Martinique. Are you contemplating it again?"

"Possibly, though of course it takes two to make a reconciliation, doesn't it."

The plan was really more marvelous than she had first thought. As a prominent politician Alexandre held a social position which, while living apart from him, she was unable to share. Being one of the three secretaries, he might even attain the presidency some day and then the social position would expand tremendously. That Alexandre might be poor scarcely mattered. In fact, it was almost certain that the success of her plan would depend entirely on that one significant factor.

"By the look of your face," her aunt said, "you're planning mischief."

"Indeed I am!" Marie-Joseph-Rose laughed. "Indeed I am!"

* * * * *

Alexandre, she thought, had aged a little and had a lean, important look. *Every day he makes yet another patriotic speech*, Aunt Marie had said, *every day he swells a little more*, and certainly he seemed to strut like a peacock while his voice held more than a hint of self-satisfaction. Oh yes, in his own eyes he was undoubtedly a very great man.

"So very kind of you to call on me," he said, for a second time, and added, a little regretfully, she thought: "I had begun to think that the rest of your life would be spent in Martinique."

For a few moments they discussed Hortense and Eugene and then, when the right moment came, Marie-Joseph-Rose turned the conversation to the political situation.

"I hear that you might soon become President of the Assembly," she said.

He tried to look modest but the process of 'swelling' mentioned by Aunt Marie betrayed itself instantly in his voice.

"There *is* a possibility," he smiled.

"*More* than a possibility, Alexandre, or so I should imagine. No one, I feel sure, is better suited for the position."

"I'm delighted to hear you say that, my dear."

"I say it in all sincerity," she said earnestly, "and do you know, I have been forced to come to the conclusion that in the old days I failed lamentably to value you at your true worth."

"Very handsome of you to admit it," he murmured.

('If I stroke him a little harder,' she thought, 'he'll begin to purr.')

"Of course," she added thoughtfully, "I was young and inexperienced. I do see now that if I had been cleverer and more understanding the separation need never have taken place."

He gave a little start. "Er—you——?"

Unwarned by this reaction she ran on quickly: "A woman can almost always save her marriage from disaster if she really wants to, if she really *tries*. Oh yes, Alexandre, during the last few years I have learned quite a lot. As a matter of fact——"

"One moment, Rose!" he said sharply. "I happen to know enough about women to know that when they talk as you are talking now they are hatching some cunning little scheme." He smiled at his own cleverness and added: "Pray proceed, my dear. I am all attention."

She was so taken aback that for a moment she was unable to speak. He smiled again, a most irritating smile.

"Are you by any chance about to suggest a reconciliation?" he asked.

She shrugged and forced herself to laugh. "I see that you're much too clever for me, Alexandre."

"Ah, then you *are* suggesting a reconciliation!"

"Yes, Alexandre. Does such a suggestion—" she paused, dropping her voice. "Does such a suggestion by any chance appeal to you?"

He shook his head decisively. "Not in the least."

There was a pause. She forced herself to laugh again.

"Alexandre," she said earnestly, "a man in your position has certain social obligations which only a wife can dispense."

"Perhaps," he admitted, "but do you really imagine yourself capable of dispensing such obligations? *You* of all people?"

The contempt underlined in the stressing of '*You* of all people,' was very marked. Marie-Joseph-Rose flushed angrily but judged it wiser to ignore the insult.

"That isn't quite fair," she said quietly. "You don't know me as I am today."

He dismissed this with a lofty gesture. "We came to a legal agreement, my dear Rose. I, for my part, intend to maintain that agreement."

"I see." Her voice was still quiet, still admirably controlled, but there was a hint of challenge in it. "Then let me point out, Alexandre, that you aren't really doing so."

He looked at her sharply. "What the devil do you mean?"

"The agreement was that you should provide me with five thousand livres a year for myself and maintain Hortense. In two years I have received only two thousand livres."

"I—!" he began, and fell suddenly silent.

"We are entering the third year," she went on, "and you are eight thousand livres in arrears, to say nothing of Hortense's maintenance."

"I may be a prominent politician," he snapped, "but that has failed to make me a rich man!"

"In other words, Alexandre"—she almost laughed aloud in her satisfaction—"you find it impossible to meet your obligations?"

He rose to his feet and strode to the window.

"I can let you have a thousand livres next week," he said, without looking at her.

"I want eight thousand, *now*."

He swung round on her. His self-assurance was gone and she found herself looking at the face of a harassed and indeterminate man.

"It is out of the question," he said.

She rose to her feet also. "Then I will make a bargain with you, Alexandre."

"A—bargain?"

"Yes. Dissolve the legal separation. Make a home for me here at the rue de l'Université. Make it possible for me to establish a fashionable *salon* of my own. Do that, Alexandre, and I shall forget that you owe me anything. Refuse and I shall have a writ issued against you."

Speechless, his mouth slightly open, he stared at her.

"By heavens!" he cried at last. "You are trying to threaten me!"

She laughed gently. "I am trying to threaten you, Alexandre."

"But do you realize that this amounts to blackmail?"

"Blackmail?" She laughed again. "My dear, I'm merely suggesting a little agreement between us."

"I refuse to discuss the matter. You are trying to coerce me and I loathe coercion."

"I suggest an easy way out of your difficulties and you call it coercion."

"There is no other name for it!"

"Let me put it a little differently," she said patiently. "Living apart as we are, Eugene is in your care, Hortense is in mine. Don't you agree that it would be better for them if they were together, like any other brother and sister?"

"You will never trap me," he said pettishly, "by an appeal to my emotions!"

"I want a position in society," she went on. "I have been your wife, the Vicomtesse de Beauharnais, too long to be denied the position which should rightfully be mine. Do you realize that you have never yet presented me at court?"

"Do you want to be presented? Is that part of the bargain you are trying to drive?"

"Hardly. The court no longer exists, does it? The King and Queen, I understand, are little better than prisoners in Paris, waiting for an opportunity to flee. You know what I want. My own *salon*. A position in the new society which is springing up. If you become president of the Assembly I want to hold the social position due to the president's wife."

"By God," he said, his voice shaking with anger, "you're very cunning!"

She dismissed this with a disdainful shrug. "Well, Alexandre, what is your answer?"

"My answer is no."

"Do you realize what would happen if I caused a writ to be issued against you? You would be forced to flee or go to prison. It would ruin your political career. A pleasant prospect, don't you think, for a future president of the Assembly?"

She thought, by the queer noise he made, that he was going to choke.

"Give me a few days to consider the matter," he said weakly.

"A few days? Oh no, I couldn't think of it."

"Two days, then! *One* day!"

She moved quietly to the door. "Very well, Alexandre, one day. We leave for Fontainebleau this afternoon. Come there tomorrow afternoon and give me your answer. One other thing, you say you can let me have a thousand livres next week. A small sum for a woman so embarrassed as I, but acceptable. Would you be kind enough to obtain it tomorrow instead of next week?"

"But you said you'd forget I owed you anything if——"

"Ah, but you haven't made up your mind yet, have you?"

And with that she bade him a polite *au revoir* and took her leave.

✳ ✳ ✳ ✳ ✳

"Is it true," the Marquis de Beauharnais asked his son anxiously, "that the King is planning to bring in foreign military aid as a counter-revolutionary measure?"

Alexandre, despite his preoccupation with the reason which had brought him to Fontainebleau, was pleased, for the moment, to air his views. Nothing, he said, was more certain, though it was the Queen who was making the plans, not the helpless, hag-ridden King. Her Majesty, an Austrian, was even now in negotiation with her brother, the Emperor. Just what the negotiations embodied was a closely guarded secret, but the plan he imagined, was that the Emperor should mass his troops on the French border, thus giving the impression that he was about to make a warlike advance into France.

"Louis," Alexandre continued, "will then put himself boldly at the head of our army and dash forward to defend his country. Naturally there'll be no real engagement. The Austrians will obligingly withdraw and Louis will return to Paris posing grandly as the savior of the nation."

"I can imagine nothing more preposterous," the marquis said.

"Nor can I, Father. Nobody would be deceived, and the King, instead of countering the revolution, would help it forward by showing himself to be a weaker fool than everybody believes him to be already."

"But hasn't it occurred to you," the marquis pointed out, "that if the Emperor actually masses his troops on the border and moves forward there might be no *voluntary* withdrawal?"

"Naturally it has, and that, if it comes about, will be the signal for the complete downfall of the monarchy. However, I am not here to discuss the political situation, but—" he coughed—"something a little more personal."

"Indeed?"

"As a matter of fact, Father, I—er—I am in a rather difficult position —er—financially."

The marquis laughed cheerfully. "Ah, that is a very common complaint with many of us these days."

Alexandre, though he felt like shaking the old idiot, made an effort to control his impatience.

"I need money," he said. "I need money badly."

"My dear boy, who doesn't? I was only saying to Rose this morning that——"

"Father, *please*! This, I assure you, is not a joke!"

119

"I'm sure it isn't, dear me yes, and I do understand what you're trying to say. You want me to help you."

"Yes, Father, if you would. I—er—I am in urgent need of eight thousand livres."

"Eight thousand livres!" the marquis echoed in an awed whisper. "And you think I might be able to lend you such a sum, eh?"

Alexandre looked at the old man doubtfully. "Well yes, if you would be so kind. After all, have I ever come to you for money before?"

"My poor boy," the marquis said earnestly, "I couldn't lend you one thousand, let alone eight."

"Pah!" Alexandre cried, and swung hurriedly from the room.

In the hall he met Marie-Joseph-Rose who had seen his arrival from an upstairs window and had heard some of the conversation while standing as close as she dared to the half-open library door.

"Ah, you were looking for me, Alexandre," she said, with a sweet smile.

"Nothing of the kind!" he snapped, and tried to push past her.

"Dear me, how vehement you sound."

He turned to face her furiously. "You she-devil," he raged. "It might interest you to know that I have tried every means in my power to raise eight thousand livres, but presumably such a sum, small as it is, is not to be found."

"Then you agree to my terms?" she asked innocently.

"Yes, confound you, I agree to your terms!"

She inclined her head gravely. "If you were a little more polite, my dear, I would say thank you."

"I fail to see the need for pretence, for hypocrisy, madame! This is a business agreement. You shall take up residence at the rue de l'Université. You shall have your fashionable *salon*. It is a business agreement. The world shall know you as my wife again—the world, mark you, but not I myself. Oh yes, a business agreement it is and shall remain!"

"Take care, Alexandre, or you'll give yourself a stroke."

"Pah!" he cried again, and rushed headlong from the house.

CHAPTER XV

THE MARQUISE DE BEAUharnais who, with the marquis, had made the journey from Fontainebleau in order to be present at the musical evening, surveyed her niece's *salon* with a little smile of approval.

"Charming, my dear Rose, charming."

"Everything is new, Aunt Marie. The furniture, the carpets, the hangings—everything!"

"So I perceive. What a veritable orgy of spending you must have enjoyed."

Marie-Joseph-Rose sighed happily. "Indeed, yes!"

"What was the total account?"

"I never troubled to ask. It would have seemed so—so *plebeian*."

The marquise chuckled. "Financial worries are Alexandre's concern now, of course."

"Of course!" She glanced at the clock. "Merciful heavens, the guests will begin to arrive in a moment. Excuse me, Aunt Marie, I must have a word with Alexandre."

She found him in his study, pretentiously busy with a number of important-looking documents.

"Well, madame," he said, without looking up, "you seem to have wasted no time in launching yourself into society."

"There's little time to waste, Alexandre."

She spoke lightly, hiding as best she could a growing uneasiness. Would Alexandre make an appearance tonight, or would he remain in his study, pretending to work, but in reality sulking? For from the moment of her arrival at the rue de l'Université he had remained aloof and ill-tempered, though, to his lasting credit, he had tried to hide it when the children were present.

"How many guests have you invited?" he asked.

"Twenty—including yourself, for my husband, naturally, is invited."

He looked up at last, the lines of his face marking an exaggerated sneer.

"You require my presence, of course, in order to maintain the fable of a reunited and loving couple."

"Of course."

"Let me remind you that it was not part of our business agreement."

"It was part of it that I should have a fashionable *salon*," she reminded him, and added sweetly, "and how could that be possible if my important husband were to absent himself from the first?"

"I see you laugh at me," he said sourly.

"I do indeed, but there is more than a grain of truth in what I say. You *are* important, Alexandre. So important that your wife's first real launching into society would hardly be a social success without you."

He looked at her acidly. "I must be grateful to you for recognizing the fact."

"You will come out and receive my guests with me?"

"Certainly not!"

"Charlotte Robespierre and her brother will be among them. I asked the brother, much as I dislike him, especially for your sake. I also asked the Marquis de la Fayette and M'sieur Bailly in order to please you."

"Bailly?" he said, showing a reluctant interest.

"Ah, so you *will* come, Alexandre."

"Later in the evening, perhaps—if I have nothing better to do."

"I see," she said quickly, "so that is what I am to tell M'sieur Bailly. He will naturally ask where you are and I shall be forced to say, 'My husband, m'sieur, has promised to join you later if he has nothing better to do'."

Alexandre's face turned red. "You—you—!" he stuttered.

"She-devil?" she supplied.

"I have another word in mind," he said coldly, "a word that is never used in polite society."

She laughed lightly. "Thank God you're a gentleman, Alexandre."

She returned to the *salon*. The musicians had arrived and were setting up their stands and arranging their music, while Signora Sarsati, a singer who was all the rage in Paris at the moment, could be heard striving to achieve her top C in a nearby reception room.

"Sarsati appears to be in good voice tonight," the marquise laughed.

"I hardly care, Aunt Marie, providing Alexandre is in good voice."

The marquise frowned. "Your husband, I presume, is still furious at having been forced into this reconciliation?"

"*Very* furious."

"In that case, my dear, how can you and he live happily together?"

"A place in society is all I seek, not happiness with Alexandre. And if he should ever become president of the Assembly——"

"If that should happen," the marquise said roughly, "it will mean little. In these times any guttersnipe might be expected to become president of the Assembly."

Her niece pouted. "Really, Aunt Marie, are you trying to discourage me?"

"No. All I'm trying to do is warn you. By all means establish this fashionable *salon*; by all means amuse yourself with the social side of politics. But remember what Alexandre is—pretentious, and underneath, weak. If you can really make use of him, do so. Who knows, having served his purpose, he may some day slip out of your life, leaving you to find a greatness he himself could never attain."

"And now, having warned me, you are tempting me to dream!"

"As far as I can see you are likely to gain one thing only from

122

this reconciliation. Alexandre, politically, is on the right side. The monarchy is finished. We still have a King and Queen, I admit, but every move they make to re-establish themselves places them in greater difficulties. Therefore, keep on your husband's side and the fact that you are an aristocrat by birth may not weigh too heavily against you in the dark days ahead."

Marie-Joseph-Rose shuddered. The conversation was beginning to depress her. Things, surely, were not so serious as Aunt Marie seemed to believe. The outcry against the monarchy and the aristocracy would die away completely in the near future and the full enjoyment of life, according to the standards of *le monde*, would be possible once again.

"Ah," said the marquise, "here comes your charming husband."

Marie-Joseph-Rose went forward to meet him. "Thank you," she said simply.

Aloof and reserved at first, he began to unbend when the guests were announced and presently he was moving among them with a languid grace and was charming to everybody.

"A miracle," the marquise commented drily.

Her niece nodded happily. Sarsati had just concluded an encore, the polite applause was dying away and general conversation was springing up again.

"Doctor Guillotin?" Marie-Joseph-Rose echoed, catching the words uttered by M'sieur Bailly who, with Alexandre, was standing in a little group nearby. "Not a second Doctor Mesmer, I hope!"

Bailly turned to her with a grim smile. "Dear me no, madame. A much more dangerous man than Mesmer, I fear."

"Mesmer," Alexandre laughed, "though a quack, has never been known to kill his patients; Guillotin, without exception, will kill all of them."

"The man," Bailly explained, "is the inventor of a beheading machine."

"Hardly the inventor," Alexandre corrected. "Such machines were used in England a hundred years ago and are still used in Italy."

"Then the perfector of the invention," Bailly amended. "The guillotine, for Doctor Guillotin has given his name to the infernal contraption, is swift, extremely efficient and allegedly painless."

"Since experiments up to now have been confined to those made with dead bodies at the Bicetre," Alexandre laughed, "whether it is painless or not is a debatable question."

Marie-Joseph-Rose gave a little cry of mock horror. "Really, gentlemen, do you wish to ruin the success of my evening by discussing such a gruesome subject?"

"One final comment, madame," Bailly smiled, "and then enough.

Doctor Guillotin's name, in being given to the machine, has been wittily turned into the feminine gender."

"And rightly too," Alexandre said, staring fixedly at his wife. "Women, I assure you, are invariably more cruel than men."

"Then beware of a mere wife," Marie-Joseph-Rose laughed lightly, returning the stare just as fixedly.

And naturally, everybody within earshot laughed merrily.

Late that night, when the last guest had taken his leave, she asked Alexandre if he had enjoyed himself.

"Well yes," he said grudgingly, "a little."

"And you thought it a success?"

"A surprising success," he was obliged to admit. "Confound it all, you were a splendid hostess."

Rightly or wrongly she suspected that he was looking at her now with an amorous speculation in his eyes. No, no, she thought, *that* would be insupportable, and was not, as he himself had insisted from the first, a part of their bargain.

"Perhaps you'll come to my next musical evening," she said quickly.

He smiled, and for the moment seemed almost human. "Perhaps I shall, Rose, if only for the look of the thing."

$$* \quad * \quad * \quad * \quad *$$

Marie-Joseph-Rose was spending a few days at Fontainebleau when the news reached her. In a high state of excitement she went in search of her aunt.

"Alexandre has been elected to the presidency," she cried. "I, the Vicomtesse de Beauharnais, am now the wife of the president of the Assembly!"

She hurried back to Paris to find the streets crammed with shouting people and the whole city in a state of tumult, and learned, when she succeeded at last in forcing her way through the crowd to the rue de l'Université, that it had been Alexandre's first duty to announce to the Assembly that the King and Queen had left the Tuileries secretly in an attempt to make their escape from France.

From that moment, until their Majesties were pursued to Varennes and brought back in strict custody, Alexandre's position, or so it seemed to Marie-Joseph-Rose, equalled that of a reigning monarch. He was cheered in the streets and his son, Eugene, was spoken of in many *salons* as the 'young dauphin.'

'At last the prediction has come true,' she thought, 'to all intents and purposes I am now the Queen of France.'

Unhappily, after a 'reign' of only fourteen days, and before the 'queen' could even celebrate her new position by giving a grand *fête*, Alexandre was succeeded by another president and was obliged to accept the comparative ignominy of a civil position at Loir-et-Cher where, while his wife remained in Paris, he contented himself with the writing of political pamphlets.

Three months later, after the Constituent Assembly had given place to the Legislative Assembly, Alexandre was ordered to rejoin the army, the order making it clear that his political services, in spite of his many speeches and hotly written pamphlets, were no longer required by the new rulers of France.

With the country at war with Austria he was elevated to the rank of lieutenant-colonel and posted to the twenty-first division, which was stationed temporarily at Valenciennes. *En route* to join the division he passed through Paris where he found it possible to break his journey for several days.

The change in him was surprising. He was still pompous, still inclined to self-importance, but there was, Marie-Joseph-Rose felt sure, a lurking fear in his eyes.

"The revolution is going too far and too quickly," he said. "We are caught up, you and I, in a tide that will sweep away the Legislative Assembly itself, and then God help France and all who love her."

"But surely you'll be safe!" she cried. "You, a republican and an anti-monarchist!"

He sighed heavily. "I am still an aristocrat by birth, Rose. The fact that I turned republican many years ago will never quite hide that if the riff-raff of Paris gain control of affairs. They'll cry out for my blood, just as they now cry out for the blood of the King."

There was silence for a moment.

"Rose," he said, breaking it, "it will now be necessary to relinquish my title, to show my contempt for the aristocracy by calling myself plain Citizen Beauharnais."

She looked at him in astonishment and horror. "Great heavens, are you serious, Alexandre?"

"The sacrifice is a small one," he said airily. "To insist on my title when all people in France are now supposed to be equal, would be foolish—a childish challenge of public opinion. In future, when anybody addresses you as the Vicomtesse de Beauharnais, correct them instantly. From this moment you must be the Citizeness Beauharnais. You quite understand?"

She nodded dumbly. The sacrifice was a small one, he said! No, no, it was great, *great*! Citizeness Beauharnais instead of Madame la Vicomtesse de Beauharnais! It would have been better to have remained in Martinique and died there.

"You quite understand?" he repeated.

"Yes," she said, "I quite understand, but if things are as bad as you think, we will have to make deeper plans than this to save our lives."

To save our lives! The words had slipped out unthinkingly, without any real significance, and it was silly to attach any significance to them now, for the King was still alive and the only political execution that had taken place was that of Collenot d'Angremont, the man who had brought into being the National Guard.

"Not only must we be plain Citizen and Citizeness Beauharnais," Alexandre said, with a sudden, eager little laugh, "but we must behave like ordinary, humble people. You, my dear, must begin by doing your own marketing."

"My own *marketing*? Merciful heavens, Alexandre, do you mean that I must carry a basket on my arm and go to such dreadful places as the rue au Fer and the quai de la Valée?"

"I do indeed, Rose."

"But I should be terrified!"

"Take your maid with you, if you wish." And then, his vision of what it meant to become an ordinary citizen of Paris expanding widely, he said briskly: "You shall make your first shopping expedition today and I myself shall accompany you."

"*You?*"

"Why not?" said Citizen Beauharnais.

*   *   *   *   *

The carriage, an open one, turned right from the rue de l'Université into the rue du Bac, crossed the juncture of the quai d'Orsay and the quai de Voltaire and so over the Pont Royal to the Tuileries Gardens in which Marie-Joseph-Rose had sometimes walked with the children during her stay in the marquis's house in the rue Thévenot.

"To give you a little courage," Alexandre said condescendingly, "we shall drive first in the gardens."

"Whatever you wish," she said stiffly, lowering her eyes from his stupid face and at the same time endeavoring not to look at the cumbrous shopping basket balanced precariously on her silk-covered knee.

They passed through the gardens in silence, Marie-Joseph-Rose hoping mournfully that none of the carriages they met and overtook would contain people known to her. (*If they were to see my basket!*) The ordeal having passed without a single encounter, she breathed her relief when the carriage entered the newly named place de la Revolution, and there, for the first time, she saw Doctor Guillotin's beheading machine. To her horror Alexandre ordered their coachman to bring the carriage as close as possible and stop.

"Is this dreadful thing to remain here," she asked, "like some horrible monument?"

"Hardly," he told her. "By order of the Government the guillotine is being exhibited for a few days in various parts of Paris."

Standing up in the carriage, and pointing, he began to explain how the machine worked.

"The condemned man," he said, "is laid out on the form and his head, face down, is placed in the slot. The knife is drawn to the top of the runners by the rope—it runs through a pulley, you see— which is then released. The descent is swift and the head, they tell me, falls instantly into the basket beneath."

"A head that may some day be yours, M'sieur le Vicomte," a voice said harshly.

Marie-Joseph-Rose saw that a crowd had gathered about the guillotine and that it was a woman, a wretched creature in a coarse apron, who had spoken. There was a laugh from the crowd, a laugh that sent a shiver of terror down Marie-Joseph-Rose's back.

"Madame—" Alexandre began, and then remembered.

"Citizeness," he tried again, "my name is certainly Beauharnais, but not M'sieur le Vicomte, merely citizen. This—" he forced Marie-Joseph-Rose to stand at his side—"is my wife, Citizeness Beauharnais."

"And a pretty neck she has," the woman remarked, at which the crowd laughed again.

The woman came closer and spat.

"I give you that," she said, "for the Citizen Beauharnais."

Alexandre flushed deeply, made an angry gesture and then, after a quick glance at the faces staring up at him, ordered the coachman to whip up the horses.

"*That*," he cried indignantly, "after the way I have worked and talked for the good of the common people!"

She was glad he had added 'and talked,' but instead of taunting him with it she merely asked if he was still determined, after so unpleasant an experience, to take her to the markets.

"Naturally," he said shortly, but there was fear in his eyes.

They drove back through the gardens in silence and at the Pont Neuf Alexandre again ordered the coachman to stop. He sprang down and gave Marie-Joseph-Rose his arm.

"Come, my dear. An ordinary citizen and his wife don't go to the markets in a vicomte's carriage. From here we walk."

"O *no*, Alexandre! My shoes were never designed for rough pavements. They——"

"Since you will be making many such shopping excursions," he said, "you may as well buy a more suitable pair. Come!"

"I shall only come," she said, with a little stamp of her foot, a stamp that made her painfully aware of the hard cobbles through the thin leather of her shoe, "if you carry the basket for me."

He looked askance at the basket, but without a word he took it from her.

By the time they had reached the rue la Tour, which led directly to the principal marketing center of Paris, she was already footsore and very much out of temper.

"Please! You walk too fast!" she protested.

Alexandre's nostrils were twitching. "Fish," he said, "first we shall buy some fish."

Never in her life had Marie-Joseph-Rose seen so much confusion nor heard such a deafening babel of ill-bred voices. Fish-stalls, egg-stalls, vegetable-stalls—all were crowded together and surrounded by female shoppers of all ages.

"It will be necessary," Alexandre said, fastidiously, "to—er—push our way forward."

"Then use the basket," she told him viciously, "like everybody else seems to be doing."

"Er—yes, of course."

She clutched at his arm and was dragged forward in a series of little jerks until she found herself pressed painfully against the nearest fish-stall. And the smell! Dear heaven, the smell!

"Fresh plaice, citizeness," the fishmonger, a handsome young man in a striped apron, said cheerfully.

She held her nose. "*Fresh*, did you say, citizen!"

"Careful," Alexandre cautioned, in a whisper, "it would never do to offend these people."

"You should have thought of that before you dragged me here!" she snapped.

"*Sacré nom*," the young fishmonger exclaimed, "not a little visitor from the rue Saint-Denis, surely!"

"And why not, m'sieur?" she snapped, "since those of the rue Saint-Denis must eat like anybody else."

Alexandre nudged her sharply in the ribs. "Not 'm'sieur,' " he whispered, "but 'citizen.' "

The fishmonger's exclamation had caused a momentary silence.

"Aristocrats!" a woman shouted, breaking it. There was much delighted laughter and surging forward of the crowd.

"Stand back! Give our visitors elbow room!" the woman cried.

She was young, not more than twenty, Marie-Joseph-Rose was quick to notice. Her clothes were poor—the *fichu* round her neck was hanging in shreds—but they clung to a body that was rounded and shapely. She reached forward and slapped Alexandre heartily across the shoulders. Then, with both arms about his waist, she swung him round.

"Music!" she commanded. "For once in my life I would dance with an aristocrat!"

The crowd applauded and made a clearing. Somebody began to strum a guitar. Alexandre, whirled almost off his feet for a moment, steadied himself and with a sickly smile began to dance. Marie-Joseph-Rose giggled suddenly at the sight and turned away to find herself confronted by the fishmonger. He made a sweeping, exaggerated bow.

"If the citizeness has no previous engagement——?"

She hesitated. These people, unlike the crowd at the guillotine, were in a happy, playful mood, but a mood which, if one offended them, would possibly become ugly and threatening. She looked into his bold clear eyes. He could be scarcely more than eighteen and was a great deal more handsome than she had first thought.

"The pleasure, m'sieur," she said prettily, "is mine."

He caught her in his arms, and what amazingly strong arms they were. He was taller and broader and very much stronger than Tercier.

"A marquise, perhaps?" he questioned.

"Merely a vicomtesse," she apologized.

"Ah, but a pretty one!" he shouted.

She laughed gaily. Such gallantry from a mere fishmonger! Other couples had joined in the dance, but she and the young man had not yet moved a step. There they stood in a veritable embrace, and there, such was his strength, they seemed likely to remain. He was smiling down at her and his lips, though a little too full, were beautifully moulded.

Alexandre and the young woman brushed against them in passing, and Alexandre, she noticed, was no longer wearing a sickly smile. He was holding the girl closely and leering, positively *leering*.

"If I know the little Elise aright," the fishmonger laughed, "there'll be a discreet retirement soon."

His face was close to her own and the warmth of his body and the strong pounding of his heart were most alarming. What was it that Tercier had said about her finding somebody in Paris just as efficient as he? But not a fishmonger, surely not a fishmonger!

"You invited me to dance, m'sieur," she said. "Therefore, shall we —dance?"

With a shrug and a grin he moved forward with her into the midst of the dancing couples. She caught a glimpse of Alexandre. His hat, to which a tricolor cockade had been attached, was now on his partner's head and his leer had become disgustingly revolting. The guitar player, with a final strum, stood back to rest. The crowd applauded and the dancers broke up. She found herself led to the back of the fish-stall and craned her neck for another glimpse of Alexandre, but he and the girl had disappeared. To abandon her like this! Really, it was carrying revolutionary patriotism too far!

The fishmonger, one arm round her waist, laughed loudly.

"What is sauce for the goose," he said, "is surely sauce for the gander."

"You have your genders mixed," she told him pertly. "My husband is a gander, not a goose, and the sauce you suggest, as far as I am concerned, smells a little too strongly of fish."

His face clouded and she wondered anxiously if she had gone too far.

"I came to the markets to do a little shopping," she said. "Oblige me, please, by giving me three of your fresh plaice."

"Very well," he said sullenly.

She found the basket discarded by the wretched Alexandre and held it out for the fish to be placed in it.

"What is the price?" she asked, taking some coins out of her reticule.

"Payment in money was hardly what I had expected," he said, still sullenly.

He told her the amount. She gave him a *louis d'or* and watched him in amusement while he counted out the change.

"Being new to the markets and needing some meat and vegetables," she said, "I wonder if I could ask you to accompany and help me?"

With a grunt he took the basket from her. "Very well, citizeness."

When the purchases had been made she said: "One more request. The basket is too heavy for me. Please carry it to my carriage."

He hesitated, scowled, but finally, with a shrug of his shoulders, agreed. At the Pont Neuf he helped her into the carriage, placed the basket at her feet and leaped in beside her.

"Some day," he said, "I too shall own a carriage. Meanwhile a little jaunt in yours will suffice."

She giggled. A very forceful young man and certainly more masculine than Tercier. She frowned. Tercier! Why must she continually think of Tercier and the cruel things he had said to her?

When the carriage drew up at the rue de l'Université she said: "Not the rue Saint-Denis, you see; merely the rue de l'Université."

She waited for him to spring down and help her alight. She waited in vain, being obliged, in the end, to lean forward and open the door herself. As she did so she felt herself caught in a vice-like grip. A moment later she was sitting awkwardly on his lap and his hot face was buried in her breast. She felt herself grow weak and help-less. That cursed Tercier! Been given a taste for such things, had she! The smell of fish, either from the basket or the person of the young man himself, filled her nostrils. *Revived*, she thought—*not by smelling-salts, but by fish!* Revived and saved! She freed herself with a great effort and tumbled from the carriage.

To the grinning coachman she said haughtily: "Take the Citizen Fishmonger back to the markets and wait there for the Citizen Beau-harnais."

The moment the carriage had turned she felt sorry, and later, when she was safe in the house, the feeling, strangely nostalgic, persisted.

"But no," she told herself sternly, "the smell of fish would have been insupportable, utterly insupportable."

CHAPTER XVI

THE MARQUISE, UP FROM Fontainebleau for a few days, surveyed the crowded *salon*.

"A somewhat mixed gathering," she commented.

"The Citizeness Beauharnais," Marie-Joseph-Rose said lightly, "opens her doors these days to many people she would have shunned before the King was brought back from Varennes."

"At Alexandre's request, perhaps?"

"No, Aunt Marie, at the dictates of my own good sense."

Since Alexandre's departure for Valenciennes, and with an eye to safeguarding herself and her children, she had begun to give a series of what she secretly termed 'possibility' evenings. The guests, her 'possibilities,' were all people of strong political aspirations. They all knew just what ought to be done to make the revolution a last-ing success. Any single one of them might rise overnight to political power. To flatter them all, to make them think she loved them dearly and supported their separate views, would give her a chance of survival if the coming changes turned out to be as drastic as everybody seemed to expect.

Meanwhile the children had been sent out of Paris to the comparative safety of Saint-Martin, in Artois, where the Princess Amalie owned a country house. This was contrary to Alexandre's wishes. He thought that Hortense should remain with her mother and insisted on Eugene being sent to the National College at Strasbourg, but since he was kept busy at Valenciennes she had no scruples in disregarding his wishes.

"Come," she said, taking her aunt by the arm, "I must introduce you to Citizen Pierre Réal, a man of considerable influence."

The marquise raised her eyebrows quizzically.

"No," Marie-Joseph-Rose laughed, in reply to the unspoken question, "not yet my lover, but later, if necessary, I shall accept his quite charming advances."

During one of the 'possibility' evenings a few weeks later there was a disturbance in the street and all the guests ran to the windows. A mob of people was moving in the direction of the rue de Bac, cheerful people, it seemed, for they were singing lustily. The song was new and so catchy that Marie-Joseph-Rose found her feet tapping out the time.

"What is it?" she asked Citizen Tallien, a man Pierre Réal had brought with him, "a new marching song?"

He nodded. "They call it the Hymn to the Army of the Rhine. A young fellow by the name of Rouget de Lisle wrote it. Those people you see down there singing it are rebels from Marseille. It's been a long march from the south and they've sung it, I'm told, the whole way."

"I like the swing of it," she said, still listening attentively. "It makes me feel oddly excited, almost as if—" she laughed negligently— "almost as if it were to mean something of great importance in my life."

The next morning she heard that the rebels from Marseille, their ranks swelled by countless hysterical Parisians, had stormed the Tuileries in an attempt to tear the Royal Family limb from limb, and had only been prevented from doing this by the Swiss Guards, most of whom had been shamefully slaughtered. She wished then that she had never heard the Hymn to the Army of the Rhine, which everybody was now calling 'La Marseillaise,' for she knew in her heart that this, for the world she loved, was the beginning of the end.

Alexandre, handsome and smug in his new uniform, strode up and down in front of his wife, obviously begging for a little admiration. She had seen him only three times since he had rejoined the army and now, by a series of rapid promotions, he was the Citizen-General Beauharnais, Commander-in-Chief of the Army of the Rhine.

"Sit down," she said irritably. "I know you look beautiful but I'm not a young girl whose head is likely to be turned, even by such a splendid sight."

His mouth fell open and remained open for a few moments.

"Forgive me," she said quickly. "My nerves are a little on edge."

A *little* on edge! They'd been like that and worse since the attack on the Tuileries and the trial and execution of the King. Many of her friends had urged her to leave Paris, but she had felt that only by remaining would she have any chance of saving herself and the children. Her mother, writing from Martinique to tell her of the sudden death of her father and sister, had begged her to visit the West Indies once more, but sad as she was at the thought of her mother all alone at Trois-Ilets she had still felt that she must remain in Paris.

"What brings you to Paris?" she asked Alexandre.

He threw out his chest and smirked. "I come, my dear, because I happen to have been offered the Ministry of War."

"I knew that such an offer was going to be made," she said, "but unfortunately it has come sooner than I expected."

"You *knew*, Rose?"

"Pierre Réal told me."

"Ah yes," he sneered, "your latest lover, I believe."

"Don't be a fool, Alexandre!" she snapped.

It had been necessary, of course, to accept Réal's advances, but why admit it to Alexandre?

"Why," Alexandre demanded, "did you say that *unfortunately* the offer had come sooner than you expected?"

"How many enemies have you in Paris?" she asked.

"Quite a number," he admitted, showing uneasiness for the first time.

"Robespierre being the greatest, I imagine?"

"Well, yes."

"Frankly, Alexandre, he thinks you a fool, a *dangerous* fool. Had he been able to wield the power he now wields at the time of your promotion——"

"I quite understand that he objected to my being given the command of the Army of the Rhine," Alexandre broke in, "but such a fact is hardly likely to make me afraid of the man."

She brushed this aside with an impatient gesture. "Be advised by me, Alexandre. Refuse the offer of the Ministry of War."

"Oh come," he cried, taking up a dramatic attitude in the middle of the room, "a grateful country, remembering my past political services and taking into account the work I've done in the army, offers me the Ministry of War and you——"

"A grateful country, but not a grateful Robespierre."

"Robespierre has not yet attained full power. Once I become the Minister of War he may never attain it. This is an opportunity for which I have waited ever since the Constituent Assembly fell."

"You aren't safe anywhere," she said, "but you're safer with the Army than anywhere else."

"Do you really imagine that I care for personal safety?" he demanded grandly. "As a soldier did I ever put *that* consideration before my duty?"

"Death on the battlefield," she said quietly, "is rather different from death on the guillotine."

She saw that she had penetrated his armor of conceit at last.

"The—the guillotine?" he stammered.

"Yes, my dear, brave Alexandre, the guillotine."

"You—you mean that you have a sound reason for advising me to refuse the Ministry?"

"A very sound reason. According to Réal a plot is afoot to get you back to Paris by making you this apparently splendid offer. When the time is ripe it will be a simple matter to accuse you of negligence, treachery or some such thing and—dispose of you."

"Dear Heaven," he said softly, and she saw that his hands had begun to tremble.

"I can hardly believe it," he whispered.

He began to pace the room again, this time in pitiful agitation. Finally he collapsed into a chair and stared vacantly before him.

"Well," she asked, "do you feel inclined to take my advice?"

He nodded. "Yes. Yes, of course!"

"Did you come straight here," she asked, "or visit army headquarters first?"

"I came straight here. I've been nowhere else, seen nobody else."

"Then I suggest that you return to Strasbourg at once and from there write a letter to the Government making some plausible excuse for declining the offer."

"Yes, yes, but *what* excuse?"

She laughed drily. "Letter-writing was always a strong point with you. You ought to be able to compose a suitable letter after a little calm thought."

He blushed swiftly. "You suggest that I am anything but calm now?"

"Why not stress the fact," she said, ignoring his question, "that while the enemies of France threaten our peace and safety the honor of defending your country means more to you than anything else in the world?"

He rose to his feet with a confident laugh. "Yes. Yes, I'll do that! The honor of defending my country! By heavens yes!"

Once more he was pacing the floor, this time with a jaunty air.

"My enemies may be clever," he cried, "but I, as I shall show them, am cleverer. Cleverer and capable of beating them at their own game. By heavens yes!"

✳   ✳   ✳   ✳   ✳

Soon after Alexandre's return to Strasbourg and his refusal of the Ministry of War, the Marquis de Beauharnais came to Paris on a short visit. By this time the Convention had established itself grandly in the Tuileries, the notorious Commission of Twelve had been formed and the Constitution of 1793 issued. Commenting on these things the marquis pressed her once more to return with him to Fontainebleau.

She shook her head decisively. "Alexandre's affairs are quickly coming to a climax. Only by remaining in Paris till a definite move is made against him will I be able to warn him in time."

"I sometimes think," the old man said quietly, "that considering the trouble my son has caused you in the past you worry too much about his safety."

She laughed drily. "His safety is my safety and the children's. Should Alexandre fall our own danger will become acute."

Life in Paris during the next few months grew increasingly perilous. The murder of Marat, instead of putting an end to what people were beginning to call the Reign of Terror, lent greater fervor and fury to its perpetrators. The Girondin leaders were outlawed and the Revolutionaries, not content with the old-established calendar, invented a new one. Twenty-first October, 1792, having seen the abolition of royalty, now became the only accepted beginning of time. Twenty-second October, 1793, opening Year Two of the Republic, became Vendémiaire the First. Vendémiaire, the month of the vintage—a pretty thought, but in its deeper significance, blood having the same color as wine and being likely to flow more freely, an ugly one too.

Concerned as Marie-Joseph-Rose was at these events, not the least of them being the execution of the Queen on Vendémiaire the twenty-fifth, a lesser one which took place at Mayence in the following month of Brumaire was of greater personal significance to her. Alexandre, ordered to march to the relief of the town, which was held by the Austrians, was forced, even though his army numbered sixty thousand men, to retreat in disorder. In alarm she saw that this would give his enemies the opportunity for which they had waited. He would be recalled to Paris in disgrace, recalled and undoubtedly court-martialed.

For three anxious weeks, weeks during which the churches of Paris were closed and the Revolutionary Government was formed, she waited for news. Alexandre, she learned from Réal, was back in Strasbourg. No actual move had been made against him.

"In the course of time," Réal told her, "a move will naturally be made. In the meanwhile, if your husband is wise, he will attempt an escape from France."

First she decided to write him a letter warning him of his increased danger, then, realizing that letters could easily be intercepted, she thought it best to pay a hurried visit to Strasbourg.

Alexandre seemed both surprised and embarrassed at the sight of his wife. The embarrassment puzzled her until she recollected some gossip she had heard on her arrival in the town concerning Alexandre and the daughter of a commissariat officer. She brushed this aside with a laugh of amusement and told him the reason for her visit. To her surprise his self-confidence was amazingly strong.

"Really, my dear, much as I appreciate your concern on my behalf, I must say that I think you are showing a little too much alarm."

"But Alexandre, the danger of your position——!"

"The danger of my position is not so great as you think. In any case I have already dealt with the situation in the way I thought best. I have written to Paris resigning my command."

"You don't expect that to help much, do you?"

"Perhaps not," he admitted, "but apart from keeping away from Paris, what else could I do?"

"As I suggested a moment ago, you could leave the country."

"Leave the country?" He drew himself up with a ridiculous show of dignity. "My dear Rose, that would be running away."

"You could return as soon as a change of government made it possible."

"I prefer to remain," he said, with finality.

"But why?" she cried desperately. "Why?"

"Because it is the right, the *honorable* thing to do."

"Having resigned your command you could at least leave Strasbourg and retire to some secluded part of the country."

"Never!"

"Has your idiotic stubbornness," she asked, her anger getting the better of her, "anything to do with the daughter of a certain commissariat officer?"

He rose to his feet with a show of temper. "My private affairs have nothing to do with it!"

Rather than make a scene which he would ascribe to jealousy she tried another line of argument.

"For the children's sake, Alexandre, make some attempt to save yourself."

"I am yet to be convinced," he said loftily, "that I am in any real danger. The Government knows me for what I am, a good republican patriot."

"The Government knows you for something else, Alexandre—a former aristocrat who, at the head of sixty thousand men, failed to relieve Mayence."

He flushed with anger. "By heaven, Rose——!"

"I'm sorry," she said wearily, "but those are the two facts which the Committee of Public Safety will even now be taking into account."

It was useless, however, to continue the argument. Nothing, apparently, would move him, and with a feeling of frustration she returned to Paris to watch, listen to the many rumors of her friends and wait for what she now considered was the inevitable.

The first thing she learned during this further and much more anxious period of waiting was that Alexandre's resignation had been refused, and then, some weeks later, that it had been accepted. Even then it was not until the second of the following March (Ventôse the twelfth, if you please, citizeness!) that the Committee of Public Safety decided to act. Alexandre was arrested on that date, his papers were confiscated and he was brought to Paris where, with many other 'enemies of the Republic,' he was confined in the prison of Les Carmes.

* * * * *

Marie-Joseph-Rose looked at Citizen Pierre Réal with big, piteous eyes. "Is it possible, my friend, that your silence means one thing only, that you can do nothing whatever to help me?"

He looked at her miserably. "Though it will cost me your friendship to admit it," he said, "that is precisely what it does mean."

She felt sorry for him instantly and gave his arm a motherly little pat. She had never been in love with him, of course, but he was a sincere and earnest man and during her now quite long association with him she had grown to like and respect him.

"My friendship will always be yours," she said gently.

She saw the tears spring to his eyes but that, though gratifying, was hardly what she wanted.

"When will Alexandre be brought to trial?" she said briskly, hoping thereby to avoid a tiresome emotional scene.

"No one seems to know," he said. "He may remain in prison for months, a forgotten man like so many others."

"What do you suggest that I should do?"

"One thing only. Leave Paris in the hope that you, his wife, will remain forgotten too."

She had already thought of this herself and had half decided to close up the house in the rue de l'Université and go to Fontainebleau. Later, while still unable to make up her mind, she became friendly with Madame Hosten, a young widow and, like herself, a Creole by birth. Madame Hosten, it seemed, had recently taken a small house in the country at Croissy. If Marie-Joseph-Rose felt so disposed she could join her there and share the expenses of the establishment.

And so it was arranged, and for a time, though the shadow of the guillotine hung over both of them, life at Croissy was not unpleasant, especially when the children, no longer safe with the Princess Amalie, were brought to join them.

During this short stay at Croissy, Marie-Joseph-Rose made a bold attempt to establish herself as a good republican by applying for what was called a Certificate of *Civisme*. And in order to lend weight to her application she apprenticed Eugene, who was now twelve, to a carpenter at Croissy, and Hortense, who was almost eleven, to her old maid Marie, now established in the village as a dressmaker.

When the certificate was miraculously granted she felt confident enough to carry her fight for survival one step farther by attempting to intervene on Alexandre's behalf.

"Nothing could be more foolish," Madame Hosten said, trying to dissuade her. "You will only draw attention to the fact that you are his wife."

"Nothing could hide that deplorable fact," Marie-Joseph-Rose retorted. "Should he be brought to trial and condemned my own arrest will quickly follow."

Accordingly she wrote a letter to Citizen Vadier, president of the Committee of Public Safety, being careful to inscribe the date according to the dictates of the new calendar. "Greetings, esteem, confidence, fraternity," she opened grandly, tongue none the less in cheek, and went on to say that though he was known throughout France for his severity she felt that it was a severity moved only by a spirit of pure and virtuous patriotism. She pointed out that her husband, born an aristocrat through no fault of his own, was at heart a patriot of the deepest republican convictions, and reminded the Citizen Vadier of the services which Alexandre had rendered the country while a member of the Constituent Assembly. In closing the letter she declared that he, Vadier, was the only man in France capable of rectifying the sad error of Alexandre's arrest and pleaded for a personal interview.

"A personal interview," she chuckled—"that is all I need."

Vadier, they said, though old, had a lecherous turn of mind. Therefore she would wear the prettiest, most feminine dress she could buy and would steel herself to make the age-old bargain with him, nauseating as it would undoubtedly be.

"If you actually knew what he looks like," Madame Hosten said, well aware of Marie-Joseph-Rose's intent, "you would prefer the guillotine."

A week after the letter had been dispatched there was a knock at the door and the harsh cry which she had feared and dreamed of more than once echoed in her ears.

"Open! Open in the name of the Republic!"

So this, she thought, when they told her that she was to be taken to Les Carmes, is Vadier's reply.

CHAPTER XVII

A VOICE SAID: "DO YOU feel better, my dear?"

Marie-Joseph-Rose opened her eyes a second time and looked about her.

"Where am I?" she asked faintly.

"In a cell in the prison of Les Carmes," said the young woman who was bending over her. "You fainted when they were bringing you in."

"Ah yes, I remember now."

She noticed that she was lying on a straw pallet, and that there was another pallet at the opposite side of the small cell. She remembered that Les Carmes had been a Carmelite monastery until religion had been dispensed with and the monks driven out, not only driven out, but many of them massacred.

"I know who you are," her companion said. "You are the Vicomtesse de Beauharnais."

Marie-Joseph-Rose laughed hysterically. "Oh no, not *that*, I beg of you! Merely plain Citizeness Beauharnais. We now have liberty, equality and above all else fraternity." She looked fixedly at the other woman. "Your face is familiar but your name eludes me."

"I am Citizeness Augillion, formerly——"

"But of course. Formerly the Duchesse d'Auguillon. I met you once at a ball given by the Princess Amalie."

The other nodded gravely. "Do you feel recovered?" she asked.

"Thank you, yes."

"Lie quietly for a little while longer."

"I really feel quite able to get up."

"You may please yourself, but what is there to get up for?"

Marie-Joseph-Rose shuddered at the restrained hopelessness in her companion's voice. Indeed yes, what was there to get up for! Sitting up she looked about the cell again.

"Those marks there on the wall," she cried in horror, "are they blood marks?"

"Yes. During the September massacres the Archbishop of Arles and several others were murdered in this cell. Afterwards somebody left three dripping swords against the wall. It has been known as the Chamber of the Three Swords ever since."

"How ghastly!"

"Oh, you'll grow accustomed to it. At first I had a nightmare whenever I went to sleep, but I never think about it now."

Marie-Joseph-Rose was sure that she would have a nightmare too. She tried not to look at the marks on the wall, but since they were illuminated by the patch of sunlight which streamed through the small barred window her eyes were constantly drawn back to them.

"How long have you been in Les Carmes?" she asked.

"Perhaps months; perhaps only a few weeks. I forget."

"And you've been alone in this cell the whole time?"

"No. Until last night there were six of us."

"Six! In a cell as small as this!"

"There are usually six hundred prisoners in Les Carmes, living in an area which formerly housed only sixty monks."

Later she learned that the prisoners within the walls of Les Carmes were permitted a certain amount of liberty. The cell doors were often left unlocked, thus enabling everybody, both men and women, to mingle freely. Social calls were paid, gossip was exchanged and even love-affairs were not uncommon.

140

"Love-affairs," she exclaimed, "in an area as congested as this?"

The duchesse laughed for the first time. "Certain of us place our cells from time to time at the disposal of those who need them more desperately than we do."

Thinking of Alexandre, Marie-Joseph-Rose asked if he was known to the duchesse and if he was still a prisoner in Les Carmes.

"Why yes. I saw him for a moment only this morning. If he is still here tonight you will no doubt find it easy to see him yourself."

"You think he might be removed before tonight?"

"Who knows?"

"To—to the guillotine?"

"Where else?"

Marie-Joseph-Rose fell silent. Silence, frightening as it was in this terrible place, was preferable to the still calm horror of the duchesse's voice.

During the afternoon there was a light tap at the cell door and a young woman entered. It was obvious at once that she was a woman of distinction and self-assurance.

"I heard," she said gaily, "that Les Carmes had taken in yet another guest and I remembered my social obligations."

Introductions were made by the duchesse. The newcomer, Teresia, Marquise de Fontenay, declared herself charmed to meet the Vicomtesse de Beauharnais.

"Welcome to Les Carmes," she said. "I see you have been honored with the Chamber of the Three Swords. You stare at me, my dear Vicomtesse. May I ask why?"

Marie-Joseph-Rose apologized.

"I find it hard to believe that you, Teresia de Fontenay, should be a prisoner here. I had always understood that you were—shall we say, a very good friend of Tallien."

The marquise laughed. "And so I am, as you so delicately put it, a very good friend of Tallien."

"Then—? Surely it isn't possible that Tallien himself has fallen from power?"

"No. Tallien, in spite of his opposition to Robespierre, is still at liberty. It was Robespierre who sent me here. He did it in order to show Tallien that he was the more powerful of the two, and as a threat, I think, that Tallien himself might follow soon."

"Do you mean that Tallien can do nothing for you?"

"Not at present. Of course, if he and his friends win the struggle with Robespierre I shall be released. Otherwise I shall go to the guillotine."

"How dreadful for you, imprisoned here, waiting!"

"Dreadful?" The marquise laughed again. "It might be dreadful but it is also quite exciting."

"The part I hate the most," the duchesse remarked, "is when a jailer reads out the names of those who are to be transferred to the Conciergerie."

Marie-Joseph-Rose looked puzzled. "The Conciergerie?"

"Prisoners go there before standing trial," the marquise explained, "but since trials usually result in one thing only, the Conciergerie is a certain step towards the guillotine. Personally I listen to the jailer with the greatest of interest."

"Teresia," the duchesse said, in her monotonous voice, "would go to the guillotine laughing."

From what little Marie-Joseph-Rose had seen of the exquisite young woman she believed that she would. Since it was easier to die these days than to live, this heroic attitude, which was becoming something of a tradition among certain aristocrats, was quite understandable. Or was it? An icy hand gripped her heart. Easier to die than to live, yes! But she wanted to live, she wanted to live more desperately than ever before, and she knew that she possessed neither the courage nor the bravado to laugh in the deepening shadow of the guillotine.

Teresia de Fontenay chatted pleasantly for a while, and when finally she took her leave she remarked that her own cell was three doors along the corridor on the left.

"Pay me a visit soon," she said. "You and I must become better acquainted."

* * * * *

Marie-Joseph-Rose, overcome by a feeling of nausea, leaned heavily against the rough stone wall. This, the last corridor she had entered in her search for Alexandre's cell, was darker than the rest. The air was heavy with the smell of stale perspiration and the floor was as filthy as the street of a Paris slum. She stumbled forward again and gave a little cry as she found herself clutching at the coat of a man who had entered the corridor silently from the other end. He uttered a short, hearty curse.

"A thousand pardons, citizen," she said.

"Ah," he cried, "a woman. If she looks as sweet as she smells my visit to Les Carmes won't have been entirely wasted."

He loomed above her in the dark corridor, a giant of a man with a deep, musical voice, a good voice but hardly that of an aristocrat. Warmed by the little gallantry and stirred by a curiosity which battled valiantly with her former misery, she looked up into his face. Dim as the light was she thought it a handsome face, and was especially struck by the eyes which flashed merrily as they looked down at her. What had the Duchesse d'Auguillon said about love-affairs not being uncommon?

"I am new to Les Carmes," she said demurely. "I came in search of my husband, Citizen Beauharnais, but I appear to have lost myself."

"Beauharnais's wife, eh?" he said, and laughed as if at a great joke. "You know him, citizen?"

"Yes, I know him." He took her by the arm, not with intentional roughness, she felt sure, but with the bone-shattering grip of a man who was quite unaware of his own strength. "Come, I'll take you to him," and he laughed again.

They emerged from the corridor into a hall that was both well-lit and well-ventilated, and she saw then that the man was a soldier attired in the uniform of a general. Her curiosity deepened. Not an aristocrat, a republican general, yet a prisoner in Les Carmes. A prisoner? More likely the commandant, or whatever one called such a person, in charge of the prison.

He turned the handle of a studded door.

"Ah," he cried, "locked, as indeed it would be."

"This is my husband's cell?"

"No, citizeness, but for the moment he enjoys the use of it. However, since the matter is urgent I think I know a way of gaining immediate entry."

He rapped sharply on the door.

"Open!" he roared. "Open in the name of the Revolution!"

A moment later the door was flung open and Marie-Joseph-Rose found herself face to face with a startled Alexandre, while behind him she caught a glimpse of a woman's skirt.

"Really, Hoche," Alexandre complained, "your sense of humor is sometimes a little more than I can sustain."

Hoche, still holding her firmly by the arm, dragged Marie-Joseph-Rose into the room, for a room it was, not a cell.

"Why," Alexandre asked her, "did they arrest you?"

She shrugged. "I happen to be your wife."

Her eyes were on the woman. She was young, pretty, and confused. Her clothing was considerably disarrayed, and so was Alexandre's, Marie-Joseph-Rose noted, flashing him an amused glance.

"Pray introduce me to your friend," she murmured.

Alexandre cleared his throat. "M'm'selle de Custine—my wife."

Marie-Joseph-Rose inclined her head. "Charmed, m'm'selle, charmed."

With a quick cry, M'm'selle de Custine slipped between Alexandre and Hoche and fled from the room. Alexandre hesitated for a moment, uttered a hurried excuse and went in pursuit.

Hoche closed the door with a laugh.

"Disconcerting as your sense of humor might be to my husband," Marie-Joseph-Rose murmured, "I myself appreciate it."

He laughed again. "A brave little woman, I see." He looked at her for a long moment, then added softly: "And one, perhaps, who has long been aware of her husband's weakness and has not been slow to find an adequate compensation?"

Her eyes were searching the room. There was a bed in it, not a straw pallet, two comfortable chairs and a slender table on which stood a bottle of wine and two glasses.

"This is your room, Citizen General?" she asked.

He nodded. "It is."

"Not the room of a prisoner, surely!"

"Unfortunately, yes."

She was still puzzled. "A very privileged prisoner, then!"

"True," he admitted, "but that is only because the Committee of Public Safety, though brave enough to arrest me by a trick, is still afraid of me, or rather, afraid of the anger of the men I commanded."

"You think—" her mind was working quickly—"you think you might eventually gain release?"

"I do." He took up the bottle of wine and filled the two glasses. "Shall we drink to ourselves, citizeness, or to your husband?"

She took the glass he offered her and watched him thoughtfully as he closed the door with a kick and shot the bolt into place. Rapidly she was comparing him with Alexandre, with Lacoste, with Tercier, and finally with Réal. He was the largest man she had ever seen and —she thought of the grip of his hand on her arm—the strongest. Large and strong, and not a gentleman. 'Helpless,' she thought, 'I'd be helpless. He'd laugh at any protest I might make and if I screamed, who would take notice in *this* place?'

"Well," he repeated, "do we drink to ourselves or——"

She looked at him frankly. "Let us drink, Citizen General, to your freedom and——"

"And," he said, understanding her instantly, "to your own."

*　　*　　*　　*　　*

"Robespierre," Alexandre said, "is aiming at complete dictatorship, but fate, I assure you, will overtake him one of these days. The murderers of the present are the murdered of the future."

This was the evening of Marie-Joseph-Rose's first day of imprisonment. She had come out to the main hall of the prison with Teresia de Fontenay and was now standing with Alexandre among a large group of other prisoners, waiting for the jailer to read out the names of those to be transferred to the Conciergerie.

Alexandre's appearance, now that she was able to study him more closely, shocked her. He was unshaven and haggard and his dress showed every sign of neglect. The Alexandre she remembered, the jaunty, self-confident, conceited Alexandre had given place to a man who, if not completely broken, had permitted hopelessness to enter his soul. For a moment her mind dwelt on the young girl, M'm'selle de Custine. Poor child, she must be in very desperate straits indeed to have found him even remotely attractive.

"My only worry," Alexandre was saying, "is the children. What is going to happen to them with both of us in prison?"

The question brought quick tears to her eyes. In a choking voice she reminded him that his father and her aunt were still at liberty, and that Hortense, apprenticed to her old maid, Marie Lannoy, would surely be free from serious danger.

"Yes, but they'll be penniless," he said. "Our property will have been confiscated by now."

"When we obtain our release—" she was thinking of Hoche—"we will get our property back."

He laughed bitterly. "Our release! As if we dare to look forward to that!"

The jailer appeared and began to read out the names from his list, which was brief.

"Only four tonight," Teresia de Fontenay remarked. "The Conciergerie must be crammed to the very doors."

Marie-Joseph-Rose breathed her relief. She had waited in an agony of suspense for the jailer to say "Alexandre, *ci-devant* Vicomte de Beauharnais," and could hardly believe that the name, heralding the reading of her own perhaps tomorrow night, had not been spoken. Teresia took her kindly by the arm.

"My dear," she said, guessing the thoughts that had been passing through Marie-Joseph-Rose's mind, "try to believe that fate has a brighter future in store for you than you imagine."

*　　*　　*　　*　　*

After a week in Les Carmes Marie-Joseph-Rose began to lose what little hope her association with Hoche had brought her—he was still a prisoner, he still enjoyed his exclusive privileges, but there was every sign that he would still be in Les Carmes when all the other prisoners had been transferred to the Conciergerie. After the second week she felt that she was losing count of time. "I shall die," she told herself, "before they decide to bring me to trial."

She saw Alexandre and M'm'selle de Custine frequently and to the latter's embarrassment was charming to both of them. She also saw much of Teresia de Fontenay, but there were times when even Teresia's optimism and gaiety showed signs of a hint of desperation.

"Tallien is weak," she would say in such moments, "too weak to organize a revolt against Robespierre. If only I were free to stand at his side and give him the courage he lacks!"

News from the outside world was brought to the prisoners with the arrival of new 'enemies of the Republic,' and to Marie-Joseph-Rose and Alexandre by Eugene and Hortense who were permitted to visit Les Carmes once in ten days. They were brought by the sympathetic Marie Lannoy, who, on the third visit, held a pet dog in her arms.

"He's mine," Hortense said. "Marie bought him for me. Isn't he beautiful?"

"Beautiful, darling. What do you call him?"

"Fortuné, Mama."

Through Fortuné, a little mongrel pug with an appealing nose and liquid brown eyes, it was possible to elude the watchfulness of the guard who stood over the visitors and establish a correspondence with Aunt Marie and the marquis. Brief notes were written and taken in and out of Les Carmes in the thick hair beneath the dog's collar.

After three months in captivity Marie-Joseph-Rose began to regain a little optimism. The news from outside, it was true, had grown worse—scores of heads were falling daily—but she and Alexandre, along with Teresia and Hoche, remained in Les Carmes like forgotten people. Hoche! How stupid to have expected any help from him, but a habit had been formed and a habit, especially this sort, was the hardest thing in the world to break.

Less than a week later, however, the feeling of security was destroyed. An order dated Thermidor Fourth, Year Two of the Republic, announced Alexandre's impending removal to the Conciergerie. To her surprise Alexandre who had remained apathetic from the first, appeared to gain new life from the Committee of Public Safety's decision.

"At all events," he declared, "I shall be given a trial and the long-awaited opportunity of defending myself."

Marie-Joseph-Rose looked at him in astonishment. Surely he knew that his trial would be little more than a mockery.

"What charge has been laid against you?" she asked.

"Conspiracy. I am to be charged, along with several others, with having conspired, here in Les Carmes, against the present leaders of the Revolution."

"And have you really been doing that?"

"No."

"What hope have you of proving your innocence?"

"Every hope! I shall make a grand speech, the grandest of my life. I shall begin by declaring myself innocent and then I shall draw the court's attention to my many years of service and sacrifice in the interests, the *best* interests, of republicanism."

She sighed lightly. It was the old Alexandre again. He was even beginning to strut. His chest was thrown out and his eyes were flashing arrogantly. She let him run on for a while and then stopped him with a gesture of impatience.

"Alexandre, we must try to face the truth. How many men have been known to prove themselves innocent at these trials?"

"Not many," he admitted, unshaken, "but I shall be one of them."

She gave way to a sudden flood of tears.

"Deceive yourself if you must, but please don't try to deceive me. They'll condemn you, and then they'll condemn me. Within a week you'll be dragged to the guillotine; within another week I shall be dragged after you."

He took her in his arms awkwardly but his unexpected attempt at gentleness only made matters worse. Pressing herself against him she sobbed uncontrollably.

"Poor little Rose," he whispered. "You were meant for a better fate. Life has rarely been kind to you, has it?" He laughed harshly. "By that I mean that *I* have rarely been kind to you. I see it all now, far more clearly than ever before."

She drew herself away from him. "Please say no more, Alexandre."

"No, no," he protested. "Let me speak. Let me admit, while I am still able to, that the fault has almost always been mine. I could have made you happier had I chosen to. I—I was too intolerant."

She tried to smile through her tears. "I must have been a very trying wife."

"I behaved badly," he insisted. "Have you forgotten what I accused you of before we separated?"

"No, Alexandre. One doesn't forget that sort of thing, but it means nothing to me now."

"I must have been a little insane. I don't think I ever really doubted that Hortense was mine." He paused for a moment, struggling with himself, and finally, in a low voice, he added: "Do you forgive me, Rose?"

147

"What else can I do now," she said sadly, "but forgive you?"

He took her hands in his. "You are kind and good. If the worst happens I shall remember you in my last moments."

If the worst happens! She knew in her heart that it would, that nothing could prevent it.

She turned from him in despair. There was little more for either of them to say except good-bye.

Early the next morning, without being permitted to see his wife again, Alexandre, *ci-devant* Vicomte de Beauharnais, was removed to the Conciergerie.

* * * * *

The children, standing close together in the crowded main hall of the prison, gave a glad cry when they saw their mother approaching them. She embraced them quickly and asked where Marie was.

"The Citizeness Lannoy," Eugene said, "was not permitted to enter with us. The guard said that only two visitors were now permitted to see one single prisoner."

"Fortunately," Hortense said with a sly laugh, "Fortuné was not regarded as a visitor."

"Why, 'fortunately'?" Marie-Joseph-Rose asked, wondering at her daughter's laugh.

"Because of the important message he carries," Eugene said, lowering his voice.

He then told his mother that having heard of his father's removal to the Conciergerie he and Hortense had gone there before coming to Les Carmes.

"We pleaded for permission to see him," he said, "and in the end we were allowed to enter for a few moments."

"You're the bravest children in the world," Marie-Joseph-Rose cried, taking them into her arms. "This important message you speak of, does it come from your father?"

Eugene nodded and Hortense took up the little dog in her arms. Her mother pretended to fondle him for a moment until her fingers found the folded scrap of paper.

"Stand close about me," she said, taking the dog from Hortense and bending down to place him on the floor. "Shield me while I read the message."

She glanced hurriedly at the hastily scrawled words, gave an exclamation of surprise and quickly hid the note down the neck of her dress.

"Stay here for a moment," she told the children, and went in search of Teresia de Fontenay. She found her talking to a group of newly arrived prisoners.

"Teresia," she whispered, "I must see you at once. Come to my cell."

Once in the cell she gave Teresia Alexandre's note. "Read this. It concerns you more than it concerns me."

A fellow prisoner here, Teresia read, *a man who had better remain nameless, tells me on good authority that Teresia de Fontenay's friend Tallien is now among the proscribed. His name has been placed on a secret list made out by Robespierre. It can only be a matter of days before Tallien is arrested unless he can be persuaded to act, and act boldly.*

"What a cunning fiend that Robespierre is!" Teresia exclaimed. "He picks off his enemies one by one." She looked thoughtfully at Marie-Joseph-Rose. "The children brought this message in; therefore they can take another message out, a message to Tallien."

"Yes. That's why I wanted you to know immediately."

"The risk will be great for them. Are you prepared to let them take it?"

Marie-Joseph-Rose was silent for a moment. Fear gripped her heart and betrayed itself in her eyes.

"If they are discovered," Teresia said, "we shall be sent to trial a little earlier. If they pass out with the message without discovery we may yet escape the guillotine."

Marie-Joseph-Rose hesitated no longer. "They shall take the message to Tallien but let them take it by word of mouth."

Both women went back to the main hall. The children were still waiting, each trying to hide anxiety beneath a cloak of childish gravity. It brought tears to their mother's eyes to see them standing there, hand in hand and silent.

Taking them to a corner Teresia told them quietly and earnestly what she wanted them to do.

"Two memories are better than one," she said, "but you Eugene, must be the one to take the message to Citizen Tallien."

Eugene nodded gravely.

"I want you to remember three things," Teresia went on. "The first, that Citizen Tallien's name is on a secret proscription list. The second, that he must act at once and boldly. The third, that due to his cowardice I am imprisoned here and threatened with death at any moment."

She had barely time to make the boy repeat these three terse messages before a guard came to take the children out. When they had gone she turned excitedly to Marie-Joseph-Rose.

"We must pray that Tallien will act in time, not only to save us but to save your husband too."

Next day, however, they learned that Tallien would need to act swiftly if he were to save Alexandre, for the news reached them through a new prisoner that Alexandre had already stood his trial.

"It was a mockery of a trial," said the new prisoner, a man with wild, fanatical eyes. "By Robespierre's latest order prisoners are now being sentenced in batches of six or more. There is no real trial, merely the sentence. Alexandre de Beauharnais was in one of yesterday's batches."

"Poor Alexandre," Marie-Joseph-Rose said softly. "He planned to make such a grand speech."

"The news from outside is terrible," the man went on. "Forty, fifty, as many as sixty heads are falling in a single day."

Marie-Joseph-Rose asked him if he knew when Alexandre would go to the guillotine.

"Within the next two or three days," he replied. "There must be more than a hundred condemned men and women waiting in the Conciergerie."

"Surely Paris will sicken of this bloodshed!" she cried. "Surely Paris will turn on the butcher himself and send him to the guillotine!"

"Tallien," Teresia said confidently, "may be acting even now."

"Tallien!" the new prisoner mocked, and spat. "That is what I think of men like Tallien!"

Three days later a news-sheet was smuggled into the prison. It carried a list of the latest executions. At the top of the list Marie-Joseph-Rose read her husband's name. . . .

*   *   *   *   *

It was now the second week of Thermidor, the last of July, according to the old calendar. No further news from the outside had reached Les Carmes. If Eugene had succeeded in carrying Teresia's message to Tallien it was obvious that no concentrated action had yet been taken against Robespierre. Teresia still believed that Tallien would act swiftly, if only to save his own head, but Marie-Joseph-Rose had reached a state of utter despair.

"Nothing you can say will give me hope," she wailed. "Now that Alexandre is dead I have no chance whatever of escaping the guillotine."

150

"Try not to give way like this," Teresia pleaded. "Presently, when you recover from the shock of your husband's death——"

"It wasn't such a terrible shock, Teresia. I knew all the time that there was no hope for him. The news upset me, not for my own sake, but for the children's. We were never happy together, but he was, I suppose, a good father. The children will be inconsolable. If only I could be with them!"

"In a few days you *will* be with them."

Marie-Joseph-Rose shook her head. "You're sweet and kind but I can't bring myself to believe you."

The two women were sitting together in Teresia's cell which had now been emptied of all occupants but Teresia herself. After a moment of silence Teresia sprang to her feet.

"Listen! I thought I heard singing in the distance. Listen!"

A moment later the singing she had heard grew closer.

"The 'Marseillaise,'" she cried, "a crowd of people singing the 'Marseillaise'!"

A great deal of shouting and cheering was also audible which, with the singing, gave the impression that the prison was being stormed by a clamoring, joyous mob. Teresia dragged a table beneath the high window, climbed up and, clinging to the bars, looked out. There was a courtyard beneath and beyond that, the street. She could see the heads of a huge crowd and as she looked a number of excited people broke past the guard into the courtyard itself. They shouted and cheered, called the name Robespierre derisively at the top of their voices and drew their fingers sharply across their throats.

"Robespierre is dead!" Teresia cried. "Either that or he has fallen!"

There was a sound at the cell door and a jailer entered. His manner was oddly friendly and a trifle sheepish. Teresia leaped down from the table, exchanged a rapid glance with Marie-Joseph-Rose and waited breathlessly for the man to speak.

"Which of you women is the Citizeness Fontenay?" he asked.

Teresia stepped forward. "I am. What do you want with me?"

He glanced at a paper in his hand. "There's an order here from the Committee of Public Safety——"

"The Committee of Public Safety!" she exclaimed and stared at him in horror.

"Not the usual sort of order," he assured her. "You're to be released at once."

"Who signed the order?" she demanded.

He looked at the paper again. "Citizen Vadier and also Citizen Tallien."

"I knew it," she cried, "I knew it!"

Marie-Joseph-Rose, sick with relief, asked him if the demonstration meant that Robespierre had fallen.

He nodded briefly. "Yes. Tallien and Fouché, Barras and a few others have got the better of him at last. They say he tried to kill himself but failed, leaving the job to Sanson and his dear little Madame Guillotine." He shrugged his shoulders eloquently. "Yesterday I said 'Long live Robespierre.' Today I say 'Long live Tallien.'" He gave a little smirk and added: "Long live Tallien and the Citizeness Fontenay."

The two women fell into each other's arms and wept for a few moments. Then Teresia said briskly: "The moment I see Tallien I shall have an order written out for your release. Tomorrow or the next day you will be free."

Marie-Joseph-Rose felt dazed. "Free," she whispered. "I shall be able to walk in the daylight again and feel the warmth of the sun on my face. I'm afraid to believe it, Teresia, yes afraid!"

Teresia laughed gaily. "Forget your fears and remember your old hag of a fortune-teller in Martinique." (During the past few months together they had told each other many stories of their childhood.) And with a suspicion of mockery she added: "Remember, my dear Rose, that you're to be Queen of France some day."

Part Three
Josephine

TERESIA PLACED ONE FOOT on a low chair, squared her shoulders and threw back her head.

"Well, Rose," she said, "what is your opinion?"

Marie-Joseph-Rose, her head a little on one side, surveyed her friend with that depth of criticism which only a woman can employ when surveying another woman's clothes.

"But aren't you cold?" she asked.

"Cold? Not in the least," Teresia lied.

Marie-Joseph-Rose shuddered. "I'm sure *I* should be in such an amazing costume, even in midsummer, and this is still only spring and as bitterly cold as if it were the very depths of winter."

The first thing she had noticed on being released from Les Carmes was the increased simplicity of women's clothing. The Revolution, with its deflation of the currency, had replaced silks and satins with cottons and lawns and cheap Indian prints, and at the time of her arrest dressmakers had been insisting on the economy of straight lines and narrower skirts. She herself was now wearing a dress of fine white cotton, a dress which was short at the front, allowing her feet to be seen—a dress, heaven forgive the dressmakers, which was waistless, being caught up sharply beneath her bosom by a narrow girdle.

Such a dress Teresia herself had worn only yesterday, but now . . . !

"Rose," Teresia said sharply, "I'm still waiting for your opinion."

"Is it Roman," Marie-Joseph-Rose inquired, "or Grecian?"

"Grecian, of course."

"Ah yes!"

The dress was in reality a tunic and extended no farther than the center of the calf. It was caught up in the middle by a buckle, thus

153

exposing Teresia's knees. There were no sleeves and Teresia's fine arms and rounded shoulders, Marie-Joseph-Rose could have sworn, were covered in goose-pimples.

"You notice the sandals?" Teresia said.

Marie-Joseph-Rose nodded. Not only were Teresia's feet shod in slender sandals, but on each toe was a jeweled ring. The whole effect was striking but surely vulgar.

"I stopped my carriage at the Tuileries," Teresia said, "and walked in the gardens while everybody gaped. And then I walked the whole length of the Champs Élysées. A week from now every woman of fashion in Paris will have copied my dress."

Marie-Joseph-Rose frowned. She had quite forgotten that possibility. Now that Teresia had become the wife of Tallien, one of the men who had brought about the downfall of Robespierre and the end of the Reign of Terror, whatever eccentric gown she chose to appear in would immediately become the latest fashion. It even meant that she, Marie-Joseph-Rose, would have to array herself in this wretched tunic if she wished to avoid being spoken of as dowdy and old-maidish.

"Must I ask you again," Teresia said sharply, "what you think of my dress?"

"Very smart," Marie-Joseph-Rose conceded with a bad grace, "but I still think it inadequate for cold weather. How much did it cost you?"

Teresia laughed gaily. "How much did it cost Tallien, you mean!"

The two women were in the boudoir of the house in the rue Chantereine, the house which Marie-Joseph-Rose had taken soon after her release. It was, despite its faint air of genteel distinction, a small shabby house, but it was at all events in Paris and more convenient than the house which she had previously shared with Madame Hosten at Croissy. At first the children had come to live with their mother, but now Eugene was at the College Irlandais, while Hortense had been admitted to Madame Campan's fashionable Academy for Young Ladies—though heaven alone knew how the bills would be met at the end of the first term! A cook, a maid, and a stable-boy who attended the two ancient horses and on occasion acted as coachman, made up the entire staff.

The end of the Terror had been a signal for a reckless borrowing from relatives, friends, bankers—anybody who was rash enough to lend against the possibility of the Government's restoring Alexandre's confiscated estates. Citizen Barras, of course, was a certain source of help, but Citizen Barras, unfortunately, seemed to have less access to the Treasury than Citizen Tallien.

Thinking of Barras she wondered if she had been wise in encouraging him and in finally becoming his mistress. A charming man, this former aristocrat who had been clever enough to survive the many violent changes of the Revolution, but undoubtedly a rogue. Wise? But of course she'd been wise. Wasn't he, like Tallien, one of the five directors, the men who had seized power on the fall of Robespierre? They were answerable, of course, to the new Council of Five Hundred and the smaller Council of Ancients, but though they were denied a real share in legislation they had acquired and still held an executive power greater than that of any king. Directors, they called themselves! Why, as Aunt Marie had remarked in her dry manner, they were in reality dictators! Wise or not, she had done the best she could to keep a roof over her head and provide money for the children's education. Her mind returned to Teresia's tunic.

"How much *did* it cost Tallien?" she asked.

"Possibly a thousand livres."

"A *thousand*!"

"In paper money, of course. In real money, only a fraction of that amount, I imagine. About twenty-five, I should say."

"Even so, Teresia——"

"Oh come," Teresia laughed, "you often say yourself that it's not what a thing costs that matters, but the thing itself."

"Yes, I know, but—" Marie-Joseph-Rose sighed deeply—"when one is hard-pressed, and the cost of living is continually rising, and so many of the tradespeople are refusing to accept paper money—" and her voice trailed away.

"So things are bad with you again," Teresia remarked.

Marie-Joseph-Rose nodded grimly. "I have known many stages of financial embarrassment in my life, but none so desperate—" She broke off suddenly. "Teresia, what are you staring at?"

"How old are you, Rose?" Teresia asked.

Marie-Joseph-Rose flashed her friend a defiant look. "A great deal younger than my present troubles are making me feel. Why do you ask? Do you—" alarm seized her—"do you think I'm beginning to look a little worn and haggard?"

"A little," Teresia said frankly, "but what really made me ask was the state of your teeth."

"My teeth? Heavens, Teresia, is a woman to be judged by her teeth as if she were a horse?"

"Two of your front teeth at the top," Teresia said calmly, "are beginning to decay."

Marie-Joseph-Rose's hand went quickly to her mouth. What a bitch Teresia was. And all because little enthusiasm had been shown for the ridiculous tunic.

"The dreadful food I was forced to eat in Les Carmes is the cause," she said tearfully. "Before that I had perfect teeth. In any case—" she turned quickly to the mirror—"they only show when I smile." She gave a little wail. "And yet a woman *must* smile, even when she feels like crying."

"Perhaps you could smile in the future without opening your lips too much," Teresia suggested, dismissing the subject. "To return to your financial troubles, why don't you try squeezing Barras a little more?"

"Unhappily Barras is not the sort of man who enjoys being squeezed."

"Pooh! He's there to be used, isn't he? You don't find his personality sufficient in itself, do you?"

Marie-Joseph-Rose laughed shortly. "Indeed no. Barras is a good lover, but that is all I can say in his favor. I never met a meaner man."

"Then what a fool you were to become his mistress."

"But I didn't suspect it until it was too late. He gave me a little money to begin with, but now the only way he helps me is by introducing me to other people who *might* be able to help me."

"And few of them are?"

"Very few indeed."

"Poor Rose," Teresia said sweetly, "how very unfortunate you've been in your choice of men."

"Very," Marie-Joseph-Rose admitted sadly, too deeply depressed by now to resent Teresia's condescending attitude.

Alexandre (God rest his miserable soul!), Lacoste, Tercier, Réal, Hoche and now Barras—in each case, even that of Tercier of whom she had sought nothing but love, an unfortunate choice.

"Oh, Teresia," she cried, "what is going to happen to me? What in the world is going to happen to me?"

✳   ✳   ✳   ✳   ✳

"Your friend Teresia," the Marquise de Beauharnais said, "is it true that people are beginning to call her the uncrowned queen of Paris?"

Marie-Joseph-Rose nodded and a little scowl clouded her face. "Yes, Aunt Marie."

"They tell me that she married Tallien as soon as she came out of prison. Is that true?"

"Oh yes, it's true, but Tallien is so rough, so uneducated. Nobody could possibly envy her."

Aunt and niece were walking in the garden of the marquis's house at Fontainebleau. Marie-Joseph-Rose had driven out from Paris that afternoon, intending to remain at Fontainebleau for several days if the mission on which she had come met with failure, and to return in the early evening if it met with success.

"Tell me about this man Barras," her aunt asked suddenly. "I hear your name and his linked quite frequently."

"You probably know as much about him as I do," Marie-Joseph-Rose said listlessly.

"I know this much, my dear Rose—" (How harsh and cracked Aunt Marie's voice had become in old age!)—"he was a rake in the days of the Monarchy, an ex-noble during the early days of the Revolution and today—today he is a spendthrift living on the country's resources, small as they are."

"He did play a part in bringing about the end of the Terror," Marie-Joseph-Rose put in mildly.

"Bah! In order to serve his own ends, not the people's. It may be necessary for you to associate with such men in order to exist, but the day will come when you will regret ever having set eyes on them. You don't propose to marry him, do you?"

"He hasn't asked me, Aunt Marie."

"And if he does?"

Marie-Joseph-Rose sighed deeply. "I doubt if he ever will, now."

"Barras, as you say," Aunt Marie went on, "played a part in bringing about the end of the Terror, but the end was already in sight, and in place of the Terror all we have now is an age of senseless spending and even more senseless debauchery. The lot of the people themselves is no better. Many of them are still workless and many more hungry. Am I boring you, Rose?"

Marie-Joseph-Rose stifled a yawn. "Of course not, Aunt Marie."

"What a bad liar you are, my dear!" the marquise laughed. "But just one more question. Tell me what you know about this new man, this Buona-parté."

"Buona-parté? I don't recall the name. What is it—Italian?"

"I believe it is. He's a soldier, a general, somebody told me. He played a leading part in putting down the royalist rising a few weeks ago."

The royalist rising—Marie-Joseph-Rose had forgotten all about it. She had been in Paris at the time, certainly, but her interest in the premature attempt to overthrow the Directory had been slight. Straining her memory she recalled that an Italian-sounding name— quite possibly Buona-parté—had been brought to her attention at the time. Barras, she seemed to remember, had brought the man from

Toulon after the English siege of that port had been lifted, and had given him an appointment with the Army of the Interior.

"I remember the name now," she said, "but I'm sure he's a man of small importance."

The matter thus dismissed she began to talk of the children and finally, Hortense's progress at Madame Campan's Academy having been reported, she brought the subject round to the real purpose of her visit.

"I absolutely shudder," she said, with a little laugh, "at the thought of the fees I owe Madame Campan and am quite unable to pay."

Her aunt looked at her shrewdly. "The old old story, Rose. Debts and still more debts. I wondered how long it would be before you found the courage to speak of them."

"Money," Marie-Joseph-Rose said sadly, "goes nowhere at all these days."

"A little economy might help."

"I economize wherever possible, Aunt Marie, really I do. I buy hardly any food, but even if a woman is strong enough to go hungry she simply *must* keep up appearances, and clothes are more costly than ever today."

The marquise laughed slily. "Why not come and live at Fontainebleau? Clothes, fashionable clothes, are hardly necessary here. We live very simply, and cheaply."

Her niece shuddered delicately. "Dear me, but I couldn't possibly bury myself in the country!"

"Are you desperately embarrassed?"

"Oh yes, *desperately!*"

"You owe me quite a lot of money already. Or had you forgotten?"

"No, Aunt Marie, I hadn't forgotten, but half of what you lent me I sent to poor Mama in Martinique. I—I shall pay you back every single sou some day. I swear I shall!"

"Would twenty-five thousand livres be any use to you?" the marquise asked casually.

"Twenty-five *thousand*, Aunt Marie?" Her head was beginning to whirl. "Is this some sort of cruel joke?"

"Twenty-five thousand livres," the old lady added, "in paper money."

Her niece's face fell. "Oh. . . ."

Little that she knew of business, unskilled as she was at totting up a column of simple figures, she was well aware of the negligible and ever-decreasing value of the *assignat*.

"How much would that be in real money?" she asked.

"Today, possibly six hundred livres; tomorrow or next week, possibly only four hundred. It's the most I can do for you and I only offer it because it will soon be almost useless. Blame your precious friends of the Directory for the currency depreciation and take it or leave it."

"Oh, I'll take it, Aunt Marie, *gladly!*"

She felt suddenly light-hearted. Worth six hundred today, possibly only four hundred tomorrow or next week. That meant that it must be spent without a moment's delay. A little for the children's schooling, a little for the servants who hadn't been paid for weeks and the rest—the rest for one of Teresia's Grecian tunics, of course!

*   *   *   *   *

A ball, given by Citizen Director Tallien, was in progress at the Luxembourg. The guests, Marie-Joseph-Rose was able to discern at a single glance, were a lamentable mixture of returned emigrants, ex-nobles, ex-terrorists, army officers and newly rich tradespeople. Half of them, as their hostess, Teresia Tallien, had just remarked behind her hand, were plainly impossible, while the other half were impossibly plain. All were present for the same reason, to make merry and forget.

"Though I must admit," Teresia laughed, "that there's one young man here who doesn't seem to be making merry, or if he is he must be a very solemn creature."

Marie-Joseph-Rose glanced casually round the ballroom. Her eyes came to rest on a young man in a shabby uniform. He was talking to Barras, who seemed to be paying him a very marked attention. After a moment the young man looked in her direction, appeared to start in surprise, and caught her eyes.

"If that's the man," she said, turning to Teresia, "I'm forced to agree with you."

At that moment Tallien joined them.

"Ah," he said, giving her a little bow, "one of the few women present whose clothing gives her adequate protection from the cold."

She wondered for a moment if he was mocking her because of her old-fashioned dress, but she soon saw, from the angry flash of Teresia's eyes, that he was actually mocking his wife, who was wearing a tunic even shorter than the one Marie-Joseph-Rose had first seen her in.

"Rose," Teresia said sweetly, "lacks the courage to adopt the new fashion."

That, as Teresia knew very well, was not the truth. One of the new tunics had been ordered, but the dressmaker had refused delivery until a settlement of older debts had been arrived at. And

so, here she was tonight in an old cambric dress which, while revealing much of her still firm bosom, exposed nothing else but her shapely
toes.

She glanced at the young soldier again. He was staring at her
now. Returning the stare she wondered whether she should be
pleased at his attention or angry. Angry, surely, for he was obviously
an ignoramus as well as a nobody. A nobody, with Barras fussing
over him? Not that, perhaps, but still an ignoramus. She tried to
look away but found his eyes surprisingly compelling. A sudden
and inexplicable weakness overcame her.

"Who is he?" she asked Teresia. "Do you know him?"

Teresia nodded. "Why yes. He's the little Corsican artillery officer,
Napoléoné Buona-parté, whom Barras found so useful during the
royalist rising. He now gives his name the French spelling, I believe,
and calls himself 'Bonaparte.' "

"The rudest man I ever saw!" Marie-Joseph-Rose commented.

"But a clever soldier," Tallien told her warmly. "He seems to be
interested in you. Would you like to meet him?"

"Certainly not," she said with decision. "I've met too many rude
men in my life to want to take the risk of meeting another."

*　　*　　*　　*　　*

The door burst open and Eugene bounded into the room. His
mother raised her hands in mock horror.

"These school holidays, they'll be the death of me one of these
days!"

The boy apologized for his rudeness, bowed hurriedly to Teresia
Tallien (who had come to the rue Chantereine for the purpose of
displaying her latest acquisition, a neat blonde wig) and stood waiting impatiently for permission to speak. Something, his mother decided, was obviously the matter. His face was flushed and his eyes
were wild. He looked from her to Teresia, then back again.

"Well, Eugene," she asked, "what is it?"

"A terrible thing has happened, Mother!" The words tumbled out
incoherently. "Father's sword has been stolen. It was hanging in my
room beside his picture this morning. Now it's gone! Do you hear,
Mother—*gone!*"

Eugene's concern was intense. The sword and the picture, they
were all he had to remind him of his father, his father who had
died a martyr's death on the guillotine. And now the sword was
gone, the sword of a gallant gentleman, his father, the Vicomte de
Beauharnais!

160

"My most valued possession," he cried, choking, "I must get it back!"

Marie-Joseph-Rose looked at him sympathetically. "My poor Eugene, the sword has been confiscated."

"*Confiscated?*"

"Some soldiers came while you were out and searched the house for arms. The sword was all they could find so they took it away."

"But why?" He turned to Teresia. "*Why?*"

"It's a new order since the royalist rising," Teresia told him. "A sort of general disarmament."

"But the sword was my *father's!*"

"If you like," she said kindly, "I'll speak to Citizen Director Tallien about it."

"Thank you, citizeness, but—*when?*"

"Really, Eugene," his mother reproved, "your impatience is anything but polite. Teresia will speak to the citizen director in a day or so."

"In a day or so!" he repeated aghast. "But anything might happen in a day or so. I think I ought to go to the authorities myself, now, without another moment's delay." He turned to Teresia again. "Citizeness Tallien, by whose order was my father's sword removed? Can you tell me that?"

"The second-in-command of the Army of the Interior was responsible, I expect."

"General Buona-parté, you mean?"

"Yes."

Eugene thanked her hurriedly and rushed from the room.

Marie-Joseph-Rose watched him go with a puzzled expression on her face. General Buona-parté— Now where had she heard that name before? She searched her memory for a moment. But of course! The thin, rather intense young man in the shabby uniform who had stared so rudely at Tallien's ball. So he had been made second-in-command of the Army of the Interior. Most extraordinary, surely! He had seemed to be such an uncouth little man. Heavens above, it was like a return to the days of the Revolution when the more untidy, the more *shabby* a man was the greater his chance of promotion. Buona-parté! An odious person with an odious name.

With a shrug she dismissed the man from her mind and returned to a contemplation of Teresia's wig.

"Why blonde?" she asked, trying to disguise her envy with an air of disapproval.

"Why *not* blonde?" Teresia retorted.

"But why a wig at all, Teresia?"

"Short hair," Teresia snapped, "has been fashionable too long, and is too great a reminder of the Terror when one's hair was cropped down to the very roots to make the guillotine's work easier. Until my own hair grows again a wig is naturally the only solution."

Marie-Joseph-Rose glanced at her own head in the mirror. Until yesterday the very latest hair-style had been the Titus Coiffure, which, with the short hair brushed forward to expose the ears, suited her very well. Shapely ears she had, and how delightful they looked with their little gold rings.

"Admitting that you judge wigs essential," she said, returning to her first question, "why *blonde* wigs?"

And so a little argument was begun, during which it was revealed that Teresia had already ordered twenty separate wigs varying in shade from blonde to light brown. From wigs the argument extended to tunics, which were growing shorter and shorter each day, and from tunics to the absolute necessity, if the shortening process was to continue, of wearing under-breeches.

"I have an unhappy memory of under-breeches," Marie-Joseph-Rose said with a frown, "but still, if a woman is to preserve her respectability——"

"Wait!" Teresia cried, and taking her tunic by the hem, lifted it as high as the jeweled corset-belt would allow.

"See!" she said, "not the old-fashioned under-breeches, but something neater, something that fits like a sheaf and is flesh-colored."

"Very cunning indeed," Marie-Joseph-Rose was forced to admit.

"Very!" Teresia laughed. "Only yesterday Barras was completely deceived by the color and wagered a thousand livres that beneath my tunic I was completely naked."

"Mother!"

It was Eugene again, and this time he was carrying the cherished sword.

"Look!" he cried. "Look!"

"Ah," Marie-Joseph-Rose said absently, thinking bitterly that mean as he was Barras had plenty of money to waste on silly wagers, "so you found your precious sword."

"Yes! General Bonaparte saw me at once and——"

"Bonaparte? I thought it was Buona-parté?"

"No, Mother, he corrected me, telling me to say 'Bonaparte.' He was very kind and understanding. He said he knew just how I felt."

"Did he indeed."

"A splendid man, Mother. A real soldier and a hero."

She frowned heavily. Until recently Eugene had always called her 'Mama.' His new and persistent 'Mother' was all very well for a boy who wanted to sound grown up, but when the parent in question was still young and attractive—

"A hero," Eugene repeated. "And he knew all about Father too, how he was a general and how he was murdered by Robespierre during the Reign of Terror. Because of that he understood that it was no ordinary favor I asked of him. As a soldier himself he knew how much the sword meant to me. 'Sir,' I said, 'I appeal to you as a soldier's son appealing to another soldier who has been more fortunate.' He was moved so much that for a moment I thought he was going to embrace me and certainly there were tears in his eyes, just as there were in mine."

Marie-Joseph-Rose tried not to smile. What a touching little scene it must have been, and what sentimental idiots men could be. And all because of a rusty old sword.

"When I thanked him," Eugene went on, "he said, 'Thank me, young man, by using your father's sword some day in the interests of your country should the need ever arise!'"

"And what did you say to that?" Teresia asked.

"I said, 'And under the command of General Bonaparte if fate is kind to me!'"

This time it was impossible not to smile, but she turned her head away so that he wouldn't see her amusement.

"Mother," he said eagerly, "I think you ought to call on the general and thank him."

"Call on him?" she exclaimed in horror. "But don't you think that the man has been thanked enough?"

Eugene looked disappointed. "At least you could write him a letter and——"

"Your mother detests letter writing, Eugene," Teresia said. "I'm sure she would rather call on the general than write him a letter."

Marie-Joseph-Rose gave her friend a sharp look.

"Run along to your room," she told Eugene, "and for pity's sake let us hear no more of General Buona-parté."

"Why not pay the man a visit?" Teresia said, when Eugene had gone. "It might amuse you to meet him."

"It might, Teresia, but——"

"Besides, my dear, since the old style is certainly dignified, it would give you a last opportunity of playing the gracious lady before finding it essential to bow to my decree and affect the tunic."

And with this parting shot Teresia Tallien took a leisurely departure.

*   *   *   *   *

Standing in the ante-room at the headquarters of the Army of the Interior, Marie-Joseph-Rose heard the orderly say quite clearly:

"A lady to see you, sir. All dressed in white and the most beautiful sight I ever saw."

"Her name, you fool!" she heard the general snap.

"Beauharnais, sir, Citizeness Beauharnais, the mother of the boy who came for his father's sword."

"Very well—" the voice sounded reluctant—"bring her in."

But by this time Marie-Joseph-Rose, her heart warmed by the orderly's description of her, had moved towards the open door and, conscious that she was making a perfect stage entry, was now glancing curiously about the bare and cheerless room. The orderly, seeing her first, bowed low and stood aside, his mouth agape. The general rose awkwardly and dismissed him.

"Forgive this intrusion," she said, and stood waiting for him to speak.

For a moment, recognition in his eyes, he stared at her. Then he recollected himself and pushed a chair forward roughly.

"Sit down," he said harshly.

She hesitated.

"Sit down!" he repeated. "Chairs are made to be sat on, surely!"

She sat—with dignity, she hoped. What an abrupt manner. He had spoken like a bad-tempered schoolmaster, and that stare of his! So direct, so very disconcerting! It made one feel quite guilty, really it did!

"I know your face well," he remarked, still staring at her. "I saw you at a ball given by Tallien at the Luxembourg. The room was full of attractive, partially dressed women, but I recall little save your face. I spent most of my time staring at you, staring rudely." His voice sounded as if he were angry about something. "Do you remember?"

"I remember perfectly," she said, struggling to retain her dignity. "You stared, as you say, rudely."

"I stared in the first place," he said, "because your dress made you almost the only woman present whom I would have cared to present to my mother. Had you been dressed as the Citizeness Tallien was I would never have noticed you." He looked at her searchingly. "You are, of course, well used to being stared at."

"Perhaps," she admitted, and added with a roguish impulse—"but not by famous soldiers."

He brushed the flattery aside. "You were in white then. Small wonder my orderly thought you a beautiful sight." He frowned. "You danced frequently with Barras." A faint contempt came into his voice. "Is the man a friend of yours, a close friend?"

"A friend, yes," she admitted, "but one could hardly call him a close one."

"So much the better. A man with an unsavory reputation."

"Citizen Director Barras," she said, rising from the chair, "has always been the soul of honor as far as I have been concerned."

The general laughed. Surprisingly enough it was a gay, almost boyish laugh.

"When I used the word 'unsavory,'" he said, "I referred to his political reputation, not to his morals. But sit down, please, sit down!"

She sat again, rather like a soldier obeying the command of a superior officer. During the short silence which followed she noticed that the general was even more untidy and shabby than she had previously thought. She decided to bring the interview to a close as soon as possible.

"Citizen General," she said briskly, "I came to apologize for my son's impetuous behavior. Much as he values his father's sword he had no right to intrude on you as he did."

"It was nothing, I assure you. I was happy to restore the sword. I understood perfectly."

"You are too kind." She rose determinedly. "And now——"

"No, no!" He leaped across the room, placed his hands on her shoulders and forced her back into the chair. "Remain a little longer and talk to me. If my manner seems rude, ignore it." He smiled faintly. "I have had little experience, up to now, in dealing with women of the French aristocracy."

She raised her eyebrows. "You have little love for the French aristocracy—is that what you mean?"

"Good lord no!" He drew himself up with ridiculous hauteur. "I bear an old and honorable name myself. I spring from a race of worthy Italian noblemen."

"Italian?" she queried. "I understood that you were from Corsica."

"And so I am. My family settled in Corsica." He looked at her critically. "I thought you were French but I see my mistake now. What are you? Spanish?"

She told him that Martinique was her birthplace.

"Ah, a Creole!" he cried. "That accounts for your gracefulness. You're the most graceful woman I ever saw."

She was obliged to smile. It was not a compliment, merely a statement of fact. Had he looked at her feet he would have remarked, in the same tone of voice, that her shoes were made by the best shoemaker in Paris. Looking at her closely he began to ask her a series of searching questions which issued from his mouth—quite a pleasant mouth, she decided—in short, abrupt sentences for all the world like military orders.

165

"How long have you been in France?"

"Since I was sixteen. I came here to marry my late husband. The marriage—" she sighed gently—"was not a success."

"Your late husband must have been a fool. How many years have you spent in France?"

She laughed lightly. "Citizen General, you are trying to discover my age!"

"Rubbish! If I wanted to know your age I would ask you outright."

"I do believe you would!"

"How many children have you beside the boy Eugene?"

"One. A daughter."

"Younger than the boy, or older?"

"Younger."

"And the boy is—thirteen? Fourteen?"

"Fourteen."

"Fourteen. Mmmm. You came to France at the age of sixteen. You married as soon as you arrived?"

"Soon afterwards."

"Ah! You were sixteen. Eugene is now fourteen. You must be at least thirty-one."

She felt inclined to rise to her feet once again, but what would be the use? She had a distressing feeling that she was a prisoner in this cold bare room, a prisoner undergoing the first stages of the inquisition.

"Citizen General," she laughed weakly, "you said that you would ask outright if you wanted to know my age."

"So I did. Very well, how old are you?"

"Actually I am thirty-two."

"Thirty-two," he mused, "and a brave woman. You look little more than twenty-six."

She inclined her head. "You are too kind."

"I," he said, looking at her thoughtfully, "am twenty-six."

"Is that all? You look at least thirty."

"Thank you, madame!"

She looked at him in surprise. "You call me 'madame,' you a general in the Republican Army."

"I prefer 'madame' to 'citizeness.' Don't you?"

"But of course. How long do you think 'citizeness' will remain in vogue?"

"Not a great deal longer." He got up and clasping his hands behind his back balanced himself lightly on his toes. "Not a great deal longer if I have anything to do with it!"

"You?"

"I see you smile!"

166

"Well, naturally."

A brooding look came to his eyes. He looked at her with a scowl. For a moment she thought him the ugliest man she had ever seen.

"I have faith in myself, madame," he said, speaking almost in a whisper. "Faith in myself to rise to greater heights and more lasting power than your friends Barras and Tallien. I have a star, a glorious star which I will follow to the end, whatever that end might be."

"You are an ambitious man," she murmured, thinking him quite ludicrous.

He made her a clumsy little bow.

"I shall watch your career," she added, "with the greatest of interest. Let me see, your full name is Napoléoné Buona-parté, isn't it?"

He frowned at her pronunciation.

"My full name *was* Napoléoné Buona-parté, but now I give it the French spelling and the French pronunciation."

"Napoleon Bonaparte?"

"Yes," he said, obviously pleased.

She repeated it again. "I shall do my best to remember." And she added that Teresia Tallien had said something about it.

He laughed shortly. "So you woman have been discussing me among you. Discussing me and—praising me, perhaps?"

"Praising you? Really, the vanity of the man!"

"Vanity, madame?" He sounded really shocked. "I assure you," he added earnestly, "there is no man in Paris less vain than I."

How quaint he was! In all Paris there was probably no man with such a high opinion of himself. She pursed her lips for a moment. After all, she admitted unwillingly, he had good reason for vanity. A general and second-in-command of the Army of the Interior at the age of twenty-six.

"Madame," he said, with characteristic suddenness, "you have the most beautiful voice in the world. I think I like your voice even more than your utter gracefulness."

"General Bonaparte!" she protested.

"When you grow old and ugly," he went on, "when you are no longer able to hide those very bad teeth of yours by the clever way you smile, your voice will still make you one of the world's most fascinating women."

Her hand instinctively at her mouth, she sprang to her feet. White with rage she was too furious to utter a single word. He crossed to the door and opened it.

"Madame, I was deeply occupied when you called, yet we have

talked, it seems, for hours. I have therefore hours of work to make up. Be off about your business and leave me to mine!"

Without further thought of dignity, without a word, without a look in the general's direction, Marie-Joseph-Rose gathered up the skirts of her dress and fled. Shaking with anger she climbed into her carriage and fell back on the cushions. Her rage was so great that she felt as if her heart would burst. The insolence of the man! The uncouthness!

"If ever I see him again," she said aloud, "I think I shall want to spit on him!"

CHAPTER XIX

CITIZEN DIRECTOR BARRAS, lounging elegantly in a chair, watched Marie-Joseph-Rose as she sat before her mirror making one of her endless *toilettes*.

"And so," he said, with a chuckle, "you have made the acquaintance of my little general."

She turned in surprise. "You seem remarkably well informed about my movements, Barras."

"My dear Rose, there are few things of importance that escape my attention."

Her surprise increased. "Surely my visit to General Bonaparte's headquarters can hardly be classified as a thing of importance."

"That remains to be seen."

His manner began to puzzle her. She turned fully from the mirror and looked at him. His self-satisfied smile irritated her. Worse still it alarmed her a little. What new scheme was taking shape in that agile, cunning brain of his?

"You're not angry about my visit, are you?" she asked.

His smile broadened. "On the contrary, I am delighted." He looked at her searchingly. "What do you think of Bonaparte, my dear?"

She turned back to the mirror. "I think him rude—the rudest man I have ever met. If fate brings us together again I shall ignore him."

"That's a pity, because fate, or to be more precise, Citizen Director Barras is going to bring you together again, not once but many times."

She forgot the *toilette* completely and swung round on him in consternation. "What do you mean, Barras?"

"I particularly want you to be sweet to him."

"But—but *why*?"

"My reasons are based on the intricate business of politics. Bonaparte has been useful to us recently. He's a very fine soldier and we want to keep him on hand for future emergencies. Therefore, my dear Citizeness Beauharnais, you will do your duty to your country and be sweet to General Bonaparte."

"I shall do nothing of the kind, Barras!"

He laughed at her wilful, sulky expression. "Oh come, Rose, he's young and not particularly experienced. You are undoubtedly the first smart woman of the world he has come across. You see, the poor young man has spent his life in study. He's what you might call a natural Spartan and therefore something of a simpleton."

"But his rudeness! His insolence! I could never tolerate him, never!"

"His rudeness and insolence are nothing but a protection, a barrier set up to hide his inexperience. Believe me, I know my man. At heart he is a simple soldier and will never be anything else. I assure you, I wouldn't give him a second thought if that wasn't just what I want—a simple soldier ready and eager to obey orders."

Marie-Joseph-Rose frowned slightly. She remembered the general as anything but a simple soldier ready and eager to obey orders.

She recalled his words: *I have faith in myself to rise to greater heights and more lasting power than your friends Tallien and Barras.* Boastful as those words had sounded she felt now that a great ambition, a great purpose, had prompted them. Instead of suggesting this to Barras she smiled a little secret smile, a vindictive smile. Much as she disliked the general it would hardly distress her deeply to find him setting himself up in opposition to the self-satisfied Citizen Director Barras.

"I shall be giving a big reception at the Luxembourg next week," Barras was saying. "Begin your campaign then. Set out to win the general over to our side completely with that special charm of yours."

She hesitated for a moment, then she said: "I make no promise, Barras, but I'll think about it."

* * * * *

Citizen General Bonaparte stood in the middle of the room with his hands stiffly behind his back. He was, Marie-Joseph-Rose noticed at this second meeting, a smaller man than she had first imagined. He was little taller than she herself, and amazingly thin. His hair was long and hung lankly about his ears. His face was pale and his eyes, with their penetrating stare, burned with an almost frightening intensity. As for his dress, it was even more untidy than at their first meeting.

"You are no doubt surprised, madame," he said, "to find me calling on you."

She noticed something else that had eluded her before. He spoke French with a slight accent.

"Surprised?" she said. "I don't think I am. Ought I to be?"

"You certainly ought." He glanced about the room. "May I sit down?"

"Please do."

He selected a chair and leaving her standing in the middle of the room seated himself. The manners of the man! There was only one way to treat him, coldly and with contempt.

"Madame," he said, "you have been in my mind constantly since last I saw you. Instead of working I have found myself thinking of nothing but you. I came to see you today so that tomorrow I might be able to get on with my work. Your name is Rose, I believe?"

She nodded. "Most people call me Rose. My full name is Marie-Joseph-Rose."

"Marie-Joseph-Rose," he repeated, with evident distaste. "I don't like it. I think I shall give you a new name."

"Give me a *new* name?"

"Yes, madame. I shall rechristen you."

"Really, General, I find my present name quite satisfactory!"

"I like Joseph," he went on, unheedingly. "I have a brother called Joseph, but naturally I can't call a woman by that name."

His face broke into a sudden smile. "I know! I shall call you Josephine! Yes, Josephine!"

Still standing in the middle of the room she drew herself up with considerable hauteur.

"Has it occurred to you, General," she said freezingly, "that you are taking a considerable liberty?"

He burst into amused laughter. "Frankly, madame, it hadn't. Do you really mind?"

"Would it matter if I did?" she asked helplessly.

"Of course it wouldn't." He looked at her steadily. "Are you a little indisposed today?"

"Indisposed?" she questioned, and added in alarm: "Do I look indisposed?"

"You don't smile, madame. That is what I mean. You haven't smiled once. Are you angry with me? Is it because I was sharp enough to notice your bad teeth? Are you trying to hide the fact more than ever?"

"Really, General—" she said weakly.

"Ah!" he cried. "For a moment it came, a dim, watery smile. And again! Oh beautiful! A really sweet smile. One of the sweetest I have ever seen."

Weak and helpless she shrugged her shoulders and began to laugh.

"You are hopelessly incorrigible, General," she said, and added mischievously, "as no doubt many a woman has discovered before now."

"You think me something of a ladykiller, madame?" he cried, almost preening himself. "You get *that* impression?"

"You were going to call me Josephine," she reminded him.

"So I was. I assure you, Josephine, that I have found no lady worth killing—until now."

"Until—*now*? Then you have some poor creature in view?"

"I have!"

"I pity her, General," she said gaily, "I pity her from the bottom of my heart."

"Because of my rude manner, or my unpleasant appearance?"

"Because of both."

'Merciful heavens,' she thought, 'I'm flirting with the man!'

"So you think my appearance unpleasant," he mused.

She looked at him critically. "Yes, but I feel sure you would be a much more presentable young man if you made more of yourself."

"More of myself?" he echoed.

"Your hair and your clothes are lamentably untidy, and you're so thin I can't help thinking you neglect to eat properly. Your mother, if you have a mother, would never permit you to neglect yourself so badly."

"You are perfectly correct," he agreed, with a frown, "my mother would never permit it."

With that he told her something of his family history. His father had died ten years ago. His mother, at the moment, lived in Marseille with his sisters Eliza, Paulette and Caroline. He had also four brothers, Joseph, Louis, Lucien and Jerome. Originally there had been thirteen children, but five had died in Corsica.

"Joseph is the eldest," he said, "but I am naturally the head of the family."

"Naturally," she murmured.

The conversation then turned to Italy and the campaign which the Government was planning against that country. She asked him if he hoped to take part in the new campaign.

"I hope to take the chief part," he said. "If Italy is to be conquered, *I* must be given complete control."

"Highly as Tallien and Barras think of you," she remarked, "they are hardly likely to replace the present commander-in-chief."

Ignoring the latter part of her remark he seized upon the first.

"They have every reason to think highly of me!" He frowned—she had never seen a man whose mood was reflected more swiftly in his face. "Unhappily they are inclined to patronize me, to treat me as if I were in need of their protection." The frown deepened. "*Their* protection! Some day they will be only too happy if I grant them mine!"

"Really, General!" she protested, with a little laugh.

He rose from the chair. "You think me over-boastful?"

"What else can I think?"

"You will change your mind when you know me better."

He came forward and took her hands in his. He looked into her eyes intently. "I am determined, you see, that I shall be able to make you know me better. I liked you when I first met you. I like you a thousand times more at this second meeting. Since I shall be leaving for Italy soon I must see you as often as possible before then."

She smiled. He had obviously made up his mind that he was to go to Italy, and go as commander-in-chief. It was really preposterous. She freed her hands.

"I hate to appear to dismiss you abruptly," she said, "but I have an appointment with my dressmaker and——"

"A thousand pardons," he cried, with a semblance of suddenly remembered good manners, "but when I like people I do my best to monopolize them. Forgive me."

She inclined her head graciously. "Your monopoly is not entirely unpleasant."

"Then I may call again soon?"

"You actually *ask* if you may! This is too much, General. Surely you are the sort of man who would call again soon, with or without permission."

Smiling boyishly, he agreed.

"Nevertheless," he said, "I should feel more encouraged if you granted your permission. *Do* you grant it, Josephine?"

"Perhaps I ought to think about it."

"Very well, madame! With or without your permission I shall call again tomorrow at the same hour."

He nodded briefly, turned sharply on his heels and strode from the room. His steps were swift and long, uncomfortably long for a man of his small stature. "He is just a *poseur*," she decided. "He will never get the better of Tallien and Barras." She remembered that during the entire period of his visit he had permitted her to stand.

"Not only a *poseur*," she said aloud, "but a pig, an ill-bred Corsican pig."

Citizen Director Barras, watching the progress of Bonaparte's growing interest in Marie-Joseph-Rose, decided that he had every reason to be satisfied. In commanding his mistress to encourage the little general, Barras was acting from a personal as well as a political point of view. He wanted both to free himself of Marie-Joseph-Rose, of whom he was rapidly tiring, and to bind Bonaparte, simple soldier that he was, to the political machine of the Directory. With this double motive well in mind he eventually brought up the subject with Bonaparte himself.

"Permit me to congratulate you," he said genially, "on your singularly good taste in women." There was a flash in Bonaparte's eyes which ought to have warned him, but unheeding it he went smoothly on. "Citizeness Beauharnais is a charming, accomplished creature. You do well to seek her friendship." He paused, smiled suggestively and added: "Or perhaps you seek more than her friendship?"

"Perhaps I do," Bonaparte admitted coldly.

Barras was mildly amused. Not only a simple soldier, he noted, but something of a puritan too!

"She is the sort of woman," he murmured, "who is made for happiness and luxury, yet up to now she has enjoyed little of either. She lost her husband, as you probably know, during the Reign of Terror. In fact, she was very nearly guillotined herself. Between you and me, Bonaparte, what she needs most is an understanding friend in whom she can confide." He looked at Bonaparte obliquely. "Any man who marries her will have much to gain from such a union. She belongs both to the old society and the new. You see the advantage of that, of course?"

"Of course."

Barras nodded vigorously and expanded still further. "Her house, small and ill-appointed as it is, is one of the best in Paris. Anybody of importance is to be met there sooner or later. Certainly, as I just remarked, any man who marries her will have much to gain."

"In short," Bonaparte said drily, "Napoleon Bonaparte would have much to gain."

"Precisely!" Barras said, trying to hide a slight start of surprise. "I was beginning to think," he added, with a little chuckle, "that you were a trifle dull-witted. I do believe you were baiting me, leading me on to make even broader hints."

There was a pause. Bonaparte refused to commit himself one way or the other.

"Is it possible," Barras asked, "that I have overestimated your interest in Citizeness Beauharnais?"

Bonaparte laughed shortly. "No man alive could do that, Barras."

"Ah! Then a final word. Marriage with Rose would bring you stronger political support, if only through myself. It would also rid you of your Corsican background and make you completely French."

"I take it," Bonaparte said softly, "that I have your permission to marry Citizeness Beauharnais?"

Barras forced himself to laugh pleasantly and decided that it would be wiser to say no more. Looking back on the interview a few hours later he realized that Bonaparte's attitude had shaken him considerably. Was it possible that he had underestimated the man, that he was not so great a simpleton after all? Surely not! He, Barras, had always been an excellent judge of men and owed his present position to the excellence of that judgment.

That evening, carrying the matter further, he paid a call at the rue Chantereine. Marie-Joseph-Rose received him coldly and still refused to commit herself in respect of the coming reception. Angered by this he made the grave mistake of speaking of marriage by remarking that Bonaparte would undoubtedly make some woman a very good husband.

Marie-Joseph-Rose looked at him suspiciously. "By 'some woman' you mean me?"

He laughed lightly. "Why not, my dear?"

"Are you tired of me?" she demanded.

"Frankly, my dear, I am, but before putting you out of my life I want to see you secure yourself for the future."

"General Bonaparte," she said flatly, "has nothing but his army pay."

"His army pay shall be increased. If you marry him I shall see that he becomes commander-in-chief of the Army of Italy. In addition he will have many opportunities of making money out of the Italians."

"*If* I marry him! I can think of nothing more revolting than marriage with General Bonaparte. I—yes, I would rather drown myself!"

"Nonsense, Rose!"

"It isn't nonsense," she said tearfully. "In any case, what makes you think that he might want to marry me?"

"Whether he does or not, a clever woman like you would find it easy to make up his mind for him." He laughed pleasantly. "Better take the little general, my dear. You are thirty-two. You have two children. Soon it will be too late to think of marrying anybody."

"You beast, Barras!"

He laughed again. "Take him, Rose, and consider yourself fortunate."

On the point of tears she found a wisp of a handkerchief and sniffed delicately into it. She was sure, of course, that Bonaparte, without any encouragement from her, would eventually speak of marriage, and what a lot of cruel truth there was in what Barras said. Soon it would be too late to think of marrying anybody, and if Barras was to withdraw his protection, such as it was, what in the world would happen to her? At the best, starvation; at the worst, arrest for debt. She shuddered. Those debts of hers! The terrible way they had grown! Her one hope of salvation was marriage, even marriage with a man who had nothing but his army pay.

"Are you sure," she asked, "that Bonaparte will have many opportunities of making money out of the Italians?"

Barras was anything but sure. It was hardly a question of Bonaparte making money out of them; it was simply and soberly a question of whether or not he would be able to prevent them from crossing the frontier and invading France.

"My dear," he said cheerfully, "Bonaparte will come back from Italy a rich man."

That was certainly something. She blew her nose and put away her handkerchief. Nevertheless she recalled the failure of her first marriage. It had almost made her too afraid to risk marriage a second time. True, General Bonaparte had little resemblance to Alexandre, but he was so rude, so very uncouth. She felt a sudden resentment against Barras.

"You are making me hate you!" she cried.

"Oh, nonsense. You are too incapable of really deep emotion to hate anybody."

"What a horrid mood you're in today!" She felt for the handkerchief again. "I hope you never flattered yourself that I was in love with you!"

"But of course I didn't! I know exactly why you have always been —shall we say 'gracious' to me. You have been attracted by my influence and position."

"Naturally! What else is there about you to attract a woman?" She sniffed into the handkerchief. "You possess a certain amount of shrewdness and political cunning, but as a man, five minutes of you would sicken any woman."

"Be careful, my dear," he warned.

"Careful? What in the world have I to be careful of?"

He chuckled unpleasantly. "Bonaparte, my dear sweet Rose, is a surprisingly virtuous young man, and will expect the woman he marries to be virtuous too. I could easily change his interest in you by passing on one or two little stories that——"

"Pass them on!" she shouted. "Why should I care? For the last time I tell you that nothing will ever induce me to marry General Bonaparte!"

Barras bowed ironically. "Very well, my dear. After all, why should I care what happens to you?"

And with that he left her.

*　*　*　*　*

When Barras had gone Marie-Joseph-Rose was seized with something akin to panic. She saw herself deserted by Barras, hounded by creditors, unwanted by any man except an untidy, boastful, conceited little general of the Republican Army. Perhaps that was why, when Bonaparte called the following afternoon, she permitted him to linger until the shadows deepened and an intimate twilight settled about the room.

Her natural indolence always more pronounced at this hour of the day, she barely protested when, seizing her hand, he kissed it. A moment later, much to her astonishment, his arms were about her and his lips were hotly against her own.

"Really, Bonaparte!" she protested, pushing him away.

"A cursed fever has fired my blood," he said, "a fever called Josephine!"

She felt inclined to giggle. What a quaint little man he was, and how Barras, with his cynical sense of humor, would chuckle if he were listening behind the curtains.

"Only one thing," Bonaparte said passionately, "can cure me."

With a little sigh she turned her head away. *Ah, she thought, the moment has come, he is going to speak of marriage.*

His arms were about her again. Surprisingly enough they were strong arms, so strong that she felt helpless in their grip.

"In case you don't know," he murmured in her ears, "I locked the door a few moments ago."

Something in his voice made her look at him sharply. What was that he had said?—*Only one thing can cure me.* Puzzled, suspicious, she tried to free herself but found it impossible. Then, with a laugh, she dismissed her suspicion. Whatever the 'one thing' might be, and even if he *had* locked the door, they were in the bare little anteroom which possessed only three chairs and the small, impossible couch on which they were sitting so uncomfortably at this moment. He re-

176

leased her suddenly and she laughed again. After all, what had Barras said?—*Bonaparte is a surprisingly virtuous young man.*

She looked at him with a little mocking smile playing about her lips. He was on his feet now, gazing searchingly about the room. He crossed to the chair beneath the window and picked up a cushion. He turned to the chair by the door and picked up his military cloak. He came back to her. He dropped the cushion and spread the cloak at her feet. Her smile faded.

"Bonaparte—!" she said.

"As you know," he remarked, "I am by no means a patient man."

"But great heavens," she cried, "the floor, of all places!"

"A soldier," he said, "is well acquainted with the floor."

CHAPTER XX

Barras, his legs straddling a chair and his chin resting lightly on the high back, looked at Marie-Joseph-Rose with a twinkle in his eyes.

"According to your note," he said, "you wished to see me urgently."

"Yes, Barras, very urgently."

She was still shaken by her experience of the night before. Bonaparte a surprisingly virtuous young man! What utter nonsense! He was little better than the rest. He required one thing of a woman, one thing only. True, he had professed to love her, repeating over and over again that he adored her and couldn't live without her, yet what mention had he made of marriage?

She was still unable to make up her mind whether or not she liked him, and as for ever being able to fall in love with him, that would surely be impossible. His love-making had disturbed rather than satisfied her. It was too direct, too relentless, though its very energy and impatience were so characteristic of the man. She shuddered delicately. What an exhausting man to live with! Barras, whom she still hated, of course, was much more to her taste in that respect—so polished, so much the man of the world, so much the epicure. If only Bonaparte had the *finesse* of Barras she would feel almost happy about marrying him.

This thought reminded her again that marriage had not been mentioned and the panic which had caused her to send for Barras gripped her again. Deserted by Barras, harassed by her countless clamoring creditors, there was no man in the world to turn to except Bonaparte—Bonaparte who had nothing but his army pay. There would, of course, be the opportunity of his making money out of the

Italians, but what use would that be to her, what *lasting* use, if Bonaparte was now regarding her as a mistress rather than a future wife? Pleasant as it might be to be a rich man's mistress it would be infinitely more satisfactory to be a rich man's wife. Besides—distressing thought!—what if he met somebody else in Italy?

"Tell me one thing, Barras," she said, "will you make Bonaparte the new commander of the Army of Italy even if I don't marry him?"

He laughed in that irritatingly shrewd way of his. "All I can reply to that, my dear Rose, is that the moment you do marry him I will give him the command."

"I don't think I trust you, Barras."

"I give you my word, Rose."

"Your word is not enough."

"It will have to be," he said cheerfully.

A new thought seized her. "If I marry him and he fails in Italy my position will be intolerable."

"Divorce," Barras said, "is very easy."

Divorce. She hadn't thought of that.

"If you wanted to free yourself," Barras went on, "I could probably help you."

"How?" she asked.

"You know the new law. Husband or wife can obtain a divorce if either partner has been away from home for more than six months. It would be easy enough for me to keep Bonaparte in Italy for six months." He chuckled. "Lots of soldiers who have been away for more than six months are returning to Paris to find another man in possession." He paused, trying to read her face. "Well, does that make things any the more attractive to you?"

"Perhaps."

"Then I shall leave you to think about it, but let me advise you not to delay too long before deciding to marry the little general."

Even as he spoke her mind was made up. If she could induce Bonaparte to propose she would accept him. *If* she could induce him! What a fool she'd been! She should have made it clear to him that in spite of the age in which they lived she was a woman of rigid moral principles. She should have kept him gently but firmly at bay. She should have said: 'Bonaparte, above all things I value my purity.' She should have said: 'Bonaparte, helpless widow that I am, I must think of my children.' She sighed gently at the loss of such a splendid opportunity but decided optimistically that it might not yet be too late. After all, it had only happened once and need not happen again.

Accordingly she left Paris for a few days, sending him a note before departing to the effect that she was going to spend a week or so with her aunt at Fontainebleau. She spread out the visit for ten days during which a number of passionately worded letters reached her, each pleading with her to return at the earliest possible moment. She made no attempt to reply. On returning to Paris she learned that Bonaparte had called at the rue Chantereine only that morning.

"The Citizen General," the maid told her, "said he would call again tonight."

When he called she received him in the ante-room, taking care first to remove the key from the lock. She saw with surprise that his dress and his hair were tidier, that in fact he was almost presentable. He took her in his arms immediately. She turned her face away and gently pushed him to arms' length.

"Ah!" he cried, "you have changed, you have fallen in love with somebody else!"

"No," she said, "but while at Fontainebleau I realized how weak I had been and I was deeply ashamed."

"But——!"

She silenced him quickly. "My poor Bonaparte, helpless widow that I am, I must think of my children. I—" she dropped her voice and looked away—"I should die if Eugene and Hortense were to grow up ashamed of me."

He pleaded with her. He scolded her sharply. He attempted to take her in his arms. She freed herself with an effort and pulled the bell-rope. When the maid came she said:

"The Citizen General is leaving. His hat and cloak, please."

She expected a passionate letter the next morning, but to her surprise none came. She waited for three days, a week. Still no letter came. She began to feel wretched and was half inclined to write herself. While she was still undecided Barras came to see her.

"My dear Rose," were his first words, "what have you done to the little general?"

"What have I done to him? I don't understand, Barras."

"He has locked himself in his room. He refuses to see anybody. I doubt if he is even eating. Since he is so fantastically in love with you there can be but one explanation. You have quarreled with him."

Marie-Joseph-Rose giggled.

"Come, my dear," Barras said, "you may as well tell me all about it."

With a shrug she told him everything. He listened with a smile and when she had finished he laughed until the tears rolled down his cheeks. For a very different reason tears were rolling down her own cheeks.

"You devil, Barras!" she said.

There was a pause.

"What am I to do?" she cried. "He may never come and see me again."

"You must write to him."

"Write to him? Never! It would be undignified."

"Undignified or not, that is exactly what you are going to do. Come, get your writing materials and I will tell you what to say."

She shrugged. "Very well."

And so, with Barras at her elbow, chuckling while he dictated, she wrote a short note to Bonaparte.

Dear Friend,

You come no longer to see a friend who loves you. You have altogether deserted her. You do wrong, for she is tenderly attached to you. Come tomorrow. I want to talk to you about your affairs. Au revoir, my friend, I embrace you.

"How shall I sign it?" she asked, and she told Barras how Bonaparte had insisted on calling her Josephine.

"Sign it 'Josephine,'" Barras decided.

The letter was dispatched at once, by hand. Instead of taking his departure Barras remained, chatted idly about affairs in Paris and from time to time recalled the letter with a chuckle of amusement.

"I wonder what Bonaparte would say if he knew that I had dictated it?" he said.

"He must never know, Barras!" she cried.

Barras rose. She watched him with relief. Thank heaven he was going at last. He strolled across the room to her. With a little laugh he lifted her to her feet, put his arms round her and kissed her softly on the mouth. A light shot into his eyes.

"By heavens," he said, "nuisance that you are I still find you an attractive woman."

He kissed her again, by no means lightly this time. She loathed the sight of him. She hated him with all her heart, but the touch of his lips and the warmth of his breath on her cheeks melted all thought of resistance. She put her arms round his neck and lifted her lips to his.

"You rat," she said.

*   *   *   *   *

"The Citizen General Bonaparte," the maid announced.

Bonaparte waited for the maid to go.

"Josephine!" he cried.

180

Marie-Joseph-Rose smiled and held out her hands. He came quickly to her and took them in his.

"I read your letter a hundred times yesterday," he said. "I read it a hundred times this morning. Does it mean that you have given your heart to me at last?"

"Why have you stayed away from me so long?" she asked.

He released her hands. He crossed to the window and stood with his back to her.

"I stayed away," he said, in a voice barely above a whisper, "because I was ashamed."

"Ashamed, Bonaparte?"

"Ashamed because I had permitted myself to treat you without respect." He turned from the window and came back to her. "You fascinate me, Josephine. You are unique among women. Here in Paris, a city of feminine charm, you are the only charming woman. You are my life. I love you as no other man would dare to love you. I love you so much that until now I have been afraid to ask you to marry me."

"Marry you!" Hiding her satisfaction she tried to fill her voice with astonishment. "You must be joking."

"I mean it, Josephine, I mean it with all my heart. I know I am penniless now, but my future has a brilliant hue. Marry me. Rise with me to fame."

"Why are you so eager to marry me when men today think so little of marriage?"

"You know the answer. Marriage is the only thing a man can offer the woman he respects."

"Then you really do respect me, even though I have been your mistress?"

His face paled. "Never use that word again," he said.

There was a silence. He looked at her miserably.

"Is your answer no?" he asked.

"My answer is neither yes nor no. I shall think about it and make up my mind tomorrow."

"Tomorrow is a thousand years away!"

"Tomorrow is exactly twenty-four hours away."

"There are sixty minutes to each hour, and every minute a separate eternity."

"You should be a poet, Bonaparte, not a soldier."

"Every man—even the humblest soldier—is a poet when he is in love. Give me your answer now, Josephine!"

"Tomorrow," she insisted.

"Now, you wretched woman, *now!*"

"Tomorrow, Bonaparte, or not at all."

She wondered if she was a fool to turn him away like this, but a devil of perversity was in her. Besides, she felt utterly sure of him now and it really was amusing to tantalize him.

When he came the next day she greeted him with a gay little laugh.

"You are an hour too soon," she teased. "The twenty-four hours are not yet expired."

"I could think of an excellent way of passing the final hour," he said meaningly.

"Ah, but you respect me," she reminded him.

"Respect you!" he cried. "I *try* to respect you, but in your presence I know one thing only, my need of you, my hunger to possess you."

The maid came into the room.

"The Citizen Raguideau," she announced.

"By heavens," Bonaparte cried, "this is too much."

Marie-Joseph-Rose laughed. "Go to the window," she said, "and stand in the recess behind the curtain. I have a little business to discuss with Citizen Raguideau, my lawyer."

"You asked him to come today, knowing that I would be here?"

"I did. Go to the recess quickly before he enters."

"Bah!" said Bonaparte, but he went.

Citizen Raguideau was a fussy little man who bounced into the room as if he were on springs. He broke immediately into voluble, indignant speech.

"My dear Citizeness Beauharnais, you sent for me to discuss the legal aspect of a proposed marriage with a certain gentleman—" Marie-Joseph-Rose saw the curtain twitch at the recess—"but first you must allow me to protest and protest strongly!"

"*Protest*, Citizen Raguideau?"

"At the senselessness of such a marriage," the lawyer added.

The curtain twitched again.

"I think you go a little too far, Citizen Raguideau," she said mildly.

"I am your legal adviser, citizeness. The young man is, in the first place, too young for you and has his way to make in the world. I admit that he is a general, but what is a general in the Republican Army? He may be a very fine soldier, but even fine soldiers are not immune to bullets."

"In that case," said Bonaparte, stepping out of the recess, "there would always be the widow's pension."

The little lawyer almost leaped into the air. "Who is this impudent person?" he demanded.

Marie-Joseph-Rose tried to keep a solemn face.

"He is none other," she said, "than Citizen General Bonaparte."

Citizen Raguideau was by no means put out of countenance.

"Then in that case," he said briskly, "I can tell him exactly what I think of him." He turned furiously on Bonaparte. "Sir, you should be ashamed of yourself. The woman you wish to marry is a gentlewoman. Moreover, she is a widow with two children. How in the world can you hope to support her, you who have nothing but your cloak and your sword?"

Marie-Joseph-Rose expected Bonaparte to fly into a temper, but instead he laughed pleasantly and slapped the lawyer across the shoulders.

"Spoken like an honorable man," he said. "It is perfectly true, I have nothing but my cloak and my sword, but my cloak will give ample shelter to my wife, and my sword—" his voice softened and a faraway look came to his eyes—"and my sword, will give me the earth."

"You see, Citizen Raguideau," Marie-Joseph-Rose laughed, "General Bonaparte is not without self-confidence."

"Then you refuse to listen to me? You insist on marrying him?"

"I refuse to listen to you." She held out her hands to Bonaparte. "I insist on marrying him."

Bonaparte appeared to be choking with emotion, and he was certainly trembling from head to foot. She looked at him in amazement. He was the quaintest man she had ever met.

"Citizen Raguideau," she said, "all the general and I require of you now is a little assistance in the drawing up of our marriage contract. . . ."

* * * * *

The day before the marriage General Bonaparte, assuming his most abrupt manner, referred to the delicate matter of his future wife's true age. They had been discussing his mother and family, and with a thoughtful frown he said:

"Since our ages will have to be declared before we marry it might make things easier if my mother thought you were younger than you actually are." His frown deepened. "She would hate the thought of my marrying a woman several years older than myself."

"My dear Bonaparte," Josephine protested with a little laugh (she had now acquired the habit of thinking of herself exclusively as Josephine), "you know quite well that I'm not the least bit older than you."

He laughed drily. "You have a bad memory, my darling little fraud. I got your age out of you the first time we met. Surely you remember?"

She laughed ruefully. "Why yes. I believe I do remember now."

"I'm inclined to think you never really forgot."

She laughed gaily. "How clever you are, and what a pity your own memory is so excellent."

"You are thirty-two—" he was frowning again—"and I am twenty-six. We must think of a way of equalizing our ages, if only for your own sake when you come face to face with my mother."

Josephine felt a pang of alarm. Bonaparte's mother, it would seem, was something of an ogre. How very fortunate that she was still in Marseille.

"If I say my age is twenty-nine," she said, "nobody can prove otherwise—unless they send to Martinique for a copy of my birth certificate."

"And Martinique being in the hands of the English, that is out of the question!" He rubbed his hands together in delight. "You are not a day more than twenty-eight, Josephine. Please remember that. And I—*I* am not a day less than twenty-eight."

"Your mother will know that you are only twenty-six," she objected.

A shade of uneasiness crossed his face—(*Quite obviously she is an ogre*, Josephine thought)—and then he smiled.

"Providing she never learns your own true age," he said confidently, "she will put my deception down to a proper sense of pride and forgive me. Besides, if we are clever enough the subject need never be discussed."

To Josephine the actual marriage ceremony the next day was something of a disappointment. She would have preferred a religious marriage, but in this age of paganism, with religious practices frowned upon if not altogether forbidden, a religious ceremony was out of the question. True, a religious ceremony had failed to endow her first marriage with happiness and success, and in the old days she had always found church-going something of a bore, but without the blessing of a priest, how in the world was a woman to feel that she was really married?

Among the witnesses who stood with Josephine and Bonaparte before the registrar were Teresia, Tallien and Barras—Barras who remarked with a significant leer behind Bonaparte's back that if anybody had a right to give Josephine away in honorable marriage it was certainly he. Furious as it made her she chose to ignore this little pleasantry. Barras, after all, had kept his word. General Bonaparte was now commander-in-chief of the Army of Italy.

"And now, Citizeness Beauharnais," the registrar said, "if you would kindly repeat after me. . . ."

With that the cold, barely impressive ceremony began. Instructed by the registrar Josephine repeated the alarmingly few words and fell silent while Bonaparte, similarly instructed, did likewise. His voice, in spite of its intensity, was almost inaudible, and his hands, she noticed, were shaking.

In a moment, to the accompaniment of a series of suspicious little throat-clearings from Citizen Director Barras, the whole inadequate business was over.

"Surely it should take longer than this!" Josephine exclaimed. "My first marriage seemed to take hours and hours!"

The registrar raised his eyebrows at the bad taste of this surprising remark, while Bonaparte, with a strained laugh, assured everybody in general that a civil marriage, thank heaven, was the simplest in the world.

"But to be over and done with in little more than a minute!" she persisted.

Barras cleared his throat again.

"A very important and momentous minute," he said solemnly. "Congratulations, my dear. No one is more certain than I that you have done the right thing."

He embraced her briefly and kissed her chastely on both cheeks. His ear being against her mouth for a moment she whispered the one word "*Rat!*" He turned from her with a fatherly smile and embraced the bridegroom.

"You're a very fortunate man, General," he said.

"And a happy one too," Bonaparte said warmly.

Barras turned to the others.

"Ladies and gentlemen," he cried. "Long live General Bonaparte! Long live Citizeness Bonaparte!"

Everybody raised their voices and echoed: "Long live General Bonaparte! Long live Citizeness Bonaparte!"

"And now," Barras said, "an appropriate celebration is surely indicated. The carriages are waiting. Shall we go?"

The wedding party drove merrily to the Luxembourg where Barras, a little too obvious, Josephine thought, in his delight at the success of his plan, proposed a number of toasts and spoke at length of the brilliance of General Bonaparte's military ability. Josephine passed an hour of acute uneasiness, while Bonaparte himself was clearly fretful and impatient.

It was Teresia who finally broke up the party by declaring roguishly that the bride and bridegroom would doubtless prefer to celebrate their nuptials alone.

"A final toast!" Barras insisted. He raised his glass: "To success in Italy!"

Every glass was raised.

"To success in Italy," everybody cried.

*   *   *   *   *

The carriage was waiting—had been waiting for an hour—and the ante-room below was full of soldiers who had come to bid farewell to Bonaparte, yet the man himself still seemed to find it impossible to tear himself away. Josephine sighed faintly. It was a little touching, of course, but such a prolonged farewell was also irritating.

Bonaparte took her hands roughly in his. His face was pale and drawn, his eyes full of misery.

"How can I ever forgive myself for rushing away after only two days," he said passionately. "To leave you so soon tears my heart. Believe me, I shall live only for my return, or for the day when you will join me in Italy."

"*Join* you?" she questioned.

"Naturally. If I find it impossible to return I shall send for you and give you a palace to live in."

A journey to Italy, even if there *was* a palace at the end of it, was more than she had counted on. All she wanted was to remain in Paris and, in the manner of most grass-widows, enjoy herself.

"Travel," she said flatly, "especially over such bad roads, would kill me. I could never undertake such a journey, never!"

"The prospect of being received like a queen will make you change your mind," he said.

"You have yet to make that possible," she said lightly.

"Give me time and I will make it more than possible!"

She laughed. His boastfulness was really quite preposterous.

"I see that you have little faith in me," he said with a scowl, "but I give you my word that within three months Italy will be at my feet."

He took her by the arm and led her from the room. At last, thank heaven, the exhausting scene was nearing its end.

In the crowded ante-room a watchful and cynical Barras was waiting, on behalf of the Directory, to bid Bonaparte farewell, and after embracing Josephine, Bonaparte turned to him impulsively.

"Barras," he said brokenly, "I commend my most precious possession to your care. For my sake, watch over her."

Barras inclined his head gravely. "You honor me, General."

Bonaparte embraced Josephine again, then flung himself from the house and into the waiting carriage. Above the clatter of the horses' hoofs he shouted a final message. Most of it was inaudible, but three words rang out clearly: "Palace . . . three months. . . !"

Once alone with Josephine, Barras permitted himself an amused chuckle.

"The amiable simpleton, asking me of all people to watch over his most precious possession!"

"Hold your stupid tongue!" Josephine cried, but there was laughter in her voice.

"Not one tear," Barras went on, "not one single little tear. You might at least have pretended you were sorry to see him go."

Josephine pouted. "I tried to cry, really I did, Barras."

"No one would have thought it. And you a woman who can cry so freely when she really wants to!"

"Pig!"

"Fortunately Bonaparte was too stricken with his own grief to be aware of the lack of grief in you."

Josephine's pout turned to a frown. "I don't think your attitude amuses me. You're laughing at Bonaparte and at me too. That's all you ever do, laugh. You even laughed when you gave me your congratulations at that dreadful marriage ceremony."

"Dreadful?" he took her up. "Oh come, for a woman of your complaisant virtue it should have been a purifying experience."

"It was cold, and over in a moment. I shall never be able to feel properly married to Bonaparte, really I shan't."

"Well, well," he said soothingly, "if religion is ever fashionable again you may be able to persuade him to seek the blessing of the church. By the way, what were those last few words he called from the carriage? I merely caught something about a palace and three months."

Josephine laughed scornfully. "He intends to conquer Italy in three months and is going to give me a palace to live in."

"You mean he wants you to join him in Italy?"

"Yes, but naturally I shall remain in France, in Paris. Naturally I shall, for in Paris I can now spread my wings and be free. Imagine it, Barras—*free!*"

CHAPTER XXI

A PARTY WAS IN PROGRESS at the house in the rue Chantereine. Most of the guests, prominent among whom was Teresia Tallien, were hilariously engaged in that latest craze, the victim game. A mock guillotine stood in the middle of the room. One of the guests was dressed to represent an executioner while one by one the others approached the guillotine, made lengthy last-minute speeches and, amid shouting and cheering, went bravely to their 'deaths.'

"A trifle gruesome, don't you think?" Teresia remarked.

"Oh yes," Josephine agreed, "but it's very popular just now and all it costs is the price of the mock guillotine."

Teresia looked at her friend shrewdly. "So you're still harassed by debts, my dear."

Josephine nodded and made a face. "My stupid creditors refuse to believe me when I assure them that they will be paid in full some day. So very tiresome, isn't it!"

"But doesn't the fact that you are General Bonaparte's wife make them a little less pressing?"

"Surprisingly enough it doesn't. Most of them don't seem to have heard of poor Bonaparte." She chuckled suddenly. "Actually I succeeded in running up a considerable number of bills before the tradespeople discovered that Citizeness Beauharnais and Citizeness Bonaparte were one and the same woman, but now that the truth has come out my credit has been stopped almost everywhere."

"How much do you owe?" Teresia asked.

"My dear, what a question to ask—unless, of course, you are thinking of making me a loan."

Teresia laughed and shook her head. She was a little in debt herself. Like Josephine she had long ago discovered that money went absolutely nowhere these days.

"I can only hope," she said gaily, "that Bonaparte will take an easy view of the matter when he returns and the bills start pouring in."

Josephine looked thoughtful but after a moment her face cleared. "I'm sure he will, Teresia. He worships me, he absolutely worships me. You should see his letters!"

"Then he writes frequently?"

"As many as five letters arrive by the same courier."

"Are they very passionate?" Teresia asked curiously.

Josephine nodded casually. "Yes, I suppose so." Her eyes were on Hyppolyte Charles, a particularly witty guest who was mounting the 'guillotine' at that moment. "We must listen to this," she said. "Hyppolyte should make a really amusing speech."

While they listened Teresia watched Josephine curiously. She gave her entire attention to the slightly inane and to Teresia's mind anything but witty speech of that fop of fops, Hyppolyte Charles, and when it came to an end she clapped loudly and shouted "Bravo!"

"Josephine," Teresia said, "how long have you known Citizen Charles?"

"How long? Now let me see, I met him for the first time a week ago. Don't you think he's amusing?"

Teresia conceded that he might be, providing you liked that type of man. Then she said:

"Josephine, people are beginning to gossip, to link your name with his. Are you really having an *affaire* with him?"

Josephine looked at her friend with wide eyes. "My dear, what nasty minds people have. Why, as I just told you, I've only known him a week!"

Teresia, not entirely satisfied, was obliged to accept this as a denial and turned the conversation once more to Bonaparte.

"What amazes me about your husband," she said, "is that he should find time to write so many letters. According to reports reaching Paris he is spending every moment of every day reorganizing his army and preparing for battle. He must love you to desperation."

"Oh, he does! He tells me so over and over again in his letters."

With a little laugh Josephine recalled some of the phrases of the letter that had reached her the day before. *You are the constant object of my thoughts. Every moment separates me farther from you, my adorable one, and every moment I find in myself less strength to bear the separation.* What a quaint little man he was, to be sure!

"Teresia," she said, "you know more of military matters than I. Tell me, do you think Bonaparte will be defeated in Italy?"

Teresia pondered for a moment. She knew, just as Tallien and Barras knew, that Bonaparte's army was a mere ragged remnant of what a real army should be. He was working hard, of course, organizing and planning, and his dreams, like those of most little men, were extravagant and large, but even so. . . .

"My dear," she said kindly, "the most I can say is that nothing short of a miracle will enable him to give you that Italian palace he so rashly promised."

Josephine sighed, and in spite of the gaiety and laughter about her, she fell victim to a sudden fit of depression. What a fool she had been to marry Bonaparte! A braggart, that was all he was. Not that she wanted a palace in Italy. Paris was her home and in Paris she intended to stay.

At that moment she saw Barras, who had promised to attend the party, entering the room in what for him was a high state of excitement. She went forward to meet him.

"You're late, Barras," she said. "Is anything the matter?"

He smiled mysteriously and crossed to the mock guillotine in the centre of the room. He held up his hands and called loudly for silence.

"Ladies and gentlemen," he said, in a ringing voice, "Murat has arrived with dispatches from Italy. There has been a battle at Monte Notte." He paused dramatically. "A battle and a glorious victory."

There was a moment of silence and then a burst of cheering. Somebody cried: "Long live Bonaparte!" and the rest took it up. Both Josephine and Teresia ran to Barras's side.

"Well," he said to Josephine, "your clever little husband is showing greater promise than we dared to expect."

"It is a really important victory, then?" Teresia asked.

"If it is followed by others, yes. And Bonaparte certainly expects it to be. In fact he promises to smash down the gates of Italy within a month."

"It seems," Teresia remarked, "that I shall have to take back what I said just now."

Josephine nodded absently.

"Tell me, Barras," she said, "will this make any difference to Bonaparte—financially?"

Barras chuckled. "How typical of you, my dear!"

She brushed this aside impatiently. "When you were trying to persuade me to marry him you said that he would have many opportunities of making money out of the Italians. You said he would come back from Italy a rich man."

"If Monte Notte is followed by other victories," he assured her soothingly, "he will certainly have many opportunities."

"You mean it?" she pressed. "You really mean it?"

"I really mean it."

"Ah!" She smiled up at him serenely. "Then perhaps you would be kind enough to advance me twenty thousand francs until Bonaparte is able to send me a little money."

For once Barras was completely taken aback.

"My dear Rose—" he protested.

"Fifteen thousand, Barras, or even ten!"

"You are the most extravagant woman I know," Barras said, now fully recovered. "Your husband would hardly thank me for encouraging a wild spending of money."

"But I don't want to *spend* money. I only want to keep my creditors at bay. Please, Barras, just ten thousand!"

"You might as well ask for ten million. Monte Notte may be a great victory but it is by no means a decisive victory. In other words, my dear, I'm not prepared to gamble on Bonaparte, yet."

"But——"

"If your husband succeeds in his claim, if he smashes open the gates of Italy within a month, my attitude may be different. Till then your creditors will have to wait."

With that Barras excused himself and took his departure. This, though the hour was still early, was a sign for a general breaking up of the party, and in twos and threes the guests left the house to spread the news of Monte Notte in the streets of Paris. With a gesture of anger Josephine turned to the single remaining guest.

"A great French victory is all very well," she told him, "but it has completely ruined my party."

Hyppolyte Charles bowed graciously.

"Dear lady," he said, in his most charming manner, "it has at all events cleared your house of rowdy guests and left us alone together, a pleasure I had failed to anticipate quite so soon."

A look of complete understanding passed between them. She softened instantly and permitted him to take her in his arms.

Presently he said: "I think it would be wise if you sent your maid to bed."

She nodded her agreement and gently freed herself. Going to the hall to call Louise she laughed softly at an amusing thought. Bonaparte little knew what he had been about when he had won the battle of Monte Notte!

*   *   *   *   *

A few days after the news of Monte Notte reached Paris an unexpected visitor presented himself at the rue Chantereine.

"Citizen Joseph Bonaparte," Louise announced.

This elder brother of Bonaparte's being the first of her relatives-in-law to come to her notice, Josephine received him with a guarded curiosity. He entered the room with a stolid tread and seemed to bring an air of gloom with him. Before he spoke she knew instantly that he would disapprove of her. She tried to get the advantage of him immediately by greeting him with a little lie.

"I heard you were in Paris, m'sieur, and wondered when you would call. Do be seated please."

He seated himself and faced her with a frown. "You were misinformed, madame. I reached Paris less than an hour ago and came here at once."

"Ah, then your fame must have preceded you." She smiled disarmingly. "Do you mind if I call you Joseph?"

"You may if you wish, madame." The frown was still on his face. "We are, after all, brother and sister-in-law."

"And you," she went on, still smiling, "must call me Josephine, just as your brother does. 'Madame' has such a cold unfriendly sound."

She noticed then that Joseph had at least one thing in common with her husband. His stare was just as rude though perhaps not quite so penetrating. Did the rest of the family stare like that, she wondered. Since they were Corsicans and therefore barely civilized they probably did.

Making conversation she inquired politely about the health of the Bonaparte mother. She was in good health, it seemed, and sent her regards.

"She hopes," Joseph said, "to have the pleasure of meeting you in the very near future. To be perfectly frank, the news of Napoleon's marriage surprised her, as it surprised us all, and left her anxious to meet his bride."

There was a little pause. Joseph transferred his stare to the various objects of the room. Presently his eyes came to rest on Josephine again.

"Our mother wrote to you. I presume you received her letter?"

Josephine remembered the letter with its stiff, uncompromising phrases and its somewhat masculine hand.

"When I left Marseille," Joseph went on, "our mother was under the impression that you would be joining Napoleon very soon in Italy. Perhaps you could tell me just when you intend to do that?"

A coldness gripped her heart. So this was the object of her brother-in-law's visit. He was here to harry her into leaving for Italy.

"No plans have yet been made," she said stiffly. "It would be unwise, I imagine, to leave Paris until Bonaparte has something more settled to offer me than a military camp."

"You could journey to Marseille, which would bring you closer to him, and stay there with our mother. She would consider it the best thing for you to do. A wife's first duty is to be as near to her husband as possible. Our mother," he added heavily, "has strong views on a wife's duty."

"Oh, so have I," Josephine assured him airily. "I have been a wife before, and a mother. I can scarcely be called a novice."

Joseph's face clouded. "Speaking of that, madame, I think I ought to mention that our mother was disappointed when she learned that Napoleon had married a widow with two children. However, as I told her, the damage has been done and there is little else we can do except make the best of it."

A flush of anger came to Josephine's face. Joseph rose stiffly.

"Please excuse me now, madame. I have much business to attend to. I shall call again soon, and by then, I trust, you will be able to give me the definite date of your departure from Paris."

Her anger increased as she watched him leave the room. The pig, the surly ill-mannered pig. And the impudence of it all. Shaking with fury she mimicked his tone of voice. "And by then, I trust, you will be able to give me the definite date of your departure from Paris." As for journeying to Marseille to stay with 'our mother,' nothing was farther from her mind. If Madame Bonaparte was anything like Joseph they would be enemies at sight. She thought of the other Bonapartes she had yet to meet, of Louis, Lucien, and Jerome, Eliza, Paulette and Caroline. The women, naturally, would be worse than the men. What a dreadful family to have married into, and how cruel of God to have created so many of them!

She was determined, too, that she would never join Bonaparte in Italy. As if she could live in a military camp, or a bivouac, or whatever they called it! The very idea! Not even the promised Italian palace would tempt her. She thought of Hyppolyte Charles, gay, witty, the most charming man in Paris and the most amusing companion any woman of fashion might hope to find. No, not even the promised Italian palace would tempt her away from the delights of life in Paris.

With characteristic abandon she had contrived by now to forget her creditors, but even they, as the weeks passed, and news of further victories reached Paris, grew less pressing. Indeed, the most substantial result of her husband's rapid climb to military fame showed itself in a gradual change of front on the part of the tradespeople, until in the end she found it possible to obtain as much credit as she wished.

Another pleasant result was the way in which crowds began to gather when she drove through the streets of Paris, crowds who not only cried 'Long live Bonaparte,' but also 'Long live Citizeness Bonaparte!' and later the more intimate 'Long live Josephine!'

Of a certainty, Paris was a place in which to remain these days, not a place to leave for the rigors of a long and comfortless journey.

Paris, the cheering crowds, the attentive Hyppolyte. What a glorious existence life was proving itself to be!

* * * * *

Hyppolyte Charles was lounging elegantly in a chair in Josephine's boudoir, smiling condescendingly over Bonaparte's latest letter which Josephine had given him to amuse himself with while she completed her usual lengthy *toilette*.

"This husband of yours," Hyppolyte sneered delicately, "he should write love stories, not lead armies."

"I merely glanced through it when it came this morning," Josephine said, dabbing a final smear of rouge on her cheeks. "Read it aloud."

With elaborate emphasis Hyppolyte began to read: "My sweet Josephine, you have done more than rob me of my soul. You are the only thought of my life. If I am weary of the turmoil of battle, if I fear the outcome, if my men disappoint me, if I am ready to curse life, I place my hand upon my heart and feel your portrait there and love fills me with absolute happiness once more."

Josephine turned from the mirror with a laugh: "Oh, Hyppolyte, what a scream you are!"

"The words are your husband's, dear lady, not mine." He folded the letter and gave it back to her with a languid sigh. "But I confess that I could hardly do better myself."

"You could do a great deal better, darling, and you know it."

"You may be right but I should find it much too boring."

Footsteps were heard on the stairs, the door was flung open and Barras, unannounced, walked into the room. Seeing Hyppolyte Charles his eyes twinkled and he looked at Josephine with a knowing smile.

"I thought you might like to know," he said, without preamble, "that Bonaparte has fulfilled his promise. The gates of Italy have been smashed. His adjutant, Colonel Junot—a handsome young man, by the way—is here with standards, twenty-one of them, taken from the enemy, and the draft of a treaty made with the King of Sardinia."

There was a pause. Josephine's brows had wrinkled thoughtfully.

"Well," Barras asked, "have you nothing to say?"

"But of course I have," she cried. "Apart from my natural delight at the news I want to remind you——"

He interrupted her with a laugh. "But of course, you want to remind me of my promise to lend you money if Bonaparte smashed open the gates of Italy within a month."

"Precisely, and it wasn't an actual promise, but I'm happy to know that you regard it as such. How much will you lend me? Twenty thousand francs, or dare I ask for more?"

"My dear," he said, "your credit will be even better than ever when I release this news to the public. The loan of a paltry sum like twenty thousand francs will be quite unnecessary."

"You mean you will lend me more?"

"I mean I will lend you nothing whatever, not a single sou."

He nodded agreeably to Hyppolyte Charles, with whom he had exchanged no conversation at all, and took a leisurely departure.

"A rat and a pig," Josephine commented, and gave herself up once more to the intricacies of the unfinished *toilette*.

*   *   *   *   *

After the signing of the treaty with the King of Sardinia it became obvious to Josephine that sooner or later she would be obliged to join Bonaparte in Italy, unless, of course, she could think of some very clever excuse. Both young Colonel Junot, who was still in Paris, and the unsympathetic Joseph Bonaparte called frequently at the rue Chantereine with personal messages from Bonaparte urging her to start out at once for Italy, and Bonaparte's letters, though still ardent, repeated one imperative phrase over and over again: "You must come to Italy, a palace is waiting for you." Finally, when she had given up all hope of finding a convincing excuse for remaining in Paris, she hit upon the idea of a suspected pregnancy. "If this is actually true, if I am really about to make you a father," she wrote to Bonaparte, "you will naturally agree that travel over the dreadful roads that separate Paris from Italy would be the worst thing in the world for me." To this she received an almost hysterical reply by special courier. To be a father, to see a child of his own in her arms, that was the dream of his life. "Send me word immediately you are positive of this," he wrote, and agreed that for the time being she had better remain in Paris.

Happy once more she threw herself wholeheartedly into the gaiety of a Paris now wild with joy. At the theater, at the numerous public receptions, people stood up when she entered and cheered till they were hoarse. She appeared at every party of note, she gave numerous parties herself, and whenever a ball was held she danced with an abandon that made Joseph Bonaparte hide his righteous head in shame.

"You must find our dear Josephine's triumph a trifle irksome," Barras remarked one day to Teresia.

Teresia smiled wryly. "Naturally I do. They used to call me the uncrowned queen of Paris, but 'Our Lady of Victories,' as they're calling Josephine these days, seems to have taken my place."

"We must put our heads together and do something about it," Barras said. "You are still an intimate friend, of course?"

"Oh yes, I'm still an intimate friend."

"Perhaps you could talk to her, persuade her to join Bonaparte in Italy. Apart from our personal feelings in the matter Bonaparte is growing restless. I received a letter from him this morning. He threatens to resign his command if she delays much longer."

"Resign his command?" Teresia echoed.

"Yes. Imagine what that would mean. Italy is not completely sub-dued. If he came back to Paris now all the work he has done might be wasted. Besides, I want to keep him out of Paris as long as possible. His presence might prove embarrassing."

"You mean the people would make too much of him, and might end in forgetting Citizen Director Barras just as they are now for-getting Citizeness Teresia Tallien."

"I mean precisely that."

"Very well," Teresia agreed. "I'll talk to Josephine, I'll persuade her, if possible, to go to Italy."

Teresia, however, knew Josephine too well to have much hope of succeeding. With Paris so attentive, with the music of 'Long Live Bonaparte! Long Live Josephine!' ringing out at every public gathering, Josephine would have to be forced, not persuaded, to leave for Italy, and Teresia knew no way of forcing her.

A few days later when she visited the rue Chantereine and brought up the unwelcome subject Josephine merely laughed gaily.

"Don't be tiresome, Teresia. I'm perfectly happy in Paris."

"I know you are, my dear, but are you aware that Bonaparte is threatening to resign his command?"

Josephine was aware of that—twice he had made the threat in recent letters—but she knew in her heart that he would never take such a drastic step.

"Have you never thought," Teresia said, "that he might grow tired of waiting? There are many pretty women in Italy, you know. Even if you don't love him you want to keep him, don't you?"

"My dear Teresia," Josephine laughed, "I know exactly how to manage him. The more I deny him the more he will pursue. If I went running to him now he would tire of me in no time."

"But surely you see that you must go to him in the end."

"I'm not so sure of that!"

It was, of course, hopeless to argue, and with a shrug of resignation Teresia began to talk of the latest fashion in hats, a mutual and much pleasanter subject of conversation. From hats they passed to dresses and were arguing fiercely about the continued use of the Greek tunic when the maid entered the boudoir.

"Citizen Joseph Bonaparte," she announced, "is waiting below."

Josephine made a face. "You should have told him that I was out, Louise."

"With Citizeness Tallien's carriage at the door," the maid pointed out, "it was obvious that you were receiving visitors."

"Then next time you must say that I am ill."

She kept Joseph waiting for the best part of an hour, hoping that he would tire and go, but in the end she was obliged to go down to him. She gave him her hand and greeted him with a charming smile.

"A thousand pardons for keeping you waiting like this, Joseph. Even a few minutes must be a great waste of time to so busy a man as yourself."

"Madame," he said, with a scowl, "I have waited almost an hour."

"An hour? You astound me!"

196

"Madame," he went on, "I received a letter this morning from Napoleon. If you are not ready to accompany Colonel Junot to Italy within twelve hours I shall be obliged to tell him something of your conduct here in Paris."

She looked at him sharply. "Are you threatening me, Joseph?"

He chose to ignore this. "Napoleon," he said, "has reached the end of his patience. It is also obvious to him that your last flimsy excuse will bear not the slightest investigation."

Josephine shook her head sadly. "How you wrong a poor woman. My last flimsy excuse, you call it. It was no excuse, merely a mistake." She lowered her eyes and forced tears into her voice. "If only you knew, if only Bonaparte knew, the intensity of my disappointment——"

"Your disappointment," Joseph cut in acidly, "can scarcely equal Napoleon's. He speaks of it in his letter."

"Does he indeed! I gave him the credit for more delicacy, really I did!"

He swept all this aside with an angry gesture.

"Madame," he said, "must I remind you once more that your place is with your husband?"

"But of course it is. I agree. I have always agreed, but surely you can see that I am little suited by nature for the rough life of an army camp."

"You go to a palace, not a camp. You will be received with all the pomp and ceremony that is dear to your heart. The old nobility of Italy will be at your feet."

She sought wildly for a further excuse and happily remembered her children.

"I have Hortense and Eugene to think of," she said. "They need me here in Paris, at least Hortense does. You have seen her, Joseph. You know the tenderness of her years. More than anything else in the world she needs a mother's care and instruction."

"The care of a mother who dances till dawn," he retorted, "is not the most desirable a young girl could have."

"You have been listening to gossip," she said sadly.

"I have seen you myself and you know it!" He rose and towered over her, a black cloud of disapproval and contempt. "Madame," he shouted, "do you want to see your husband ruined?"

"Ruined? What in the name of heaven do you mean, Joseph?"

"As my brother's trustee, as his business representative, I am aware of the magnitude of your debts."

She looked at him uneasily. How in the world did he know about her debts? Was it possible that her creditors were now sending their accounts to Joseph instead of to her?

197

"Before you married Napoleon," he went on, "your one outstanding worry was not that you were in debt, but that you were unable to fall more deeply into debt."

"Dear me," she laughed, "what a lot you seem to have discovered about me!"

"I have discovered more than you think. Today your position is rather different. Due to Napoleon's military successes you have secured unlimited credit. Not a day passes without your fancy being taken by some useless but expensive trifle. If Napoleon resigns his command and returns to France, as he threatens to do, both you and he will be ruined. No more trifles. No more pretty luxuries. Nothing but inescapable debts and poverty."

"Merciful heavens!" she said, beginning to feel quite alarmed, "what a gloomy picture you paint!"

"I could paint an even gloomier picture."

"Yes, I'm sure you could!"

He crossed to the door and opened it.

"Madame," he said, "you have your choice. Go to Napoleon or remain here and face ruin and poverty. I shall now leave you to think about it, but let me warn you, make your decision quickly."

With that he muttered a surly "*Au revoir*" and left her.

Utterly miserable she burst into tears and was crying as if her heart were broken when Teresia, having heard Joseph's carriage drive away, came down from the boudoir.

"I have decided," Josephine sobbed, "that it is imperative for me to join Bonaparte in Italy." She thought of Joseph's words. *No more trifles. No more pretty luxuries. Nothing but inescapable debts and poverty.* "*Most* imperative," she added.

✳   ✳   ✳   ✳   ✳

Josephine's first thought when she had recovered from her brother-in-law's visit was that leaving Paris, which was bad enough in itself, would also mean leaving Hyppolyte. She knew, of course, that she was by no means in love with him, but he amused her and without him she would be horribly bored. She admitted to herself that she had never intended to conduct more than a mild flirtation with him, but sheer good nature had carried her farther, and happily he was a most proficient lover.

'I really need him,' she thought, 'to amuse me during the dreary journey to Italy.'

No sooner had this thought passed through her mind than she conceived a plan for taking him with her. For the successful execution of this plan she needed the help of Barras and accordingly sent him a message asking him to call on her at the earliest possible moment.

When Barras came she saw at once that he was suspicious, but then, Barras was always suspicious. In spite of this he was unable to hide his satisfaction at her decision to join Bonaparte in Italy. He even spoke of it—"My dear, permit me to congratulate you on making a very wise decision—" and in such a way that his words suggested a little mental hand-rubbing.

"Whether it is a wise decision or not," she said, "I am half inclined to change my mind."

Consternation flooded his face.

"In fact," she added, "I certainly will change my mind unless you promise to do something for me."

"And that?" he demanded.

"I want you," she said with disarming frankness, "to see that Hyppolyte Charles is included in my party."

Barras was too taken aback to laugh.

"That would be neither wise nor discreet," he said.

"I am the best judge of that, Barras. I warn you, unless you do this for me I shall remain in Paris indefinitely."

"But don't you realize how obvious it would be?"

"It would only be obvious if he went at my own invitation. You, on the other hand, could send him on a military mission, or something like that."

With a shrug Barras gave up the argument.

"Be it on your own head," he said, "and don't blame me if this leads you to disaster."

"You promise to arrange it?"

"I promise to arrange it. Your dear Hyppolyte shall be sent out to Italy as aide-de-camp to General Leclerc, but heaven help you if Joseph Bonaparte, who is to escort you to Italy, grows in the least suspicious."

"Joseph Bonaparte to escort me to Italy?" she gasped. "This is the first I've heard of it!"

"Perhaps you would rather Charles stayed in Paris after all. There certainly won't be any chance for you to flirt with him."

"No, no, he must accompany me. I shall need him in Italy while Bonaparte is busy with the army. But Joseph Bonaparte!" she threw up her arms in despair. "That is too much!"

A crowd of noisy, cheerful idlers had gathered about the door of the house in the rue Chantereine, staring up at the windows, swarming about the two carriages, patting the stamping horses, engaging in lively backchat with the waiting postilions, for the news had quickly spread that Josephine, Our Lady of Victories, was about to make her departure for Italy.

Presently a third carriage turned into the street and drew up on the opposite side. The occupant, stepping down, was greeted with enthusiasm and a passage was made for him through the center of the crowd.

"Long live Citizen Director Barras!" the people shouted. "Long live the Republic!"

Barras smiled 'his acknowledgments and made his way into the house. He found the ante-room crowded with people. Apart from the members of the Italy-bound party he recognized Teresia and Tallien. He was about to join them when Joseph Bonaparte detached himself from the rest.

"My sister-in-law," he said, in tones of disgust, "has locked herself in her boudoir and refuses to come down."

Barras merely smiled. He had expected something like this.

"Go up to her," Joseph urged. "You have more influence with her than anybody else, I believe."

Barras laughed ironically. "My dear Citizen Bonaparte, as you are the lady's brother-in-law, the duty is plainly yours."

But in the end Barras went up to the boudoir, gained admittance and found Josephine grasping her smelling-salts, reeking of lavender-water and in tears.

"I feel ill, Barras," she sobbed, "wretchedly ill. I have the most frightful headache and I know I shall never be able to stand the journey." She looked at Barras through her tears. "For heaven's sake take that insufferable grin off your face!"

He threw himself into a chair with a laugh. "You are far more entertaining than a play. I think I ought to call the others and let them see you."

"I hate you, Barras."

"I can't imagine what you have to cry about. Your little Hyppolyte is below, looking a perfect dream in his Hussar's uniform."

"What if he is? I still hate you, and I absolutely loathe that wretched Joseph Bonaparte! What an impossible family the Bonapartes must be! And the number of them! Thirteen or fourteen, or perhaps fifteen. Imagine it, fifteen Bonapartes to bully me!"

"You're exaggerating, as usual. Your husband has three sisters and four brothers. The father died years ago but the mother is still alive. That makes nine, not fifteen."

"Then where did I get fifteen from?" She searched her memory as if it were the most important thing in the world. "I know! Madame Bonaparte had thirteen children but five of them died. What a tough old Tartar she must be, and I expect she will want me to have thirteen children too."

"I shouldn't be surprised."

"Well, I refuse to go near her."

"Nonsense, my dear. You can't possibly pass through Marseille without paying your respects."

"I shall travel to Italy by another route."

"Joseph will have something to say about that, I imagine."

Josephine took a delicate sniff at her smelling-salts. "I shall be dead before I reach Marseille; that is absolutely certain."

Barras rose. He took her in his arms and kissed her.

"*Au revoir*, you little fraud," he said. "Now take my arm and do your best to stagger downstairs."

Still grasping her smelling-salts, still sobbing, she took his arm.

"Stop that sniffling," he said. "Have you no pride? Do you want everybody to see you like this?"

"Why shouldn't everybody see me like this? I am leaving Paris and my heart is broken." She looked about wildly. "My lavender-water, I must have my lavender-water!"

Eventually, carrying her lavender-water and her smelling-salts for her, he got her down to the ante-room, and from there to the street where the crowd cheered wildly.

"Josephine!" they roared. "Our Lady of Victories!"

"Smile!" Barras commanded, gripping her arm till she cried out in pain.

She choked back her sobs and smiled.

"Long live Josephine!" the crowd chanted. "Long live Bonaparte!"

The rest of the party came out of the house. Josephine took her place in the first carriage. The wretched Joseph stepped in next and seated himself opposite her, looking for all the world like the jailer he was. General Murat and Colonel Junot followed, while Hyppolyte climbed into the second carriage with the maid Louise and two other servants.

Joseph gave the word and the postilions whipped up the horses. The cheering of the crowd grew wilder. Josephine, smiling sadly, waved a damp handkerchief. Joseph leaned out of the window and inclined his head with the solemnity of an undertaker.

Josephine fell back on the cushions in apparent exhaustion, but her mind, forced into activity by the thought of having to face Joseph's saturnine countenance for the endless days of the journey, was very busy. At some stage of the journey it would surely be possible, one way or another, to evade his watchful eyes. If it was the last thing she did, she would contrive to change carriages and find a little relief in the stimulating presence of Hyppolyte Charles. Comforted by this thought and confident of success she smiled an almost happy smile.

And so the journey to Italy, by way of Marseille, began.

CHAPTER XXII

Do YOU SPEAK ITALIAN?" Madame Bonaparte asked.

Josephine shook her head. "I'm afraid I don't, madame."

Bonaparte's mother was younger than one might have expected, much younger. A woman who had borne thirteen children had no right to look so young, so barely middle-aged, nor to possess such a straight, almost slender figure. Josephine had always thought that child-bearing on the grand scale did dreadful things to a woman's body, but some women, it seemed, would remain angular however many they bore.

"You do *not* speak Italian?" the wretched woman said, in such a tone as to suggest that Josephine's ignorance in that direction was a very great offense indeed.

"It is to be regretted," Josephine apologized humbly, "but no, I do *not* speak Italian."

"It is a pity," Madame Bonaparte commented, her execrable accent more pronounced than ever. "We might understand each other better if you did."

The two women were alone in the small bare living-room of the Marseille house. Looking about her Josephine was shocked at the unmistakable signs of poverty. She had married into a poor family; nothing was more certain than that.

"I dislike the French language," Madame Bonaparte said, folding her hands uncompromisingly in her lap, "but Napoléoné—" she gave the name its Italian pronunciation—"insists that France is our country now, and therefore I try my best to speak the language of France."

"You speak it very well," Josephine assured her.

With distressing directness Madame Bonaparte said: "That is not true. I speak it very badly."

It was like saying: *You are mistaken if you hope to get around me by flattery.*

"You speak it with an accent," Josephine admitted, trying to make a better impression, "but your grammar is as perfect as mine."

Madame Bonaparte brushed this aside without a smile.

"I trust you will be comfortable," she said, "in the room we have prepared for you."

"I'm sure I shall be," Josephine murmured, knowing perfectly well that she would be anything but comfortable.

"I need hardly say," Madame Bonaparte added stolidly, "that as my son's wife you will be made welcome however long you may choose to stay."

"You are too kind," Josephine said hurriedly, "but I hope to resume my journey tomorrow."

"Tomorrow? I am happy to hear you say that. Napoléoné is anxiously awaiting you. He has waited a long time."

"My health," Josephine explained hastily, "has constantly delayed me and I was always a poor traveler." She rose, her one object being to terminate this increasingly unpleasant interview. "I think I should like to go to my room." She searched her mind for a plausible excuse. "A courier is leaving for Milan tonight. I must write a letter to Bonaparte."

Madame Bonaparte rose too. "But of course."

Joseph put in an appearance at the evening meal, which Madame Bonaparte had prepared. Two other Bonapartes were also present, Paulette and Caroline. Caroline was a child of Hortense's age. Paulette, fifteen or sixteen at the most, had the maturity of a woman. She was pretty and obviously spoiled, and her mouth was both sensuous and wilful. An instinct told Josephine that this Paulette would need watching. 'Unless I'm careful,' she thought, 'she will become a greater enemy than Joseph.'

After the evening meal, as if by a prearranged signal, Joseph and the two girls left the room. 'A plot,' she decided. 'I'm in for a bad quarter of an hour.'

Madame Bonaparte, her lips in a thin uncompromising line, came to the point immediately.

"I think I should tell you," she said bluntly, "that we were hurt by Napoléoné's marriage. To marry like that, secretly, without any of his family knowing—it was cruel."

"He was obstinate, Madame Bonaparte. Surely you know by now that your son has an obstinate nature."

"Even so, it was inconsiderate. There was nothing to hide, was there? Nothing to be ashamed of? At least one member of his family should have been present. Had I been informed I myself would have made the journey to Paris. I speak harshly, perhaps, but you will understand a mother's feelings in such a matter."

"But of course!" Josephine cried eagerly. "After all, am I not a mother myself?"

"Yes," Madame Bonaparte frowned, "and that is something which surprised us very much. We never expected Napoléoné to marry a widow, still less a widow with two children."

Before Josephine could think of a reply to this Madame Bonaparte added: "We were surprised and a little shocked."

"I may be a widow," Josephine protested, with a little laugh, "I may have two children, but surely if your son——"

"You are twenty-eight," Madame Bonaparte interrupted—"two years older than Napoléoné. I always feel apprehension when a wife is older than her husband."

So the question of age was coming up with a vengeance! What a mercy the old ogre knew nothing of the real difference in their ages!

"Two years," Josephine said weakly, "is hardly a great difference."

"That is a matter of opinion."

Having said this Madame Bonaparte changed the subject and questioned Josephine about her children. She inquired which was the elder, the boy or the girl, and under whose care they had been left during their mother's absence from Paris. When she learned that they were both at school and that Hortense was actually at Madame Campan's Academy her disapproval became evident again.

"A most fashionable establishment, Madame Campan's!"

"Well, yes."

"*And* expensive!"

"Oh, but everything is expensive these days, Madame Bonaparte, and I always think that education is the one thing in which a mother should never try to economize."

"At Madame Campan's you pay for the fashionable surroundings, *not* the education. In any case economy must be an ever-present necessity with a woman in your position."

"Er—with a woman in my position?" Josephine said weakly.

"To make myself a little clearer, your husband has nothing above his army pay. You have two children already and you will doubtless have more."

"Doubtless," said Josephine, looking down her nose.

"Children," Madame Bonaparte went on, "are a responsibility as well as a blessing. It will be necessary to count every sou when the others begin to arrive." With this she gave Josephine a look as sweeping as it was searching.

"I see you are not yet expectant. I understood Napoléoné to say in one of his letters——"

"A mistake was made," Josephine explained in her coldest tones. "Naturally I am deeply disappointed."

She rose with decision and once again made letter writing an excuse for breaking up an unpleasant tête-à-tête.

"But you wrote to Napoléoné this afternoon," Madame Bonaparte objected.

"Yes, but tonight I must write to the children."

"Ah yes, the children." Madame Bonaparte looked Josephine straight in the eye. "You say that Eugene, the elder, is—what age?"

"Fourteen."

"Fourteen. Ha!" (The wretched woman was actually smiling.) "You must have been very young when you married your first husband—a mere child."

A mere child— Looking back over the years Josephine was inclined to agree. Those early days in Martinique seemed like part of another life. She had been so enthusiastic then, so ridiculously hopeful of the life she was going to lead in France! Even the first years of her marriage with Alexandre seemed too distant to be part of her actual life. She had been the timid little Marie-Joseph-Rose then; now she was Josephine, a very different person indeed!

"I was sixteen," she said absently.

"Sixteen?" There was a grimness in Madame Bonaparte's voice. "And your son is now fourteen." She drew in a deep breath. "You must be at least thirty-one, not twenty-eight, as Napoléoné said!"

Josephine came out of her dream of the past with a start of dismay. Then, since there was nothing else to be done, she laughed lightly.

"How quick you are at figures, Madame Bonaparte!"

Madame Bonaparte, however, was not amused.

"Does Napoléoné know your true age?" she demanded.

"Oh yes, he knows."

"I begin to understand. You put your heads together and tried to deceive me. Napoléoné must have known that I would disapprove of a woman so many years older than himself. You have hurt me deeply, both of you."

"But Madame Bonaparte——"

"Not another word!" She drew herself up. Her accent became more heavily pronounced. "Deceit!—when a man begins to practice deceit because of a woman, where will he not end!"

Josephine smiled happily. What a relief it was to leave Marseille behind! Much as she hated travel, ill as it made her, if she was forced to choose between an eternity of it and a further twenty-four hours with her mother-in-law she would choose the agony of everlasting travel without a moment's hesitation.

All things considered, however, the journey from Marseille to Milan was not without enjoyment. For one thing, Joseph remained behind in Marseille, leaving Josephine to flirt to her heart's content with Hyppolyte, to flirt even with the handsome Murat and the young Junot. In fact the absence of Joseph, whose presence had cast a spell of gloom over everybody from Paris to Marseille, turned the journey into a light-hearted, frolicsome picnic which came to an end all too soon.

There was a great deal of speculation; as the party came within sight of Milan, as to whether General Bonaparte himself would ride out to meet them, and in view of such a possibility Josephine was cautious enough to place the three men—Hyppolyte, Murat and Junot—together in the front carriage, while she herself sat demurely in the second carriage with Louise and the other two servants.

As it happened this precaution turned out to be unnecessary. A league from Milan they were met, not by Bonaparte, but by a large escort of soldiers headed by an Italian nobleman, a nobleman who made Josephine a sweeping bow and introduced himself as the Duke of Serbelloni.

A duke! That was an honor, to be sure! She gave him a quick, shrewd examination. Quite a handsome man, for an Italian, and obviously a member of the old nobility. It was something, after all, to visit a country where there had been no revolution.

"Permit me to be the first to welcome you to Milan," the duke greeted her in excellent French.

She smiled graciously. "Thank you, m'sieur, but I was expecting my husband to have *that* honor." She looked at the duke anxiously. "What news have you of my gallant little Bonaparte?"

"Ah, my dear madame, General Bonaparte, he is many miles away, driving back the Austrians, performing miracles on the field of battle."

"How very uncomfortable—for the Austrians," she added quickly.

She then learned that the Serbelloni Palace had been placed at her disposal and that the duke himself had but one ambition, the ambition to serve her in every possible way. She thanked him and gave him her hand to kiss.

"M'sieur le Duc," she said, "I feel that I am going to enjoy my stay in Milan after all."

A number of letters from Bonaparte were awaiting her at the palace. He was at Verona, it seemed, and shaken with remorse because the Austrian campaign was keeping him apart from her now that she was in Italy.

I want you, I need you, he wrote. *Come to Verona.*

She merely smiled, and since Junot was leaving for Verona immediately, wrote a brief note to say that her health being what it was after the long journey from Paris it was impossible for her to move another step. That evening, wearing her gayest dress, she attended an elaborate reception given in her honor by the duke, and so enjoyed herself that when she finally retired at three in the morning she remarked to the sleepy Louise that she was the happiest woman in the world.

"They treat me like a queen," she said, her heart too full for words.

After a week in Milan, a week of flattering receptions and gay, informal balls, a week with the duke on one hand and Hyppolyte on the other, each competing for her briefest smile, Paris was almost forgotten and Milan seemed the pleasantest city in the world.

"If only Teresia and that wretched Barras could see me now," she told Louise, "they would be green with envy!"

$$*\qquad*\qquad*\qquad*\qquad*$$

Junot was back from Verona. He brought a letter from Bonaparte, a letter worded like a military order.

Come to me at Verona, she read, *you must be thoroughly rested by now. Come at once. Junot is instructed to accompany you.*

After frowning over these terse sentences she looked steadily at Junot who stood so stiffly before her.

"Poor Bonaparte must be out of his mind," she said.

Junot showed signs of embarrassment. "You mean that you intend to remain in Milan, citizeness?"

"But of course!"

Junot set his chin stubbornly. "Forgive my stressing the point, citizeness, but I am ordered to accompany you to Verona."

She gave him a woebegone look. "How stern you sound, Colonel."

"Orders," he said, half apologetically, "are orders."

"For a soldier, yes, but I am only a poor woman." She found a handkerchief. "What pitiless creatures men can be! Not content with dragging me all these hundreds of miles from Paris, Bonaparte—and you too!—wants to imperil my life on the very battlefield!"

"Verona is comparatively safe, citizeness."

She began to weep softly into the handkerchief. "Don't talk to me, Colonel! To think that I believed you a man of finer feelings and infinite understanding! The mistakes we poor women make when we put our faith in men!"

Junot coughed. His face had turned scarlet.

"Go back to Verona," she said, "and tell Bonaparte that if he wants to kill me he will continue to insist on my joining him."

"But citizeness——"

"Leave me, please," she said firmly. "I am utterly exhausted and shall go to bed immediately."

And with that Junot had to be satisfied. He bowed himself out and concluded that if Citizeness Bonaparte was going to bed at this hour—it was barely eight in the evening—she must be very exhausted indeed. Her tears had moved him and he had begun to feel that General Bonaparte was acting a little unreasonably.

Two hours later Junot heard hoof-beats in the courtyard and a moment later he found himself face to face with his general. His astonishment was so great that Bonaparte burst out laughing.

"If I can surprise Josephine as easily as I seem to have surprised you," he remarked, "I shall have nothing to complain of."

He then announced that he wished to come upon her without warning and asked if she were in her apartments.

"She retired two hours ago," Junot said.

"Two hours ago?" Bonaparte looked anxious. "Is she ill?"

"Not actually ill, sir, but a little exhausted."

"Ah, then she is probably asleep."

"I should imagine so, sir."

Bonaparte rubbed his hands together. "What a joke. What a huge joke! I shall steal in quietly, undress without a word and——"

"And leave her to discover you there in the morning?" Junot smiled.

"No, you idiot! Would you yourself do a thing like that? Think, man, would *any* husband?" and Bonaparte laughed coarsely.

The maid, Louise, who was sitting outside Josephine's bedroom reading a book, was even more surprised than Junot had been. She dropped the book and sprang to her feet in consternation.

"General Bonaparte!"

"Quietly, Louise," he whispered. "If anybody wakes her it must be I."

And then he saw the expression on the maid's face.

"Is anything the matter, Louise?"

"Why no, sir, except that——"

"Speak up, girl, speak up!"

Completely frightened, Louise said in a whisper: "The citizeness is not in bed."

"Not in bed? Then——?"

"She's gone out for the evening, sir. She's gone to a ball with the Duke of Serbelloni."

*   *   *   *   *

Louise and Junot were whispering together at the door of Josephine's bedroom. They could hear Bonaparte pacing lightly up and down inside the room. Somewhere in the near distance a clock finished chiming the quarters and struck three clear notes.

"Something must be done about it," Junot said, for perhaps the tenth time.

"Yes, but what?"

"Citizeness Bonaparte must be warned. I think perhaps I ought to go to the ball and fetch her."

"The Citizen General insists that she shall be kept in ignorance. He wants to surprise her."

"But the time! He's been waiting five hours. He must be furious by now."

"And the ball might last till four o'clock or even five. Perhaps you really ought to fetch her, after all. You could warn her to *pretend* surprise."

With that Junot slipped out of the palace hastily. Less than half an hour later he was back, bringing with him a highly excited and badly frightened Josephine. She was innocent, she knew she was innocent, but a feeling of guilt had complete control of her.

"Is he still in my room?" she demanded.

Louise nodded. "Yes, but he is very quiet now. I think he must be asleep."

"If that is the case, believe me I shall see that he remains asleep!"

"It might be wiser to wake him, citizeness."

Josephine considered this for a moment. "But of course! I could then pretend that I have been in much longer than he thinks."

"He was awake when the clock chimed three," Louise warned.

"Then I shall say nothing whatever and wake him with a kiss. That will choke his anger, surely!"

"And if he is actually awake, citizeness?"

"I shall scream. I shall scream and pretend I don't recognize him, otherwise—" she looked at Louise obliquely—"otherwise he will think I am used to having a man in my bedroom in the middle of the night and make a dreadful scene."

She placed a trembling finger to her lips and opened the door softly. Taking a candle from Louise she tip-toed across the room. Bonaparte was lying fully clothed and motionless across the middle of the bed. She held the candle high, drew in her breath and screamed. He sat up and looked at her coldly.

"Bonaparte!" she cried, putting as much surprise into her voice as she could. "*Bonaparte!*"

Louise came hurrying into the room. "Did you scream, citizeness? Is something the matter?"

Josephine sank into a chair. "No, no, Bonaparte gave me a great shock, that is all. You should have warned me he was here, really you should!"

Bonaparte rose from the bed. "Thank you, Louise, you may go."

He crossed the room. He was still looking at Josephine coldly. For a moment he reminded her of his dreadful mother. The memory of that ordeal in Marseille sent a shiver down her spine.

"What a terror you are," she said weakly, "frightening a poor woman out of her wits!"

"How utterly lovely you look," he whispered.

She sighed her relief, but a little too quickly.

"And for hours," he said, his voice rising angrily, "Serbelloni and his friends have feasted their eyes on you while I—" he seemed to choke—"while I waited here alone, desolate and impatient!"

"My poor Bonaparte!" She put down the candle and ran to him. "If only you had given me warning!"

His anger melted. He took her in his arms and embraced her roughly.

"Two days!" he said hoarsely. "That was all we had together before this Italian campaign separated us. Oh, Josephine, if only you knew how I've waited for this moment, waited for it with an eagerness that has burned up my very soul!"

She closed her eyes wearily. She was tired. To meet the demands he was about to make of her would surely kill her. And yet, what could a poor woman do? Merciful heavens, married to such a man as Bonaparte, what *could* a poor woman do?

CHAPTER XXIII

JOSEPHINE FOUND BONA-
parte's presence at the Serbelloni palace in many ways restricting.
She was still able to attend balls and receptions, but only in the
company of her husband, under whose watchful eye she was obliged
to play the part of a demure and faithful wife.

Once only during Bonaparte's stay was she able to arrange a meeting with Hyppolyte. He came to her apartments while her husband
was deep in a military conference, and since she had been obliged
to send for him she reproached him for having neglected her so
shamefully.

"A whole week," she said, with a little pout, "and you haven't
even written to me."

"Ah," he smiled, "but the general, your husband——"

"Oh come, you're not afraid of Bonaparte, surely!"

"Everybody," he mocked, "is afraid of Napoleon Bonaparte."

Josephine frowned. It did seem rather like that. There were times
when even she felt her heart turn cold with fear at the sight of those
staring eyes. It was perfectly ridiculous, of course, but there it was.
The man undoubtedly possessed a strange power, a personal magnetism, perhaps. . . .

"With Bonaparte in Milan," Hyppolyte was saying, "my watch-
word is naturally discretion."

"Discretion is one of the most tedious things in the world."

"Tedious, my dear lady, but necessary. Imagine, for instance, what
would happen if your husband were to learn the true reason for
my being in Italy."

Josephine shuddered delicately. "Undoubtedly he would kill
me."

"I hear," Hyppolyte said, "that he is planning to leave for Mantua.
Is that correct?"

"Yes, but just when he intends to leave is another matter."

"The sooner the better, dear lady, the sooner the better!"

They exchanged a glance of understanding and began to talk of
other more interesting topics than Citizen General Bonaparte. Josephine mentioned a trip she was planning to Genoa during which
Hyppolyte would naturally be a member of her military escort.

"A trip to Genoa?" he smiled. "You, who hate travel so much?"

She laughed lightly. "Since the Mayor of Genoa has issued an
official invitation I shall have no option but to accept."

The outcome of Bonaparte's military conference was his decision to proceed at once to Mantua.

"You have," he told Josephine, "exactly two hours in which to make your preparations for the journey."

Consternation flooded her face. "But you must be mad! At Mantua I shall be on the very battlefield. At Mantua my life will be in constant danger!"

He brushed this aside impatiently. "At Mantua you will be an inspiration, not only to me but to the whole army. My men have achieved miracles; with you among them they will achieve what I require of them, the impossible."

"But to leave in two hours! The rush would kill me. My health would never stand it!"

"Then follow me at a leisurely pace."

"I see you have little regard for my safety or my health!" The easy tears were beginning to flow. "You are determined to kill me. I see that clearly. You are thoughtless and cruel. I wish I had never married you!"

"Very well," he said harshly. "Remain in Milan. Go to the ball every night. Forget your husband. Forget him utterly. Your health will at least stand up to that!"

Pleased with his apparent weakening she looked at him through tear-dimmed eyes. "Now you are going to make a scene, and all because on the night you chose to arrive without warning I had the misfortune to be out till three in the morning!"

He took her in his arms. "Will nothing persuade you to come?"

"Nothing, Bonaparte. I owe it to my children to safeguard the health you would ruin."

He sighed deeply. "Very well, I shall go alone. I shall fling myself headlong into battle. Quite probably I shall be killed, but that will barely move you."

Less than an hour after Bonaparte's departure Hyppolyte Charles was admitted to Josephine's apartments. He found her in the gayest mood. With many a little chuckle she told him how she had wept her way out of the journey to Mantua. She agreed, however, that it would be unwise to leave just yet for Genoa and turned her thoughts to the ball which the Mayor of Milan was giving that night. . . .

The next day they started again, the endless stream of letters from Bonaparte. He complained that away from his precious Josephine he was constantly melancholy.

I thought I loved you a few days ago, but I know now that I love you a thousand times as much. From day to day my adoration increases. The charms of the incomparable Josephine kindle unceasingly a bright and burning flame in my heart and senses.

When she read this particular letter to Hyppolyte he remarked negligently that it was rather beautiful.

"I could hardly have done better myself," he said. "It makes me just a little envious that anybody so uncouth as Bonaparte should know anything about the charms of the incomparable Josephine."

She laughed her delight and went on to read another letter.

"Listen to this," she cried, "just listen to this!" And she read: "'Come to me here, I beseech you. Come to me so that before we die we shall be able to say, we were happy together for a little while.'"

"Rather morbid," Hyppolyte commented, "to talk of dying."

"The war is becoming too much for him, poor lamb."

"Perhaps you ought to go to him," Hyppolyte said, with surprising seriousness.

"What nonsense! If I am going to die I would prefer to die here in comfort. No, no, wild horses would never drag me to Mantua!"

A few days later Colonel Junot arrived from Mantua with a personal message from Bonaparte, who, it seemed, had left for Brescia.

"I am to join him there," Junot said, "and he wishes you to accompany me. I leave at noon tomorrow."

Josephine made a face. "So once again Bonaparte has selected you for the role of his wife's jailer. A pity, otherwise I could grow quite fond of you, Colonel."

Junot began to blush. "A courier leaves for Brescia within an hour," he said. "I am to send a message to the effect that you will leave Milan with me tomorrow."

"If you send a message at all, Colonel, it will be to the effect that I will *not* leave Milan with you tomorrow!"

Junot, being no match for Josephine, could only stare at her miserably.

"If you had a wife," Josephine went on, "would you compel her to join you under such perilous circumstances?"

"Citizeness," Junot said sternly, "I am merely the bearer of a message, not a critic of my general's conduct."

"How old are you?" she asked softly.

"I—I beg your pardon?" he stammered.

"Twenty?" she said. "Twenty-two, perhaps?"

"Twenty," he admitted.

"Ah! Then let me tell you, young man, by the time you are thirty you will be a very pompous old gentleman." She rose to her feet.

"Now leave me, Colonel—unless, of course, you have something more agreeable to talk about."

When Hyppolyte learned of Junot's visit and the message from Bonaparte he said again that perhaps Josephine ought to join her husband.

"Merely as a matter of policy," he added quickly, when he saw the anger in her eyes. "A matter of policy and nothing else."

He then went on to say that the news from the army was not the best. The French forces were hard-pressed by the Austrians, and in spite of Bonaparte's tremendous hold upon their imagination his men were likely to break up and scatter in the face of further Austrian counter-attacks.

"Your name," he said, "has become something of a legend among the soldiers. Appear dramatically in their midst and you will make them see that they have something tangible to fight for. You will remind them that at home wives and sweethearts and mothers are waiting and praying for them. You might even turn imminent defeat into glorious victory."

To Hyppolyte's surprise he saw that tears were rolling down Josephine's cheeks.

"You rat, Hyppolyte," she said brokenly, "you've made me cry. To think that I could do that for all those thousands of men!"

"Then you'll join Bonaparte at Brescia?"

She found a handkerchief and blew her nose. "Certainly not."

He smiled wryly. "What a waste of good rhetoric. Ah well, I must tell you my true reason for wanting you to go to Brescia."

"Your *true* reason? I don't understand, Hyppolyte."

"If you refuse to join Bonaparte you may try his patience too far. You may force him to quarrel seriously with you. Worse still, you may even make him think of divorce, and that is the last thing I would want to happen."

"The last thing *you* would want to happen?"

"You tell me often how deeply you're in debt, how Bonaparte would kill you if he knew."

"Well?"

"I happen to be in touch with a number of business people who are anxious to secure army contracts. While you hold a position of influence with Bonaparte you and I could do very handsomely for ourselves in the way of commission."

Understanding came to her eyes. She smiled broadly. "You rogue, Hyppolyte," she said.

"You grasp what I mean by a 'matter of policy'?"

"Perfectly."

"And you'll give serious consideration to joining Bonaparte?"

She had already given it. Her debts, which she had forgotten, were truly mountainous. To be reminded of them made her feel ill, not because of their magnitude but because she felt sure that Bonaparte, even if he did make money out of this Italian campaign, would never be able to liquidate them. In addition, imagine the scene that would follow if his impossible mother ever learned of them!

"I know it will kill me," she said, on the point of tears again, "but I will take your advice and leave with Junot at noon tomorrow." Suddenly she remembered something. The Duke of Serbelloni was giving a grand ball in a week's time. "I shall stay at Brescia," she said firmly, "just long enough to inspire the army with my presence and then I shall return to Milan."

"In time for M'sieur le Duc's ball?" Hyppolyte smiled.

"I do believe you can read my thoughts," she laughed. "Yes, in time for M'sieur le Duc's ball, and not even the Austrian army, still less my little Bonaparte, shall stop me!"

*　　*　　*　　*　　*

Josephine sat alone in the carriage which was carrying her to Brescia. She was petulent, unhappy and lonely. From time to time she sprinkled herself with lavender-water and took continual sniffs of her smelling-salts. Every jolt of the carriage increased her discomfort and fired her resentment against Bonaparte. Moreover she felt certain that the worst headache of her life was about to develop. She had been on the road less than an hour and was already regretting her rashness in having agreed to make the journey.

After a few moments she put her head out of the window and shouted to the postilion to stop.

"The citizeness requires something?" the man inquired.

"I require a rest. Every bone in my body is broken."

Presently Colonel Junot, who was riding behind with the rearguard of her miltary escort, cantered up and asked if anything was the matter.

"I happen to be bored," she said. "Have the kindness to dismount and sit in the carriage with me."

Junot hesitated.

"This is an order," she cried.

He sighed philosophically, dismounted and climbed into the carriage. She indicated that she wished him to remain at her side during the rest of the journey. He sighed again. One of the escort took over his horse and the carriage lurched forward again.

"I never imagined," she said plaintively, "that there were roads as bad as this in the whole world. Once I get back to Paris I shall refuse to move farther than Croissy or Fontainebleau."

Junot merely grunted. She looked at him with distaste.

"It will take me weeks to recover from this journey," she went on. "What a heartless beast that husband of mine is."

Junot grunted again.

"In the name of heaven," she cried, "are you speechless?"

"No, citizeness," he muttered, and even that sounded like a grunt.

And so, for the greater part of the journey, she continued to make little bursts of conversation and Junot continued to grunt.

She decided that but for his good looks she would report him for insolence and insist on a reduction to the ranks. Finally, after five hours of jolting agony, the outskirts of Brescia came into sight and she sighed with relief.

"Thank heaven we are nearly there," she said.

Before Junot could give a further grunt the sound of distant cannon fire fell on her ears. Terrified, she clutched at him wildly.

"There's no need for alarm," he said testily.

"The Austrians!" she cried. "Brescia is being bombarded."

"Several miles to the north, I think, citizeness."

"North, south, east or west," she almost shouted. "Brescia is no place for a woman!"

Junot calmed her as best he could. He held the smelling-salts to her nose, he sprinkled lavender-water on her brow, he even permitted her to rest her head on his shoulder, upon which she sighed and declared that it was something to have a strong man .there to protect her, even if the extent of his social graces was a series of pig-like grunts.

And so Josephine, and the embarrassed and uncomfortable Junot, entered the streets of Brescia and arrived at Bonaparte's temporary headquarters. By this time Josephine was determined that whether the army needed her inspiration or not she would leave Brescia first thing the next morning. Her terror increased by the continued sound of cannon fire, she flung herself into Bonaparte's arms.

"I must go back at once," she cried, "at once!"

Bonaparte looked at the flustered Junot. "What have you been doing to her, Junot?"

The young man shrugged and with a gesture indicated the distant explosions.

Bonaparte shook Josephine gently. "You silly goose. That is only our own artillery."

"You are trying to deceive me. The Austrians are about to take the town."

"My sweet Josephine——"

She shook with anger as well as terror. "It was inhuman to bring me here. Do you love me so little that you want to see me killed?"

"Your imagination will kill you, madame, not the Austrians. I admit there's a little danger. This is war, not a Sunday afternoon picnic——"

"There! I knew, I knew! Send me back to Milan tomorrow."

"Not tomorrow, but the day after. My troops are moving out tomorrow."

"Moving out! Retreating, you mean, retreating!"

He almost lost his temper. "Confound you, no! I happen to be maneuvering for a more favorable position."

At that moment an aide-de-camp approached. Bonaparte turned to the man in relief.

"Well, what is it?"

The aide-de-camp stated briefly that the *proveditore* of the town wished to give a *fête* in honor of the Citizen General's wife. Bonaparte remarked that the news of Josephine's arrival had got about amazingly soon and asked when the *fête* was to be.

"Tomorrow," the man told him.

"We move out tomorrow. You know that well enough. The *proveditore* knows it well enough." He looked at Josephine. "You would like a *fête* in your honor? It would please you?"

"Since you intend to keep me here I may as well celebrate my death with a *fête*."

She and Bonaparte dined alone that night. He was in his most boyish mood and interrupted the meal continually to make love to her. He almost convinced her, with his light-hearted playfulness, that Brescia was as safe as Milan. Almost, but not quite.

When he was called away for a few moments on military business she sent for Junot. At last a plan for getting out of Brescia the following morning had begun to form in her mind.

"Junot," she said, "this *fête* for tomorrow night, is it definitely arranged?"

"As far as I know, citizeness."

"Tell me about the *proveditore*, is he an Italian?"

"Yes."

"And friendly towards the French?"

Junot laughed shortly. "He can hardly please himself in the matter, can he?"

"But if he *could* please himself?"

"That is hard to say, citizeness. Why do you ask? Have you heard something about the man?"

"Of course not. I was merely curious, merely curious. . . ."

After going to bed that night Josephine took her plan a step farther by remaining awake until Bonaparte at last fell asleep. By a tremendous effort, for she was very sleepy, she remained awake an hour longer. Then she sat up in bed with a violent jerk and began to scream. Bonaparte awoke instantly.

"Josephine, what's the matter!"

She changed her screaming to a wild, hysterical sobbing.

"A dream," she said, "a dreadful dream," and clung to him.

He began to laugh. "What happened? Did the Austrians take my little Josephine prisoner?"

She controlled her sobbing but still clung to him. "How odd that you should ask that. They took not only me prisoner, but you and your entire staff."

"Well, it was only a dream."

Noting a slight uneasiness in his voice she began to enlarge her story. "It was more than a dream, Bonaparte. You see, I wasn't really asleep. It makes me shudder to recall it. It was—" she sought for the right word—"it was something *psychic*."

"Psychic?" The uneasiness increased. She had imagined all Corsicans to be superstitious and apparently she was right. "You're a silly little goose," he said. "Go back to sleep."

"Wait till I tell you. At first I thought I was at a ball. There was music. Then things began to take more definite shape and I knew that I was at some sort of reception. You were there too, and Junot, and some other staff officers——"

"Well? Go *on*, Josephine!"

"There was a lot of speech-making and then suddenly hundreds of soldiers, strange soldiers, burst in on us and—well—we were all taken prisoner."

"And that was the end of your dream."

"No. A man I knew instinctively to be the *proveditore* came forward and the strange soldiers thanked him. I knew then that we had been invited to the reception in order to be trapped in Brescia."

Bonaparte began to laugh. "How badly my little Josephine has set her heart on going back to Milan!"

She sighed tragically. "I expected you to say that, to think I was trying to deceive you. Very well, remain in Brescia and prove the truth of my dream. When you are held in an Austrian prison you will be able to reflect bitterly, but too late, that your wife, had you permitted her, would have saved both France and you from disaster."

With that she turned from him and settled down to sleep. The next morning she saw from Bonaparte's face that he had passed a bad night.

"Josephine," he said, "do you give me your word of honor that you were telling the truth last night, that your dream wasn't an invention?"

She looked at him steadily. "I give you my word of honor."

"Very well, we shall leave Brescia at noon. Whether you were telling the truth or not you have had your way with me."

* * * * *

By noon the army had moved out of Brescia. Bonaparte had decided to pay Milan a short visit and he and Josephine were sitting side by side in the carriage which had brought her to Brescia. An escort of twenty men accompanied them.

They had been on the road less than an hour when Junot, one of the last officers to leave Brescia, overtook them at a furious pace and signaled for the carriage to stop. It was clear from his face that he was the bearer of grave news.

"Brescia," he gasped, "is in the hands of the Austrians. The *proveditore* was evidently in league with them. Aided by him they entered the town in swarms. Had we remained for the *fête* tonight we might have been taken prisoner or even killed."

"Great heavens!" Bonaparte exclaimed softly, and looked at Josephine. "Your dream, Josephine, your dream!"

She nodded dumbly. Actually she was so shaken by this news that she was almost frightened. The course of events had turned her lies into grim reality. She reached for her smelling-salts. What if, in spite of herself, she had really been telling the truth? What if she were actually psychic? It was a thought that filled her with awe. Psychic! She shuddered. *Psychic!*

"You would do well," she told Bonaparte, "to be guided by me in the future."

He brushed this quickly aside.

"The Austrian occupation of Brescia," he said, "is serious. The obvious plan is to cut off our retreat to Milan. Therefore while we remain near Brescia our position is precarious."

"*Bonaparte!*" she cried, and dropped her smelling-salts. He picked them up and held them to her nose.

"I shall accompany you as far as Lake Garda, and there I shall leave you in Junot's care."

"Lake Garda?" Junot questioned. "But that is in the opposite direction!"

"I know. We shall turn in our tracks, branch off at the cross-roads several miles back and make for Verona via Lake Garda. Once in

219

Verona it will be possible for you to reach Milan by a roundabout route."

With that he gave the word, the carriage was turned and the party was *en route* once more. They reached the cross-roads without a sign of the Austrians and raced along the road to Lake Garda. An hour later, after a brief halt, they were crashing and jolting forward again.

"The pace is killing me," Josephine wailed.

Bonaparte merely smiled. "Better the pace than the Austrians." He leaned forward to pinch her cheek. She averted her head.

"I think I shall always hate you for exposing me to all this danger."

"Danger? Pah, what's a bit of danger? You're a soldier's wife. You should keep that well in mind."

"I keep it in mind always. I get little chance to forget it."

"Take another sniff of your smelling-salts and give me one of your charming smiles."

"What an impossible man you are, Bonaparte!"

"But naturally! Out of all the months of our marriage we have been together perhaps seven days. Think of it, *seven short days!* Is it any wonder I'm impossible!"

"Impossible," she said, making her voice break, "and also c-cruel."

He looked at her blandly. "And now you are going to weep."

"You would make a saint weep."

"I would never be in love with a saint."

There was a long pause. The postilion whipped up the horses to greater fury until the carriage began to rock dangerously from side to side. Josephine clutched at the seat.

"It will overturn," she cried, "I know it will!"

Bonaparte put his arm round her shoulders. The pressure of his fingers, warm and firm, made her writhe.

"Bonaparte, *please!* You're crushing my dress."

"What of it? A fragile thing like this was meant to be crushed."

"I shall scream in a moment!"

His grip tightened. "Scream to your heart's content. I have an excellent way of silencing you."

She tried to twist away from him but he drew her closer.

"Bonaparte, you're hurting my arm."

"Put it round my neck." His voice suddenly became low and caressing. "Oh, Josephine, if only I could make you know how much I love you."

She laughed weakly. "Really, what a place for love-making—" the jolting of the carriage threw her against his chest—"and what a time."

"Place and time mean nothing when I'm alone with you. I know only one thing—life is short and you are the most desirable woman in the world."

A wave of helplessness overcame her. "You're mad, Bonaparte, utterly mad!"

"Blame yourself. Your presence fires my blood."

"You're crushing me to death, really you are. What with the pace and the lurching of the carriage and——"

He released her suddenly and leaned out of the window. "We'll stop the carriage, then; we'll stop it for one little moment. This, I admit, is love-making under extreme difficulty."

He shouted to the postilion to stop.

"But the Austrians!" Josephine cried.

"To the devil with the Austrians!"

The carriage drew up with a final lurch. Josephine began to laugh hysterically.

"Bonaparte, you great idiot——!"

He flung open the door. "Our twenty men shall form a guard of honor about us." He dropped lightly to the ground and looked right and left. "Junot! *Junot!*"

"But it's hardly *decent*," she protested weakly.

"Nonsense, madame! We're man and wife, aren't we?"

Her shoulders came up in a little shrug of resignation. "You're incorrigible, really you are!"

He gave her his most boyish smile. "I love you, Josephine."

Half dolefully, half admiringly, she held out her arms to him. "There's no other man in the world like you, Bonaparte."

Junot came up and received his instructions. The twenty men, their backs to the carriage, were placed in a watchful circle about it. The doors were closed, the curtains were drawn, the Austrians, for the moment, were completely forgotten.

*   *   *   *   *

True to his promise Bonaparte accompanied Josephine as far as Lake Garda. Here, taking Junot's horse and leaving Junot to continue in the carriage, he bade her good-bye.

She called him back for a moment. "Must you really leave me, Bonaparte?"

"I must. My place is with my men. Junot will see you safely to Milan."

"I shall be afraid without you," she said prettily.

"Nonsense! Junot is a brave soldier. You will be in excellent hands."

Josephine smiled coquettishly at Junot. "Ah yes, in excellent hands and safe hands too."

Bonaparte looked at her searchingly, kissed her, gave Junot a slap across the shoulders and said good-bye a second time.

No sooner was the carriage under way again than Josephine attempted once more to flirt with Junot. Her success was negligible. She had never found a young man so difficult, so unresponsive. 'Poor dear,' she thought, 'his loyalty to Bonaparte is really quite touching.' She sighed. At any rate she was *en route* for Milan, and even if it meant a short halt at Verona she had every hope of being there in time for the Duke of Serbelloni's ball. In addition the knowledge that she would soon be with Hyppolyte again made her feel almost gay. She looked at Junot. He was staring stolidly out of the window.

"It is naturally more interesting," she teased, "to gaze fixedly at the lake than listen to a poor woman's gossip."

"There is a boat on the lake," he said.

"Really, Colonel, a boat! Perhaps you would like to stop and wave to it!"

"A gun-boat," he added. "Moreover, a gun-boat flying the Austrian flag."

She clutched his arm with one hand, and her throat with the other. "Dear heaven!"

Junot leaned out of the window and called: "Faster, faster!" to the postilion. A little puff of smoke, rising from the gun-boat, was followed by a loud explosion. The horses reared and plunged forward again.

"Down on the floor," Junot cried. "They're aiming at us."

There was a second puff of smoke, a second explosion. To Josephine, cowering in terror on the floor of the carriage, the world went suddenly black. Out of the blackness came streaks of light. She opened her mouth to scream but before a sound could leave her lips a merciful blankness descended upon her and she knew no more.

Hours later, it seemed, she opened her eyes. She was lying on her back, looking up at the sky and Junot's voice, somewhere near, was saying over and over again: "Thank God you're safe, thank God you're safe!"

Presently she found that she could stand. She was badly shaken but no bones were broken. Both Junot and the postilion were unhurt but the horses had been killed. The gun-boat was no longer in sight. A farm cart had been brought up and stood close at hand.

She pointed a shaking finger. "Do I have to travel in that?"

It seemed that she had. Junot gathered her up in his arms and carried her to it. The postilion took his place and cracked his whip. The broken-down farm horse moved gingerly forward.

"The things I do for Bonaparte!" she cried. A terrible thought came uppermost in her mind. "Colonel Junot, my smelling-salts!"

"I searched the wreckage," he said curtly, "but they were nowhere to be found."

That, perhaps, was the cruelest blow of all.

Verona was eventually reached without further mishap, and finally Milan. At the Serbelloni palace, surrounded by the duke, Hyppolyte and a whole host of admiring males, she told the story of her adventurous journey, omitting nothing, not even the delay caused by Bonaparte's love-making.

The duke bowed low and kissed her hand.

"Madame," he said, "is the bravest woman in the world."

"My dear man," she laughed, "I simply *had* to be brave. It was only by gritting my teeth and trying my poor best to be resolute that I knew I could reach Milan in time for your ball."

She gave him her hand to kiss again, and kissing it the gallant duke murmured: "Madame is the bravest woman in the world and General Bonaparte the most romantic of lovers."

"Not the most romantic," she said with a shudder, "but without doubt the most relentless."

CHAPTER XXIV

THE DUKE OF SERBELLONI'S ball was followed by a series of *fêtes* and receptions, so that it was some time before Josephine remembered the mayor of Genoa's invitation and was able to make plans for her visit to that city. When at last it was possible to do this, she decided that her traveling party should be small. There would be her maid, Louise, and a military escort of six men—a military escort led by the indispensable Hyppolyte, who would naturally do his 'leading,' not on horseback, but sitting at her side in the carriage to amuse her with his witty conversation and his subtle compliments.

Thinking of Hyppolyte reminded her that she had not been too busy with her social engagements to use her influence in the matter of the army contracts, and already she had benefited largely in the way of commission. As she had remarked to Hyppolyte, it was something of an accomplishment to achieve so much success in combining business with pleasure.

On the eve of her departure for Genoa, Junot arrived with dispatches from Bonaparte who, after defeating the Austrians once more, was now back at Verona. Junot, full of renewed admiration for the military genius of his general, gave her a full and enthusiastic account of the three battles of Arcola. It seemed that at the first battle Bonaparte himself had led the charge against the bridge of Arcola, had led it with his wife's name on his lips.

"How touching," Josephine murmured, stifling a yawn.

The first charge had been unsuccessful. Bonaparte had been thrown from his horse into a bog and surrounded by Austrians. Everybody had cried "Save the General!" and another charge had been launched, a charge which carried the bridge.

Josephine shuddered delicately. "Poor Bonaparte, how nasty for him, being thrown into a bog."

Junot glanced at her suspiciously and went on with his story. With wearisome detail he described the second battle of Arcola, and then the third. Finally, recollecting himself, he gave Josephine a letter which for the moment he had forgotten. Josephine looked at it with slight distaste. She had received two the day before. One would have thought that what with charging bridges and getting himself out of bogs Bonaparte would have little time for letter writing.

She opened the letter, which was brief, more difficult than usual to decipher (the effects of the drenching in the bog, no doubt), and which ended: *I hope soon to be in the arms of her whom I love to madness.*

She looked up with a frown. "Colonel Junot, when does my husband expect to return to Milan?"

"Within two days, citizeness."

Within two days! Why, that would interfere with her little jaunt to Genoa!

"Is that absolutely definite?" she asked.

"Nothing is absolutely definite in time of war," Junot said.

"Ah!"

She thanked him for his news and dismissed him. Then she gave her attention to the letter again. *I hope soon to be in the arms of her whom I love to madness.* The words gave her but one picture, the picture of Bonaparte arriving like a whirlwind and shattering her—absolutely shattering her—with his tremendous and somewhat cruel energy. She came to a quick decision, rang for Louise and wrote a little note to Hyppolyte which read:

Darling, I find that I am now ready to leave for Genoa immediately.

Josephine's reception by the civic authorities of Genoa was one of the most flattering experiences of her life and amply repaid her for the discomforts of the journey. Once again she was forced to remark that in Italy she was being treated exactly as if she were a queen.

After two days in Genoa a courier arrived from Milan with a letter from Bonaparte. Her first thought was: 'Ah, I escaped in the nick of time!' Then she read the letter.

I reached Milan. I hastened to your room. I have, left everything to see you, to press you in my arms—and you were gone.

Josephine giggled. Poor lamb, he sounded quite angry!
She read on:

You fly from me when I come. You no longer think of me. Caprice caused you to marry me. Inconstancy makes you indifferent to me.

Angry, most certainly, and also sorry for himself.

The letter was naturally too priceless to keep to herself. She read it, with dramatic emphasis, to Hyppolyte, but Hyppolyte, instead of laughing, listened with an expression of seriousness clouding his face.

"Why *did* you marry him?" he asked thoughtfully.

She shrugged. "Perhaps, as he himself suggests, out of sheer caprice."

"Does that mean that you care little whether you remain married to him?"

"Are you suggesting," she teased, "that I leave him and marry you?"

Hyppolyte raised his hands in mock horror. "Heaven forbid!"

"How very ungallant of you," she pouted.

"I am much too disturbed just now," he said, "to resort to gallantry. Much too disturbed on *your* account," he stressed.

She asked him to explain himself. Laughing wryly he pointed out that here he was in Genoa with her while her husband, fuming in Milan, was becoming more impatient every day, every hour. She merely laughed. Obviously he was concerned on his own account, not hers. The *affaire*, menaced by the threat of discovery, was becoming too much for him.

"There's nothing whatever to worry about," she told him gaily. "Angry as Bonaparte might be, he nonetheless adores me. I am a divinity. He tells me so over and over again." She chuckled softly. "I should be a most inexperienced woman if I were unable to hold a man like Bonaparte."

"Time, dear lady," Hyppolyte remarked, "will answer that."

During the next few days a number of similarly worded letters arrived from Bonaparte. Josephine tossed them aside with a laugh and would never have written even one letter herself but for Hyppolyte, who nagged her into it.

"Really, Hyppolyte," she complained, "you are beginning to bore me."

She half expected Bonaparte to follow her to Genoa, but to her relief she learned that the military situation made his presence in Milan imperative.

"Thank heaven," she said, "for the military situation!"

She continued to throw herself wholeheartedly into the festivities organized for her by the city of Genoa, but presently Hyppolyte was the bearer of news which even she was wise enough to view with complete seriousness.

A friend of his who had just reached Milan from Marseille had written hastily to say that on the road he had passed a carriage bearing three members of the Bonaparte family.

"*Three* members?" Josephine asked sharply.

"Yes, dear lady, your brother-in-law, Joseph, your little sister-in-law, Paulette, and also that old ogre your mother-in-law."

"*Heaven protect me!*" Josephine whispered.

"They were undoubtedly *en route* for Milan to pay your husband a visit."

"Will they have arrived by now?"

"I should imagine so."

It was alarming news indeed. Both Madame Bonaparte and Joseph disapproved of her. Worse, they almost certainly hated her. By now, with Bonaparte to themselves, they would be poisoning his mind against her. She might have married him out of caprice, she might regard him as something of a joke, but as his wife she had become a woman of social, even political, importance and had no wish to find herself seriously estranged from him.

"Hyppolyte," she said, "I must return to Milan at once!"

*　　*　　*　　*　　*

On her arrival in Milan, Josephine was met at the Serbelloni palace by Junot. She immediately asked him two questions.

"Have the Bonapartes arrived? Is my husband still here?"

226

To each of the questions Junot coldly replied: "Yes."

"Where is he? In his study?"

"Yes, citizeness, and I must warn you that he is very busy."

She raced wildly to the room on the ground floor which Bonaparte· had turned into a study. At the door she was met by the secretary, Bourrienne. Instead of standing respectfully aside Bourrienne barred her way and said curtly:

"General Bonaparte cannot see you, citizeness."

Frantically she tried to push him away.

"He sends his apologies," Bourrienne added, "but regrets that he will be extremely busy for the rest of the day."

"But this is monstrous," she cried, "*monstrous*! What do you think I am—a serving maid to be kept waiting in an ante-room? A poor relation to be refused admittance to the great man's presence? Stand aside, Bourrienne!"

He stood aside. She grasped the handle of the door.

"Why, the door is locked! He not only refuses to see me, he locks the door in my face!"

She began to hammer violently on the panels of the door.

"Let me in, Bonaparte!" she shouted. "*Let me in!*"

"Go away, Josephine," Bonaparte's voice came from within the room.

She raised her voice still more. "How can you be so cruel! I travel from Genoa at breakneck speed! I almost kill myself with fatigue! I do that and you sit there behind a locked door like a coward! Yes, that is what you are, a coward!"

"You are growing hysterical," the voice said. "Go away."

"I shall hammer at the door till you open it!"

"I can work in the din of battle," he said, "a woman's feeble tapping is hardly likely to disturb me. If you're still there, Bourrienne, take her away. Find some smelling-salts for her and a gallon or so of lavender-water."

"Pig!" she screamed. "Beast! Ill-bred Corsican bandit!"

"And when she is sufficiently rested to control herself," Bonaparte went on calmly, "see that she pays her respects to my mother."

"Your mother!" she repeated. She turned to Bourrienne. "His mother! I have *her* to thank for this! How right I was when I suspected that she would poison his mind against me!"

"For the last time," Bonaparte said, "go away."

"Very well," she sobbed. "I'll go, oh yes, I'll go, but you'll be sorry Bonaparte, and so," she added with a very different inflection, "will that wretched mother of yours!"

Josephine made no attempt to pay her respects to Madame Bonaparte. She retired to her apartments and stayed there. Prostrate on her bed, with Louise in attendance, she gave way to real and bitter tears. Refusing all food but taking a little wine, which went instantly to her head, she made the most of her misery. After two hours of this the door was thrown open and Bonaparte walked in. She sat up in bed and gave a half-tipsy giggle at the sight of his stern, uncompromising face.

"Leave me alone with your mistress," he told Louise.

The moment Louise was out of the room Josephine flung herself into Bonaparte's arms. He pushed her roughly away.

"Bonaparte!" she cried, with a sob in her voice.

"It might interest you to know," he said, "that I have ordered the arrest of Hyppolyte Charles."

She tried to speak but her mouth remained open in complete and dumb amazement.

"I think you have broken my heart," Bonaparte added, making a tragic gesture.

"Is this some sort of horrible joke?" she forced herself to ask.

"I wish to God it were." He turned and stood with his back to her. "You have been found out, Josephine."

Keep your wits about you, she urged herself.

Still with his back to her he said: "I will give you a chance to defend yourself, but you must tell me the truth. It will be better for you in the end."

"The truth?"

He swung round. "The truth of your unfaithfulness with this man Charles."

She forced herself to laugh. "You mean to say—? You actually believe—? Oh, but this is too much! This is utterly ridiculous!"

"Your excellent acting doesn't deceive me, Josephine. What a fool I've been! What a blind fool!"

"But Bonaparte——!"

"Silence, madame! I have a full record of your deceit. You began your *affaire* with Charles in Paris, a few days after I left for Italy, a few days after we were married!"

"This is intolerable, Bonaparte!" She was forcing herself to sound angry and indignant, and was amazed at her own success. "Some malicious person has evidently gossiped in my absence and you immediately accuse me of something too infamous for words!"

"Yes indeed, too infamous for words!"

"I knew Hyppolyte Charles in Paris," she admitted. "I knew him—" (a judicious lie might help!)—"I knew him even before I knew you. I saw him many times at public functions after you left. I make no attempt to deny it. Hyppolyte Charles is a very witty man. He amused me immensely when I was feeling sad and lonely."

228

"So immensely that when you were finally obliged to join me he left Paris with you."

"That was the merest coincidence."

"Oh, you did your best to disguise your plans. You persuaded Barras to appoint him aide-de-camp to Leclerc. A very subtle way of gaining your desire. Permit me to compliment you on your shrewdness."

She made a weary, hopeless gesture. "I see there is a conspiracy afoot to ruin our marriage."

She saw doubt reflected in his eyes for a moment, but before she could seize on it he brushed it aside quickly.

"In addition," he said, "you have been using your influence to gain army contracts for Charles. Do you deny that also?"

"Why should I?" she was wise enough to say. "I always like to help my friends."

"Since you admit that, the rest may be taken for granted!"

She shook her head sadly. "And I believed you to be a just man, Bonaparte, a *fair* man."

There was a pause.

"Tell me one thing," she begged. "Who is responsible for turning you against me?"

"That is beside the point."

"It is very much to the point! Is it your mother? Your wretched brother, Joseph? Your sister, Paulette?"

"If you must know, Joseph performed the unpleasant duty of making known to me what was already known to everybody in Milan."

"Joseph!" she breathed. "Thank you, Bonaparte! That is all I wanted to know." She had begun to think that it was time to faint, but she changed her mind and drew herself up proudly. "Please leave me, Bonaparte, but first let me tell you this: within a week I shall have shown you just how false your brother's accusations are!"

It was a rash thing to say; she knew that well enough, but by some means, fair or foul, she intended to prove that black was white. She was determined to get the better of Joseph, determined to get the better of the whole Bonaparte brood.

Had she but known it, the private war, the war which was to last for many years between Josephine and her relatives-in-law, was entering its first phase. . . .

$$* \quad * \quad * \quad * \quad *$$

During the first three days of her return to Milan, Josephine isolated herself in her apartments at the palace. Making an outwardly dignified stand against the whole world she refused to see not only her husband but also the other three members of his family. Her only contact with the outside world was Louise and through her she learned that Hyppolyte had indeed been arrested. However, when she also learned that, like her, he had denied everything except the matter of the army contracts, she contrived to remain undismayed.

At first she was inclined to believe that Joseph Bonaparte had established his charge on nothing more substantial than gossip, but in the end she saw that he must have received some definite information to be able to state so boldly that she had persuaded Barras to appoint Hyppolyte aide-de-camp to Leclerc.

Could Barras be at the back of her troubles? He was quite capable of such a thing, certainly, but Joseph, she knew, had not been in communication with him since she had left Paris. Leclerc himself? Surely not. She had flirted with him on more than one occasion and had always found him charming and friendly. Murat, perhaps? She had flirted with him too on more than one occasion, and he also had always been charming and friendly. Barras, Leclerc, Murat—it must be one of them.

There was only one thing to do, and that was make a few discreet inquiries. She assumed that Joseph had gained his information since his arrival in Milan with his mother and sister. Could Paulette be concerned in the matter as well as Joseph? She recalled her first impression of the spoiled and wilful Paulette and her conclusion that the girl would need watching. 'I shall begin my inquiries with Paulette,' she decided. Accordingly she took Louise more fully into her confidence, tempted her with the promise of a small diamond bracelet and sat back with as much patience as possible to await results.

A day later Louise reported that Paulette Bonaparte and Citizen General Murat were behaving in a suspicious manner.

"Suspicious?" Josephine questioned. "You mean——?"

"I mean, citizeness, that the child—for that is all she is, is obviously weaving a spell of fascination about the Citizen General, who appears to be most susceptible."

"Ah! And how long has this been going on?"

"As far as I can gather, since the day of her arrival in Milan."

Josephine smiled happily. "I may be wrong, Louise, but I feel sure that you have found out exactly what I wanted to know."

"And the bracelet, citizeness?"

"If I am not wrong the bracelet will be yours in the very near future. In the meantime, find General Murat for me and tell him that I would like to see him immediately."

Josephine had been lying in bed. She rose quickly, selected her most daring *négligé* and seated herself before the mirror in her boudoir. When Murat was shown in by Louise she half turned to smile at him and with a languid gesture indicated a chair.

"Please sit down, Murat."

He sat and looked at her with frank and evident appreciation. This was noted by Josephine, noted with complete satisfaction. He was no more in love with the vapid, ill-bred Paulette than she herself was in love with Bonaparte, and when she had finished with him he would be well aware of the fact.

"Murat," she said, "I want you to help me."

He made her a gallant little bow. "Nothing would give me greater pleasure, citizeness."

His look of appreciation had increased. He was leaning forward. He was even breathing a little heavily. (Disgusting, the way suddenly aroused passion did that to even the handsomest man!) A move from her and he would have her in his arms in a moment. Most certainly a daring *négligé*!

"I have always imagined," she said, "that you, above all my husband's comrades-in-arms, are the one he can call his friend."

Murat looked puzzled and remarked lightly that he was certainly deeply attached to Bonaparte.

"Too deeply attached," Josephine smiled, "to be a mere place-seeker, like so many who surround him."

"I hope so, citizeness."

"You would never do anything to hurt him. I feel sure of that."

"But of course not!"

"Nor anything that would hurt me, his wife, I trust!"

"My respect for you, citizeness, is second only to my respect for Bonaparte."

She smiled sweetly. "I knew I wasn't mistaken in you, Murat."

"Has something happened?" he asked. "Has my loyalty been called into question?"

She shook her head. "Your loyalty has not been called into question, but I suspect that something you have done, unwittingly and in all innocence, has hurt not only me but Bonaparte."

Murat sprang to his feet. "Citizeness!"

"Sit down, Murat. I only said that I *suspect*, not that I know for certain."

He sat again and in his agitation brought his chair closer. Turning from the mirror she brought her own chair closer and leaned earnestly forward so that the *négligé*, which had never been designed to conceal, fell open still more at the neck.

"Have patience," she said, "with my inability to express myself clearly. Remember, I said that I need your help."

He cleared his throat but there was a hoarseness in his voice when he murmured, "Tell me what is troubling you."

She sighed tremulously. "To begin at the beginning, perhaps you know that there has been considerable gossip concerning me and Hyppolyte Charles."

She saw that he did.

"Naturally," she went on, with another sigh, "people will always gossip." She smiled disarmingly. "I gossip myself. Unfortunately, in this case, somebody has taken the story, with gross exaggerations, to Bonaparte, and he is so angry that—" (a little lie would help at this stage)—"that he threatens to divorce me."

"Divorce you!" Murat echoed. He reached out and took her hands in his. "My dear, this is terrible."

"I admit," she said frankly, "that I have been a little indiscreet in my association with Hyppolyte, but there is nothing, absolutely nothing, between us. I need hardly assure you of that, need I, Murat?"

His grip on her hands tightened. "Of course not, citeziness."

"The really unfortunate part of this unhappy business," she went on, "is that Bonaparte has been given certain facts which, on the surface, appear compromising. Please don't take offence at what I am about to say, but I have reason to believe that those facts have come from Leclerc to you and from you to somebody else."

His eyes gave nothing away, but when he echoed: "From me to somebody else?" she recognized an uneasiness in his voice.

"And that somebody else," she added, "is Paulette Bonaparte."

He let her hands fall and stood up again. There was a little silence. Josephine rose also. Standing thus they were less than a pace apart.

"Is it possible," she asked softly, "that I have made a horrible mistake?"

He looked down at her. His breath was warm on her face.

"You've made no mistake," he said.

She put her hands lightly on his shoulders. "My poor Murat, to think that a man of your experience could be used so shamelessly by an impudent child like Paulette!"

His arms came round her. They stood for a moment in a half embrace.

"I quite see," she said, "that Paulette gave you no peace until you told her all you knew. Or rather, all you *thought* you knew." She let her head drop to his shoulder with a little sob. "Oh, Murat, how glad I am that I sent for you. But even so, will it be possible to right the wrong already done?"

He held her closer.

"We must make it possible," he whispered.

Absentmindedly she permitted him to kiss her, permitted him even to take liberties with the ridiculous inadequacy of the *négligé*. Presently she freed herself gently.

"I imagine," she said thoughtfully, "that Leclerc told you that Barras was responsible for Hyppolyte's being appointed his aide-de-camp."

Murat nodded.

"And also that Barras did it to please me?"

Murat nodded again.

"Barras," she said, "has reason to hate me and is jealous of Bonaparte. Barras was lying. You see that, surely!"

"But of course, you tantalizing woman!"

Josephine laughed softly. Murat might be fascinated by silly virgins of sixteen (Paulette *was* a virgin of course?), but his real preference lay in the direction of women of experience such as herself.

"Having wormed the story out of you," she went on, "Paulette repeated it to her brother, Joseph, who has hated and disapproved of me from the first, and Joseph, in his turn, carried it to Bonaparte."

Another interlude, attended by further by-play with the *négligé*, followed.

"You want me to contradict the story," Murat said at last.

"If you would, Murat, but discreetly, of course. You might tell Bonaparte that you feel concerned at the story going about Milan of my supposed unfaithfulness with Hyppolyte, and that you know it to be absolutely untrue."

"That I know it to be absolutely untrue," he repeated, with a cynical laugh.

"You rogue," she said, and precipitated a third interlude.

"I will also add," Murat volunteered, "that Barras, out of enviousness and jealousy, has been trying to make trouble between you and Bonaparte."

"Thank you," she said warmly, "thank you from the bottom of my heart."

There was a pause. With Josephine in his arms once more Murat whispered hoarsely: "And my full reward for the little fairy story I am about to tell?"

"That," she assured him, "will come later."

* * * * *

Josephine had talked to Murat in the late afternoon. In the early evening Louise brought her a short note from Bonaparte.

It seems, she read, *that I have misjudged you. If you can find it in your heart to see me, I would like to talk to you and ask your forgiveness.*

With a chuckle of satisfaction she said: "Louise, go down and tell the Citizen General that I will see him at once."

When Bonaparte came he was a trifle pompous and very uncomfortable.

"Two members of my family," he said briefly, "have been trying to make trouble between us. Barras also appears to have had the same intention. I was foolish enough to listen to gossip. In my anger I misjudged you. Remember that I have a vivid imagination, a jealous nature and a quick temper, and try to forgive me."

Josephine smiled bravely and forced the tears to her eyes.

"I will try, Bonaparte, but it won't be altogether easy."

"Thank you. There is one other matter. The army contracts you secured for Charles, that was wrong of you. Please refrain from actions like that in the future."

"Whatever you say, Bonaparte. My sin, at worst, was merely a generous impulse. What of Hyppolyte? He will be released, of course?"

"Naturally, but he will be sent straight back to Paris."

There was little more to be said. Before Bonaparte left her, Josephine promised to pay her long-delayed respects to his mother. When he had gone she recalled that Murat's name had not been mentioned, and that, all things considered, was no doubt just as well.

She thought of the Bonaparte family, of Joseph and Paulette in particular. How they must hate her, and how furious they must be at the turn of events! She chuckled at the thought. It was delightful to have got the better of the Bonaparte brood at the first encounter. Of course there would doubtless be more encounters. After all, they were Corsicans! She shuddered at the name. Vindictive people, Corsicans. Vendettas, and distressing things of that sort.

'Dear me,' she thought, 'they will probably do their best to make things difficult for me.'

Later that same evening Bonaparte came to her again. His embarrassment at having been proved in the wrong was less pronounced.

"I shall make amends," he said, "I was never the man to act ungenerously. I have it in my power to see that you receive honors never yet bestowed upon a general's wife. For the last hour I have been in torment. *What if she never forgives me?*—that has been the theme of my tortured thoughts."

"My poor Bonaparte."

"You pity me? You are both compassionate and magnanimous?"

"What am I," she said, with a sob in her voice, "but just a— woman?"

"Then you do forgive me!"

"From the bottom of my heart."

"You will never regret this," he said emotionally, "never!"

She flung herself into his arms and the reunion was complete. Graciously, she permitted him to remain with her for the rest of the night. When at last he fell asleep she remained awake and thoughtful, staring into the darkness. His words, *I have it in my power to see that you receive honors never yet bestowed upon a general's wife,* had impressed her. The conqueror of Italy had gone far since his early days in Paris and would undoubtedly go farther. As his wife she had shared much of his glory, and in the future there would be much more glory in which to share. Whatever she might feel in her heart for Bonaparte she decided that it would be diplomatic to show him at least a semblance of respect. Boring as it might be at times, it would pay, undoubtedly it would pay.

Having made this resolution she closed her eyes and went happily to sleep.

CHAPTER XXV

FOLLOWING THE RETURN of Hyppolyte Charles to Paris, Josephine behaved herself with a studied propriety. She fulfilled her obligation, certainly, in respect of Murat's 'full reward,' but she made it perfectly clear that under the ever-watchful eyes of the Bonaparte family too much repetition would be risky. In any case, military duties soon took Murat away from Milan, thus removing what might have become an embarrassing temptation.

Meanwhile the war, interesting her only in the abstract, went steadily forward to its spectacular climax. Bonaparte, haughtily refusing to wait for instructions from the Directory, dictated the Treaty of Campo-Formio and Josephine's little court, as her circle of friends had come to be called, moved from Milan to Montebello. From here, much to her relief, Bonaparte went alone to Rastadt, where a congress was to be held, and her return journey to Paris was undertaken without him.

At Vincennes, after a leisurely journey from Italy, during which she, General Bonaparte's wife, had been cheered at every halt, she was met by Barras, Tallien and Teresia.

"Why, Barras," she said, "you make me feel as if I had suddenly become a woman of considerable importance."

"And so you have, my dear," he said, his teeth bared in a smile but his eyes inscrutable.

Tallien and Teresia smiled too, but not with their eyes. Quite clearly, though they were giving her a state welcome, they were filled with a personal resentment that amounted almost to hatred. She pursed her lips shrewdly. Bonaparte's victories had made him a hero. To the people he had become the savior of their country and they loved him. Therefore the Directory, though its members, all five of them, feared his popularity, was obliged in public to pretend a similar love.

The crowd that had gathered at Vincennes broke into cheering again.

"Our Lady of Victories!" a man cried, and his cry was taken up. Josephine turned graciously to Teresia.

"I may be wrong," she said sweetly, "but it almost seems as if I am about to take your place as the uncrowned queen of Paris."

"Yes, doesn't it," Teresia said softly, but she showed her teeth like a mongrel dog at bay.

From Vincennes, Josephine traveled to Paris in Barras's open carriage. She sat next to Barras and faced Teresia and Tallien. The Champs-Élysées was crammed with people, people who cheered wildly, people who called Bonaparte's name over and over again, then her own.

"Dear me," she said, as if gravely shocked, "Barras and Tallien seem to have been completely forgotten."

"Forgotten or not," Teresia snapped, "Barras and Tallien are still the rulers of France!"

The crowd was thickest at the rue Chantereine, or rather, the rue Victoire, as it had been renamed in honor of Bonaparte's campaign.

"One thing seems clear," Josephine said, in bidding Barras, Teresia and Tallien good-bye, "my credit with the tradespeople will now be unlimited."

Bonaparte's arrival in Paris followed quickly on her own and the warmth of the public welcome was even more spectacular. Barras, while the watching crowd cheered lustily, embraced him with apparent enthusiasm, kissed him on both cheeks and looked (as Josephine noticed at close quarters) as if he would gladly murder him.

When husband and wife finally found themselves alone together at the rue Victoire, Josephine said: "Well, Bonaparte, and what now?"

"Ah yes," he murmured, his eyes holding a dreamy look, "that is the question."

"You have an answer to it, of course?"

"Of course. For the time being I shall settle quietly here and prepare myself to watch and wait. In the meantime I would like very much to know what is in the minds of Barras and his fellow directors."

"Then why not let me find out for you?"

He looked at her thoughtfully. "You? But how?"

"Simply by renewing my old friendship with Barras."

She saw that the suggestion both attracted and repelled him.

"I have no wish," he said, "for you to associate with such people as Barras, Tallien and Tallien's wife, but—" he paused, frowned, looked at Josephine doubtfully and finally came to a decision. "Very well, since the only thing of real importance is the end, not the means, I give you permission to cultivate Barras again."

With that, Josephine began to entertain on a modest scale at the rue Victoire—modest only because Bonaparte insisted on modesty. Choosing her guests she gave her first party 'to celebrate our return.' Among the guests were Tallien, Teresia and Barras—Barras for whom the party had in reality been given. Though he was amiable enough Josephine was well aware of the resentment behind the mocking light in his eyes and wondered if he was thinking of his earlier opinion of Bonaparte—*A natural Spartan and therefore something of a simpleton. . . . A simple soldier ready and eager to obey orders.* Hardly a simpleton, surely, when he had conquered Italy, cowed Austria and matched his wits against the best diplomatic brains of Europe!

During the course of the evening Josephine made it possible to talk alone with Barras. He complimented her on her dress ("In better taste than Teresia's, my dear"), remarked on her poise ("Quite gracious but by no means haughty"), and spoke lightly of her social triumphs in Italy.

"But tell me about your marriage," he said. "You and Bonaparte had been man and wife only two days when he left you in Paris. Is he agreeable to live with?"

She smiled. "The most agreeable man in the world."

"How very loyal of you!" he mocked. "And speaking of loyalty, we heard in Paris that you had been caught in the lamentable act of unfaithfulness. There was quite a lot of talk here, I assure you."

"Paris being Paris there must have been."

"There was nothing in the gossip, of course?"

"Nothing, Barras."

Their eyes met and both were obliged to laugh. For a moment the old understanding was apparent between them.

"Naturally," he said, "you are no more in love with Bonaparte now than on the day you married him."

"Ah, but I have learned to respect him."

"You have? If you said that you had learned to respect his *achievements* I might be more inclined to believe you."

"Perhaps that is what I really mean," she said candidly.

He smiled broadly. "I once flattered myself that you were in love with me. May I still flatter myself that you are, at least a *little*?"

She was instantly on her guard. *Watch him!* she told herself.

"Unless I'm very much mistaken," she said, "you want me to do something for you."

He laughed lightly. "What a shrewd woman you are."

"Does it by any chance concern Bonaparte?"

"Naturally." He looked at her thoughtfully, hesitated, then appeared to come to a deliberate decision. "I'll be frank with you, my dear. The man I was at such pains to make you marry has become something of a problem. When I secured him the command of the Army of Italy I never dreamed that it would lead him to the extraordinary position he holds today."

"You begin to regard him as a political embarrassment, perhaps?"

"Yes." A look of irritation flashed across his face. "His success has fired the imagination of the people—fired it *damnably*. Should his views differ from mine he could, if he chose, wield a power too dangerous to contemplate."

He paused. Waiting for him to continue she reflected that in his resentment he had betrayed himself pitifully, and that behind the resentment was fear.

"Bonaparte is a soldier, not a politician," she said lightly.

"He *was* a soldier, but now—" He broke off. "Josephine," he said earnestly, "should this husband of yours show a disinclination to fall in with my plans, whether they be military or political, it will be your business to use your influence with him. Your business, you understand, as a good friend of the Directory."

"That sounds remarkably like a threat, Barras."

"You may regard it as such if you wish!"

No more was said, and during the rest of the evening Barras, making himself agreeable to everybody, paid especial attention to Bonaparte. When the last guest had departed Josephine reported Barras's conversation to her husband. Not in full, of course: to have included the more personal aspects would have been stupid.

"One thing is clear," she said. "Barras suspects that your ambitions are now political as well as military."

"A child would suspect that," he laughed. He rubbed his hands together, a sure sign that he was pleased with himself. "The events of the next few weeks," he said, "should prove most interesting."

* * * * *

"Talleyrand?" Bonaparte said, in response to a remark Barras had made. "Up to now I've had few dealings with him."

"Ah, but if the man succeeds in getting his way you'll have many with him."

"Indeed?"

Barras was entertaining Bonaparte and Josephine at dinner. There were no other guests. The invitation, Josephine knew, had been issued with a purpose: Barras, at last, was about to reveal his hand. She had seen him several times since the night of her party at the rue Victoire, but had learned nothing, save the obvious fact that his irritation was increasing. The cry of a large section of the Army— "Down with the Directory, put General Bonaparte at the head of affairs!"—had naturally reached his ears. Oh yes, he was about to reveal his hand; that was perfectly clear.

"Having sold his king and his God," Barras was saying, "Talleyrand, unless I misjudge him sadly, is now about to sell the Directory."

"To whom?" Bonaparte asked.

"To the Citizen General Bonaparte, of course."

"To me, Barras? But why to me?"

"Talleyrand, having become our foreign minister, has every intention of increasing his power still further. In his own opinion he is not a leader but a maker of leaders. A king-maker, for want of a better word."

"Surely," Josephine laughed, "Talleyrand has no wish to make a king of Bonaparte!"

"I use the word 'king' figuratively, my dear. Talleyrand has heard the cry of a handful of your husband's soldiers, whose loyal enthusiasm, by the by, has got the better of their sanity, and it has given him something to think about."

"Talleyrand," Bonaparte said brusquely, "will have to learn that I'm a soldier, not a politician."

"Nevertheless he is determined to make himself indispensable to you, and you to him. Indeed, I happen to know that he is planning to win your friendship, or at least your initial interest, by giving a great public reception in your honor."

Josephine saw Bonaparte raise his eyebrows as if in surprise, but he had already heard—she herself had told him—that such a move was being planned by Talleyrand. His great Paris house, the Hotel Gallifet, was being stripped and redecorated—a fabulous amount was being spent on that alone. A large orchestra had already been engaged and preparations were being made for four thousand guests, who would take supper at midnight while a special guard of soldiers stood about the tables.

"Talleyrand," Bonaparte said, "should I know that I am not to be won by public receptions, great or small."

"Precisely, my dear Bonaparte. That is why I myself am content to honor you with nothing more imposing than a humble little dinner party."

"Honor me? Why should you honor me, Barras? Whatever my achievements, I am merely a soldier who takes his orders from the Directory."

Barras made a gesture which seemed to say: *Enough of this fencing,* and said: "A soldier who has, I trust, greater achievements before him in the very near future."

The way he stressed 'in the very near future' satisfied Josephine that the purpose of the 'humble little dinner party' was about to be made clear at last.

"You have plans for me then?" Bonaparte asked.

Barras nodded. "New plans, and a new command. Henceforth you will be known as the Commander of the Army, not of Italy but of—England."

"Then the rumors of a coming invasion of England are more or less correct."

"Indeed they are."

"The invasion of England is no light matter, Barras. Much as I favor it I think we ought to patch up our quarrel with that country until we are fully prepared to cross the English Channel."

"We are fully prepared now, Bonaparte."

Bonaparte rose. "I beg to differ."

Barras smiled almost gleefully and rose too. "We thought you might, and in deference to your military experience we wish you to take the precaution of thoroughly investigating the project. You will begin by making a survey of the coastline nearest to England."

"When do you want Bonaparte to leave Paris?" Josephine asked.

"Immediately, my dear."

"Not before Talleyrand's reception, surely!"

Barras smiled. "Ah yes, Talleyrand's reception." He turned to Bonaparte. "Well, what do you say, General? Is it duty first, or pleasure?"

"I think," Bonaparte said smoothly, "that duty and pleasure, as you call it, can be made to fit in nicely together. I shall leave Paris tomorrow and slip back for a day or so at the time of the reception. You have no objection to that, of course?"

Barras's face had become a mask.

"I—!" He checked what was obviously a hasty rejoinder and said quietly: "Why no, my dear Bonaparte, none at all."

✳   ✳   ✳   ✳   ✳

During the first week of Bonaparte's absence at the coast Josephine brought the children from their respective schools and took them for a short visit to Aunt Marie at Fontainebleau. Hortense and Eugène enjoyed this but on the whole Josephine was glad to return to Paris where she learned that the date of Talleyrand's reception had been officially announced. Knowledge of this was followed by a visit from Barras. He came to the point at once.

"Josephine, you remember that I said I would want you to use your influence with Bonaparte if he refused to fall in with my plans?"

"I remember. What of it?"

"The time has now come for you to act. Talleyrand's reception must fall through."

She had expected this, of course.

"But why come to me?" she asked curiously. "What can I do about it?"

"You can join Bonaparte at the coast and be so sweet to him that he will forget the reception."

"Oh come, Barras," she laughed. "You know what Bonaparte is like when his mind is made up."

"After all this time you should be capable of making up his mind for him when you want to."

She sighed. "I have barely recovered from the journey from Italy. Another journey now, however short, would kill me."

"Ah, I understand you!" Barras was angry and made no attempt to hide it. "You refuse to help me!"

"No, no, my friend, I merely refuse to kill myself by undertaking another journey."

"Bah, do you think me a fool? You make it clear whose side you are on!" His rage was almost pitiful. "Bonaparte!" he cried—"I made him and I can break him. Remember that, my dear, I can break him and you with him!" He turned to the door. "You shall hear more from me, much more, I assure you!"

When Bonaparte returned for Talleyrand's reception, which was considered one of the most elaborate and successful Paris had seen for many months, he also gave the Directory a full report on his survey of the coast. He pointed out that in attempting an invasion of England it was essential to consider the possibility of the French being thrown back and invaded themselves, in which case, in his opinion, the French coastal fortifications would be inadequate. He also pointed out that a considerable amount would have to be spent on improving French shipping facilities.

"In short, gentlemen," he said, "I advise against an immediate invasion of England. At a later date, when we are fully prepared, there will be no one more willing and eager to lead an army to London, but in the meantime——"

"Yes, General," Barras said, "in the meantime——?"

"I will have no hand in a premature attempt."

"And should the Directory decide that it is not premature?"

"Should the Directory be foolish enough to do that," Bonaparte said, "a new commander of the Army of England will have to be found."

Presented by this ultimatum, which deeply impressed the other members of the Directory, Barras was obliged to forget the projected invasion. To force Bonaparte to resign, to follow up the resignation by appointing a new commander, would, instead of solving the problem of Bonaparte, intensify it by keeping him inactive, and therefore dangerous, in Paris.

Following this first crossing of swords with Barras, Bonaparte decided that for the present he would return to civilian life. He took up a studious life, went out rarely and from time to time prowled (as Josephine put it) like a lion in her *salon* and frightened all the ladies. As for politics, his interest in that, deep as it was, appeared on the surface to be superficial.

When Josephine told him what Barras had said about having made him and being able to break him, he laughed scornfully.

"Having made me! Bah, all he did was appoint me commander of the Army of Italy. It was I, not Barras, who conquered Italy. It was I, not Barras, who brought the Austrians to their knees. It was I, not Barras, who dictated the Treaty of Campo-Formio. I made myself and if Barras imagines that he can break me now I should like to see him try!"

The first hint that Barras was planning a new move came when he invited Bonaparte and Josephine to a second dinner party. His chief topic of conversation was the coming anniversary of the execution of Louis the Sixteenth.

"The Directory," Barras told Bonaparte, "has decided that this year you shall take the place of honor at the public celebrations."

"The place of honor? In God's name, Barras, what will the Directory decide next?"

Having discussed this anniversary earlier with Bonaparte, Josephine knew what was in his mind. The most important anniversary of the Republican calendar, it was formerly celebrated in Paris with wild enthusiasm, but of late it had grown unpopular with the people who, for the most part, preferred not to be reminded of the Revolution. As Bonaparte had said, if the members of the Directory were forced to take the lead in the celebrations the action might throw much discredit upon them. How shrewd of Barras to give Bonaparte the place of honor, to make sure that if discredit was thrown upon anybody it would be thrown upon Bonaparte!

"Oh come," Barras was saying, "we thought it would be a nice gesture to make and one which would meet with great public approbation."

Bonaparte smiled amiably. "How very thoughtful of you, Barras. However, I regret that I find it impossible to accept the place of honor."

"Preparations have already been made," Barras objected. "Our decision was announced this afternoon. By tomorrow all Paris will know that you are taking the place of honor."

"Then on the day itself all Paris is going to be disappointed!"

Barras began to show signs of anger. "An order has been issued," he said. "Kindly understand that you are not requested but *ordered* to appear at the festival." With that he laughed apologetically. "But come, I invite you to dinner and am rude enough to discuss a matter which should be reserved for a meeting of the Directory." He offered his arm to Josephine. "Come, my dear, dinner, I believe, is served."

There was naturally no meeting of the Directory to discuss Bonaparte's threatened disobedience, but on the eve of the anniversary a message came from Barras suggesting, in the friendliest language, that Bonaparte should reconsider what could only have been a hasty decision. With a chuckle, and to Josephine's surprise, Bonaparte sent a reply to the effect that he had already reconsidered his decision and would appear at the festival. When Josephine protested he merely told her, with a secret smile, to wait and see just what he had up his sleeve.

The celebrations were apathetic and there was very little cheering. The Parisians, unable to resist the appeal of a public gathering, crowded into the streets and squares, but what little enthusiasm they betrayed was severely restrained.

Driving in a private carriage with Josephine, and dressed in civilian clothes, Bonaparte made his appearance unnoticed at first by the people. Realizing by now what was in his mind Josephine was not surprised when he refrained from taking his place with the other directors. Presently somebody cried "Bonaparte!" The cry was taken up. With seeming reluctance he showed himself and beckoned to Josephine to do likewise. Wild cheering greeted him, during which the name "Josephine!" was called as frequently as "Bonaparte". Finally, when the anniversary had been turned into a *fête* in his own honor, he nodded to the postilion and he and Josephine drove away.

"And that," he remarked cheerfully, "is that."

$$* \quad * \quad * \quad * \quad *$$

Events moved slowly until the early spring of 1798, when talk of an invasion of England gave place to talk of an invasion of Egypt. It became generally understood in Paris that France, unable at the moment to strike at the heart of England, could seriously embarrass that country by striking at her elsewhere. General Bonaparte, everybody said, had long been of the opinion that France should seize Malta and invade and completely occupy Egypt, after which it would be a simple matter to deal with the rich prize of India. And General Bonaparte, of course, was right.

Bonaparte, as Josephine knew, had indeed spoken frequently in this strain, but she never guessed that his words would be turned into a weapon against him by Barras.

"We have," said Barras, at a meeting of the Directory, "the already well-equipped Army of England idle in our military camps. We propose, therefore, to rename it the Army of the East and give it something to do. The English are expecting an invasion. Let them continue to expect it. Their surprise will be all the greater when we strike at Egypt. Our concentration of shipping at Toulon will merely give them the impression that we intend to transport more men by sea to Boulogne. However, full details will be discussed later. The important business of the moment is this: General Bonaparte has been unanimously appointed to the command of the Army of the East and will leave for Malta and Egypt at the earliest possible moment."

Barras was quite unable to hide his delight at the cleverness of his latest move, but Bonaparte, to Josephine's dismay, remained completely unmoved and even a little amused.

"To accept the appointment," Josephine said, "will be playing right into the wily fox's hands."

"You think so? It will remove me, a political embarrassment, from

Paris, but when I return the conqueror of Egypt I shall be stronger than ever."

"But what if you fail to conquer Egypt?"

"Failure is not a habit of mine!"

"I know, Bonaparte, but why not remain in Paris and conquer the Directory before leaving to conquer Egypt? Besides, Barras has little faith in this Egyptian venture. He expects you to fail. He thinks he is sending you to your death."

"Undoubtedly, but a year from now I shall be back and in a strong enough position to deal with Barras and his precious Directory once and for all."

Josephine tried to argue further but Bonaparte refused to listen. He told her that his mind was made up, that nothing would change it, and he warned her to prepare herself for a hurried departure.

She looked at him in amazement. "Are you proposing to take me with you?"

"Naturally."

Panic seized her. Egypt was so far away. It would mean a journey by sea, a journey menaced continually by English warships. The danger she had faced in Italy would be nothing to the danger she would be forced to face during a voyage across the Mediterranean.

"I have good reason for wishing to take you with me," Bonaparte was saying playfully. "I want to keep an eye on you, and all the young men who wish to flirt with you. If I leave you alone in Paris you will have a dozen lovers within a week."

She knew what was in his mind. He was thinking of Hyppolyte Charles who was at large in Paris.

"Really, Bonaparte," she protested weakly.

"So to Egypt you shall come, my love, and remain a faithful wife."

She pouted. "I must say you always choose the wrong time to make your jokes. Take me to Egypt by all means—if you want to bury me there."

"Oh, I would never do that." He pinched her chin. "If you die in Egypt I shall have you embalmed and brought home for burial."

It was impossible to argue with him, she saw that clearly, but she was determined that she would find a way of remaining in Paris. However, when the date of departure was settled her ingenuity had failed her and she found herself *en route* for Toulon with Bonaparte and Eugene who, realizing the ambition of his life, had now been made his stepfather's aide-de-camp.

Fortunately Josephine and Bonaparte had a carriage to themselves during the greater part of the journey to Toulon. Fortunately that is, since an idea, a veritable last hope, came to her almost as soon as the carriage had left Paris.

"Bonaparte," she said, nerving herself to lie as convincingly as she could, "did I tell you that I went to see a new doctor last week?"

"Really," he said, barely interested.

"You're not in the least concerned about my health," she complained. "I do believe you're the most heartless man in the world."

For a moment he gave her his undivided attention and chuckled. "One moment, Josephine! This new doctor, if I'm not very much mistaken, warned you solemnly that you were in no fit condition to travel——"

"Bonaparte——!"

"He further warned you that sea travel more than any other sort of travel would kill you. He even declared that if you ventured as far as Egypt he would not be responsible for your safety."

She drew herself up with dignity. "You are quite wrong, Bonaparte."

"Then he can hardly have earned his fee."

"Joke if you must, but I went to see him for a very special reason, a reason that should interest you and your family very much."

He looked at her oddly. "My heavens, Josephine, do you mean that you are going to have a child at last?"

"Well—well no."

"Bah! To raise a man's hopes and then——!"

She interrupted him quietly. "Please listen to me, Bonaparte. I went to this new doctor because I was so distressed at not being able to grant you your dearest wish. I went in the hope that he would be able to suggest a course of treatment."

Bonaparte leaned eagerly forward. "Go on, go on! What did he say?"

"I told him that I was on the point of making a sea voyage——"

Bonaparte made an impatient gesture. "Bah! We are back to the same thing. He said a sea voyage would be the worst thing in the world for you."

"On the contrary, he said that a sea voyage would do me good. It would restore my impaired health but naturally it would never guarantee that—" she hesitated and looked down.

"I appreciate your delicacy," Bonaparte said, "but please continue!"

"There is little more to tell you, except that he suggested a definite course of treatment for a woman who, like myself, has had children in her early life, her *very* early life, and is unable to have more a number of years later."

"Well?"

"He said that he had cured a similar case a few months ago by

sending—" her nerve failed her and she avoided Bonaparte's eyes—
"by sending the patient to Plombiéres."

"Why to Plombiéres?"

"It seems that there are some perfectly nauseating waters there,
mineral waters which you take baths in and drink. That is what I
should have to do if I went to Plombiéres, hideous as it sounds.
I never," she added plaintively, "liked the taste of mineral water."

She ventured a look at him. His face was convulsed with excitement. There was even the ridiculous light of hope in his eyes.

"I trust," he said, "that for my sake you are willing to try anything, anywhere!"

"Well yes," she conceded, "naturally I am willing to try anything,
anywhere, for your sake."

There was a pause. She waited in a fever of anxiety for him to
make up his mind. At last he said:

"Very well, you shall proceed to Plombiéres as soon as I have
left for Egypt."

Her heart almost missed a beat.

"As soon as you have left for Egypt?" she whispered.

"Yes. You will remain in France. You will go to Plombiéres and
take a course of the waters. Later I shall send for you to join me.
Plombiéres first, you understand, and then Egypt; and by heavens,
if that doctor of yours has made a fool of me I shall have him
hounded out of Paris!"

She hid her delight in a tremulous little sigh. It had been easy—
easy! But what a mercy Bonaparte had never thought of asking the
name of her mythical new doctor! And as for going from Plombiéres
to Egypt, well, time alone would tell, but she had a shrewd idea
that it would be Paris after Plombiéres, not Egypt.

CHAPTER XXVI

THERE ARE TWO THINGS I
wish to discuss with you," Bonaparte said, during the afternoon
of their arrival in Toulon. "The first is the political situation in Paris.
If by any chance events delay you in France and you return to Paris
before following me to Egypt, you will join my brother Joseph in
keeping a close watch on Barras and his friends."

Josephine scowled at the mention of Joseph.

"I should be able to watch Barras easily enough without the need
to ally myself with your wretched brother," she objected.

"Perhaps," he admitted, with an irritating smile, "but while you watch Barras I intend Joseph to watch you."

"Really," she protested, "anybody would think me a child!"

"In many ways, my love, you are."

She knew, of course, that he was still thinking about Hyppolyte and tried not to smile. As if Joseph, however watchful he might be, could keep her from seeing Hyppolyte if she wanted to see him!

"You mentioned two things, Bonaparte. What is the other?"

He looked thoughtfully into space. "It will not be long before the treasures of Egypt begin to reach Paris in a steady stream. We shall therefore need a larger house if we are to make full use of our own share."

She was all attention. "You actually intend to buy a larger house?"

"Yes, but not in Paris. Before we left for Toulon I went to inspect a château near Reuil, a château called Malmaison. I was taken with the place at once and made the owner an offer."

"And you never told me!"

"I was keeping it as a surprise. I offered the man two hundred and fifty thousand francs, but since I happen to be General Bonaparte he refused to sell for that price."

"I begin to understand. You want me to negotiate with him."

"Yes, but remember, my limit is three hundred thousand."

"You will leave me credits big enough to cover that amount?" she asked, quite excited at the prospect of having so much money to play with.

"I have already left large credits with Joseph. Come to terms with the owner of Malmaison but leave the actual financial arrangements to Joseph."

Her excitement melted away. Joseph was the meanest man in the world. With him in charge of Bonaparte's affairs she would be lucky if she were able to lay her hands on a single sou.

"You may scowl as much as you like," Bonaparte said, "but Joseph, much as you dislike him, is an excellent man of business. That is why—" he paused and chuckled—"that is why I have ordered him to pay you your allowance."

This was too much. She flew into an instant rage.

"You might consider my feelings a little," she cried. "I know Joseph. He will play the miser. He will dole out my allowance a livre at a time and ask for an account of every miserable sou I spend. You may not be dragging me to Egypt but you are condemning me to a life of misery and embarrassment, really you are!"

But Bonaparte refused to listen and dismissed the matter abruptly. She began to sulk and declared that she had a headache when he wanted to take her on a tour of inspection of the transports in the harbor.

The following day, however, when Bonaparte and Eugene embarked on the *Orient*, and the time came for Josephine to say goodbye to both of them she wept with suitable abandon.

"My son," she sobbed, "my husband! If only I could be sure I shall see you again!"

With a band playing the 'Marseillaise' and thousands of soldiers cheering themselves hoarse, there was real drama in the parting, and for the moment Josephine felt a sincere regret that she was being left behind.

"You must be brave," Bonaparte told her, his voice breaking with emotion.

"I am a coward," she said. "I always was."

He kissed her tenderly.

"You tear my heart, Josephine. I would gladly face a million enemies than part with you like this."

Later, when the fleet of transports led by the *Orient* was under way, Josephine stood on a balcony waving a dutiful handkerchief and sobbing spasmodically.

The next day, in high spirits, she set out for Plombiéres. She would have gladly returned straight to Paris, but for the sake of appearances it was necessary to take the waters, if only for a day or two. . . .

$$* \quad * \quad * \quad * \quad *$$

Due to an accident Josephine's stay at Plombiéres was dragged out interminably. A balcony on which she was seated one day, taking the sun and sipping at a glass of revolting mineral water, collapsed without warning. From the balcony to the ground was a drop of fourteen feet. (Twenty feet, she told Bonaparte, in a letter.) Fortunately she escaped without serious injury but she was badly shaken and went to bed for a week.

While playing the invalid with a doctor (such a handsome young man) in constant attendance, it occurred to her that the accident was nothing more or less than a happy stroke of fate. A pity, of course, that she hadn't sustained at least one tiny little fracture, but even so her nerves had been left in such a state that it would be impossible for her to travel for months and months—as far as Egypt, that is; she would be able, if she were very brave, to reach Paris by easy stages.

To give her 'illness' greater reality she sent for Hortense and caused a daily report of her 'condition' to be issued in Paris. When the doctor declared her 'out of danger' the civic authorities of Plombiéres came in a deputation to congratulate her on her 'escape' and a band played patriotic airs beneath her window.

Meanwhile news, and a stream of Bonaparte's letters, began to arrive from Egypt. Malta, it seemed, had been taken easily after only slight opposition by the Knights of St. John, and the disembarkation east of Alexandria had been accomplished without any opposition at all. Alexandria had been taken, the Battle of the Pyramids fought, and Bonaparte was now in Cairo. All this glorious news was marred a little by rumors of England's sea victory in the Bay of Aboukir, but official bulletins hardly referred to it and Bonaparte's fame barely suffered. As for Bonaparte's personal letters, each of which urged Josephine to join him in Cairo the moment she was well enough to face the voyage, she put them aside with a smile. Nothing in the world could make her leave France now.

Back in Paris she celebrated her return with a discreet little reception at the rue Victoire. Among the guests were the five directors, Teresia (whom she patronized sweetly) and, most important of all, Citizen Hyppolyte Charles. . . .

*   *   *   *   *

"Do sit down," Josephine said, smiling plaintively, "we must have such a lot to talk about."

Joseph Bonaparte, summoned reluctantly, had come to discuss the purchase of Malmaison, Josephine's part of which had now been completed. He seated himself without a word. His face was long and his scowl of disapproval most pronounced.

"I trust," Josephine said, "that your mother is in good health?"

"Thank you, yes."

"Ah, splendid. Madame Bonaparte is really marvelous for her age."

"Our mother," Joseph reproved her, "is not as old as you would make her out to be."

"But still, my dear Joseph, any woman who has borne so many children—thirteen, wasn't it? Or perhaps *fifteen*. The number always eludes me!"

Joseph's frown deepened.

"And the rest of your family?" she went on, suppressing a giggle. "All are well?"

"Thank you, yes."

"The little Paulette, she must be quite a young lady by now."

"Quite," Joseph agreed. "Marriage has certainly given her a more mature appearance."

"Marriage?" Then she remembered. Paulette, having flirted with every officer on Bonaparte's staff, had finally, and after certain maternal opposition, made a hasty marriage with Leclerc.

"A more mature appearance, you say? How delightful—for Leclerc, I mean. A happy event is anticipated, perhaps?"

"Not as far as I know," Joseph said, glaring at her.

"No? Ah well, no doubt I misjudged your sister, but a marriage made so hastily——"

"By heaven!" Joseph exclaimed, half rising in his chair.

Again Josephine suppressed a giggle.

"Please convey my respects to your mother," she said, changing the subject quickly. "As soon as I am well enough to leave the house I intend to pay her a short visit."

Joseph, sinking back into the chair, looked at her coldly. "Taking into consideration the fact that you gave a reception on the second day of your return, that you drove out to Malmaison two days ago, and that you were at the opera last night, such a message is hardly likely to——"

"Dear me," Josephine interrupted, "you Bonapartes have a way of knowing everything, really you have!"

There was a pause, during which she realized that her delay in calling on her mother-in-law, who was now in permanent residence in Paris, must have caused the dispatch of many complaining letters to Egypt.

"I asked you to call today," she went on quickly, "to discuss the purchase of Malmaison. I think my lawyer has already given you a report on my negotiations with the owner."

Joseph inclined his head. "He has, and I must say that the employment of a lawyer was both unnecessary and needlessly expensive."

Needlessly expensive! Trust Joseph to look at it like that!

"I imagine," he continued, in an aggrieved tone, "that I am a good and scrupulous brother. If you feel dissatisfied with my stewardship you may complain to Napoleon."

She almost giggled. The ridiculous pomposity of the man!

"What figure," he asked, "have you agreed to pay for Malmaison?"

"Three hundred thousand livres—or francs, as we now call them."

Joseph gave a visible start.

"Three hundred thousand!" he repeated. "Preposterous!"

"Bonaparte gave me permission to go to that amount."

"I see! And being a woman with no idea of the value of money you immediately came to terms with the owner."

Josephine smiled. "As a matter of fact I agreed to pay three hundred and twenty-seven thousand altogether."

His mouth fell open in astonishment.

"The extra twenty-seven thousand," she added, "covers the furniture."

"Napoleon said nothing whatever to me about furniture!"

"Why should he, my dear Joseph? He naturally expected me, and you also, to have a little intelligence. What use would an unfurnished château be?"

Joseph shook his head stubbornly. "I refuse to take the responsibility for paying out a franc more than three hundred thousand, which in all conscience is far too much."

She dismissed the matter with a shrug. "The responsibility shall be mine."

"I shall see the owner at once," Joseph declared. "The deal shall be held up until I have written to Napoleon."

Josephine rose with dignity. "Your interference is beginning to bore me, Joseph. Shall we talk of something else?"

"If you wish."

"My allowance, for instance. Bonaparte was inconsiderate enough to leave it in your hands. I am entitled, I believe, to forty thousand francs a year."

"Yes, and a very generous allowance too!"

"I am not complaining, Joseph!"

"You surprise me! Especially since you have spent a matter of twenty thousand francs, your allowance for six months, in a little under *three* months."

"Dear me!" She was really appalled. "Ah well, money goes nowhere at all these days. Just because I'm the wife of Napoleon Bonaparte the tradespeople charge me more than anybody else. 'Bonaparte,' they say, 'lined his pockets in Italy and is lining them afresh in Egypt. His wife can afford to pay more.' Anyone would think I was the wealthiest woman in France, really they would!"

"You certainly behave as if you were. If you were to ask the *price* of a thing before you——"

She stamped her foot impatiently. "Please, Joseph, *please*. I am not a peasant's wife. Instead of lecturing me, kindly make arrangements for the balance of my year's allowance to be paid to my banker before the end of the week."

"But—!" Joseph began, rebelliously.

"Do as I say," she commanded, "unless, of course, you want to see me overdrawn."

"Very well, but let me warn you, it will be nine months before I am able to make any further payment."

"Bonaparte will be back before then, thank heaven!"

"I sincerely hope he will, but for a very different reason!"

Something in his tone filled her with suspicion. "What precisely do you mean by that, Joseph?"

"I am thinking of your renewed friendship with Hyppolyte Charles."

Josephine, hiding her surprise that he should know of Hyppolyte's visits, walked sharply to the door and flung it open.

"Please go, Joseph," she said. "Or would you rather I called my maid and asked her to show you out?"

An angry flush reddened his cheeks.

"Some day," he threatened, as he marched past her and out of the room, "you will regret this attitude, you will regret it deeply."

The moment he had gone she began to regret her hastiness. She felt sure that he knew nothing of Hyppolyte's visits—he had been groping in the dark, baiting her—and now she had given herself away. Finally she shrugged and dismissed the matter. What she did was, after all, her own affair, and unless Joseph actually caught her in the act of unfaithfulness, nothing he could tell Bonaparte would matter, and naturally she was much too experienced ever to be caught. . . .

*　　*　　*　　*　　*

"Things," Hyppolyte remarked, "are going anything but well in Egypt. The English fleet seems to have cut our communications rather badly."

"Be that as it may," Josephine said, "a letter reached me from Bonaparte this morning."

"A letter beseeching you to join him in Egypt, of course?"

"Of course!" she laughed.

They were seated in Josephine's boudoir and Louise had been instructed to inform any possible visitors that her mistress, suffering from one of her headaches, was unable to receive anyone. Josephine, one of her scantiest *négligés* thrown about her shoulders, was leisurely painting her cheeks. Hyppolyte, now fully clothed, was adjusting his latest and most fashionable cravat. These early afternoon assignations were very pleasing for two reasons: if the Bonapartes were really watching her they would expect her to choose nighttime for her little experiments in adultery; and (in spite of the fact that the hours of darkness were the accepted time for such things) she found the afternoon more physically delightful.

Hyppolyte gave his cravat a final little pat. "Pessimistic stories are being spread in Paris, mostly by Barras, I admit, but unless good news comes from Egypt very soon Bonaparte's Italian triumphs will be quickly forgotten."

"You mean that the people will hiss instead of cheer?"

"Quite possibly."

"And that, of course, is exactly what Barras would like."

Further conversation was interrupted by the sound of voices outside the door. One, a man's, was indistinguishable; the other, obviously Louise's, was raised in protest.

"Merciful heavens!" Josephine whispered, "do you hear that?"

"I do!" Hyppolyte listened intently for a moment. "And the man's voice, I think, is your brother-in-law Joseph's."

Josephine caught a glimpse in the mirror of her half-naked reflection and gasped in horror. She clutched at the *négligé*, drawing it more fully about her.

"Hide, Hyppolyte, for mercy's sake!"

He looked round helplessly. Afraid to speak she signaled to the only possible place, beneath the bed. He hesitated, distaste written clearly on his face, but the sound of the door handle turning decided him. Quickly as he moved Josephine could still see his feet protruding from beneath the bed when Joseph Bonaparte walked into the room. Worse still, he was followed by Madame Bonaparte.

"Really, Joseph," she cried, "an intrusion of this sort is unforgivable!"

"They insisted, citizeness," said a tearful Louise from the door. "There was nothing I could do."

Josephine dismissed her with a nod and pretended to see Madame Bonaparte for the first time.

"You too, Madame Bonaparte! This is indeed an honor!"

Madame Bonaparte inclined her head coldly. "Good afternoon, Josephine."

Joseph gave his mother a chair and glanced curiously about the room.

"Your maid," he said, "assured us that you were too ill to receive callers, but seeing a carriage at your door we concluded that she was making a mistake."

"A carriage at my door?" Josephine echoed. (She had completely forgotten Hyppolyte's carriage.) "You must be mistaken. Somebody must be calling next door. That—er—quite often happens." She turned to Madame Bonaparte. "I was just about to dress. If you would care to wait downstairs I shall be ready to join you in a few moments."

"We are not staying," Madame Bonaparte replied. "Merely calling in passing."

Looking at Joseph she said something rapidly in Italian. He replied briefly and continued to glance about the room. Josephine, afraid to look at the bed, wondered if Hyppolyte's feet were well enough hidden.

"While we are here," Madame Bonaparte went on, in French, "I may as well say something that has been on my mind for some time. To be brief, we are all a little perturbed by the company you are keeping."

"Madame Bonaparte!" Josephine protested.

"I would make no mention of it," the exasperating woman went on, "if I had not my son's interests so much at heart. In Napoléoné's absence you are living wildly and extravagantly, and are consorting with some of the worst and most depraved characters in Paris, many of whom are your husband's enemies."

"If, as you say, I am consorting with some of the worst and most depraved characters in Paris," Josephine said, unconsciously mimicking Madame Bonaparte's studied accents, "I am doing so because, having Bonaparte's interests at heart as much as you have, it is my business to watch these people."

"You were always a resourceful liar, Josephine," Joseph sneered.

"Such a remark is worthy of a man who spies on me at every turn!" she retorted.

There was a pause. She found that Joseph was staring at her with a peculiar light in his eyes. Puzzled, she watched him closely. After a moment she realized that his eyes were fixed on the open neck of her *négligé*. In a flash she understood and almost laughed aloud. It would seem that she had been dealing with Joseph in the wrong way. She thought of her success in Milan with Murat. All men, after all, were the same underneath. Perhaps if— But no, merciful heavens no! Joseph would be enough to revolt even the least fastidious woman. She shuddered. Not even to save herself would she stoop to *that*!

Madame Bonaparte rose. "Joseph, I think we had better go."

"I think we had, Mother," he agreed. "To stay longer would be to invite even more insults."

He held out his arm. Madame Bonaparte took it. Josephine, breathing a sigh of relief, watched them leave the room. She flew to the door on tip-toe and peeped out. Joseph was assisting 'our mother' down the stairs. Satisfied, she closed the door softly.

"You may come out, Hyppolyte," she whispered.

Hyppolyte emerged, legs first. He was covered in dust and his beautiful hair was badly disarrayed.

"I wanted to sneeze," he said. "I had the greatest difficulty in controlling myself." He began to dash the dust from his clothes. "The indignity of it," he complained.

"Ah!" cried a voice, loud with triumph, "exactly as I thought!"

Josephine swung round. Standing at the door, which had been silently opened, was Joseph Bonaparte. He turned and called over his shoulder.

"You may as well come in for a moment, Mother. Two witnesses will be better than one."

Madame Bonaparte entered. Her face was frozen with horror. For a moment she gabbled rapidly in Italian and appeared to choke.

"I would never have believed it!" she said at last, in French.

Joseph began to strut.

"Well, Josephine," he said, "I think we have sufficient proof this time. Napoleon will be very interested, very interested indeed. You were able to fool him in Milan, but this time it will be a different story." He gave his mother his arm again. "Come, Mother, this is no place for you." He bowed ironically. "*Au revoir*, Citizen Charles. *Au revoir*, Josephine. We now have you both exactly where we want you."

CHAPTER XXVII

JOSEPHINE UTTERED A LITtle scream of alarm.

"It can't be true," she said aloud, "it *can't* be!"

Then she read the really important part of her son's letter a second time.

Much as I love and respect my stepfather I have found it necessary to protest at his continued association with Madame Fourés, the wife of Lieutenant Fourés of the 22nd Chaseurs. He pointed out, reasonably enough, that it was his own personal affair and that Madame Fourés would never have interested him had it not been for your own conduct in Paris. 'For your mother,' he said, 'Citizen Charles; for me, Madame Fourés.' And he added, 'Your mother herself has forced me to it.'

Both furious and a little terrified, Josephine threw the letter aside. That wretched Joseph Bonaparte, she had *him* to thank for this!

There was a tap at the door and Louise, entering, announced that the Citizeness Tallien had called and was waiting below. Josephine frowned. Teresia never called these days. Therefore

Teresia must have heard rumors from Egypt about Bonaparte and this Fourés person and was eager to pass them on.

"Tell the citizeness," she said, with decision, "that I am ill and unable to receive anybody today."

Not twenty-four hours later the fact that rumors had indeed reached Paris from Egypt was made woefully apparent. Everybody was gossiping, even the very servants of the rue Victoire, and it was from Louise that Josephine learned the story which was being carried from *salon* to *salon* by Teresia and her friends.

Lieutenant Fourés, it seemed, had been sent away from Cairo leaving the field clear for Bonaparte, and Madame Fourés was now living openly with him at army headquarters.

"The soldiers are beginning to call her 'Our Lady of the East,' " Louise said, with wide eyes.

Josephine's hands went to her throat. *Our Lady of the East!* The name that would have been hers if she had accompanied Bonaparte to Egypt!

"The Citizen General," Louise added boldly, "is reputed to have said that he refuses to be made a laughing stock throughout the length and breadth of France as a complaisant husband twice deceived."

Josephine gave a little moan. That Joseph Bonaparte, a thousand curses on his wretched Corsican head!

"The Citizen General is also reputed to have said——"

"Enough," Josephine screamed, "for pity's sake enough!"

A week later it was learned in Paris that a strong English blockade of the Egyptian coast was making communications between the Directory and the Army of the East difficult and well-nigh impossible. That, Josephine tried to tell herself, was the reason why Bonaparte's usual flood of letters had ceased, but she knew in her heart that no letters would have come in any case.

Shortly after this, when the gossips of Paris had found something else to talk about, Joseph Bonaparte paid a visit to the rue Victoire. He had come, he said, on business, and under instructions from Bonaparte, from whom he had received a letter only that day.

"One ship," he said, "has managed to break through the blockade. You received a letter yourself, no doubt?"

She shook her head, hating Joseph, hating Bonaparte, hating even herself.

"Ah, times have changed," he murmured. "I can remember the day when as many as five couriers arrived one after the other with letters for you."

"Have the kindness to state your business and go," she said sharply.

"As you wish, and it can be stated in a few words. Since Lieutenant Fourés has divorced his wife Napoleon is eager to be in a position to offer Madame Fourés marriage."

"Marriage?" This was something she had never dreamed of. "You lie, Joseph, you lie!"

He smiled gleefully. "I speak the sober truth, Josephine. Napoleon has decided to divorce you and has asked me to arrange the matter for him."

This was too much.

"Since when has a man, even a Bonaparte," she demanded indignantly, "been able to divorce his wife without being present himself?"

"Oh, I am only to make the preliminary arrangements so that the divorce can be carried through swiftly the moment Napoleon returns to France."

Terror gripped Josephine's heart. "Does that mean that he is returning soon?"

"Possibly. The Directory, as you know, have destroyed all the work Napoleon did in Italy. They have made enemies everywhere and brought France within danger of immediate invasion. If Napoleon wants to strike at the Directory, if he wants to put himself at the head of the government, he must return without delay."

Josephine had taken little interest in the political situation lately, and now that it was brought to her attention the critical state of her own affairs still reduced it to insignificance.

"You were in a great hurry," she said bitterly, "to bring me this news of divorce."

Joseph smiled happily. "I thought it my duty to let you know where you stood."

"How very noble of you! And now, having performed your duty so righteously, please go while I am able to speak civilly to you!"

When Joseph had gone she gave a little more thought to what he had said about the Directory. If Bonaparte were actually on the point of striking at Barras and putting himself at the head of the government, the last thing in the world she wanted was to be divorced and put aside. She repeated the phrase in her mind. *To be divorced and put aside.* Dear heaven, no!

Less than a week later the news reached Josephine that Bonaparte had landed unannounced in the south and was rapidly approaching Paris. Hard on this came Hyppolyte with the information that Joseph Bonaparte and one of the other Bonaparte brothers had left Paris hastily with the obvious intention of meeting Bonaparte *en route*.

"They apparently want to reach him," he said, "before you have a chance to see him alone. I think they must be afraid that you might still be able to exert your old influence over him."

Josephine's mind was working quickly. *Her old influence over him* —the only thing on which she could count to avert divorce.

"Has he brought that woman with him?" she asked.

"Madame Fourés? There's no mention of her, but I understand that your son is with the party."

"In that case Madame Fourés has been left behind. Eugene would have refused to travel with her." She began to feel a little happier. "Tell me, Hyppolyte, is there any way I could reach Bonaparte before Joseph gets at him?"

"Well—" Hyppolyte began, but she stopped him. A plan had formed in her mind and she was ready for action, but she must know one thing first.

"Which route are the Bonaparte brothers following?"

"The Bourbonnais route to Lyons, where they expect to meet your husband."

"You're sure of that?"

"Yes, quite sure."

"Splendid!" She laughed aloud. "The Bourbonnais route is shorter, but Bonaparte is a great admirer of the countryside of Burgundy and is almost sure to take that route. I shall leave at once for Lyons, *by the Burgundy route!*" She laughed again, a little hysterically, Hyppolyte thought. "I shall fight the Bonapartes, I shall fight them and win!"

But Hyppolyte only shook his head. This, he felt sure, was the end. . . .

* * * * *

"Mother," Hortense said, "why are you in such a hurry to meet General Bonaparte?"

Mother and daughter were seated opposite each other in the carriage. It had been a stroke of genius, Josephine thought, this last minute decision to bring Hortense with her. The presence of both her children, young and innocent, would appeal to Bonaparte's emotions and might even restrict the development of a reproachful scene. At all events, it would certainly soften him against the final moment of reckoning.

Hortense repeated her question. Her mother looked at her thoughtfully. The girl was no longer a child and it would be nice to have somebody sympathetic in whom to confide.

"If it has anything to do with the divorce," Hortense went on, "I think I know your reason without asking."

This glib mention of 'the divorce' gave Josephine a mild shock. So the rumors had even reached Madame Campan's and the school had been gossiping. The Bonapartes were to blame for that, of course. The youngest of them, Caroline, was now at Madame Campan's and must have had her instructions.

"My dear," Josephine said, "I think I ought to take you completely into my confidence."

"Thank you, Mother," Hortense said gravely.

"The Bonapartes, as you know, have always hated me. Nothing would please them more than to see your stepfather and me permanently estranged. That is why we must meet him first and prevent Joseph Bonaparte from poisoning his mind completely with *his* side of the story."

A little frown appeared on the girl's brow. "But isn't it true about you and Citizen Charles?"

"Really, Hortense!" Josephine protested, and added, with the defiance of a child: "I have a right to enjoy myself, haven't I?"

"I am only trying to help you, Mother," Hortense said patiently. "Everybody knows about Citizen Charles and you. The Bonapartes have already written and told the general. The general has already written and asked his brother to arrange a divorce. Therefore——"

"Really, my dear," Josephine interrupted angrily, "you seem to be in little need of my confidence!"

Hortense nodded her agreement. "True, Mother, but I was about to say that it would be useless for you to pretend to the general that you are innocent."

"I have pretended before," Josephine chuckled.

"Perhaps, but could you do so with any chance of success this time? That is what I am trying to say."

There was a pause in the conversation. Josephine, more shaken than she cared to admit by her daughter's attitude, relaxed in her seat and pretended to fall into a little slumber. Watching Hortense through half-closed eyes she saw that the girl was still brooding over the same subject, and presently she said:

"Mother, why did you marry General Bonaparte?"

"Oh, for a number of reasons," Josephine yawned.

"But not because you loved him?"

"What makes you think that?"

"The way you sometimes speak of him."

"You seem to be a very observant young woman!"

"Do you—" Hortense hesitated—"do you love Citizen Charles?"

"Merciful heavens no! He amuses me, that's all."

"Did you—" Hortense hesitated again—"did you love my father?"

"Really, my dear," Josephine complained, "why this inquisition?"

"Forgive me, Mother, but I'm very curious."

Josephine sighed. "Your father was an unusual young man when I married him. I was only sixteen. The marriage was arranged by our families. Whether I loved him or not had little to do with it."

Hortense was silent for a moment.

"Thank you for telling me, Mother. When I marry I want to be in love with my husband. I think it would kill me if I were not."

Josephine laughed weakly. How preposterous, Hortense to be contemplating marriage already. And yet, was it? She was sixteen, though not so mature as she herself had been at that age. Why, if Hortense married now she, Josephine, would be a grandmother within a year. The idea was utterly fantastic. Tears came to her eyes. To have her age emphasized to that extent! A grandmother! Besides, it would embarrass Bonaparte and make him angry too. Bonaparte! The thought of him brought all her troubles back with a rush. She sat up suddenly.

"At the next halt," she said, "we must tell the postilion to drive the horses to the utmost limit!"

Trying to relax again she remembered something Hortense had said: *It would be useless for you to pretend to the general that you are innocent.*

"You seem," Josephine said, reminding Hortense of this, "to have been thinking out the matter for yourself."

"Well, yes," Hortense admitted gravely.

"And you've come to a definite conclusion, no doubt, as to how I ought to plead my case?"

"A very definite conclusion, Mother."

"Tell me what it is."

Hortense leaned forward earnestly. "Simply this, since it would be fatal to make denials, your only hope of salvation is to admit your guilt."

"My guilt?" Josephine echoed indignantly. "Are you trying to make me feel like a criminal?"

"No, Mother, but I think you ought to feel sorry for what you've done."

So taken aback was she that she hardly knew whether to laugh or to scold her daughter.

"You *are* sorry, aren't you, Mother?" Hortense said anxiously.

"What a strange child you are," Josephine said, and added lightly: "You ought to know very well that I'm sorry."

The girl looked at her mother unhappily. "That's just the trouble. I ought to know, but——"

"But what?" Josephine encouraged.

"But I suspect," Hortense got out miserably, "that you're only sorry because you've been found out."

Josephine looked at Hortense in astonishment. Merciful heavens, was her daughter growing up to be a wretched little prig?

"When you're a little older," she said, "you might learn that being found out is the only thing a woman is ever sorry about."

"What a horrible thing to say, Mother!"

"At your age I thought much the same—" (Did she, though? She couldn't really remember.)—"But later I learned the truth of it."

"I still think it's horrible."

Josephine leaned forward and kissed Hortense. "How sweet you are. I pray you will always be able to keep your idealism."

The rest of the journey was a nightmare of anxiety. If only she could be sure of reaching Bonaparte first! Everything depended on that. Over and over again she thought: *'Please God I've chosen the right route!* To be kept in suspense much longer would drive her raving mad. What a wretched life it was! In the name of heaven, why were the Bonaparte brothers ever born!'

They arrived at Lyons without meeting Bonaparte, or even a single courier. The town was decked out in festive array. Flags were flying and swarms of excited people filled the streets. From time to time as they drove to the center of the town Josephine heard the familiar phrase: *Long live Bonaparte!*

"He must be here," she cried, "he must be here!"

At the town hall the mayor received her with every mark of respect. She cut short his flowery greetings.

"My husband—where is he?"

"General Bonaparte left for Paris several hours ago."

"By—by the Bourbonnais route, you mean?"

"Why yes, citizeness, by the Bourbonnais route."

There being nothing else to do, she uttered a little moan and fainted. . . .

*　　*　　*　　*　　*

There were still dozens of people in the rue Victoire, waiting undoubtedly for another glimpse of Bonaparte, but within the house itself all seemed very still and quiet.

"Go to my room and wait," Josephine told Hortense. "I might need you later."

Wearily she followed Hortense up the stairs. Tired as she had been when reaching Lyons she had insisted on traveling through the night on the return journey to Paris. Now she was utterly worn out and in no state to face the scene with Bonaparte which lay before her.

"Ah," said a voice, "this *is* a surprise."

She gave a great start of surprise. Joseph Bonaparte, of course, was standing guard at Bonaparte's door like the evil spirit he was.

She almost spat in his face.

"Let me pass, Joseph!"

Without moving, and in obviously high spirits, he said: "May I ask what you want?"

"May you ask what I want!" she shouted. "This is my own house, isn't it? Let me pass. I want to see my husband."

"My dear Josephine, Napoleon has no wish to be disturbed. Take my advice. Go away. You are wasting your time."

"Ha! You're afraid to let me see him!"

"When he first arrived I was afraid. But now—" Joseph laughed confidently—"Oh no, not now. 'Josephine is finished, utterly finished.' Those were Napoleon's own words." He leaned forward with a leer. "Be a sensible woman. Take your punishment with dignity and go."

"Stand aside," she said, in a quivering voice, "or I shall have you thrown out of the house!"

She pushed past him and tried the door. It was locked.

"Bonaparte!" she shouted. "Bonaparte, I want to speak to you!"

"Shouting like that will only disturb him," Joseph said.

She swung round on him furiously. "Pig of a Corsican! Hold your interfering tongue!"

She was about to throw herself on the door when the bolt was drawn back. A moment later Bonaparte was looking at her through a slit of not more than three inches. His face was deadly pale.

"Joseph," he said, "how do you expect me to work with a hysterical woman screaming at the door? Take her away."

The door closed. The bolt was shot into place.

Joseph took Josephine by the shoulders. "Come, you heard what he said."

She twisted violently out of his grip. "How *dare* you touch me!" She turned back to the closed door. "Bonaparte, let me in! I promise to be calm. Let me in for one little moment."

"Go away," he replied.

"Then promise to see me tomorrow. Promise that and I'll go away at once."

"I refuse to see you now, tomorrow or any day. Let that be clearly understood. All is over between us."

She threw herself against the door, but instead of screaming she pitched her voice low and succeeded without difficulty in making it break with a little sob.

"Ah, how you must loathe me! How you must hate me! And how I deserve it! My conduct has been shameful." Out of the corner of

263

her eye she saw a look of alarm cross Joseph's face. Encouraged, she went on sadly: "I am everything you think—wicked, neglectful, faithless. I come to you in sorrow—" of its own accord her voice broke this time and the words died in her throat. "I come to you in sorrow," she went on, "asking your forgiveness. Grant it, Bonaparte, grant it, I beseech you!"

Joseph stepped forward and at the same time Bonaparte's voice came clearly from within the room.

"Go back to Hyppolyte Charles. You chose him, now you shall stay with him."

The look of alarm left Joseph's face. He relaxed and folded his arms.

"Go *back* to him!" Josephine wailed. "But Bonaparte, I have never——"

"Must you lie?" the voice took her up. "Where have you been since I returned to Paris? Why do you trouble to come to me now? Has Charles turned you out?"

In a sudden rage Josephine flew at Joseph, forced him against the wall and hammered madly at his face and chest with her clenched fists.

"This is your doing!" she shouted. "You told Bonaparte that I had fled with Hyppolyte Charles! You told him that, and yet you must have known that I was hastening along the Burgundy road to Lyons!"

Joseph, guarding his face with his hands, slid back along the wall and out of her reach.

"She-cat!" he cried.

She turned to the door again. "Listen to me, Bonaparte, for pity's sake! The moment I heard you were in France I set out to meet you on the Burgundy road. I——!"

"A most ingenious story."

"Hortense was with me!" (Thank God for Hortense!) "Ask her! Only ask her!"

There was a pause. Josephine waited breathlessly, hopefully.

"Are you still there, Joseph?" Bonaparte said at last.

"Yes, Napoleon."

"Kindly see that Josephine's belongings are packed and sent away."

"Where shall I send them, Napoleon?"

"Ask Josephine. She knows Citizen Charles's address."

"My belongings shall remain here!" Josephine cried. "If Joseph dares to touch them——!"

A little sigh was audible from within the room.

"Very well," Bonaparte said, "have them placed in the street, Joseph, and leave me in peace. You understand, both of you, leave me in peace."

Joseph, watching Josephine closely, edged closer to her.

"You hear?" he said.

"Yes, I hear!" She raised her voice so that Bonaparte would catch every word. "I hear and I forgive him. It isn't he who is responsible, but you. However—" and here she lowered her voice to a fierce whisper—"I am not defeated yet. Smile if you must, Joseph Bonaparte. Hurry to your mother and your brothers and your impossible sisters with this story of my shame, but—*I am not defeated yet!*"

And then, with the gesture of a drowning woman, she fell against the door and slid to the floor. 'This is no pretence,' was her last clear thought; 'this, God pity me, is a *real* faint.'

$$* \quad * \quad * \quad * \quad *$$

Josephine opened her eyes and stared up at the ceiling. Joseph, heartless beast that he was, had gone and the house seemed deathly quiet. She struggled to a kneeling position and leaned against the door for support.

"Bonaparte," she said softly.

There was no response.

"Bonaparte!" she said in a louder voice.

There was still no response.

She rose to her feet and turned the handle of the door, but the door was still locked. She tottered away, regretting that Bonaparte, hiding like the coward he was behind a locked door, was unable to witness the spectacle of her misery and dejection.

Upstairs she found Eugene with Hortense. From the look on their faces and the quick way they drew apart they had obviously been discussing the family crisis. Eugene came forward and kissed her. She noticed vaguely that his absence in Egypt had turned him into a man. Had she met him in the street she would hardly have recognized him. She wondered if he had experienced his first *affaire* yet. Egyptian women were said to be most passionate.

She held him away from her and looked at him sadly. "My poor Eugene, in my sorrow I had completely forgotten you."

He looked embarrassed. "Have you seen the general yet?" he asked.

"No, Eugene. The door is locked against me."

His embarrassment deepened. "He is very upset."

"Upset? *Bonaparte?* Never! His voice was cold and cruel."

"I think you wrong him, Mother."

She looked at her son in utter amazement. "You think I wrong him! So this is what comes of your spending so many months alone with Bonaparte!"

Hortense took her brother's hand. "I think I know how Eugene feels, Mother."

The tears came to Josephine's eyes. "Oh, but this is too much! This is indeed the end! My children against me now—my children in league with the Bonaparte brood!"

"You are overwrought, Mother," Hortense said, and her voice, to Josephine, seemed cold and unsympathetic.

Eugene put his arm round his mother's shoulders. "We're not against you, Mother. Don't think that. It's just that I, for my part, am placed in an unpleasant position. The general has always been kind and good to me, more like a father than anything else. This quarrel grieves me for his sake as well as yours. I would do anything to bring you together again, anything."

Josephine, now sobbing on her son's shoulder, began to feel a little happier. Hortense came closer and there were tears in her eyes. For a moment, mother and children were caught in a wave of contagious emotionalism.

"I too," Hortense said, "would do anything to bring you and the general together again."

Josephine, shaken by a final spasm of sobbing, took them both in her arms.

"I believe you, my children, I believe you!"

Then she found a handkerchief, blew her nose in a businesslike manner and said: "Come with me, both of you." Her voice was calm and practical. "Two innocent children should be more than a match for that pig of a Joseph."

Eugene and Hortense exchanged a startled glance.

"Come with me at once," Josephine said, unaware of the effect of her change of manner on the children. "The longer we leave it the worse it will become. Give me your arm, Eugene, and you too, Hortense. You must appear to be supporting me, just in case Bonaparte should come out of the room."

("I can hardly believe it," Eugene whispered to Hortense.)

("She is really very upset," Hortense whispered back.)

"Besides," Josephine said, eyeing them obliquely, "I really am too weak to walk alone."

"Of course, Mother," Hortense agreed, soothingly.

Josephine clutched suddenly at Eugene's arm. "Eugene, tell me about that woman in Egypt, that Madame Fourés! Was Bonaparte's interest in her serious?"

Eugene coughed. "Well, it *appeared* to be, Mother."

Josephine's fingers bit deep into Eugene's arm. "Is it *still* serious?"

266

"I—" Eugene's embarrassment became intense. "You see, Mother, after the general heard about you and Citizen Charles he——"

"Never mind that, Eugene! Answer my question! Is Bonaparte's interest in Madame Fourés still serious?"

"Yes," Eugene said briefly.

"Yet he left her behind in Egypt."

"She's going to follow soon. Colonel Junot is to bring her."

"Tell me the worst. Is it true that he wants to marry her?"

"Yes, Mother."

"I see." Josephine's face cleared. "Ah, well, she can be taken care of when she arrives. The only trouble now is Bonaparte himself. Come, both of you, we are wasting time. Your arm, Eugene, your arm, Hortense!"

Supported by Eugene and Hortense, drooping gracefully between them, Josephine returned to Bonaparte's door. There still being no sign of Joseph, she concluded that he had left the house. So much the better! His absence would give her plan greater chance of success.

She tapped lightly on the door. "Bonaparte!"

There was no reply.

"Bonaparte," she said quietly, "bear with me for one little moment."

Something like a grunt came from within the room. Encouraged, Josephine tried again: "Listen, Bonaparte, there's somebody here who wishes to speak to you." She gave Hortense a little pull towards the door and whispered fiercely: "Go on, speak to him, *speak to him!*"

"General Bonaparte," the girl said, "it is I, Hortense."

There was a moment of dead silence.

"Say something else!" Josephine urged.

Hortense glanced quickly at Eugene, who shrugged.

"General Bonaparte," she said, "please open the door."

Not even a grunt came from within the room.

"Something else," Josephine whispered. "Something more touching!"

Hortense cleared her throat. "Please open the door and listen to my mother. You can't dismiss her unheard. That would be unjust and cruel."

Josephine listened eagerly. The sound of a chair scraping on the floor reached her straining ears.

"Now you, Eugene!" she whispered. "Quickly, quickly!"

Eugene squared his shoulders.

"General Bonaparte," he said, "it is I, Eugene. Please open the door. For my sake, give my mother a chance to defend herself."

Josephine uttered a heartrending moan. She pressed herself close against the door and repeated it.

"Are you completely heartless?" she demanded. "Have you no love in your heart for these innocent children who plead for their repentant mother?"

Footsteps were now heard within the room. They came to the door, turned and receded. They came back to the door, turned and receded. This went on for several moments.

"He's pacing the room," Josephine reported, trembling with excitement. "He's trying to make up his mind. I think perhaps if I began to weep. . . ."

At that point the footsteps reached the door and paused. After a moment the listeners heard Bonaparte clear his throat.

"Oh, Bonaparte!" Josephine sobbed.

The door was flung open but Bonaparte remained in the shadows, hiding his face.

"Hortense," he said, "Eugene, you had better both come in."

His voice told Josephine nothing. Hortense and Eugene passed into the room. The door was closed in her face. She sank to the floor and pressed her ear against the lower panel, but only an indistinct murmur of voices reached her. She strained her ear still more. Bonaparte was speaking. She caught a few phrases spoken in a voice shaking with emotion.

"Your young voices, pleading like that, tore my heart. . . . If I insist on divorce . . . fatherless again . . . not right . . . the victims of your mother's faults . . . blame myself for the rest of my life. . . ."

Josephine almost shouted for joy.

"Eugene," she heard Bonaparte say next, "go and fetch your mother."

Josephine threw herself away from the door. Quickly she arranged herself on the floor in a tragic pose. In her present condition there was hardly any need to pretend to faint. Now that she was within sight of victory she began to think about her appearance. She knew she looked an absolute wreck. Her eyes were swollen. Her cheeks were stained with tears. Her dress was crumpled. She looked forty-five if a day. Bonaparte would be revolted, and in heaven's name, what was she going to say to him?

The door opened. She closed her eyes and let her head fall limply back.

"She's fainted, sir," she heard Eugene say.

"Poor Mother," Hortense murmured.

She felt somebody picking her up. It was Bonaparte, and she heard him say: "See that we're not disturbed, Eugene." The next moment the door slammed and she felt herself carried forward across the room. With that she thought it judicious to open her eyes.

"Oh, Bonaparte," she said tremulously.

He lowered her gently to a chair.

"My poor Josephine," he said—tenderly, she imagined.

"Ah, you forgive me," she whispered, "you forgive me!"

His eyes narrowed. "I haven't said so, Josephine!"

"Not with your tongue, no, but with your eyes, Bonaparte, with your eyes!"

"Bah!" he cried, angry with himself. "I am weak and foolish. In God's name, what is it that you possess above all other women?"

"A deep and lasting love for you," she said promptly.

He stared at her intently. "You have never loved me, never! When I married you it was I alone who loved. It is the same now."

She felt that he wronged her. She had been wanton, thoughtless, careless of his love; she had taken all and given little, but he had played a greater part in her life than she had realized. With genuine emotion she saw all this, now.

"I love you now," she said sincerely, "even if I never loved you before. You must believe me, Bonaparte."

For a moment he looked at her intently.

"Yes," he said sombrely, "I think I do believe you. You love me now, Josephine, now when it is too late."

She sprang up in alarm.

"You bring me here," she cried; "you encourage me to believe that you're about to forgive me, and then you speak of it's being too late! Oh, how cruel, how cruel!"

He took her gently in his arms. "You alarm yourself unnecessarily, my dear. You shall remain my wife, but the tearing passion I once felt for you has gone."

"But love remains, Bonaparte? Love remains?"

"Yes. Unhappily for me, love remains."

"Unhappily for you!" she repeated. "Ah well, I deserve that, oh yes, I deserve that." She brought a faraway look to her eyes and sighed profoundly. "Yet in the future you will see how repentant I can be. I promise you never to look upon another man again."

He shook her half playfully by the shoulders. "I shall see that you keep your promise. I don't think I blame you altogether for what has happened. I blame the weakness of your sex. I shall see that strict watch is kept on you in the future."

"Only take me back and no watch whatever will be necessary!"

He released her and turned to his desk. Over his shoulder he said: "We have talked enough. Go to your room and rest. If you are as exhausted as I am by all this waste of emotion you'll need all the rest you can get."

She went obediently to the door, where she turned and looked back at him.

"You will join me later, Bonaparte?"

He was studying some papers. "Yes," he said, without looking up, "but I must be at my desk by eight in the morning. Joseph is coming then, and Lucien too. A busy day lies ahead of us tomorrow."

"Very well."

With a little secret smile she left the room, closing the door softly behind her. It would be the easiest thing in the world, she felt sure, to keep him in bed well after eight. If necessary she would even put the clock back.

Chuckling maliciously she went in search of Louise.

"Louise," she said, on finding the maid, "my husband and I will take breakfast in bed tomorrow. Serve it promptly at nine."

"Very well, citizeness."

Josephine chuckled again. "One other thing— We expect an early visit from Joseph and Lucien Bonaparte. The moment they arrive, show them straight to my room."

She laughed aloud. The sight of Joseph's face in the morning when he found her and Bonaparte in bed together was going to be worth more than a diamond necklace.

Happily she went to her boudoir, selected a flimsy night-dress, and, seated before the mirror, began to repair the damage which 'all this waste of emotion' had left on her face.

"Faithfulness," she said aloud, as she gazed at her reflection in the mirror. "Well, why not?"

She was thirty-two—no, better admit the truth, if only to oneself!— she was thirty-six and had lived a full, if not always satisfied life, in *that* direction. Alexandre, Lacoste, Tercier, Réal, Hoche, Barras, Bonaparte, Hyppolyte, Murat, Hyppolyte again—

"Merciful heavens!" she cried, "what a long list!"

Her eyes met their startled reflection in the mirror, wavered, and fell.

"I refuse to believe it," she whispered.

Her chin stiffened, her head came up. She looked into the mirror again, catching her reflected gaze and holding it bravely.

"It happened to somebody else, not to me. In any case, whoever the wretched woman was, the past is the past and I shall *never* remember it, no *never!*"

She thrust out her right hand, as if holding a wineglass.

"To Citizeness Bonaparte," she said, "a good and faithful wife!"

Part Four
The Faithful Wife

J OSEPHINE," BONAPARTE said quietly, "how much money do you owe the tradespeople? What, exactly, is the extent of your debts?"

Josephine's heart missed a beat. She looked at her husband in undisguised alarm and sighed deeply. A week had passed since their reconciliation, a week during which she had convinced herself that the problem of her by now quite fabulous debts had slid quietly into obscurity.

"Come, come," he said testily, "how much money do you owe?"

"Joseph," she remarked tartly, "has been telling you dreadful stories about my extravagance."

"Joseph has given me nothing more than a plain, unvarnished report, but there must be numerous small debts of which Joseph is completely unaware. Come, my dear, tell me the truth, how much money do you owe?"

She sighed again. "I was never very good at figures, Bonaparte."

"Give me a rough estimate of the total amount. That is all I ask."

He spoke impatiently, not angrily, and noting this Josephine began to feel a little happier.

"I think the total amount must be about a hundred thousand francs," she said bravely.

He looked at her in amazement.

"A hundred thousand francs!" he echoed.

"Is that a very great amount?" she asked innocently.

"Great enough, at all events, to stagger even me!"

"Everything is so expensive," she sighed. "The cost of living has simply *soared* during the past year. You have no idea, Bonaparte, the number of difficulties that beset a poor woman living alone in Paris."

Bonaparte smiled grimly and pinched her ear. "Ah well, I have forgiven you a greater sin than extravagance. Be a little more careful in future and I will find it in my heart to forgive your quite mountainous debts."

"You're the kindest man in the world, Bonaparte."

"The most foolish, you mean."

She threw her arms round his neck. "From this moment, darling, I shall be a model wife."

He freed himself and laughed drily. "My dear Josephine, no woman could reach your age and change her character overnight. Fortunately, however, I know you too well to expect too much from you."

She pouted girlishly. "What a poor opinion you have of me!"

"I have a better opinion of you than you think, otherwise Joseph and Lucien would never have found us breakfasting in bed together a week ago."

Josephine chuckled. The chuckle became a roar of laughter. In a moment she was holding her sides in uncontrollable mirth. The sight of Joseph's face when he'd found her and Bonaparte sitting up in bed eating breakfast was a sight she would never forget. When she was a very old lady, when memories were neither bitter nor sweet, memory of Joseph's face would remind her that life in many respects had been well worth while.

"You exult a little too much," Bonaparte remarked.

"You were vastly amused yourself," she told him.

"Yes, yes, but please remember that Joseph, whatever his faults, is a good man. And remember also that you have at least one thing in common with him—in common with him and in common with the rest of my family. After all, their future as well as yours depends largely on the success of my career."

"You know that I'm eager to help you in any way I can, Bonaparte."

"Yes, my dear, I know you are, and you must begin at once. In a way your recent extravagance has yielded certain advantages. Your lavish way of entertaining means that you are in touch with Parisian society, such as it is. You are, I believe, on intimate terms with three out of the five directors. You are also friendly with the leaders of the various factions. It is not an exaggeration to say that you are the most attractive and popular hostess in Paris."

"You flatter me, Bonaparte," Josephine said humbly.

He took her hands in his and looked intently into her eyes.

"I want and need your help," he said. "I have never agreed with the interference of women in politics but in your case I intend to make an exception. Therefore I say this to you, Josephine: open your *salon* to all the prominent people of the day; gather together the deputies, the Jacobins, the Royalists, the out-and-out Republicans; entertain them with your incomparable graciousness and I—" he paused to take in a deep breath—"and *I* will do the rest."

Awed by his manner she could only whisper: "You may rely on me, Bonaparte."

A smile came to his lips. "Whatever expenditure you make will be amply repaid. For soon, Josephine, unless I'm sadly mistaken, I shall make you the first lady of Paris."

"The first lady of Paris!" she echoed.

He laughed aloud. "No, better still, the first lady of France. In all but name I shall make you queen."

✻   ✻   ✻   ✻   ✻

During the exciting weeks that followed, Josephine, taken completely into Bonaparte's confidence, gained a thorough understanding of his aims and plans. Not only did she preside, with her 'incomparable graciousness,' over her crowded *salon*; she was present at many secret meetings between Bonaparte and his growing band of supporters.

"The Republic of France," he repeated over and over again at the meetings, "is in grave danger, and I intend to save it. Indeed, I am the only man who *can* save it!"

His plan, it seemed, was to get at each of the five directors separately and either force them to join him or resign. Two of them, Ducot and Sieyes, were easy; almost immediately they agreed to join him openly the moment he gave the word. Two others, Barras and Moulins, he had little use for and wished only to make them resign. The fifth, Gohier, he considered a good man and intended, if possible, to secure his services.

"What is in your mind?" Josephine asked him. "Do you propose to become chief director of a new directory, or do you want to make yourself a sort of absolute dictator?"

"I want to and shall make myself a sort of absolute dictator," he replied, "but the word 'dictator' must not be used. It would frighten many of my more timid supporters."

"You could form a council," she suggested, "and make yourself president."

"Yes, I could do that," he agreed, "but what I favor most is a consulate, with myself chief consul."

"And that," she smiled, "would make me a consuless."

"And that," he laughed, "would make you a consuless."

273

"It sounds like a fairy story, a dream," she said.

"It *is* a dream, the dearest dream of my life. Soon it will be a reality."

"When do you intend to strike?"

"Not before I feel that the right moment has arrived."

"And not, I trust, without military support," she said.

He laughed heartily at that. "My dear, I shall have all the military support I need. The moment I returned from Egypt three regiments of dragoons petitioned for the honor of being reviewed by me. I have delayed the review. I shall continue to delay it until the day I strike. In addition forty adjutants of the National Guard have asked leave to wait on me. That too I have delayed until the day I strike. Finally, all the officers of the garrison have expressed a wish to come to me in a body and admire me. They shall do so, God bless them, on the day I strike. Oh yes, I shall have all the military support I need!"

During the weeks of preparation the members of the Directory, though they must have been aware that a certain amount of plotting and planning was afoot, made no attempt to interfere with Bonaparte. "They're afraid of me," he said; "at least, they're afraid of my popularity with the people of France." To test the depth of this alleged fear Bonaparte accepted an official invitation to dine with the Directory at the Luxembourg and there, challenging Barras, he made an arrogant speech.

"I sit here this night," he said, "at this public dinner given so lavishly in my honor, with a heavy heart, a sad heart, and moreover an angry heart! After an absence of sixteen months I find the Republic in an amazing condition. What have you done, Citizen Directors, with the fair and prosperous France which I left in your keeping? In place of peace I find you at war with Austria. In place of the wealth of Italy which I secured for you I find misery and taxation. Where are the hundred thousand Frenchmen whom I knew and loved—the companions of my glory and triumph in Italy? They are dead or forgotten! If I were a politician instead of a plain soldier of the Republic I would ask for—nay, I would *demand* your resignation!"

Even this speech brought no open move against him, not even from the watchful, cunning Barras.

"Their inaction," he confessed to Josephine, "worries me a little. I want to know what is going on in that agile brain of Citizen Director Barras. I want to know what he is thinking, planning. I want to know if it's possible for me to force him to resign."

"That should be simple," Josephine said. "Let me go to him. Let me question him."

Bonaparte frowned and shook his head.

"I played the same game once before," Josephine urged. "I played it with considerable success. Besides, nothing would give me greater pleasure than to cross swords with my dear friend Barras."

Bonaparte looked at her thoughtfully. "Very well," he said at last. "Go to him. Cross swords with him by all means, but if you succeed nobody will be more surprised than I."

✳   ✳   ✳   ✳   ✳

Barras greeted Josephine with a disarming smile.

"My dear Josephine," he said, "this is indeed a surprise."

"Yes, isn't it?" she laughed gaily. "We see very little of each other these days, don't we?"

"Too little," he assured her. "However, news of your activities reaches me from time to time." He bowed mockingly. "Permit me to congratulate you on getting the better of the Bonaparte brood once more. You showed amazing skill in averting the threatened divorce, amazing skill."

"Thank you, Barras," she said.

"It is to be hoped," he went on smoothly, "that you will be just as skilful next time."

"Next time?" she echoed coldly. "There'll be no next time, Barras."

"No?" he laughed. "My dear, you must be losing your zest for life. You must be getting old."

"I have merely learned a little wisdom," she said, determined not to lose her temper with him.

"Wisdom? But how splendid! It did you a lot of good, apparently, when Bonaparte began to play your own game."

"My own game? What on earth do you mean?"

"I was thinking," he said softly, "of his little digression in Egypt with the attractive Madame Fourés."

"Madame Fourés," Josephine snapped, "was precisely what you say, a digression and nothing more."

"Ah, but didn't he plan to marry her? Isn't she even now on her way to Paris to join Bonaparte and take your place?"

"Oh *that*," she said airily. "Bonaparte *did* implicate himself, I admit, but happily he is in his right mind again. In any case the wretched woman is now in the hands of the English. Her ship was intercepted. She will, I trust, remain a prisoner for many months."

"In the hands of the English, eh?" Barras laughed. "How very convenient!" He looked at her steadily for a moment and his face changed. "But enough, Josephine. You haven't come here to discuss

275

the chances of your lifelong devotion to Bonaparte. You've come, if I'm not very much mistaken, on a little political mission."

"Correct," Josephine admitted, with a little start of surprise, "but how did you guess?"

"I still have a number of sources of information. Shall we—" he hesitated, and for a moment she recognized doubt and indecision in his manner—"shall we be frank with each other, Josephine?"

She inclined her head. "By all means, Barras."

He made an indeterminate gesture. "Proceed, my dear. You have come, I think, to issue an ultimatum. Issue it, then. I am all attention."

She looked at him steadily. This was undoubtedly better than she had expected, but as for issuing an ultimatum, nothing had been farther from her mind. If only she knew what to say, what line of action to take!

"I'm waiting," he said, with an elaborate attempt at patience. "Personally I can't believe that you have anything very incriminating to hold over me. As a member of the Directory I have always used my office with one object only in view, the good of the Republic. Therefore——"

"Not the good of the Republic!" she broke in, "but the good of one person only, the good of Citizen Director Barras!" She almost laughed aloud: Barras, having talked too much, had unwittingly given her a cue. "You have a very large private fortune, a very large private fortune indeed. The people of France would, I'm sure, be interested to know just how you managed to accumulate it."

Barras laughed uneasily. "The people of France have never thought of asking me."

"No, but they might, Barras, and in the very near future."

He looked at her oddly. She returned his look coolly and saw, to her gratification, that his hands were trembling.

"It would be most unpleasant, don't you think, if Bonaparte were to make close inquiries?"

"Unpleasant and very indelicate," Barras admitted.

"I think I ought to warn you," she went on, "that Bonaparte has impeachment in mind."

"Impeachment?" Barras rose to his feet quickly. Josephine had never seen him so deeply moved. A moment later, but a little too tardily, he shrugged with apparent negligence and said: "Impeachment is hardly a pretty word."

"No," she agreed. "'Resignation' has a happier sound."

"Resignation?" He sat down heavily, and then, in a final attempt to pull himself together, he laughed pleasantly. "My dear Josephine, I do believe you're bluffing."

She rose. "Is that what you want me to tell Bonaparte, that you believe I'm bluffing?"

He laughed again, but this time wryly. "I should like you to tell him to go to the devil, but I see that the game is up. Very well, tell your cunning husband that I'm a little tired of political life and intend to vacate my seat on the Directory. Tell him that I propose to retire, a sadder and wiser man, to my country estate where, in due course, I shall embarrass a number of people, yourself not excepted, by writing my autobiography."

This last gave Josephine a pang of apprehension but she steadied herself quickly.

"When," she demanded, "will you send in your resignation?"

"At once, if you like." He turned to his desk. "If you care to wait I'll write it for you now and give you the pleasure of carrying it to Bonaparte."

"Thank you," Josephine said gravely.

When the brief document was completed Barras folded it and gave it to Josephine.

"You know," he drawled, "there's really a bit of comedy in all this. Josephine, the social butterfly, Josephine the most unsatisfactory mistress any man could ever be cursed with, turned politician! It's screamingly funny, my dear, screamingly funny."

She took a furious step towards him.

"No, no, control that temper of yours," he said, "all I wanted was the last word, and having had it, I'm perfectly happy." He held out his hand. "I shall say good-bye, not *au revoir*. Good-bye, Josephine, and God protect you from the Bonaparte brood!"

*   *   *   *   *

With something of a flourish Josephine handed Barras's resignation to Bonaparte.

"Read this," she said.

"From Barras?" he questioned.

"From Barras," she chuckled.

Bonaparte unfolded the sheet of paper and glanced at the few lines which Barras had written.

Since the destinies of the Republic will shortly rest in the hands of her young and invincible general, I gladly resign the office which I have held since the Reign of Terror. My work in the interests of liberty, fraternity and equality is now completed.

277

"Well," Josephine demanded, "are you pleased with me?"

"Pleased! My dear, you fill me with admiration."

"Thank you, Bonaparte. It's good to know that I am no longer under a cloud. Is there anything else I can do?"

He looked at her thoughtfully. "I think perhaps there is. Barras is disposed of, but there's still Gohier to be dealt with."

"Gohier is a different proposition from Barras."

"I'm well aware of that. He has always been a model of virtue. There's nothing in the world we can hold over him. We must either come to terms with him or trick him."

"It would be easier to trick him, Bonaparte."

"You have an idea, then?"

"Yes, but tell me first, when do you plan to strike your blow?"

"Three days from now," he replied promptly.

"Then three days from now I shall invite Gohier and his wife, who have accepted my hospitality many times in the past, to breakfast."

"Splendid, Josephine, splendid! And the moment the Gohiers are at the table the house shall be surrounded by my men. He will realize then that his choice lies between imprisonment and resignation."

In his excitement he took her in a rough embrace. She screamed in mock alarm, but he only laughed.

"My dear," he said, "I've lived to be proud of you. You're a better wife than I imagined."

"Since you're in such a good humor," Josephine said, "I think I'd better tell you that my debts are nearer a hundred and fifty thousand than a hundred thousand."

"I don't care if they're half a million!" he cried and kissed her passionately.

"Thank you, Bonaparte," she said. "That is, I think, the exact amount, half a million."

*　　*　　*　　*　　*

Late in the afternoon of Brumaire the Nineteenth, Bonaparte's mother came to call on Josephine. When announced she entered the room stiffly. She smiled in a watery fashion, hesitated just within the door and finally broke into voluble Italian. With a wild gesture and another watery smile she corrected herself.

"Forgive me," she said in her stilted French. "I am so worried I hardly know what I am doing."

Josephine, watching her with secret amusement, inclined her head gravely.

278

"Please sit down, Madame Bonaparte," she said.

Madame Bonaparte said "Thank you," and sat on the edge of a chair. During the uneasy silence that followed, Josephine reflected that this was the first time she and Madame Bonaparte had been alone since the wretched woman and her interfering pig of a son Joseph had discovered poor Hyppolyte beneath the bed in the boudoir upstairs. Since then a truce had existed between them, but it had been, and still was (Josephine imagined) the most rigid of armed truces.

"I came to see you," Madame Bonaparte said at last, "because I could bear the suspense no longer."

Josephine smiled graciously. "You're very welcome, Madame Bonaparte."

"Thank you, Josephine. You see, I know nothing of what is happening, nothing except that Napoleon is attempting some political *coup* and that his life is in danger. Where is he, and what is he doing? If you know, for pity's sake tell me!"

Briefly Josephine told her the little she knew. Bonaparte, with his brother, Lucien, had left that morning for St. Cloud. He knew that the members of the Council of Five Hundred had assembled there and his intention was clearly to dismiss them and set up a provisional Consulate which would consist of himself, Siéyes and Ducos.

"And if he fails?" Madame Bonaparte cried. "What then?"

The words gave Josephine a sudden stab of fear.

"Failure," she asserted, "is out of the question."

"How calm and sure you sound!" Madame Bonaparte said, with grudging admiration.

Josephine, beginning to enjoy herself in spite of the gravity of the situation, smiled graciously again. It then occurred to her that since Madame Bonaparte was evidently laboring under an agony of suspense (as she herself was, of course!) a heaven-sent opportunity was presenting itself for a morsel of revenge. She'd make the old harridan suffer a little more, by heavens she would!

"It is easy to *sound* calm and sure," she said, "but not so easy to *feel* calm and sure. In my heart there is nothing but doubt and fear. I *tell* myself that failure is out of the question, but that is bravado, sheer bravado."

Madame Bonaparte sprang to her feet in alarm. Her face seemed more drawn than ever and all that Josephine could see of her eyes was the whites. She smothered a chuckle in her throat and added, with a suitable break in her voice:

"You see, Madame Bonaparte, I have experienced too much political intrigue in my life to believe that Bonaparte can succeed in this venture, this *insane* venture."

"He is over-ambitious," Madame Bonaparte said shrilly, "that is the trouble, he is over-ambitious!"

She began to pace up and down the room. In delight, but with a suitably grave countenance, Josephine sat back in her chair and watched her.

"There's nothing we can do," she murmured, "but wait and hope."

Madame Bonaparte halted in her tracks. "You do not mind if I wait here with you?"

"Of course not. Why should I mind?"

Madame Bonaparte looked at her steadily. "We have not been friends, you and I. We have never seen eye to eye."

"Well, no," Josephine admitted.

"I well remember our first meeting. We almost quarreled then. Later we *did* quarrel. I will not hide from you the fact that I, as well as my children, were bitterly disappointed when Napoléoné refused to divorce you. But now, Napoléoné has told me that you are a different woman, that you are helping him, as a good wife should."

"I hope I shall always help him," Josephine said, trying not to smile, "as a good wife should."

"One more thing I must say, and then I have finished," Madame Bonaparte went on. "Let us both try to be friends in the future, for we are two women with one interest in common: *my* son, *your* husband."

"*Your* son," Josephine echoed, looking up with wide, innocent eyes, "*my* husband."

For a moment a look of suspicion crossed Madame Bonaparte's face.

"I hope," she said, "that you are as sincere as you sound."

Josephine's first impulse was to leap to her feet in a temper. For a moment she struggled with herself, bit her lip and remained silent. The woman was impossible, utterly impossible. They would never be friends, never in a thousand years!

Further conversation was, of course, out of the question. Josephine settled down to a grim silence; Madame Bonaparte resumed her pacing. From time to time she stopped, glanced questioningly at Josephine, appeared to shrug and went on pacing. 'The old bitch,' Josephine thought, 'she's dying to ask if I'm pregnant yet!'

An uneasy stillness fell on the room. It was almost as if, beneath the volcanic surface of their mutual resentment, the lava was bubbling faster and faster, and that at any moment an eruption might take place. Fortunately, after only a few moments of silence, the sound of racing hoof-beats became audible.

"Listen!" Madame Bonaparte cried.

Both women rushed to the window. The hoof-beats were drawing rapidly closer and a crowd, which seemed to have appeared from nowhere, a shouting, gesticulating crowd, was milling about the door. In a moment a number of horsemen were among the crowd and the foremost, quite unmistakably, was Bonaparte.

The crowd cheered and began to call his name.

"Bonaparte! Long live General Bonaparte!"

"Long live the First Consul!"

"Long live the savior of France!"

And finally somebody cried: "Long live the Republic!"

"The Republic comes last, it seems," Madame Bonaparte remarked drily. "Napoléoné first. That, undoubtedly, will be symbolical. Ah well, we must be thankful that he is safe, that he returns to Paris a free man."

Bonaparte, fighting his way through the crowd, entered the house. Josephine and Madame Bonaparte hurried forward to greet him.

"Why, Mother!" he said, in surprise and pleasure. "*You* here!"

"I came for news," she said. "I was anxious. I see now that you were able to look after yourself."

Josephine threw herself into his arms. If the old harridan thought she was going to take first place at a moment like this she was badly mistaken!

"Oh, Bonaparte!" Josephine cried. "Is it true? Have you really succeeded?"

He pushed her away from him. He was flushed and excited and breathing heavily. He made a grandiloquent gesture.

"You can hear the crowd," he shouted. "*There* is your answer. The Directory is dead. The destinies of France are now in the hands of the Consulate." He threw out his chest. "Remember, if you please, to address me in the future as First Consul Bonaparte." He threw out his chest still farther. "Tomorrow we sleep, you and I, at the Luxembourg!"

*   *   *   *   *

Josephine, wearing a new dress and the latest fashion in hats, stood in her boudoir at the house in the rue Victoire for the last time. Everything was packed and the dust covers were already in place over the furniture. She shuddered delicately; an almost death-like silence had fallen over everything. 'I died during the Revolution,' she thought, 'and came back to earth with the fall of Robespierre; I have died again today and will come back to earth again when I enter the Luxembourg.'

The Luxembourg! If anyone had told her a month ago that she would leave the rue Victoire for a palace she would have thought them mad. The Luxembourg! It was too fantastic!

A sudden thought made her chuckle. Those Bonapartes, divorce was what they'd wanted, not the Luxembourg. Obscurity and disgrace, not honor and the cheering approbation of the crowd.

"They'll be jealous, insanely jealous!" she said aloud.

She heard footsteps in the passage.

"Ah," said Bonaparte, looking into the room, "I see you're ready."

She went to him gaily. "Bonaparte, I can't believe it all. The Luxembourg! No, no, it's too fantastic!"

"Rubbish! After a few weeks, when we get the Parisians used to our greatness, we'll move on to the Tuileries."

"The Tuileries?" she gasped. "But you must be joking!"

"I'm perfectly serious," he said, with affected calmness. "You approve, surely?"

"Oh yes, I approve," she said quickly, "but there are many who won't. Your mother, for instance, she will shake her head and say—" (here Josephine imitated Madame Bonaparte's voice and gestures perfectly)—"she will say: 'That Napoléoné, his vaunting ambition frightens me.'"

Bonaparte frowned. "Well yes, no doubt she will, but like everybody else she will have to accommodate herself to my vaunting ambition." His frown melted away and for a moment he smiled. "And speaking of my mother, Josephine, let me say how delighted I was to find her and you together yesterday, how delighted and how surprised."

"I was a little surprised myself," Josephine admitted.

"It was a fine gesture she made, coming to you like that."

"Yes, wasn't it!" Josephine said tartly.

"Does it mean," he asked, apparently missing the tartness, "that you and my family are about to reach a more amicable understanding at last?"

"I don't see why it shouldn't," she murmured, looking down her nose.

"Splendid! Your past relations, to say the least, have been stormy. That you and they should be good friends now is the best thing in the world, for you will naturally be brought into much closer contact."

Josephine sighed delicately. "Ah yes, I feared that something like that would happen."

"You *feared*, madame?" he said sharply. "Let me tell you, Josephine, you will be wise, very wise, if you endeavor to avoid all the differences of opinion you can with my family."

"And let me tell *you*, Bonaparte, *they* will be wise, very wise, to avoid all the differences of opinion they can with *me*."

"They shall be warned," he said stiffly, "but I naturally expect you to meet them half-way. In the past, the fault, I admit, has been theirs as much as yours, but you must agree that had you used even a little discretion——"

"Really, Bonaparte," she interrupted, "must you commence yet *another* lecture on that most tiresome subject, the Bonapartes versus your wife?" She stamped her foot and brought on a flood of tears. "What a hard and cruel man you are, and how you make me hate you!"

He looked at her coldly. "Come, my dear, you might at least spare me a scene on such a day as this."

"A scene!" she cried. "If *this* is a scene, who started it? I ask you, Bonaparte, who started it! Oh, your family, your wretched interfering family. How I wish they'd never been born!"

"Enough of this nonsense," he said, and she saw that his face had turned very pale. "The carriage is waiting below, waiting to take us to the Luxembourg. Are you ready to accompany me, or do I go alone?"

Her tears ceased and she gave a final sniff.

"I'm ready," she said.

"Then take my arm," he commanded, "and try, even if you feel like murdering me, to look like a faithful, loving wife."

"You beast, Bonaparte," she said sweetly, "you ill-bred Corsican beast!"

They went out to the carriage. A little crowd had gathered about it. Smiling graciously Josephine allowed Bonaparte to help her in. The people began to cheer. "Long live Bonaparte!" they shouted. "Long live Josephine!" As the carriage drove away she leaned out and waved happily.

At the Luxembourg there was a larger, noisier crowd, and it was some time before Bonaparte and Josephine could make their way through the clamoring, shouting people. The cries of "Long live Bonaparte!" and "Long live Josephine!" were deafening.

"We might be king and queen!" Josephine whispered.

"In all but name we *are* king and queen," he replied.

They were received at the Luxembourg by the other two consuls Siéyes and Ducos who, it seemed, were taking up residence there also. Josephine made a face at this news.

"I thought," she remarked pettishly, "that we were to have the place to ourselves."

Bonaparte pinched her cheek playfully. "My sweet little Josephine, some day we shall have a greater palace to ourselves, but not just yet. Try to realize that Siéyes and Ducos are of little consequence but for the moment are very necessary window-dressing. The people would never accept my dictatorship at one blow, they must be brought round to it gradually. Siéyes and Ducos will go the way of Barras and the rest when the time is ripe."

When the ceremony of their arrival was completed, when hysterical speeches had been made and the people had dispersed, Bonaparte led Josephine to his suite of rooms on the ground floor of the palace. The furnishings were few and simple; the rooms, Josephine thought, had the look of a prison.

"We must be modest to begin with," Bonaparte pronounced. "You may, of course, be a little more lavish in your own rooms."

"My own rooms, Bonaparte? Then I'm not to share your suite?"

"No, my dear. A separate suite is waiting for you on the next floor directly above here."

"So you wish to keep me at a distance," she said, and added sadly, "Times have changed, Bonaparte. You make that very clear."

"You won't be as far away as you imagine, you little goose. A private staircase connects the two suites."

"A private staircase!" she exclaimed. "That sounds like something out of a novel."

"I thought it might fascinate you." He took her by the arm. "Now come and sit down, I want to talk to you."

She allowed him to lead her to a chair and sat down obediently. What was coming, she wondered—another lecture? She looked at him cautiously. He had folded his arms and was gazing dreamily out of the window.

"As you know," he began, "I am on the eve of instituting a new political era; but quite apart from that I am also on the eve of instituting a new social era. The political era I can take care of myself; but the social era, that is where *you* come in."

She sprang up in delight. "Anything I can do, Bonaparte, I will do gladly, *gladly!*"

"There is plenty for you to do. The society of the old monarchy is something of a mystery to me. If I dealt with it in the same manner in which I propose to deal with the clergy I'd find myself bogged in a morass of prejudice. Therefore——"

"Just one moment, Bonaparte!" Josephine interrupted—"do you mean that you're going to restore the old society?"

"I do, but gradually of course, and only in proportion to its usefulness. You, my dear, are an aristocrat. Before the Revolution you, the wife of the Vicomte de Beauharnais, were a leader of fashion. Your *salon* was frequented by the *right* people."

The emphasis on 'right' brought a pout to Josephine's mouth.

"I think you're trying to be sarcastic," she complained.

"By no means," he smiled. "The point I'm trying to make is this: no one better than you can act as an intermediary between me and the returning emigrants, courtiers and noblemen."

"Thank you," she said, quite deeply flattered.

"Knowing you as I do," he laughed, "I feel sure that you will find your part in helping to restore the old order both pleasing and exciting."

"Oh, I shall, I shall!"

"You will have a completely free hand, without interference from me—providing," he added with a grin, "you aren't *too* extravagant."

"Ah, so there's to be at least *one* condition!"

"The condition is merely a matter of policy. My position is not yet as secure as I wish it to be. The Directory made the fatal mistake of openly squandering public money. I've no wish for people to point at me and say: 'Look at the way his wife spends our money, look at the lavish scale on which she entertains.' Bear that in mind and all will be well."

She nodded vigorously. "Very well, Bonaparte."

"Entertain modestly while we're here, modestly and with dignity. Choose your friends carefully. Keep a strict watch for imposters. Undesirables must be sternly turned away. One other point," Bonaparte went on, "I have long abhorred the use of 'citizen' and 'citizeness,' even as you have. Set the fashion once more of addressing a man as 'monsieur' and a woman as 'madame.' That, as much as anything else, will give the touch of dignity I wish to establish."

She made him a pretty little bow. "I'll do it gladly, m'sieur."

He returned her bow, though a trifle clumsily. "Thank you, madame!"

"When do you wish me to give my first dinner party?" she asked.

"At the earliest possible moment."

"Tomorrow, then."

"Can it be arranged at so short a notice?"

"It can, providing the list of guests isn't too long."

"Shall we say a dozen?" he mused.

"A dozen would be excellent."

"Say a dozen, then. Include Siéyes and Ducos, of course, and Talleyrand, and also Fouché."

"Fouché?" she questioned, thinking of all she knew about the man.

"He's a rogue, I admit," Bonaparte smiled, "but a valuable rogue, and the very man for the Ministry of Police. Choose the rest of the guests yourself, and be sure to invite your Aunt Marie, who, after all, is a dignified old aristocrat."

Josephine hid a smile. Poor Aunt Marie, how she'd laugh at such a description!

Bonaparte began to pace the room. After a moment he turned to Josephine. His chest was thrown out and his eyes shone with pride and self-satisfaction. He seemed, Josephine thought, to have grown at least three inches in stature.

"Remember," he said, "that the keynote of the dinner party must be modesty and dignity."

"I'll remember, Bonaparte."

He sighed deeply and balanced himself lightly on his toes.

"Ah, my dear," he said, in a whisper, "you and I together, we're going to change the face of this sorry and bewildered Paris! And after the face of Paris, the face of France herself!"

CHAPTER XXIX

JOSEPHINE, SITTING AT HER mirror and completing a lengthy *toilette*, was bored. She was now in residence at the Tuileries, occupying apartments formerly occupied by Marie Antoinette, but nevertheless she was bored. For one thing, Bonaparte was away with the army. (News had reached Paris a few days ago of his spectacular crossing of the Alps with thirty-five thousand men, and news was hourly awaited of his entry into Milan.) This meant, of course, that she was now in a position to enjoy a limited amount of freedom, but she was not the sort of woman who could enjoy a *limited* amount of anything. In the old days Bonaparte's absence would have been the signal for a new flirtation, or a brief and refreshing *affaire*, but now— She sighed tremulously. "But now," she said aloud, "I've learned my lesson. I'm a faithful wife, God pity me!"

There was a tap at the door and her maid entered. Hovering behind her was Aunt Marie. Josephine turned from the mirror with a smile of welcome. A little gossip with Aunt Marie would be better than nothing and would round off the afternoon quite pleasantly.

Aunt Marie collapsed into a chair and complained that rheumatism was making life something of a burden. She went on to chat about this and that, to inquire after Eugene and Hortense, but Josephine, who knew her aunt so well, felt perfectly sure that the visit had been prompted by something more serious than the desire for an exchange of gossip. And presently she had the satisfaction of knowing that she was right.

"My dear," Aunt Marie said at last, "I want to have a talk with you about politics."

"Politics? *You*, Aunt Marie?"

Aunt Marie smiled and went on: "Josephine, before you married Bonaparte you were an aristocrat and the widow of an aristocrat. You were also a royalist who had served a term of imprisonment."

A frown gathered on Josephine's brow. Aunt Marie smiled again.

"Bear with me for a moment longer, my dear. I shall get to the point at once. I have been approached recently by Bourbon agents. They want me to use my influence with you to bring their cause, the royalist cause, to Bonaparte's notice."

"You mean that you want me to persuade Bonaparte to use his power for the purpose of restoring the monarchy?"

"Yes."

"What makes you think that he would be interested in a restoration?"

"The way he makes returning emigrants welcome here at the Tuileries, for one thing."

"Ah, but he's just as hospitable to the republicans."

Aunt Marie frowned. "Yes, I've noticed that. The whole thing, of course, depends on your own attitude. You don't favor the republicans more than the royalists, do you?"

Josephine shuddered delicately. "God forbid."

Aunt Marie's face brightened. "Then I may count on your help?"

Josephine was silent and thoughtful for a moment.

"The time," she said at last, "is not yet ripe."

"Does that mean that you don't want to help the royalist cause?"

Josephine laughed lightly. "Perhaps."

"And yet, you certainly don't want to help the republican cause!"

"No, Aunt Marie. I want to help one cause only, my husband's."

"I can quite understand that," Aunt Marie said, "but sooner or later Bonaparte will be obliged to make up his mind one way or the other. He will have to choose between the royalists and the republicans, and you, with your influence, can help him to make the right choice."

Josephine's mind went back to the placards which had filled the streets of Paris shortly after the fall of the Directory. They'd been headed 'Political Subtraction' and the problem had read: 'From five directors take two; there remain three consuls; from three consuls take two and there remains Napoleon Bonaparte.' With a laugh she reminded Aunt Marie of this.

"Well, what of it?" Aunt Marie said.

"There are still three consuls," Josephine smiled, "but the only one that counts is Napoleon Bonaparte, who is now installed at the Tuileries. Do you really think that he's going to vacate this fine palace for a Bourbon prince?"

Aunt Marie was silent.

"Whatever title you might choose to give him," Josephine went on, "Bonaparte is the ruler of France and intends to remain the ruler of France. A little while ago his mother shook her head and muttered that Napoléoné was like a big fish who had swallowed up all the little fish. She was right, and Bonaparte, I feel sure, will always do precisely that—swallow up all the little fish, whether they be republican fish or royalist fish. Go back to your royalist agents, Aunt Marie, and repeat Madame Bonaparte's words to them."

Aunt Marie rose with a sigh. "Very well, Josephine, but I'm disappointed in you, sadly disappointed. I only hope that this game you're playing, you and Bonaparte, this game of king and queen, won't carry you too far."

Josephine smiled and shrugged.

"I don't think it will," she said confidently.

Before more could be said there was a tap at the door. "Come in," Josephine called, and Bourrienne, Bonaparte's secretary, entered. She saw, by a glance at his face, that he brought good news.

"Well, Bourrienne, what is it?"

He smiled broadly. "Madame, the First Consul has made a triumphant entry into Milan and has re-established the Cisalpine Republic."

Josephine turned to Aunt Marie. "The big fish again, you see."

"Yes," Aunt Marie agreed gravely, "the big fish again."

"When do you expect Bonaparte to return home?" Josephine asked Bourrienne.

"Very soon, madame, though no definite date has yet been mentioned."

"I suppose," Josephine said thoughtfully, "that I ought to do something to celebrate this latest victory. Something personal, I mean. Have you any suggestions, Bourrienne?"

"Why not a grand reception, or possibly a ball?"

"That would mean spending too much money and might displease Bonaparte," she said, with unaccustomed prudence.

"Perhaps a private dinner, then, with the First Consul's mother the guest of honor?"

Josephine frowned. "Not *that*, Bourrienne!"

"It would please the First Consul more than anything else," he said. "It would show him that you were making an attempt to—well——"

"To be friendly and sociable with her relatives-in-law?" Aunt Marie supplied.

"Well, yes, madame."

"Very well," Josephine said, "I'll make a martyr of myself once more. A private dinner party it shall be, with Madame Bonaparte the guest of honor. Let me see, how many Bonapartes are in Paris at the moment?"

"Apart from Madame Bonaparte there is only Joseph, Caroline and Paulette."

"Paulette? But I thought *she* was in the country!"

"She returned this morning, madame."

Josephine sighed elaborately. "Oh well, I suppose we must send out the invitations. See to it, Bourrienne."

Bourrienne bowed. "For tomorrow night, madame?"

"That would be rather short notice. Saturday, I think, would be better. Stay, though!" For a moment she smiled happily. "Make it tomorrow night, after all. At so short a notice it's just possible that they'll all have other engagements. In that case I shall have done my part and no further invitations will be issued. That will be all, Bourrienne."

Bourrienne bowed himself out of the room.

Josephine turned to Aunt Marie, who was grinning broadly.

"You'll come, of course, Aunt Marie?"

Aunt Marie shook her head. "My dear, I'm far too old and full of rheumatism to be referee at what might turn out to be a pitched battle between you and Paulette Bonaparte."

And with that she took her leave, shaking her head sadly and murmuring once again: "I only hope that this game you're playing won't carry you too far. . . ."

* * * * *

While Josephine was making her morning *toilette* on the day of her proposed dinner party three notes of apology were delivered at the Tuileries. They came from Madame Bonaparte, Joseph and Caroline. Each regretted that a previous engagement made it impossible to be present at the dinner party.

"Splendid!" Josephine cried. "That leaves only Paulette and she won't come alone, I'm sure!"

After luncheon, when no note of apology had arrived from Paulette, Josephine began to grow a little anxious. By the middle of the afternoon she was on tenterhooks and by six in the evening, when it seemed obvious that Paulette intended to present herself for dinner, Josephine was storming up and down her boudoir in a furious temper.

To be forced to dine alone with Paulette, the most hated (next to Joseph) of the Bonaparte brood!

"Intolerable!" she shouted, "*intolerable!*"

In due course Paulette was announced and swept into Josephine's drawing-room as if she were mistress of the Tuileries. She was wearing a new and very scanty dress which clung with a disgusting frankness to the curves of her perfect figure. Josephine, looking at her, felt sick with envy. No wonder they called the wretched girl the Bonaparte Venus!

"I suppose you're a little surprised to see me," Paulette remarked, looking about her arrogantly.

Josephine made an admirable attempt to control herself. "Surprised, my dear? But why? I sent you an invitation and you didn't refuse it."

"Oh yes, but when the others were unable to come you must have been just a little surprised that I should choose to come alone."

"Well, perhaps I was," Josephine admitted, "but since we so rarely have a little chat together these days I welcome the opportunity of dining alone with you."

Paulette, staring at her, laughed rudely.

"Have I said anything amusing?" Josephine asked mildly.

"You certainly have, Josephine! *You* welcome the opportunity of dining alone with me! How prettily you lie!"

"Really, Paulette!—" Josephine said weakly.

"Why don't you tell the truth? Why don't you say you hate the thought of it as much as I hate it myself?"

"My dear child," Josephine said, trying to gain command of the conversation, "if this is your idea of a joke——"

"I'm not joking, Josephine."

Josephine looked at the girl steadily. No, she didn't appear to be joking. Her lips might be smiling but her eyes were cold and calculating.

"Then you came," she said, "for the pleasure of insulting me."

"No. I really came to give you some news of Napoleon."

"I think I know all the news of my husband there is to be known, thank you, Paulette!"

"I wonder if you do. I wonder, for instance, if you've heard anything about the concert given in his honor when he entered Milan?"

"A concert? Yes, Bourrienne mentioned it this morning."

"And did he mention the two famous Italian singers who took part in it—Marchesi and Grassini?"

Josephine shook her head. There was something in Paulette's voice that alarmed her. She watched the girl's face intently. She smiled and said softly:

"Grassini is the more interesting of the two, of course. Are you sure you've never heard the name Grassini before?"

"What are you trying to tell me, Paulette?" Josephine demanded.

"Simply this, Josephine. Napoleon is beginning to pay you back in kind, and with a vengeance. Grassini, I understand, has a splendid voice. She has also, I understand, a splendid figure."

"*She!*" Josephine exclaimed.

"Ah, you thought Grassini was a man." Paulette smiled and turned to the door, where she paused for a moment. "Napoleon, so they say, is listening to Grassini's voice on every possible occasion. His interest, I admit, might go no farther, but time, of course, will tell. *Au revoir*, Josephine. I trust you enjoy your solitary dinner."

"Brat!" Josephine shouted, but Paulette, slamming the door behind her, was gone.

After a moment's hesitation Josephine called her maid and sent for Bourrienne. She came to the point the moment he entered the room.

"Bourrienne, what do you know about this Italian singer, Madame Grassini?"

"Well—" he hesitated.

"Is she young? Is she attractive?"

"That, madame," he said diplomatically, "is a matter of personal taste and judgment."

"She possesses, I believe, a ravishing figure."

"Ravishing?" he murmured. "A little massive, I think."

"Then you've actually seen her, Bourrienne?"

He nodded. "Two years ago. Her eyes are black and rather brilliant. Her skin is olive and her hair, of course, is dark. One might call her typical of the Italian idea of beauty."

"Is that all you know?"

"Well, yes."

"Be frank with me, Bourrienne. Is Bonaparte having an *affaire* with her?"

"As far as I know, madame, the First Consul merely admires her voice."

"Thank you, Bourrienne," she said, and dismissed him.

The First Consul merely admires her voice. Nothing very alarming in that, of course, and yet—! Josephine's heart gave a leap of dismay. Bonaparte had once admired *her* voice, and look what *that* had led to—a rough and tumble on the floor with nothing more comfortable beneath them than an army cloak and a cushion. Why, even at this moment—!

"Stop this nonsense," she told herself aloud, "stop it!"

After all, Paulette had probably exaggerated, her intention being

to create havoc in her—Josephine's—sensitive mind. *The little bitch,
I'll pay her out at the first opportunity!*

* * * * *

"M'sieur Foncier," the maid announced.

Josephine sprang to her feet with a cry of pleasure as Foncier,
a dapper little man who looked more like a diplomat than a jeweler,
bowed himself into the room. She held out her hand. He made a
final sweeping bow and kissed it.

"And what does M'sieur Foncier bring me this time?" she asked.
"Diamonds, pearls, emeralds or——"

"Pearls, madame," he said, and drew from an inner pocket a flat,
velvet-covered jewel case. He opened it with a flourish. "There!"

Josephine caught her breath. "Oh, Foncier, how very exquisite!"

"They were brought to my establishment not an hour ago. I
strongly suspect that they were once the property of her late Majesty, Queen Marie Antoinette. Ah, I tell myself, what more fitting
than that they should first be submitted to Madame Bonaparte, her
Majesty's successor at the Tuileries."

"What more fitting indeed!" Josephine cried. She reached out to
take up the pearls with trembling fingers. "May I, Foncier?"

"Permit me," he said, and adjusted the string about her neck.

She turned to the mirror and, sick with longing, gazed in silence
at her reflection. Diamonds and emeralds she had by the score, but
pearls—pearls such as these—she had never even dreamed of possessing.

"If General Bonaparte could see them now," Foncier murmured,
"he would agree with me that though a queen once wore them they
were destined for no other woman but his wife."

"I doubt it," she sighed. "My husband is generous, I admit, but
the Bonapartes, at heart, are all very saving. No, no, Foncier, he
would merely ask the price."

"Ah yes, the price. A little high, naturally, but for such a string
of pearls, who would hesitate to pay even a million francs?"

"A—a *million*, Foncier?" she gasped.

"To you, madame, the price is only *half* that."

Her heart sank. A bargain, undoubtedly, but where in the world
was she to find five hundred thousand francs? Her fingers went to
the catch, wavered, and fell away. There must be some way, surely
there must!

"It would hardly be necessary for madame to make immediate
payment," Foncier murmured.

"But I owe you so much money already, Foncier."

"A hundred thousand francs only, madame. The credit of the First Consul, I feel confident, was never better."

Josephine pursed her lips. That was all very well, but what of her own credit? Her allowance, certainly, had been doubled, but she was already deeply overdrawn and Foncier was not her only creditor. Her fingers, feeling as heavy as lead, went up to the catch again.

"Madame," Foncier said promptly, "could retain the pearls on approval for two weeks."

"You would expect payment by that time?" she questioned.

He nodded regretfully and shrugged. "I am, after all, and unfortunately, a man of business."

"Very well," she said briskly, "I accept your offer, Foncier, and thank you from the bottom of my heart."

✳　　✳　　✳　　✳　　✳

Bourrienne, not without trepidation, placed a copy of the latest Army Bulletin on Josephine's escritoire. He bowed hastily and made to withdraw, but she stopped him.

"This was issued in Milan, of course?"

"Of course, madame."

"Is there any mention in it of Madame Grassini?"

"Well yes, madame," he was obliged to admit.

"Then save me the trouble of searching for it. Find it and read it out to me."

Bourrienne picked up the bulletin, turned the pages, traced the paragraph with his forefinger and cleared his throat.

" 'The First Consul,' " he read, " 'along with the Commander-in-Chief, General Berthier, attended another concert last night and was charmed by some fine examples of Italian singing. The famous singers, Mrs. Billington, Madame Marchesi and Madame Grassini delighted both the First Consul and the Commander-in-Chief.' "

"Is that all, Bourrienne?"

He cleared his throat. "I'm afraid not, madame."

"Read the rest then."

" 'These three singers,' " he went on, " 'after concluding their series of concerts in Milan, expect to proceed to Paris.' "

"Ah!" Josephine cried.

"Things might not be as bad as you imagine, madame," Bourrienne ventured. "In any case, little can be done till the First Consul returns to Paris."

293

"No, I suppose not," Josephine was obliged to agree.

"And in any case, madame, you may be alarming yourself over nothing. All you have to go on is gossip and the fact that the First Consul is attending concerts at which one of the singers is Madame Grassini."

"And also the fact that Madame Grassini is coming to Paris."

"Along with the other two singers, madame."

"That, my dear Bourrienne, is a blind. However, as you say, little can be done till Bonaparte returns to Paris."

"And even then, madame, it would be wise to refrain from letting the First Consul know that you are suspicious of his interest in Madame Grassini."

"I can't agree with you there, Bourrienne."

An anxious week passed, with more gossip of Bonaparte and Grassini filtering through to Paris each day. He was devoting all his time to her. Not content with attending every concert, he was conducting her home afterwards and insisting on private auditions in the middle of the night. He was sending her jewelry and expensive furs. He had written a poem about her voice and had been heard to declare in public that he was her slave for life.

"Jewelry and furs!" Josephine muttered darkly. "Most certainly I shall keep my pearls whether I can pay for them or not!"

By the time Bonaparte was *en route* for Paris she was half crazy with jealousy. When at last he arrived she suspected coldness in his greeting and only restrained herself by a miracle of self-restraint from hurling the name Grassini in his face.

While not agreeing with Bourrienne's advice she tried, during the first day, to follow it. On the second day she sent for General Berthier, who had always been polite and friendly towards her, and questioned him closely. Grassini, she learned, was now in Paris and was expected to give a concert in the very near future. Also, she was to sing a duet with Bianchi at the Feast of the Concord.

"For which," Josephine snapped, "she will undoubtedly be well paid."

Berthier smiled. "Very well paid indeed, as I myself have reason to know."

"Why you yourself?"

"As Commander-in-Chief I have complete control of army funds and——"

"Merciful heavens!" she exclaimed, "do you mean that the wretched woman's expenses are a drain on army funds?"

He nodded. "And a substantial drain too."

Josephine had never been more shocked in her life. Here she was, scraping here and pinching there in an effort to find a paltry five hundred thousand francs while a screeching Italian singer—! It was intolerable, intolerable!

"Madame Bonaparte," Berthier was saying, "I wonder if I dare ask a favor of you?"

"A favor?" she said vaguely, her mind still seething with indignation. "Why not?"

"It concerns Madame Visconti," he said, with an awkward little laugh. "She—er—she happens to be a very dear friend of mine with certain social ambitions. In short, madame, she would like to see herself established in the inner circle of the Consular Court."

Josephine frowned. "By a very dear friend you naturally mean that Madame Visconti is your mistress."

"Well yes, but also my future wife. To be frank, madame, her one condition before accepting marriage is the social establishment of which I spoke."

Josephine pursed her lips. Berthier, it seemed, was madly in love; not only madly but foolishly. Berthier would therefore pay a good price to gain for his mistress the social elevation she so badly desired.

"How much would it be worth to me?" she said frankly.

Berthier looked startled. "In actual money, madame?"

"In actual money, Berthier."

He smiled ruefully. "I'm afraid that in spite of my position I am a very poor man."

"Ah yes, but a man who controls, completely controls, the funds of the army."

He looked at her in amazement.

"Does my husband," she asked, "ever inquire deeply into your administration of those funds?"

"Well no," he admitted.

"Ah!"

There was a silence. Berthier ran the tip of his tongue round his lower lip. Josephine, watching him, felt sure that she was about to get her way. And why not, merciful heavens, why not! If Madame Grassini could acquire furs and jewelry and heaven knew what else at the expense of army funds, surely the wife of the First Consul, desiring nothing more than a little string of pearls, could expect—no, no, could *demand*—!

"What *is* your price?" Berthier asked.

Josephine smiled brightly. "Merely half a million francs."

"Half a million!"

"Let us say five hundred thousand, then; it sounds much less ambitious."

There was another silence. The tip of Berthier's tongue was busy again.

"If Bonaparte were to discover the expenditure," she said softly —"and a man as clever as you could surely put it down to ammunition or general supplies—but if he *were* to discover it you could easily point out that a wife has as much right to benefit from the army funds as a mistress."

Berthier laughed shakily. "Yes, yes, I could."

"We make a bargain, then?"

He hesitated no longer. "Very well, madame, we make a bargain."

"Thank you," she said warmly. "Madame Visconti will be received at the Tuileries immediately. As for the money, on my behalf you will pay it to Foncier the jeweler."

And then, in case he changed his mind, she bade him a hasty *au revoir* and hustled him out of her apartments. 'And now,' she thought grimly, 'my next concern is Grassini.'

*   *   *   *   *

Bonaparte was dictating a letter to Bourrienne when Josephine burst into the room. The latter sprang up hastily at the sight of her face and Bonaparte half rose in his chair.

"Grassini!" she cried.

The word came out of her mouth like a minor explosion.

"Grassini!" she cried again, with greater venom.

Bonaparte coughed and, for the moment, looked helpless.

"What have I done to deserve such treatment?" she demanded. She turned to Bourrienne. "What have I *done*?"

At a gesture from Bonaparte, Bourrienne went hurriedly from the room. Bonaparte sank slowly back into his chair. Josephine, flinging papers right and left from the desk began to hammer on it wildly.

"Beast!" she cried. "Beast!"

His face grew pale but he remained silent.

"Bonaparte, the most heartless man in the world!"

He still remained silent, staring at her.

"How little you care for your poor wife's feelings!"

His eyes caught and held her own.

"It must be either Grassini or I. Make your choice, Bonaparte! Either she goes or I do!"

He sprang to his feet and flung open the door. "What is your destination, madame? Malmaison, or possibly Martinique?"

She uttered a piercing scream. "*Bonaparte!*"

"No fainting, I beg of you!"

For the first time she was aware of alarm in his voice. No fainting indeed! She clutched at her throat, slumped against the convenient desk to break her fall and slipped to the floor.

"Bourrienne!" Bonaparte shouted. "Water!"

Bourrienne—she could see him through her half-opened eyelids —came running with a carafe and a glass goblet. He got down on his knees at her side and began to fill the goblet.

"Pah!" Bonaparte said, snatching up the carafe. "This is what I meant you to do with it!"

And tipping up the carafe he slopped its contents over her face and head and neck. She sprang up with a squeal of rage.

"Pig! Ill-bred Corsican pig!"

He took her roughly by the shoulders and forced her into a chair. Bourrienne, with a backward glance, left the room again. In the ante-room she could hear excited voices, one of them, high and clear, being that of the wretched Paulette.

"You behave foolishly," Bonaparte said harshly. "You would be better advised to ignore the things in my private life which you are powerless to obstruct."

She shivered violently. Little streams of ice-cold water were running down her back and chest.

"How little you care whether you hurt my feelings or not," she sobbed.

"You had little concern for *my* feelings when I was in Egypt."

"Ah, you propose to hold that one small indiscretion against me for the rest of my life!"

"Nonsense. I merely refer to it because it was the thing which made me feel justified in seeking diversion myself when and where and as often as I choose."

"But a singer, Bonaparte, a common singer!"

"Grassini is by no means a common singer. Her voice is incomparable, enchanting, magnetic."

"Magnetic!" she cried.

"The sweetness and pathos of it—" a dreamy look had come to his eyes—"are almost heartrending."

She closed her eyes with a little moan. "And to think that you once said that my voice was the most beautiful in the world."

"I had not then heard Grassini's."

Josephine sneezed suddenly.

"There!" she cried. "Your cruelty has given me a cold."

He knelt quickly at her side.

"Sweetheart," he said, contritely, "forgive me."

"Why Bonaparte, of course!" Her face had broken into a watery smile and her heart began to sing happily. "Grassini will be sent from Paris immediately?"

He shook his head. "No. She has an engagement to fulfil at the Théâtre de la Republique, and others of a more private nature here at the Tuileries."

Her smile faded; her heart felt heavy again in her breast.

"But you asked me to forgive you!"

"For half drowning you; not for anything else." He took her hands in his. "My dear, in Milan, after the strain of battle, Grassini's voice calmed my nerves and warmed my heart. It gave me new life and new hope; it intensified my dreams and ambitions. That is the reason for my interest in her, an interest which is concerned more with the singer than the woman."

She withdrew her hands and rose unsteadily to her feet.

"I think I begin to understand," she said quietly. "But tell me, am I expected to receive the woman here at the Tuileries?"

"Of course not. Her visits will naturally be secret."

"Naturally." She nodded her head sadly. "How very silly of me."

He reached out and kissed her swiftly on the cheek. "Thank you, Josephine, for having decided at last to be sensible."

Sensible! She could have laughed in his face.

"It was the cold water," she murmured, and now she did laugh, for the idea, the scheme for ridding herself of the Italian singer which had begun to form in her mind the moment she'd sneezed, was now complete in every detail.

*　　*　　*　　*　　*

"General Berthier," the maid announced.

"Ah, Berthier," Josephine cried cheerfully, "come in, my friend, come in."

She was seated in a low chair in her boudoir. A shawl was wound tightly round her neck and shoulders; her bare feet were thrust deeply into a footbath of steaming water.

"Mustard and water," she explained, when she saw Berthier's look of amazement, "as hot as I can possibly bear it."

"But why?" he asked.

"I suspected that I might be catching a cold and am doing my best to avert it. But sit down, sit down."

Berthier, chuckling, obeyed.

"Well, madame," he asked, "why did you send for me?"

"Because I need your help—your help in the matter of disposing of Grassini."

He shook his head quickly and rose. "My dear madame, I value my career too highly to endanger it by meddling in my master's private affairs."

"Don't be tiresome, Berthier," she said. "And remember, please, that though Madame Visconti has now been received at the Tuileries I may yet decide that it would not be in the best of taste to continue to receive her."

"But we made a bargain!" Berthier cried hotly. "The money has passed. The money has been paid to Foncier!"

Josephine lifted her feet from the water, drained them thoughtfully and replaced them.

"Oh come, Berthier," she said sweetly, "be sensible."

"What do you want me to do?" he asked sulkily.

"First," she said, "pour a little more hot water into the footbath for me."

He took up the large copper kettle which was standing nearby and obeyed.

"Not too much!" she cried, withdrawing her feet again hurriedly.

He put down the kettle and stood back, waiting. She tried the water with her toes, held her breath and immersed her shapely feet slowly, inch by inch.

"It has reached my ears," she said, "that Madame Grassini has certain political ambitions. Is that correct?"

"Why yes. At least, she wants to intervene with the First Consul on behalf of some of her fellow countrymen. Merely a matter of presenting petitions; nothing more serious than that."

"They haven't actually been presented yet, I hope?"

"No. As a matter of fact, she is afraid of offending the First Consul and is waiting till she feels more sure of him. Of course, when what she considers a favorable moment has arisen——"

"Precisely," Josephine chuckled, "precisely!"

Berthier was looking at her curiously. "What have you in mind, madame?"

"Bonaparte," she said, with another chuckle, "hates a woman to interfere in politics. I, you know, have been the only exception." Her voice became suddenly brisk. "Berthier, I want you to go to Grassini tomorrow afternoon and tell her that the long-awaited favorable moment has at last arrived. You might even say that you have prepared the ground for her, and that she must present her petitions tomorrow night. Meanwhile I will do my best to put Bonaparte in the worst possible humor."

Berthier chuckled. "Quite a good scheme, I admit, but more than likely he will merely tell her to put aside her petitions and sing an aria."

"I'm sure he will!" Josephine said promptly.

"Then——"

"Patience, Berthier, patience. If you were Bonaparte and you said to Grassini, 'Sing an aria,' and you discovered then that she had lost her voice, what would you say?"

"I should probably tell her to go to the devil and take her petitions with her."

"Of course you would!" She took him by the hand and looked at him with big, appealing eyes. "Berthier, my friend, you and I together are going to do our utmost to see that before tomorrow night Grassini has lost her beautiful, enchanting and so very magnetic voice!"

*   *   *   *   *

Josephine's apartments at the Tuileries, like those she had occupied at the Luxembourg, were above Bonaparte's and connected with them by a small, narrow staircase. Warned by her maid that Bonaparte's valet, the discreet Constant, had already entered the palace with a heavily veiled Grassini, Josephine was now at the bottom of the staircase with her ear pressed tightly against the door. Her heart was beating an excited tattoo but her head was clear. The threatened cold, thanks to the hot mustard and water, had been averted. "I can only pray," she whispered to herself, "that Grassini has never heard of mustard and water."

A murmur of voices reached her ears. A door closed in the distance and the murmur grew louder. A moment later she heard a distinct sneeze and almost laughed aloud. Then, his voice raised in annoyance, she heard Bonaparte say clearly:

"Petitions, madame? Did you say—petitions?"

"But yes, my own Napoléoné," Grassini replied (her voice was hoarse, Josephine would have sworn to that), "little petitions on the behalf of my oppressed countrymen in Milan. It rests with you, First Consul of the great and magnificent France, to make their miserable lot more comfortable. Therefore I——"

"Silence!" Bonaparte roared. "Silence, I say!"

"But Napoléoné, I do not comprehend. You are angry, and yet all I ask——"

"Madame," he shouted, "feminine meddling in politics is something I will never tolerate, even from you."

"But my own Napoléoné——"

"Not another word. You have displeased me enough as it is. I brought you here tonight, not to irritate me, but to soothe me. If you wish to please me, sing to me."

"No, no!" Grassini protested. "I am not in good voice tonight."

"Nonsense. You're merely sulky."

"Oh no, my friend, it is you who are sulky."

"You refuse to sing, then?"

"It is not that I refuse, it is my voice—she absents herself. Only listen and you will realize that I speak the truth."

Quivering with delight Josephine pressed her ear more closely against the door. A few appalling notes, ascending the scale and cracking lamentably, shattered the silence.

"There! You see!" There was another sneeze. "I have taken cold!"

"That was utterly stupid of you, madame."

"But the fault was not mine. Only listen and I will tell you the story. Last night, very late—midnight, as you say—when I am in bed one, two hours, a message is brought to me. 'Come immediately,' it say, 'First Consul very ill.'"

"Ill? *Me?*"

"I dress hurriedly. I throw on this and that, so. My own Napoléoné ill! I am desolated. My hands tremble. I rush to the street where a carriage is waiting. There is a long drive. I begin to shiver. It is winter and I am cold to the bone. The carriage, I realize, is open and I have forgotten my furs."

"Proceed, madame," Bonaparte said grimly.

"Presently the carriage stop. I imagine I am at the palace, but no! No, no, no! The road is empty. The postilion, he who bring the message by word of mouth, departs. There is a long wait. I shiver, oh how I shiver. Then he returns. A mistake has made itself. The First Consul is not ill. We drive back, I collapse, and sneeze and sneeze and——"

Josephine, chuckling softly to herself, heard another sneeze.

"An incredible story," Bonaparte said.

"You do not believe me?"

"I do not believe you, madame."

"But Napoléoné, my own, I assure you——"

Bonaparte's voice faded but was still audible. "Constant shall call your carriage and take you home. But first a word of advice. If the climate of Paris is so bad for you, why not return to your native Italy?"

Josephine, clapping her hands together and jumping up and down like a delighted child, heard a door open. This was followed by a little shriek from Grassini and Bonaparte's voice shouting: "Constant, Constant, Madame Grassini is leaving!"

A few moments later, when Josephine had hurried back up the stairs, the bottom door was flung open.

"Josephine!" she heard him call.

She rushed through the boudoir to the bedroom and leaped into bed.

"Josephine!"

He was in the boudoir now. She threw her head back on the pillows and, composing her features, pretended to be asleep. A moment later the bedclothes were dragged back sharply and Bonaparte was standing over her.

"As I suspected," he said, and pointed to her feet, which were still shod in slippers.

She looked him straight in the eye and giggled.

"You were listening, of course, madame?"

She made her eyelids flutter. "Of course."

He bent and kissed her, not on the cheek but full on the lips and warmly.

"You're a clever little witch," he said, smiling.

"Why, Bonaparte," she demanded, wide-eyed, "what in the world do you mean?"

"Is your door locked?" he asked.

"Why no, but Louise, having heard your voice, will see that we are not disturbed."

"Splendid."

Josephine looked at him slily. "I could never sing, Bonaparte, but my voice, I think, is still a pleasant one."

"The pleasantest in the world, Josephine."

He pinched her cheek and laughed loudly.

"What is it, Bonaparte?"

"I was wondering," he said, "if you'll be as clever next time."

"N-next time?"

"Yes, next time, for since I have found a taste for such things, there'll be many more Grassinis, many more, I promise you!"

She sniffed loudly. "And meanwhile, having nothing better to do, you turn to your wife."

He roared with laughter. "Precisely, sweetheart, precisely!"

CHAPTER XXX

IN MANY WAYS JOSEPH FOUché reminded Josephine of the now almost forgotten Barras. She looked at the man as he lounged in the most comfortable chair in her drawing-room, lounged there as if he, and not Bonaparte, were the First Consul of France. Short in stature he was, but well-proportioned, so that at a distance he had the appearance of a much taller man. His face in repose was pleasanter than Barras's, and his eyes, when he smiled, as he so often did, were like separate living entities. Oh yes, not unlike Barras but more agreeable to look at, though probably just as untrustworthy. She remembered what Bonaparte had once said of him: "A profligate and a liar, but the only man capable of controlling the Ministry of Police and making it the powerful instrument I require it to be. He alone has a full knowledge of all the factions the intrigues of which have spread misery and dissension in France. He alone, then, is the man, who, above all others, I need." A profligate—yes, she could well believe that. A handsome, appealing profligate. What a pity, what a great pity, that circumstances had made her a faithful wife!

"And so, madame," he remarked, "the Grassini affair may now be regarded as closed."

"It may indeed," she assured him.

He chuckled, his eyes danced merrily. "Madame la Consulesse, in my humble opinion, is the cleverest woman in the world."

"Thank you for the compliment, Fouché," she murmured.

"Let me see now, she caught a cold and lost her voice, I believe."

"Why yes. A misfortune, poor thing, that could have happened to anybody."

"I wonder," he said softly, "what caused the cold?"

Josephine shrugged. "Really, Fouché, how should I know?"

Fouché rose and began to stroll about the room.

"Madame," he said, without looking at her, "let me compliment you again on your cleverness. For I know, you see, almost all the details of your little plot."

"*You* know almost all the details—?" she stammered.

He bowed. "Am I not the Minister of Police, the chief spy, as your husband often calls me, of the Republic?"

"What a dangerous man you are," she laughed.

"I agree, madame." He sat down again. "I might know a great deal about the Grassini affair, but there are many other things concerning your husband that I don't know—things that I want to know, that I *must* know. And that, my dear Josephine, is why I decided to call on you this afternoon."

Josephine! So he intended their relations to be as intimate as that, did he!

"I don't understand what you mean," she said.

"I want to know, for instance, not only what your husband does but what he *thinks*, thus making myself fully acquainted with his latest political moves before he actually makes them."

She laughed at him in amazement. "Are you seriously asking me to spy on my husband?"

"Indeed I am."

"Really, Fouché—" she tried to infuse a convincing indignation into her voice—"what sort of a woman do you think I am?"

"My dear," he protested smoothly, "if I were to tell you that you might conceive a lasting dislike for me."

"Well!" Beyond which exclamation she was temporarily speechless.

"If I were to tell your husband all I know of the Grassini affair," he murmured—

"Ah," she burst out, "a hint of blackmail!"

"As you say, a hint of blackmail."

She leaned forward and tapped him on the knee. "My poor Fouché, Bonaparte knows everything already."

"He does?" Fouché was completely unperturbed. "A pity." He examined his finger-tips carefully. "However, I have another trick up my capacious sleeve, a trick which might be called the 'Half-million Franc Necklace.'"

Her hands went to her throat in horror. "*Fouché!*"

"I thought *that* might possibly interest you."

"I don't know what you're talking about."

Fouché sighed gently. "Foncier brought you a pearl necklace, which incidentally was never the property of Marie Antoinette. You desired it immediately you saw it, but you had no money. You then learned that Berthier was anxious to establish his mistress in Consular society. A bargain was struck and army funds are now depleted to the extent of half a million francs." He raised his left eyebrow quizzically. "Well, Madame la Consulesse?"

"I would gladly have you drawn and quartered!" Josephine raged.

"I'm sure you would, my dear."

"Are you working for the royalists? Are you plotting Bonaparte's downfall?"

"Heavens, no. I'm working for one man only—myself. I'm merely the same sort of man as Talleyrand, who worked for Louis the Sixteenth, yet survived the Revolution; who now works for Napoleon Bonaparte, yet will no doubt survive the fall of Napoleon Bonaparte when, and *if*, such a thing is brought about."

"I see." She looked at him with an interest that bordered on respect. "What do you want me to do, Fouché?"

"I thought I'd already made that quite clear."

"I—" She was about to capitulate when she thought of Berthier and hesitated. "I should like a little time to think the matter over," she said.

He rose. "You may have twenty-four hours. Tomorrow at this time I will call again. By then, I feel sure, you will have decided to make the best of an unavoidable situation."

"We shall see," she said coldly.

He smiled and bowed himself from the room.

"A rat," she said thoughtfully, when the door had closed, "but a charming one."

*   *   *   *   *

"Are you suggesting, madame," Berthier demanded indignantly, "that I was foolish enough to confide in a man like Fouché?"

"Naturally I am," Josephine cried tearfully. "How else could he have gained his information?"

"My dear Madame Bonaparte," Berthier protested, "I——"

She stopped him with a dramatic gesture. "You, Berthier, you whom I was sure I could trust!" Having liked the gesture, she repeated it. "What an ill-fated woman I am! On every hand I am face to face with faithless friends, sycophants and vindictive relatives-in-law."

"I assure you madame," Berthier said impatiently, "that Fouché's discovery is as distressing to me as it is to you. It makes me realize that the man is far more dangerous than I ever believed him to be."

Her mouth fell open in amazement. "You really told him nothing?"

"I told him nothing."

"Then what am I to do? Merciful heavens, Berthier, what am I to do?"

"The alternative is clear, madame. Either you confess to the First Consul or——"

"Confess?" she shrieked. "But Bonaparte would kill me, I know he would!"

"In that case——"

"But to spy on him. To *spy* on my husband!"

"Does the suggestion shock you so very much?" Berthier asked quietly.

"Really, Berthier," she protested sadly, "you're as bad as Fouché. You think me an unscrupulous woman."

"Whatever I think, this much is clear; you may be able to use Fouché even more than he hopes to use you."

305

"What do you mean, Berthier?"

"The Bonaparte family, with the exception of the two younger members, dislike you intensely and would do all they could to bring about your disgrace."

She shuddered delicately. "Indeed they would."

"You—" here Berthier chuckled softly—"you, if only in a spirit of self-preservation, would do all *you* could to see *them* disgraced."

"I most certainly would!" she agreed cheerfully. "But what are you trying to tell me?"

"I discovered something this morning that even the clever Fouché is still in ignorance of. The Bonapartes seem to be of the opinion that your husband is established at the Tuileries for life, and are so sure of it that they are looking round for a successor."

"A successor?"

"Yes, and one, since you and the First Consul are still childless, to be recruited from their own ranks."

"Interesting as this information is I don't see how it can benefit me in my struggle with the Bonaparte brood."

"Ah, but wait, madame. The Bonapartes fear that if the First Consul were to learn of their scheme he might grow angry and accuse them of being anxious to get him out of the way. The suggestion, therefore, will first be made by an outsider who will start a public agitation. You begin to understand me now?"

Josephine laughed shortly. "I do indeed, Berthier. If I act cautiously it should be simple for me to induce Fouché to expose the scheme."

"Precisely, but have the patience, madame, to wait until the Bonapartes have committed themselves more deeply."

"Never fear, I shall." She rose, dismissing him. "Thank you, Berthier, and forgive me for having misjudged you. . . ."

$$* \quad * \quad * \quad * \quad *$$

The twenty-four hours had expired and Fouché, without having been invited to sit, was lounging once again in the most comfortable chair in Josephine's drawing-room. A decanter of wine was at his elbow. Seeing it he reached out for it and withdrew the stopper. "Ah," he said, sniffing the aroma delicately, "a very fine madeira," and taking up a glass he poured out a liberal helping.

"To a long and amicable association," he said, raising the glass.

"You seem very sure of me," Josephine snapped.

"I *am* very sure of you, Josephine."

"Bah!" she said, but was obliged to laugh.

('I'm too good natured,' she thought. 'That is my chief failing, nay, my only failing!')

"Fouché," she said, "I have given your proposition quite a lot of thought since yesterday. As Minister of Police you have considerable money at your disposal."

"I have," he agreed.

"The use of which you are not obliged to give a very detailed account."

"Ah," he chuckled, "I might have suspected something like this."

"Something like what?" she demanded.

"You're about to ask for payment for services yet to be rendered."

"And why not, Fouché? Doesn't the ministry pay its spies a salary?"

"Always, and sometimes generously."

"For a thousand francs a week," she said boldly, "I will do everything in my power to help you."

He raised his glass again. "To a woman who is cleverer than I gave her the credit of being."

"You agree?"

"Why not? The money won't be coming out of my own pocket."

So delighted was she with her success that she could have clapped her hands for joy. A thousand francs a week, why that was over fifty thousand a year! Not a very large sum, perhaps, but a help, a considerable help.

"Take another glass of wine," she said generously. "Here, let me pour it for you myself."

While Fouché was sipping the second glass she broached the subject of the Bonapartes. She mentioned the mutual hatred which existed between herself and the majority of her relatives-in-law, speaking finally of the thing that Berthier had told her. Fouché listened attentively until her voice had trailed away and then he chuckled.

"So you want me to help you strike a blow at the Bonapartes."

"Oh, please, Fouché, if you would be so kind!"

"In other words, I'm to pay you a thousand francs a week, not to help myself, but merely to help you."

"You *could* put it like that," she laughed, "though seriously, to discover and expose such a scheme would help you as much as it would help me."

"Indeed?"

"But of course it would. The discovery would prove to Bonaparte that you're a very alert and very clever Minister of Police and more indispensable than ever."

He smiled and put down his glass.

307

"I think that has already been proved, my dear."

He took a folded sheet of paper from an inner pocket and gave it to her. She unfolded it curiously. It was a printed handbill headed: NAPOLEON BONAPARTE—*Should His Successor Be Named?*

"Thousands of these," Fouché said, "are now being distributed in Paris. I myself obtained one of the first copies and took it to Bonaparte."

"Was he angry?"

"So angry that for a moment he was speechless. He then ordered me to have every available copy secured and destroyed. I pointed out that it was a question of great interest to all the people who loved him, but he said that politically it was very dangerous. Both the royalists and the republicans, he said, would accuse him of attempting to found a dynasty."

Josephine read through the briefly worded pamphlet quickly.

"Anonymous, I see," she commented. "I wonder who wrote it?"

"From what you told me a moment ago I would suspect one of the Bonaparte brothers."

"But *which* brother? Joseph, perhaps, or Louis? Or possibly Lucien?"

"Lucien, since that young man has been giving himself airs ever since Bonaparte made him Minister of the Interior—yet this pamphlet is too cleverly worded to be Lucien's work."

"Perhaps all of them had a hand in it."

"If they had Bonaparte himself is not in the least suspicious."

"Are you sure, Fouché? My husband is hardly as great a fool as that."

"Your husband knows nothing of his family's deep interest in the matter. But apart from that he ordered me to discover the author and place him under arrest. If he suspected one of his brothers would he have given such an order?"

"Dear me, no," Josephine agreed, "and what a joke, what a delightful joke, if you *did* arrest a Bonaparte brother!"

"A joke, I'm sure, that would please Madame la Consulesse more than any other person in France!"

"Naturally!" she chuckled, and then grew suddenly grave. "Fouché, I have an idea. Lucien Bonaparte is the weakest member of the family. He also has a very poor head when it comes to drinking wine. Therefore I——"

"Propose to get him drunk?"

"Yes, and tonight. Tonight because Bonaparte is holding a council meeting with Berthier, Junot and several other officers and won't be free till well after midnight."

"You'll give a little party, perhaps?"

· "Yes! I shall invite the whole Bonaparte brood, with the exception of the old lady, who rarely touches wine. I shall set them talking; I shall, God forgive me, be especially sweet to them. I——"

"God forgive you indeed, Josephine."

"He will, I know He will!"

"Am I to be present?"

"Of course. Two pairs of ears are better than one, aren't they?"

"Usually, Josephine," he laughed, "though in this case yours, I imagine, would be sharp enough."

* * * * *

Lucien Bonaparte, standing in the middle of Josephine's drawing-room, held his glass high and gazed rapturously at the amber liquid, a third of which had already been spilled on the carpet.

"I am," he pronounced, "quite drunk."

"A man," Fouché assured him, "who can stand as firmly as you at this moment is very sober."

"Ah," Lucien asked archly, "but what would happen if I were to move? I ask you, what would happen?"

Josephine, smiling sweetly, felt nothing for him but disgust, possibly because, for the first time, she noticed in him a striking resemblance to her first husband, Alexandre de Beauharnais. He was not so tall as Alexandre, not so handsome, but he had the same mannerisms, the same weak arrogance.

"I confess," he went on weightily, "that I was a little drunk when I left the ministry, otherwise I would never have come."

"Even the visit of a drunken Bonaparte," Josephine assured him, "is an honor."

She ignored Fouché's quick frown and thanked heaven that the other Bonapartes, claiming previous engagements, had refused her invitation. To have invited them in the first place was madness. Knowing Lucien's weakness they would have hustled him away before either she or Fouché had had time to set him talking.

"Sister-in-law," Lucien said, after draining his glass, "one thing only is wrong with this little party of yours."

"And that?" she asked.

"Your own presence!"

"Come, come," Fouché said, taking Lucien's glass and refilling it, "we mustn't be rude to our hostess."

Lucien swayed dangerously and was only saved from falling by Fouché, who caught him swiftly by the arm. More wine was spilled on the carpet.

"Hic!" said Lucien, leering at Josephine.

Fouché raised his own glass. "I give you a toast, my dear Lucien. A toast to Napoleon Bonaparte's successor."

Lucien roared with laughter, caught Josephine's watchful eye and leered again.

"To Napoleon Bonaparte's successor," he pronounced owlishly.

"A somewhat ticklish subject, eh?" Fouché suggested.

"Damnably ticklish, my dear Fouché—hic!—damnably!"

"You've seen the pamphlet, of course?"

Lucien raised his glass to his lips; it rattled against his teeth, spilling the wine down his chin and onto his white, already-disarranged stock.

"What pamphlet?" he asked blankly.

Fouché shrugged.

"A ticklish subject," he went on smoothly, "but a most important one."

"The most important subject," Lucien responded heavily, "that the Consulate has yet been called upon to deal with. On the question, 'Should Napoleon's successor be named?' hangs the very existence of the Consulate."

"Oh, I think you exaggerate a little there," Fouché murmured.

"I speak the solemn truth, Fouché, the solemn truth." Lucien's words, though thick and painfully mouthed, were clearly of great importance to him. "Can you deny," he went on, "that—hic!—that France owes her present greatness to the Bonaparte family? Can you or anyone else deny that if her greatness is to be maintained it can only be maintained by the rule of a Bonaparte dynasty? I tell you, Fouché—hic!—I tell you, it is absolutely imperative for Napoleon's successor to be named—hic!—and named now."

He shook himself free of Fouché's supporting grip. The glass fell from his fingers and was crushed beneath his feet as he staggered forward. Fouché caught him as he fell and lowered him into a chair which Josephine dragged across from the fireplace.

"Now a cushion," she said.

The two conspirators stood back and gazed at their victim.

"Asleep?" Fouché questioned.

A snort, followed by a gentle, rippling snore, was sufficient answer.

"I only hope," Josephine said, "that he won't wake up and be sick."

Fouché, taking the pamphlet from his pocket, unfolded it and handed it to Josephine.

"Glance at the second paragraph," he said with a smile, "and feel as satisfied with tonight's work as I do. Lucien, though he pretended to know nothing of the pamphlet, quoted from it just now, quoted from it almost word for word."

Josephine, having thought Lucien's words vaguely familiar, read the second paragraph.

"The question of the First Consul's successor is the most important question facing the Consulate today, the question upon which its very existence hangs. Can any one deny that if the greatness of France is to be maintained it can only be maintained by the rule of a Bonaparte dynasty? Citizens of France, it is absolutely imperative for the First Consul's successor to be named and named now!"

"I think you will agree," Josephine cried triumphantly, "that Lucien is the author of the pamphlet. Arrest him, Fouché, arrest him at once!"

Fouché shook his head. "A drunken utterance, even made before witnesses, could hardly be regarded as complete and irrefutable proof."

Josephine considered for a moment.

"I know!" she cried. "If Lucien is the author, the original copy, in his own handwriting, might still be in existence."

"It might; we can only hope that it is."

Fouché bent over the snoring Lucien and began deftly to search his pocket. Lucien stirred slightly and giggled. "Ticklish!" he mumbled, "ticklish!"

"Nothing here," Fouché was forced to admit.

"We must search his rooms at the Ministry of the Interior," Josephine decided.

"Now, you mean?"

"Lucien is likely to sleep for hours. We could never have a better opportunity than now."

"Lucien may be absent from the ministry, but what of his servants?" Fouché objected.

"Tell them that you have an appointment and have been instructed to wait for Lucien in the study."

Fouché hesitated. "Nevertheless——"

"Oh, come," Josephine cried in exasperation, "timidity on the part of the Minister of Police is ridiculous."

Fouché shrugged. "Very well, Josephine, I'll do as you say, but——"

"Not another word," she shouted. "Go to the Ministry of the Interior at once, find the original copy and bring it back to me!"

Josephine glanced at the clock again. An hour had passed and Fouché had not yet returned. She looked at Lucien. He had slumped farther down in the chair and was still snoring. 'Pig,' she thought, 'Corsican pig!' Impatiently she sprang to her feet and began to pace the room. A moment later the door was flung open.

"Ah!" she cried, turning eagerly, and then, "Oh!" for it was Bonaparte, not Fouché, who had entered.

He saw Lucien instantly.

"In the name of heaven," he demanded, "what have we here?"

She laughed nervously. "Not a very pretty sight, is it, Bonaparte! He was disgustingly drunk when he came. Three more glasses of wine and he collapsed into helplessness."

Bonaparte strode over to Lucien, caught him roughly by the lapels of his coat and shook him.

"Wake up, you fool!" he shouted

Lucien grunted. His eyes remained closed but his mouth began to work.

"Imperative," he muttered. "Absolutely imperative. A Bonaparte dynasty."

Bonaparte began to shake him again, and was still shaking him when Fouché, breathing heavily and half running, burst into the room. At the sight of the First Consul he came to a startled halt.

Bonaparte looked at him coldly, and from him to Josephine.

"Since when," he asked, "has Fouché had the *entrée* to my wife's apartments?"

Josephine's hands went quickly to her throat. Dear heaven, Bonaparte would now accuse her of conducting an *affaire* with Fouché.

"Sir," Fouché said swiftly, "knowing that your brother was here, and finding it necessary to have speech of an official nature with him, I permitted zeal to get the better of good taste."

"Speech of an official nature?" Bonaparte questioned.

Fouché bowed. "I regret to inform you, sir, that Lucien Bonaparte is the author of the pamphlet entitled NAPOLEON BONAPARTE— *Should His Successor Be Named?*"

Holding her breath Josephine watched Fouché as he took a soiled and crumpled piece of paper from his pocket.

"The original copy," Fouché said, passing the document to Bonaparte. "The handwriting, as you will see, is your brother's."

Josephine's eyes were now on her husband. He took the document hesitantly, opened his mouth to speak and then, with a forced smile, remained silent. Queer, very queer indeed.

"Since you don't seem inclined to examine the handwriting," she said, "may I look at it myself?"

He shrugged and passed it to her.

"Revive him, Fouché," he said, pointing a finger at his brother.

Diffidently, Fouché began to shake the sleeping man.

"You'll have little success that way," Bonaparte said. "Slap his cheeks; sprinkle him with cold water."

"Take this," Josephine said quickly, and passed a carafe of water to Fouché.

Bonaparte laughed shortly. "Why not do it yourself, sweetheart? I'm sure it will give you a lot of pleasure."

"Very well," she said promptly.

She took the carafe from Fouché, tipped it up over Lucien's head and held it there until the last drop had been drained out. By now Lucien was sitting up in the chair, shaking himself. Josephine returned to her study of the document.

"These corrections in the margin," she cried suddenly, "they're in *your* handwriting, Bonaparte."

"They are," he admitted, smiling inscrutably. He turned to Fouché. "I gave you orders to arrest the author of the pamphlet; therefore arrest him."

Fouché looked nonplussed. "But, sir, if the corrections were made by you——"

"Lucien has failed me. Lucien has shown himself a fool by preserving a document I instructed him to destroy. You have your orders, Fouché, carry them out. Arrest my brother. Take him to the Ministry of the Interior and place a guard about the building."

Fouché shrugged.

"The First Consul," he murmured, "is like the Almighty. He moves mysteriously his wonders to perform."

* * * * *

Josephine glanced idly at the faces of her relatives-in-law. She herself was seated on Bonaparte's right; on his left was his mother. Next to her was Joseph, and next to him, Louis. The Bonaparte girls, thank heaven, were absent, but even so the room seemed overfull of Bonapartes. A family conference, and called by Madame Bonaparte herself—could anything be more ridiculous!

There was a knock at the door and Bourrienne entered carrying pen, ink and paper. He seated himself next to Josephine, having been summoned, it seemed, to take notes of the proceedings. Beyond the stiff formal greetings when the gathering had assembled a few moments ago, no conversation whatever had taken place.

Josephine looked anxiously at Bonaparte. His fingers were beating an impatient tattoo on the table; his eyes were raised to the ceiling so that all she could see was their whites. Though three days had passed since the arrest of Lucien, Bonaparte had offered no explanation. Why, Josephine asked herself for the hundredth time, had Bonaparte, knowing all about the pamphlet from the beginning, ordered Fouché to discover and arrest the author?

"Where the devil," Bonaparte burst out suddenly, "are Fouché and Lucien?"

A second knock at the door and the entry of Fouché and Lucien Bonaparte answered his question.

"You're late," he barked.

Fouché shrugged. "You brother was unwilling to leave the ministry. It was necessary to employ a little force."

Fouché seated himself next to Bourrienne. Lucien, scowling, moved indeterminately to the chair at the bottom of the table.

"You will remain standing, Lucien!" Bonaparte commanded.

"Really, Napoléoné," Madame Bonaparte protested, "Lucien is your brother, not a criminal."

"Shall we proceed?" was all Bonaparte would say.

Madame Bonaparte turned to Lucien. "Your brother has been persuaded to hear whatever explanation you may care to make. It is even possible that he will make an explanation himself."

Avoiding his mother's eyes, Bonaparte said: "No explanation Lucien may make will excuse him. My disappointment in him is as great as ever."

"Lucien," Joseph pronounced heavily, "has served you well in the past. Surely——"

"It is the present that interests me, Joseph, not the past."

"You have grown hard, my son," Madame Bonaparte said. "The acquisition of power has done that to you."

"The acquisition of power has nothing to do with it, Mother. Lucien has failed me. I have no further use for him."

There was a little silence.

"To my mind," Madame Bonaparte said at last, "you also have failed Lucien. You and he, I imagine, have been concerned in some intrigue which reflects credit on neither of you. Before I can permit you to condemn Lucien unheard I demand a full explanation."

Bonaparte, making an impatient gesture, stared at her in silence.

"Come," she said quietly, "I am not to be intimidated by your glaring. I am not one of the people who bow to your wishes and tremble at your glance. I am your mother."

Josephine, forced in spite of herself to admire her mother-in-law, was watching Bonaparte's face closely. It had grown pale, as it always did in extreme anger.

"Very well," he said, in a low voice, "you shall hear my own quite simple explanation. When it reached my ears that Joseph and Lucien and Louis were eager to have my successor named I sent for Lucien, who has always been clever when it came to expressing an idea in writing. At my suggestion he composed the pamphlet, but for obvious reasons I bound him to absolute secrecy."

"For *obvious* reasons, Napoléoné?"

"I wished to test public opinion before betraying any personal approval of such a move. I wanted to know how France as a whole would receive the idea of a new reigning family, a family by the name of Bonaparte."

"But when the pamphlet was issued," Joseph said mildly, "you ordered every copy to be secured and destroyed."

"I knew by then, you great idiot, that the whole of Paris was talking about it. Its purpose had been adequately served. My apparent anger was merely to safeguard myself if the suggestion was badly received."

"And it was badly received?" Madame Bonaparte demanded.

"Yes," Bonaparte growled, "very badly."

"I still fail to see why Lucien should have been arrested," Joseph complained.

"I ordered the author's arrest; not Lucien's. I ordered it as yet another means of safeguarding myself; I ordered it feeling perfectly sure that Lucien would never betray himself. He undertook a delicate and extremely important commission and he failed. I have no use for a man as unreliable as Lucien, even if he *is* my brother."

"He failed through no fault of his own," Joseph said acidly, "but, as far as I can gather, through the interference of Josephine."

Josephine caught her breath sharply. How much did Joseph know of her association with Fouché? She looked at Bonaparte with big, innocent eyes. Ridiculous, surely, to imagine that he knew anything at all.

"She and Fouché," Joseph went on, "have been working together against Lucien."

Bonaparte smiled for the first time. "I know they have."

"Why, *Bonaparte!*" she exclaimed weakly.

"I even suspect them," Joseph went on, "of having reached a financial agreement."

Josephine caught her breath again. This was really uncanny.

"You mean," she said shrewdly, "that I might have been paying Fouché to work for your brother's disgrace?"

"Something like that," Joseph muttered.

She smiled happily. The danger, thank heaven, had passed.

"No," Bonaparte remarked smoothly, "the financial agreement is quite different. Where would my extravagant wife find money to make such payments? Josephine is receiving money from Fouché in return for information about my possible political moves."

Josephine gave a little cry and half rose in her chair.

"Josephine," Madame Bonaparte demanded, "is this the truth?"

Bonaparte laughed merrily. "Of course it is, Mother."

"And you are in no way disturbed, Napoléoné?"

"No," he said cheerfully. "It amuses me to know that Josephine is clever enough to obtain money from as shrewd a man as Fouché, though I imagine that the payments will now cease."

"They will indeed!" Fouché agreed.

"How did you discover all this?" Josephine asked weakly.

"Fouché may be my chief spy," Bonaparte explained, obviously very pleased with himself, "but I also employ other spies to keep a watch on all such dangerous men as he."

Madame Bonaparte rose to her feet majestically. "One thing has been overlooked. Your wife is a spy, a spy on your own actions."

"Not a very dangerous one," Bonaparte laughed. "She will never be in a position to learn my political secrets, nor, for that matter, will you, Mother."

Joseph Bonaparte rose also.

"You must be mad, Napoleon," he said, "to make light of her conduct. Lucien might have failed you, but Josephine has been willing to betray you."

"Nonsense," Bonaparte said sharply.

"Thank you, Bonaparte," Josephine murmured. She turned to Madame Bonaparte. "Having become a faithful wife," she explained, "I have much time on my hands and must do *something* to amuse myself."

Bonaparte frowned but was obliged, in the end, to laugh heartily.

"Thank you, Josephine," he said, "for bringing a little comedy to a very tragic situation." He turned to Lucien. "You will relinquish your position at the Ministry of the Interior and you will also leave Paris."

"Leave Paris?" Lucien cried shrilly.

"You would actually send him into exile?" Joseph asked.

"You *could* call it that, Joseph. He shall go to Spain as an Ambassador Extraordinary. He shall go there and remain there until I feel that he has learned his lesson."

"But you said just now," Josephine murmured, "that you had no use for a man as unreliable as Lucien."

"Oh, come," Bonaparte chided her, "be gracious to a fallen enemy. Be generous enough to grant him the chance of re-establishing himself."

"Very well, Bonaparte." She turned to Lucien with a sweet smile.

"The climate of Madrid, they tell me, is excellent, and the senoritas not entirely uninteresting. Make the most of your stay in Spain and if you find the time, do please send me a Spanish shawl." She inclined her head, including all the others in the gesture. "Will you be kind enough to excuse me?"

"One moment," Madame Bonaparte said, in her harshest tone. "Your part in bringing about Lucien's disgrace has been shameful. We Bonapartes have a long memory. Some day, perhaps, you will have reason to regret it."

Josephine inclined her head again but her heart missed a beat. She had always known it, of course. Her struggle with these wild, unrelenting Corsicans was no ordinary quarrel between relatives-in-law, it was—horrible but exciting thought!—it was a *vendetta!*

CHAPTER XXXI

W AS IT HELEN OF TROY," Josephine asked, "or Cleopatra?"

The maid Louise shrugged. "It might have been either, madame."

"Well, whoever it was, Louise, I've always wanted to try it."

"I myself," Louise said severely, "consider it a shameful waste of milk."

Josephine chuckled. "That, Louise, is precisely what my wretched mother-in-law would say."

She rose to a sitting position in the bath and watched the little lines of white liquid drain down her arms and chest. She wasn't quite sure whether or not she was enjoying this new experience. December was hardly the month during which to take a cold bath in anything, whether it be water or milk, but if, as it was claimed, a weekly bath in milk preserved the youthfulness of one's skin, then a weekly bath in milk she would certainly take. She stood up and stepped out of the bath. Louise came forward with a towel.

"Don't rub," Josephine said. "Just pat me gently all over till I dry."

"Very well, madame."

After patting stolidly for a moment Louise giggled.

"What is it, Louise?" Josephine asked.

"Forgive me, madame, but madame smells so like a baby."

"Or else a wet-nurse," Josephine decided, and giggled too.

317

When the patting operation had been completed Josephine surveyed herself critically in the mirror.

"Tell me frankly," she said, with a little frown, "do you consider that my figure is as good as it used to be?"

Louise looked at her solemnly. "Frankness, madame, is not the thing that any lady approaching her fortieth year should ask of her maid."

Josephine's frown deepened. Her breasts, of which she had once been proud, drooped heavily, and her buttocks—she turned sideways on to the mirror, twisting her neck to gain a clearer view—merciful heavens, how they *sagged*!

"Madame understands what I mean," Louise murmured.

"My wrap," Josephine commanded coldly.

Louise brought it and adjusted it in silence.

"And I've been so kind to you," Josephine complained, "so very kind."

"Madame," Louise said earnestly, "is still the most graceful lady in the whole of France."

A smile broke on Josephine's face. "Thank you, Louise. After all, Bonaparte always says that I do everything gracefully. He said only last night that I even go to bed gracefully."

Happy again, she went to her boudoir and set purposefully about the first stages of the lengthy *toilette*. A few moments later the door opened and Bonaparte strode into the room.

"What?" he cried, "not ready yet?"

"Ready, Bonaparte? Ready for what?"

He reminded her gently that a consular party was to make an appearance that evening at the opera where a special performance of Haydn's 'Creation' was to take place.

"I give you an hour, madame," he said, "an hour and not a moment longer."

He drew up a chair and sat down to watch her.

"The intricacies of my wife's *toilette*," he teased, "will never cease to amaze me."

"Ah," Josephine said, "Bonaparte is in a good humor tonight." She was looking at his reflection in her dressing-table mirror. Strange, but not until now had she really noticed the change in him. His face, once so thin, had filled out and the formerly emaciated body had gathered a little flesh about its bones. It was even possible, by the look of the slight bulge beneath his waistcoat, that he would soon have a large stomach, and what, in so short a man, could be more ludicrous!

"My dear," he said lightly, "I want to talk to you about Fouché."

"Fouché?" she echoed guardedly. "What has he done now?"

"Nothing. I merely want to warn you against entering into any further intrigues with the man."

"Don't be cruel," she cried. "As I told your mother I must do *something* to amuse myself."

"What I really object to," Bonaparte frowned, "is your giving him the *entrée* of your apartments. Confound it all, Fouché has been coming and going as freely as I myself."

"Why, Bonaparte, I do believe you're jealous!"

"Nonsense! I trust you implicitly."

The tone of his voice told her instantly what the trouble was.

"Is it possible," she asked, "that your family has been gossiping —suggesting that Fouché and I——?"

"Yes," he said shortly.

"Bonaparte," she said earnestly, "it not only amuses me to ally myself with Fouché, but it gives me the chance to keep a strict watch on a man whom you yourself admit is dangerous." She threw her arms round his neck and kissed him quickly but warmly on the lips. "Be generous, Bonaparte, and permit me to serve your cause as I have always served it, and that is faithfully."

"You little witch," he said, "you still have power over me!"

His arms were about her and his breath on her neck was hot. Gratifying, of course, but also a little alarming, especially when one had taken a bath and settled down to enjoy the vast pleasures of a long *toilette*. She pushed him away gently.

"You gave me only an hour, Bonaparte, and time is flying."

He rose stiffly. "Very well, madame."

He bowed and turned.

At the door he said: "You may continue to intrigue with Fouché if it really pleases you."

"Thank you, Bonaparte." She caught his eyes for a moment and said meaningly: "Tonight, if you wish it."

He opened the door. "Tonight, madame, the mood may not be upon me."

And with that he was gone.

She laughed softly. "Louise," she called, "the new white cambric, I think."

An hour later there was a knock at the door and Eugene entered.

"Mother," he said, "the First Consul is waiting."

Josephine, holding her breath, was carefully applying white paint to her blown-out cheeks. Still holding her breath and watching him in the mirror, she beckoned him to come forward. He did so awkwardly, his every movement betraying embarrassment. Poor lamb, it was always the same, now that he was grown up, though as a child he had often sat at the dressing-table with her and prattled happily. *Now that he was grown up. . . .* The words had slipped into her mind without warning. Nineteen, he was, and old enough to marry and—horrible thought!—make a grandmother of her. A grandmother, *she!*—how the Bonapartes would gloat over such a great misfortune!

The white paint applied to her satisfaction she relaxed and turned to her son with a smile.

"Tell your stepfather that I shall be ready in half an hour."

"Very well, Mother, but I'm sure it won't please him."

He turned and bowed himself out of the room. She sighed gently. How straight and handsome he was, and how well he looked in his uniform. A better figure of a man than any of the Bonaparte brothers, an aristocrat not only by birth but in his every look and movement. If Bonaparte ever did decide to form a dynasty and name his successor, who better could he choose than Eugene?

"Great heavens," she said aloud, realizing the full significance of this thought, "I must speak to Bonaparte about it. What a triumph, what a glorious triumph over the Bonapartes!"

Half an hour later there was another knock at the door and this time it was Hortense who entered the room. Thinking how pretty the child looked, Josephine turned to greet her with a smile. After taking one look at her mother Hortense began to laugh. Holding her sides in anything but a ladylike manner she collapsed helplessly into a chair.

"What is it, child?" Josephine demanded suspiciously.

Hortense pointed a quivering finger. "Your face, Mother, your face!"

Josephine looked hastily in the mirror. She saw nothing amusing in the fact that her left cheek had been painted with rouge while the right was so far untouched. Nevertheless she began to attend to the right cheek at once.

Hortense began to sniff. "Can you smell anything peculiar, Mother?"

Josephine sniffed also. "Why, yes. What is it, I wonder?"

"It smells like stale milk," Hortense decided.

"Merciful heavens, so it does!"

She began to dab perfume on her neck and arms. Not only was the milk which her pores had absorbed beginning to smell strongly, it was sticky too, most uncomfortably sticky. She squirmed uneasily. She really needed another bath to wash it off. Never again would she order Louise to fill the bath-tub with milk.

The door opened again. This time it was Bonaparte.

"Madame," he said, "unless you come down within five minutes I shall be forced to leave the Tuileries without you."

"Men," Josephine sighed, as he slammed the door in departing, "will never understand the importance of a woman's *toilette*."

She rose from the dressing-table, linked her arm through her daughter's and drew her round to face the mirror. Despite the fact that Hortense's youth was emphasized by her own over-painted face, she said guilelessly:

"Why, child, we look more like sisters than mother and daughter."

They went below, only to find that Bonaparte had now left with Eugene, Berthier and Junot. A second carriage, however, was waiting. Josephine and Hortense were helped into it, furs were wrapped about their knees and the order given to the coachman.

"Bonaparte," Josephine laughed, "will sulk all night because of this."

"You could scarcely blame him, Mother," Hortense said.

Josephine laughed again; then she grew suddenly serious. "I wonder how many of the wretched Bonapartes will try to push into the box?"

"None of them," Hortense assured her. "Another box has been reserved for the family."

"You and Eugene—you'll be in the box with me and Bonaparte?"

"Oh yes, Mother. The First Consul told me so himself."

"Splendid!" Josephine cried. "Naturally my own children should take precedence over old Madame Bonaparte and the others."

The carriage turned into the rue Saint-Nicaise where, despite the cold and a fall of sleet, a little crowd had gathered and was still cheering.

"Ah, we can't be very far behind Bonaparte's carriage," Josephine said.

Her own carriage came to a sudden halt, throwing Josephine roughly forward. A moment later there was a deafening explosion. Josephine and Hortense were thrown together on the floor and the windows of the carriage were shattered. The horses took fright and broke into a wild gallop, and were not brought under control until the carriage reached the other end of the street. Josephine was helped to the seat of the carriage by Hortense whose face was bleeding from a cut. The carriage was instantly surrounded by a large and highly excited crowd.

"Josephine! Josephine, are you safe?"

It was Bonaparte, pushing his way through the crowd. He was recognized, a path was made clear for him and the people began to cheer.

"In the name of heaven," Josephine moaned, "what happened?"

Bonaparte was in the carriage now.

"Thank God you're not hurt," he said. "They shall pay for this with their lives, by heaven they shall!"

"Was it an attack on your life?" Hortense asked.

Bonaparte nodded. "When my carriage turned into the rue Saint-Nicaise we found the way blocked by a carriage and a farmer's cart. My escort cleared a path for us. The cart was apparently full of gunpowder. Had my carriage been a moment later in arriving, or your own a moment sooner, we might all have been killed."

"Eugene—" Josephine cried.

"Quite safe, but several people in the street were killed." He took a deep breath. "This attack on my life has convinced me that though it might be a little premature the name of my successor must now be announced."

Josephine looked at him quickly. "Does this mean that Lucien will be recalled from exile?"

"By no means. In any case I would never have named him."

"Who *do* you intend to name?" she asked anxiously.

He looked at her for a long moment.

"Since you have never given me a son, Josephine, I shall be forced to make up my mind between Joseph, Louis and Jerome."

"And—and Eugene, perhaps?" he said.

"Much as I love Eugene my successor must be a Bonaparte."

She tried to hide her disappointment, but sitting back in the carriage when the journey to the opera was resumed she fell victim to a fit of deep depression. *One thing is clear*, she told herself a dozen times, *the moment a Bonaparte is named to succeed him, my fight with the family will become a losing one.*

* * * * *

"My dear Rose," said Aunt Marie, one of the few people who still called Josephine by her proper name, "sit down and try to relax."

Josephine made a wild gesture and obeyed. Aunt Marie, increasingly trying in her old age, had come on one of her infrequent visits to Paris and, at Bonaparte's invitation, was spending a few days at the Tuileries. The Marquis de Beauharnais, still in reasonably good health, had remained at Fontainebleau. Paris, he said, was not the same these days, and Napoleon Bonaparte, though a fine soldier, was going much too far politically.

"I received a letter from Martinique last week," Aunt Marie said. "Your mother seems to be well and happy."

"Quite well," Josephine agreed. "Fortunately I can send her enough money these days to keep her in comfort but I do wish she would come to France." Her mind returned to the vexing problem of the Bonapartes. "A family council!" she cried, in disgust. "These days that is all Bonaparte seems to think of, family councils!"

She sprang to her feet again and began to pace the room.

"This dreadful question of heredity," she moaned, "is driving me crazy, really it is! Once it is decided that one of Bonaparte's brothers shall succeed him my position will become dreadfully insecure."

"You alarm yourself unnecessarily," Aunt Marie said. "Your position could only become 'dreadfully insecure' through your husband's death. In any case, to talk of a successor is ridiculous. Napoleon is not the King of France, only chief consul, and not even that for the duration of his life."

Josephine waved this aside. "Bonaparte is clever. Fouché told me only this morning that a move is afoot to make him chief consul for life with the right to name his successor."

"Why not Eugene?"

"I suggested Eugene but these stupid Corsicans are so clannish. The successor must be a Bonaparte."

"Then the only solution to your problem, my dear, is to have a child by your husband."

Josephine turned furiously on her aunt. "So Bonaparte keeps on telling me, but the fault is surely his, not mine. 'The woman is barren,' his impossible family say. Barren!" She snorted. "Have I not borne two children already? Quite obviously I've been cursed by a sterile husband."

"Is that what the doctors say?"

"The doctors! There isn't one of them brave enough to tell Bonaparte the truth. All they can do is recommend treatment at Plombiéres and other equally nauseating spas. Treatment for me, that is! One of them had the effrontery to suggest that I had suffered a miscarriage at some time and thus rendered myself incapable of bearing other children."

"And have you ever suffered one?" Aunt Marie asked curiously.

"Certainly not!"

Nevertheless Josephine recalled the suspected pregnancy which had followed the Lacoste *affaire* and which had ended with that terrible bout of seasickness during the voyage to Martinique. Ridiculous, of course, but at times it did make one wonder.

There was a knock at the door.

"Come in!" she barked.

A servant entered.

"The First Consul is waiting, madame," he announced.

"To say nothing of the rest of the family," she muttered.

She excused herself and went, by way of the private staircase, to

Bonaparte's apartments. There, to her surprise, she found only Madame Bonaparte and Joseph with him.

"Where," she asked sourly, "are the others?"

"The decision," Bonaparte assured her, "can be made without them."

She gave him a bleak smile. "Thank heaven for that."

Bonaparte cleared his throat. There was an uneasy silence.

"Shall we proceed," Joseph suggested, "with the vexing question of heredity?"

"Why 'vexing'?" Bonaparte challenged darkly.

"I call it vexing, Napoleon, because of your wife's unfortunate childlessness."

"Really, Joseph," Josephine almost shouted, "if you have come to the Tuileries to insult me——"

"You must admit, Josephine," Madame Bonaparte interrupted harshly, "that your persistent childlessness *is* vexing, not only to Napoléoné but to the rest of his family."

Josephine turned on Madame Bonaparte with flashing eyes. "I was under the impression that it pleased the rest of his family, and certainly I feel sure that none of you would be pressing him now to name his successor if a son had been born to me!"

"Ah," Joseph said, "but a son has *not* been born to you, nor is likely to be." He laughed unpleasantly. "As Paulette remarked only yesterday, you will soon be past the age for child-bearing."

"Pig!" Josephine screamed. "Ill-bred Corsican pig!"

"In the name of heaven," Bonaparte shouted, "let us discuss this matter calmly." He waited for a further outburst, took a deep breath of relief when none came and continued in a quiet but eager voice: "The first obvious question at this stage of my political career is: 'Should the consulate, with I myself as First Consul, be prolonged?' Assuming that it should the next obvious question is: 'For how long should it be prolonged, a period of five or ten years, or for my lifetime, with one of my family named as my successor?' "

"I beg you to think well before embarking on anything so rash," Josephine said. "Remember that France has just passed through a dreadful revolution the chief aim of which was to destroy the reign of a single family."

"Napoleon's family is wiser," Joseph said smugly, "than Louis the Sixteenth's."

"I fail to see," Madame Bonaparte remarked drily, "why you have called this family council together when your mind is already made up and you have no real intention of taking advice from any of us."

Bonaparte chuckled. "How well you know me, Mother."

"Yes, how well I know you, and because of that, how uneasy I am for you."

"Uneasy?"

"Josephine is afraid of your ambition for a very selfish reason; I am afraid of it because I love you. Try to listen to a mother's advice. Find strength in your heart to set aside this madness that is eating into your soul. The lust for power, your father once said, is the only thing that prevents a man from becoming really great."

Bonaparte looked at his mother coldly. "My mind is made up. Nothing you say will change it. Resign yourself to the inevitable. Make the best of what it pleases you to call my lust for power."

"Which of us," Joseph asked quickly, "do you intend to name?"

Josephine looked at Bonaparte in horror. Joseph, her most hated enemy among the Bonaparte brothers, was the eldest. Would *he* be the one?

"Why not Louis?" she suggested hastily, and it was not until after she had spoken that she saw, through Louis, an excellent way of saving herself.

Bonaparte looked at her thoughtfully. "Louis?"

She remembered then that Louis had always been his favorite brother, that he had supervised his education, denied himself in many ways in the past for the wretched boy, had regarded him more as a son than a brother. Besides, she and Louis had never come to actual blows.

"In my opinion," she went on, trying hard to control her mounting excitement, "Louis is the most suitable choice you could make. More suitable, certainly," she added sweetly, "than Joseph, who would be plainly impossible."

Joseph jumped to his feet angrily. "By heaven, Josephine——!"

"Oh come," she said, as if reasoning with a child, "excellent man of business that you *might* be, nature has designed you to be a follower, not a leader."

Bonaparte laughed heartily. "Fool that many people think her, my wife, on occasion, is given to uttering priceless words of wisdom."

"There, you see!" Josephine cried. "Joseph is out of the question, Lucien, poor fellow, is in disgrace; Jerome is too young even to be considered. Therefore——"

"Wait!" Bonaparte commanded, looking at Josephine curiously. "Why have you suddenly withdrawn your opposition and begun so eagerly to sponsor Louis?"

She looked at him sadly. "I am merely doing my poor best to resign myself to the inevitable and make the best of—of your lust for power."

Bonaparte laughed shortly. "I know my Josephine very well indeed. There's a great deal more in this extraordinary attitude of yours than meets the eye."

"I too believe that," Madame Bonaparte said, "but I agree with her suggestion. Louis is clever, at times even wise, and not so headstrong as the rest of you."

Josephine went quickly to Madame Bonaparte's side, and though it made her flesh creep to do it she took her by the hand.

"We agree, you see, your mother and I. Louis, who has none of the faults of his brothers, is the only man to succeed."

Joseph was on his feet again. "Your attitude is becoming insufferable, Josephine. It——!"

"Wait!" she said, and went on sweetly: "I was about to add that while Louis has none of the faults of his brothers he has many of their good qualities, though I must confess, Joseph, that *your* good qualities are sometimes hard to find."

"You—you—you—!" Joseph spluttered.

"Careful," she warned, "you're growing purple in the face. I should be most distressed if you fell victim to a fit of apoplexy." She turned to Bonaparte who was smiling broadly. "Is it Louis, then?"

"Yes," he said, "though I may as well tell you that I had decided on Louis before you mentioned him."

"How gratifying," she murmured, "how very gratifying."

With that she excused herself and made her way back to her own apartments. She paused at the top of the private staircase to laugh aloud at the memory of Joseph's face. She was still smiling when she entered the drawing-room and laughed even more at the amazement Aunt Marie betrayed.

"You went as if to your execution," the old lady said. "You return as if from a play at the Comédie Française."

A trifle exhausted, Josephine sat and began to tell her aunt what had happened. At the end of it all, when Joseph and Madame Bonaparte had been cruelly mimicked, Aunt Marie remarked that like Bonaparte himself she believed that there was more in Josephine's attitude than met the eye. Josephine nodded energetically and chuckled.

"Come," the old lady demanded, "tell me the truth."

"Louis," Josephine said slyly, "is a bachelor."

"Undoubtedly, but——"

"As soon as I realized that I could do nothing to prevent one of the Bonapartes being named my husband's successor I thought of Hortense."

"Hortense?"

"My daughter is nearly eighteen and unmarried. Louis, you must admit, is the best of the Bonaparte brood. If he and Hortense marry, and especially if they have children to carry on the Bonaparte succession, my position will be absolutely secure."

Regardless of the fact that her aunt was staring at her in horror she laughed triumphantly. "Well, Aunt Marie, don't you think I'm a very clever woman?"

"Clever, yes, but also heartless."

"*Heartless*, Aunt Marie?"

"Not only heartless but selfish."

"Really," Josephine cried indignantly, "are you trying to hurt me?"

"Perhaps it would be kinder if I merely said that you must have taken leave of your senses."

"I was about to say that of you, indeed I was! Why, it would be a splendid match for Hortense. The prospects are marvelous. Some day, if she marries Louis, she will be the first lady of France."

"In these days of political instability no one could count on that." The old lady looked searchingly at her niece. "Are you prepared to sacrifice your daughter's happiness in order to gain what you believe will be security for yourself?"

Josephine saw clearly what her aunt meant but she refused, after this one flash of insight, to admit it, even to herself.

"I see no reason," she said stubbornly, "why Hortense should not be happy with Louis Bonaparte."

"Happy with a young man she has been taught to hate ever since you married Bonaparte? I think not, Rose!"

"Oh, I doubt if Hortense really does hate the Bonapartes," Josephine said airily. "She's very fond of Caroline. I do know that."

"You yourself are very fond of Louis, perhaps?"

"I dislike him less than I dislike the others, and I know him to be very clever and—er—capable."

"And also vain and surly, or so I gather from what little I know of him. Hortense would be unhappy with him, desperately unhappy, and in your heart of hearts you know it."

"I know nothing of the kind, Aunt Marie!"

There was a little silence while Josephine scowled resentfully at her aunt and wished that she had remained quietly at home at Fontainebleau.

"Fortunately," the old lady said at last, "there's still a little hope for the child. I know that her own wishes will never be consulted, but I also know that the marriage you plan will never be made without Bonaparte's consent. Louis may be as reluctant to marry Hortense as she, I'm sure, will be to marry him."

"When do you propose to return to Fontainebleau?" Josephine asked quietly.

"Ah, you want to get me out of the way."

"I do," Josephine said frankly, "indeed I do."

The old lady rose and reached for her stick. "I shall remain in Paris—" each word was emphasized by a thump of the stick on the floor—"until the matter has been settled one way or the other."

*   *   *   *   *

"Bonaparte," Josephine said, "I'm a little worried about Hortense."

Bonaparte looked up from his papers anxiously. "Worried about her? She's not ill, I hope!"

"Not *physically* ill, but—" She broke off suddenly, as if in distress. In opening her campaign with Bonaparte it was essential to approach him skilfully, to choose her words with caution. "No, not *physically* ill," she went on, "but so very quiet of late, so—what is the word I want?—ah yes, so *introspective*. You must have noticed it yourself, Bonaparte."

He shook his head. "She always seems singularly light-hearted and happy to me."

"How unobservant you are, Bonaparte. But then, being a mere man——"

"Don't be a fool, Josephine. If anything was the matter with Hortense I should know it instantly."

"There are things," she said solemnly, "that only a mother would notice. Have you never realized that Hortense is no longer a child? The real trouble is probably that all her friends are marrying and making her feel like an old maid."

"Ah, so you want to get her married and off your hands!"

Josephine sniffed and began to fumble for a handkerchief. "What a cruel thing to say! Hortense is everything in the world to me. It would *kill* me to lose her. You *know* it would. And yet——"

"And yet you feel it your duty to arrange a good match for her, eh?"

"If by a good match you mean a happy one, yes, Bonaparte, I do."

"Do you suspect her of showing any especial preference?"

"Well—yes." (*Carefully, now, carefully*, she warned herself.) "To be frank, I once suspected her of an interest in your brother Lucien. Indeed, it is only since Lucien went away that her distressing quietness has become pronounced."

"But good lord," Bonaparte exclaimed, "Lucien, whom I would never choose for her in any case, is already married."

"Yes, I know. And that naturally worries me."

Lucien's wife, Christine, whom Josephine had met on two or three occasions only, was a sweet girl, but had always been kept in the background of her husband's life, possibly because he was a little ashamed of her, a daughter of a country inn-keeper. Lucien had married her many years ago before there had been any sign of the Bonaparte family attaining a position of consequence in France. Nineteen at the time, and aware that his mother and eldest brother Joseph would have forbidden the marriage, he had stolen Bonaparte's birth certificate and presented it to the registrar as if it were his own.

"Just imagine," Josephine said, "how we should all feel if Hortense really was in love with a married man!"

"If the man in question were Lucien," Bonaparte laughed, "I certainly know how *you* would feel, hating him as you do."

"How you wrong me," she sighed, "how you wrong me. The hatred is all on Lucien's side."

"We won't go into that," he said hastily. "Lucien is in Spain, and however Hortense might feel about him, he's well out of reach and will soon be forgotten."

Dismissing the subject he returned to a study of his papers.

'So far so good,' she thought. 'Now for the next step.'

"If Lucien were single," she said thoughtfully, "and a marriage *could* be arranged between him and Hortense, the unhappy circumstances which have always existed between me and your family might eventually vanish."

Bonaparte looked up quickly. "That is possible," he admitted, "but what can we do about it? Nothing. Nothing at all."

He gave his attention once more to his papers. She looked at the top of his head anxiously. Was the ground as well prepared as she imagined?

"Bonaparte," she said softly.

"Well?" he said, without looking up.

"Would you *really* look favorably upon an alliance between Hortense and one of your brothers?"

"Why, yes—" he was looking at her now—"I do believe I would, but, not, as I said a moment ago, an alliance with Lucien. He——"

"Oh, but I'm not thinking of Lucien. I—I'm thinking of Louis." It was out now, and to keep him from dwelling on the suggestion too much at first she went on quickly. "They would make a very handsome couple, don't you think?" She laughed pleasantly, as if at herself. "I can't imagine why I never thought of Hortense and Louis before, really I can't!"

"Hortense and Louis—" Bonaparte echoed, reflectively. "Strange that I too had never thought of them in that way before."

"Your favorite brother," Josephine said, sentimentally, "and the step-daughter you love as dearly as if she were your own."

The lines of Bonaparte's face had softened and his eyes, she saw, were shining. She held her breath and waited.

"A wife will have to be found for Louis some day," he declared, "especially now that I have decided to name him my heir and successor, and who better could we find than Hortense? All things considered——"

He broke off suddenly and rose to his feet. The light, for no apparent reason, had gone from his eyes. He came swiftly round the desk, took Josephine by the shoulders and shook her.

"You shrewd little devil!" he cried. "You shrewd little devil!"

She freed herself with difficulty. "Please, you hurt!"

He stood back from her and laughed shortly. "Now I understand the reason why you urged me to make Louis my successor. What a fine plan that little head of yours had already hatched."

Knowing how hopeless it was she nevertheless thought it wise to make at least one little protest. "A fine plan? Really, Bonaparte, you absolutely bewilder me!"

"Then let me bewilder you still more by explaining the details of your plan. When you realized that nothing would shake my determination to make one of my brothers my successor you suggested Louis because he is a bachelor. You said to yourself: 'If Louis marries Hortense and they have a son I shall be safe from the threat of divorce. You even——'"

"Divorce?" she shrieked. "Dear heaven, Bonaparte, *is* there a threat of divorce?"

"There *was*," he said smoothly, "and a very strong threat, I assure you."

This was the first time since the Hyppolyte Charles *affaire* that the word had passed between them, though it had hovered, unwanted and sternly shunned, at the back of her mind on more than one occasion.

"A very strong threat," she questioned, "because you and I have no children, or—or because you've grown a little tired of me?"

He took her in his arms, roughly. "I could never grow tired of you, Josephine, and though I fell out of love with you long ago I can still find love and affection for you in my heart."

She wriggled free. This was no time for stupid sentimentality.

"How can you blame me for our childlessness when I have had two children already? How can you blame me when neither Madame Fourés nor Madame Grassini bore you children? The fault is yours, not mine, and that would be quickly proved if you set me aside and married some other poor woman."

His face had grown pale and his eyes had the look of a hurt animal. *So much the better*, she raged to herself, *so much the better*!

"We were discussing a possible marriage between my brother and Hortense," he said quietly.

Her attitude changed instantly.

"You really favor it?" she asked eagerly.

"Yes. The more I think of the idea the more I like it. I think it would make me happy and bring a little compensation for our own childlessness."

"It would make me happy too, Bonaparte, *very* happy."

He went back to the desk and sat down. "We must do what we can about it, and soon."

"You—you would like me to speak to Hortense immediately?"

"Yes, though quite possibly—" his eyes twinkled wickedly—"the poor child might find it difficult to transfer her affections from Lucien to Louis."

"From Lucien to Louis?" Josephine demanded, deeply puzzled.

He slapped his hands on the desk in delight and laughed triumphantly. "Ah-ha! I caught you out there, sweetheart. Liars should try to cultivate good memories."

There was nothing she could do, of course, but laugh with him. "Yes, they should, shouldn't they!" She went round the desk to his side and kissed him lightly on the brow. Looking down she saw that the papers he had been studying were headed: *Memorandum for speech to be made by Allier in the Tribunate concerning the making of Napoleon Bonaparte First Consul for the term of his life.* "How frightening it is," she said, "to know that as far as you are concerned even my thoughts are not my own!"

She touched his brow with her lips a second time. Now for the next move in her campaign of safety and security for Josephine. Now for Hortense herself. . . .

CHAPTER XXXII

"SIT DOWN, HORTENSE," Josephine said. "I have something of the utmost importance to discuss with you."

Without showing even a little curiosity Hortense did as she was told and, with her hands folded in her lap, waited patiently for her mother to continue.

Josephine laughed wryly. "Dear me, what an old woman it makes me feel to see you looking so grown up."

Hortense smiled affectionately. "Does it really, Mother?"

"Yes." Hortense being a very different proposition to Bonaparte, it was a simple matter to come to the point at once. "I hardly know what I shall do, darling, when you make me a grandmother in a year or so."

"Oh, Mother, it might be years before I marry," Hortense protested, blushing.

"Years? Nonsense! When I was your age I had been married almost two years and Eugene was born." She reached forward and took the girl's hands in hers. "My dear, Bonaparte and I have found a husband for you."

Hortense withdrew her hands. "Oh."

"Really, is that all you can say? You should be delighted. Wildly excited. You——"

"May I ask the young man's name, Mother?"

"But of course, you quaint child. His name is Louis Bonaparte."

Hortense was silent for a moment, but the horror she felt was written plainly in her face.

"You must be joking, Mother," she said, in a low voice.

"Joking? In heaven's name why should I be joking?"

"But a Bonaparte— A Bonaparte, after the terrible way the family has always treated you."

"I—" At a loss for the moment, Josephine broke off.

"You're not serious, Mother." The girl's voice was trembling now. "You *can't* be serious!"

To mask the uneasiness she was beginning to feel, Josephine decided to speak sharply, even angrily, if necessary.

"Try to realize," she said, "that if you marry Louis you will be the most envied girl in France. Louis is soon to be named as Bonaparte's heir and successor. As his wife you will some day become the first lady in France, and your children and your children's children will carry on the Bonaparte succession. No girl in her right mind would refuse such a high honor."

In silence Hortense, now deadly pale, looked down at her folded hands.

"Well?" Josephine demanded.

"I'm sorry, Mother, but I dislike Louis and could never love him."

"Am I asking you to love him?"

Hortense looked up, understanding her mother perfectly. "I could never love him or marry him. I—" her voice faltered—"I'm sorry, Mother, but I love somebody else. But even if that were not the case I would rather die than marry a Bonaparte."

Josephine half rose in her chair. She could scarcely believe her ears. "Who is he? Tell me his name!"

"No, Mother," Hortense said firmly. "If I did that you would only have him sent away from Paris."

"How far has it gone? Has he asked you to marry him? Has he dared to do that?"

"No, Mother, but I had hoped, stupidly enough, that he would soon be able to approach my stepfather and you."

"Well!" was all Josephine could say, and annoyed with her temporary inability to cope with the situation she repeated it. "Well!"

"Mother, why are you so eager for me to marry Louis Bonaparte?"

The girl was on her feet now, trying to catch her mother's eyes and staring at her in a most disconcerting manner. 'The image of her wretched father,' Josephine thought, 'the very image!'

"Is it to save yourself from divorce, Mother?"

Josephine gave a little scream of horror and fell back in her chair.

"Please don't faint, Mother," Hortense begged earnestly, "just answer my question."

"Faint?" Josephine screamed. "What a horrible, ungrateful child you are. Why, you're as bad as the Bonapartes. You ought to be married to one of them, certainly you ought!" She began to weep. "I wish I was dead. Yes, I wish I was dead!"

Half in exasperation, half in tenderness, Hortense said: "Please don't cry, Mother."

"What if I do want to make my position secure?" Josephine ran on. "Can you blame me after so much sorrow has crowded my very short life? Could *anyone* blame me? If you imagine that I'm thinking only of myself you're badly mistaken. If Bonaparte were to divorce me what would happen to you? Tell me that! *What would happen to you?*"

"Nothing very serious, Mother. The First Consul would probably let me marry the man I love."

"*Hortense!*" Josephine wailed. "Your selfish attitude breaks my heart. You—you would actually stand by unfeelingly and see me divorced!"

Hortense found her own handkerchief and gave it to her mother.

"Use this, Mother. It's larger than your own."

Once more all Josephine could say was "*Well!*" Involuntarily she took the proffered handkerchief and blew her nose. "*Well!*" she said again.

"You upset yourself unnecessarily, Mother," Hortense said quietly. "The First Consul will never divorce you."

Josephine looked at her sharply. "You mean you really will marry Louis?"

"Have I any real choice in the matter?" Hortense said sadly.

"Naturally you have. I can only beg you to marry him, I can't *force* you to."

"No, Mother," Hortense agreed.

"Then you agree? You agree, darling?"

Hortense shrugged her shoulders. "Yes——"

"Ah," Josephine laughed, "you were only teasing me, trying to give me a fright!"

"Providing," Hortense concluded, "that Louis himself is willing."

"Wretch!" Josephine shouted. "I see what you're thinking, hoping! But let me tell you, Louis will do exactly what Bonaparte orders him to do."

"I wonder if he will," said Hortense softly. "Louis is a Bonaparte and as stubborn as the First Consul. I think he will refuse to marry me. Nay, I feel sure he will."

And with that, there being nothing else to do, Josephine began to weep again. . . .

✳ ✳ ✳ ✳ ✳

There was a knock at the door.

Bonaparte took Josephine by the shoulders, spun her round and gave her a push towards the window.

"That will be Louis. Hide behind the curtains."

"But Bonaparte—" she protested.

"Yes, yes," he said, "I know I said you could be present, but it was foolish of me. Louis might be difficult to handle. Your presence would only complicate matters. *Hide behind the curtains!*"

There was a second knock at the door. Bonaparte waited until Josephine was out of sight and then said: "Come in!"

From her position Josephine could hear Bonaparte and his brother quite clearly, and by dividing the curtains slightly at the side she could see their faces. Louis, she was delighted to admit, was the best-looking of the Bonaparte brothers. His nose was a little too long, of course, and his cupid-bow lips too thick, but there was something about the heavy-lidded eyes and the high cheekbones that would have set her heart racing in excitement if she had been a girl as young as Hortense.

Bonaparte, employing no *finesse* at all, came to the point at once. The moment he pronounced the words 'marriage' and 'Hortense' Louis began to laugh. Bonaparte told him angrily that it was anything but a laughing matter, and that the sooner he married and had children the better.

"But why Josephine's daughter?" Louis demanded. "Surely any other girl would be just as capable of bearing the required children."

"I happen to have chosen Hortense," Bonaparte said. "You will therefore marry Hortense."

334

"*You* happen to have chosen her? I begin to suspect that the choice was made by Josephine."

"The choice was mine, and it is my hope that when you and Hortense are married the feud which exists between my wife and my family will give place to friendliness and—er—understanding."

"I doubt if it will," Louis scoffed. "And you say *when* Hortense and I are married——"

"Whatever you doubt, Hortense is a sweet and intelligent child and will make you an excellent wife."

"Why not divorce Josephine and marry her yourself?"

"No levity, I beg of you, Louis. Surely you like Hortense a little, surely you find her an attractive girl!"

"Hortense," Louis murmured, "is a great deal better than her mother, but even if I were drawn to her, which I'm not, I could hardly come between her and the man she is already in love with."

"The man she is already in love with? What man is this?"

Josephine held her breath, and waited for Louis's answer.

"One of your *aides-de-camp*, Captain Duroc."

"How do you happen to know this, Louis?"

"Duroc himself told me. He came to me and asked my advice only this morning. He wanted to know how you would take it if he approached you for Hortense's hand."

Bonaparte was silent for a moment, then he came to a swift decision.

"Go to my dressing-room, Louis," he said, "and remain there."

"But——"

"Do as I say. I mistrust you, naturally I mistrust you."

Louis shrugged and obeyed.

Josephine came from behind the curtains on tip-toe just as Bonaparte opened the door and called "Constant!" When the valet came Bonaparte said: "Find Duroc, and also M'm'selle Hortense. Tell them that I want to see them at once."

"Bonaparte—" Josephine whispered.

"Back behind the curtains," he commanded, "and remain there."

"But Bonaparte——"

"Do as I say, Josephine."

"Very well, but may I suggest that if the outcome warrants it Louis and Hortense shall be left alone here later? Neither of them being aware of my presence, it might help us to know——"

He stopped her from saying more. "As you wish. If the outcome warrants it they shall be left here alone."

With that she retreated to the window and took up the position once more behind the curtains. A few moments later Duroc knocked and was told to enter. He was followed quickly by Hortense. Once again, employing no *finesse*, Bonaparte came straight to the point.

"Duroc, it has reached my ears that you are in love with my stepdaughter and want to marry her. Is that correct?"

Duroc hesitated.

"Come, come, man—is that correct?"

"Yes, sir," Duroc said faintly.

Bonaparte turned to Hortense. "Tell me, my dear, do you imagine yourself to be in love with Duroc?"

"It isn't a question of imagining it," Hortense said quietly. "I *am* in love with him."

Bonaparte sighed elaborately. "Ah well, I was never the man to stand in the way of true love—once I am convinced that true love really exists." He moved slowly forward until he was close to Duroc, who instinctively drew back a little. "Perhaps I should tell you, Duroc, that I want my stepdaughter to marry my brother, Louis. Now Louis, good fellow that he is, and animated by the tenderest of sentiments, is unwilling to enter upon such a marriage while knowing —or *suspecting*—that you want Hortense for yourself."

Bonaparte turned and strode across to the window, parted the curtains an inch to wink at the watching Josephine and swung back on Duroc again.

"To continue, Duroc. As I remarked a moment ago, I am not the man to stand in the way of true love, *once I am convinced that true love really exists*. On the other hand, this marriage which I plan for Hortense and Louis is a matter of political as well as family—er— necessity, and must, if humanly possible, be brought about. You follow me, Duroc?"

Duroc licked his underlip unhappily. "I—I think I do, sir."

"Splendid!" He gave Duroc a playful little punch in the ribs. "Now I very much doubt, Duroc, if, in your case, true love *does* exist."

"I assure you, sir—!" Duroc began.

"It does, Father, I know it does!" Hortense broke in.

Josephine saw a gleam of pleasure shoot through Bonaparte's eyes. Hortense rarely addressed him as 'Father,' but when she did it delighted him immensely. *And she knows it*, Josephine told herself angrily, *she knows it, the clever little wretch*!

"Very well," Bonaparte said, "I shall give him the benefit of the doubt and agree with you that it does. I shall even go as far as to say, my dear Duroc, that if you love Hortense as deeply as you claim you will prove it by sacrificing yourself on the—er—the altar of political necessity."

Josephine began to breathe more freely. Bonaparte was not to be defeated by sentiment, thank heaven!

"Let me make myself a little clearer," he continued. "I have long marked you for promotion, Duroc. If you remain in Paris an important and useful career lies before you, but unhappily, if you marry my stepdaughter, I shall be obliged to send you to one of the provinces. You begin to understand, I hope?"

"I—well yes, sir," Duroc admitted, unhappily.

"An intelligent man, I see— One more point. If Hortense marries my brother she will be the wife of my heir and successor. If she marries you she will be the wife of a small and unimportant provincial official. Married to Louis, her children will play a large part in the destiny of this new France of ours. Married to you they will be nobodies till the day they die."

Josephine, glancing beyond Bonaparte's shoulder, saw the door of his dressing-room open quickly.

"You cunning devil!" Louis cried, as he sprang forward.

Bonaparte ignored him.

"I think I have put the matter before you, Duroc," he said softly, "with the utmost clearness and—er—fairness. I shall make no further attempt to influence you, one way or the other, but I want your decision *now*."

Josephine pressed forward against the curtain. She saw Duroc turn hesitantly to Hortense; she saw Hortense take one step forward, pleadingly. 'What a drama,' she thought, 'what a powerful drama!'

"Well, Duroc?" Bonaparte said.

Duroc looked at Hortense for a long moment, then lowered his eyes.

"Forgive me," he said, "but there is only one decision I *can* make."

Josephine saw that Hortense understood, perfectly.

"I take it, Duroc," Bonaparte purred, "that you refrain from standing in the way of my stepdaughter's marriage with my brother Louis?"

Duroc bowed his head—*In shame, of course!* Josephine decided—begged to be excused and went hurriedly from the room. Louis began to follow him.

"Louis!" Bonaparte commanded, "where the devil are you going?"

Louis turned for a moment. "I propose to leave Paris at once, Napoleon. Possibly I shall join Lucien in Spain. Nothing you do or say will make me marry Hortense."

Bonaparte went to him quickly. Taking him gently by the arm he said: "Why not discuss this matter quietly and sensibly with Hortense herself?"

Louis tried to shake himself free.

"Please," Bonaparte pleaded, "for her sake as well as your own." He went quickly to the door. "I shall leave you alone with her. Call me the moment you reach the decision I want you to make."

Leaving Hortense and Louis to stare helplessly at each other, he went softly from the room and closed the door behind him. For one horrible moment, as she watched them, Josephine wondered if Louis suspected her presence, but presently, as he and Hortense began to talk together, she reassured herself that he didn't.

"We find ourselves in a most unfortunate predicament," Louis remarked.

"Yes," Hortense agreed bitterly, "a most unfortunate one."

"I shall, of course, leave Paris, just as I said I would."

"What use would that be?" Hortense asked. "Your brother will have you followed and brought back."

"You think it might be simpler—I won't say *wiser*—to remain and submit to his wishes?"

"Well, yes, Louis, I think perhaps it would."

"Bah! You must be mad! When I told Napoleon that nothing would make me marry you I meant it. I meant it, I say!"

Hortense laughed shortly. "I told my mother that I would rather die than marry a Bonaparte. And I meant that, too."

"Did you indeed!" Louis cried indignantly. "Well let me tell you that whatever that interfering mother of yours might say, we Bonapartes are much less poisonous than you Beauharnais!"

Only by a great effort did Josephine restrain herself from flinging the curtains aside and revealing herself.

"Oh, Louis, Louis," Hortense was saying wearily, "what good will it do us to quarrel?"

"None at all," Louis admitted.

"If only we could think of a way of escaping this marriage, but I feel so helpless."

"The only way is for me to leave Paris and try to evade pursuit."

Suddenly Hortense said: "Louis, a few weeks ago I heard some gossip about you and a young girl. I forget her name but I think she was the daughter of an inspector of bridges."

"Oh, you mean Blanche Leroy," Louis laughed. "What of it?"

"I thought perhaps you were in love with her."

"So I am, a little," he said casually.

"Had you ever thought of marrying her?"

"Marrying her? Good lord no!"

Ah, Josephine muttered to herself, *I know exactly what you're about, my fine Hortense, I know exactly*!

"But Louis," Hortense pressed, "if you had to choose between Blanche Leroy and me——?"

"What are you trying to say?" Louis asked curiously.

"Simply this. You could avoid marrying me by eloping with her and marrying her before your brother was able to interfere."

"Hortense," Louis said warmly, "in spite of myself, in spite of the fact that you are Josephine's daughter, I'm beginning to like you."

"Then you'll do as I suggest?"

"Yes. I shall leave Paris tonight with Blanche. Tomorrow at this time I shall be well beyond the reach of Napoleon and his ambitions!" He went to the door. "Napoleon!" he called.

"Be careful," Hortense warned, and when Bonaparte entered she said: "Louis and I have had a very interesting talk. I—I can't promise anything now but we do understand the situation a little better."

'Merciful heavens,' Josephine thought, 'the image of her father did I say! No, no, the image of her mother!'

The moment Louis and Hortense were out of the room Josephine rushed to Bonaparte's side.

"Much better than I could have hoped," he said, with a smile.

"Much worse, you mean!"

She told him quickly what Louis and Hortense were planning.

"This," she said with decision, "is clearly a matter for Fouché."

"It is," Bonaparte growled, "by heaven it is!"

*　　*　　*　　*　　*

When Louis had been overtaken with Blanche Leroy and brought back to Paris Josephine went in search of her daughter. She had no real intention of reproaching her. It would be sufficient punishment for the scheming little wretch simply to say: "Louis has been brought back."

She found Hortense in her room. She was standing by the window and turned as Josephine entered.

"Louis," Josephine said, "has made an attempt to leave Paris. He was overtaken by Fouché's men and brought back. When Bonaparte has finished with him he will be perfectly willing to marry you."

Hortense, betraying no surprise, making no comment whatever, turned listlessly back to stare out of the window.

"Rose," a voice said sharply, "I want to talk to you."

Josephine swung round. Aunt Marie, sitting on a chair in a corner of the room and leaning forward on her stick, had evidently been there all the time.

Josephine sighed. "I can see by your eyes that you're going to be tiresome," she smiled.

"Hortense, child," Aunt Marie said, "you know how things stand and will always stand between your mother and the Bonaparte family. Do as I say. Resist this marriage. Resist it with all the strength you possess."

339

Hortense turned to look at Aunt Marie but remained silent.

"Hortense," Josephine said sharply, "is too young to know her own mind in such a matter."

"Too young, Rose? She is two years older than you were when you came to France to marry Alexandre."

"The child has led a very sheltered life, Aunt Marie. You know she has."

"I wonder," Aunt Marie said, reflectively, "if you remember those early days in Paris as well as I do?"

"I—" Josephine's voice dropped. "I remember them perfectly."

Aunt Marie turned to Hortense. "My dear, neither you nor Eugene have ever been told the whole truth about your mother and your father."

"Aunt Marie—!" Josephine began in alarm, and then fell miserably silent.

"Your father," Aunt Marie went on, "had the hardest nature I have ever come across in any man. From the first he treated your mother as if she were a half-witted pupil and he a school-teacher. He began by correcting her grammar and on their wedding night he forced her to read aloud to him from the unutterably dull essays of Montaigne."

"For pity's sake—!" Josephine begged, and again fell silent.

"During their honeymoon," Aunt Marie went on, "he set her lessons in geography and history, and scolded her mercilessly when she found it impossible to remember an unimportant date. In the end he was repeatedly unfaithful to her, and then, when he wanted to free himself of the marriage ties, he accused her of conduct even worse than his own, and to his lasting shame he suggested that you——"

"Aunt Marie," Josephine cried, "I forbid you to go on!"

"To his lasting shame, Hortense, he suggested that you, his second child, were the offspring of an illicit love *affaire.*"

Hortense was staring at Aunt Marie in horror. "He suggested that? He, the man I always loved and respected?"

"He suggested that."

Josephine went quickly to her daughter's side. "She exaggerates, darling, I give you my word she does."

"I do not exaggerate, Hortense, and your mother knows it."

Hortense took her mother's arm tenderly. "Mother, you should have told me this yourself long ago."

Josephine laughed shakily. "Nonsense, and for heaven's sake don't look so—so *tragic.* The story belongs to the past, and the past, happily for all of us, is dead."

"But what of the future, Rose?" Aunt Marie said. "Hortense's future?"

Josephine made a gesture of annoyance. A fox, that was what Aunt Marie was, a wily old fox!

"Why did you tell me this about my father?" Hortense asked.

"What I told you was really meant for your mother who prefers to forget the past." She turned to Josephine. "Have you forgotten, Rose, that I was responsible for your marriage with Alexandre? The things you suffered left a lasting and terrible impression on my mind. I have never forgiven myself for causing you so much unhappiness. Now *you* are in the position I was in. Think well, Rose, before you make a marriage for Hortense which may well prove as disastrous as your own first marriage."

Josephine looked about her for a chair, found one and collapsed heavily into it. She had never felt so unhappy in her life. Aunt Marie had tried to frighten her before; now she had succeeded. Yet surely Louis Bonaparte at his very worse could never be as bad as Alexandre had been. Those dreadful essays of Montaigne! She could remember some of the ponderous, meaningless phrases even now! On a sudden thought she looked shrewdly at her daughter. Yes, the expression of tenderness was still in her eyes; it was even a little more pronounced. She rose quickly and took Hortense in her arms.

"Hortense," she said, "you may please yourself about this marriage. I shall make no further attempt to force you. It was wrong of me ever to think of forcing you, very, very wrong."

She caught Aunt Marie's eyes, which held a suspicious look, then looked down, waiting for Hortense to speak.

"Thank you, Mother," the girl said, in a voice that was deeply moved. "Thank you, but my mind is made up. If I can give you happiness by marrying Louis, if I can make up a little for the unhappiness you knew with the man who was my father——"

"In heaven's name, Hortense—!" Aunt Marie shouted.

Triumphantly Josephine's eyes met the old lady's. *Too late,* she almost said aloud, *too late, Aunt Marie!*

"Please, Aunt Marie," Hortense said quietly, "I know what I am doing. I said before that if Louis were agreeable I would marry him, but I didn't mean it. I say it again now and this time I do mean it."

Josephine kissed her. "You dear, sweet child," she murmured.

Entering the room (at a very suitable moment, Josephine considered) came Bonaparte. He was followed by Louis, a red-faced, angry Louis who flashed her a challenging look and remained near the door, waiting for his brother to speak.

"Louis and I," Bonaparte said softly, "have reached an understanding. He realizes, intelligent young man that he is, that if he wishes to remain my heir and successor he must marry a girl of my own

341

choosing." He turned to Louis. "Come, Louis, tell Josephine about our agreement."

Louis advanced into the room looking more challenging than ever.

"Nobody," he said, with a confident laugh, "would be more willing to marry your daughter than I, providing her own consent is given freely, without any compulsion whatever."

Hortense stepped forward. In a low but distinct voice she said: "Thank you, Louis. I accept your offer of marriage. I accept it gladly."

Josephine looked at Aunt Marie and smiled, and the smile said clearly: *Thank you, Aunt Marie. You, and you alone, have made this possible.*

CHAPTER XXXIII

MALMAISON, JOSEPHINE thought, as she strolled through the grounds of the country house, had never looked more beautiful. The army of gardeners, it was true, still had the larger part of their task before them, but the outline of the English park she desired was at last discernible.

"How much," Fouché asked, "has all this cost?"

She laughed easily. "Very little, up to now. A mere six hundred thousand francs, I believe."

Josephine had been at Malmaison for a week, having come alone to gain a slight respite from the watching eyes of the Bonapartes, and also to superintend the alterations being made to the château itself. Fouché, surprising her with the unexpectedness of his visit, had arrived less than an hour ago, and up to now he had made no mention of the reason for it.

"Well, Fouché," she said, curiosity finally getting the better of her, "what brings you to Malmaison?"

Fouché smiled slily. "I fancied a drive in the country and I wanted to talk to you without fear of being overheard by your husband's spies."

"Ah," Josephine cried, in delight, "an intrigue is in the making!"

"Two intrigues, to be precise. The first concerns your little sister-in-law, Paulette Leclerc."

Josephine's hands went to her throat. "Merciful heavens, what is the wretched girl planning now?"

"You needn't alarm yourself," Fouché laughed. "I am the one who is planning something, not Paulette. I happen to have discovered a way of disposing of her and thought you might be interested."

"You thought! You only *thought!*"

"Very well, I knew. I knew for certain. However, before I give you my suggestion I want you to promise to do something for me, which incidentally is also something for yourself."

"Tell me what it is," Josephine said cautiously, "and let me be the judge of it."

Fouché, despite the fact that no workmen were closer than twenty yards, lowered his voice to a whisper.

"What," he asked, "is your attitude to the possibility of a Bourbon restoration?"

She looked at him in amazement. "What makes you think I might be interested in such a thing?"

"Oh, a number of reasons, including the fact that you, a member of the old aristocracy, can have little love for republicanism."

"Republicanism," she shrugged, "is not without its advantages. As for royalism, Bonaparte often speaks of it as a lost cause."

"Am I to understand, then, that you decline the honor of interesting yourself in a Bourbon restoration?"

"You are," she said warmly, "and a shrewd man like you would be well advised to decline it too."

"What a pity," he sighed, "that my scheme for sending Paulette into exile is to be wasted."

"Exile?" Josephine questioned sharply.

"A sort of exile, at all events. But to return to the Bourbons. Bonaparte is very powerful at the moment, and will become more powerful still if he succeeds in having himself declared First Consul for life, and yet——"

"Yes, Fouché? And yet——?"

"At heart the people of France are still too conservative to tolerate such a dictatorship as he would set up for very long. I firmly believe that the only way he can retain his power is by making it the power behind the throne of the restored Bourbons. Your husband has won his place in the hearts of the people through the sheer force of his military genius. His armies are regarded as invincible, but once that myth is disproved his loss of personal prestige will be tremendous."

The tone of his voice made her ask him uneasily what he was suggesting.

"I happen to have received secret information from Egypt. The English have not only landed there but are pressing on to Alexandria. I know the signs. The fall of Egypt is close at hand. That is why I feel that Bonaparte might be persuaded to discuss a Bourbon restoration and so free himself of the responsibility of what I choose to regard as inevitable military reverses."

Josephine shook her head. "Bonaparte has set his own stubborn and ambitious course. Nothing I could ever say would turn him from it."

Fouché looked at her speculatively. "Let me make my appeal more personal. You know, of course, that if your husband turns his back on the Bourbons he will attempt to make himself king."

"Yes, I do know that."

"Should he succeed your own position, since a king must have an heir, will be sadly menaced."

An icy hand gripped her heart but she tried to laugh confidently. "Once Hortense and Louis Bonaparte are married I shall have nothing whatever to fear."

"Bonaparte the First Consul might be satisfied with a brother for his heir and successor, but Bonaparte the King—" Fouché laughed easily. "Oh, come, Josephine, take his ridiculous vanity into consideration. King Bonaparte would want a son to follow him on his stolen throne."

The icy hand closed about her heart in a colder grip.

"What do you want me to do?" she asked, making up her mind immediately.

"No one has ever had more influence with Bonaparte than you. All I ask on behalf of my royalist friends is that you talk to him about a restoration. I know the difficulty of the task, but you're a clever woman and, remember, you will be fighting for the preservation of your own personal security."

Josephine shook her head sadly. "The difficulty, I think, will be unsurmountable, but I shall do my best." Her manner changed and her voice became brisk. "Now tell me your scheme for disposing of Paulette."

"Saint Domingo," Fouché murmured.

"Saint Domingo? What do you mean by that?"

"You must have heard of the native risings there. Bonaparte is sending an expedition of twenty thousand men to Saint Domingo but can't make up his mind who to place at the head of it."

Josephine saw what Fouché meant. "Leclerc!" she cried, and then her face dropped. "But Paulette would never accompany her husband."

"You think not? Bonaparte always says that a wife should stand at her husband's side. Don't you think he could be persuaded to insist?"

Josephine chuckled, then, remembering the uncomfortable journeys she herself had been forced to make because of Bonaparte, she frowned.

"They tell me," Fouché said softly, "that yellow fever is very prevalent in Saint Domingo."

The frown vanished and she chuckled again.

"Yes, Fouché, *very* prevalent!"

* * * * *

Josephine, on returning to Paris, had ascertained that Junot's presence in France was considered necessary by Bonaparte. Therefore, approaching her object with characteristic deviousness, she said:

"Why not place Junot at the head of the expedition?"

Bonaparte shook his head. "I need Junot in France."

"Duroc, then?" (He, too, she had discovered, was needed in France.)

"Duroc could be spared even less than Junot."

Josephine pondered for a moment. "I can make only one other suggestion. Why not Leclerc?"

"Leclerc? But of course! The very man! How stupid of me not to have thought of him before."

Josephine hid a smile. So far so good. Now for the more ticklish part of the scheme.

"I'm afraid," she said, "that there might be one difficulty when it comes to sending Leclerc to Saint Domingo."

"Indeed?"

"Paulette—" she tried to make her voice sound innocent—"will hate the thought of leaving Paris."

Bonaparte raised his brows. "I fail to see why she should."

"But I should hate it myself, Bonaparte. Surely, when it comes to the point, you won't be so cruel as to send her abroad with Leclerc?"

"Cruel? Why the devil should it be cruel to send her? Her place is with her husband. You know that as well as I do."

"No doubt it is, but all the same——"

"Really, Josephine," Bonaparte cried angrily. "I want your help in this, not your opposition. I shall have enough trouble with Paulette without *you* taking her side. I should have thought you would be only too glad to see Paulette leave France—" He stopped in mid-sentence and looked at her suspiciously. "What," he asked softly, "would you have done if I had agreed to send either Junot or Duroc?"

She saw that his eyes were twinkling and felt sure that though he had seen through her subterfuge he was more amused than angry.

"Had you done that," she said promptly, "I should have tried to persuade you that Leclerc was the only choice."

"Fortunately for you," he laughed, "Leclerc, in my opinion, *is* the only choice."

Three hours later Paulette, followed by an angry-faced Bonaparte, burst into Josephine's boudoir. In the act of applying rouge to her cheeks, Josephine, eyeing the wrathful girl in the mirror, proceeded quietly with the delicate operation.

"I might have known," Paulette stormed, "that *you* were at the bottom of this vile plot to get me out of France. First Lucien, then me. Your intention to pick us off one by one is very clear."

"Keep your temper, Paulette," Bonaparte warned. "When I first suggested that you should accompany Leclerc, Josephine opposed the idea."

"Naturally she did. Josephine is cunning. Josephine knows that to oppose a thing is to strengthen your determination."

Bonaparte's eyes met Josephine's in the mirror. She saw him wink and coughed to cover up an involuntary giggle.

"A wife's place," Bonaparte pronounced, "is at her husband's side."

"But the *danger!*" Paulette screamed. "You seem to want to send me to what might well be certain death."

Josephine turned from the mirror. "As a matter of fact, Paulette, I felt as you now feel when I joined Bonaparte in Italy. Yet join him I did, and countless times I risked my life in order to be at his side."

"You went to Italy with the greatest reluctance," Paulette shouted, "and when Napoleon was in Egypt did you join him there?"

"Had my health been better at the time," Josephine said virtuously, "I should have joined him there gladly, nay—eagerly!"

"And what of *my* health? A long and hazardous sea voyage might easily kill me!"

'If not the sea voyage,' Josephine thought, 'the fever, let us hope.'

"Enough of this arguing," Bonaparte said. "Leclerc sails two weeks from today. You, Paulette, will sail with him."

"And if she refuses?" Josephine questioned softly.

"If she refuses she shall be sent to live quietly in the provinces as befits a person in her delicate state of health."

"Beast!" Paulette stormed. "Beast, beast, *beast!*" With an effort she controlled herself and turned on Josephine. "We shall meet again, Josephine, and under very different circumstances, if *I* have anything to do with it!"

"Dear me," Josephine drawled, "that sounds remarkably like a threat."

"It was meant to be a threat. Lucien has been sent into exile, and now *I* am to be treated in the same way, but only temporarily, I assure you. We have long memories, we Bonapartes, and nurse our hatreds jealously. Remember that, Josephine, remember *that!*"

"Dear me," Josephine murmured, "what dreadfully uncivilized people these Corsicans are."

*　　*　　*　　*　　*

Shortly after the departure of Leclerc and Paulette, and while Josephine was still awaiting a favorable opportunity to approach Bonaparte on the subject of a Bourbon restoration, a family conference composed of Bonaparte himself, Madame Bonaparte, Joseph and Josephine was called to discuss the coming marriage of Hortense and Louis. Before an actual discussion could take place, Bonaparte was put in a bad humor by Joseph's asking if the stories of reverses in Egypt were founded on fact.

"Because if they are," Joseph added, "steps should be taken to contradict them until a French victory has been won."

"Steps have already been taken," Bonaparte muttered darkly.

"These stories of English successes," Madame Bonaparte was imprudent enough to ask—"They are true, Napoléoné, or false?"

"The English," Bonaparte said, his face pale and set, "have enjoyed a few minor successes but the main battle is yet to be fought."

"Then the English have made landings," Joseph asked, "and are in a position to give battle?"

"You fool, Joseph!" Bonaparte exclaimed, suddenly losing his temper. "Can't you see that Egypt is a subject I have little wish to discuss except at a military conference?"

Joseph turned red, stammered that he was sorry and fell silent.

"I called you here today," Bonaparte went on, in a calmer voice, "to discuss the coming marriage of Louis and Hortense. The contract will be drawn up on January third—" already the employment of the Revolutionary Calendar was falling into disuse—"and the ceremony itself will take place on the following day."

"Is it to be a civil ceremony," Madame Bonaparte asked, "or a religious one?"

"Why do you ask that, Mother?" Bonaparte demanded sharply.

"Mother asks," Joseph said, "because of the rumors now going about that you intend to restore religion to France."

"Is this true?" Josephine asked, her mind suddenly busy with a new possibility of increasing her own security.

"Perfectly true," he admitted. "But please don't imagine, any of you, that I am suddenly becoming religious. The restoration of a national faith is a matter of policy. A matter of policy because religion is a principle which cannot, at this stage of our evolution from superstition to the far-off age of enlightenment and knowledge, be eradicated from the hearts and minds of the people as a whole."

Madame Bonaparte frowned disapprovingly. "That, Napoléoné, is a very cynical thing to say."

"Nonsense, Mother! I understand the people, that is all. Most of them want a national faith again. Therefore they shall have it and thank me for giving it to them."

"Have you actually opened up negotiations with the Pope?" Joseph asked.

"Yes, I have."

"And you intend to come to an agreement soon?"

"That, naturally, rests with the Pope."

"Ah," Josephine laughed, "I understand perfectly. The terms of the agreement will be *your* terms. Otherwise—no agreement."

"Precisely, my dear, though I see no reason why the concordat I have drawn up should not be acceptable to the Holy Father. In the first place I propose that the Roman Catholic religion shall once more become the national faith of France. In the second, that the Pope, in concert with the French Government, shall make a new division of dioceses. In the third, that vacancies shall be filled by the Pope, but only on nominations made by the French Government."

"In other words," Josephine chuckled, "on nominations made by Napoleon Bonaparte."

He leaned forward and pinched her cheek. "How well you understand me, sweetheart."

"Really, Napoléoné," Madame Bonaparte exclaimed, "you shock me."

"Do I, Mother? And why, pray?"

"Because of your arrogance, your attempt to dictate terms to His Holiness the Pope."

Bonaparte laughed gleefully and rubbed his hands together. "The Holy Father may dislike my terms, but I feel confident that he will accept them rather than permit France to remain a pagan country."

Her mind having developed the new scheme for increasing her own security, Josephine turned to her mother-in-law with a sweet smile.

"Whatever we might think of Bonaparte's methods," she said, "one thing about the restoration of religion is pleasing to both of us. I speak, of course, of the religious ceremony which Louis and Hortense will now be able to enjoy."

"You go too fast," Bonaparte laughed. "I made no promise of a religious ceremony, but since it will please the clergy, and if I'm not mistaken my mother also, by all means let us have a religious ceremony."

"You are not mistaken, Napoléoné," Madame Bonaparte said. "It has always hurt me to think that when Caroline and Joachim Murat were married the marriage remained unblessed by the Church."

Josephine could hardly believe her ears. Here was Madame Bonaparte, a sworn enemy, innocently preparing the ground for her. Swiftly, but not too swiftly, she said:

"Then why not let Caroline and Murat marry again when Hortense and Louis are married?"

The hard lines of Madame Bonaparte's face softened for a moment. "It warms my heart, Josephine, to hear you make such a suggestion."

Josephine turned eagerly to Bonaparte. "You agree, Bonaparte?"

He laughed shortly. "I think it a lot of nonsense, but if you women really want it, I agree." He laughed again. "The more display and ceremony you can attach to a wedding the better you like it, eh?"

"It is not a question of display and ceremony," Madame Bonaparte said severely, "it is a question of religious principle. A marriage that is not blessed by the Church is only half a marriage."

Josephine smiled. For the moment she almost loved her mother-in-law, and could have embraced her warmly for her additional help.

"That is just how I feel," she said humbly. "It would break my heart to see Hortense and Louis married without the blessing of anything more than a cold civil contract." She sighed deeply and looked at Bonaparte with big, soulful eyes. "I shall never forget how I felt at our own wedding, Bonaparte. The civil ceremony was so short, so swift, so—so *soulless*."

Madame Bonaparte gave Josephine an understanding smile. "It could hardly have been a happy experience, Josephine."

"Of course at that time," Josephine went on, making her voice sound as reasonable as possible, "a religious ceremony was out of the question, but I have often regretted——"

Bonaparte interrupted her with an uneasy laugh. "You're not about to suggest, I hope, that you want me to make good the omission now."

"We—ell——"

"That is what is in your mind, Josephine?" Madame Bonaparte asked.

"To be perfectly frank, it is. Oh, I know that Bonaparte is hardly likely to agree to such a course, but if only he would, if only he *would*!"

"Bah!" Bonaparte cried, "I can see that if I don't you will pester me and nag at me until life becomes unbearable."

"I will, Bonaparte, I declare that I will!"

He smiled indulgently. "Then the best thing I can do is agree at once."

Josephine ran quickly to his side and embraced him warmly. "Oh, Bonaparte, how happy, how very happy, you make me!" And she thought: 'Divorce, after a civil marriage, is one thing; after a religious one, quite another!'

"Really, Napoleon," Joseph was saying acidly, "have you taken leave of your senses?"

Bonaparte's temper flared up instantly. "What the devil do you mean by that, Joseph?"

"Looking into the future, Napoleon," Joseph went on, "I can see you King of France, but a king without a direct heir. However satisfied you may feel at this moment to be succeeded by Louis, the time will come when you will want a son of your own, a son destined to be known as Napoleon the Second."

"Napoleon the Second—" Bonaparte echoed, savoring the words. Josephine shot a quick look at Joseph. She knew what his next words would be, and powerless to prevent him uttering them, she felt suddenly lost and desperate.

"And when that time comes," Joseph said, holding Josephine's eyes for a moment, "you will be forced to divorce Josephine in order to marry a younger woman, in order, perhaps, to marry the daughter of some royal house."

"Well," Bonaparte said harshly, "what of it?"

"A national faith is to be restored to France. The Church is to regain its old place of dignity and honor. Think what that will mean if, having married Josephine again before the altar, you decide to divorce her."

"What *will* it mean, Joseph?"

"It will mean that the heart of France, a religious country once more, will be shocked, and shocked justly. Public opinion might force you to remain married to Josephine whatever you might want to do yourself."

An uneasy silence fell on the room. Bonaparte had folded his arms and was staring unhappily at Joseph. With black hatred in her heart Josephine looked from Joseph to Madame Bonaparte. It was clear that she, in spite of her earlier sympathy, would support Joseph now. Finally Bonaparte, looking at Josephine miserably, said gently:

"You must forgive me, my dear, but——"

She interrupted him quickly. "No more need be said, Bonaparte. I quite understand. You break my heart between you, you and your family, but does that really matter?"

She went slowly from the room. Only one hope remained to her now, a Bourbon restoration, but that, she knew, was a very faint hope indeed. . . .

CHAPTER XXXIV

J OSEPHINE, SPENDING MORE
time than ever at her dressing-table these days, was subjecting
her face to the critical examination she normally reserved for other
women's faces. She had just come from the bath which, in addition
to the morning bath, she had fallen into the habit of taking in the
late afternoon. The Bonapartes, and indeed most of the ladies of the
Consular Court, were inclined to snigger behind her back and declare that a woman who immersed herself in water so frequently was
surely mad. "Your health will suffer," Aunt Marie often warned,
while Elisa Bacciochi, Bonaparte's eldest sister, had reminded her
that the late Queen of France, whose apartments she occupied, had
rarely done more than wash the parts of her body not covered by
clothing. "In spite of the perfume she used," Josephine had retorted
smoothly, "there must have been times when Marie Antoinette
smelled like a dead rat."

She leaned closer to the mirror and what she saw reflected there
both alarmed and depressed her. Lines, lines, nothing but lines!
What a blessing that nobody save her maid ever saw her face as it
was now, temporarily innocent of its habitual layers of cosmetics. A
hag, that's what she was, a raddled old hag. And whose fault was it?
The Bonaparte family's, of course, for they were lines of worry, not
dissipation or age. Certainly not age, she was only thirty-five—well,
thirty-nine then, but not until June, which meant that she was still
thirty-eight. Thirty-eight, and an expectant grandmother. Ridiculous,
and also heartbreaking.

Hortense and Louis had now been married two months and were
living together at the house in the rue Victoire which Bonaparte
had insisted on Josephine making over to them. With a frown Josephine recalled the wedding ceremony. Hortense, betraying no
emotion whatever, had been so quiet, so unnaturally restrained, and
all she would say when asked if she was happy was: "Of course,
Mother." No reproaches, no tears, no understandable hysteria, just
"Of course, Mother." And now, with a somewhat indecent promptness she was going to have a baby. Josephine made a rapid calculation. Yes, the very minimum, which of course was fortunate, otherwise
the Bonapartes would raise a great outcry and make an unpleasant
scandal. . . .

The door opened and Bonaparte walked into the room. She gave
an exclamation of annoyance. What an impossible man he was, catch-

ing her like this without a vestige of paint or rouge on her face.

"Splendid news!" he cried, after kissing the back of her neck. "The Pope has finally agreed to the terms of my concordat."

"Splendid news indeed," she agreed promptly.

Bonaparte threw himself into a chair. "Bourrienne, fool that he is, thinks the concordat a little premature."

"Why premature?" Josephine asked, busying herself with the white paint.

"He imagines that the republicans will regard the restoration of religion as a definite step on my part towards the re-establishment of the monarchy."

Josephine smiled at herself in the mirror. This, surely, was the opening for which she had waited so long and so patiently.

"And is it?" she asked.

"It might be," he said airily. "On the other hand, it might not be." She turned from the mirror to face him.

"I have always thought," she said earnestly, "that your wisest policy would be to come to terms with the royalists and give your upmost support to the restoration of the Bourbons."

He tweaked her nose playfully and refused to be drawn further, and she, satisfied for the time being, was wise enough to refrain from pressing him. He chatted for a few moments about Hortense and Louis—"Just think, Josephine, a nephew for me, a grandson for you!" —and then spoke of the great procession he was planning to celebrate the return of religion to France.

"And after the procession," he said, "a solemn service in Notre Dame itself."

"Am I to ride in the procession with you?" Josephine asked, wondering instantly what she ought to wear for such an occasion.

"No, my dear. There's no place for a woman in a military procession."

She pouted. "How you love to keep me in obscurity, Bonaparte."

"Obscurity?" he cried, "when a place of honor will be reserved for you at Notre Dame?"

"Oh, in that case—I shall, of course, need a new dress."

"Of course," he laughed, "being Josephine the need of a new dress will be imperative. Wear something white. You always look your best in white." And he added drily: "It disguises your true age; for some strange reason white always gives you the look of a young girl."

"Pig," she said, but on the whole she chose to accept his words as a compliment.

"A triumph of simplicity and extravagance," Fouché chuckled, glancing admiringly at Josephine's dress.

Josephine laughed gaily. "I don't mind admitting, Fouché, that it *did* cost a small fortune!"

The procession and the impressive service at Notre Dame were over and the reception which had been planned to follow them at the Tuileries was now in progress.

Looking about him Fouché said: "All this display must be very dear to your husband's heart."

"Dear to his heart or not," Josephine assured Fouché, "you may take it as a sign that he is beginning to look favorably upon a Bourbon restoration."

"You have spoken to him about a restoration?" Fouché asked eagerly.

She nodded briefly, lowered her voice and told him what Bonaparte had said about a re-establishment of the monarchy.

"But he admitted nothing," Fouché pointed out, "he admitted nothing whatever."

"That might be true, Fouché, but if he were as strongly against a restoration as you think—as I myself thought until recently—would he have spoken as he did?" She looked at Fouché earnestly. "I want to help the Bourbons in every way I can. Tell me what you would like me to do next."

Fouché looked casually about to make sure that nobody was within earshot, then he told her that a petition was being prepared by certain royalists.

"All we ask of you," he said, "is the presentation of it yourself. If it goes to him in the ordinary way through Bourrienne it will be thrown aside, possibly by Bourrienne himself. If *you* present it——"

Josephine laid a hand on his arm. "Let me have it the moment it's completed. A restoration is assured. I give you my word, Fouché, a restoration is assured."

*   *   *   *   *

Bonaparte began to read the petition a second time while Josephine, watching him in a fever of anxiety, wondered what he was thinking. From time to time she saw his lips silently form a word or a phrase, but though an occasional smile flitted across his face his expression told her little. The petition had been brought to her the night before when Fouché, accompanied by the Bourbon agent, the Marquis de St. Bernard, had paid a secret visit to her apartments. She had thought the terms proposed by the royalists exceedingly reasonable and hoped with all her heart that Bonaparte was thinking the same thing now.

Presently he looked up from his second reading. "Am I permitted to ask the name of the man who delivered this interesting document into your hands?"

Having been warned against betraying the marquis she said: "He wishes to remain anonymous. Not even I know his name."

"Dear me, what a ridiculous air of mystery," he laughed. Then he grew thoughtful. "So they would make me a peer of the realm, and in addition, Constable of France."

"Next to the King," Josephine said eagerly, "you would be the most powerful man in France."

Bonaparte laughed gently. "Oh, come, do you really believe that the man who has followed his star through years of strife and adversity, the man who has made France the greatest country in Europe, would willingly take second place in the ruling of the realm?"

"Ah, but as king-maker the real power would be yours. You know that, Bonaparte, as well as I do."

"Do I?" He laughed again, still gently. "Napoleon Bonaparte, Constable of France!"

"You find the idea amusing?"

"A little." He looked at her steadily. "Why are you so eager for me to open up negotiations with the Bourbons?"

"Because I think France is ready for a king once more," she said promptly, "and possibly because I am a royalist at heart."

"Perhaps France will have a king once more," he said softly, "and soon."

"You mean—you yourself?"

He tweaked her nose. "I merely mean that I am perfectly willing, if you wish it, to open up negotiations with the Bourbons."

She looked at him suspiciously. "I can hardly believe it, Bonaparte."

He laughed shortly. "No?"

"When you laugh like that it generally means that you're joking."

He grew immediately serious. "I give you my solemn word, Josephine, negotiations with the royalists shall be opened up immediately. Tomorrow I shall invite the Bourbon agent, the Marquis de St. Bernard, to come to the Tuileries."

"The—the Marquis de St. Bernard?" she exclaimed, taken by surprise.

"You know the man?" Bonaparte inquired innocently.

"Oh no, no," she denied, "but naturally I've heard of him. Somebody—I forget who it was—remarked recently in my hearing that the marquis was in Paris."

"Strange, very strange," Bonaparte murmured. "The name is fictitious, and in any case the man's visit to Paris is supposed to be a very deep secret."

Josephine remembered then that Fouché, chief spy though he was, was spied on continually by other spies. 'Bonaparte,' she thought in alarm, 'knows perfectly well that Fouché and I are intriguing together.'

"By the way," Bonaparte said, frowning, "I think I ought to tell you that Louis has left Paris."

"Left Paris? But why?"

"He feels—" Bonaparte hesitated—"he—er—feels that he must rejoin his regiment."

Josephine gave a little cry of dismay. She remembered how Alexandre, in wishing to desert her, had found it necessary to rejoin his regiment.

"You mean," she said faintly, "that your brother has grown tired of Hortense and deserted her?"

"I know no more than I have told you," Bonaparte said harshly. "Louis has rejoined his regiment." His voice softened. "It would be kind, I think, if you brought Hortense to the Tuileries during Louis's absence." He folded the petition and placed it in his pocket. "Tomorrow at three in the afternoon. That is the hour at which I shall receive the Marquis de St. Bernard, and you, my love, shall be present at what, I feel sure, will prove an interesting and edifying interview. . . ."

* * * * *

Josephine, though she smiled sweetly and inclined her head graciously, felt a distinct pang of uneasiness when the Marquis de St. Bernard was ushered into Bonaparte's study by Bourrienne. The night before she had sent for Fouché, told him that he was being carefully watched by Bonaparte and had been alarmed at the sight of his face when he had admitted that he was deeply disturbed.

"M'sieur le Marquis," Bonaparte was saying, "permit me to present you to my wife."

The marquis bowed deeply. "Charmed, madame. Your kindness to returning emigrants is well known. It delights me to make your acquaintance."

"I think, my dear," Bonaparte declared, his eyes twinkling, "that M'sieur le Marquis would like to kiss your hand."

The marquis, somewhat flustered for a moment, made an effort to regain his dignity. "If madame would permit——?"

Josephine held out her hand. He bowed over it and kissed it.

"Delightful," Bonaparte commented, "delightful."

"You must forgive my husband's manners," Josephine said. "They are seldom as bad as they seem. His sense of humor is often a little inopportune."

"It has always been my belief," Bonaparte pronounced, scowling meanwhile at Josephine, "that the so-called gentlemanly graces and insincere formalities of the Bourbon court contributed not a little to the fall of that court."

'Fool,' Josephine thought, 'I should have held my silly tongue.'

"M'sieur le Marquis," Bonaparte went on harshly, "I sent for you because I have been given to understand that you are an accredited Bourbon agent."

"My husband," Josephine explained to the surprised marquis, "has many ways of discovering the most closely guarded secrets."

"To continue," Bonaparte said, "since you represent the Pretender Louis——"

"I beg your pardon, m'sieur," the marquis interrupted warmly, "my master is the King, the rightful King, not a mere pretender!"

"I repeat," Bonaparte said insistently, "that since you represent the Pretender Louis I wish you to inform him that I have read your petition with interest. I am, you might also add, quite willing to open up negotiations between him and my government."

The marquis bowed low and stammered his thanks. Josephine, watching Bonaparte carefully, waited anxiously for him to continue.

"You have my wife to thank for my attitude," he said, showing his teeth in a smile which Josephine thought forbidding. "Her persistence in preaching the cause of your master has led to this interview and to the—er—terms which I propose to lay before him."

The marquis turned to Josephine. "Madame, in the name of his Majesty the King I thank you. When his Majesty returns to France and his throne is restored to him, he himself——"

"Throne?" Bonaparte echoed. "You say—*throne*, m'sieur?"

"But—but naturally, M'sieur Bonaparte. Why, you yourself——"

"I myself, I fear, have not yet been permitted to make my attitude clear. Your master shall have a throne, if he really covets one, but not —dear me no!—not the throne of France."

"Is this some ill-timed joke?" the marquis demanded indignantly. "Is this another example of your inopportune sense of humor?"

Bonaparte placed his hands behind his back and balanced himself lightly on his toes.

"When a man comes on a beggar's errand," he murmured, "he should practice a little humility. But to continue—the terms of the negotiation I wish to make with your master are simply and solely that he shall execute a formal deed resigning for himself and his heirs all pretensions to the throne of France."

"M'sieur!" the marquis gasped.

"Whereupon, M'sieur le Marquis, the Pretender Louis, a pretender no longer, shall be given independent dominions in Italy, over which he may reign for as long as he might be capable of reigning."

"By heaven," the marquis cried, "so you brought me here today in order to insult the House of Bourbon! Never before in all my vast experience of diplomatic affairs have I come upon a proposition so outrageous. Never before——"

"I take it, m'sieur," Bonaparte said softly, "that you refuse to convey my suggestion to your master?"

"I not only refuse but I give you the answer that he himself would give."

"And that, m'sieur?"

"Napoleon Bonaparte is mistaken if he imagines that the rights of Louis the Eighteenth of France can ever be made the subject of bargain and compromise."

Bonaparte laughed happily. "I spoke of no bargain or compromise. I merely expressed the wish of the French people, though naturally I myself would be generous enough to grant your master a small pension."

The marquis, turning swiftly on his heels, had reached the door. As he opened it Bonaparte said: "One moment, m'sieur. You have forgotten to bid my wife good-day."

Speechless, the marquis bowed stiffly, flung open the door and was gone. Bonaparte rubbed his hands together and chuckled.

"I know what you are thinking, Josephine," he laughed. "You are thinking that I am as ill-bred and ill-mannered as ever."

She shook her head sadly. "You said that perhaps France will have a king once more, and soon. All I was thinking was that what you meant when you said it has now been made most clear."

"Most clear," he repeated softly. "Napoleon Bonaparte, Constable of France—No, no, my sweet little Josephine, Napoleon Bonaparte, *King* of France. Either that or France will never know a king again."

"Bonaparte's behavior was so dreadful," Josephine told Fouché, "that I could have killed him. Really I could."

Fouché looked at her out of half-closed eyes and said softly: "And are you still angry enough to feel that you could kill him?"

The tone of his voice gave her a little shock. "What do you mean, Fouché?"

"Let me ask you a question. What would you do, Josephine, if you discovered a plot to assassinate your husband?"

"You know quite well what I would do," she said sharply.

"But supposing the plot, if successful, would result in the restoration of the Bourbons?"

"I would still expose it without a moment's hesitation. I don't want Bonaparte to die; I only want to keep him from the throne."

Fouché chuckled. "You love him very dearly, then?"

She looked at him obliquely. "Very dearly indeed."

"The position Bonaparte has given you and the inexhaustible supply of money that goes with it mean nothing, of course."

"Nothing whatever, Fouché."

"You could even live with him happily in a hovel in a small Corsican village, eh?"

This was too much for her.

"You rat," she said, laughing quietly.

A moment later, and serious again, she said: "This talk of assassination, have you discovered a plot?"

Evidently pleased with himself he smiled broadly. "I have—or to be more explicit, I've had a hand in it myself."

"*Fouché!*"

"Let me explain before you run to Bonaparte and expose me. Have you never thought that my interest in a Bourbon restoration, when you consider my past record, is a remarkable phenomenon?"

"Frankly, no. In all your intrigues you work for one person only, Fouché, Minister of Police. You probably imagine that you might gain more from serving Louis the Eighteenth than from serving Bonaparte."

"Precisely, but now, realizing that Bonaparte would do anything rather than restore the Bourbons, I have suffered a convenient change of heart. Unfortunately, however, it has recently reached my ears that your husband, who never really liked me, is looking about for a means of replacing me."

"And so you plan an attempt on his life!"

"No, no, the dastardly royalists are responsible for that. I myself will discover it, thus proving that I am still invaluable to the First Consul of France."

Josephine laughed drily. Fouché, entirely to serve his own ends, was planning an assassination with the royalists whom, at the last moment, he would betray.

"As a matter of fact, Josephine," Fouché was saying, "you too have a hand in the plot."

"I?" she exclaimed, dumbfounded.

"Oh, your part is merely that of a decoy, an unconscious, innocent decoy. M'sieur le Marquis will invite you to visit him at a country house he has taken near Saint Cloud. You will be asked to persuade Bonaparte to go with you."

"As if Bonaparte *would*!"

"You will merely tell him that you want to inspect the palace, which has been shut up since the revolution, and during the drive you will remember that an old friend has taken a house nearby. Since that is all you will be told you are meant to assume that Bonaparte is to be tricked into a second meeting with the marquis. Actually a cart filled with gunpowder will block a country lane."

Josephine clutched at her throat in horror. "But merciful heavens, Fouché, if the plot were successful I too would be killed!"

"Yes. A pleasant prospect, isn't it! But calm yourself. The plot, as I have already explained, will not be permitted to succeed."

"Why," she asked abruptly, "have you taken me into your confidence?"

"Oh, I thought that if we discovered the plot between us Bonaparte would be touched by your concern for his safety and love you more than ever."

She frowned. "I wish I could convince myself that that is your real reason."

"The trouble with you," he told her, "is that you plot and intrigue so much yourself that you find it almost impossible to give anybody else the credit of occasionally speaking the truth."

"You may be right," she laughed. "When can I expect a visit from the marquis?"

"Tomorrow at three in the afternoon, but remember, you know nothing of what I have told you, nothing whatever."

*　　*　　*　　*　　*

"Why do you keep glancing at the clock?" Hortense asked. "Is anything the matter?"

"At three o'clock," Josephine told her daughter, "I expect a visitor, an important visitor. It is now five minutes to the hour."

She looked searchingly at Hortense. The child, meeting Bonaparte's wishes half-heartedly, had arrived from the rue Victoire that morning and had agreed to stay at the Tuileries during her husband's absence from Paris. Apart from looking pale, which could be ascribed to her condition, she showed little sign of distress. After all, it was quite possible that no quarrel had taken place. A sense of duty and nothing else could easily have been Louis's reason for rejoining his regiment.

"Why did Louis leave Paris?" Josephine asked, her curiosity getting the better of her.

"You know the reason as well as I do," Hortense said quietly. "You must have expected him to desert me sooner or later."

Too late now to regret having spoken, Josephine said: "Was there a quarrel?"

Hortense considered this gravely for a moment.

"No," she said at last, "Louis had been silent and sulky for days, but there was no quarrel."

"But you told me you were happy with him!"

Hortense laughed shortly. "That was what you wanted me to tell you, wasn't it?"

Josephine squirmed uneasily. What cruel and disconcerting frankness. She glanced at the clock. If only M'sieur le Marquis would hurry and bring an end to this stupid conversation.

"Why was Louis silent and sulky?" she asked.

"Probably because he found me less satisfactory than one of his mistresses."

Josephine squirmed again, but brightened considerably at the more interesting turn the conversation was taking.

"Than *one* of his mistresses?" she queried. "He has several then?"

"Three, he told me."

"And you don't mind?"

"What good would it do me if I did?"

Hortense, still speaking quietly, seemed barely interested in the subject. A queer girl, Josephine decided, a very queer girl indeed. She leaned forward confidentially.

"Three at the same time!" she exclaimed. "What a formidable young man. Did you—" she lowered her voice but spoke eagerly— "Did you find him a good lover?"

Hortense blushed suddenly and looked down.

Josephine laughed gaily. "But what a stupid question for me to ask. How could you judge whether he is good or bad? You went to him an innocent child. A woman must enjoy a number of experiences before she can say with any certainty that this man is good, or that bad, or someone else indifferent. Your father, for instance——"

Hortense looked up quickly. Her face was hot with shame.

"Please, Mother, must we talk about things like that?"

"But you're a married woman now, darling," Josephine protested. "I could help and advise you so much if you really wanted me to."

"I don't think I do, Mother."

Josephine shrugged elaborately. In a hurt voice she said: "Just as you wish, then."

There was a little silence between them, during which the clock began to chime.

Still curious, and too unwise to leave well alone, Josephine said: "Didn't Louis give you any explanation for rejoining his regiment?"

Hortense smiled faintly. "Yes. He said that since I was going to have a baby the main purpose of the marriage had been fulfilled and the First Consul would now be as happy as if the baby was going to be his own."

There was a knock at the door. Josephine sprang to her feet and flung it open. Hortense rose as the Marquis de St. Bernard entered and excused herself.

"No, no," Josephine said, "I want you to remain."

Introductions were made and the marquis, having been assured that he could speak freely in front of Hortense, spoke briefly of his desire to meet Bonaparte a second time. He mentioned the country house he had taken near Saint Cloud, and giving no hint of the planned assassination, outlined his scheme for a second meeting just as Fouché had said he would. Finding it hard to contain her rising indignation—('Dear me,' she thought, 'my love for Bonaparte must be deeper than I imagined!')—Josephine asked him when he wanted her to visit the country house.

"Just as soon as you can persuade your husband to drive with you to Saint Cloud," he said.

"That might be at very short notice," she pointed out. "In which case I would have no chance of warning you."

The marquis smiled. "I assure you, madame, that you will be carefully watched. A courier will be ready to precede you to Saint Cloud."

There was a knock at the door and before Josephine could tell the marquis to hide, Bourrienne entered. He was followed by three soldiers.

"Madame," he said, "the First Consul is anxious to see you at once."

To the marquis he said: "Forgive me, m'sieur, but I have been ordered to place you under arrest."

✳   ✳   ✳   ✳   ✳

Josephine sat trembling in the chair in which Bonaparte, taking her by the shoulders, had flung her. Bourrienne, standing behind Bonaparte at the desk, stared at her coldly.

"Bonaparte—" Josephine began, trying for the third time to speak.

"Hold your tongue, madame," Bonaparte snapped. To Bourrienne he said: "Bring in the prisoners, but make sure that they are not permitted, even for a moment, to speak together."

Bourrienne left the room and returned with the marquis and Fouché. Catching sight of Josephine, Fouché stared at her oddly.

"So you, madame," he said, "are responsible for this."

"No, no," she protested. "I too have been brought here as a prisoner!" She turned to Bonaparte. "The least you can do, Bonaparte, is give me some explanation of your conduct."

"Nothing could be easier. The three of you are charged with conspiring to bring about my death."

"Oh, Bonaparte, how could you include me, your *wife*, in anything as vile as that!"

"You are no longer my wife. The legal tie shall be dissolved at the earliest possible moment—either by divorce or death at the guillotine."

Divorce or death at the guillotine! She tried to cry out, but no sound escaped her; she wished with all her heart that she could faint, but for once in her life even the power to simulate a convincing faint seemed to have left her. Fouché, watching her cynically, appeared to think otherwise, for he said:

"Forgive my drawing your attention to the fact, Bonaparte, but your wife is on the point of fainting."

"What of it?" Bonaparte said. "It's a woman's prerogative, I believe."

"You beast!" she cried, finding her voice at last.

Bonaparte rose from the desk and bowed. "Permit me to congratulate you, madame, on a remarkably swift recovery."

She flung herself out of the chair and ran to his side. "Oh, Bonaparte, surely you're not going to condemn me unheard!"

"On the evidence I hold I could condemn you all unheard, but in the interests of justice you shall each make whatever defense you choose."

"May I ask," Fouché said smoothly, "how you came by this evidence, and also what proof you have of its reliability?"

Bonaparte smiled. "You know quite well that I have means other than your Ministry of Police of guarding my interests. But to enlarge

362

on the charge I make, let me give you the details of your plot. You, Fouché, and you, St. Bernard, were overheard planning that my wife should invite me to drive to Saint Cloud. During the drive I was to be murdered; blown up by gunpowder."

"One moment, Bonaparte, *please!*" Josephine begged.

"Well?"

"Will you grant me one favor before this terrible misunderstanding goes further?"

"I might. What is it?"

"Give me a few moments alone with you. That is all I ask. A few moments alone with you."

He hesitated. "If you imagine, madame, that you will be able to get round me by making one of your violent scenes, by storming and weeping——"

"I shall neither storm nor weep," she assured him quickly. "I give you my word."

"Very well." He turned to Bourrienne. "Take these men away but keep them separated."

At a gesture from Bourrienne, Fouché and the marquis left the room.

"Well?" Bonaparte said. "But remember your promise!"

She smiled faintly. He was still afraid of her tears, but this was too serious a matter for mere weeping. He must be convinced by the truth, not softened by a few easy tears.

"One question first," she said. "When were Fouché and the marquis overheard planning your assassination?"

"Yesterday afternoon, after which Fouché visited you in the evening."

She repressed a sigh. Bonaparte was far too well-informed. It was useless, it seemed, to attempt to prove that she had had no meeting with either Fouché or the marquis until this afternoon. At a loss for a moment she suddenly remembered Hortense and her heart sang joyously.

"Fouché came to me last night," she said quickly. "I make no attempt to deny it. He told me about the plot. I make no attempt to deny that either. For he came, you see, not to make me a party to it, but to warn me of it. He and I together were to *pretend* to agree to it, and then, at the last moment, expose it and so cause the arrest of a dangerous enemy."

Bonaparte laughed drily. "An ingenious story, madame."

"Ah, but wait! When the marquis approached me this afternoon, all he asked of me was that I should trick you into a second meeting with him. He told me nothing of the plot. And would I have agreed to it if he had? Why, even if I hated you, would I want to murder you at the expense of my own life?"

"At the expense of your *own* life?"

"I would have been in the carriage with you when the attack was made. Remember that, Bonaparte, remember that!"

She saw his face change and his eyes soften.

"Hortense was present," she said eagerly, "while the marquis talked to me. Ask her what was said and decide for yourself whether I speak the truth or not."

He made a helpless gesture. "Really, Josephine, I hardly know what to think."

"Go to her at once," she urged—(It was 'Josephine' now, not 'madame,' and that was an excellent sign)—"and then question Fouché alone. If my story differs in any way from his I shall go to the guillotine gladly." She made a dramatic gesture with her arms. "Yes, *gladly!*"

"I believe you," he said gruffly. "It won't be necessary to question either of them."

"But I insist," she said. "I insist. Unless you question them the doubts might easily return to your mind some day and I shall be condemned or suspected all over again."

He went to the door. "Very well, then. Remain here."

Ten minutes later he returned, followed by Fouché.

"Both stories," he said, "are identical with your own."

She inclined her head gravely. "Fouché, of course, will be released?"

"Of course."

"And the marquis?"

"I shall have him escorted to the border. Should he be unwise enough to enter France again—imprisonment for life." He turned to Fouché. "And now, my little master of intrigue, be kind enough to sit down at the desk and write out your resignation."

"My resignation?" Fouché gasped.

"Yes. A man as dangerous as you is something of a liability to me. Josephine is innocent, but what proof have I that you were not prepared, in spite of what you said, to carry out the plot? Your resignation, please, quickly."

When Fouché had complied with the demand and taken his leave, Josephine threw herself into Bonaparte's arms.

"Oh, Bonaparte—!" she sobbed.

"And now the long-delayed tears, eh?" he laughed.

"I can't help it," she said brokenly. "What I did—it was inspired by my love for you and—and my fear of divorce. I only listened to the wretched royalists in the first place because I was fighting in the only way I knew to keep your love. To—to protect myself against your terrible ambition."

He soothed her gently while, with many repetitions and intervals to blow her nose, she told him the whole story. In the end he kissed her gravely on the brow.

"Let me tell you something," he said quietly. "In spite of my *terrible* ambition, as you call it, I have been forced, at last, to realize that our childlessness is my fault, not yours. What would I gain, then, by setting you aside and marrying somebody else?"

And that, naturally, was the signal for a further outburst of weeping, but, as she tried to tell him while smiling dimly through her tears, they were the happiest she had ever shed in her life.

"Goose," he said huskily, and to her great delight she was able to detect a glint of tears in his own eyes.

Giving her nose a final blow she had a triumphant thought: 'If only the Bonapartes could have heard and seen all this!'

CHAPTER XXXV

Bonaparte's study seemed uncomfortably full of Bonapartes. *Seemed!* Josephine grunted under her breath. It *was* uncomfortably full of them. Even with Lucien and Paulette and Louis out of the way, Paris, when the rest of the family gathered together like this, was still a city of Corsican bandits with danger lurking in every square and alley. And what airs they were giving themselves, now that the government had at last made Bonaparte First Consul for life and the appointment had been confirmed by a general plebiscite. She had always known that they were too big for their humble Corsican boots; it was evident now that those same boots would never fit them again. Everybody's attention was centered on Joseph. He was flourishing an imposing-looking document in his hand and clearing his throat before speaking. After the first few words—"In order to express—" he checked himself.

"Perhaps I should begin," he said, "by telling you all that this is a communication from the government."

"They know that already," Bonaparte said testily.

"Very well, Napoleon." He cleared his throat again and began to read. " 'In order to express the confidence, love and admiration of the French nation we, the Government, pray that you, the First Consul, will accept the gift of the former royal château of Saint Cloud to be used by you and your family as a summer residence.' "

Joseph's words were greeted with loud cries of satisfaction from the Bonapartes. Even Madame Bonaparte, always afraid that her son's ambition would take him too far, permitted herself a broad smile and a grunt of approval.

"Well, Josephine," said Bonaparte, rubbing his hands together like a tradesman who had bought some useless article for next-to-nothing and sold it for a huge fortune, "does it please you to know that you will now be mistress of a third residence?"

"Oh yes," she cried eagerly, envisaging already the delightful task of redecorating and refurnishing the château, "but it does stagger me a little to think of having a place as big as Saint Cloud for a mere summer residence."

"Nothing should stagger you these days," Bonaparte reproved. "The acquisition of Saint Cloud should be taken as a matter of course."

"Naturally," Joseph agreed, puffing out his chest. "The whole family takes the gift as a matter of course."

"They say," Elisa Bacciochi put in shrilly, "that Saint Cloud was originally bought by Queen Marie Antoinette for five million francs."

"*Six* million," Josephine corrected her softly. "And in those days it was livres, not francs." She turned to Bonaparte, knowing by his sudden frown that her words had made him fear the outbreak of a little family quarrel. "When do we take possession, Bonaparte?"

"Not for some time, I imagine. Saint Cloud was badly damaged during the revolution and the furnishings were either stolen by the mob or destroyed."

"Ah, then the task of putting it in order and refurnishing it will undoubtedly fall upon my shoulders."

Joseph coughed. "If it is left to Josephine the expense will be terrific."

"What of it?" Bonaparte demanded. "Extravagant as Josephine is her taste is admirable. In any case the expense will naturally be borne by the government."

"Even so, Napoleon——"

"Oh, Joseph," Josephine cried, "must you sound so disapproving? Like the rest of your family, with the exception of my husband, you are far too tight-fisted when it comes to spending a little money." She glanced at each of the family in turn and went on sweetly: "You should try to accustom yourself to the fact that you and your family are living in the most luxurious city in the world these days, not merely *existing* in poverty-stricken Corsica."

"You see, Napoleon," Joseph complained bitterly, "one word from me and your spoiled wife flies into a silly rage!"

With that everybody was talking at once, shrilly, indignantly, and staring at her with hostile eyes. She glanced anxiously at Bonaparte.

He, fortunately, was suddenly smiling, but even had his earlier frown deepened the pleasure of continuing to bait Joseph would still have got the better of her.

"Take care, Joseph," she laughed, "or I may forbid you entry to my little Palace of Saint Cloud."

"Yes," Bonaparte warned his brother playfully, "take care, take great care!"

Josephine clapped her hands in delight. "Thank you, Bonaparte, for taking *my* side for once. I find it unusual, but most encouraging!"

"If he continues to take your side, as you call it," Joseph muttered sulkily, "I shall probably find myself banished to Spain, or some such place, just as poor Lucien was."

"Or possibly," Josephine chuckled, "to Saint Domingo."

Since Bonaparte was now frowning again, and since it was wiser to withdraw while one was in command of a situation, she rose languidly and, including the Bonapartes with a single, sweeping inclination of her head, excused herself.

"I must," she murmured, "get in touch with the decorators and furnishers at once."

Even when she had closed the door behind her the strident babble of anger and indignation which filled the room was clearly audible and followed her for some way down the corridor. She laughed aloud. Poor Bonaparte, what a time he would be having, trying to pacify them!

In her own drawing-room she found Hortense sitting quietly in a chair, reading a book. She looked up patiently while Josephine, too full of her recent triumph to keep silent about it, and mimicking Joseph skilfully, gave a full and gleeful account of the whole scene.

"If only you could have seen poor Joseph's face!" she cried. "If only you could have seen it!"

"I can well imagine how furious he was," Hortense said gravely.

"He could cheerfully have killed me, darling. Well, hardly *cheerfully*. Never in his life has Joseph had the spirit to do *anything* cheerfully. Oh, dear, but I mustn't laugh too much, it will only ruin my figure and make me too fat." She looked at her daughter anxiously. "Have I put on very much weight lately, Hortense?"

Hortense smiled affectionately. "Do you want me to answer candidly, Mother?"

Josephine gave a little squeal. "What a wretched child you are!"

"Why not take a little exercise?" Hortense suggested.

"Exercise? *Exercise?* But enough. Let us talk of something else. Yourself for instance. You look pale today, much too pale, and not so pretty as formerly. However heavy with child a woman might be she should remember to take great care of her appearance. Let me see now, when *is* your child to be born?"

Hortense pretended to be reading her book again. "In less than a month, Mother."

"And that impossible husband of yours is still away. I shall speak to Bonaparte about it. He must be ordered back to Paris in time for your confinement."

"Please don't do that," Hortense begged. "If Louis chooses to return of his own accord I shall be glad to see him, but if my step-father forces him to return Louis will hate me more than ever."

"But, *darling—*" Josephine began, and then fell silent. Her daughter's words, dissipating in an instant her high spirits, filled her with a black depression. She argued that Hortense's unhappiness was more Louis's fault than hers, and in arguing very nearly convinced herself. After all, had Hortense ever admitted to being unhappy? And if she really *was* unhappy, had she ever made the *slightest* accusation? That, of course, was the trouble. No accusations were ever made; no tears were ever shed. An occasional scene, a few wild recriminations, and one could have forgotten more easily that one had ruined forever the poor child's hope of happiness. Unreasonable, that's what her daughter's attitude was, unreasonable and also cruel——

There was a knock at the door.

In relief Josephine said: "Come in."

The door opened and Fouché entered.

She ran forward in delight to meet him. "Fouché!"

It was weeks since Fouché had visited her. Nay, months. For since his resignation he had thought it wise to keep away from the Tuileries until Bonaparte's anger had melted a little.

"I've missed you," she cried. "Rogue that you are, I've missed you!"

Fouché bowed. "Madame, I myself was about to say much the same to you."

She invited him to sit down but he refused.

"I can spare only a moment," he said, "and I bring you very sad news." He paused, smiled and added softly: "Lucien Bonaparte has returned to Paris."

"*What?*" she almost shouted.

"He has returned, my dear Josephine, vowing vengeance and declaring that this time it is you who will be sent into exile, not he."

Josephine collapsed heavily into a chair.

"I was beginning to feel," she wailed, "that my troubles were over. How wrong I was, merciful heavens, how wrong I was!"

*   *   *   *   *

Lucien, it turned out, had returned to Paris without Bonaparte's permission. Apart from this one act of defiance, as Josephine discovered to her intense alarm, her husband was not ill-pleased with his brother's activities in Spain, chief of which, it seemed, had been the successful negotiation of a treaty with Portugal. Fearing the worst she asked Bonaparte uneasily if Lucien was to be permitted to remain in France.

"Certainly not," he said.

Josephine breathed her relief. "You will have him escorted to the Spanish border at once?"

"Well, no. Joseph has prevailed on me to receive Lucien at the Tuileries and listen to his explanation before sending him away again."

Josephine's heart fell. If Lucien's explanation was plausible and his manner sufficiently persuasive Bonaparte might weaken. In something of a panic she made up her mind that though there might be little she could do she would be present when Bonaparte received the irritating and troublesome Lucien.

"His return was secret," Bonaparte was saying, "yet I suspect that you knew about it before I did. May I ask how that came about?"

Josephine smiled frankly and utter one word only. "Fouché."

Bonaparte scowled. "Fouché, though no longer my Minister of Police, appears to be just as well informed as ever."

"Spying," Josephine laughed, "has become a habit with Fouché."

"The man is more dangerous than he ever was. I think perhaps I should forbid you to receive him at the Tuileries."

"Oh no, Bonaparte, that would be cruel! I find him amusing as well as useful, and by receiving him openly I can still guard your interests by keeping a strict watch over him."

Bonaparte laughed shortly. "As you wish, then. Whatever happens my little Josephine must be kept amused."

Lucien came to the Tuileries the following afternoon. Informed by one of Fouché's men of his departure from Madame Bonaparte's house (where he was staying), Josephine was able to reach Bonaparte's study a few moments before he arrived.

He entered jauntily, gave a slight start at the sight of Josephine and then, ignoring her rudely, went quickly to Bonaparte's side and embraced him warmly. Josephine giggled, for Bonaparte, submitting to the display of brotherly affection, had the startled look of a spinster in the arms of a village Don Juan. With an awkward gesture he freed himself.

369

"Your explanation, Lucien, if you please."

"You expect me to make it in the presence of Josephine?" Lucien cried hotly.

"Why not?" Josephine asked sweetly. "Up to now you have barely acknowledged it!"

"What do you want me to do?" Lucien sneered. "Kiss your hand, or possibly your cheek?"

Josephine held out her hand. "Not the cheek, I beg of you, but the hand, if you wish it."

Bonaparte came between them quickly. "Enough of this nonsense. Come, Lucien, your explanation."

Lucien shrugged. "Very well. My chief reason for returning was to put a certain proposition to you on behalf of the King of Spain."

"Any proposition from the King of Spain should come through the usual diplomatic channels."

"Not a proposition as personal and delicate as this, Napoleon."

"Personal, you say?"

"It concerns you and the Infanta Isabella."

Bonaparte exchanged a glance with Josephine. She knew instantly, and suspected by the glance that he knew also, what Lucien was about to say next.

"What the devil are you talking about?" Bonaparte demanded.

Lucien smiled broadly. "A man in your position, Napoleon, should be married to the daughter of a royal house. Should you decide to divorce Josephine, who is surely too old now to bear you a child, the King of Spain will gladly offer you the hand of the Infanta."

Josephine's temper flared up at once. "Merciful heavens, Bonaparte, am I to be subjected to an indignity as great as this? Have I no rights? No protection from the continued insults of your family?"

Bonaparte took her hand in his and patted it reassuringly. To Lucien he said, his voice dangerously low:

"Is this proposition made with the knowledge of the King of Spain, or is it a little invention of your own to give you an excuse for returning to Paris?"

"With the full knowledge of the King of Spain," Lucien smiled.

"Who is the author of it? The King himself, or you?"

"In all modesty," Lucien confessed, "I admit that I am the author."

Bonaparte dropped Josephine's hand and advanced slowly on his brother. Lucien stepped back hastily.

"Do you expect me, sir, to compliment you on your ingenuity?"

"You may please yourself, Napoleon—" Lucien, still moving backwards, stumbled against a chair and cursed softly—"you may please yourself but you must admit that the proposition has much to recommend it."

"Rubbish, Lucien. If I were interested in divorcing Josephine, which I am not, I should have more sense than seek an alliance with a royal house which has already begun its decline."

Bonaparte was standing over Lucien now.

"You fool," he said.

He turned quickly and flung open the door.

"Go."

Thoroughly intimidated Lucien went quickly from the room.

The moment the door had closed behind him, Josephine ran to Bonaparte's side. Her heart was singing joyously and she was remembering what Bonaparte had said after the dismissal of Fouché: *I have been forced, at last, to realize that our childlessness is my fault, not yours. What would I gain, then, by setting you aside and marrying somebody else?*

"Thank you, Bonaparte," she said simply.

✳   ✳   ✳   ✳   ✳

Though no longer seriously disturbed by Lucien's return, Josephine nonetheless felt a pang of misgiving when she learned that Bonaparte, hard-pressed by his mother, had given the young man permission to remain in Paris. He would need watching, of course, but she told herself confidently that she had the upper hand.

Several days later, while busy with her plans for Saint Cloud, she learned that Lucien had decided to buy the Hotel de Brienne, a large house in the rue Dominique.

"But how can he afford such an expensive place?" she asked.

"His stay in Madrid was quite profitable," Bonaparte told her. "The King, hoping that the scheme to get me married to his daughter would succeed, presented Lucien with a number of valuable paintings from the royal collection. Lucien sold most of them to great advantage. Also, while arranging the treaty with Portugal, he acquired two hundred thousand crowns' worth of Brazilian diamonds."

"In short," she cried indignantly, "he took advantage of his position as your brother to make a fortune for himself!"

"He did, sweetheart, and you would have done the same yourself, so why blame him?"

A week later, still busy with her plans for Saint Cloud, she was reminded again of Lucien. Fouché came to her and, smiling as cynically as ever, told her that Lucien and Joseph were intriguing for the removal of Louis from the Bonaparte line of succession.

"Lucien," Fouché said, "is cunning. He began by suggesting that it had been an insult to pass over Joseph, the eldest brother, the legitimate head of the family, and nominate Louis."

"I should have thought he would have wanted to have himself nominated."

"Oh, he has the sense to realize that Bonaparte would never do that. He will be well content to replace Louis with Joseph and thus strike a blow at you by removing Hortense's child from the succession."

"Of course!" Josephine acknowledged. "How stupid of me not to have seen that at once."

But once again, as she told herself afterwards, her alarm was unnecessary. Joseph approached Bonaparte on the subject but, as Bonaparte himself told her later, he was received coldly and sent away in bitter disappointment.

"However, angry as I was," he said, "Joseph's suggestion that Louis is proving himself unreliable and irresponsible was very much to the point. While Joseph was speaking I made up my mind that unless Louis returns to Hortense and treats her kindly, her child, should it be the boy I want it to be, will then become my heir."

Josephine, delirious with joy, could scarcely believe her ears. "Bonaparte, you mean, you actually mean——?"

"I actually mean that your grandson, and not Joseph, or Lucien or Jerome, will be the one to replace his father."

Josephine had only one thought. 'Security, at last security!'

"I might even go farther," Bonaparte added, "and legally adopt the child as my own."

"Oh, Bonaparte, would you really do that?"

He laughed gently. "I would, but the issue, remember, rests entirely with Hortense."

"Why with Hortense?"

"If she presents us with a girl my plans will have to be revised. Therefore, let her be clever and present us with a boy."

Josephine closed her eyes and gave a little moan. All thoughts of security had vanished. Heaven forgive her, but if the child turned out to be a wretched girl she would never speak to Hortense again, no never!

*   *   *   *   *

A week before Hortense's confinement could, according to the doctors, be safely expected, Louis Bonaparte returned to Paris and presented himself at the Tuileries. He was announced while Josephine and Bonaparte were taking breakfast together, an occurrence which rarely happened these days and had only been brought about by Josephine rising earlier then usual and Bonaparte later.

On entering the room, Louis stood hesitantly just within the door. Though his face had a sheepish look the set of his chin was not without a surprising determination. He looked from Bonaparte to Josephine and when neither spoke he said, in a very low voice:

"Would it be possible for me to see Hortense?"

Bonaparte rose stiffly from the table. "Tell me first why you want to see her."

Louis came forward a few steps. "She's my wife, isn't she?"

"Undoubtedly, but that, after your long absence, is hardly sufficient reason."

"My absence is something which I regret. I—" his voice was almost inaudible now—"I want to tell her how sorry I am for any unhappiness I might have caused her."

Bonaparte went to him impulsively and embraced him. "Thank God you've come back to your senses at last."

Josephine, watching this sentimental little scene, hardly knew whether to be glad or sorry. She should be glad for Hortense's sake, she supposed, but for her own— After all Louis, though never an active enemy, was still a Bonaparte.

"What has made you so suddenly repentant?" she asked him curiously.

He gave her a wry smile. "I might be a Bonaparte, Josephine, but I also have a conscience. I was tricked into marrying your daughter, but she was tricked into marrying me. I grew to feel sorry for myself, but later I grew sorry for her too." He laughed drily. "It's just possible, isn't it, that if we feel sorry for one another we might be able to console each other?"

Josephine, feeling distinctly uneasy at his words, feeling, in short, an inescapable guiltiness, looked at him sourly.

As if divining her thoughts Louis said: "Oh, I've ceased to blame you, so why not give me your blessing and help me to make the best of a situation that can hardly be altered now?"

"Yes, Josephine, why not!" Bonaparte cried emotionally.

Josephine shrugged, endeavored to set aside the feeling of guilt and held out her hands to him. He took them in his and held them for a moment. He laughed lightly, and just a little maliciously, she thought.

"I know that it is often difficult for a man and his mother-in-law to be friends," he said, "and when the man is a Bonaparte and the mother-in-law is Josephine——"

"Really, Louis," Josephine interrupted him sharply, "it would be kinder to think of me as a sister-in-law."

"Much kinder," Bonaparte laughed. "And if you should dare at any time to call her 'mother' even *I* would resent it."

Hortense accepted Louis's return with no show of surprise or emotion, and when Bonaparte said that she and Louis would need a larger house, now that they were to have a family, she agreed with him gravely that they would.

"Aren't you pleased to have Louis back again?" Josephine asked her.

Hortense pondered for a moment. "I'm neither pleased nor sorry. Were you pleased when father returned to you after one of his absences?"

Josephine frowned. Though she always told herself that the past was dead and forgotten she remembered as clearly as if it were yesterday how she had felt when Alexandre had returned after his first absence.

"It was much the same with me," she admitted, "but Louis, I think, is a kinder, more human man than your father ever was. For my sake, please try to find a little happiness with Louis."

Hortense put her arms affectionately about her mother. "I shall do my best. I could never fall in love with him, but I do think that he and I might become friends."

*   *   *   *   *

Bonaparte, summoned hastily by Josephine, stared intently at the child in the nurse's arms.

"A boy, of course?" he cried.

Josephine, hovering at his side, nodded happily. "Of course."

"And Hortense—is she in any danger?"

"None whatever. It was a perfectly normal birth."

Louis, returning from a few moments with Hortense, joined the little group. He looked at Josephine and laughed slily.

"I hope you will be able to forgive a Bonaparte for having made you a grandmother."

"I may have become a grandmother," she said, with dignity, "but the very youngest one, I'm sure, in the whole of France!"

Later she questioned Bonaparte about his intention of replacing Louis with his newly born son. He reminded her that he had only proposed to do that if Louis had continued to neglect Hortense.

"While Louis behaves himself," he said, "he shall remain my heir, but in any case the child will be the next in the line of succession."

When the question of choosing a name for the child arose, Bonaparte made it clear that whatever anybody else might suggest his own mind had been made up.

"He shall have two names, Napoleon and Charles. Napoleon after myself, of course; Charles after my father. I take it that nobody objects?"

"Nobody," Josephine assured him, "would dare to object, not even his parents."

"Louis and Hortense may be his parents," Bonaparte said gravely, "but I am the one who will endow him with the cloak of greatness." The familiar faraway look came to his eyes. "Some day he may even be spoken of as Napoleon the Second."

For Bonaparte to speak of Napoleon the Second would once have filled Josephine's heart with dread, but now, the fear of divorce being no longer present, the most she felt was a thrill of anticipation. Grandmother she was, and forty, but she had never felt happier than at this moment. The troubled part of her life, she told herself, was at an end. There would, inevitably, be many little encounters with the Bonapartes, but on the whole tranquility and security lay pleasantly ahead of her.

"I *hope!*" she said aloud, and fervently.

Part Five
The Empress

JOSEPHINE, SEATED AT THE dressing-table in the boudoir once occupied by Marie Antoinette, was at Saint Cloud. After many months of feverish activity and what the Bonaparte family spoke of as 'an orgy of money-spending,' the château had been completely redecorated and refurnished. An orgy of money-spending indeed! The Bonapartes were the sort of people who expected you to make a silk purse out of a sow's ear and show a profit while doing so. Not that Saint Cloud had ever been a sow's ear, but still, that was the sort of people they were.

Tonight, Josephine was alone with Eugene, Hortense and the little Napoleon-Charles, but tomorrow Bonaparte, accompanied by his mother and the rest of the wretched family, was to come to Saint Cloud for the official opening of the château, or *palace*, as he now insisted on calling it. Applying the habitual heavy coating of rouge to her cheeks with a little more care than usual she reflected that she had been right in assuming, after the birth of Napoleon-Charles, that tranquility and security lay pleasantly before her—security at all events, if not exactly tranquility. Bonaparte was almost always in a good humor these days and there had been little trouble with her Corsican relatives-in-law. Joseph was still surly, of course; but then Joseph would always be surly. Madame Bonaparte, save for shaking her head at the expense of making Saint Cloud habitable, was less disapproving than formerly, and inclined on occasion to show a slight if frigid friendliness. Lucien, naturally, still sulked a little but made no active move against her, while Louis, treating her with politeness and Hortense with consideration, was showing promise of becoming a model son-in-law. Jerome, busy like Eugene with his army career, she rarely saw, and Caroline and Elisa, immersed in a sober domesticity, had always counted for little, if nothing at all. There remained only Paulette, but she, thank heaven, was still in Saint Domingo with the gallant but unfortunate Leclerc. As Aunt Marie had remarked in a letter—Aunt Marie who, since the death of the Marquis de Beauharnais, rarely left Fontainebleau these days —the Bonapartes seemed to have been tamed at last.

The maid entered quietly.

"Captain Tercier," she said, "is waiting."

Josephine looked up eagerly. "Tell him that I will receive him immediately."

The maid gave Josephine a pert glance. "Save for what, by courtesy, is called a wrap, madame is naked."

Josphine's eyes twinkled. "Captain Tercier is a very old friend, Louise."

Louise gave her a look of complete understanding. "In that case, madame——"

At the door she turned. "If by 'a very old friend' madame means that she and the captain have not met for many years it might be just as well if——"

"Pig!" Josephine cried.

Nevertheless, while Louise left the room with a chuckle, she drew the wrap more closely about her and admitted to herself that in the intervening years her figure had deteriorated somewhat.

Tercier, having arrived from Martinique a few days ago, had sent her a bulky parcel of tropical plants. In the accompanying note he had said that since somebody had told him that she was collecting tropical plants for Malmaison he thought she might be glad to receive his little offering. Old, almost forgotten memories having been revived by this, she had replied at once, thanking him for his thoughtfulness and suggesting that he might care to present himself at Saint Cloud. And now, here he was—he, Tercier, the only man she had ever really loved.

She had thought a lot about Tercier during the last day or so. Curiosity had caused her to issue the invitation and caution had prompted her to name a time when there would be no fear of Bonaparte's catching them together. Now that she had been reminded of him again it seemed clear to her that she was still in love with him, and in resuming the old association it would be ridiculous to say that she was being unfaithful to Bonaparte—of course it would be ridiculous: Tercier, after all, had preceded Bonaparte. Not that she had any intention of a *prolonged* resumption. One or two meetings, or perhaps three—that would be the most she would be able to arrange without fear of discovery. She sighed ecstatically. After the brief ruthlessness of Bonaparte's love-making, what a delight was in store for her! Tercier would renew her youth, would give her something to look back on in delight when the horror of old age finally claimed her. . . .

The door opened and Tercier entered. For a moment Louise hovered behind him, leering, and then she closed the door with a steady firmness that was even more suggestive than her leer. Her heart beating like a young girl's, Josephine rose slowly and turned to greet her visitor.

"Oh, Tercier," she cried, "after all these years!"

He came forward purposefully, took her hands in his and kissed them. It came as a mild shock to her to see that he was not so handsome as she had always imagined him to be. His hair had grown thin and as he bent over her hands a distinct patch of baldness was visible. He was older than she, of course, and must now be forty-five. Not that baldness really mattered, though Samson, having been shorn of his hair. . . .

"Many years might have passed," he said, releasing her hands, "but to me your beauty is as tempting as ever."

He spoke smoothly, a man long-practiced in the art of flattery. Normally her heart would have warmed to such an approach, but the words, for some odd, disappointing reason, merely made her shudder.

Searching for something to say she thanked him for the tropical plants. He told her easily that the plants having survived the rigors of the voyage was surely proof that their love, likewise a thing of tropical growth, had also survived. She saw that he had grown fat and gross as well as bald, and shuddering again drew the wrap more closely about her. *A rake*, she decided, *an odious elderly rake.*

He seated himself without invitation and looked at her speculatively.

"You seem to have done very well for yourself since you returned from Martinique," he said. "A queen, they tell me, a queen in all but name."

She suspected at once what he really wanted.

To test her suspicion she said lightly: "In short, my dear Tercier, a woman whose position makes it possible for her to grant favors and promote the interests of her old friends."

"Precisely, my dear Rose."

He sprang up quickly and with confidence took her in his arms. 'Now,' she thought, 'it will surely happen. The old delight will return, in spite of his grossness, in spite of his true reason for coming to see me.' She waited, but all she felt was a slight revulsion. So great was the disappointment that tears came to her eyes. At the sight of them he laughed triumphantly.

"Ah, you love me still, you remember me as the greatest lover any woman could ever know."

His arms tightened about her. He kissed her, slowly at first, then demandingly, and all she felt was the revulsion which rose in her breast, sickening her. She thought sadly how different it had been in Martinique, and then, angrily, how he had tired of her and hurriedly persuaded her father that it was imperative for her to return to France. She remembered too the horrible things he had said to her. *You've fallen in love with love, have even been given a taste for it.* And now here he was, a nauseating little elderly rake, sure that seduction would be the simplest thing in the world, and confident that she, the queen in all but name, would secure for him some lucrative position at the Consular court.

Too self-satisfied to have noticed her utter lack of response, he cast his eyes reflectively about the room until they came cunningly to rest on the door which led to her bedroom. The revulsion rose from her breast to her throat, choking her.

"My son and daughter are at Saint Cloud," she said quickly, "and Bonaparte is expected at any moment. It—well, it isn't really safe for you to remain much longer."

He grinned horribly. "I quite understand, but in Paris, perhaps—? After all, a woman as clever as you should have no more difficulty in arranging such matters than in arranging some suitable appointment for a very old and very dear friend."

The moment he had gone she sank weakly into a chair. In Paris he would be forbidden entry at the Tuileries. He would have no hope whatever of approaching her again. And as for a suitable appointment, he should have that at the earliest possible moment, and one so suitable that it would take him out of France again and back to the colonies. She would write to Berthier whose discretion, thank heaven, could be relied upon. . . .

Suddenly she had an appalling thought. Many handsome men deteriorated when they grew older. Tercier today was little different to look at than Barras had been, and though she had never been in love with Barras she had always enjoyed his love-making. Was it possible that she had lost all desire for love? It certainly seemed like it, since, even with Bonaparte himself, it had long been little more than a duty, and an irksome one at that. True, she had always blamed him for his lack of understanding and consideration, but even so there had been odd times when, purely by accident—

"Dear heaven," she said, in a horrified whisper, "I must be on the brink of the greatest tragedy that can happen to a woman; I must be on the brink of my change of life!"

* * * * *

The elaborate dinner demanded by Bonaparte was nearing its end, but Josephine, still brooding over the discovery which Tercier's visit had brought about, had scarcely eaten. Nor had she taken much notice of the conversation which the Bonapartes had carried on incessantly since the soup had been served. Such was her inattention that when Madame Bonaparte said: "And what do you think of the idea, Josephine?" she started guiltily and was forced to say, "I beg your pardon, I'm afraid I wasn't paying much attention."

"We were discussing Lord Whitworth, the newly appointed English Ambassador," Bonaparte told her. "I was saying that we must make his reception at the Tuileries as grand and impressive as possible. Mother, I suspect, was hoping that you would disagree. That, of course, would be stupid. We must do our best to intimidate the English with a full display of power, military or otherwise."

"From what I know of the English," Joseph remarked, "they are too stubborn and blind to be intimidated by anything."

"And when were you last in England?" Bonaparte demanded. "And how many English people of importance have you met?"

Joseph scowled and remained silent.

"I may as well tell you all at once," Bonaparte went on, "that I have decided that the unofficial court I have been in the habit of holding at the Tuileries shall become a real court."

All attention now Josephine asked eagerly: "Does this mean that I shall have a recognized position at last?"

"It does, my dear little blue-blooded aristocrat, it does! When Lord Whitworth presents himself at the Tuileries he will find a court etiquette and a court household equal in every way to what he has left behind him in London."

Josephine, forgetting the biological tragedy that was overwhelming her, gave a little squeal of delight.

"Shall I have ladies-in-waiting?"

"Naturally."

"How many?"

"Four to begin with; more later if I judge it necessary." He turned to his mother. "And before I forget, Mother, at our new court you shall be known as Madame Mère. It will give you more standing, more dignity." His eyes twinkled. "Unhappily it is impossible to call you the Queen Mother, so Madame Mère will have to suffice."

Madame Bonaparte sighed deeply. "I think you are very vain and very foolish, Napoléoné, but you shall have your way."

380

"Thank you," he said, avoiding her eyes. "One other thing. I want you to remember to call me Napoleon, not Napoléoné."

She rose from the table. "In the language of your birthplace, which some day we may all regret having left, you are Napoléoné. To me, that is what you will always remain."

On the return to Paris, Josephine learned that the ladies-in-waiting selected by Bonaparte were all members of the old aristocracy. Actually they were to be known as Ladies of the Palace, though, as he hinted meaningly, the time would come when the more royal appellation would be employed.

"They shall attend you for a week at a time, turn by turn," he told her, "but on special occasions, when we want to make a splash, all four shall attend you at the same time."

She smiled. "Lord Whitworth's reception will be a special occasion, of course?"

"Of course!"

Following the appointment of the ladies of the palace the names of the governor and the prefects were announced and the consular servants were put into a livery of green and gold. Finally, when these and other details had been scrupulously attended to, Bonaparte spoke of religion.

"Now that religion has been fully restored to France," he told Josephine and a gathering of the family, "I want to see it recognized, *actively* recognized by my wife and family."

"What do you mean by that?" Josephine asked.

"Simply, my dear, that I want to see you all going to church, and going regularly."

"Oh, dear," she protested, "but since the revolution I've got out of the way of going to church."

Bonaparte laughed drily. "You were eager enough for me to sign the concordat with the Pope, and you were eager enough to see your daughter's marriage blessed by the Church. Therefore you should make no complaints when I ask you to make church-going a regular habit."

"Do you intend to make it a regular habit, Napoléoné?" Madame Mère demanded.

"I shall go to church if and when I choose," he said coldly, "but you, Mother, and you, Josephine, shall attend mass every Sunday morning."

"Not *early* mass, I hope!" Josephine wailed.

"You may please yourself about that," he laughed, "but by going to mass you will be setting a new fashion. That, surely, will give you adequate compensation for getting down on your knees once a week."

Before Lord Whitworth paid his official visit to the Tuileries word came from Saint Domingo that hundreds of Leclerc's men had been struck down by yellow fever and that Leclerc himself had died of it. Worse still, as far as Josephine was concerned, Paulette, bringing her husband's remains with her for burial in France, had already sailed from Saint Domingo. With a little shudder Josephine recalled the threat her sister-in-law had made before leaving Paris. Bonaparte must have remembered it also for he remarked, a trifle uneasily, that if Josephine wanted to please him she would do her best to make a friend of Paulette.

"Treat her kindly," he begged. "Remember how young she is to be a widow."

Josephine tossed her head. "I shall only treat her kindly if she treats me kindly, and that, I feel sure, is more than we can expect. The old quarrel will be resumed, you can rely on Paulette for that, and when it is the fight this time will be a fight to the death. No quarter will be asked, and as far as I am concerned, none will be given!"

*　　*　　*　　*　　*

"I assure you, Josephine," Fouché said, "that the Bonapartes are plotting nothing whatever against you, not because they have grown to love you, of course, but simply because there is nothing for them to plot."

"Ah, but with Paulette in Paris," Josephine cried, "an attack of some sort is bound to be launched. That is why I want you to keep a watch on them, a stricter watch than you have ever kept on anybody before."

"You forget," he told her, "that I am no longer Minister of Police."

She laughed shortly. "I know my Fouché. He still employs his personal spies. He still contrives to know everything that is going on in Paris."

Fouché bowed gracefully and murmured: "Thank you, madame." On a sudden thought she said: "Fouché, please kiss me."

He gave a little start and stared at her unbelievingly. She chuckled happily. It was something to bring a look of surprise to the face of a man like Fouché.

"Come," she commanded, "put your arms round my neck and kiss me. Kiss me as if you really meant it. Kiss me passionately."

He laughed pleasantly. "Ten years ago I should have been glad to, and I should have been loath, I assure you, to have stopped at a kiss."

She chuckled. "I always suspected that you were something of a rat where a young girl was concerned."

"Ten years ago," he murmured, "you were thirty."

She came close to him. "Pig!" She turned up her face to his and pressed herself against him. He looked at her queerly and, to her intense satisfaction, his breath became a little labored. She reached up and put her arms round his neck.

"You little harlot," he said, and kissed her.

She endured it for a few moments, noting abstractedly that he certainly had a way with him when it came to kissing. Then, her fears confirmed, she released him and pushed him away.

"Well?" he demanded.

She shook her head sadly. "It's no use, Fouché, it's no use at all. Even if I were to let you take the matter farther, as apparently you would have wanted to do ten years ago, it would still be no use."

"What the devil do you mean?"

"Oh, it isn't your fault, Fouché, it's mine. You see—" She stopped herself. Why tell him the truth and make him laugh? "You see," she wound up, on a sudden inspiration, "it so happens that in spite of myself Bonaparte has become the only man who means anything to me *that* way." She chuckled at the queer look he was giving her and said briskly: "Remember, keep a strict watch on Paulette, for my sake keep a strict watch on her."

Paulette had been back in Paris for a month and was, in Josephine's opinion, making the most of her widowhood. She wore mourning on all occasions; she had followed the latest fashion of cutting her hair short, and at her husband's impressive military funeral she had wept as if her heart was broken. Of course it wasn't broken, as Josephine had proved to her own satisfaction by telling the girl that Bonaparte had recently restored the old etiquette in respect of mourning. "The old etiquette?" Paulette had asked, completely mystified. "One is now required to wear mourning," Josephine murmured, "for a period of a year and six weeks." To which Paulette, in horror and indignation, had exclaimed: "But how barbarous!"

On her return Paulette had stayed with Lucien at his new house, but after two weeks, tiring of this, she had bought a house of her own in the fashionable rue Saint Honoré out of money, Josephine discovered, made available by Bonaparte. "Much too generous," Josephine had sniffed. "If I were to spend as much as that what a scene you would make." But Bonaparte, laughing, had drawn her attention to the fortune she had spent on Saint Cloud, and before that the other fortune she had spent on Malmaison. "You spend as much in a year on clothes," he had murmured, "as Paulette has spent on her new house."

Once established in the rue Saint Honoré, Paulette announced that she would like to give a dinner party. Bonaparte pointed out at once that such frivolity in a widow in mourning would be unseemly, but when she told him sadly that she would go mad unless she indulged in a little relaxation and added that the party she proposed would be private with only the family invited he agreed to permit it.

It was at this party that the first battle of precedence took place. When the whole family had gathered in the drawing-room and dinner was announced Lucien, at a nod from Paulette, offered his arm to Madame Mère and began to lead the way to the dining-room.

"One moment!" Bonaparte said sharply.

Paulette, a pathetic sight in her mourning, looked at him innocently. "What is it, Napoleon?"

"I think it is high time," he said sternly, "that you began to realize the importance of precedence."

"Precedence?" Paulette questioned, her manner more innocent than ever.

"You know quite well what I mean. Josephine is the first lady of France. This may be no more than a family dinner but the newly established etiquette must nevertheless be observed. Lucien, I gather, is acting as your host. Lucien will therefore lead the way with Josephine. I will follow with Madame Mère. The rest of you, in order of seniority, will line up behind us."

There was a little silence. Josephine, taking in the indignant faces of the Bonapartes with one sweeping glance, repressed a giggle.

Finally, Paulette said warmly: "This is my house, Napoleon, and in it no other person shall take precedence over our mother."

"By heaven, no!" Lucien cried, and began to move forward with Madame Mère.

"Stop!" Bonaparte roared, and with such suddenness and fierceness that Lucien dropped his mother's arm and stood back like a sulky schoolboy.

Joseph, his gloomy face contorted in anger, was the next to join in the battle.

"Paulette is right," he said hotly. "In my house, as you will live to discover, no woman will ever take precedence over our mother."

Bonaparte looked at him coldly. "You must be out of your senses, Joseph. Either that or your insane jealousy of Josephine is getting the better of you."

Joseph wriggled uncomfortably. "Forgive me, Napoleon, but all I am doing is trying to take a dignified stand on our mother's behalf."

Bonaparte threw up his hands. "Dignified!"

"For the sake of peace," Madame Mère boomed, "let Napoléoné have his way."

"Certainly not, Mother. Too great a principle is involved."

Bonaparte looked at Paulette. "Well?"

She sighed gently. "I'm sorry, Napoleon, but I must insist on Lucien leading the way with mother."

"Very well. In that case Josephine and I will return at once to the Tuileries."

Josephine, watching Paulette's face, was surprised to see it change suddenly. For a moment her eyes were filled with alarm. Nonplussed she stared at Bonaparte, then, with a shrug, nodded briefly to Lucien. Reluctantly he came to Josephine and offered his arm.

"Thank you," she said graciously, and took it.

Bonaparte offered his to Madame Mère. There was some argument among the others about seniority. Bonaparte settled it by turning his head and saying sharply:

"Male seniority first, then female, but since Paulette is our hostess she may as well follow immediately behind me."

"With whom?" Paulette demanded.

Bonaparte looked puzzled. Josephine repressed another giggle. Paulette was the only one without an attendant and it would be ridiculous to separate Eliza and Caroline from their husbands. Of course had Jerome been present, though that would have raised another arguable point: he, the youngest Bonaparte male, would never have been permitted to take Paulette's arm and precede Louis and Hortense.

"Bah!" Bonaparte exploded, "the best thing you can do, Paulette, is bring up the rear."

And so, with anger, indignation and sulkiness written on all faces but Josephine's, the battle ended and the little party entered the dining-room.

The meal was hardly a success. The number of the guests was small enough for general conversation, but that being out of the question, in spite of Josephine's own gallant efforts, the Bonapartes, silent for the most part, muttered occasionally among themselves.

When the meal was over and the Bonapartes were sitting uneasily about the drawing-room, glaring into space or at each other, the *major-domo* entered and whispered something in Paulette's ear. She nodded eagerly and turned to Bonaparte with a brilliant smile.

"Napoleon," she said, "I have a surprise for you."

The *major-domo* had left the room and was now at the door again.

"M'm'selle George," he announced.

"Of the *Théâtre-Français*," Paulette added.

Instantly suspicious, Josephine looked sharply at Paulette, and then at the young woman who was entering the room. She was probably eighteen, large rather than tall, and though in a few years time she would be massive her figure was beautifully proportioned. She had dark, flashing eyes, a full sensuous mouth and a deep chest which proclaimed her a powerful singer. Josephine thought instantly of Grassini and shuddered. Then she saw the girl's hands and feet. They were large, so large that any man of refinement would shrug regretfully and dismiss her attractive body as a cruel paradox perpetrated by a cynical nature. But Bonaparte, was *he* a man of refinement?

Scrupulously observing the order of precedence, Paulette introduced the company one by one.

"Though M'm'selle George is new to the *Francais*," Paulette remarked, "her voice, in my opinion, is one of the best I have ever listened to."

"You specialize in tragedy, I hope?" Bonaparte demanded of the girl.

"But of course she does," Paulette said quickly. "I know your fondness for tragedy. Presently she shall sing something from *Othello* for you."

Josephine shuddered delicately. "Tragedy, I'm afraid, is inclined to depress me. Comedy, that is what I prefer, or a light drama."

"Comedy!" Bonaparte scoffed. "And as for drama——"

"That, m'sieur," M'm'selle George interrupted boldly, "is a mongrel art."

Bonaparte shot her a look of intense interest. "Precisely, m'm'selle. Only tragedy is real art. If I could I would make it the school of kings and people alike. Tragedy fires the soul, elevates a man's heart, creates heroes in the true sense of the word. But come, we must hear you sing. *Othello*, by all means some rendering from *Othello*."

Paulette clapped her hands. Musicians entered, took up a position reserved for them at the far end of the room and began to tune their instruments. A few moments later the conductor tapped his baton commandingly. M'm'selle George, standing immediately in front of him, took a deep, easy breath and threw out her formidable chest. The first notes were a blast in themselves and made Josephine want to thrust her fingers deep into her ears. But worse was to come. The room was much too small for such swelling notes. Both Elisa and Caroline clutched instinctively at the sides of their chairs and Paulette herself, standing close to Bonaparte, took a quick step backwards.

"Are you ill?" Josephine asked her.

"Sssst!" Bonaparte cried fiercely.

He was leaning forward in his chair, one hand cupping his chin.

"Magnificent," he murmured rapturously, not once but a dozen times, and when M'm'selle George had finished and was bowing deeply he clapped his hands together madly and shouted: "Encore, encore!"

The rest of the company, with the exception of Josephine, politely supported him.

"Something from Corneille this time," he commanded.

Once again he listened rapturously, when Josephine coughed, he cried: "Ssst!" and once again, when M'm'selle George had finished, he clapped his hands madly. Not content with that he sprang to his feet, went quickly to the girl's side and took her hands in his.

"M'm'selle," he shouted, "you surpass Grassini."

"But naturally," she agreed. "Grassini is old and I, m'sieur, am young."

Paulette laughed softly and glanced mockingly at Josephine. Josephine leaned forward and pinched the wretched creature sharply in her left buttock. *"Bitch!"* she hissed.

Bonaparte linked an arm through M'm'selle George's and lead her towards the door which opened into Paulette's private sitting-room. "You and I," Josephine heard him say, "must discuss your amazing voice and—er—possibly your brilliant future."

Without a word of excuse, without even a backward glance, he flung open the door, ushered M'm'selle George into the intimate little sitting-room and closed the door firmly on the somewhat startled company.

"Well!" was all Josephine could say.

Paulette laughed shrilly. "I knew Napoleon would appreciate her voice."

"A doubtful blessing, the voice," Josephine snapped, "when one considers the size of her hands and feet."

"Ah, but Napoleon's interest is surely in her art," Lucien murmured.

A moment later the singer's voice rose again, muffled certainly, but still very distinct. Josephine sat bolt upright in her chair and tapped her foot angrily on the floor. At the conclusion of this third rendering, which was mercifully short, she looked about her ironically.

"Do we applaud?" she asked.

For the next hour Bonaparte remained closeted with M'm'selle George whose voice, never once losing its power, continued to rise and fall. A long silence followed the final rendering. Paulette chortled; Lucien looked at Josephine and leered. The rest of the Bonapartes, less blatant in their delight, contented themselves with throat clearings and nose blowings.

Josephine laughed with forced gaiety. "What in the world can they be doing now?"

"Discussing her brilliant future, I imagine," Lucien sniggered.

Madame Mère rose abruptly. She thanked Paulette for her hospitality, gave Josephine a pitying glance and took her solemn departure. Hortense, flushed and embarrassed, was the next to rise.

"If you wish to go, Mother," she offered, "Louis and I will be glad to accompany you to the Tuileries."

Josephine, fighting back her tears, shook her head firmly. "I shall wait for Bonaparte. If necessary I shall wait till four in the morning."

After that, one by one, the others excused themselves, until only Josephine, Paulette and Lucien were left. No sound, except one deep laugh from M'm'selle George, had come from Paulette's sitting-room during the last tortured hour.

It was close to midnight when Josephine, unable to endure another moment of waiting, stumbled weakly to her feet.

"Not going, Josephine?" Paulette asked.

Josephine nodded dumbly.

"You found our little party enjoyable, I hope?" Lucien said.

"I found it as enjoyable as you both intended me to." She drew a deep breath and added with uncertain dignity: "I never suspected the use to which you intended to put this house. I should have imagined that even the most ambitious madame would hesitate before setting up an establishment in the rue Saint Honoré."

So taken aback was Paulette that her mouth fell open and remained open.

At the door Josephine turned for a final thrust. "With my husband for your first customer you should attract many wealthy gentlemen and make a quite handsome profit."

*　　*　　*　　*　　*

"I presume," Bonaparte said jauntily, "that you expect me to beg your forgiveness."

"I was never so humiliated in my life," Josephine said sadly, "but for you to beg my forgiveness is the last thing I would expect of you."

She was sitting up on the pillows, her face red and swollen after a night of ceaseless weeping. Bonaparte, who had entered the room a moment ago, was standing at the foot of the bed, staring at her moodily.

"As you wish," he said curtly. "But let me attempt to excuse myself by telling you that her entrancing voice made me forget everything."

"Her voice, her entrancing voice!" Josephine stormed. "She was silent for hours before I was forced to leave."

Bonaparte coughed and grinned sheepishly.

Josephine wailed suddenly. "And a woman with such big feet and such coarse hands! Grassini was certainly massive but all her members were at least shapely!"

"If M'm'selle George were as big as an elephant and as ugly as a rhinoceros I would still find her attractive."

Josephine gave a moan and covered her head with the sheet. Bonaparte moved round the side of the bed and sat on the edge. He patted her shoulders gently and withdrew the sheet.

"Sweetheart, why do you take this thing so seriously? Why do you torture yourself with the thought that I might fall in love with one of these women who attract me for an hour, or a day or so, and are then forgotten?"

"But you might," she wailed, "you might!"

"Nonsense! Love is not for me, Josephine, and never has been since you yourself cured me of the disease by your own unfaithfulness. What indeed *is* love?" He sprang up and began to pace the room. "A passion, perhaps, that casts aside the whole world in favor of one beloved object? I wonder, though that is what I thought it when first I fell in love with you."

Josephine sprang out of bed and flung herself into his arms.

"Oh, Bonaparte, I'm so miserable, so miserable!"

He held her gently against him. "You should know by now that such exclusiveness was never in my nature. You should know it and refuse to make yourself unhappy and desperate about amusements in which my affections have no part."

"But how can I? How *can* I?"

"Simply by remembering that you and you alone have something more valuable than my love."

"And what is that, pray?"

"My friendship, my deepest affection. Surely I proved it last night by insisting on your taking precedence over the rest of my family!"

"Yes, yes, but the thought that we are nothing more than friends——"

He tweaked her nose. "You little idiot, 'Nothing *less* than friends,' you should say. Come, dry your eyes, and remember in the future when M'm'selle George has been replaced by somebody else equally unimportant, that you, the mistress of the Tuileries, are irreplaceable."

He picked her up in his arms, staggered a little under her weight and laid her on the bed.

"Try and get a little rest," he advised, and went quickly from the room.

The moment the door had closed on him she sat up and uttered an unladylike phrase.

"You may not think it, my fine Paulette, my sniggering Lucien," she said aloud, "but I shall get the better of you for this."

And for a second time she uttered the unladylike phrase.

CHAPTER XXXVII

A RECEPTION WAS IN progress at the Tuileries, but since Bonaparte considered it an occasion of small importance Josephine was attended by only one of her ladies of the palace, her favorite, Madame de Rémusat. Indeed, of such small importance did he consider it that, sprawled on the floor playing with the six-month-old Napoleon-Charles, he was completely ignoring his guests. As she watched him Josephine smiled serenely. He and the child made such a pretty picture, and the fact that each day his love for his little nephew (or step-grandson, if you liked to put it that way) grew deeper was a source of increasing satisfaction.

"M'm'selle George," one of the ushers announced.

Josephine looked up sharply. She had heard from Fouché that the singer had been recently dismissed—dismissed and replaced by a certain Madame Larue, also the possessor of a beautiful voice, but a speaking, not a singing voice; according to Fouché she had been commissioned (among other things) to soothe Bonaparte at night by reading to him.

Watching M'm'selle George, Josephine was quick to notice how confused and unhappy she looked; the girl, she suspected, had presented herself today without invitation. After a slight hesitation she made her way through the guests to Bonaparte's side. He took no notice of her as she stood above him, waiting. Eventually she coughed, or spoke a few low words, for Bonaparte, looking up casually from the child, failed to recognize her and yawned widely in her face. She drew herself up to her full height and, red in the face, made a hurried retreat from the room. Josephine chuckled softly. Poor thing, she knew exactly how she felt.

Since the humiliating night at Paulette's house Josephine had learned painfully to reconcile herself to these casual *affaires*. For one thing Bonaparte, clearly a little conscience-stricken, had tried to show her greater consideration, even a surprising tenderness; for another, he had generously increased her allowance. More surprising still he had summoned her to his apartments more frequently. Last week, for instance, the call had come on three nights in succession, and on the third night as early as ten o'clock. Amazingly enough she had enjoyed these unlooked-for interludes; it almost seemed as if Bonaparte, more restrained in his passion, had gained a little useful knowledge from his experiences with actresses, readers and the like. Change of life or not, the desire of which she had bewailed the loss had returned, not so much physically as spiritually. It was a solemn thought that Bonaparte himself should have been the cause of this, and a gratifying one too, indicating as it did that the tiresome years of respectability and faithfulness had brought the reward of a single-minded and single-hearted love for the man who was her husband. Nevertheless, as she thought of all this now, a slight uneasiness assailed her at the recollection of Bonaparte's ridiculous little homily on love and friendship. A difficult man to understand, this humble Corsican who had risen so high; a man others would never really understand; a man indeed, who would never understand himself.

She turned with a smile of pleasure as Fouché approached her. Fouché, almost always present at the consular court these days, was viewed with greater favor by Bonaparte, who often complained that Fouché, rogue that he was, was badly missed at the Ministry of Police.

Fouché paid his respects with an easy flattering phrase and a deep, mocking bow.

"Later, if madame is so disposed," he said, "I should like to discuss the war."

Josephine, now that war had broken out again with England, had little interest in its progress. Earlier, at Bonaparte's command, she had been set the task of negotiating with the English Ambassador, and since Lord Whitworth, conscious of the fact that he was dealing with a born aristocrat, had shown her a proper respect, she had enjoyed herself very much indeed. She had even believed at one stage that through her intervention the threatened war would be averted, but Bonaparte, losing patience, had shattered that belief. She shuddered now as she recalled the embarrassing *finale*. Lord Whitworth, gracious of bearing, listening politely, Bonaparte, striding up and down and shouting like a fishmonger in the *Halles*. And as a result, war.

"I know nothing of Bonaparte's plans," she told Fouché, "and would hardly care to discuss them if I did."

"I'm not referring to the war with England," Fouché laughed, "but to your own more personal war with the Bonaparte family."

Josephine's eyes lit up instantly. "You've learned something to my advantage at last?"

"I have, my dear."

"Concerning the wretched Paulette?"

"Not Paulette but Lucien."

"Splendid. To dispose of them one at a time is by far the best plan." She looked quickly about the room. "The reception is about to break up. Come to my apartments in half an hour's time."

Fouché smiled, bowed and withdrew.

Half an hour later with Madame de Rémusat dismissed, Josephine was alone with the man who was still the cleverest spy in France. She leaned forward eagerly in her chair.

"Well, Fouché?"

"You still wish to strike a crippling blow at Lucien?"

"What a stupid question to ask. Of course I do!"

"Have you heard of Madame Jouberthou?"

"Madame Jouberthou? No, never."

"An attractive young woman, I assure you, and quite new to Paris. She arrived a few weeks ago from Plessis."

"Plessis?" Josephine began to understand. "Lucien has a country estate at Plessis."

"Precisely. The young lady, by the way, now occupies a small house in a quiet alley off the rue Saint Dominique."

"Ah! And Lucien's town house is in the rue Saint Dominique! Quite a coincidence, isn't it!"

"Yes, quite."

Josephine frowned. "How does this obvious liaison give me the opportunity of striking a crippling blow at Lucien?"

Fouché smiled mysteriously. "That is something which you will discover later. Tonight at eight you will come with me to Madame Jouberthou's house. You will wear a veil, assume the name of Madame Trappini and speak with an Italian accent."

Josephine blinked. "But in the name of heaven *why*?"

"Madame Trappini is a widow who wishes to adopt a child before returning to Milan."

"A child?" Josephine said sharply.

Fouché laughed pleasantly. "It gives me the greatest pleasure in the world to puzzle an inquisitive woman. Therefore I shall tell you no more now, except that I, for the purpose of allaying Madame Jouberthou's suspicions, have assumed the name of Doctor Randeville."

He rose and bowed. "Until tonight at eight, madame."

Fouché made the introductions graciously.

"Permit me to present Madame Trappini of Milan, the lady I mentioned during our conversation yesterday. Madame Trappini—Madame Jouberthou."

Josephine inclined her head; Madame Jouberthou, a pretty little thing with big startled eyes, a beautiful skin and a shapely body (though over-large breasts, Josephine decided) stammered that she was pleased to make Madame Trappini's acquaintance.

"As I told you, madame," Fouché went on, "Madame Trappini is eager to adopt a child of good parentage. Therefore I took the liberty of bringing her here tonight to see your child and discuss the possibility of its adoption."

Madame Jouberthou blushed hotly. "That was kind of you, but the child, I should tell you, is my sister's, not mine. My sister has been—unfortunate. You are fond of children, Madame Trappini?"

"But yes, so very fond," Josephine gushed.

"Could we see the child?" Fouché asked.

Madame Jouberthou hesitated. "Well—well yes, but please understand that I—that my sister is by no means happy at the thought of parting with him and will do so only with the greatest reluctance."

She hurried from the room, a small and gloomy place with dark panelled walls and heavy curtains.

"The child," Josephine remarked in a whisper, "is hers, of course, hers and Lucien's."

"And since they want to dispose of it by a discreet adoption Lucien is afraid of the story reaching Bonaparte's ears. Silly, of course, but there it is."

Josephine chuckled. "Silly indeed, but now that the Bonaparte family is the first family of France not even the slightest hint of scandal must touch it." She took a deep breath through her veil. "Thank you, Fouché. I shall never forget what you've done for me."

Madame Jouberthou returned carrying a young baby in her arms. She held it lovingly and gazed at it with tender adoration. For a moment Josephine's heart melted at the sight and she felt ashamed. *Fool*, she told herself fiercely, *war is war and when the enemy is a Bonaparte one must grasp at every weapon.*

She looked intently at Madame Jouberthou's over-large breasts. "You are still feeding him, I see. How old is he?"

Madame Jouberthou's easy blush came again. "Madame is mistaken. The child is my sister's."

"But of course. How stupid of me. May I take him in my arms?"

Madame Jouberthou hesitated and before she could either acquiesce or refuse, a man's voice, slightly muffled, called: "Alexandrine!"

Both Josephine and Fouché swung round to face the direction from which the voice had come. One of the panels in the wall was open and Lucien Bonaparte was stepping into the room.

"Fouché!" he cried. "By heaven, *Fouché!*"

Fouché bowed. "A dramatic but hardly surprising entry. I already suspected that a secret passage connected your house with this. But come, I find myself faced with a little difficulty here, but one which you, I imagine, will be able to simplify."

Lucien came forward and turned roughly on Madame Jouberthou.

"Alexandrine, how many times have I warned you against admitting strangers to this house? Bah, if only you knew what a stupid thing you've done! This man here, this grinning ape, is Fouché, former Minister of Police."

"I—I understood that he was a doctor," Madame Jouberthou stammered. "A doctor by the name of Randeville."

"And this veiled woman? Who is she?"

"Madame Trappini, my dear Lucien," Fouché said easily. "A widow from Milan."

"You brought her here?"

"Yes."

"Why?"

"Madame Trappini would like to adopt a baby."

"Much as I hated the thought of it, Lucien," Madame Jouberthou broke in, "I—I thought it would be best for you. That is why I tried to do it without your knowledge. You see, I—I was under the impression that you had gone to Plessis and so I——"

"Oh, Alexandrine," Lucien cried, "why must you give everything away to Fouché?"

"I'm sorry," she said miserably, "but if Madame Trappini is suitable and would like to adopt him——"

"Suitable! I very much doubt it. This, obviously, is some intrigue engineered by Fouché. However, Madame Trappini, if that is really her name, shall speak for herself. She has been remarkably silent ever since I entered the room, hiding there behind her veil."

He reached out suddenly and plucked at Josephine's veil.

"My God," he shouted, "Josephine."

The baby, restless during the last few moments, began to cry.

"Quietly, Lucien," Madame Jouberthou begged. "You're frightening Jules."

"Jules?" Josephine said. "You refrained, I see, from choosing a family name."

At a signal from Lucien, Madame Jouberthou left the room with the baby.

"Quite a handsome young man," Josephine remarked. "Do you propose to deny that he is yours?"

Lucien, scowling, was silent.

"You are completely in our hands," Fouché told him. "You may as well make the best of it and come to terms as agreeably as you can."

"Terms?"

Fouché turned to Josephine. "There will be terms, of course?"

"Of course!"

"You must be insane," Lucien blustered. "Why should I come to terms with you or anybody else because you happen to have discovered that I am the father of Madame Jouberthou's child?"

"Ask yourself that question," Josephine murmured.

"What do you want me to do?" Lucien demanded.

"Nothing very much. All I ask is that you should relieve me of the embarrassment of your presence in Paris."

"And if I refuse?"

"I shall tell Bonaparte all I know about this—" Josephine giggled over the word—"about this *shameful* liaison."

Lucien laughed shakily. "But good lord, Napoleon was never a very strict moralist."

"He has one rule for himself, another for me and his family." It was plain from Lucien's face that he recognized his defeat. "Give me a few days to think the matter over," he begged.

"Not even one day, Lucien. You must decide at once."

He scowled again. "I have never asked a favor of you in my life, Josephine, but circumstances force me to it now."

Josephine smiled happily and almost purred. "How gratifying to find a Bonaparte humbling himself before me like this, how very gratifying. You shall have twelve hours. I shall expect you at the Tuileries tomorrow morning."

Fouché laughed shortly. "Twelve hours from now will be a little after nine in the morning. You rarely rise before eleven."

"I shall expect Lucien at midday, then." She gave her arm to Fouché. "In the meantime, Lucien, *au revoir*."

*   *   *   *   *

Back at the Tuileries Josephine learned from Madame de Rémusat that Paulette was with Bonaparte and that, if the screams of rage which had come from his apartments were anything to go by, an argument was in progress. Delighted at the knowledge that Bonaparte and Paulette were quarreling, but alarmed at the thought that she herself might be the subject of the quarrel, Josephine hurried down the private stairway to her husband's apartments.

She found Paulette lying face downwards on the floor of Bonaparte's study. She was kicking her heels wildly and sobbing hysterically. Bonaparte, his arms grimly folded, but a look of helplessness on his face, was standing over her and telling her, almost begging her, to control herself. At the sight of Josephine a smile of relief broke over his face.

"Dear me," Josephine murmured, "what an undignified posture."

Paulette leaped to her feet. "I warn you, Josephine, I want no interference from you!"

With interest Josephine glanced from Paulette to Bonaparte.

"A nincompoop," Bonaparte exploded. "That is all the man is, a nincompoop!"

"But handsome," Paulette retorted, "and rich, and a prince!"

"I repeat," Bonaparte shouted, "that when the time comes for you to marry again I shall choose a man, whether he be a prince or a commoner, who will be of some little political advantage to me."

"May I ask," Josephine inquired sweetly, "what all this storming and shouting is about?"

With an angry gesture Bonaparte explained that Paulette had been flirting outrageously, and in complete disregard of the fact that she was still in mourning for Leclerc, with Prince Camillo Borghese.

"Prince Camillo Borghese?" Josephine echoed.

She had met the young man on one occasion only. He had come to Paris from Rome as Joseph Bonaparte's guest and had duly made his bow at the Tuileries some weeks earlier. Josephine recalled what little she knew of him. He was handsome, as Paulette had claimed, even elegant, with a manner of speech which had reminded her for a moment of Hyppolyte Charles. An excellent match for Paulette, surely, save for the fact that, as Bonaparte had indicated, he was politically useless.

"Do you want to marry him?" she asked Paulette.

"Whether she does or not," Bonaparte complained wearily, "she threatens to."

Josephine pursed her lips. Married to the prince, Paulette would eventually leave Paris and take up residence in faraway Rome. Rome would be even better than Saint Domingo where Paulette could hardly have been expected to remain permanently.

"No good will come of continuing this silly argument tonight," she said wisely. "Why not agree to call a truce and then discuss the matter more calmly tomorrow?"

With a sigh of relief Bonaparte agreed. He gave Paulette a little push and hurried her from the room. A moment later, after he had thrown himself heavily into a chair, Bourrienne entered.

"A dispatch by special courier from Etruria," he said.

Bonaparte took the dispatch and began to read it.

Yes, Josephine told herself, *by fair means or foul Paulette must marry Camillo Borghese.*

"Good Lord!" Bonaparte cried, "the King of Etruria is dead."

"Poor man," Josephine said sympathetically, "but is it of any great consequence?"

"His death could have unpleasant repercussions at this stage of my affairs. The Queen of Etruria is young and childless and might easily make a foolish second marriage."

"By foolish you mean of no advantage to the First Consul of France."

"Naturally."

"The poor girl is hardly likely to be thinking of marrying again just yet."

"Possibly not, but I must be prepared for anything in this matter. I think—" he paused, playing with the idea that was forming in his mind—"yes, I think I shall send Lucien to Etruria."

"Lucien? Merciful heavens why Lucien of all people?"

"Lucien is a Bonaparte, and a widower. Also, he is well acquainted with the young Queen. She was, remember, the Infanta of Spain, the same princess—" he chuckled, looking at Josephine slily—"he wanted to marry to me before I arranged her marriage with the King of Etruria."

Not unconscious of the fact that this would remove Lucien from France, Josephine asked Bonaparte if her suspicion that he was planning a marriage between his brother and the Queen of Etruria was correct.

He nodded eagerly. "He shall go to Etruria as French resident, commiserate with the young widow, act as her chief adviser and, after a decent interval, marry her."

"Thus becoming the King of Etruria?"

"Why not? I have the power to make him that if I wish."

No more was said, but the more Josephine thought of Lucien becoming a king, even an insignificant king, the less she liked it. Gratifying as it would be to see him permanently removed from France she would rather he remained to plot against her than gain a position as elevated as that. Besides, hadn't she the power to remove him herself? Not permanently, perhaps, but for a considerable length of time. And then, as she brooded over all this, an idea, perhaps the best she had ever thought of, occurred to her.

"Poor Lucien," she said, maliciously, and began to chuckle. The chuckle developed into a laugh, the laugh into a roar of such intense mirth that a pain shot into her sides and the tears rolled down her cheeks.

"Poor Lucien," she gasped, "poor, poor Lucien!"

*   *   *   *   *

It was ten o'clock in the morning, two hours before Lucien was expected at the Tuileries. By a tremendous effort, and one which had left her utterly exhausted, Josephine had risen at eight instead of the usual hour of eleven. To Madame de Rémusat she had said: "I shall require a carriage at ten and your attendance on a little visit I find it necessary to pay." It being essential to her plan that Lucien and Bonaparte should have no meeting before the pressure she was about to bring to bear had been applied, a note had been sent to Lucien's house warning him not to come to the Tuileries. "I myself," she had written briefly, "shall come to the rue Saint Dominique."

If Lucien felt surprise to find Josephine calling on him at so early an hour he betrayed it in no way.

"This is indeed an honor," he said drily.

"Yes, isn't it," she agreed.

"May I ask the reason for it?"

She smiled sweetly. "I came to tell you, my dear Lucien, that I have changed the price of my silence."

"Really?"

She laughed easily. "You may think me a sentimental idiot, but I feel so sorry for Madame Jouberthou that I think you ought to marry her."

"*What?*" Lucien exclaimed.

"Marry her, Lucien, and I shall say no more about your leaving France."

Lucien clapped his hands to his sides and began to laugh. His mirth was as violent as her own had been the night before. She waited uneasily for him to finish and then asked him as mildly as she could what he found so amusing.

"I can't pretend to know what you're planning," he said, "but it is quite safe, I feel, to tell you that Madame Jouberthou and I are already married."

"When," she demanded, "and why?"

"When? Last night, not an hour after you left. Why? Because I happen to be in love with her."

"I can hardly believe that, since you waited for an illegitimate child to be born before making an honest woman of her."

"Alexandrine was a widow but before we could marry we had to obtain a certificate of Jouberthou's death and there was considerable delay."

There was a silence between them. Josephine, though things had turned out as she wanted, felt as if she had been shamefully cheated.

"I naturally want to keep my marriage a secret from Napoleon," Lucien said presently. "Is it too much to expect you to respect my wishes in that?"

"Providing you behave yourself," she murmured, "the secret shall be kept."

He looked at her oddly. "And you don't propose to force me into exile?"

"No."

"I'm afraid I don't understand you, Josephine."

"Then what a dull young man you are, and how sorry I feel for your new wife."

She rose to take her leave.

"Your brother," she was unable to resist saying, "will summon you to the Tuileries soon, so it won't be long before we meet again. Until then, my poor Lucien, *au revoir.*"

✳   ✳   ✳   ✳   ✳

"Napoleon," Paulette said, "will obviously do his best to keep me from seeing Camillo, and then, let me warn you, I shall make such a scene that the whole of Paris will be gossiping about it within half a day."

On returning from the rue Saint Dominique Josephine had found Paulette waiting in her sitting-room. Since the girl had greeted her with a smile that was faintly friendly she was curious to know the reason for this unexpected visit and was about to utter a cautious leading question when the girl broke out again.

"I know why he objects to my wanting to marry Camillo. I would then become a princess, you see, and Napoleon would hate any member of his family to attain royal rank before he has had time to make himself a king in name as well as in fact."

Josephine smiled at Paulette's ignorance. It would serve no good purpose to point out that in Rome princes were as common as Capuchin monks and that Camillo Borghese was anything but royal when it came to rank.

"I must say," she ventured, "that a visit from you is not only a surprise but an honor."

Paulette frowned at this blatant sarcasm, but instead of flaring into a rage she said hesitantly that she had come in the hope that Josephine, who had so much influence with Napoleon, might feel disposed to intervene on her behalf.

"I love Camillo," she said simply. "I want to marry him. Will you help me if you can?"

Josephine almost laughed aloud. Here was one of her most hated enemies stupidly and blindly playing into her hands. Love, it would seem, had made her desperate, for clearly, though she coveted the title of princess, she was madly in love with the handsome Camillo.

"My dear," Josephine said earnestly, "if it is humanly possible Bonaparte shall be persuaded to consent to your marriage."

Paulette laughed shortly. "With you the most impossible things often turn out to be humanly possible. If only I could believe in your sincerity in this I would be very happy indeed."

"Watch that hasty tongue of yours," Josephine said darkly, "or I shall wash my hands of the whole affair."

Paulette looked instantly contrite. "Please forgive me, Josephine."

"Willingly," said Josephine, exultantly.

She assured the girl that she would speak to Bonaparte at the first favorable opportunity, but without approaching him at all she sent for her the next afternoon and told her that she had had a long and calm discussion with him.

"You found him more reasonable?" Paulette cried.

Josephine shook her head sadly. "You should know that your brother is always more difficult when calm than in a temper."

Paulette's face fell. "You achieved nothing, then?"

"Nothing at all, but try, I beg of you, to cultivate a little patience."

"Patience! What a silly remark to make to a Bonaparte!"

"Silly or not, I suggest that you wait till your period of mourning for poor Leclerc is over before you do anything hasty."

"The period of mourning is a year and six weeks," Paulette stormed. "Could anything be more ridiculous! And why does one have to add six weeks to the year in any case!"

"I often wondered about that myself."

"Would Napoleon wait as long as that if he were in my place?"

"Dear me no, he would have gone to bed with Camillo—er—presuming he were a woman and in your place, I mean, long ago."

A sly look crossed Paulette's face. "When you want to catch a husband as important as Camillo you must make him wait. However much you might want it yourself you must make him wait."

Josephine cleared her throat. "As a matter of fact, my dear, I didn't make your brother wait and he was still crazy to marry me."

Paulette's eyes flashed. She began to utter an unpleasant word, checked herself quickly and said: "What did you mean when you warned me to wait before doing anything hasty?"

"I merely thought you might decide to elope with Camillo, to marry him secretly in defiance of Bonaparte."

"And so I shall," the girl said promptly, and gratifyingly, "if no other way is possible."

"Such a marriage," Josephine warned, "could be declared null and void by Bonaparte who is the First Magistrate as well as the First Consul."

Paulette's mouth dropped open. Josephine repressed a giggle. It was, of course, a common failing with the Bonapartes, a lasting reflection on their poor breeding.

"The consent of the head of the family is necessary," she went on. "Without that all marriages can be dissolved." Then, innocently, as if the idea had suddenly occurred to her, she added: "But I was forgetting. Paulette, my dear, I was forgetting!"

"Forgetting what?"

"Joseph is the eldest. Joseph, legally, is the head of the family."

Paulette rose to her feet with a triumphant laugh.

"Thank you, Josephine. Joseph and Camillo are good friends. Joseph often resents Napoleon's insistence on being the head of the family. Thank you indeed. No more, I feel sure, need be said."

*   *   *   *   *

Josephine had never laughed so much in her life. It might make her fat but she didn't care. When one had three reasons for hearty and prolonged laughter one was a fool if one didn't take advantage of them. First of all there was Lucien. He had refused to discuss Etruria with Bonaparte and then, after thanking her for not betraying his secret, had lost his temper and betrayed it himself. And now, after a terrible scene, he was to be banished from France.

Secondly there was Paulette. Having pleaded with Joseph and taunted him with being afraid of Bonaparte she had obtained his consent and made a hasty marriage with her dear Camillo, and Fouché, discovering it, had taken the story, after only a little prompting, to a Bonaparte already smarting from the shock of his disappointment in Lucien. And now she, though not actually banished, was to leave soon for Rome.

And thirdly there was Joseph, who had been soundly castigated by his brother and had retired to brood and sulk at his country house.

Laugh! She would laugh for years to come. Two of the wretched Bonaparte clan disposed of almost at one blow and a third put out of countenance! Incredible, almost impossible!

"Whatever happens now," she chortled, "I shall surely die a happy and well-contented woman."

CHAPTER XXXVIII

JOSEPHINE GLANCED proudly at Eugene. Could it be possible, she asked herself, that this distinguished-looking but quiet and unassuming young man was really her son? So occupied had she been with her consular duties and her quarrels with the Bonapartes that for months on end she had almost forgotten that she possessed a son as well as a daughter. She thought his small, slightly drooping mustache very striking and particularly admired his large clear eyes. He caught her glance as he sat watching her make a belated breakfast and smiled affectionately. She returned the smile and wondered idly how many *affaires* he had had, and if one was in progress at the moment. Bonaparte's stepson, he was one of the most eligible young men in France. Unless he made a move himself it would soon be necessary to find him a wife.

"When you were in Italy," she asked, "did you see anything of Lucien Bonaparte?"

"I saw him once or twice, Mother."

"Was he—friendly?"

Eugene smiled faintly. "Would you expect him to be friendly?"

She giggled. "Well no, I'm afraid I wouldn't. Is he staying with that impossible Paulette?"

"Why, yes, he is."

"Was *she* friendly?"

"Hardly, but at all events polite."

Josephine giggled again. "You amaze me. The wretched little brat must have learned a few manners since last I saw her."

Eugene laughed softly. "Poor Mother, will you and the Bonapartes never be friends?"

Josephine pursed her lips thoughtfully for a moment, then she broke into hearty laughter.

"How dull life would be, Eugene, if the Bonapartes and I were ever to become friends!"

He gave her another of his pleasant, affectionate smiles and asked when she would be returning to Paris.

Josephine was at Boulogne where a little court composed of her ladies of the palace and Bonaparte's staff had now been in residence for several weeks. She had pouted and made a dozen excuses about accompanying him on this irksome tour of the coastal defences, but in the end she had been forced to comply. At every halt Bonaparte had made vaunting speeches about the glory and prosperity which he had brought to France, and had claimed that the war would end with the complete defeat of England and a triumphant march on London. She had thought him boastful, but the enthusiasm of the people and the solemn singing of the *Marseillaise* had stirred her heart and brought tears of pride and emotion to her eyes.

"Tell me, Eugene," she said thoughtfully, "when is the invasion of England to begin?"

Eugene shrugged. "Nobody but the First Consul knows that."

"But surely you have *some* suspicion. You came here as his *aide-de-camp*. You must be as close to him as anybody else where military matters are concerned."

"The only suspicion I have," Eugene said quietly, "is that the invasion plans will be canceled. English sea power has been underestimated badly. English warships are blockading our harbors and sometimes even sailing right in to destroy our flotillas."

Josephine laughed lightly. "Poor Bonaparte, how furious he must be, but between you and me, Eugene, I can't say I'm really sorry. How I should hate to be dragged all the way to London with him!"

She finished her breakfast and stretched lazily.

"Eugene," she said, her curiosity getting the better of her at last, "have you ever been in love?"

He blushed faintly. "Once or twice, perhaps, but not seriously."

"Dear me, you mean you've never even had a mistress?"

He rose quickly and his face was now crimson. "Please, Mother, I would rather not talk of such things."

"Ah," she cried, "you are I see a discreet young man— Your father, now, would have been inclined to boast of his conquests."

"I'm afraid I have none to boast of, Mother."

"Oh, come," she coaxed, "I could never bring myself to believe that. It isn't natural for a young man of your age not to have had at least *one* mistress."

He smiled for a moment. "I'm sorry to be such a disappointment to you, Mother."

She gave his hand a little pat. It was very touching to think that he was keeping himself pure for the girl he would eventually marry, but if the marriage was to be a success he really ought to approach it with a little experience behind him. A sudden thought made her giggle. Merciful heavens, was it possible that she, of all people, was the mother of a puritan!

The door opened and Bonaparte came briskly into the room.

"We leave Boulogne tomorrow," he announced.

"Thank heaven for that," she cried fervently. "I never knew it would be possible to miss Paris so much."

"Who said anything about Paris? We go to Ostend, then Bruges, and possibly to Ghent and Brussels."

Josephine's face fell and she gave a little moan. "You'll kill me, Bonaparte, really you will!"

It so happened that the consular party left Boulogne that afternoon instead of the following morning, and hurriedly. And to Josephine's delight it left, not for Ostend, but for Paris.

"Why did you change your mind?" she asked Bonaparte, as she sat in the carriage which jolted and swayed on the bad road.

"Need I give you a reason for everything I do?" he snapped.

"Why, Bonaparte, what a temper you're in!"

Later, at the first halt, she had time to question Eugene, who, beseeching her to keep the story to herself until Bonaparte felt inclined to speak of it, told her that a serious plot had been discovered by Fouché. The republicans and the royalists, it seemed, had joined forces for the purpose of assassinating the First Consul, the republicans because they hated the policy which had made him First Consul for life, the royalists because they saw little chance, while he remained alive, of a Bourbon restoration.

"Have the conspirators been arrested?" she demanded.

"All I know, Mother, is that the plot has been discovered and foiled."

"And by Fouché."

Eugene smiled. "And by Fouché, who has every hope now of regaining the lost Ministry of Police."

Josephine gave a little chuckle. "Since the plot is taking us back to Paris, all I can say is thank heaven for the republicans and the royalists."

*   *   *   *   *

Josephine and Bonaparte, with Joseph and his wife and Madame Mère, were taking dinner with Louis and Hortense, who in spite of her second pregnancy seemed in excellent health. During the meal, which was now nearing its conclusion, Bonaparte had maintained a strange silence. Watching him anxiously Josephine wondered what was in his mind. There was nothing actually *brooding* about his silence, for from time to time the mild expression on his face had melted into a little secret smile. Whatever his thoughts were he was obviously feeling very satisfied about something. It could hardly be the war, for the ambitious plan to invade England had been openly abandoned. Possibly it was the discovery of the recent plot, the leaders of which, due to Fouché's skill, had been arrested and were now awaiting trial, or possibly——

"Ladies and gentlemen!"

Bonaparte was on his feet and rapping the table with his hand. Everybody looked at him in surprise. *Ladies and gentlemen!* What an extraordinary way of addressing one's wife and relatives!

"Ladies and gentlemen," he went on, "the pear is now ripe and I propose to pick it at once before it becomes full-blown."

"The—the *pear?*" Josephine exclaimed. "What in the world are you talking about?"

Joseph Bonaparte, suddenly flushed with excitement, laughed wildly.

"Some months ago," he said, "when I asked Napoleon when he was going to make himself King of France, he told me that the pear was not yet ripe. That, Josephine, is what your husband is talking about."

Madame Mère gave a grunt—whether of approval or disapproval it was impossible for Josephine to decide.

"That Napoléoné has decided at last to make himself King Napoléoné the First," she pronounced, "hardly comes as a surprise to any of us."

Bonaparte frowned at her pronunciation of his name.

"Napoleon the First, yes," he agreed, "but the title 'King' will not be used. At best it is outworn. The title 'Emperor' is greater, more fitting. It appeals to the imagination. It suggests infinitely more than the limitations of a kingdom; it suggests vastness, and that is what my empire shall be, *vast.*"

A little silence fell on the room. Josephine, though she had expected this move for many years, was frightened now that it had come. Madame Bonaparte was shaking her head gloomily and even

405

Joseph, now that his first excitement had passed, was staring at his brother uneasily.

"What is the matter with you all?" Bonaparte cried. "Why shouldn't I become Emperor of the French? Why shouldn't my glory eclipse the power of all the kings of Europe put together? Why shouldn't the crown of France be worthy of me, since by my sword I have made myself worthy of that crown?"

"I think," Madame Mère said sadly, "that we are all a little afraid for you."

"Afraid? Nonsense, Madame Mère, nonsense! Am I not the idol of France, hailed everywhere as a guardian god? My seizure of the throne of Charlemagne, the throne which is rightly mine, will be my final answer to the royalists and republicans who have tried to murder me. Once I am Emperor their plots and conspiracies will melt into nothingness and I shall stand before them and the whole world untouchable and unassailable."

Madame Mère rose slowly and deliberately.

"Napoléoné," she said, "turn and look at the wall behind you, at the portrait of your father, there in the shadows, ignored and forgotten by all but me."

He looked at the portrait. "Well?"

"Look at it well, my son. That man bore your name. As his portrait is hidden in the shadows, so did the man himself live in peace apart from the noise and strife of the world. You see upon his garb none of the ensigns of power or greatness. The world could say little of him except that he was happy."

"What are you trying to say, Mother?"

"Are *you* happy? And if you are, which I doubt, can you expect to remain happy, once you bear the title of Emperor?"

"Happiness," he said harshly, "has nothing to do with it. Happiness and ambition are things apart. I turn my back upon the portrait of my father, who was a happy man."

"Then I have nothing more to say to you, Napoléoné."

With that she asked to be excused and withdrew from the dinner party with a dignity of bearing which Josephine would never have thought possible in a Bonaparte. But then, when you came to think of it, Madame Mère was only a Bonaparte by marriage, wasn't she!

Joseph cleared his throat and asked Bonaparte if, as Emperor, he still intended Louis to be his heir and successor. Bonaparte stared thoughtfully at his favorite brother.

"No," he said at last, "but I have a proposition to put to him."

"And that is—?" Josephine asked, half suspecting what was coming.

"I want to adopt Louis's son and name him my heir, which will one day make him Napoleon the Second."

"But that," Joseph objected warmly, "would give Josephine's grandson precedence over all of us. It would even, if he has children himself, omit the rest of us from the succession."

"It would," Bonaparte said smoothly.

"Then I for one object to your following such a course!"

"Your objection counts for little, Joseph." Bonaparte turned to Louis who had made no attempt to speak. "I take it that you have no objection to my adopting Napoleon-Charles?"

"I have every objection," Louis said. "Why should I take second place to my own son?"

Joseph had sprung to his feet. "I am eldest brother and head of the family. As such I demand my rights!"

Josephine laughed gently. "Poor Joseph speaks as if my husband hadn't won a throne for himself, but as if his father had been king and Bonaparte had usurped his rights in the matter of legitimate succession."

"He does," Bonaparte cried, "by heaven he does!"

"What have I done," Louis asked querulously, "to deserve this threat of disinheritance?"

"Nothing," Bonaparte told him, "but in my opinion none of my brothers is fit to follow me on the throne of France. I select Napoleon-Charles because he is a baby and can be trained from his earliest years for the position which awaits him. Come, be sensible, Louis. Make it possible for me to adopt your son."

Louis shook his head stubbornly. "I would rather renounce all my hopes of the future. I would rather leave France and take the child with me."

Bonaparte turned to Josephine in exasperation. "Oh, Josephine, Josephine, why have we no son of our own to protect us from the pettiness of my family?"

"A very apt question," Joseph sneered.

Josephine felt herself turn pale.

"You will be suggesting next," she cried, "that the old question of divorce should be revived!"

Bonaparte laughed shortly. "I doubt it! I doubt if any of my brothers will ever suggest such a thing again."

Josephine smiled suddenly. "I understand what you mean. While you remain childless they will each make plans for following you on the throne. And dear me, how much they are going to grow to hate each other!"

"Precisely!"

He turned to Louis again and pleaded with him to reconsider his decision, but Louis remained adamant.

"I insist," Joseph said, "on the strict order of heredity."

Bonaparte threw up his hands in despair.

"Come, Josephine," he said, "we may as well go home to the Tuileries. To continue this argument would be futile. I shall make my own arrangements about the succession later."

She rose and took his arm sympathetically.

"Poor Bonaparte," she said, "you might have been a happier man if your mother had borne no other sons but you."

With this last thrust she smiled sweetly, bowed to Joseph and Louis, dropped her eye in the suspicion of a wink in Hortense's direction and withdrew with the fuming Bonaparte.

*   *   *   *   *

On reflection Josephine had thought that it was one thing for Bonaparte to decide that he would like to be Emperor of France, but quite another for the Government to meet him in his desire. If he felt any uneasiness himself he masked it with an admirable show of confidence and busied himself with the preparation of a speech which Curée, one of his most ardent supporters, would make in the Tribunate.

When Curée, suitably bribed and admirably coached, was ready to bring forward the motion it became pressingly necessary for the question of the succession to be decided. In the end, after Louis had refused once more to agree to the adoption of Napoleon-Charles, Bonaparte, making a hasty decision, named Joseph and Louis as his immediate successors. "I shall outlive Joseph, who is childless," he said, "and though Louis might outlive me he would probably reign for only a few years before Napoleon-Charles succeeded him."

Curée's motion, though hotly opposed by the ex-director, Carnot, passed the Tribunate with only one dissentient voice and was sent to the Senate for debate. Long speeches were made in Bonaparte's favor, the measure was enthusiastically adopted and an impressive *senatus-consultum* was eagerly prepared which declared Bonaparte Emperor of the French, the Empire to descend in the male line of his body. Should no male heir be born to him, the document proclaimed, he had the right to adopt any son or grandson of his brothers, while in default of such adoption Joseph and Louis Bonaparte would come to the throne one after the other.

"You made no mention earlier of this right to adopt any son or grandson of your brothers," Josephine said, in surprise.

"It was an after-thought," he chuckled, "and should give both Joseph and Louis many uneasy moments in the years to come."

While the Senate was occupied with the *senatus-consultum* Bonaparte and Josephine withdrew to Saint Cloud and there, in the country residence of the former Queen of France, they stood side by side to receive the senators when they hurried to Saint Cloud to make their decision officially known to the new Emperor. Arrayed in full uniform Bonaparte listened graciously to the address which Cambacérès read aloud in ringing phrases, and when everybody cheered and cried: "Long live the Emperor, Napoleon the First!" a smile of triumph crossed his face.

Cambacérès then called for silence and with the emperor looking approvingly on he addressed himself to Josephine.

"Madame, there remains an agreeable duty for the Senate to perform—the duty of offering your Imperial Majesty the tribute of its respect and the gratitude of France for the good you have always done and will continue to do."

Tears of emotion came quickly to Josephine's eyes. *Your Imperial Majesty!* This, surely, was nothing more than a dream!

"It is clear to us and to the whole of France," Cambacérès continued, "that your Majesty's name, linked with that of his Imperial Majesty, Napoleon the First, will endure forever. The Senate congratulates itself on being the first public body of the nation to greet your Imperial Majesty, and prays humbly that they will ever be numbered among the ranks of your most faithful servants."

He raised his voice to a shout. "Gentlemen of the Senate, long live the Empress!"

"Long live the Empress!" the senators roared.

Bonaparte took her arm in his and gripped it till she winced. "Long live the Empress," he whispered.

The tears were running freely down her cheeks.

"And the Emperor," she said brokenly, "long live the Emperor!"

*   *   *   *   *

The Imperial Family was at dinner.

Josephine, sitting at her own end of the long table, looked at each of the Bonapartes in turn and smiled derisively at the varying shades of self-importance on the faces of her relatives-in-law. The only absentees were Lucien and Paulette, and Madame Mère, who had departed suddenly for Rome, where she proposed to spend a long holiday with Paulette and Borghese. Bonaparte had just announced that his brothers were to be created Princes of the Empire and would henceforth bear the title of Imperial Highness, and as a result everybody was now laughing and talking at once. Josephine suppressed a contemptuous snort. His Imperial Highness Prince Joseph!

"Our wives, of course, will now be Princesses of the Empire," Joseph was saying.

"Of course," Bonaparte assured him.

"What of your sisters?" Caroline Murat asked suddenly.

"Paulette is already a princess. You and Elisa, I am afraid, must remain plain Madame Murat and Madame Bacciochi."

"You mean," Elisa demanded hotly, "that while strangers are loaded with honors Caroline and I are to be condemned to obscurity?"

"Strangers? And who, pray, are the strangers?"

"The poor girl," Josephine said sweetly, "is probably referring to Joseph's wife, Julie, and Hortense. And possibly to me also."

"Have the goodness to keep out of this, Josephine!" Elisa cried.

Bonaparte rapped heavily on the table with a clenched fist.

"Kindly remember, Elisa," he said, "that you are addressing the Empress of France."

"Empress or not the woman is still Josephine, the widow of questionable reputation you were stupid enough to marry."

Bonaparte sprang to his feet. "You go too far, Elisa. You shall apologize to her Majesty at once."

Elisa burst into tears.

"In the name of heaven," Bonaparte groaned, "why should I have such a family?"

"The poor child is overwrought," Josephine said. "Try not to be angry with her."

The words were no sooner out of her mouth than she wondered what on earth had made her utter them. Instead of speaking kindly to the little beast she should have slapped her soundly. The only explanation she could think of was that her new dignity was making her gracious, and of course she could afford to be gracious to a Bonaparte, now.

"I'm not overwrought," Elisa sobbed. "I'm merely shocked and hurt by Napoleon's unfair treatment. That's all it is, isn't it, Caroline!"

"Yes," Caroline agreed, on the point of angry tears herself.

"When you come to think of it, Bonaparte," Josephine said gently, "your treatment *is* a little unfair."

"You would actually take her side when she has been so rude to you?"

"Why not? To return good for evil, that will surely shame her a little." And feeling mightily virtuous she added: "I can understand her point of view quite easily. She and Caroline are your sisters and as such, important members of the Imperial Family. Your Majesty should remember that and take it into full account."

She saw him melt with pleasure at her form of address, but

410

with a short laugh he said: "So important that they would have everybody think that I had stolen their inheritance from their late father the King!"

Josephine giggled. "Yes, it does seem a little like that, doesn't it!"

"While the subject is under discussion," Joseph said heavily, "what of our mother, Madame Mère?"

"At her own request," Bonaparte said, "she will remain Madame Mère."

"And Elisa and Caroline?" Josephine pressed.

Bonaparte laughed shortly. "Would you have me make princes of Murat and Bacciochi, then?"

"I hadn't thought of that complication, sire—" again she saw him melt with pleasure—"but it really was thoughtless of you not to arrange for Elisa and Caroline to be recognized equally with Hortense and Joseph's wife."

"For Murat and Bacciochi to become princes," Joseph remarked acidly, "would be preposterous."

"It would indeed!" said Louis, speaking for the first time.

"You beast, Joseph!" Elisa sobbed.

"Pig," Caroline cried, pointing a finger at Louis, "jealous pig!"

"My God," Bonaparte shouted, "this is more than I can bear."

"For the sake of a little peace and goodwill," Josephine pleaded, "grant them their wish."

He threw up his hands in despair. "Very well. Caroline and Elisa shall henceforth be granted the courtesy title of Princess of the Empire. I only hope they will eventually prove themselves worthy of it."

"Oh, they will. I feel sure they will."

"I very much doubt it," he snapped. "The dignity, graciousness and high breeding suggested by such a title has not been in evidence this evening. Her Imperial Highness Caroline! Her Imperial Highness Elisa! Look at them, everybody! And their Imperial Highnesses Joseph and Louis! Look at them! Dignity, graciousness and high breeding— Can you see it? I ask you, can you see it? Can you see it in any of them? A fine story tonight's petty jealousies would make in the foreign newspapers. The Imperial Family of France at dinner! You sicken me, all of you, you sicken me!"

He strode rapidly to Josephine's end of the table and offered her his arm.

"Come, your Majesty. In a belated attempt to preserve our own dignity the best thing we can do is withdraw."

The *senatus-consultum* had been sent from the Senate to the Departments, and now the desire of the people themselves, thus given the opportunity to vote on the question, was about to be made known. Waiting in an ante-room with Bourrienne while Bonaparte conferred with the assembled prefects, Josephine began to betray a little anxiety. The plebiscite, she thought, had been something of a risk, and what a ticklish problem the newly appointed emperor would be faced with if the peoples' decision was at variance with that of the Tribunate and the Senate!

"Listen!" she cried, for a sudden burst of cheering was heard. Bourrienne smiled. "That, your Majesty, is all we were waiting to hear."

The door was flung open and a flushed and triumphant Bonaparte strode into the room.

"There are," he cried, "only three thousand votes in opposition. Without the slightest exaggeration I can say that I have received the unanimous approbation of the French people."

He dismissed Bourrienne.

"Ten years from now," he cried, striding up and down in his excitement, "I shall be monarch of the whole world. Nothing on the earth or in the heavens above can resist me, no nothing!"

He came and took her in his arms. "And now, my little Empress, we come to the question of our coronation."

"*Our* coronation, Bonaparte?"

"Yours and mine, for you too, I am determined, shall be crowned."

Her knees felt suddenly weak and her eyes filled with tears of gratitude. To stand by Bonaparte's side at a solemn coronation, to receive a crown of her own! For this she had come to France and married Alexandre de Beauharnais; for this she had passed through the Revolution unscathed; for this she had endured the hatred and jealousies of the Bonapartes; and by this, whoever might whisper the word 'divorce' in the future, she would remain secure, Empress of France in her own right.

It is the decree of fate that you will become the Queen of France. The Crown of France will be placed on your head, but you will die, perhaps in sorrow, and without your crown.

Coming out of the past it was the voice of the old hag in Martinique, but though a little shudder ran down her spine at the latter part of the prediction, she told herself eagerly that the glory she had now attained, however brief its duration, would be sufficient in itself.

"Where will the coronation take place?" she asked.

"In Notre Dame, of course. Where else would you have it take place?"

"Who will officiate? Who will place the crowns on our heads? The papal legate, Cardinal Caprara, perhaps?"

Bonaparte gave a great laugh. "Cardinal Caprara? Oh no, my dear, his holiness the Pope himself!"

CHAPTER XXXIX

THE VERY SUGGESTION," Joseph cried, "is preposterous."

Josephine chuckled. His Imperial Highness, Prince Joseph, was purple in the face.

Bonaparte looked at his brother in distaste.

"I see nothing preposterous," he said mildly, "in my desire to be crowned by the Holy Father."

Joseph made a gesture of impatience. "The suggestion to which I refer is that Josephine herself should be crowned by him, though I doubt if His Holiness will ever be persuaded to crown either of you."

"And why not, pray?"

"He might consider it if you go to Rome for the ceremony but he will certainly never come to Paris for it."

"I think he will," Bonaparte said.

"But not willingly. You must be mad if you think he will come willingly."

"Willingly or unwillingly the Pope shall come to France. Please remember that I am the man who drew up the concordat, the man who restored religion to France."

"But on your own terms!"

"I nonetheless restored it, and even if the Holy Father should frown on my desire, he will, if wise, recognize the advantages which religion will gain in France by his visit."

Joseph shrugged and returned to his original protest.

"For your own sake and the sake of your Empire," he said, "I beg you to think well before permitting Josephine to be crowned Empress of the French."

"By heaven," Bonaparte cried, "if you try me much further I shall be obliged to send you after Lucien into exile!"

Joseph grew pale but he stood his ground. "I would willingly risk exile rather than see you take a step which you may live to regret."

"It is not my habit, Joseph, to indulge in regrets."

"Very well, you force me to speak frankly. If you permit Josephine to be crowned, divorce, however much you may some day want it, will then be impossible."

Divorce! So that was what was at the back of Joseph's pig-headed attitude. She looked quickly at Bonaparte. Catching her anxious eye he gave her a reassuring smile and came to her side. He put his arm about her and turned his head to look at Joseph.

"Before you go, Joseph, look at this picture of your Emperor and Empress. Look at it well and carry it away in your mind. Here we stand, inseparable, and there in Notre Dame we shall stand, still inseparable, to receive our crowns from His Holiness the Pope."

Joseph's mouth worked unpleasantly but the words he was trying to frame remained unuttered. "Bah!" he said, and went hurriedly to the door. Bonaparte called him back.

"Your Imperial Highness," he said, "should wait for leave to retire and should know that the proper way to withdraw from a sovereign's presence is backwards. One other thing. You made several disrespectful references to the Empress as 'Josephine.' In future try to remember the proper form of address. You—er—you may now withdraw."

His face more purple than ever, his eyes flashing hatred, Joseph backed clumsily to the door, fumbled for the handle and fell out of the room. Josephine giggled like a schoolgirl but her smile, when she turned to Bonaparte, was beatific.

"Does your Majesty," she presently asked, "intend to force the Pope to come to Paris against his will?"

"I hope to persuade him to come willingly, but if all reasonable argument fails come he shall, whatever his attitude."

She shook her head at this. If force in any degree was used, she pointed out, it would not be long before every son of the Church would be leagued against him, not only in France but in the whole of Christendom.

"Why not approach the subject tactfully?" she suggested.

"Tactfully?"

"I know the papal legate well. He and I are good friends. He—" she giggled—"he even considers me a devout daughter of the Church. I could easily broach the matter, broach it discreetly, before you make a move yourself."

Bonaparte pondered for a moment.

"Very well," he said. "Send for Cardinal Caprara at once."

"I shall be glad to, sire."

Bonaparte smiled and tweaked her nose playfully. "I love you when you call me 'Sire' or 'Your Majesty' but such formality is scarcely necessary when we are alone together."

The affection in his voice warmed her heart and she remembered the picture he had commanded Joseph to look well at. She referred to it hesitantly and asked him if he had really meant what he had said about their being inseparable.

"With all my heart," he said warmly. "Whatever public policy may some day demand I shall never have the heart to set you aside. You shall be crowned when I am crowned. Standing at my side you shall receive from the hands of the Pope the divine conse-cration."

Whatever public policy may some day demand. . . .

The words lingered in her mind for a moment, but she quickly forgot them, and the emotion with which Bonaparte had uttered the reassuring words that had followed them lulled her into the now familiar feeling of complete security.

*   *   *   *   *

So sympathetically did Cardinal Caprara listen to Josephine's cautious approach to the subject of the Pope's possible visit to Paris that she was able to tell Bonaparte that whatever happened the papal legate was their ally.

"The cardinal," she said, "suggested that I should send some little gift to His Holiness and accompany it with a suitably worded letter."

"Splendid!" Bonaparte cried.

"I wonder what sort of gift I should send?" she mused.

"A difficult question, certainly," Bonaparte frowned.

Difficult indeed it was. She knew nothing whatever about His Holiness, but supposed that his tastes would naturally be very austere. A Bible, perhaps, handsomely bound and beautifully printed? Or possibly some holy painting crowded with saints and angels wearing bright yellow haloes? She sighed. How much easier the decision would be if this was the Middle Ages when the Popes of Rome had been less virtuous and much more human. One could then have settled the whole tedious question by sending a bottle of expensive perfume or a ravishing new hat to the Holy Father's favorite mistress.

"Why not a rochet?" Bonaparte suggested.

"And what, pray, is a rochet?"

"Though the Empress of France goes to mass every Sunday morning," Bonaparte chuckled, "it is evident that she will never be a very religious woman. A rochet is a vestment of fine linen or lawn."

"Speaking of vestments," Josephine said brightly, "we ought to be busying ourselves with designs for our coronation robes."

"Dear me, what an exciting time you are going to have and what a lot of money you are going to spend."

"You surely don't want me to economize in anything so important as a coronation?"

"You shall spend as much money as the occasion demands."

She sighed happily. "As you say, what an exciting time I am going to have!"

A rochet of the finest lawn was made, submitted to Cardinal Caprara, who approved of it, and sent to Rome by the hand of a devout son of the Church who also bore a humbly worded letter from her Imperial Majesty, the Empress Josephine. It was drafted by Bonaparte, copied laboriously by Josephine, and expressed the hope that the gift would be well received. Addressing her as his beloved daughter in Christ, the Pope replied that the rochet was a very handsome one indeed. He thanked her warmly and urged her to do all in her power, which he knew was considerable, to complete the restoration of religion in France, and he ended by granting her an apostolic benediction.

"Upon which," Bonaparte remarked drily, "you will no doubt conclude that you need go to mass only once a month instead of once a week."

Josephine felt an odd sensation in her breast. To have been addressed by the Pope as his dearly beloved daughter in Christ. . . . It made her want to giggle and at the same time it made her want to cry.

By this time Cardinal Caprara had written privately to Rome and it was felt that what he had had to say would be well received. It was then that the Papal Secretary of State (feeling slighted, Bonaparte said, because the Pope had not been first approached through him) began to make difficulties and cause exasperating delays. The matter was then taken up by the Sacred College of Cardinals, which resulted in more difficulties and more delays. Finally, when Bonaparte was beginning to lose patience and was talking darkly of issuing an Imperial command, Cardinal Caprara brought word that His Holiness was prepared to receive an official invitation if the Emperor Napoleon cared to send one. And so an invitation was sent, was frowned upon because it was conveyed by an Imperial *aide-de-camp* instead of a French bishop, was considered lengthily and at last accepted.

"The rochet no doubt helped," Josephine remarked, "but if we were living in the Middle Ages I feel sure the matter could have been concluded much more speedily."

*   *   *   *   *

Josephine's carriage had been brought to a halt on a little rise in the road so that, without inconveniencing herself in any way, she could obtain a clear view of the hunting field. Seated next to her was Madame de Rémusat, carefully nursing the Imperial smelling-salts and lavender-water, while opposite her were Eugene and Fouché, now Minister of Police once more.

It was the 24th of November in the year 1804 and His Holiness Pope Pius the Seventh, with whom negotiations had begun eleven months ago, was at last approaching Paris in a solemn and impressive cavalcade. So busy had Josephine been with the negotiations and plans for the coronation that she had had little time to think of Hortense's second pregnancy, though naturally she had been delighted at the birth of the second grandson, Napoleon-Louis.

"What a farce this hunting party really is," Eugene remarked.

"A farce no doubt," she agreed, "but an ingenious one."

"A most ingenious one," Fouché chuckled. "I myself was the one to suggest it."

Josephine smiled. When it was known that the Pope had left Rome, Bonaparte had been faced with the necessity of designing some suitable ceremony to mark his reception. Unable to find a precedent to his liking he had been delighted when Fouché had suggested an 'accidental' meeting. As a result the court had come to Fontainebleau, a grand hunting party had been organized in the forest and here, at the Cross of Saint-Herem, everybody was waiting excitedly for the papal outriders to make their appearance round the bend in the road.

"I do hope no mistake has been made," Josephine said. "The Emperor will be furious if the Pope arrives tomorrow instead of today."

Fouché glanced at the heavy watch hanging from his waistcoat.

"The Holy Father will make his appearance in less than ten minutes."

At that moment Bonaparte rode up on a white horse. He was in full hunting costume and attended by two of the newly created Marshals of the Empire similarly dressed. He signaled to them to withdraw and placed his head within the carriage.

"Eugene, a word with you if you please."

Eugene got out of the carriage and stood in the road bareheaded, looking up and waiting for Bonaparte to speak. By craning her neck

417

and straining her ears Josephine, devoured by curiosity, was able to hear what Bonaparte had to say.

"We have a few moments to spare," he said. "I want to discuss something that has been on my mind for some time. Namely, your future."

"My future?" Eugene echoed.

"Yes. Your sister, through her marriage with Louis, is now a princess. My own sisters are princesses and my brothers, unworthy as they are, are princes. I myself am an Emperor and your mother—" he cocked a twinkling eye at Josephine—"unworthy as *she* is, is an Empress. But you, my stepson whom I love as dearly as I could ever love a son of my own, are still plain Monsieur de Beauharnais."

Eugene smiled in his unobtrusive way. "I find it no disgrace to be plain Monsieur de Beauharnais, even if my mother is an Empress."

"I know, Eugene, and I admire your attitude, but if you were a Bonaparte this shameful neglect of mine would have driven you crazy by now. Be kind enough, please, to accept the office of Grand Chamberlain."

Eugene looked troubled. "Such an office, I'm afraid, sire, would suit neither my taste nor my character. My vocation, I feel absolutely convinced, is entirely military."

Bonaparte smiled and leaning down clapped Eugene heartily on the shoulder. "If I myself were not an Emperor I would want nothing but to be a soldier. Some day, whether you like it or not, I might make you a prince, but for the present I shall content myself in promoting you to the rank of colonel-general with a personal allowance of a hundred and fifty thousand francs."

There was a sudden shout and Josephine saw that the papal outriders had come into view. "Ah!" Bonaparte cried. He signaled to the two marshals and rode forward at a sharp trot.

Josephine turned to Fouché. "I presume that the Pope himself is unaware that an accidental meeting is to take place?"

"Quite unaware."

The cavalcade itself was now within sight. For a moment Josephine thought that it was going to ride past at full gallop, and what then would poor Bonaparte do? Fly after it, perhaps, commanding the Holy Father to stop? While she quaked with inward mirth at this amusing possibility the cavalcade was brought to a halt and the Pope, resplendent in his white robes and white silk shoes, stepped from his carriage to the muddy road. Bonaparte flung himself from his horse and went quickly to the Pope's side. For a moment both men hesitated and then, at a move from Bonaparte, they fell into each other's arms.

"Touching," Fouché murmured, "*most* touching."

"But what will His Holiness think of Bonaparte!" Josephine cried. "He should have bowed deeply or—or fallen at the Holy Father's feet!"

"The Pope," Fouché chuckled, "must have formed an opinion of your masterful husband long ago. In any case, I can't imagine Napoleon the First, Emperor of France, falling at anybody's feet."

By now the male members of the hunting party—the Imperial Princes, the Arch-chancellor, the High-constable, the Grand-admiral and all seventeen marshals—had crowded about the central figures of the drama. For a moment all was confusion, but only for a moment, for at an angry signal from the Emperor they all fell quickly back. At another signal from him an Imperial carriage which had been held in readiness made its appearance. Bonaparte climbed in first, taking the seat on the right; the Pope followed, taking the seat on the left. Josephine gave a little shudder of horror, but Fouché only smiled.

"In France," he said, "etiquette is dictated by a little Corsican who has now become an Emperor."

With the Imperial carriage leading the papal cavalcade, and the hunting party following it, a move was made on the road to Fontainebleau where the Pope was to rest that night before proceeding to Paris.

A reflective smile had come to Fouché's face.

"I wonder," he said thoughtfully, "what His Holiness would say and do if somebody told him that he has been brought to France to crown and consecrate an Emperor and an Empress who were joined together in marriage by a mere registrar—an Emperor and Empress, in short, who, in the eyes of the Church, were never married at all?"

"Merciful heavens!" Josephine cried.

She looked at Fouché in horror, and then at Madame de Rémusat and Eugene whose faces revealed a horror as marked as her own.

"Madame de Rémusat," she said faintly, "my smelling-salts, for pity's sake my smelling-salts!"

While Josephine lay back in the carriage the smelling-salts were held to her nose and lavender-water was sprinkled on her brow. She moaned as if in acute physical agony. If the truth were ever revealed to the Pope, she, the woman he had addressed as his beloved daughter in Christ, she, the woman he had granted the apostolic benediction, would be regarded, not as Bonaparte's wife, but as his concubine. Worse, His Holiness would surely refuse to officiate at the coronation, and then what would Bonaparte say!

She sat up suddenly, thrusting aside the smelling-salts, knocking

419

the lavender-water to the floor of the carriage. She sat up and she began to laugh.

"Control yourself, Mother," Eugene begged. "The Pope is hardly likely to discover it."

"You think I'm hysterical but I'm not," she said. "And I *want* him to discover it. *I want him to discover it!*"

"Your Majesty is distraught," Madame de Rémusat soothed. "The smelling-salts again, perhaps?"

Josephine leaned forward and gripped Fouché's arm. "It surprises me that my enemies the Bonapartes have never thought of telling the Pope. You will therefore go to one of them—to Joseph, I think—and drop a little hint."

He looked at her in amazement. "You must be out of your mind."

"I was never more sane than I am at this moment. The opportunity for which I have longed ever since Hortense was married has come at last. Give me your word, Fouché, that you will drop a hint to Joseph."

His amazement gave place to a look of complete understanding. "Her Majesty, I see," he chuckled, "has lost none of her cunning."

"Your word, Fouché, your word!"

"You have it gladly." He laughed aloud at the puzzled expressions worn by Eugene and Madame de Rémusat. "What an intrigue, what a masterly intrigue!"

✳ ✳ ✳ ✳ ✳

Cardinal Caprara stood before the Empress. His face was long and solemn and his eyes were troubled.

"The story is true," he said, "not merely an unpleasant rumor spread by your Majesty's enemies?"

She bowed her head sadly. "The story is true, your Eminence. Had others not gone to His Holiness with it I should have been forced to confide in him myself. Splendid and awe-inspiring as the coronation might be I had begun to dread it with all my heart. How, I ask myself a hundred times a day, could I, with my guilty secret, stand before the high altar in Notre Dame and receive from the Holy Father that greatest of all sacraments, the Triple Unction?"

"How indeed!" the cardinal breathed.

"But what fault of mine was it," she went on, "that when the Emperor and I were married shortly after the fall of Robespierre there was no such thing in France as religion?"

The cardinal frowned. "Has the Emperor never suggested rectifying the wrong he did you?"

420

"No," she whispered, "never."

"Your Majesty bewilders me. The Emperor is the man who restored religion to France. His first act after signing the concordat should have been to insist upon a marriage before the altar."

"It should. Oh yes, it should!"

For a moment a silence fell between them.

"Was the Emperor present," she asked, "when the dreadful truth was made known to His Holiness?"

"No. The Holy Father was alone when his Imperial Highness Prince Joseph found it necessary to make it known to him."

"What did he say?" she asked curiously. "The Holy Father, I mean."

"In his distress and anger, his very righteous anger, he cried out against the Emperor for having so wilfully deceived him. He spoke of your Majesty as the Emperor's concubine, a woman living with him in a state of mortal sin. He declared it his intention to return to Rome at once."

Josephine thought it judicious to weep a little. She groped for a handkerchief and began to sob quietly into it. The cardinal averted his eyes and murmured sorrowfully that she must indeed be the most unhappy of mortals.

"Oh, I am," she cried, "I am!"

Her ears caught the sound of a familiar step in the corridor and a moment later the door was flung wildly open. She looked up cautiously. The news had been broken to Bonaparte and he was in a furious temper.

"I have," he shouted, "just come from an interview with His Holiness the Pope. The nature of that interview, I imagine, has already been made known to you by Cardinal Caprara."

"Yes, sire, it has." And she added: "His Holiness, of course, is deeply grieved."

"If Joseph were not my brother," Bonaparte said, "I would wring his neck."

She smiled sadly. "You know why he did it, of course. He wanted to prevent me from taking my rightful part in the coronation."

"The Pope," Bonaparte said, "is even now preparing to return to Rome. Not only has he refused to officiate himself, but he has forbidden any bishop to take his place."

"That, of course, was to be expected."

"The coronation," Bonaparte said, "is an essentially religious ceremony. Without the Pope, or without a bishop, it would be little more than a farce, a farce that would shake the whole world with laughter—laughter at my expense!"

"Oh, sire, what a terrible situation!"

Bonaparte's face was paler than she had ever seen it and his eyes were black with rage.

"It would be one of the greatest scandals in history," he said, "if, after coming to France to crown me, the Pope returned to Rome without having done so—a scandal which I, master of France and potential master of the world, am powerless to avoid."

Cardinal Caprara cleared his throat and spoke for the first time—spoke, Josephine praised heaven, before she herself, in desperation, had been forced to introduce the ticklish subject.

"I feel confident," he said, "that the Holy Father will remain and officiate at your Majesty's coronation providing you agree to what, after all, is a very simple expediency."

Bonaparte waved his hand irritably. "I know, your Eminence, I know! The simple expediency of a belated marriage before the altar."

"Ah," Josephine cried, "then the scandal can be averted after all."

"Bah!" Bonaparte said.

"Would a marriage before the altar be a very terrible thing?" Josephine pleaded.

"Since I would be forced into it against my will, yes!"

"Ah, well," she said reasonably, "you must take a few days to think it over. Some sort of compromise might yet be found."

"No compromise is possible. The date of the coronation has been announced and cannot be postponed. Delay, even until tomorrow, is out of the question. I must make up my mind at once."

She saw the struggle written plainly on his face and knew exactly what was passing through his mind. If he set aside the religious aspect of the coronation and went forward with the mockery of a civil ceremony he would be admitting to the Roman Catholic world that he had tricked, or tried to trick, the Pope. Thus, if he were foolish enough, he would antagonize a large majority of his subjects. But worse still, when you considered the pride and vanity of the man, he would, as he had pointed out himself, shake the whole world with laughter. She smiled to herself and waited patiently, without the slightest feeling of anxiety, for him to make up his mind.

"Very well," he said, addressing Cardinal Caprara, "I agree to a religious marriage with the woman who, by the laws of France, is already my wife. I will agree providing it is performed in secret."

The cardinal bowed and left the room.

Five days later, and two before the announced date of the coronation, the religious marriage took place in the little chapel at the Tuileries. It took place in the late evening, with only two witnesses present, Marshal Berthier and Foreign Minister Talleyrand, both of whom were sworn to secrecy. At the conclusion of the ceremony Bonaparte took Josephine by the arm.

"Remember this," he whispered fiercely, "my hand has been forced. I have acted against my will, against my better judgment. Some day, Josephine, somebody is going to pay and pay dearly for this."

CHAPTER XL

IT WAS THE EVENING OF the 1st of December and tomorrow was Coronation Day. Within the Tuileries Palace the excitement had mounted feverishly and the scene, though gay and colorful, was one of utter confusion. Chamberlains in their long silk stockings, soldiers in multicolored uniforms bristling with gold lace, ladies-in-waiting in full dress and lackeys in silver-embroidered coats bustled hither and thither rubbing shoulders with the numerous members of the papal party who, except for the Capuchin friars arrayed in rough serge robes, rivaled in their black and purple cassocks the splendor of the ladies and gentlemen of the Imperial court.

Josephine, surrounded by her ladies, whose high-collared Catherine de Medici dresses she had designed herself, was eagerly preparing for the full-dress rehearsal which Bonaparte had ordered. Not an hour ago she had paid a visit to the Pavilion de Flore which had been set aside for the use of the Pope and his attendants. Here, a concubine no longer but the Holy Father's dearly beloved daughter in Christ once more, she had been received with kindness, sympathy and understanding. Kneeling humbly before him but staring up at him in irresistible curiosity, she had been deeply impressed by the nobility of his countenance and the angelic sweetness of his smile. The touch of his hand on her shoulder had filled her with a feeling of peace, and she had left the holy presence ready to love the whole world, including every single member of the Bonaparte family.

"There," Madame de Rémusat cried, standing back with the other ladies to view the effect, "not even the Emperor himself will have a single fault to find."

Josephine turned slowly to view herself in the long mirror. The white satin gown with its gold and silver embroidery, despite the simplicity of design, was truly regal. She took a few steps forward, allowing the train to drag out to its full length.

"Exquisite," Madame de Rémusat murmured.

The other ladies took up the coronation mantle of red velvet lined with ermine. It was covered with gold bees and had a deep hem of heavy gold embroidery. They adjusted it about her shoulders and spread out the long train behind her. She staggered under its weight and faltered as she tried to take a step forward. What a blessing she was to have five train-bearers!

The door opened and Bonaparte entered. She gave a little gasp at the splendor of his appearance. He wore white velvet breeches, white silk stockings and white velvet shoes, all embroidered in gold and with the Imperial coronet conspicuous on the clocks of the stockings. Even his vest was of white velvet decorated with gold buttons. His crimson coat, again with white velvet on the facings, glittered with diamonds, and the short crimson cloak which hung from his left shoulder was caught on his right breast with a double clasp of diamonds. She suppressed a giggle. Poor Bonaparte, magnificent as he looked he had almost succeeded in turning himself into the sort of fop one might have seen at court in the old days.

Foncier the jeweler had followed Bonaparte into the room. He came forward now, bearing the crown which he had been commissioned to make for Josephine. Falling on to one knee before her he held it out for her inspection. She caught her breath sharply at the sight of it. There were eight branches rising to the center to support a shimmering golden globe on top of which was a cross. The branches, four resembling myrtle leaves and four palm leaves, were worked in fine gold and studded with diamonds. The encircling band beneath the branches was of emeralds, amethysts and pearls.

"Try it on," Bonaparte commanded.

She hesitated. "Oh, but that might be unlucky, sire."

"Nonsense!"

He took the crown from Foncier and placed it on her head. Foncier's assistant, hovering in the background, came timidly forward with the Imperial girdle, a golden ribbon sparkling with a bold array of rose diamonds. Bonaparte took it and adjusted it about her waist.

"Now the necklace."

Foncier took the necklace from its case and Bonaparte clasped it round her neck. Some of the diamonds in it were larger than any she had ever seen.

"Your train-bearers—where are they?" Bonaparte cried.

There was a stir at the door and the five Imperial princesses entered the already crowded room. Paulette, summoned to Paris for the coronation, led the way with a sulky expression on her face. Elisa and Caroline, equally sulky, followed, with Hortense and

Joseph's wife Julie close behind. Julie looked uneasy and Hortense plainly distressed.

"Take your places," Bonaparte commanded.

"Wait!" Paulette said, as the others moved hesitantly towards Josephine.

All eyes were turned on Paulette's wilful, rebellious face.

"On behalf of the others who are afraid to speak for themselves," she said, "I want to protest against this indignity which you would impose upon us."

"Indignity? What indignity?"

"The indignity of carrying Josephine's train."

"When referring to the Empress," Bonaparte almost shouted, "be kind enough to use the proper form of address." He swept the others with a swift, contemptuous glance. "So, with the exception of Hortense, you would like to refuse the honor of bearing your Empress's train in Notre Dame tomorrow!"

"Honor," Elisa cried, "when, Josephine——"

"For the last time," Bonaparte thundered.

"Honor," Elisa corrected herself hastily, "when her Majesty has always been our greatest enemy!"

Josephine smiled sweetly. "Personally, your Majesty, I would prefer to recruit my train-bearers from the slums of Paris. I would then feel sure of being faithfully served."

There was a titter from her ladies and loud screams of wrath from the Bonaparte sisters. Josephine looked at them distantly, at Paulette and Elisa and Caroline. Anybody else, she thought, would have looked magnificent in the finery they wore but all *they* had achieved was the look of over-dressed washerwomen bedecked in their flashy best for a village fair.

"Either you carry her Majesty's train," Bonaparte warned them, "or you stay away from the coronation tomorrow. Either you carry it or you go into immediate exile."

Elisa and Caroline burst into tears; Paulette, still sulky but much less rebellious, stamped her foot angrily.

"How could we bear the weight of the train," she asked, "and manage our own trains successfully?"

"An officer of the Imperial household," he conceded, "shall stand behind each of you and hold your train."

Paulette looked a little happier.

"Let us compromise," she said, with a glint in her eyes that only Josephine saw, "and agree that we are to *hold*, not *carry*, the train."

"Merciful heavens, and what is the difference between holding and carrying it?"

"If it is written in history," she pointed out, "that we held, not carried it, our dignity will be preserved."

"Then for the sake of your precious but barely perceptible dignity," he shouted, "let it be written in history that you *held* her Majesty's train. And now, for pity's sake let us proceed with the rehearsal!"

* * * * *

Josephine, rising earlier than she had ever risen since her childhood days in Martinique, had been up since seven o'clock. At that hour a heavy mist had covered Paris and those who understood, or claimed that they understood the signs, had predicted that the mist would turn to rain. Now, at eight o'clock, the mist was lifting and a watery sunshine was filtering through the north-east windows of the palace.

Madame de Rémusat, chatting with Josephine as the long and painstaking *toilette* was undertaken, reported that the army of a thousand workmen who had been employed for weeks at Notre Dame had been dismissed at last and that the Master of Ceremonies, having inspected the cathedral, had declared himself satisfied.

"Paris," she said, "is in a state of tremendous excitement. Even as early as two o'clock this morning many of the people were up and making their preparations, and at daybreak the streets were thronged with sightseers. The route to Notre Dame is already impassable and cavalry will be forced to clear a path. Some people, they tell me, are doing a rare trade out of letting their windows. Three hundred francs is being charged for a single window and seats in the double windows are being sold at a hundred francs each. Nothing is left but standing room, and for that one is obliged to pay fifty francs."

"Even the best rouge these days is rubbish," Josephine said. "My greatest fear is that if I grow too hot during the ceremony it will begin to peel off my face."

Hortense, fully dressed and flushed with excitement, came in at that moment to pay her respects and wish her mother well. Josephine thanked her absently.

"Has there been any more bickering," she demanded, "about the carrying of my train?"

"None, Mother. Paulette seems quite content with the change of words but there is something I don't quite trust about her manner."

Josephine remembered the glint which had been in Paulette's eyes the night before and wondered anxiously if she and the others could

426

be planning anything. Stupid, of course, for what *could* they be planning?

The door opened and Bonaparte, wearing a short dressing-gown which revealed his bare ankles and calves, strode into the room.

"It occurred to me," he said, "that the bodice of your coronation gown would look better if sprinkled with a liberal number of diamonds. See to it at once."

With a smile for Hortense and a nod for Madame de Rémusat, he strode out again.

"Such an impossible man!" Josephine wailed.

The order was given to Madame de Rémusat who hurried away in search of the Imperial dressmaker.

"He would have me look as vulgar as his wretched sisters," Josephine complained.

At nine o'clock there was a great confusion in the palace as His Holiness the Pope and the papal cavalcade set out for Notre Dame. From a window Josephine caught a glimpse of this solemn departure. The Pope's carriage, decorated with papal emblems, was drawn by eight handsome dapple-grey horses, and was preceded by the papal chamberlain who rode on a mule and carried a heavy wooden cross. Many of the sightseers, she learned later, never having seen the like of this before, and caring little for the ancient customs of Rome, jeered and laughed and shouted crude comments at the top of their voices.

At eleven o'clock Josephine, miraculously on time for once, went down with Bonaparte to the Imperial carriage, the panels of which were entirely of glass. As she stepped into it she caught a glimpse of the four golden eagles on the roof; their wings were outstretched and above them they held a golden crown. A prearranged signal had evidently been given, for as the horses were set into motion the batteries placed along the quays fired salute after salute. The sun, shining brightly now, increased with its wintry rays the brilliance of the uniforms of the ten thousand cavalry troops who followed the Imperial carriage.

"Look at the sun flashing on the breastplates and the swords!" Bonaparte cried. "Never has a king of France gone to his coronation attended by a train of followers as magnificent as mine! Never since the days of Caesar has such a spectacle as this been seen!"

The crowded route—half a million people were in the streets, Bonaparte claimed—was lined with another ten thousand mounted soldiers, and the cheering which rose and fell was deafening. "Long live the Emperor!" "Long live the Empress!" The two separate cries were repeated frantically over and over again, while in the distance military bands played the *Marseillaise*.

427

"Why do you smile like that?" Bonaparte demanded.

"I was thinking," Josephine told him, "of the first time I heard the *Marseillaise* played."

"And when was that, my dear?"

"During the Revolution. They called it the Hymn to the Army of the Rhine, then. I heard it the night before the rebels from Marseille stormed the Tuileries. I liked it instantly and I even felt it was going to mean something of importance to me some day."

"And how right you were!" he cried. "And how grateful you must feel to the rebels who cleared a path for you when they stormed the palace that is now ours!"

"Oh no, sire, not grateful to them, but to you!"

He slapped her knee with his open hand. "By God, Josephine, if we weren't on show in this glass case I would give you a kiss to remember for the rest of your life."

It took almost an hour to reach Notre Dame. So stiff was she with sitting straight and still that she almost fell when she got down from the carriage. There was a pain in her back and her head was beginning to throb. Worse still, a hot, suffocating sensation was rising from her legs and through her abdomen to her throat. It was intolerable that her change of life, which had never troubled her *very* much, should evince such distressing symptoms at a moment as important as this. 'Merciful heavens,' she thought, 'my rouge!' and she wondered anxiously if the thick layers could possibly survive the coming ordeal.

Her attendants were busy adjusting her coronation mantle while Bonaparte's were likewise occupied adjusting his, which though short, was so heavy that four gentlemen were needed to support it. At last, with the cheering of the crowd echoing behind them, they moved slowly forward into the cathedral. A hasty glance over her shoulder gave her a glimpse of the five princesses 'holding' her train. Paulette's face, wickedness personified, alarmed her for a moment, but Hortense's gentle, affectionate smile seemed to assure her that all was well.

The Cardinal Archbishop came forward to attend the Imperial couple to their thrones. He made a little speech of welcome and sprinkled them with holy water, while the Pope, rising from his own throne, sang the *Veni Creator* in his rich and pleasantly modulated voice.

With a sigh of relief, and hoping fervently that the holy water hadn't spotted her rouge too much, Josephine sank down on her throne. Bonaparte, his head high, his chin thrust out, was glancing arrogantly at the scene within the cathedral. From the church door to the choir was a solid and colorful mass of army officers, senators, magistrates and civil members of the Imperial Court. With a faint smile Josephine thought of the half-forgotten Aunt Marie, now dead like poor Mama, and wondered how many caustic remarks that sharp-tongued lady would have made about the waste of public money, the play-acting and the somewhat clumsy members of the new aristocracy now crowding Notre Dame.

The long ceremony, which was to last three hours, went forward on its slow and impressive course. Within the cathedral the air was chilly and grew so intensely cold that Josephine had little fear of any disaster befalling the carefully applied layers of rouge. During the purely civil part of the ceremony—the administration of the constitutional oath—the Pope and all the church dignitaries withdrew, and when they returned the spectators were busy munching the refreshments which they had bought from the businesslike hawkers who had gained the Imperial permission to sell their goods within the cathedral. Meanwhile, at a respectful distance, military bands entertained them with stirring, patriotic renderings.

It was late afternoon and the shadows were lengthening by the time the climax of the ceremony was reached. With a cry of satisfaction Bonaparte, who had done little to hide his yawns of increasing boredom, even during the solemn anointing and the blessing of the insignia, leaped to his feet and ascended the altar. A startled hush fell on the congregation as, with a gesture of impatience, he snatched his crown from the hands of the Pope and placed it on his head himself. A moment later, coming quickly down the altar steps with Josephine's crown in his hands, his next action was clear to all. She fell on her knees before him, and with tears in her eyes and a gratitude that was both shocked and amazed in her heart, she held herself motionless while he crowned her Empress of the French.

At a sign from him she rose, the train-bearers fell into place behind them and they stepped forward towards the Grand Throne. Together they climbed the first five steps and it was then that Josephine felt a distinct tug and a downward pull on her train. She stumbled, grasped at Bonaparte's arm and glanced round quickly.

"My *dear*," Bonaparte reproved her quietly.

"Your wretched sister Paulette, she and the others, with the exception of Hortense. . . ."

He understood instantly. Paulette, Caroline, Elisa and Julie, no longer even 'holding' the heavy train, had allowed it to drop over the foot of the Grand Throne.

"Paulette," he hissed sharply, "behave yourself!"

Steeling herself Josephine made a supreme effort and continued to mount the Grand Throne unaided. A cunning wretch, Paulette. However savagely Bonaparte might castigate her afterwards she would draw his attention to the length of the train and point out reasonably that neither she nor any of the other train-bearers was meant to mount the steps, and naturally she would deny, while the others supported her denial, that she had actually *tugged* at the train.

Breathing heavily and a little painfully Josephine endeavored to preserve a gracious and queenly bearing, and the enthronement ceremony concluded, she looked on hazily while the Pope kissed Bonaparte on the cheek and intoned the *Vivat Imperator in aeternum.* A herald sprang forward and in a loud and ringing voice cried:

"The most glorious and august Emperor Napoleon, Emperor of the French, consecrated and enthroned!"

Bonaparte gave her a little poke with his sceptre.

"Over at last," he whispered.

The return to the Tuileries was made in the early darkness of the winter's night. There was wild cheering from the people and the route was illuminated by the flickering, smoking light of ten thousand torches held bravely in the air by the mounted soldiers.

As they entered the Tuileries Bonaparte said: "Well, my little Empress, consecrated and enthroned, what do you think of your clever husband now?"

She laughed shakily. "I think he must be very hungry—the hungriest man in France."

* * * * *

It was eleven o'clock in the evening. The noise of a still-excited and still-delirious Paris rumbled like thunder about the Tuileries Palace, while within the building the laughter and somewhat intoxicated cries of the courtiers penetrated the sacred confines of the Imperial apartments where, at the Emperor's request, he and Josephine were taking supper alone.

"What a remarkable woman you are," Bonaparte said. "This must have been the most trying day in your life, and yet you still look radiant. Not a royal lady in Europe could have looked more regal than you looked today. You were grace and majesty personified."

Josephine inclined her head gravely. "Thank you, sire."

Her satisfaction was deeper than he could ever guess. His words were not those of a love-sick young man intent on flattering her; they were the words of a shrewd observer whose sharp eyes rarely missed the smallest detail, yet he had never suspected that an aching back and a throbbing head had weighed her down with a feeling of unutterable weariness. It was a greater triumph, surely, than her coronation itself.

"You look twenty-five today," he said, "I can scarcely believe that your true age is forty-two."

She thanked him again.

He raised his wineglass. "To the most radiant woman in the world."

She sighed happily and began to feel as radiant as he claimed she looked. Consecrated by the Pope, crowned by her husband the Emperor himself—what more could she now ask or expect of life, what greater guarantee of future happiness and security?

She raised her own wineglass. "To the kindest and most generous man in the world, the Emperor, Napoleon the First!"

CHAPTER XLI

WITH TWO *FEMMES DE chambre* in attendance, Josephine lay back in her bath and tried, after the exertion of rising, to find a little relaxation.

"The water is too cool," she complained. "Please heat it."

Two copper kettles were brought and the steaming water poured into the bath.

"For pity's sake do it *gradually*," she wailed. "Would you scald your Empress to death?"

The maids raising their eyebrows a little at her Majesty's tone, apologized and emptied the rest of the water more slowly into the bath.

"Forgive me," Josephine said contritely. "I am, as you see, a little out of temper this morning."

She had, now that she came to think of it, been a little out of temper much too frequently of late. Not that anyone could blame her, for the last nine months since the coronation had been a period of intensive, even hectic activity. Long before she had been allowed to recover from the celebrations, which had extended for weeks, she had been dragged by Bonaparte on the long and tiring journey to Milan for a second coronation, and back again at breakneck speed almost before she had had time to realize that in addition to being Empress of France she was now Queen of Italy. She squirmed uneasily in the bath. What a nightmare life was going to be if Bonaparte decided to reach out for the other thrones of Europe, one after the other!

A discreet little cough made her turn her head lazily.

"Ah, Madame de Rémusat," she said. "Good morning, my dear."

"Good morning, your Majesty. If your Majesty is ready——?"

"Very well, but I feel so comfortable here that I should like to lie in my bath all day."

Madame de Rémusat helped her out of the bath and the two *femmes de chambre* came forward with warm towels to dry the Imperial body. Then, with a thin silk wrap about her shoulders, she went to the boudoir. She shivered slightly.

"A very cold September this year," Madame de Rémusat suggested.

"Yes." She shivered again. "I think I shall dress this morning before attending to my face."

"Your Majesty is very wise. Would it be too indiscreet of me to suggest that your Majesty——"

"It would indeed," Josephine said firmly, well aware of what Madame de Rémusat had in mind. "If I were foolish enough to wear under-breeches in September I should be obliged to wear them for the rest of the winter. At the end of December, perhaps, but not before."

Save for an occasional involuntary grunt she was silent while the *femmes de chambre* laced up her corset, which she always wore next to her skin instead of over a chemise. Madame de Rémusat disapproved of this, she knew, but since she changed her chemise twice a day she preferred (except when she took a second bath in the late afternoon) to avoid the agony of a second corset-lacing in one day. She was silent, but her mind was busy trying to recall the name of the man who had said: *Only old ladies wear under-breeches; a young lady of fashion should be prepared to suffer a few draughts.* Tercier, Barras, Lacoste? Réal, perhaps, or even the pompous and fastidious Alexandre himself?

"Wait," she said, when the corset had been tightened as much as possible and the lawn chemise placed carefully over her head, "I shall be warm enough now."

She put on the wrap again and sat down at the dressing-table.

"M'sieur Deschamps is waiting," Madame de Rémusat told her. "Is your Majesty prepared to receive him *en deshabille*?"

"Good heavens, why not?"

"M'sieur Deschamps is new to your Majesty's service. I merely thought that if his Majesty were to enter, as he so often does, suddenly and unannounced——"

Josephine laughed drily. "The Emperor himself chose my new secretary. He chose him well. However bored I might feel, Deschamps would be less attractive to me than any eunuch."

Madame de Rémusat opened the door and Deschamps, carrying

a sheaf of papers and his writing materials, bustled in to take his place at the desk on the right of the dressing-table.

"What are my duties for today?" Josephine asked.

"His Majesty wishes you to proceed as usual," he told her. "There are no special duties for today, except, however—" he looked down his plump little nose—"the necessity of receiving Madame Mère at luncheon."

Josephine scowled. "Madame Mère, but none of the others, I sincerely hope!"

"None of the others, I assure your Majesty."

Her face cleared. "Madame Mère herself is almost harmless these days. How many people am I to expect in the audience chamber today?"

"Possibly twenty, your Majesty—including at least three—er—creditors."

She looked at him uneasily. "Merciful heavens, Deschamps, is it possible that my debts are mounting up again?"

The little man cleared his throat and tried to look stern.

"During the last nine months your Majesty has spent almost eight hundred thousand francs, which is three times the Imperial dress allowance for a full year."

Josephine turned imploringly to Madame de Rémusat. "I know nothing of arithmetic. How much money do I really owe?"

"More than half a million francs, your Majesty."

"Ah, then when it reaches a million I shall be forced to confide in his Majesty. His Majesty will then reduce the figure by half and the wretched tradespeople, knowing his habit and having provided against it with exorbitant profits, will be well content. To whom do I owe the largest amount?"

"The dressmakers, your Majesty, from whom your Majesty has purchased a matter of two hundred and forty dresses this year."

"Two hundred and forty? What utter nonsense. I swear I don't possess more than a dozen dresses at this moment."

"The majority of them, your Majesty, have been stored at Malmaison and Saint Cloud and have been—er—forgotten."

"Forgotten? I should hope so, since I looked a fright in most of them!"

"The next largest account," Deschamps went on, "is from the shoemaker. Your Majesty has purchased a matter of five hundred and twenty pairs of shoes, three hundred and thirty of which, happily, have been paid for."

"I see you have a list of my purchases there. Let me look at it."

Deschamps gave her the list. She glanced at it casually. *Twenty cashmere shawls, seventy-seven hats, sixty pairs of stockings, forty-*

eight rolls of cloth, fifty corsets, five hundred pairs of gloves. . . .
She grew weary of the list, which extended to the bottom of the long sheet, and threw it aside.

"I couldn't possibly have bought so many things," she said, as she reached for the rouge-pot. "Everybody is conspiring to rob me."

She leaned forward to the mirror suddenly and then withdrew just as suddenly in horror. The continual application of cosmetics over a period of twenty years was beginning to tell; the skin on her cheeks and beneath her chin had grown loose and flabby.

"Which dress will your Majesty wear this morning?" Madame de Rémusat asked.

"How many times have I worn the new yellow muslin?"

"Twice, your Majesty."

"Twice? Have I really? What a pity, but I think I like it enough to wear it just once more."

When Madame de Rémusat had helped her with the dress she surveyed herself thoughtfully in the long mirror. The basic design which had come into vogue during the Directory and, with minor alterations, had survived the Consulate was still plainly evident, though in this latest creation the drawstring at the high waist had been replaced with a long blue cord knotted a little to the left, the neck was square and the sleeves, reaching almost to the elbows, were a fraction longer. The hem at the front, embroidered in green, barely revealed her toes, while the train was the longest that had been worn this year with such a dress.

"I like the color," she said. "It seems to bring out the chestnut in my hair. My gloves, if you please, Madame de Rémusat."

Madame de Rémusat helped her with the long gloves, which reached above the elbows, and gave her the clean lace handkerchief without which she never ventured forth.

"Merciful heavens," Josephine cried, "we have quite forgotten my stockings and shoes. What a wretch you are, madame!"

The fine silk stockings, pink in color and so close fitting that garters were quite unnecessary, were carefully adjusted, the white velvet shoes were laced and the new cashmere shawl, which had cost ten thousand francs, was draped over the still graceful shoulders.

"Your Majesty is content?" Madame de Rémusat asked anxiously.

"Thank you, yes." She turned to the door. "And now—breakfast."

* * * * *

"Dear me," Josephine said, as she entered her sitting-room and caught sight of her daughter, "did I really invite you to breakfast?"

Hortense smiled faintly. "No, Mother. I took the liberty of inviting myself."

"Ah, then we shall take it tête-à-tête and have a pleasant little gossip. But I warn you, all I can offer you is thin bread and butter and an infusion of orange flowers. I must do *something* to keep myself from growing fat."

A lackey brought in the frugal meal on a silver tray.

"This new infusion," Josephine said, "is guaranteed to purify the blood, clear the skin and take pounds, literally *pounds,* off a poor woman's weight."

"Doesn't the Emperor ever take breakfast with you nowadays?" Hortense inquired.

"Very rarely, I'm thankful to say."

Bonaparte, during the last few weeks, had been extremely difficult to live with, and the less she saw of him the happier she was. At first she had feared that he was absorbed in a fresh love affair, but happily, as careful inquiry had revealed, all that was troubling him was his latest plan for the invasion of England.

Hortense, sipping with distended nostrils at the orange flower infusion, asked if there was any news of Eugene who, now that Bonaparte had made him Viceroy of Italy, was in residence in Milan.

"None," Josephine complained. "The wretched boy is either working too hard or spending too much time with the Italian signorinas to write to his lonely mother." She took up a third slice of bread and butter, gazed at it longingly and then put it down regretfully. "The children are well, I hope?"

"Napoleon-Charles has a slight cold but Napoleon-Louis is in excellent health."

Josephine cast a quick but penetrating glance at her daughter's figure.

"Are you by any chance—" she began.

Hortense, who still blushed easily, had gone red in the face under her mother's penetrating scrutiny.

"No, Mother. Nor am I likely to be."

"Dear me, I was under the impression that Louis was the most attentive of husbands these days."

"Then you can't have been paying as much attention to gossip as you usually do," Hortense said drily.

435

Josephine avoided her daughter's eyes. She had heard the numerous stories of Louis's unfaithfulness, but for her own peace of mind she had tried to ignore them.

"Whatever your more private relations with Louis might be," she said, "I was sure that you and he were at least friends."

"For a time we were friends, but apparently he has a conscience. The sight of me seems to infuriate him, and when I try to tell him, as I did again last night, that I am willing to tolerate his many love affairs, he flies into a temper. He even asked me last night if I was finding consolation in the same way myself."

"And are you?" Josephine asked curiously.

"*Mother!*"

"Well if you're not you are very silly. You must have many opportunities, and if I were in your position I would certainly take them."

"What a horrible thing to say, Mother."

Josephine shrugged impatiently. Not only Eugene, but Hortense also, was a puritan. It was enough, surely, to make poor Alexandre turn over in his grave.

"Ah, I remember," she cried suddenly. "It was Lacoste!"

"Lacoste?" Hortense asked blankly.

"Never mind," Josephine laughed. "It's a very old story and I doubt if you would appreciate it. But tell me one thing, do you wear under-breeches?"

"Why yes, Mother, I do."

"Does Louis know that you do?"

"I imagine so."

"Ah, then cease to wear them and your husband will come back to you without the slightest hesitation. You may laugh, but I give you my word. Without the *slightest* hesitation!"

* * * * *

The routine of Josephine's normal day at the Tuileries was divided into six distinct and now familiar sections—the morning *toilette*, breakfast (sometimes taken with Bonaparte, more often without him), the hour in the audience chamber, luncheon, the afternoon *toilette*, and dinner, the most formal meal of the Imperial day.

Having listened to a number of petitions, some of which she had granted on her own initiative and others she had promised to pass on 'to his Imperial Majesty, my husband,' and having distributed a matter of twenty thousand francs to people she suspected were less in need than she herself, she was now making her way to one of the smaller dining-rooms to preside at the luncheon table.

Since Bonaparte rarely took luncheon the meal, taken with her ladies and a few court idlers of her own choosing, was usually a leisurely affair with plenty of gossip and a few good stories from the obscene pages of the latest novel. Today, unhappily, with Madame Mère present to cast a blight over the one hour of the day to which Josephine looked forward, the meal would be short and the conversation nothing if not formal.

When she reached the dining-room she found seven people waiting for her—Madame Mère, looking ridiculous in a dress twenty years too young for her, Madame de Rémusat and two other ladies-in-waiting, Fouché, the Arch-chancellor Le Brun and Prudhon, the witty painter who was working at present on a new portrait of Bonaparte. She sighed regretfully. What a happy gathering it would be if only Madame Mère would fall suddenly ill and relieve them of her unwanted presence.

With a grim face she sat at the head of the table and rang the bell. The *Major-domo* made no move. She rang it again sharply.

"Napoléoné," said Madame Mère, refusing as usual to say 'His Majesty the Emperor,' "has announced that he will join us. We must therefore wait."

"It isn't often the Emperor who keeps us waiting," Fouché remarked, "but the Empress," and everybody, with the exception of Madame Mère, laughed half-heartedly.

Half an hour passed, passed without real conversation, before Bonaparte joined them. Everybody rose respectfully while he seated himself. As she sat down again Josephine noticed that his face was dark with anger. She thought instantly of her debts. Was it possible that the tradespeople had gone to him in a body to present their accounts? The soup came. Bonaparte tasted it and sent it back. The fish came, and though he scowled at it, it was allowed to remain. He had addressed himself to no one, he had looked at no one. Josephine shuddered. The atmosphere, accentuated by the deadly silence, was intense, and only Fouché, catching her eye, was brave enough to smile. How much had she spent? What was the figure Deschamps had quoted? Half a million? Or was it a million and a half?

Bonaparte pushed his plate aside. He had barely touched the fish.

"If it is your Majesty's pleasure," the *major-domo* began, tremblingly, "the duck has been cooked to a turn and——"

Bonaparte rose suddenly. "I want no more. You may clear the table."

He folded his arms and swept the faces which were turned anxiously up to him with a contemptuous glance.

"I suppose I may as well tell you my news. God knows it will be made public soon enough."

Josephine waited, holding her breath. It hardly seemed that the thing which was troubling him was her debts, but still, one never knew. She looked at his face anxiously, searching it.

"A coalition," he said, "has been formed against me. England, Russia, Sweden and Austria have joined forces. In their stupidity they challenge me, all four of them."

"Does this mean that the invasion of England will be delayed?" Fouché asked.

"It does. The Grand Army will be withdrawn from the coast immediately and will march to the Rhine. I have already drawn up a new campaign. First I shall subdue and conquer every state in Europe, then I shall turn on England. Europe first, then England."

"Do you intend to lead the Grand Army yourself, sire?" Le Brun asked.

"That is something which I have yet to decide, but whether I lead it or not my star is in the ascendant and my new campaign will be the most glorious in the history of the world."

With that he turned and strode from the room.

Josephine gave a deep sigh of relief. So that was all it was. Not her debts, but a new campaign. . . .

She signaled to the *major-domo*.

"The Emperor may not be hungry," she said, "but we, I feel sure, are ravenous."

$*$ $*$ $*$ $*$ $*$

While Josephine was busying herself with the afternoon *toilette* an order came from Bonaparte commanding her to prepare herself for a military banquet that night. She shrugged unconcernedly. She was well used, by now, to Bonaparte's sudden decisions, and while banquets, receptions and balls were the most important items on her list of duties as Empress, they were also the most pleasurable.

"I think," she told Madame de Rémusat, "that I shall wear the new pink tulle."

This dress, which had arrived from the dressmakers only that afternoon, was powdered with silver stars of varying size and was cut very low in the bodice. With it she wore a cluster of diamonds in her short, curly hair.

"Never," Madame de Rémusat enthused, "have I seen your Majesty look more beautiful."

Josephine nodded approvingly at her reflection in the mirror.

"I feel inclined to agree, madame," she said guilelessly.

A second message arrived at that moment from Bonaparte. His Majesty, the lackey informed her, had canceled the banquet. Her Majesty was to proceed to the Emperor's apartments at once and there take dinner with him alone.

"His Majesty," Madame de Rémusat laughed, "is as unpredictable as ever."

As Josephine entered Bonaparte's apartments he was giving an instruction to his valet, Constant.

"Inform M'm'selle Dénuelle of my decision," he was saying, "and make it clear to her that adequate provision will be made for her during my absence."

She saw then that Bonaparte was dressed in the simple uniform he wore when making a long journey, and that his cloak and sword were lying on a nearby chair.

"And who," she asked sweetly, when Constant had gone, "is M'm'selle Dénuelle?"

Bonaparte shrugged. "What! Gossip has not yet informed you of my latest *affaire*?" He looked at her with slight uneasiness. "You entered at an unfortunate moment. I sincerely trust that you don't propose to make me a scene."

"A scene," she laughed, "would be exhausting as well as futile. You like my new dress, I hope?"

He looked at her critically. "On a younger woman I would find it enchanting. The neckline is too low. It reveals the lines which are beginning to form on your chest. Be wise in future, my love, and wear a higher bodice."

She gave a little sniff. "What a cruel husband I have!"

"I merely draw your attention to the truth."

"And to the fact that you don't love me any more!"

"On the contrary, to the fact that I do, since the truth which stares me in the face in no way dismays me. All I ask of my Empress is that she shall be graceful, elegant and obedient. Graceful she will always be, but if she wishes to remain elegant she will wear higher bodices."

She fought back the tears which had come to her eyes.

"Are you going on a very long journey?" she asked.

"I am, and so, my dear, are you. We shall make a quick meal, you will change into a suitable traveling costume and, in an hour's time, will be *en route* with me for Strasbourg."

439

All the misery she had endured during the long journey to Milan and back flooded her mind.

"But I can't leave Paris," she protested. "Think of my duties at court."

"The court will follow us to Strasbourg. You will preside over it there during my absence with the army."

"But Bonaparte the journey will kill me!"

"No journey has killed you yet. You will have your precious smelling-salts and lavender-water to sustain you."

She began to cry as if her heart were broken.

"Kindly remember," he said coldly, "that of the three things I demand of you obedience is the most important." He laughed shortly. "Would you prefer me to leave you in Paris and take M'm'selle Dénuelle with me?"

"You beast!" she cried.

But an hour later, a few hastily packed trunks on the roof, she was seated in the swaying carriage with Bonaparte, holding a handkerchief soaked in lavender-water to her brow and a bottle of smelling-salts to her nose.

"The things I do for the Emperor of France," she wailed, "merciful heavens, the thing I do for him!"

CHAPTER XLII

THREE MONTHS HAD PASSED and the Imperial Court, presided over by Josephine, was now in temporary establishment at Munich where the Emperor's arrival was expected daily. Even Josephine, immersed in the festivities which surrounded her, and of which she was the gracious and elegant pivot, was deeply impressed by the military triumphs which Bonaparte had crowded into the three short months. The surrender of Ulm, the occupation of Vienna, the glorious victory at Austerlitz and now the treaty which Bonaparte was dictating so imperiously at Presburg. It was the first Italian campaign of General Bonaparte all over again, but on a grander and much more shattering scale. Only one thing troubled her. Having been hustled from Strasbourg to Munich, it seemed likely that she might now be hustled to Vienna.

Bonaparte's arrival in Munich was preceded, two days earlier, by the joint arrival of Joseph Bonaparte, who had been playing the soldier lately, and her son Eugene. Both, she learned, had been summoned to Munich by their Emperor, though neither had been acquainted with the reason for the summons. She was delighted to see Eugene, but the sight of Joseph, thankful as she was that he was the only Bonaparte present in Munich, filled her with misgiving. "Possibly I am growing old, or at all events tolerant," she confided in Eugene, "but all I desire now is to avoid trouble with my wretched relatives-in-law."

"Don't be silly, Mother," Eugene teased her. "Nothing gives your Majesty so much pleasure as a little encounter with them."

On the night of his arrival Bonaparte commanded Josephine, Eugene and Joseph to take dinner with him. Since no other members of the court were present Josephine suspected that a family conference was about to take place, and wondered anxiously how any decision that Bonaparte might be about to make could possibly concern both her old enemy Joseph and her son.

With characteristic abruptness Bonaparte came to the point without preamble.

"Eugene," he said, "it will interest you to know that I have found a wife for you."

Showing no surprise Eugene gave his stepfather a mild look. "I trust the lady in question is young and pretty, sire."

Bonaparte laughed pleasantly. "She is seventeen. She possesses a figure that would make your Imperial mother sick with envy. Her face, though not particularly beautiful, is lively and intelligent."

"And her name, sire?"

"Her name is Augusta. She is the daughter of the Elector of Bavaria."

Joseph Bonaparte, who had shown little interest until now, gave an exclamation of annoyance.

"Quite naturally," Josephine laughed, "his Imperial Highness, Prince Joseph, objects to a royal princess being chosen for my son."

"Has the Elector agreed to the marriage?" Eugene asked quietly.

"He has neither agreed nor disagreed. The Princess Augusta is apparently betrothed to Prince Charles of Baden, but I shall soon find some other girl for Prince Charles. Whatever the Elector may think at the moment he is hardly fool enough to refuse the honor of being allied by marriage with the Imperial Family of France."

"Strictly speaking," Joseph pointed out, with a deep frown, "Eugene is not a member of the Imperial Family."

"That, my dear Joseph," Bonaparte said, "can be remedied easily. I have made up my mind to adopt Eugene and to create him a Prince of the Empire. He will add 'Napoleon' to his name and become Prince Eugene-Napoleon of France."

In her delight at this Josephine almost clapped her hands like a child. She gave Joseph an impish look.

"Poor Joseph, how distressed he is at the thought of my son becoming a prince!"

"Not only distressed, but shocked," Joseph cried, *"deeply, shocked."*

"And half crazy with jealousy also, eh!" she teased him.

Joseph turned eagerly to Bonaparte. "Surely it is hardly necessary to adopt him."

"For political reasons it is more than necessary. My plan is to bind the kingdoms of Europe to my dynasty by as many marriages as possible with members of my family. Eugene, therefore, must become a legal member of the Imperial Family, and, by his marriage with the Princess Augusta, secure Bavaria for me."

"But think of the implications!" Joseph almost shouted. "As a legal member of the family Eugene will be admitted to the succession."

"Ah, you fear that after my death he might compete with the rest of the Bonapartes for the throne of France."

"And so he might!"

"Make your mind easy, Joseph. The decree of adoption will read something like this—" Bonaparte leaned back in his chair, his eyes half closed. "Yes, something like this—*We have determined to adopt as our son the Prince Eugene-Napoleon, Viceroy of our Kingdom of Italy. In no case or circumstance can our adoption authorize him or his heirs to make any pretensions to the throne of France, but we call him, after ourselves and our natural and legitimate children, to the throne of Italy.*"

"Merciful heavens," Josephine cried, "so my son may yet become the King of Italy!"

"Since I have no natural and legitimate children," Bonaparte said, broodingly, "only an early death will keep him from the throne of Italy."

"You must be mad," was all Joseph could say, "yes, mad!"

"So mad," Bonaparte smiled, "that I have decided to make you yourself a king, and not *some* day, but in the very near future."

"A king?" Josephine squealed. "Joseph a king?"

Joseph's anger had melted in a moment.

"King of where?" he demanded eagerly. "King of *where*?"

"Naples. I made up my mind some time ago that the Bourbons should relinquish the throne of Naples. If you act swiftly you should find it a simple matter to take possession of your new kingdom. My victory at Austerlitz has already shaken the Neapolitan Court to its very foundations. Once it is known that you have crossed the frontier with an army the Bourbons will flee for their lives."

"You—you want me to lead the army myself?"

"Yes, my valiant Joseph, but have no fears. At the most you will

442

be a mere figurehead. An experienced commander will be placed in charge of the campaign."

Bonaparte rose. "Come, Joseph, we shall discuss this matter at once, and fully."

When Bonaparte, with an excited Joseph following at his heels, had left the room Josephine laughed quietly.

"And so, at a wave of the hand, he creates kings and princes and decides the destinies of nations. I sometimes feel that I am living in a fairy story, really I do."

Eugene was silent.

"How bewildered you must feel," she said, watching his face narrowly.

Still he was silent.

"I know you may feel a little loath to marry a girl you have never even seen," she rushed on, "but think of the honor and the position that will be yours. I know that Hortense's marriage has been unhappy, but for you, a man, it will be quite different. If you don't succeed in falling in love with the Princess, or even if you do, you can always find yourself a good mistress and——"

"You talk too much, Mother," Eugene said quietly.

She saw that he was blushing, just as he always did when she spoke to him about such intimate things as love and marriage.

"My poor Eugene," she said, mischievously trying to embarrass him a little more, "is it possible that you are still a virgin?"

His blush deepened but with something of her own spirit he said: "I shall say neither yes nor no, Mother, but keep you in doubt."

"What a cruel boy you are," she cried. "You know there's nothing I should love more than a little gossip on the subject."

"Really," he protested faintly, "is nothing sacred to you, Mother?"

"Nothing," she chuckled. "But seriously, Eugene, if your innocence is as pronounced as I suspect there are many things I could tell you, many little hints I could give you, that might help you and the Princess to fall deeply in love with each other."

His embarrassment more evident than ever, Eugene rose hastily from the table. She sighed gently. Poor boy, what a handicap his reticence really was.

"For both your sakes," she said, "let us hope that the Princess, young as she is, is more experienced than you."

And with that, but very regretfully, she dismissed the subject from her mind. . . .

Bonaparte had said: "The man is pig-headed; he has refused to give his consent to the marriage between his daughter and Eugene; you must take a hand in the matter yourself." And so, fluttering her eyelashes a little and smiling her most gracious smile, Josephine was opening her campaign by making herself pleasant to Maximilian Joseph, Elector of Bavaria. He was a fussy little man, and middle-aged, but still she fluttered her eyelashes and still she smiled, and chatted, not without a hint of menace in her voice, about the growing and irresistible power of her husband, the Emperor.

When the interview was over she was able to report to Bonaparte that the reason for the Elector's pig-headedness was his wife, the Electress Caroline. She was a second wife and only the stepmother of the young Princess. The engagement which existed between the stepdaughter and Prince Charles of Baden had been brought about by the Electress, for the Prince was her brother.

"The poor Elector," she said, "is at least twenty years older than his wife and is clearly afraid of her."

"Send for her," Bonaparte commanded. "Reason with her. If necessary threaten her. Make it clear that it will be all the worse for Bavaria if she continues to flout the wishes of the Emperor Napoleon."

The Electress Caroline, Josephine decided, was twenty-nine or thirty years of age. A handsome woman with a mouth that was both bad-tempered and spoiled, she wore her clothes (obviously the latest Paris fashions to reach Bavaria) with an air of self-assurance, and she was inclined, Josephine suspected, to look down her long aristocratic nose at the regal pretensions of the Bonaparte family. The first thing she said, after making a condescending bow, was that she greatly admired the shawl which Josephine was wearing.

"I sometimes think it makes me look like a peasant," Josephine said, "but I assure you it cost almost ten thousand francs."

"Being cashmere," the Electress assured her, "it would be worth twice that amount in Bavaria. They are, of course, unobtainable here."

"I have several in Paris," Josephine murmured, "but unfortunately I only brought one with me, otherwise I would gladly have made you a present of it."

From shawls Josephine turned the conversation to dresses and hats, but the Electress, interested as she undoubtedly was, cut her short.

"I believe," she said, "that your Majesty has brought me here

444

for the purpose of discussing the proposed marriage between your son and my stepdaughter. Let me tell you at once that whatever you say the marriage will not eventuate. Augusta has been promised to my brother Charles, a fact which is well known to your husband the Emperor."

"Ah yes," Josephine laughed, "but my husband the Emperor, as you undoubtedly know, is——"

"Is accustomed," the Electress concluded for her, "to riding rough-shod over other people's feelings and would like, if he could, to sweep the engagement aside."

"Really, your Highness—" Josephine protested weakly.

"Emperor though he may be," the Electress said contemptuously, "he is nothing but a Corsican adventurer and shall not be allowed to interfere."

"Your Highness may change her mind," Josephine said softly, "if she forces that same Corsican adventurer to cross swords with her."

"I doubt it!"

"But consider the advantages of such a marriage," Josephine reasoned. "My son will soon be a Prince of the Empire. He is already the brother-in-law of several Imperial Princes, the uncle of the child who will some day be Emperor of France, the stepson of the present Emperor, and, on the death of this same Emperor, will be King of Italy."

The Electress smiled thinly. "I admit that the advantages are impressive—on the surface, but what guarantee can you give me that the Empire will endure and that the Bourbons will never return to France?"

Taken aback for a moment, Josephine could only nod dumbly when the Electress rose abruptly and asked permission to withdraw. A Corsican adventurer indeed! True as that might be it would hardly please poor Bonaparte when she told him. Surprisingly enough he merely laughed, and then grew reflective.

"Quite a woman of spirit, this Electress Caroline," he murmured.

"No, Bonaparte, merely unpardonably rude."

He laughed quietly. "Ah well, I have dealt successfully with unpardonably rude women before today. We have, I think, been dealing with her in the wrong way. It would have been better if I had interviewed her myself." The reflective look deepened. "Yes, much better. Let me see, you described her as handsome! A Corsican adventurer, am I? And why not where women like Caroline of Bavaria are concerned? Indeed, why not!"

"You actually intend to flirt with her?" Josephine asked uneasily.

"Flirt? Dear me no! The Elector is over fifty and could never have been a romantic figure. I am thirty-five and vigorous. I am also,

I think I may say without boasting, a *very* romantic figure. Flirt, did you say!" and he laughed coarsely.

"But, *sire*," Josephine cried, "the humiliation would be terrible. For me, I mean. I never object these days to your seducing actresses and women like that, but a woman of my own station! Besides," she added nastily, "you're not thirty-five, but nearly thirty-seven."

He tweaked her nose. "The *affaire* will be conducted discreetly, and please don't alarm yourself. It is not my intention to lose my head. It will be quite sufficient for my purpose if *she* loses hers."

During the next week Josephine learned that Bonaparte had sent the Electress expensive presents, including diamonds and furs which the Elector was much too poor to give her. "She melts a little," he reported. "I was permitted last night to kiss her once and fondle her a little." Josephine shuddered and recalled in alarm that the Electress was the possessor of two firm little pointed breasts.

Another week passed and Bonaparte gave a ball for the wretched creature. It was a very gay affair, but not for Josephine, who received the guests with a tight little smile and in speaking of the Electress to Eugene used one of the rudest words she had ever used in her life. "And as for Bonaparte . . . !" she muttered, searching her mind for another equally appropriate word in the male gender.

During the earlier part of the evening she watched Bonaparte covertly. In spite of his talk of discretion the exclusive attention he was paying the Electress was attracting considerable notice.

The look on his face reminded her painfully of the look that had been there when he had been first attracted by that singer, the George woman. As for the Electress, she was cool, exceedingly sure of herself, and tantalizingly aloof. There was no doubt about it, Bonaparte, in spite of what he had said, was perilously close to losing his head.

She turned as the Elector himself approached and greeted him with a stiff smile. His own smile was sickly and as he made spasmodic conversation, turning the while to look at his wife and Bonaparte, she felt the depth of his unhappiness. During an interval in the dancing, while a German woman sang a dreary song in a dreary mannish voice, Bonaparte came hastily to Josephine's side.

"My dear," he said, without a word or even a glance for the Elector, "give me your shawl."

"My shawl?" she echoed, for she was wearing it, partly because not another could be obtained in Bavaria, partly because she wanted to tantalize the Electress with it.

"Yes, yes," he said testily, "Caroline admires it and covets it more than anything else I could give her."

446

She clutched stubbornly at the shawl and turned to smile glassily as Eugene went by with the Princess Augusta on his arm.

"Come," Bonaparte commanded. "Do you give it to me or do I take it by force?"

"Sssst!" she hissed. "For a man who professes to love singing as much as you do your rudeness is deplorable."

He took one end of the shawl and twitched it sharply. She gave a little scream, but further resistance was useless. Besides, people were beginning to crane their necks and stare openly. A moment later she saw Bonaparte place the precious shawl about the Electress Caroline's shoulders with loving care. She also caught the woman's eyes and the sneering message they conveyed.

At her elbow the Elector cleared his throat and began to applaud half-heartedly as the German woman, her song finished, bowed drearily to the company. His face was pale and his smile more sickly than ever.

"Your Highness," she said, on a sudden inspiration, "are you by any chance perturbed by the conduct of your wife and my husband the Emperor?"

"Really, your Majesty, I—er—" he stammered.

"Answer my question!" she commanded in fierce whisper.

"To be perfectly frank, your Majesty, I am deeply perturbed."

"Ah!" She began to feel that there might be a little hope of success. "Do you wish to see yourself turned into a laughing-stock? Do you wish to set the people of Bavaria laughing behind your back and pointing the finger of scorn at you? Do you wish to be known as one of those weakling elderly husbands who, unable to exert even a little control over their wives, must always stand helplessly aside while a younger and stronger man takes what he fancies before passing on to a further adventure?"

The Elector, a flush staining his pale cheeks, looked deeply embarrassed.

"It is hardly possible," he stammered, "for me to challenge the Emperor of France to fight a duel."

"Of course not, but you can, if you wish, get the better of both the Emperor and a wilful wife by calling for silence and announcing to the company that my son Eugene and your daughter Augusta have become engaged."

He hesitated in alarm, but there was a promising gleam in his eyes.

"After which," Josephine went on, "you could take your wife to the country for a few weeks of quietness and rest. Better still, you could send her there alone, in disgrace."

"Yes, yes," he agreed, "I *could*, but bless my soul——"

"Which do you fear the most," she demanded. "The laughter of the people or your wife's temper?"

He took a deep breath and a hesitant step forward.

"Be strong, your Highness," she urged, "and the shrew will be tamed for the rest of her miserable life."

He took another deep breath, squared his shoulders and stepped forward boldly.

"Ladies and gentlemen!" he cried.

He made a short but quite charming speech to which Josephine, once the words 'engagement between her Highness my daughter and Eugene, prince-elect of the Imperial Family of France' had been uttered, paid no further attention. By the time he had finished she was standing, a graceful and elegant figure, at Bonaparte's side.

"I think," she murmured, "that we should congratulate the young lady's stepmother."

"You little fiend," Bonaparte grunted, but there was a twinkle in his eyes.

"My shawl, if you please," she smiled. "The night is a little chilly, don't you think?"

*　*　*　*　*

Lying wearily back in the Imperial carriage on the last lap of the return journey to Paris—they had traveled, she and Bonaparte, by way of Stuttgart and Carlsruhe—Josephine was listening, as she had listened so often during the long journey over well-nigh impassable winter roads, while Bonaparte, in high spirits, boasted of the increased power which his military genius and shrewdness had brought him.

They had left Paris towards the end of September; it was now the last week of January in what, Bonaparte said grandly, would be known to history as the Emperor Napoleon's glorious king-making year of eighteen hundred and six. Joseph was now firmly established on the throne of Naples; Eugene, his adopted son and a Prince of the Empire, was ruling Italy with wisdom and intelligence; Elisa was soon to be granted the sovereignty of Lucca, Massa Carrara and Garfagnana, and Paulette the sovereignty of Guastalla; the Confederation of the Rhine, with himself named Protector, was being brought firmly into being, and as for Holland——

"Holland?" Josephine questioned.

He chuckled and slapped her rug-covered knee. "I have a surprise for you in respect of Holland, a surprise, however, that will have to keep a little while longer."

Not only had Eugene been made a member of the Imperial Family, but also Stephanie de Beauharnais. Stephanie, a pretty child of seventeen, was the grand-daughter of Madame Fanny whose kindness in earlier years Josephine had never forgotten. In memory of this kindness Josephine had brought Stephanie to court once or twice but had never really taken a personal interest in her, and nor for that matter would Bonaparte have done so now, had his political schemes not made it necessary for him to find a wife for the jilted fiancé of Princess Augusta. "Stephanie," he had said, "is pretty, intelligent and an aristocrat. Summon her to Munich. I intend to adopt her, marry her to Prince Charles of Baden and so bind another German state to my Empire." Josephine would have protested a little, except for the thought that the elevation of another Beauharnais would infuriate the Bonapartes.

"Do you think that Eugene is happy with Augusta?" Bonaparte asked thoughtfully.

Josephine pondered for a moment. Before the wedding she had suffered a slight misgiving at seeing her son forced, like her daughter had been, into a marriage that might not bring him happiness. She had questioned him cautiously, and he had replied that he quite liked the girl and had added that in any case he knew his duty to his general and Emperor.

"Yes," she said confidently, "I feel sure that he is."

They reached Paris just before midnight on 25th January, and late as the hour was, and uncertain the day of their arrival, they found Hortense waiting to greet them. Josephine threw herself into her daughter's arms and burst into tears of happiness. Bonaparte himself was touched and with tears in his own eyes reproved Hortense gently for having taken so much trouble.

"It is more," he said, "than any of my own family would have done."

"Apparently!" Josephine remarked, "since Louis himself is absent. Where is your wretched husband, Hortense? Tucked warmly in his bed at the rue Victoire, I imagine!"

Hortense hesitated, distress plainly written on her face.

"By heaven," Bonaparte cried, "is it possible that he has left you again?"

Hortense nodded dumbly.

"Where is he?" Josephine demanded.

Hortense smiled faintly. "He complained of rheumatism and said he was going to Plombiéres to take the waters."

Bonaparte laughed shortly. In a moment all three were laughing, but not with very much humor.

"Louis's behavior," Josephine said, "is shameful. It always *has* been shameful."

"So shameful," Bonaparte said, "that if he were not necessary to my plans I would disown him immediately. However, since I need him in Paris he shall be brought back immediately."

"What are those plans, sire?" Josephine asked.

"You shall learn them in good time, I promise you!"

Curious as she was, Josephine soon forgot Louis in the resumption of her duties at the Tuileries, the first important one of which was her appearance, with Bonaparte, at the opera, where in honor of the victory of Austerlitz a grand performance had been organized. The composers, Stobelt and Esménard, had written a special cantata, which was to be preceded by an elaborate ballet representing the conquered nations of Europe.

The Imperial arrival at the Opera House set Bonaparte rubbing his hands and brought a quiet smile of triumph to Josephine's lips. The audience leaped to its feet, waved laurel branches and cheered deafeningly. Without pausing to dwell on the thought that the cheering would have been less enthusiastic if Bonaparte had suffered a recent defeat, she told herself that she was the happiest woman in the world. Before the curtain rose she caught sight of Fouché, who was a member of the Imperial party, and beckoned him to join her.

"Fouché," she cried, "what a pleasure it is to see you after all these months!"

She smiled as he bowed before her.

"I hear," she said, "that his Majesty my husband has decided to raise you to the peerage."

"Why, yes. I am to be created duc d'Otrante."

"Splendid!"

"I seem," he chuckled, "to have drawn a reasonably good prize in the Imperial lottery."

She smiled again. What a delight it was going to be to give him the full story of the Electress Caroline, and how he would chuckle and compliment her on the recovery of the cashmere shawl!

"And what new intrigue have you on hand at the moment?" she demanded.

He gave her a look that made her heart miss a beat.

"A very grave one," he said. "An intrigue, I fear, that is a direct threat to your personal happiness, an intrigue that may well result in the end of your Majesty's short reign as Empress of France."

Part Six
Finale

Realizing that she had been biting her nails, a thing she had never done in her life before, Josephine glanced impatiently at the clock. Fouché, unable to say more at the opera last night, had promised to present himself at the Tuileries at midday and it was still only five minutes to twelve. *An intrigue that may well mean the end of your short reign as Empress.* . . . The words, sometimes jumbled but always menacing, had been running through her mind ever since Fouché had uttered them. It could hardly concern the Bonapartes, for only Madame Mère and Jerome were in Paris, and Jerome, who had never lifted a finger against her, was soon to go to Wirtemburg to marry the Princess Catherine. "If Fouché is having some nasty little joke with me," she told herself viciously, "I shall never forgive him!"

The door opened. Josephine leaped to her feet.

"His Excellency the Minister of Police," Madame de Rémusat announced.

"Excellency?" Josephine barked. *"Why Excellency?"*

Fouché smiled cynically. "In respect of your gallant husband one might say, His Majesty—why his Majesty?"

Before he could sit on the chair she silently offered him she was demanding an explanation for the remark he had made the night before.

"It was a dreadful thing to say," she wailed. "For pity's sake put my mind at ease and tell me that whatever you meant you were exaggerating."

"Forgive me, your Majesty," he said gravely, "but there was no exaggeration."

"Then explain yourself, in heaven's name explain yourself!"

451

He looked at her steadily. "The matter is so exceedingly delicate that I hardly know how to begin."

"Delicacy has never rendered you speechless before," she cried, wanting to take him by the shoulders and shake him.

"What," Fouché asked, "would make the Emperor Napoleon the happiest man in the world?"

"The conquest of England, perhaps?"

"Dear me, no. Something much simpler than that."

Josephine clutched at her heart. Her voice came in a faint whisper. "A—a son of his own?"

"Precisely, a son of his own." Fouché took a slip of paper from an inner pocket and gave it to her. "This is a copy of a birth certificate. Read it."

With trembling fingers and a palpitating heart she took the paper and read the few words scribbled on it.

Léon, son of Alienor Dénuelle, spinster of independent means. Father unknown.

Dénuelle, Dénuelle. . . . Where had she heard that name before? Suddenly she remembered the night Bonaparte had announced that she was to leave Paris within an hour for Strasbourg, and the instructions he had been giving his valet, Constant, when she had entered the room. *Inform M'm'selle Dénuelle of my decision; make it clear to her that adequate provision will be made for her during my absence.*

"Your Majesty will note," Fouché said, "that the child's name is Léon, an obvious contraction of Napoleon."

"Are you suggesting," she asked miserably, "that the father is Bonaparte?"

"It seems quite possible. The girl was his mistress. She has now given birth to a male child whom she has called Léon."

"None of his other mistresses ever gave birth to a child. That was why I have always believed him to be sterile, why he has always believed it himself. Tell me about the girl. Surely she has had other lovers. Bonaparte rarely expects a casual mistress to be faithful to him. The child could easily be some other man's."

"M'm'selle Dénuelle assures me that she was utterly faithful."

"You've seen her? Talked to her?"

Fouché bowed ironically. "In guarding your Majesty's interests I judged it necessary to do both. If what she says is true, and I am inclined to believe that it is, the Emperor will realize——"

"Stop!" Josephine shouted, "for pity's sake stop!"

If it were true, and Bonaparte was satisfied that it was, he would realize that divorce and remarriage with one of the many princesses of Europe would give him the thing he wanted most, a legitimate son of his own to follow him on the Imperial throne. Not that she would ever agree to a divorce, which, now that she had been married to him again before the altar, would be difficult in any case. Nevertheless, with a man like Bonaparte, a man who overthrew ancient thrones and set up new kings of his own choosing, a man who made his own laws . . . !

"Does Bonaparte know about the birth of this child?" she asked suddenly.

"Apparently not."

"What of Constant?"

"Constant knows, but for your Majesty's sake he has agreed to make no mention of it until the girl herself comes forward."

"That was kind of Constant."

Now that she had recovered a little from the first shock of the discovery Josephine was searching her mind for a plan. Though Bonaparte had made provision for the girl he had probably forgotten her completely by now, and with Constant remaining silent it was just possible, if one acted quickly enough, that she might never be brought to Bonaparte's attention again.

"Do you think the girl can be bribed?" she asked.

"That will probably depend on the amount your Majesty is prepared to offer her."

"You shall take me to her then. In any case I want to see the child for myself."

"In the hope, of course, that he bears no resemblance to the Emperor?"

"You think he does?" Josephine cried.

Fouché rose. "Your Majesty, the child Léon is absurdly like the man whom I believe to be his father."

* * * * *

"Rheumatism!" Bonaparte cried. "Really, Louis, do you expect me to believe a story as stupid as that?"

Louis scowled. "No more than I expected Hortense to believe it, but it happens to be true."

Louis, who had returned to Paris that afternoon, was dining with Hortense and Madame Mère at the Tuileries. Josephine, having greeted him coldly, had ignored him during the progress of the meal. Indeed, preoccupied with the story which Fouché had told her earlier that day, she had ignored the others also and had done little but stare in misery at the various dishes which were placed before her and then taken away untouched.

"Louis," Madame Mère boomed, "has been suffering from rheumatism for several months now and has, I regret to say, received little sympathy from his wife."

"But plenty," Josephine roused herself sufficiently to say, "from the mistress he took with him to Plombiéres."

"I hold little brief for immorality," Madame Mère said, "but when a man is married to a Beauharnais. . . ."

She shrugged and left the rest of the sentence unfinished.

"Madame Mère," Bonaparte said, staring fixedly at his mother, "how old are you?"

"What a strange question, Napoléoné. You surely know my age quite well."

"I do, Madame Mère, but I begin to think that you yourself have forgotten it. Look at your dress. Look at its bodice, which is lower than Josephine's. Look at the girlish bows and flowers on the skirt and the feathers in your hair. You should remember the dignity of your position as the mother of an Emperor and wear clothes suited to your age."

Josephine forgot her misery for a moment and giggled.

Bonaparte rang the bell and told the *major-domo* when he entered to have the fire built up. While two lackeys were doing this he smiled about him pleasantly, his eyes coming to rest on his mother's bare arms.

"You may all think the room overwarm as it is, but at all costs we must see that Madame Mère is prevented from catching cold."

When the fire had been made up he reached out, selected a large nut and began to crack it.

"Madame Mère," he said, "from your words just now I gather that you are willing to condone Louis's unfaithfulness, not out of a sense of tolerance, but because Hortense is Josephine's daughter."

"Whatever my reason," she replied, "unfaithfulness is not considered a very great crime in France today. Committing it frequently yourself you have made it quite the fashion."

"Unfaithfulness," Louis laughed, "is the accepted thing among the men of my station in the world."

"You remind me of my first husband," Josephine told him. "He said much the same, but I think he lived to regret it."

Louis bowed over his plate. "Your Majesty is pleased to threaten me."

"Your first husband," Madame Mère said, "had more than one thing in common with Louis. They were both married to women they did not love, married to them through no fault of their own.

Your late aunt, I believe, arranged your first marriage, just as you, in your turn, arranged your daughter's marriage. In each case the object was the same. It——"

"No no, Mother," Louis broke in. "The object was not the same. In the case of Josephine's aunt it was an attempt to rescue a colonial niece from poverty; in Josephine's case it was an attempt to secure herself from divorce. She was successful, I grant you, but whether or not she will save her *daughter* from divorce is another matter."

"Louis!" Bonaparte, having flung his chair back violently, was on his feet. "Are you suggesting that I might permit you to petition the courts for a divorce from Hortense?"

Louis rose quickly but with less violence.

"Hortense and I," he said, "have never been really happy together. Our marriage has been as great a failure as Josephine's marriage with the Vicomte de Beauharnais was. The only sensible thing for us to do is admit it frankly and seek release from each other in divorce."

"Your words suggest that you speak for Hortense as well."

"I—I hope I speak for her as well."

Bonaparte turned to Hortense. "Do you want to free yourself of my brother?"

"If I spoke for myself alone," Hortense said quietly, "I would say yes, but in duty to you, the Emperor, I have only one wish, and that is to please and obey you."

"At the sacrifice of your own happiness, Hortense?"

"Part of that happiness was sacrificed long ago, sire."

Hortense spoke quietly. There was no hint of rancor in her voice, and when she caught her mother's eye she smiled reassuringly and with affection. With a pang of self-reproach Josephine remembered what Hortense had said when agreeing, after all Aunt Marie had done to turn her against it, to marry Louis. *If I can make up a little for the unhappiness you knew with the man who was my father. . . .* A fine and noble creature, this daughter of hers, a child to be proud of. . . . And yet, if the divorce which she had long ago thought impossible was brought about by the birth of the Dénuelle woman's child, what a waste Hortense's sacrifice had been.

"Only part of your happiness?" Bonaparte questioned.

Hortense smiled gently. "I found another happiness in my children, sire, a happiness that can never be sacrificed, whatever Louis may decide to do."

"The children are Louis's too," Josephine said. "Surely he can find a happiness in them as great and unselfish as your own."

Louis stirred uneasily. "Please don't try to move me to the sort of sentiment that is admirable only in a woman."

Bonaparte, with his love of family, was shocked, but a moment later the look on his face turned to one of anger.

"Louis," he said, "I shall never permit you to divorce Hortense."

"In that case," Louis cried, "I shall leave France; I shall go gladly into voluntary exile."

And with that he turned and went quickly from the room.

*　　*　　*　　*　　*

"A fine little chap, don't you think?" Fouché remarked.

Josephine, staring intently at the baby which M'm'selle Dénuelle held in her arms, was sure that she was going to faint. She raised her arm weakly and threw aside the heavy veil.

"Ah, as I suspected," the girl laughed. "Her Majesty the Empress."

Josephine had chosen a time for her visit when Bonaparte was known to be deeply occupied with a military conference. She had worn a heavy veil and a plain drab walking costume, not with the intention of deceiving the girl, but to keep her Imperial identity a secret from the passers-by in the street.

"I was not aware," she said mildly, "that you had ever been presented at court."

"And nor have I, but I was once a member of the Princess Caroline's household and saw your Majesty there on several occasions."

"Ah, so it was there that you met the Emperor."

"Yes."

Josephine gave the girl a searching glance. She was as pretty as her name, but just a little bit common—the sort of person, in short, that a Bonaparte female, common herself, would include in her household. Her glance dropped from the mother's face to the child's. There was no mistaking the resemblance to Bonaparte. As Fouché had said, the child was absurdly like him.

"A chair, Fouché," she wailed, "for pity's sake get me a chair."

He pushed one forward and she sank into it with a sigh.

"Please, Fouché," she said weakly, "confer with M'm'selle Dénuelle, on my behalf."

"Gladly, your Majesty."

"Confer?" the girl echoed.

"My dear Alienor," Fouché said, "for very private and personal reasons the Empress wishes the birth of your child and his resemblance to the Emperor to be kept a closely guarded secret."

"I can well imagine that!" M'm'selle Dénuelle chuckled.

"Under the circumstances,". Fouché continued, "which to say the least are embarrassing, her Majesty would be grateful if you could be persuaded to remain silent."

"That is impossible, m'sieur. It would be unthinkable to keep the news from him. After all—" she smiled broadly at Josephine—"his Majesty's first-born child, and more gratifying still, a son——"

"I quite understand how you feel," Josephine said acidly, "but when you consider that grave political complications might arise and——"

"Nothing will persuade me to keep silent, your Majesty."

"Not even a little monetary reimbursement?" Fouché murmured.

"Are you trying to insult me, m'sieur?"

"Oh, come, my dear," he laughed, "be a good girl and tell us the price of your silence."

"We are prepared," Josephine said, "to offer you a hundred thousand francs in instalments of ten thousand francs a month."

The girl laughed easily. "Your Majesty must be joking. Only a hundred thousand for the suppression of such momentous news? Only a hundred thousand when your Majesty must spend at least a million each year on clothes alone? Assuredly your Majesty must be joking."

"You have some figure of your own in mind?" Fouché asked.

"Yes. Not a hundred thousand merely, but a pension of that amount. I could live handsomely, I think, on a hundred thousand francs a year."

"Merciful heavens!" Josephine exclaimed.

"Outrageous," Fouché laughed.

"That is the price of my silence, m'sieur. You may consider it for a few days, if you wish, but unless you agree within a week I shall go to the Tuileries and take my son with me. The Emperor, I feel sure, will be glad to welcome us."

*　　*　　*　　*　　*

Josephine and Bonaparte were visiting Hortense and Louis, and Bonaparte, to Josephine's surprise after the last meeting with Louis, had been in high spirits when he had said: "Come, my dear, I want to call on that difficult brother of mine." He had kissed Hortense affectionately on the cheek and then, turning to his brother, had embraced him warmly.

"We have called this afternoon," Bonaparte said, "for a very special reason."

"I can see nothing 'special,'" Louis said tartly, "in what is obvi-

457

ously a good-humored attempt to talk me out of petitioning for a divorce."

Bonaparte smiled happily. "Ah, but wait, Louis."

He looked about the room and selecting the most comfortable chair settled himself deeply into it.

"No ceremony, please," he begged. "Be seated, all of you."

Louis bowed Josephine grimly to a chair, but leaving Hortense to find one for herself remained standing himself. Forgetting for the moment the more personal problem facing her—the problem of finding the ridiculous sum of a hundred thousand francs a year for Alienor Dénuelle, Josephine sat on the edge of her chair and waited anxiously for Bonaparte to continue.

"Louis," he said at last, "at the military banquet last night you met the Dutch Minister Extraordinary, Rear-Admiral Verhuell."

"I did, but what concern is the rear-admiral of mine?"

"Verhuell has come to Paris for a very special purpose. You are no very great soldier, Louis, and I doubt if either your Maker or I could turn you into one, but I think you realize that the defense of our northern border depends largely, nay entirely, on the security of Holland."

"Even a child would realize that," Josephine said sweetly.

Bonaparte smiled and nodded. "Now the security of Holland lies largely in the sympathies of the Dutch Government. That is, whether that Government is sympathetic to England or to France."

"Under the present circumstances," Louis said drily, "the Dutch Government has little choice in the matter."

"Granted, but there is, nonetheless, a strong English party in Holland. However, to return to Rear-Admiral Verhuell. Fearing an invasion from England he has come to Paris with the request that I shall exercise my influence in the coming election of the new Grand Pensionary. You see my drift, Louis?"

"I'm afraid I don't."

"Your Majesty," Josephine squealed, "is not thinking of making Louis Grand Pensionary of Holland, surely!"

"Indeed, no." He paused and chuckled. "And for the simple reason that no Grand Pensionary will be elected." He chuckled again. "Verhuell, while seeking my intervention, has been charged to resist my possible desire to establish in Holland an hereditary monarchy, and that, I might tell you all, is precisely what I do intend to establish. You see my drift now, Louis?"

Louis jumped to his feet in sudden excitement. "Great heavens, Napoleon, you—you mean you propose to make me King of Holland?"

"Yes, my dear Louis, King of Holland." He turned to Josephine

458

with a broad smile. "You look startled, my dear. You disapprove of the idea, perhaps?"

"We-ell——"

"Surely it pleases you to think of your daughter becoming a queen?"

"We-ell, yes," she said, with little enthusiasm.

"But hardly," Louis laughed, "at the expense of seeing me, a hated Bonaparte, a king?"

"You misjudge me, Louis," Josephine said lamely. "It will give me great pleasure to see you King of Holland."

"You understand, of course," Bonaparte went on, "that if you go to Holland, Hortense goes with you. A King-elect, you must put all thought of divorce or separation from your mind."

"Let me ask you a question," Louis said, "before giving my decision. Are you sure that the Dutch Government can be made to agree?"

Bonaparte rubbed his hands together and laughed happily. "The Dutch Government has already been presented with an ultimatum. Holland shall either be annexed to my Empire and occupied, or set up as an independent monarchy with you on the throne. We know quite well which choice the Dutch will make."

"One more question, Napoleon. What will you do if I refuse to go to Holland?"

"I shall send Hortense there in your place, making her a queen with all the rights and privileges of a king."

Louis flushed and leaped angrily to his feet.

"I take it, Louis," Bonaparte murmured, "that you are ready to accept the throne of Holland?"

"Yes," Louis said shortly, "quite ready."

*   *   *   *   *

"Why not sell some of your jewelry?" Fouché suggested.

Josephine shook her head. "Bonaparte would miss it instantly. He has the memory of an elephant and the eyes of a hawk."

"Two very pretty similes," Fouché laughed.

They were discussing the ways and means of raising the hundred thousand francs a year which Alienor Dénuelle had demanded. Only one day remained of the time allowed for consideration, and Josephine could still see no possibility of raising the money.

"A hundred thousand francs," Fouché remarked, "is a very small sum when one considers the amount your Majesty generally fritters away in a single year. Why not try a little economy?"

"I economize enough as it is in an attempt to meet my debts. Deschamps told me only this morning that I owed over a million francs."

"Oh, come, my dear Josephine, try to be serious. Try to remember that this may mean the loss of your throne."

"I'm not so sure that it may," Josephine said thoughtfully.

"If you are counting on the Emperor being moved by the opposition of the Pope and the Church you are badly underestimating his character."

"You beast, Fouché!" she snapped.

"Why not borrow the money?"

"Borrow it? But from whom? Tell me that. From whom?"

"From me, your Majesty—at a modest rate of ten per cent."

"You Shylock, Fouché!" she screamed.

"Oh, come, do you expect me to lend my money interest free? Any other man taking such a risk would ask twenty per cent."

"Risk? What risk is there? I am, remember, the Empress of France!"

"Assuming, then, that there is no risk," he chuckled, "how will you pay me back, and when?"

Josephine sniffed and put her handkerchief to her eyes, but for once the tears, good reason though she had for weeping, refused to come with their accustomed readiness.

"What a pitiful object I am," she wailed. "An Empress, yes, but an Empress without one true friend in the world."

There was a knock at the door and Madame de Rémusat entered. She came quickly to Josephine's side and whispered in her ear that she brought a message of great importance from the Emperor's valet.

"You may speak freely before Fouché," Josephine said.

"Very well, your Majesty. M'sieur Constant wishes your Majesty to know that a person by the name of Dénuelle has just been admitted to the Emperor's apartments."

Josephine sprang to her feet, ran stumblingly to the head of the secret stairway that led to Bonaparte's apartments and clattered down it. The door at the bottom, as she quickly discovered when she tore at the handle, was locked. She began to hammer at it with clenched fists. No movement or sound came in response except the sudden crying of a baby. Josephine continued to hammer on the door with renewed vigor. A moment later it was flung open and Bonaparte, the baby in his arms, stood glowering at her.

"I suppose you may as well come in," he said. "Otherwise you will begin to kick and scream."

With a sidelong glance at the puckered face of the baby, she slid past Bonaparte and came face to face with a smug-looking self-satisfied Alienor Dénuelle.

"So this," Josephine cried, resisting a strong temptation to slap the wretched girl's face, "is how you keep your word!"

"The Emperor sent for me," Alienor said pertly, "otherwise I would have waited another two days."

Bonaparte called sharply for silence, and began to pace the room with the baby in his arms. He jiggled it up and down, he cuddled it against his chest, he even began to soothe it with ridiculous crowing noises. Sick at heart Josephine averted her eyes.

"There!" he cried, when the child began to chortle.

He came on tip-toe to Josephine's side.

"My son," he said emotionally, "my son. And a fine, strong little fellow, by heaven!"

With an unwilling gesture he gave the child to Alienor.

"You must go now," he said, "but you shall hear from me again presently. You will, of course, receive a substantial pension."

When the girl had gone he began softly to pace the room. His eyes were sparkling and his face, usually so pale, was flushed with excitement. "My son," he kept murmuring, "my son." Finally he came to Josephine and took her hands in his.

"So we were wrong," he said. "The fault *was* yours."

Speechless, she stared at him in misery.

"It was wrong of you to attempt to bribe Alienor and wrong of her to bargain with you. I can only thank God that I intervened in time."

"Tell me one thing," Josephine said brokenly, "did you know before we left for Strasbourg that M'm'selle Dénuelle was to have a child?"

"Oh yes, I knew."

She began to take hope. "And yet you said nothing of it to me?"

He laughed drily. "I knew my Alienor. I was not her only lover, and not being in love with her, I did not expect her to practice faithfulness. That the child should be mine seemed only a remote possibility, but now, having seen him— Oh, Josephine, to have a son of my own after all these years, you can't understand how happy it makes me."

"The resemblance," she said weakly, "could be a coincidence."

"Nonsense. The Bonaparte features have been propagated too strongly for that. The child is mine. Anyone who sees him will be forced to admit it, just as you are forced to."

Unable to stand longer Josephine collapsed into a chair.

"The girl said you sent for her," she managed to say. "What made you do that?"

461

"I had always intended to see the child, but when I found that you had been to visit her I began to suspect that he might be mine after all."

"How did you know of my visit?"

"My dear Josephine, am I a fool? Ever since you became Empress a special watch has been kept on you. Oh, come, you needn't scowl. The watch is kept as a means of guarding you against a possible assassin."

"I see."

She was silent for a moment; then, with fear in her heart, she asked him what he was going to do.

"At the moment, nothing," he said. "Military affairs are so pressing that I shall soon find it necessary to leave Paris again. When I return you shall learn my wishes."

"You—you don't intend to take me with you this time?"

"No."

She rose and flung herself into his arms.

"Take me with you," she begged. "Please take me with you!"

He shook his head. "I know what you have in mind. You fear that if I go alone, thus freeing myself of the sight of your misery, I might come to a decision that will hurt you."

She nodded her head dumbly.

"Come," he said, "you must go back to your apartments."

She clung to him, still without weeping, but he freed himself gently.

"Try to remember," he joked, "that you are still the Empress of France, and that, for all we know, I might die on the field of battle."

The next day, when she crept down the secret stairway, she found workmen in Bonaparte's apartments. They were taking measurements and making calculations in preparation for removing the bottom doorway and replacing it with a solid wall of bricks.

CHAPTER XLIV

IT WAS SIX MONTHS BEfore Bonaparte left France to lead the Grand Army against the Prussian forces. So great was his kindliness during this period that Josephine's anxiety faded and she began to tell herself once again that nothing would ever menace her security. He liquidated her debts without a murmur, he even increased her allowance, and never once did he refer to Alienor Dénuelle and her child, both of whom, Josephine learned from Fouché, had been sent from Paris to live quietly in retirement in a country village the name of which even Fouché was unable to discover.

Nevertheless the wall which had been erected against her remained, not only as an unsurmountable barrier, but as a warning, had she heeded it, that her feeling of security was both false and vain. And the summons to the Imperial bedchamber for which she waited timorously was never issued.

To the best of her ability she obeyed the injunction to be graceful, elegant and obedient, but though her life as Empress of France was a long succession of the receptions and banquets dear to her heart, and the numberless conferences with dressmakers, milliners and jewelers even dearer to that same feminine heart, there were times when boredom overcame her with a greater force than ever before. Eugene was at Milan, Hortense, now Queen of Holland, was at The Hague, and only one Bonaparte, Madame Mère, was in Paris, refusing, despite Josephine's many attempts to force the issue, to enter into any new engagement. With nothing better to do she, who had always hated letter-writing, wrote long letters to Hortense whose presence she was beginning to miss with a sincerity she had never felt before.

When Bonaparte finally left France she tried to engross herself in military matters and followed his progress, probably for the first time in her life, with genuine interest. With each new victory she organized an elaborate celebration, and when news came of his triumphant entry of Berlin she went in state to Notre Dame. His victories in Poland, the taking of Warsaw and the driving back of the Russians, she took little notice of, for news had reached her privately that he was lingering over-long in Poland because he had fallen deeply in love with Marie Walewska, the wife of an elderly Polish count. It was no passing infatuation, she discovered, when shamelessly questioning an army officer who had returned to Paris on a military mission, but an obsession the romance of which was affecting and inspiring the whole army.

"He first saw her," the man told Josephine, "while changing horses at Bronia. She approached Marshal Duroc and asked if she could speak to the Emperor."

"Why, the forward hussy!"

"A very great Polish patriot, she merely wanted to thank his Majesty for liberating her country."

"A pretty ruse, I must say!"

"His Majesty was deeply touched and gave her a large bouquet which some deputation or other had presented to him."

"And then, no doubt, he invited her to get into his carriage!"

"The Emperor, your Majesty, was on horseback."

Later she learned more details from Fouché, who told her that the countess was eighteen and that a ball had been given in her honor in Warsaw. So familiar was she with Bonaparte that she was calling him Napoleon, even on formal occasions. According to one story Bonaparte was spending a holiday alone with her at a little château near Finkenstein, and it was common knowledge that he had written her a series of passionate love letters.

"It would almost seem," Fouché murmured, "that at last the Emperor has found a woman attractive enough to menace your own hitherto unrivaled possession of his heart."

"Really, Fouché, is it necessary to gloat over my unhappy position!"

Josephine wrote to Bonaparte soon after this asking him to permit her to travel as far as Berlin and from there, if he was still in Poland, to join him at Warsaw. She dispatched the letter by special courier. Bonaparte replied that the season was cold, the roads worse than ever and pointed out tartly that at her age the fatigue of so long a journey would undoubtedly kill her. In short, he told her, none too kindly, that she must remain in Paris and endeavor to be as graceful, elegant and beautiful as she had always been. *All my life,* the letter concluded, *I have sacrificed everything, including tranquility and personal happiness, to my destiny; you, my dear Josephine, must be prepared to do the same yourself.* This brought back her old fears, and also the suspicion that Bonaparte was planning to dispose of the elderly Count Walewska as a prelude to marrying the eighteen-year-old countess.

"Oh, Fouché," she moaned, for Fouché was always at her side these days, "what is there left for me to live for!"

"Probably a great deal more than you think," he said heartlessly.

"But what, Fouché, *what!*"

"You have your children, Eugene, Viceroy of Italy; Hortense, Queen of Holland. And you have your grandchildren. Napoleon-Charles, remember, is still the Emperor's choice as heir-presumptive."

This was something she had forgotten, and reminded of it she began to feel more cheerful. In the existence of this little heir-presumptive, whom Bonaparte loved to distraction, it was surely possible to find an assurance of personal security. She was still dwelling with satisfaction on this thought when, in the second week of May, news came from The Hague that Napoleon-Charles, suffering a severe attack of croup, had been too weak to recover.

Grief-stricken and sure that Napoleon-Charles's death would hasten any plans Bonaparte might have for divorce, Josephine hurried north to Laeken where Hortense, coming south with Louis and the little Napoleon-Louis, was waiting to meet her. The change in Hortense was pitiful, and though Louis showed her a surprising and touching kindness, she appeared to be inconsolable.

"She must come back to Paris with me," Josephine said, and without hesitation Louis agreed.

In Paris the doctors advised a complete change of air for Hortense, and so, while Napoleon-Louis remained at Saint Cloud with Josephine, Hortense, without a murmur of protest or any sign of enthusiasm, allowed herself to be sent to take the waters at Cauterets.

On 17th July, while Hortense was still at Cauterets, Bonaparte, with very little warning, appeared dramatically at Saint Cloud at six o'clock in the morning. Since he refrained from waking her, Josephine knew nothing of his arrival until four hours later when an *aide-de-camp* came to her apartments with an order that the Empress should rise and take breakfast with the Emperor at eleven.

She found Bonaparte's manner cold. He embraced her, certainly, but with no more warmth than he would have embraced a distant cousin. He spoke briefly of Napoleon-Charles's death, saying that it was one of the greatest blows he had ever received. This subject of conversation exhausted, he fell silent and began to eat his breakfast with an air of embarrassment.

"What a change I see in you," Josephine said sadly.

"A change? Ah yes, everybody tells me that I am growing stouter."

"The change I see has nothing to do with your appearance."

"Indeed, madame?"

She gave a low, stricken cry. "Oh, Bonaparte, after an absence of eleven months you call me 'Madame,' the word you always used to use when you were displeased with me. The change is terrible. Please make no attempt to deny it."

"Very well. I make no attempt to deny it."

"You no longer love me. That is the truth of the matter. You no longer love me!"

He rose from the table with a deep sigh.

"I admit," he said, "that I have changed in the past few months, that my love for you has changed also, but it is still here in my heart, a fire that will never be entirely quenched."

"Then this Marie Walewska hasn't really come between us? She was just a passing distraction, like so many others?"

"She was a great deal more than that, Josephine, and she still is."

Josephine clutched at her throat. "You say—is?"

"Next to you, as you were in those early days when you fascinated me and tried me beyond endurance, Marie is the greatest love of my life."

Josephine made a wild gesture with her hands. "Oh, Bonaparte, if only I had the strength to hate you!"

"Such strength will never be given you," he said sadly. "I wish with all my heart it could be. If you could find it in your heart to hate me my way would be made easier. And yet, in the end, the sacrifice will have to be made. It would be made now if I were not so great a coward."

"The sacrifice?" she asked faintly. "What sacrifice?"

"You know what I mean, even though you try to hide it from yourself. In a letter I told you that all my life I had sacrificed everything, including tranquility and personal happiness, to my destiny—to my great and terrible destiny. In the end her Imperial Majesty, Josephine, Empress of France, will be called upon to do the same."

* * * * *

"Had you noticed," Josephine said, as Madame de Rémusat attended her at a late morning *toilette*, "that there are streaks of grey in my hair?"

"Only a few, your Majesty," Madame de Rémusat said soothingly.

"Nonsense, there are so many that even the Emperor, rarely as he looks at me these days, must have noticed them."

It was no wonder, of course, that her splendid chestnut hair was beginning to turn grey. It was now the beginning of May, 1808, over nine months since Bonaparte had returned from his last campaign. Many things had happened in that time. Hortense, pregnant apparently at the time of Napoleon-Charles's death, had returned to Holland and given birth to a third son, Louis-Napoleon, and was, according to her letters, on better terms with her husband than she had ever been; Murat had led an army to Madrid, the Royal House of Spain had been deposed and Joseph, recalled from Naples—the throne of which had been given to Murat—had been set up as King of Spain; Marie Walewska had given birth to a son, thus making Bonaparte the father of two illegitimate children, and— But why, thought Josephine wearily, recapitulate these things, important as they were, when she still languished miserably under the shadow of divorce?

Bonaparte, for some reason best known to himself, had made no further reference to his great and terrible destiny. The actual word divorce had never passed between them, though at the Tuileries and among the members of the Government it was a continual topic of conversation.

"If I reach the inevitable decision at all," Bonaparte had said once, "it will be because events are greater than you and I and what little happiness we have found together in the past."

And again he had said: "Josephine, Marie's child should have been yours. He should have been yours and mine, our direct, natural and legitimate heir."

He had also said: "It is a great grief, not only to me, but to France, that I possess no legitimate son to follow me on the throne, and never will possess one while you remain my wife."

In October, when she could endure the suspense no longer, Josephine brought matters to a climax herself. She had learned from Fouché that that arch-intriguer, Talleyrand, was urging Bonaparte to give serious consideration to divorce on the plea that the Bonaparte dynasty would never endure unless Bonaparte were followed by a direct heir. Rashly and hysterically she challenged Bonaparte with this. He told her gravely that what Talleyrand had suggested was something which he had felt for many years himself.

"Josephine," he said, avoiding her eyes, "if my marriage to someone else becomes an unavoidable political necessity you must be brave—braver than you are now, braver than you have ever been—and come to my assistance."

"What do you mean by that?"

"You must give me all the help you can; you must give me the strength I need to make a sacrifice which will mean as much to me as to you. If such a thing ever comes to pass—and I warn you that there is every sign that it will—I want to count on your friendship to support me in the unhappy course of my duty."

"I don't understand what you are trying to say," she said stubbornly.

He looked at her with undeniable misery in his eyes. "When divorce becomes a necessity I want you to have the courage to decide upon a voluntary retirement."

She felt anger and indignation rising in her breast. Unable to make up his own mind he wanted her to make it up for him. More, he wanted her to make what he would call a patriotic gesture and agree to the divorce herself—to place herself in the wrong, even, and give him a legitimate reason for setting her aside.

"Your Majesty," she said quietly, "is the master. You and you alone shall decide my fate. If you order me to leave the Tuileries I shall obey at once. If you decide to divorce me I shall submit without resistance, but I shall never actually show myself to be in agreement with you. In the meantime, I am your wife, married to you before the altar, crowned by your own hands in the presence of the Pope. Divorce me if you must, sire, but if you do, all France shall know that it is you and you alone who drive me away."

Bonaparte laughed uneasily. "I really begin to fear you, Josephine, when you attack me with words instead of tears."

"You talk of your dynasty enduring," she went on, pressing her advantage, "but if you set me aside it will perish overnight. I am the star you often talk about, the woman whose presence at your side has brought you victory after victory. Marriage with me, remember, gave you your first important command, the command of the Army of Italy. Marriage with me inspired you to make the most of that command. Marriage with me enabled you to set up the Consular Court. Oh yes, I am your star. Set me aside and your good fortune, even your ability to plan shrewdly, will desert you. Set me aside, sire, and for you it will be the beginning of the end."

"This is nonsense you talk and you know it," he said harshly.

She repressed a smile. She could see that his uneasiness had increased. He was a Corsican and all Corsicans were superstitious. It had been inspiration to attack him in this manner, sheer inspiration!

"You must drive me away yourself," she said. "I will never go unless you do."

"Is that your final word, madame?"

"Yes."

He made a hesitant gesture with his hand, turned to leave the room, then paused. His manner, when he spoke again, was almost humble.

"Until I make up my mind," he said, "I should appreciate it if you would try your best to be happy and gay. Paris must know nothing of the struggle that is going on within me, must never catch us with long faces. During the next few months there will be more banquets and receptions than ever before. Paris is swarming with illustrious visitors. The world is at my feet. My court, Josephine, must have the appearance of a happy court. I—I look to you to set a fine example."

With dignity she said: "I will do my best, sire."

"You—er—you have my permission to spend a quarter of a million francs on new dresses and jewelry."

"Thank you."

"Above all," he said, trying pathetically to work up a show of anger, "no tears in public, or in private either, if you wish to please me. Be the gay and gracious Josephine who has always captivated my heart and then, perhaps, we might both forget for a while the terrible sword that hangs over our heads."

She laughed triumphantly when he had gone. She had, she felt, got the upper hand of him, and by being wise and remaining calm she would do her utmost to retain the upper hand. . . .

The next afternoon Fouché waited on her. His reason for requesting an audience, he said gravely, was one of the utmost political importance. She sensed at once that he had been sent by Bonaparte, but making no comment she invited him to proceed. He bowed and came to the point at once.

"I am here," he said smoothly, "to discuss the divorce."

"You come on your own initiative, or at my husband's command?"

"Let us say, your Majesty, that I come in the capacity of a private individual."

"If I were not a lady," she snapped, "I would thrust out my tongue at you, but being a lady I will content myself with telling you to mind your own business."

"Ah, but the divorce of the Empress of France is *my* business, just as it is the business of every loyal Frenchman."

"You must be mad," she cried hotly. "Since when has it been the business of every loyal Frenchman to interfere in my private affairs?"

"A woman in your Majesty's position," he said oracularly, "is not entitled to private affairs. She is, in a manner of speaking, a public servant."

"Merciful heavens, Fouché, how *dare* you!"

He laughed gently. "Pardon my bluntness, but that is exactly what your Majesty is, a public servant—a servant of the state whose every action must be directed towards the good of the Empire as a whole."

"I see your drift," she said contemptuously. "You want to tell me that I can serve the Empire by submitting to divorce."

"Precisely, your Majesty."

"And I thought you were my friend!" she raged. "Not, of course, that I have never been warned. I should have known from the first day I met you that you are entirely without principles, that for a little profit you would sell your soul, always providing you have a soul!"

"Let us say frankly that I would sell it," he said coolly, "whether I have one or not. But to continue. Whatever you may think or do, the consolidation of the new dynasty demands that the Emperor shall possess a son, even several sons. As you know his Majesty is unwilling to divorce you without your freely given consent. Therefore, in loyalty to the Throne, in loyalty to your husband himself, it is your duty to petition the Senate to join you in urging him to make the most painful sacrifice which his heart could ever be called upon to make."

Josephine clapped her hands. "A very long and touching speech, Fouché, but you will never convince me that it was spontaneous and entirely your own composition."

She rose and took him by the hand. She gave him a little tug as if he were a disobedient child.

"Come, Bonaparte will be waiting anxiously to know how much

success you have met with. Shall we go to him together and tell him how lamentably you have failed?"

He freed his hand with an effort.

"Spare the poor man a scene, my dear. Failure was anticipated. As he would tell you himself if you were to burst in on him now, your lack of sympathy and understanding are about to force his hand."

"You mean—?" She clutched at her throat and could say no more.

"I mean that his Majesty has made up his mind. With or without your co-operation he will now proceed to divorce you."

* * * * *

Josephine, half lying on the floor and clutching frenziedly at Bonaparte's knees, was weeping bitterly. Her resolution to be wise and calm had been swept aside. Bonaparte was afraid of her tears, had always been afraid of them. It had been madness to present him with any other form of argument, sheer madness. And yet, weeping because she wanted to weep, because there was nothing else to do, the tears she shed were the most sincere she had ever shed in her life.

He reached down and lifted her to her feet.

"Is this the behavior of a grown woman," he asked gently, "of a gracious and elegant Empress?"

She flung her arms round his neck and clung to him with all her strength. She knew she had no hope of moving him, but as sure as there was a God in heaven she was determined to make him suffer.

"Whatever my behavior," she sobbed brokenly, "I know only one thing, that I love you."

He freed himself with difficulty and made her sit in a chair.

"God," he whispered, in a voice that quivered, "what a scene for a tragedy, what a scene for the dramatists of the future."

She held back her tears for a moment.

"This much is certain," she said darkly, "the dramatists of the future will never have a greater villain to write about than the Emperor Napoleon."

He fell on his knees in front of her and took her hands in his. Her heart exulted at the sight of the tears in his own eyes.

"I love you, Josephine," he said. "I shall always love you. That is why it breaks my heart to set you aside."

"And what of *my* heart? Do you care nothing for it? Of course you don't! You care more for the wretched throne than you do for me."

"In politics," he said miserably, "a man must obey his head, not his heart. He must obey his head or fail. He must be single-minded or give up the struggle. Divorce you as I must I shall never forget you, and I shall treat you handsomely. I intend you to remain an Empress in your own right. You shall have Malmaison, and Saint Cloud as well, if you want it. Your allowance in retirement shall be five million francs a year."

"Give me the whole world and my lot will be no easier to bear. Money!" she burst out—"you seem to think that I care for nothing else."

He smiled faintly. "I know what it means to you, just as I also know that with five million francs a year you will still fall rapidly into debt."

"What a poor opinion you have of me," she wailed.

"Say rather what a *good* opinion. I long ago realized that money itself means nothing to you. You never knew the value of it. To you it is just a token with which to buy things. Buying, that is your sole pleasure. Buying, not even possessing."

Scarcely listening she said suddenly: "His Holiness the Pope will never give his consent to the divorce."

Bonaparte chuckled. "The Pope's power is at an end. I may as well tell you now what the whole world will know in a few weeks' time. His Holiness and I have rarely seen eye to eye. For many years now the Vatican has opposed me secretly, intriguing against me in Italy and in Spain. When the truth is told nobody will blame me for what I have done."

"What have you done, Bonaparte?"

"My forces have occupied the papal territory. Rome itself has been incorporated within my Empire and declared my second city. As for Pope Pius the Seventh, he is now my prisoner, held under guard at the Vatican."

Josephine gave a little cry of horror. Irreligious as she was, hating church-going as she did, she had never been the atheist that Bonaparte so obviously was. It made her flesh creep to think what would happen to him when he died.

"His Holiness," she whispered, "will surely excommunicate you."

"His Holiness has already excommunicated me."

"And—and it doesn't make you tremble in mortal fear?"

He laughed harshly and sprang to his feet.

"Nothing will ever make me do that!" he cried.

"Poor Bonaparte," she said in awe, "I shall have to spend the rest of my life praying for your soul."

He clapped his hands on her shoulders and gazed at her affectionately.

"Do so by all means," he said—"if it will give you a little happiness."

"I shall also pray for myself," she said soberly, "for my own life has not been entirely free of sin."

He tweaked her nose in the old playful way, an action which brought the tears to her eyes again and a lump to her throat.

"My dear little fraud," he said sagely, "there are greater sins in the world than sexual unfaithfulness. In my mind the petty little meannesses of human nature are deadlier sins than wantonness."

She took up her already sodden handkerchief and mopped her eyes with it.

"In that case," she said, "I have always been a very virtuous woman." A happy thought struck her and her eyes narrowed. "Without the Pope's consent the divorce will be a purely civil affair. In the eyes of the Church I shall remain your wife and the woman you marry will never be more than your concubine."

He shook his head. "In order to satisfy my religious subjects I have provided for that. In the name of the Church, Cardinal Fesch, our worthy Archbishop of Lyons, has agreed to sanction divorce."

A silence fell between them. She began to sob again, convulsively.

"Shall I call your ladies," he asked hurriedly, "and have them help you back to your apartments?"

She made an effort to control herself. "No, I—I would rather find my way there alone."

She rose uncertainly to her feet and staggered. He caught her quickly in his arms. Half supporting, half embracing her he said:

"Never forget that you will always be my best-loved friend."

She asked him for his handkerchief. He gave it to her and she blew her nose delicately.

"Sire," she said, in a low voice, "now that the end has come I want you to know that I am ready to do the only thing you have left me the power to do for you. I—I will go voluntarily into retirement. I—" she choked for a moment—"I will express myself in full agreement with divorce."

He thanked her gravely. With a suspicion of a twinkle in his eyes he said: "In anticipation of this I have already prepared the speech of renunciation which you will be called upon to make."

"Why you beast!" she cried. "You beast to be so sure of me!"

"Sure of you or not I was determined that this sacrifice shall bring you honor. France will grieve for you, France will sympathize with you, and France will honor you."

"And then," she said brokenly, "France will forget me."

✳   ✳   ✳   ✳   ✳

With an unaccustomed briskness Josephine concluded the shortest *toilette* she had ever made in her life and turned to smile faintly at her daughter's look of amazement. Hortense, like Eugene, had been summoned to Paris for the divorce. "You must have your children at your side," Bonaparte had said, "and afterwards they shall accompany you to Malmaison and remain with you as long as you wish."

"Why do you stare at me?" Josephine asked.

"I was only wondering if you knew that you had forgotten your rouge."

Josephine chuckled softly. "This is the one occasion in my life when I want to look pale. Tragic and heartbroken though I am, would I look it with rouge on my face? For the same reason my dress is white and very plain and I am wearing no jewelry. I assure you, Hortense, my renunciation shall remain in the memory of those who witness it for the rest of their lives. It is even possible that the wretched Bonapartes themselves will feel sorry for me."

The ceremony, which was to take place in a few moments, was to be conducted in the Throne Room before the Arch-chancellor and the Secretary of State for the Imperial Household, and in the presence of Madame Mère, Louis, Paulette, Caroline and her husband and Jerome. It was dreadful to think that so many of her enemies would be there to witness her defeat, but a blessing that the worst of them, Joseph and Lucien, would be absent. And after all, gloat as they undoubtedly would, it would irk them to know that she was to retain her rank and title and enjoy a pension greater than any single one of them would ever enjoy.

There was a light tap at the door and Eugene entered the room. Josephine looked with satisfaction at his pale, drawn face. It was splendid to have a son who felt his mother's sorrow as much as she felt it herself.

"The whole palace is blazing with light," he said indignantly. "Is it necessary to celebrate tonight's tragic ceremony as if it were a great military victory?"

"Bonaparte is very fond of pomp and circumstance," Josephine said soothingly. "His greatest grief, I feel sure, will be the fact that when he dies he will be deprived of the pleasure of supervising his own funeral."

She saw Eugene glance at Hortense with a shocked expression on his face. He thought, of course, that she was being unnecessarily flippant. In the distance a clock began to chime.

473

"Nine o'clock," she said, "come, children. Bonaparte will only be angry if I keep him waiting."

She entered the Throne Room with Eugene on her right and Hortense on her left. She saw Madame Mère, Louis, Paulette, Caroline and Jerome. All were in full court dress, and as usual the Bonaparte women looked cheap and overdressed. Each one of them bowed but was careful not to catch her eye. Bonaparte was nowhere to be seen, nor the Arch-chancellor, nor the Secretary of State. Louis came forward and informed her in a quiet voice that the Emperor had changed his mind and now wished the ceremony to take place in his study. She inclined her head graciously and led the way from the Throne Room.

In the study Bonaparte's secretary led them each in turn to the chairs which had been arranged in strict order of precedence. Bonaparte was already seated. His face was pale, his hands were clasped tightly in front of him, and he glanced at nobody. The secretary bowed before Josephine and gave her the paper on which her speech had been written. For a moment there was a tense silence, with everybody looking uncomfortably at the floor. The Arch-chancellor and the Secretary of State entered the room. The silence continued. Bonaparte tried to break it twice, failed miserably each time and grew paler. Finally he leaped to his feet with an exclamation of impatience. He addressed himself solely to the Arch-chancellor.

"This sacrifice which I am now about to make, formally and officially, is one which costs my heart dear, but one, unhappily, which I am obliged to make for the welfare of my beloved France."

He faltered, cleared his throat and continued.

"In this moment of sadness, a moment which will extend till the day I die, I can rejoice in the affection and tenderness of my well-loved wife. The memory of the fifteen years during which she has graced my life will remain forever stamped upon my heart."

Josephine's eyes filled with tears. It was play-acting, but play-acting at its best, sincere and heartfelt. A haze enveloped her. The faces about her changed and became those of the registrar, Barras, Teresia Tallien and all the old friends who had been present fifteen years ago at the civil marriage of Citizen General Bonaparte and Citizeness Beauharnais. *You're a very fortunate man,* she could hear Barras saying, and Bonaparte replying: *And a happy one too.*

Dimly she could hear Bonaparte the Emperor continuing his speech.

"She was crowned by my hand. I myself will never deprive her of that crown. It is my wish that she shall retain the rank and title of Empress. But above all else it is my desire that she shall never doubt my feelings and will remember me always as her dearest friend."

He sat down abruptly. "I have nothing more to say."

There was a great deal of throat clearing. Paulette, Josephine saw, was scowling down at the carpet and biting her bottom lip, and two large tears were rolling down Madame Mère's cheeks, giving the old lady so comical a look that one had difficulty in suppressing a giggle.

The Arch-chancellor leaned forward anxiously.

"If your Majesty is ready—" he faltered.

"Of course," she said brightly, "you want me to read my speech." She rose and stared at the crumpled paper in her hand.

"With the permission of our august spouse," she read, "our august and dear spouse, I declare that since I have now no hope of bearing children, it is my pleasure to give him the greatest proof of my attachment and devotion."

The haze enveloped her again. The words on the paper became hopelessly jumbled. *"You're a very fortunate man,"* the next sentence seemed to read, and that, surely, was not correct. She closed her eyes for a moment while the words straightened themselves out.

"I owe all to his bounty," she continued. "It was his hand that crowned me and seated me on this throne. I——"

Something came up in her throat, choking her. The paper fell from her fingers.

"I can read no more," she gasped.

At a sign from Bonaparte the Secretary of State took up the paper and began to complete the speech for her.

"I, the Empress Josephine, willingly urge the dissolution of a marriage which is now an obstacle to the welfare of France and deprives her of being ruled one day by the descendants of the man who, by the will of providence, replaced the ill-effects of revolution with throne, altar and social order. . . ."

She heard little more. The voice, she believed, continued, but the words were too distorted for her to follow them. And yet, though she knew the tears were rolling down her cheeks, she felt amazingly calm and even smiled when, for the first time, Bonaparte's eyes met hers. *The Empress Josephine*— Who in the name of heaven was the Empress Josephine? Marie-Joseph-Rose—Rose—Yeyette—*they* were all familiar names, but Josephine—no, she had never heard the name in her life before.

∗   ∗   ∗   ∗   ∗

The rooms in the Tuileries apartments of her Imperial Majesty the Empress Josephine were bare and empty. Everything had been dismantled. Every piece of furniture had been removed. Every single article of clothing had been packed into a well-nigh endless succession of trunks and portmanteaux which had been loaded on to a veritable cavalcade of carriages. The outer door had been locked, the key laid on the Emperor's desk. And yet, despite all this, a voice still echoed in the ghostliness of the deserted rooms.

I say farewell to this palace, which is no longer my home. . . .

I look upon these apartments, which are no longer mine, for the last time. . . .

And while the voice echoed round the bare walls those members of the court who had assembled sorrowfully in the courtyard of the palace to watch the departure of their Empress could still hear the hoof-beats of the receding cavalcade now raising the dust on the road to Malmaison.

"It puts me in mind of a funeral procession," said one.

"Yes, a funeral procession," another agreed, "but whose funeral, think you—the Empress Josephine's or the Emperor Napoleon's?"

CHAPTER XLV

JOSEPHINE REACHED MALmaison in the late afternoon of the day following her Act of Renunciation. The heavy rain, which had developed during the journey from Paris, and the early December dusk gave the place a gloomy look. She stared through the carriage window at the dripping branches in the drive. She stared, and shuddered. Once she had taken pride in Malmaison and had gaily expended several fortunes on its maintenance; now she hated the sight of it and felt that if she were condemned to live in permanent retirement here she would fall into an immediate decline and die within a year. She looked at Eugene and Hortense sitting silently opposite her.

"A graveyard," she said tragically. "That is Malmaison, a graveyard in which I, as well as all my hopes and dreams, will soon be buried."

Asking Eugene to superintend the unloading of the carriages, she retired at once to her apartments, dismissed Madame de Rémusat the moment she was undressed, refused to take food—"the smallest

476

mouthful would choke me!"—and threw herself face down on her bed with the curtains drawn tightly about it. She was, she told herself, too desolate even to find relief in tears. In any case, she thought gloomily, what was the sense in weeping with no audience to witness the tears. . . .

Later in the evening Hortense tapped lightly on the door and came hesitantly into the room. Peering through the curtains, which she opened slightly, she saw that her daughter was carrying a tray containing a bowl of steaming soup and some delicately prepared sandwiches. Her nostrils twitched. From its aroma the soup was evidently seasoned with garlic.

She closed the curtains sternly.

"Take it away," she cried, "for pity's sake take it away."

There was a silence.

"Are you still there?" she asked.

"Yes, Mother. Eugene and I are very worried about you. Please try to take a little nourishment."

"Never, unless you want to kill me!"

A moment later she heard the door close but the smell of the soup remained. Her nostrils twitched again. Her tongue felt large and dry in her mouth and her stomach woefully empty. She parted the curtains cautiously. Hortense had gone, certainly, but there, on a little table near the bed, was the tray with its steaming bowl and tempting sandwiches. She sprang out of bed, flew to the door and shot home the bolt. After all, if one were going to die it would be foolish to do so on an empty stomach. To die on an empty stomach would only give one a pinched look in one's coffin. She took up a spoon and sipped at the soup. It was a little cool, but still palatable. She lifted the top slice of a sandwich. Chicken, by the look of it. She laughed grimly.

"I can eat as much as I like now," she said aloud, "and never worry whether it makes me fat or not."

The next morning, when Madame de Rémusat woke her from a deep sleep by beating frantically at the barred door, she felt amazingly refreshed. The day was cold but the sun was shining and a few birds could be heard twittering bravely outside the window.

"We were all very concerned when we found the door barred," Madame de Rémusat told her.

"Ah," Josephine said solemnly, "you thought I had killed myself. Let me confess at once that the thought *was* in my mind, but as I lay awake during the long hours of the night, struggling with myself, I came to realize that suicide would be cowardly."

Hortense had followed Madame de Rémusat into the room. Josephine glanced guiltily at the tray with its empty soup bowl and plate.

"I shall dress at once," she said quickly, "and take a walk in the park."

Hortense, looking with a faint smile at the plate, told her mother that a message had come a few moments ago from his Majesty, who was spending a week or two at the little palace of Trianon, and proposed to ride over in the early afternoon for an informal visit. Josephine felt a thrill of excitement, but she frowned heavily.

"What a cruel man he is. Not content with breaking my heart he wants to see that it remains broken."

Resigned as she was now beginning to feel, she resolved that when he came he should find her pale, tear-stained and pitifully broken in spirit. Accordingly she arrayed herself in a simple black dress, wore no jewelry save a single string of pearls and refrained once again from putting rouge on her face.

When Bonaparte arrived, attended by only two *aides-de-camp*, he found her sitting alone on a seat in the Japanese garden. She rose slowly when he approached and stood forlornly before him. With satisfaction she took note of his air of embarrassment. He carried a shawl over his arm.

"Hortense told me that you had ventured out without sufficient clothing," he said. "This is a winter's day. Do you want to kill yourself?"

Having been determined to force tears in her eyes, she was gratified to find that they came unbidden. Her heart, after all, was as tender and loving as ever.

"Why have you come?" she asked sadly. "Does it really give you pleasure to torture me?"

He placed the shawl roughly about her shoulders.

"My dear," he said brusquely, "black is the worst possible color you could ever wear. Without rouge it makes you look ghastly."

"I care nothing for my appearance—" ('Pig,' she thought, 'nasty Corsican pig!')—"nothing whatever."

"Nonsense," he said. "You left the rouge off your face and dressed yourself in black simply to make me feel more wretched than I already am."

"Pig!" she cried.

"Ah, that's better. Much better!"

"I see no reason why I shouldn't look, as well as feel, unhappy and heartbroken."

"Dear little Josephine," he said sadly, "there isn't another woman in the world like you."

"I should hope not!"

He offered her his arm. "Shall we take a little stroll?"

"If your Majesty wishes it."

478

They moved forward slowly, and for a while in silence.

"Next time I see you," he said, "I expect you to be in a white dress, with enough rouge on your face to hide your raddled cheeks. At the moment you look your age, *more* than your age."

She freed her arm and stamped her foot angrily. Tears sprang to her eyes again, tears of vexation.

"What a beast you are, Bonaparte! And how I pity the poor woman you decide to marry."

He grasped her arm again and impelled her forward at a brisk pace.

"There are certain financial matters that we ought to discuss," he said.

"Financial matters! As if I could bring myself to talk of money when all I want to do is hide my head in sorrow from the world."

"As far as I gather," he went on, "the Senate will be glad to grant you two million francs a year. I myself will add a million from my own funds. You should be able to manage very well on three million francs a year."

"Unless my memory is playing me tricks," she said sharply, "you promised me five million. What a fool I was to trust you. I might have known that once you had disposed of me you would break your word."

He chuckled happily. "Dear Josephine, every word you utter makes my misery a little less hard to bear. In giving you three million I am well aware that you will spend at least five, and that I shall have to pay off the creditors for you. Had I given you five outright you would have spent seven."

"What nonsense!" she cried. "Life will never be sufficiently interesting again for me to get into debt."

"We shall see," he murmured, "undoubtedly we shall see. And now, your present debts. Tell me how much you owe and I will see what can be done about it."

"I shall have to ask my secretary. I couldn't possibly tell you the exact amount off-hand."

"Very well. Have a complete list prepared and send it to me. Better still, come and dine with me at the Trianon a week from today and bring it with you."

"Dine with you? But would that be proper?"

"You have no wish to dine with me?"

She smiled frankly. "Of course I have and as often as possible."

"Then today week, and bring Hortense and Eugene with you, just to prevent the people from making a scandal of our dining together."

The moment Bonaparte had gone Josephine sent for Eugene and

asked him what he knew of the Emperor's plans to make a second marriage. When Eugene, plainly shocked, showed himself reluctant to discuss the matter she told him sharply that her love for Bonaparte was strong enough to make her regard the inevitable second marriage with a disinterested calmness.

"If it is humanly possible," she said, "I want to ensure that he chooses wisely."

"You actually propose to interfere?"

"Help," she said coldly, "was the word I had in mind."

Eugene shrugged his shoulders helplessly, and told her then that Bonaparte had already approached the Tsar of Russia, asking for the hand of the Grand Duchess Catherine. On the list he had drawn up were also the names of the Grand Duchess Anne, and the Archduchess Marie Louise of Austria.

"My own choice," Josephine said promptly, "would be Marie Louise. In any case I feel sure that the Tsar, a recent enemy who has every reason to hate Bonaparte, will never give his consent."

"The same might be said of the Emperor of Austria."

"Moscow is much farther from Paris than Vienna. Austria, therefore, has more to fear than Russia. If a little pressure is brought to bear the Emperor will soon be made to give his consent."

"And you yourself propose to bring that pressure to bear?"

"Of course not, Eugene. I shall simply content myself with a discreet and diplomatic approach. Send a message to the Austrian Ambassador. Tell him that I should be grateful and honored if he would dine with me on Saturday night."

She thought of all she knew of Marie Louise. An attractive girl, she was young, seventeen or eighteen at the most, and had led an exceedingly sheltered life. She knew nothing of life at court, and though she could speak French she was ignorant of French habits and would be lost, utterly lost, in Paris. Once married to Marie Louise, Bonaparte would be forced to call upon a woman of experience to instruct and help his young foreign wife in her exacting duties as Empress.

"In short," Josephine chuckled, while Eugene stared at her blankly, "he would be forced to call on me, and the Paris which I love with all my heart would be forbidden to me no longer!"

*   *   *   *   *

Dinner was over at the Trianon, Eugene and Hortense had been dismissed on a flimsy pretext and Josephine was alone with Bonaparte. Having resolved to make him see how miserable she was by eating nothing—or at the most merely picking at the food—she had ended, so tempting were the dishes laid before her, by making a very hearty meal. "Malmaison is good for you," Bonaparte had murmured; "it has given you an excellent appetite," and then he had thanked her for wearing a white dress and putting "a whole pot of rouge" on her face.

"Have you brought the list of debts I asked for?" he said presently.

She shook her head. "I forgot it at the last moment but I can tell you the exact amount."

"Amazing," he laughed. "What *is* the exact amount?"

"One million nine hundred thousand francs," she said boldly.

Staggered for a moment, he shrugged philosophically and laughed.

"Of course the tradespeople have robbed you, as usual," he said. "The figure shall be reduced by five hundred thousand. I will make a personal advance to cover the debts. For the next two years you will receive only two million three hundred thousand, instead of three million. Thus in two years the present debts will be wiped off and, for the moment, you will be solvent again."

She sighed gently. "You should have been an international financier, not an Emperor."

She looked at him searchingly. He was, she thought, amazingly pleased with himself at having disposed of her debts so easily, and in consequence was in a very mellow mood. She took a deep breath.

"Bonaparte," she said, "I went to discuss something very special with you. I—" she looked down delicately—"I want to discuss your second marriage."

"I should have thought it would be the last thing you would want to discuss."

"But why? It was the cause of our separation. I have a deep and personal interest in it. Since for political reasons you must marry again I want to see you marry the right woman."

"And who, in your opinion, is the right woman?"

"The Arch-duchess Marie Louise."

"I rather favor her myself, Josephine, especially since the Tsar of Russia is proving himself loath to negotiate with me."

"Splendid!" she cried.

"There would, of course, be similar difficulties——"

"Similar, but not so pronounced," and without pausing to think she ran on quickly: "The Austrian Ambassador is of the opinion that the Emperor——"

"By heavens, Josephine," he cried, "have you actually been intriguing behind my back to get me married to Marie Louise?"

"Yes," she admitted faintly, taken aback by his sudden anger.

"Pah!" he cried. "Was there ever a woman more lacking in dignity! Graceful and elegant you are, but when it comes to dignity——!"

"Please don't be angry," she pleaded, and added with a sweet smile which robbed her words of all spitefulness: "I was only doing my poor best to find the most suitable royal mare for the Imperial stud."

His anger passing in a moment, he laughed coarsely.

"Have you made up your mind to marry Marie Louise?" she asked.

"Yes. The difficulties, such as they are, will be swept aside."

"I hope you will be very happy with her."

"You hope nothing of the kind, madame."

"Then let me say that I hope she will give you your wish and bear you a son."

"It will be all the worse for her if she doesn't," he said darkly.

Satisfied that Marie Louise had been selected, and never doubting that the Emperor of Austria would give his consent, Josephine returned to Malmaison in a happy frame of mind. She had been half inclined to speak to Bonaparte about the help he would need when the girl came to Paris, but wisely she refrained; the suggestion, if possible, must come from him himself.

Less than a month after her retirement she learned with pleasure that the Elysée Palace had been placed at her disposal and that, if she wished, she could use it as a town house and pay frequent visits to Paris. "Bonaparte," she told herself, "is paving the way. Very soon now he will ask me to take charge of his new wife."

Hortense and Eugene accompanied her back to Paris and Eugene, once she had expressed herself satisfied with the arrangement, returned to his wife and his duties in Milan. Hortense, for the time being, begged to be allowed to remain in France and was touched when Louis, now in Holland again, gave her permission to have the children, Napoleon-Louis and Louis-Napoleon, with her.

Now that she was in Paris again Josephine was looking forward to holding her own court and paying frequent visits to the Tuileries when receptions and balls were held. "Hold your own court if you wish," Bonaparte told her in a letter, "but hold it discreetly, and remember that when Marie Louise comes to Paris you must make no attempt to vie with her. As for appearing at the Tuileries, that, I regret, will not be possible." This was the first blow. Other blows followed in quick succession. The newspapers, she soon found, were forbidden to make any mention of her presence in Paris; she was not permitted to enter any theater when the Imperial box was occupied (clearly because the people might embarrass the Emperor by cheering her too much); a drive in the Bois de Boulogne was out of the question when an Imperial hunt was in progress, and no public celebration was open to her until she had discovered first that Bonaparte himself would not be present.

"At Malmaison," she stormed, when Bonaparte came to visit her one evening at the beginning of March, "I was my own mistress; in Paris I am kept in a palace as if I were a state prisoner. Why? Why? *Why?*"

"You should be wise enough," he said, "not to ask a question as foolish as that. Many people are protesting already at my having allowed you to come to Paris at all."

"Then I shall return to Malmaison; I shall return there at once!"

"No," he told her quietly, "you will go to Navarre."

She could have sworn that he was going to say, *You will remain in Paris,* and was therefore amazed when she heard him mention Navarre. Navarre was a small, uncomfortable château near Evreux, and Evreux was fifty miles from Paris.

"Why do you want to send me to Navarre?" she demanded.

"It is not that I *want* to send you there, but my marriage contract has been signed and Marie Louise is expected to leave Vienna for Paris within the next few days. Did you ever dream that I would permit you both to be in Paris at the same time?"

She saw then how stupid she had been to expect that he would call on her for help, and seeing it, there was nothing she could do but burst into tears, tears in which there was anger, self-pity and abject misery.

Bonaparte looked about him hastily till his eyes fell on her smelling-salts. He snatched up the bottle, withdrew the stopper and, throwing back his head a little as the pungent smell assailed his nostrils, held the bottle firmly beneath her nose. The overpowering smell, for the bottle was a new one, made her catch her breath sharply.

"What a beast you are," she gasped.

"I was afraid that your tears might be followed by a little fainting fit."

"I may as well be dead," she wailed, "as condemned to live at a place like Navarre."

"The air there is bracing and will do you good. You will leave Paris not later than today week and will remain at Navarre until I decide that you may take up residence at Malmaison again."

"Very well," she sighed, "since nothing is left to me now but the humiliation and misery of abject submission, submit to your cruel decree I must."

The château of Navarre was even worse than Josephine had imagined. The grounds were a wilderness of weeds and dank undergrowth; the roof leaked and the windows fitted badly; the passages and dimly lit halls were cold and draughty; every room was like a separate dungeon, a torture-chamber even. Residence there, save that the shadow of the guillotine was absent, was every bit as uncomfortable as residence in the prison at Les Carmes had been during the Revolution. After six weeks at Navarre, six weeks during which her household had begun to murmur discontentedly, she wrote to Bonaparte pleading to be permitted return to Malmaison where she could at least wait for death in comparative comfort. He replied that with his wife in Paris—a marriage by proxy had taken place in Vienna and another ceremony on Marie Louise's arrival in France—it would be politically unwise to permit it. "Why not make a little tour?" he concluded, suggesting Aix-les-Bains, Geneva and possibly Milan to see Eugene. And in a postscript he added gaily that all was going well in the Imperial stud. "My son," he said, "will be born next April."

"A son," she stormed, showing the letter to Hortense. "How very sure he is. Personally I hope Marie Louise gives birth to a girl, to a whole litter of girls!"

A few weeks later, after Bonaparte had agreed to send an army of workmen to Navarre, she set out tearfully for Aix-les-Bains with a little court of faithful followers. Presently she was joined by Hortense who brought the surprising news that Louis, having quarreled with Bonaparte over some matter of policy, had suddenly, and for no sensible reason whatever, abdicated in favor of his young son, Napoleon-Louis.

"Does this mean," Josephine asked anxiously, "that you will have to go back to Holland as regent and take the children with you?"

Hortense shook her head. "No, Mother. The Emperor has declared the abdication null and void. He told me that he will eventually do what he should have done earlier, annex Holland to the Empire."

"And what does Louis say to that?"

"He proposes to retire to private life."

"Dear me, does that mean that he will join us here?"

"Of course not. From now on Louis and I will go our separate ways. I, fortunately, will keep the children."

Restless and still bored, and brooding the while on Marie Louise's pregnancy, Josephine soon left Aix-les-Bains to make a tour of the towns and villages surrounding Lake Geneva. At every halt she was met with enthusiasm, and the continual cry of "Long live Josephine!" began to warm her heart. A little refreshed, but unwilling to admit to anybody that she was almost happy again, she returned to Aix-les-Bains, and with Hortense's help began to assemble a little court of admirers about her. She became a patroness of the arts, she gave numerous musical evenings, she played backgammon with the celebrities who visited her and she began, once more, to take a lively and conscious interest in clothes. "I hear that you are gay and happy again," Bonaparte wrote, "and that makes me gay and happy too." She replied that the gaiety and happiness were a pose which deceived everybody but herself, and pleaded to be allowed to return to Malmaison. In his next letter he was adamant. He urged her to go to Milan but added that since Navarre was now more habitable she could take up residence there again if she wished.

"I choose Navarre," she told Hortense, and with a cunning chuckle she added, "we shall make the journey there by way of Malmaison."

On arriving at Malmaison she professed herself too weary to continue the journey, and with the intention of remaining there in defiance of Bonaparte's wishes, ordered the servants to unload her trunks from the carriage. The next day she learned that the Emperor was at Fontainebleau with Marie Louise who, despite her condition, was in excellent health.

"Discover if you can," she commanded Hortense, "how the wretched girl is carrying the child, high or low."

"Really, Mother," Hortense said, "have you no shame? No delicacy?"

"Shame and delicacy have nothing to do with it. If low the child will undoubtedly be a boy. You were high and Eugene was low, so I know from experience what I am talking about."

Three days later a message came from Bonaparte ordering her to proceed at once to Navarre. She replied that she was too ill to move a single step. The next day, justifying her expectations, he came to Malmaison himself. He found her in bed and shook her none too gently when she pretended to be asleep.

"Why, Bonaparte," she cried, "is it really you?"

She saw that Hortense was standing hesitantly at the door and signaled her to withdraw.

"No," he said, "Hortense shall remain."

"Ah, you think we need a chaperone," she murmured archly.

"You will dress at once," he said, "and prepare to leave for Navarre."

"How cruel you are. I am much too ill to move from my bed."

"You may be forty-eight," he said, "but that is no reason why you should behave like an invalid of *sixty*-eight."

485

"Forty-eight!" She sat up suddenly. "I shall be forty-four next birthday and you know it."

"Forty-eight next birthday," he said.

"Wait," she said earnestly. "It is sixteen years since we were married and I was only twenty-eight at the time. Poor as I always was at figures twenty-eight and sixteen add up to forty-four."

"You reduced your age by four years, I advanced mine by two."

"Nonsense. All I remember about the ceremony is that my age was recorded at the time as twenty-eight."

He tore the bedclothes from her and turned to Hortense.

"A wrap for her Majesty, my dear."

Hortense obediently took up a wrap and placed it about her mother's shoulders.

"Pig of a Corsican," Josephine shouted.

He laughed shortly. His eyes, she saw, were soft and tender. If only Hortense could be got rid of— They would call it adultery, of course, but that, surely, would appeal to Bonaparte's sense of humor.

"You may return to Malmaison," he said, "the moment my son is born."

"Your son! How sure you are that the child is going to be a boy."

"I was never more sure of anything in my life."

"How is she carrying the child—high, or low?"

"That," he said harshly, "is nothing but superstition."

"Ah, so the poor girl is carrying it high."

"High or low the child will be a boy. You will dress and make your preparations—unless, of course, you would prefer to be taken to Navarre in your night-dress."

He approached her swiftly, placed a brief kiss on her brow and went abruptly from the room. Her heart swelled until she felt it might burst.

"Oh, Bonaparte," she sobbed, "I shall always love him, always!"

*   *   *   *   *

Josephine was playing backgammon with the Bishop of Evreux, one of her most constant visitors during this second residence at Navarre. He was an old man, slow of speech and a little deaf, but next to an occasional game of billiards with one of the gentlemen of her household, backgammon with the bishop was the most exciting highlight of her life these days. She watched him as he shook the dice and prepared to throw. He was a dear old man, really, and

486

with only a little dissimulation she had succeeded in convincing him that she was the most devout daughter of the Church in France.

Madame de Rémusat entered the room.

"Is there any news yet?" Josephine cried.

Madame de Rémusat shook her head. "The postmaster is waiting in the village. The moment the news reaches Evreux he will ride out to Navarre without a moment's delay."

Josephine turned to the bishop. "You must pray again, my lord, for a son."

The bishop gave a gentle grunt. Having thrown the dice he had slumped back in his chair and was snoring softly. She pursed her lips thoughtfully. The bishop reminded her of Alexandre, the only man she had ever known who snored. She took up the dice and shook them.

"Twelve for a boy," she said, and made a throw.

"Ah, only seven," said Madame de Rémusat, peering over her shoulder.

"But of course. The child, as we all know, will be a girl. I would wager all I possess. Never in my life have I known the signs to be wrong." She cocked her head on one side. "Listen!"

Racing hoof-beats were approaching. They clattered up the drive and into the courtyard. A moment later the postmaster was admitted to the room.

"Well?" she demanded.

"A boy, your Majesty," he said. "A boy decreed by the Emperor to be the King of Rome."

The bishop gave a great snort and slumped farther down in his chair. Josephine looked at him with distaste. Even Alexandre had never snored in public like that.

"For the first time in your Majesty's life," Madame de Rémusat murmured, "the signs were wrong."

Josephine nodded dumbly. Her eyes had filled with tears. In her heart she was glad; in her heart, she knew, she had always wanted the child to be a boy. And how she envied Marie Louise, how desperately she *envied* her. The tears were rolling down her cheeks now. She searched hurriedly for a handkerchief, and finding it blew her nose loudly. The bishop sat up suddenly.

"What was that?" He put a hand to his deaf ear. "What was that?"

"Our prayers have been answered," she told him. "A son has been born to the Emperor."

She turned briskly to Madame de Rémusat. "Begin to pack immediately. We leave for Malmaison tomorrow."

CHAPTER XLVI

THERE IS PEACE AT MALmaison," Bonaparte said.

He was walking in the grounds with Josephine, a thing he always insisted on doing when he paid her one of his infrequent visits. It was the month of May. In the bright sunshine the rain of a passing shower glittered and sparkled like diamonds on the fresh green foliage of a spring that had come early this year, this fatal year of 1812.

"Yes," he repeated, "there is peace at Malmaison."

"Peace," she said softly, "is something I have never sought, but now that it has come to me, replacing happiness, I am glad of it."

In the year that had passed since the birth of the King of Rome she had become more resigned to retirement. To talk of peace was of course ridiculous, as ridiculous as to talk of growing old, but since Bonaparte, strangely silent today, was in a mood to find peace at Malmaison, there was no harm, surely, in encouraging him. It might even induce him to visit her more often, and certainly it would force him to make regretful comparisons between her, the ever graceful and elegant lady, and Marie Louise, the foreign princess who still despised and hated him.

"You will soon see Eugene again," he said abruptly. "I have summoned him to Paris for a military conference."

She looked at him thoughtfully. "These rumors that I hear of war with Russia, is there any truth in them?"

"Yes. I am about to lead the Grand Army east again, this time to Moscow itself."

"Ah well, you have made war on Russia before."

"I have," he said somberly, "but to what purpose? Russia was never vanquished. She has recovered and is ready for me once more."

"Then this time you will smash her armies once and for all."

"Yes, once and for all. Russia, like the rest of Europe, must be made to see that my destiny demands that Paris shall become the capital of Europe. There must be one code, one court of appeal, one coinage, one language for the whole of Europe. The states of the continent must be melted into one single state, one single *nation*."

They walked in silence for a few moments.

"I would give half of all I possess," he cried suddenly, "to look into the future and learn the truth."

"Why look into the future," she murmured, "when you yourself are about to shape it to your own design?"

She could see by his face that her words had not been heard, that her clever attempt at flattery had been woefully wasted. He stopped abruptly and took her hands in his.

"You told me once that if I divorced you my good fortune, even my ability to plan shrewdly, would desert me. My Empire, you said, would perish overnight. Did you speak in anger, without thinking, or were you inspired by a glimpse of the future?"

She was about to say *I was inspired by a glimpse of the future*, but checked herself. It would be kinder to tell the truth, though heaven knew there was no reason why she should be kind to this man who had treated her so shamefully.

"I spoke in anger," she said virtuously, "and regretted it soon after."

He appeared to be satisfied, but the look of indecision which had come to his face remained. Still holding her hands he said:

"You once said that you would have to spend the rest of your life praying for my soul. Is it possible that you have ever had the self-discipline to get down on your knees since and do that, even once?"

"I pray for you every night," she lied.

He laughed a little but was soon serious again.

"Then please continue to do so during my Russian campaign," he said.

She looked at him in surprise. "But Bonaparte, you were never religious. You never believed in God."

"No, but when a man grows less sure of himself he sometimes begins to fear that he might be wrong."

They returned to the house in silence. Before he climbed into his carriage he took her hands in his once more.

"*Au revoir*, my friend," he said. "You have always been the most graceful woman in the world. Try, for my sake, to remain so till I see you again."

"Poor Bonaparte," she murmured sadly, waving to him as the Imperial carriage rolled down the drive, "what purgatory it must be for him, married to that Austrian mare."

She was surprised to find that there were tears in her eyes, surprised, and a little gratified too. . . .

*   *   *   *   *

A ball was in progress at Malmaison. With Hortense at her side Josephine was surveying the crowded ballroom with considerable satisfaction. It was, she felt sure, one of the gayest gatherings over which she had ever presided, a gathering, she also felt sure, the splendor of which would never be witnessed at the Tuileries these days under Marie Louise. All her guests, most of them were aristocrats of the old *régime*, were in full court dress, while she herself, she knew, was the most elegantly dressed woman present. An Empress without a throne, she was nonetheless a lady with a brighter and happier court about her than the foreigner who had replaced her would ever possess. Her dress was of pink *crêpe*, flounced with lace and embroidered with silver. Cunningly arranged in the head-dress, which was the very latest Chinese fashion, were narrow bands of silver. The only jewelry she wore was a magnificent string of pearls, the beauty of which was emphasized by the low-cut, off-the-shoulder neckline of her dress.

"Hortense," she whispered, "had you noticed my hair?"

Hortense smiled affectionately. "Yes, Mother. The silver bands completely hide the grey streaks."

Josephine pouted like a schoolgirl. "Darling, there are *no* grey streaks to hide."

"Oh, Mother, have you actually started to dye your hair?"

"I have, and for the rest of my life I shall continue to dye it. With a figure as good as mine, would you have me look sixty above my neck and thirty below?"

Hortense coughed and turned away to hide a smile.

"My figure *is* good," Josephine insisted. "I admit that I was growing a little fat before I left the Tuileries, but the worry of the divorce and the anguish of the first year of separation reduced me to a shadow. It was only when I started to eat again that I began to recover my lost weight. And that," she added challengingly, "is all I have recovered, weight, not fat."

Fouché approached and bowed deeply. Josephine greeted him with a bright and brittle smile in which there was none of the friendship she had felt for him in the old days. No longer in favor with Bonaparte, dismissed once more from the Ministry of Police, he had been invited to Malmaison tonight because she hoped to get a little pleasure out of gloating over his misfortune.

"Your Majesty," he said, "is looking younger than ever."

"And feeling younger than ever, I assure you, Fouché!"

His eyes traveled slowly about the room and came to rest on her again.

"When one is obliged to consider that this might well be your Majesty's swan song," he murmured, "one must congratulate you on a most magnificent effort."

"Swan song?" she almost screamed.

"Why, yes. The ball, I understand, is being given to celebrate the Emperor's entry of Moscow. It should, however, have been given a week ago. The Grand Army, I regret to inform you, or what is left of it, is now in retreat."

"In—retreat?"

"Yes, your Majesty, in retreat."

He bowed, smiled cynically and withdrew.

"Fouché!" she called after him.

He turned, bowed again, but continued his withdrawal and a moment later was lost to sight among the guests. Josephine clutched at Hortense's arm.

"I refuse to believe it!" she cried. "Fouché was only trying to alarm me—" she thought of his reference to 'swan song'—"and to insult me too!"

The next day a letter from Eugene confirmed Fouché's words, while a few days later the story of the retreat caused a panic in Paris, where it was said that while the Grand Army was retreating the body of the Emperor had been left behind in the snows of Russia. Loath as she was to do it, Josephine sent an urgent message to Fouché, begging him to come to Malmaison at once. It was two days before he obeyed the summons, during which time the story of Bonaparte's death had been contradicted and the bare facts of the disaster had become common knowledge. In taking Moscow Bonaparte had entered a deserted city; in setting himself up at the Kremlin he had done so without having inflicted a lasting defeat on the Russian armies. Now, after a mysterious and disastrous fire in Moscow, and defeated, not by the Russians but by the intensity of a Russian winter, he was in full retreat.

"It is estimated," Fouché told Josephine, "that out of the vast Grand Army only twelve thousand troops are left. If the Emperor returns to France with even five thousand he will be a fortunate man. The little Corsican adventurer has come to grips at last with a force greater than himself, a force which men call nature."

"You exaggerate," Josephine said stubbornly.

Though this, to a certain extent, was true, the real facts, as she learned on Bonaparte's return to a bewildered Paris, were tragic enough without exaggeration.

"A hundred and twenty-five thousand of my men were killed in battle," he told her somberly when he came to see her at Malmaison. "A larger number than that died of cold and hunger and almost two hundred thousand were taken prisoner. In the end I had only forty thousand left—thirty thousand foreign troops, ten thousand French."

"You know what a poor head I have for figures," she laughed

gaily. "All I can grasp is the fact that the numbers you quote remind me unhappily of a statement of my debts."

He smiled for the first time.

"Dear Josephine," he said.

He looked thin and haggard, but his chin was set at a more stubborn angle than ever and his eyes were stern.

"You will strike again," she said earnestly, "and retrieve your losses."

"Naturally."

"You are making plans already, of course?"

"Of course."

Less than two months later, due to a new conscription decree and the hurried arrival of regiments from Spain and Italy, a new army of over three hundred thousand men had been formed and Bonaparte was ready to march again. Before he left Paris he spent an hour at Malmaison. He insisted on inspecting the whole grounds, from the English lake to the hothouses, from the latest of a series of Japanese gardens to the newly planted mimosa, and he expressed himself delighted when she told him that through her interest in horticulture almost two hundred exotic shrubs had been imported into France.

"How fortunate," he remarked, "that horticulture has taken the place of dalliance."

She grasped his meaning at once and giggled.

"I could count the number of my lovers on the fingers of one hand," she said.

"On the fingers of only *one* hand?" he chided her.

"Well two, then, but you would need a dozen hands to count your mistresses."

Only when they returned to the house did he speak of the impending campaign.

"The country," he said, "is solidly behind me. Every single Frenchman is loyal to my cause. Every single Frenchman knows that the only reverse I have ever suffered was caused by the Russian winter, not by the Russians themselves. Through another mighty campaign I now go forward to peace—a peace that will be real and enduring, but a peace, I swear, which will be dictated by no one else but Napoleon Bonaparte, Emperor of France and future Emperor of the world."

He spoke so quietly that she could scarcely hear him; he spoke, she felt, without conviction.

"Give me your hands," he said, "let me look at you once more before I bid you good-bye."

"Good-bye?" she echoed. "You have never used that word before. You have always said *au revoir*."

With her hands in his he drew her forward and kissed her on the brow.

"You little fraud," he whispered, "you have taken to dyeing your hair."

She freed her hands and flung them round his neck.

"Oh, Bonaparte," she sobbed, "I have a dreadful feeling that I shall never see you again."

*   *   *   *   *

Josephine sat forward in the carriage as the Tuileries came into sight. She leaned impatiently out of the window.

"Hurry," she shouted to the postilion, "for pity's sake hurry."

"This," Hortense said quietly, "is madness."

News had reached Malmaison that morning that Marie Louise, now that calamity after calamity had overtaken Bonaparte, was on the point of flying from Paris with the little King of Rome. Shaken with anger and indignation at this news Josephine had decided to come to the Tuileries to plead with the girl to remain, nay to command her to remain. Marie Louise was Empress of France and the mother of a future Emperor. Her place was in Paris. No matter if the whole world, including her native Austria, was allied against Bonaparte, no matter if the Allied Armies were marching on the capital, no matter if Joseph Bonaparte (who had been called to Paris as Lieutenant-General of the Empire) had lost his head and was about to surrender the city, her place was in Paris.

In the palace courtyard a guard sprang forward and surrounded the carriage. Since both Josephine and Hortense were heavily veiled they remained unrecognized. Josephine flung open the door and made to step down.

"You will conduct me to her Majesty the Empress," she commanded.

There was a roar of derisive laughter and the captain of the detachment stepped forward.

"Madame, whoever she may be, is too late," he said. "The young Empress has fled to her father. All that remains at the Tuileries is the ghost of the old Empress who, God bless her, would have remained like the queen she was till the last."

A lump rose in Josephine's throat; tears sprang to her eyes.

"As heaven is my witness," she cried, in a choking voice, "indeed she would!"

Hortense gave a quiet order to the postilion. The guard stood back, the horses were whipped up. A moment later Josephine heard a cheer rising behind her.

"Long live the Empress Josephine!" the guard cried.

"Do you think they recognized me?" she asked Hortense.

Hortense shook her head. "They cheer your memory, Mother; just that and nothing else."

Josephine found her handkerchief and blew her nose.

"You speak as if I were dead," she complained. "I realize now that I wasn't recognized, otherwise the guard and that handsome captain would have carried me into the palace and forced me to remain."

At Josephine's command the postilion drove across the Pont Royal, down the rue du Bac and turned left into the rue de l'Université. She glanced sadly at the house where she had established her first *salon*, and insisted on the carriage being turned and driven back for a final glimpse. In the rue du Bac again the street had suddenly become blocked with wagons and carts and overladen carriages. She stared dumbly about her while the postilion waited patiently for a clearance.

"Refugees," he said, in answer to a question from Hortense. "Refugees from Meaux. They flee from the advancing enemy. Within two days Paris will be occupied."

Behind the wagons and carts and carriages came aged peasants with their wives and daughters. Some led terrified cows at whose heels mongrel farm dogs barked and snapped. A small girl, clinging to a struggling cat, was sobbing bitterly. An old man waved his stick at Josephine, shouted "Bonaparte!" at the top of his voice and spat. A young woman boxed his ears and began to sing the *Marseillaise*. Others joined her till the air was filled with the familiar words and notes, but the slow retreat of bewildered peasantry went on unchecked.

"This," Josephine whispered, "is the end. The end for Bonaparte, for you, for me, for all of us. . . ."

Back at Malmaison she found that more than half of her household had deserted her and that the remainder had already made their preparations for an early flight. Without protest she agreed that no good purpose could be achieved by remaining at Malmaison and expressed herself willing to leave the next day for Navarre. She superintended the packing of her trunks herself and with the help of one of her ladies sewed diamonds and pearls and fifty thousand francs into the folds of a petticoat.

"I shall have to scratch and save now," she said, with a wan smile. "I shall have to be as prudent as any peasant's wife."

At Navarre she waited anxiously for news of Bonaparte and Eugene. Both, she learned presently, were safe. Bonaparte was at Fontainebleau; Eugene, having made a successful retreat from the Austrians, was in Milan. She had almost made up her mind to join Bonaparte at Fontainebleau when she received news of his abdication.

"The Emperor," the messenger told her, "has signed an act of unconditional abdication. The Bourbons are to be restored; the Emperor himself is to go into exile on the Island of Elba."

*   *   *   *   *

With a feeling of unreality Josephine re-read the short letter which the Cossack officer had brought to Navarre.

To the Empress Josephine,
It is the wish of the Allies that you should suffer as little anxiety as possible regarding your future safety. Certain provisions were made for you by the Emperor Napoleon in his Act of Abdication. In order to discuss these it is suggested that you should return to Malmaison where I myself, if you desire it, would be pleased to visit you.

The letter was signed by Alexandre, Tsar of Russia.

She had heard that the Tsar was a charming, courteous man and quite the most well bred of all the kings and princes and generals now in Paris at the court of the fat and pig-like Bourbon prince whom they had made Louis the Eighteenth. She read the letter a third time. How wrong she had been when she had told herself that Bonaparte's defeat was the end.

At Malmaison, while dressing to receive the Tsar, it crossed her mind that his interest in her was probably that of a young man who had heard the countless legends of her graciousness and elegance, and that he was coming to see her, not because he was sorry for her, but because he felt a romantic urge to pay her homage. He was thirty-five, she was little more than fifty; the difference, if she dressed cunningly, would be scarcely perceptible.

Alexandre—strange that there should have been two men of that name in her life!—was striking in appearance but not good looking. He had fair skin and blond hair, which was a pleasant change from the dark skin and black hair of the Frenchmen who had usually surrounded her. His face had a friendly look and his smile was boyishly delightful. But most important of all (and exceedingly gratifying when she had been afraid of him thinking her old and raddled) his brilliant blue eyes were those of a short-sighted man who peered and squinted at everything that came within his vision.

He bowed before her; he took her hand in his and kissed it; he told her gallantly that the three portraits he had seen of her had failed to do her justice. He inquired delicately about her position, he hoped that she was not embarrassed in any way by a temporary lack of money, and he offered to make her a personal advance until the first instalment of the pension granted by Bonaparte under the Act of Abdication reached her.

"What does this pension amount to?" she asked briskly.

"A million francs a year."

Tears came to her eyes. Poor Bonaparte, even in the hopelessness of defeat he had found time to think of her, though while he was about it, and knowing how hard it had been for her to manage on three times that amount, he might have been a little more generous!

"I should be very grateful," she said, "if your Majesty could advance me a quarter of a million."

He bowed and beamed at her with his squinting eyes.

"I shall be delighted," he said.

He told her that provision had also been made for the Imperial Family. Joseph and Jerome were to receive five hundred thousand francs each, Louis two hundred thousand, Madame Mère and her daughters three hundred thousand and Hortense four hundred thousand.

"Ah," Josephine chuckled, "a hundred thousand more for my daughter than for the Bonaparte women. But what of my son Eugene?"

"No provision seems to have been made for Prince Eugene, but he will, I assure you, be well received should he decide to present himself at the Bourbon Court."

With that he brought his visit to a conclusion, assured her that he would always be ready to help her in the future, and begged her to grant him the favor of paying her another visit soon. He left her with a warm sensation tingling about her heart, and with a chuckle she told herself that she felt like a pretty country girl who had come to Paris and succeeded in finding a rich protector within the first week.

The Tsar's first visit was followed by formal visits from the King of Prussia, the Emperor of Austria and a host of German princelings who made up for their ignorance of the French language by staring at her in bewitched silence. By the time Eugene was able to join her a continual stream of kings, princes and members of the Bourbon Court was flowing down the road from Paris to Malmaison.

Her new and splendid position gave her considerable satisfaction, and in thinking of it she gloated a little as she contrasted it with that of the Bonaparte family. Joseph, who had fled with Marie Louise after his shameful surrender of Paris, was living quietly in Switzerland; Louis, rarely heard of or seen since Bonaparte's annexation of Holland, was last reported to be with Joseph; Lucien, never having been permitted to return from exile, had been taken prisoner by the English while making an attempt to reach America on an Italian vessel and was now on parole in England; Jerome, having failed to distinguish himself during Bonaparte's last campaign, was also in Switzerland; Madame Mère and Paulette were at present with Bonaparte on the Island of Elba, and Caroline and Elisa, engaged in some obscure intrigue with the Austrian Court, were last heard of at Bologna. All were in exile, and that, save for the divorce, was where she herself would be. Strange, when you came to think of it, that fate in dealing her an apparent death blow had merely been mindful of her ultimate preservation, and through her, if her newest plan met with the success she anticipated, Bonaparte's ultimate preservation too.

"I feel like a reigning Empress again," she told Eugene and Hortense. "Never in my life, not even when I was mistress of the Tuileries, have I entertained so many illustrious guests at the same time."

Eugene frowned a little and protested faintly that her attitude could hardly be called loyal to Bonaparte.

"Ah, but you don't understand," she said warmly. "I was never more loyal to him than I am today. You see, I have a plan, a last tremendous intrigue." She lowered her voice and spoke eagerly. "I want to pave the way for his return to France." She looked from Eugene to Hortense with dancing eyes. "If I succeed in bringing him back his gratitude will be so great that he will gladly divorce Marie Louise and I shall be Empress of France again and remain on my throne till the day I die."

"You must be mad to dream of such a thing," Hortense said.

"Nonsense. I have gone into the matter very carefully. There is a great deal of dissatisfaction with the Bourbons. I shall work cunningly but boldly. I—" she chuckled deeply—"I shall begin my intrigue at the Tuileries itself, once I have gained permission to make my appearance there."

"I doubt if that permission will ever be granted," Eugene said.

"We shall see. The Tsar is a very good friend. He has promised already to see what he can do about my opening a house in Paris. Believe me, children, before the end of the year the Empire will have been restored, restored, I promise you, in full!"

Her mind busy with this 'last tremendous intrigue' she gave a dinner party for the Tsar. Intending it to be an intimate little gathering she invited only twelve guests, amongst whom were the Grand Dukes Nicholas and Michael. For the occasion she wore a white tulle dress powdered with gold stars and beneath it a deep burgundy petticoat. She selected a necklet of large diamonds and some smaller ones for her hair. Hortense suggested that the dress, though delightful, was too thin.

"May is always a treacherous month," she said, "and the nights have been very chilly lately."

"I always wear thin dresses, even in the depth of winter."

"Then wear a shawl about your shoulders."

"A shawl would spoil the effect. In any case shawls are no longer fashionable."

While dessert was being served Josephine announced that an orchestra had been brought out from Paris and that an informal ball would be held during the evening.

"Your Majesty and I," she said addressing the Tsar, "will open it."

He smiled amiably and declared that nothing would delight him more.

Feeling strangely restless after the first dance and unaccountably hot, she insisted on strolling in the grounds. Squired by the attentive Tsar she brought up the subject of the house in Paris. He told her that there was some little difficulty but assured her that it would be overcome within the next few days.

"Your Majesty is shivering," he said. "Surely it would be wiser, after the heat of the ballroom, to remain indoors."

"I was much too hot indoors. I still feel warm, even out here."

He looked at her fixedly with his short-sighted eyes. He placed his hand on her brow and withdrew it in alarm.

"Your Majesty is feverish," he said. "To remain here would be foolish— Come, I insist that we go indoors."

He offered her his arm and she staggered a little as she took it. She was suddenly aware that her head was aching and that the ballroom, as they entered it, was swimming before her eyes. Later, when she found her guests grouped about her, staring down at her with anxious faces, she realized that she must have fainted. A moment later a blackness enveloped her again. She knew no more till she opened her eyes and saw a patch of sunlight streaming through the window. Her head ached abominably and though shivers ran continually down her back every fibre of her body seemed to be on fire. She could see nobody in the room, but two voices reached her

ears. One was indistinct; the other, after a moment, said clearly:
"A putrid fever, but not immediately dangerous."

* * * * *

The room was full of faces. They hovered above her in a slowly moving circle, just faces with no bodies whatever attached to them. Presently one of them detached itself, and while the others continued to circle it swam forward to leer at her. She recognized it as that of Alexandre de Beauharnais.

"*Madame Renaudin tells me that you are very fond of music,*" he said.

"Oh yes," she said, "very fond, and I play the guitar a little."

"*The guitar? But surely such an instrument is a little barbaric?*"

"You'll probably think me very lacking in education, but what does 'barbaric' mean?"

"*You don't know? My dear child, it means rude and uncivilized. Er—not in the best of taste. Lacking in refinement.*"

She tried to sit up. "But Alexandre you're dead, and that surely, is lacking in refinement too."

A chorus of male laughter filled the room. Alexandre's face stiffened, grew blurred and was replaced by one she failed, for a moment, to recognize.

"*My duty, madame,*" the face murmured.

"Why—Lacoste!"

"*Your servant, madame. I find that Madame la Vicomtesse is in the habit of wearing heavy black under-breeches.*"

The chorus of laughter burst out again. Fingers appeared with the revolving faces and pointed. Lacoste's face faded and was replaced by that of Tercier. Others crowded about it. She had a passing glimpse of Réal, Hoche, Barras, Alexandre again and then, jostling them all aside, came the thin pallid features of the Bonaparte she had first known during the Directory period.

"*Your name is Rose, I believe,*" he said.

"Most people call me Rose. My full name is Marie-Joseph-Rose."

"*Marie-Joseph-Rose—I don't like it. I think I shall give you a new name.*"

"Really, General, I find my present name quite satisfactory."

"*I like Joseph. I have a brother called Joseph, but naturally I can't call a woman by that name. I shall call you Josephine. Yes, Josephine.*"

A cushion and an army cloak had appeared behind the face.

"Bonaparte—!" she cried.

499

"*As you know, I am by no means a patient man.*"

"But great heavens, the floor of all places!"

"*A soldier is well acquainted with the floor.*"

The circle of faces was revolving faster now. The pace increased until she could feel the draught of cool air caused by the rapid movement. She closed her eyes for a moment. When she opened them again she could still feel the draught but not a face was to be seen.

"Mother——"

It was Hortense, bending over her, fanning her with a Japanese fan.

"Why Hortense, darling."

Her voice was so low she could scarcely hear it herself.

Eugene joined Hortense. His face was the saddest she had ever seen, but he smiled gently and encouragingly when her eyes caught his.

"Have I been talking a lot of nonsense, darling?" she asked.

"You were muttering to yourself," he told her, "but we were quite unable to understand a word."

She smiled weakly. "Poor Bonaparte, and poor Alexandre too. Dear me, but what a lot of dreadful men I have known during my short life."

"Please don't talk, Mother," Hortense begged. "You will only tire yourself."

"What news is there from Elba?" she asked.

"Very little, Mother."

"Does Bonaparte know that I am ill?"

"Word has been sent to him."

She felt the hot tears as they began to roll down her cheeks. "I shall never see him again. When he comes back—if he ever comes back now—I shall be dead."

She saw then that a third person was in the room. She recognized him as he stood there silently in the shadows. He was the Abbé Bertrand, the priest who had been employed as a tutor for Hortense's children.

"Really," she stirred herself to protest, "surely a bishop could have been brought to administer the last sacraments." She heard a horrible noise in her throat which she knew was meant to be a chuckle. "Bonaparte would have insisted on the Holy Father himself."

When the last sacraments had been administered and she had murmured politely that she now felt a great peace in her mind, she caught another glimpse of Bonaparte's face. If only she had really loved him when she had first married him, how different the course of their life together might have been.

"The course of our life together," she thought she heard him say, *"was of my own making. Nothing you might have done would have changed the final issue."*

The weight above her eyes, pressing down on them, was so heavy that she was forced to close them.

"Bonaparte—that dreadful island—" she heard herself murmur. "Forgive me for dying before I could bring you back——"

"Mother!"

It was Hortense's voice. She struggled to open her eyes for a moment, and half succeeding she caught a passing glimpse of the tragic faces of her son and daughter.

"Sleepy," she muttered, "so very sleepy."

She roused herself once again, forcing her stiff and heavy lips to frame the words, if not actually to speak them.

"Merciful heavens, the only man I know who is dead, the only one who might possibly be waiting for me, is Alexandre. . . ."

In all conscience it was enough to compel one to go on living.